Children of God

"A Heartbreaking Tale."
—*The Seattle Times*

"Russell's *Children of God* continues the gripping tale of Jesuit missionaries on a godless planet begun in *The Sparrow*."

—amazon.com

"*Children of God*, like its predecessor *The Sparrow*, combines a compelling story with intelligence and careful research. . . . Russell's exploration of the psychic rift and its healing is eloquent, illuminating all the dark corners of the mind in great novelistic style."

—*Cleveland Free Times*

"In terms of characters, *Children of God* is even stronger than *The Sparrow*. . . . Russell is an anthropologist by training, and her training allows her to be extraordinarily precise about culture."

—*San Jose Mercury News*

"Russell's portrait of courage and endurance [is] both moving and exhilarating."

—*Locus*

"Powerful prose and memorable characters . . . Firmly grounded in science yet informed and illuminated by an inherent spirituality, this sequel to Russell's highly praised *The Sparrow* examines the problem of faith under fire with insight and clarity."

—*Library Journal* (starred review)

"Riveting . . . Near impossible to put down . . . The story Russell tells is not only incredibly entertaining and imaginative, but intellectually, morally provocative. The speculation of *Children of God* is painfully truthful, but also, strangely, filled with hope. At the story's end, the world will witness something of a miracle."

—*BookPage*

"Misunderstandings between cultures and people are at the heart of her story. It is, however, the complex figure of Father Sandoz around which a diverse interplanetary cast orbits, and it is the intelligent, emotional and very personal feud between Father Sandoz and his God that provides energy for both books."

—*Publishers Weekly*

BY MARY DORIA RUSSELL

Children
of God

A Novel

MARY DORIA RUSSELL

FAWCETT BOOKS
The Random House Publishing Group · New York

A Ballantine Book
Published by The Random House Publishing Group

Published in the United States by Ballantine Books, an imprint of
The Random House Publishing Group, a division of Random House,
Inc., New York, and simultaneously in Canada by Random House
of Canada Limited, Toronto.

www.ballantinebooks.com
www.randomhousereaderscircle.com

Library of Congress Catalog Card Number: 98-96702

ISBN: 978-0-449-00483-8

This edition published by arrangement with Villard Books,
a division of Random House, Inc.

Book design: Fritz Metsch
Cover art (bottom front and back): Giotto, *Banquet of Herod*,
c. 1320 (Scala/Art Resource)

Printed in the United States of America

First Edition: February 1999

30 29 28 27 26 25 24 23 22

FOR

KATE SWEENEY

AND

JENNIFER TUCKER

hermanas de mi alma

Children of God

Prelude

SWEATING AND NAUSEATED, FATHER EMILIO SANDOZ SAT ON THE EDGE of his bed with his head in what was left of his hands.

Many things had turned out to be more difficult than he'd expected. Losing his mind, for example. Or dying. How can I still be alive? he wondered, not so much with philosophical curiosity as with profound irritation at the physical stamina and sheer bad luck that had conspired to keep him breathing, when all he'd wanted was death. "Something's got to go," he whispered, alone in the night. "My sanity or my soul . . ."

He stood and began to pace, wrecked hands tucked under his armpits to keep the fingers from being jarred as he moved. Unable to drive nightmare images away in the darkness, he touched the lights on with an elbow so he could see clearly the real things in front of him: a bed, linens tangled and sweat-soaked; a wooden chair; a small, plain chest of drawers. Five steps, turn, five steps back. Almost the exact size of the cell on Rakhat—

There was a knock at the door and he heard Brother Edward Behr, whose bedroom was nearby and who was always alert for these midnight walks. "Are you all right, Father?" Edward asked quietly.

Am I all right? Sandoz wanted to cry. Jesus! I'm scared and I'm crippled and everybody I ever loved is dead—

But what Edward Behr heard as he stood in the hallway just beyond Sandoz's door was, "I'm fine, Ed. Just restless. Everything's fine."

Brother Edward sighed, unsurprised. He had cared for Emilio Sandoz, night and day, for almost a year. Tended his ruined body, prayed for him, watching appalled and frightened as the priest fought his way back from utter helplessness to a fragile self-respect. So, even as Edward padded down the hall to check on Sandoz tonight, he suspected that this would be the soft-voiced reply to a pointless question.

"It's not over, you know," Brother Edward had warned a few days earlier, when Emilio had at long last spoken the unspeakable. "You don't get over something like that all at once." And Emilio had agreed that this was true.

Returning to his own bed, Edward punched up the pillow and slid under the covers, listening as the pacing resumed. It's one thing to know the truth, he thought. To live with it is altogether something else.

IN THE ROOM DIRECTLY BENEATH SANDOZ'S, THE FATHER GENERAL OF THE Society of Jesus had also heard the sudden, gasping cry that announced an arrival of the incubus who ruled Emilio's nights. Unlike Brother Edward, Vincenzo Giuliani no longer rose to offer Sandoz unwelcomed help, but he could see in memory the initial look of bewildered terror, the silent struggle to regain control.

For months, while presiding over the Society's inquiry into the failure of the first Jesuit mission to Rakhat, Vincenzo Giuliani had been certain that if Emilio Sandoz were brought to speak of what had happened on that alien world, the matter could be resolved and Emilio would find some peace. The Father General was both administrator and priest; he had believed it was necessary—for the Society of Jesus and for Sandoz himself—to face facts. And so, by methods direct and indirect, by means gentle and brutal, both alone and aided by others, he had taken Emilio Sandoz to the moment when truth could free him.

Sandoz had fought them every step of the way: no priest, no matter how desperate, wishes to undermine another's faith. But Vincenzo Giuliani had been serenely confident that he could analyze error and correct it, understand failure and forgive it, hear sin and absolve it.

What he had been unprepared for was innocence.

"Do you know what I thought, just before I was used the first time? I am in God's hands," Emilio had said, when his resistance finally shattered on a golden August afternoon. "I loved God and I trusted in His love. Amusing, isn't it. I laid down all my defenses. I had nothing between me and what happened but the love of God. And I was raped. I was naked before God and I was raped."

What is it in humans that makes us so eager to believe ill of one another? Giuliani asked himself that night. What makes us so hungry for it? Failed idealism, he suspected. We disappoint ourselves and then look around for other failures to convince ourselves: it's not just me.

Emilio Sandoz was not sinless; indeed, he held himself guilty of a great deal, and yet . . . "If I was led by God to love God, step by step, as it seemed, if I accept that the beauty and the rapture were real and true, then the rest of it was God's will too and that, gentlemen, is cause for bitterness," Sandoz had told them. "But if I am simply a deluded ape who took a lot of old folktales far too seriously, then I brought all this on myself and my companions. The problem with atheism, I find, under these circumstances, is that I have no one to despise but myself. If, however, I choose to believe that God is vicious, then at least I have the solace of hating God."

If Sandoz is deluded, thought Vincenzo Giuliani as the pacing above him went on and on, what am I? And if he is not, what is God?

Naples

September 2060

CELESTINA GIULIANI LEARNED THE WORD "SLANDER" AT HER COUSIN'S baptism. That is what she remembered about the party, mostly, aside from the man who cried.

The church was nice, and she liked the singing, but the baby got to wear Celestina's dress, which wasn't fair. No one had asked Celestina's permission, even though she wasn't supposed to take things without asking. Mamma explained that all the Giuliani babies wore this dress when they were baptized and pointed out the hem where Celestina's name was embroidered. "See, *cara*? There is your name and your papa's and Auntie Carmella's and your cousins'—Roberto, Anamaria, Stefano. Now it's the new baby's turn."

Celestina was not in a mood to be reasoned with. *That baby looks like Grandpa in a bride dress,* she decided grumpily.

Bored with the ceremony, Celestina began to swing her arms, head down, watching her skirt swirl from side to side for a while, sneaking a look now and then at the man with the machines on his hands, standing by himself in the corner. "He's a priest—like Grandpa Giuliani's American cousin Don Vincenzo," Mamma had explained to her before they left for the church that morning. "He's been sick a long time, and his hands don't work very well, so he uses machines to help his fingers move. Don't stare, *carissima.*"

Celestina didn't stare. She did, however, peek fairly often.

The man wasn't paying attention to the baby like everyone else and one time when she peeked, he saw her. The machines were scary, but the man wasn't. Most grown-ups smiled with their faces but their eyes told you they wanted you to go and play. The man with the machines didn't smile, but his eyes did.

The baby fussed and fussed, and then Celestina smelled the caca. "Mamma!" she cried, horrified. "That baby—"

"Hush, *cara*!" her mother whispered loudly, and all the grown-ups laughed, even Don Vincenzo, who wore a long black dress like the man with the machines and was pouring water on the baby.

Finally, it was over and they all left the dark church and walked out into the sunshine. "But Mamma, the baby went!" Celestina insisted, as they came down the stairs and waited for the chauffeur to bring the car around. "Right in my dress! It'll be all dirty!"

"Celestina," her mother reproved, "you yourself once did such things! The baby wears diapers, just as you did."

Celestina's mouth dropped open. All around her, grown-ups were laughing, except for the man with the machines, who stopped next to her and dropped to her level, his face a mirror of her own stunned outrage. "This is slander!" she cried, repeating what he had whispered to her.

"A monstrous calumny!" he confirmed indignantly, standing again, and if Celestina did not understand any of the words, she knew that he was taking her side against the grown-ups who were laughing.

They all went to Auntie Carmella's house after that. Celestina ate biscotti and got Uncle Paolo to push her on the swing and had soda, which was a treat because it wouldn't make her bones strong, so she could only have it at parties. She considered playing with her cousins, but no one was her age, and Anamaria always wanted to be the mamma and Celestina had to be the baby, and that was boring. So she tried dancing in the middle of the kitchen until Gramma told her she was pretty and Mamma told her to go visit the guinea pigs.

When she got cranky, Mamma took her to the back bedroom, and sat with her, humming for a while. Celestina was almost asleep when her mother reached for a tissue and blew her nose.

"Mamma? Why didn't Papa come today?"

"He was busy, *cara*," Gina Giuliani told her daughter. "Go to sleep."

·   ·   ·

THE GOOD-BYES WOKE HER: COUSINS AND AUNTS AND UNCLES AND grandparents and family friends, calling out *ciaos* and *buona fortunas* to the new baby and his parents. Celestina got up and took herself to the potty, which reminded her of slander, and then moved toward the loggia, wondering if she would get to take some balloons home. Stefano was making a fuss, yelling and crying. "I know, I know," Auntie Carmella was saying. "It's hard to say good-bye to everyone after such a nice time, but the party's ending now." Uncle Paolo simply scooped Stefano up, smiling but brooking no nonsense.

Amused by the tantrum and indulgent, none of the adults noticed Celestina standing in the doorway. Her mother was helping Auntie Carmella clear up the dishes. Her grandparents were out in the yard saying good-bye to the guests. Everyone else was paying attention to Stefano, screaming and struggling manfully, but helpless in the arms of his father, who carried him off, apologizing for the noise. Only Celestina noticed Don Vincenzo's face change. That was when she looked at the man with the machines on his hands and saw that he was crying.

Celestina had seen her mother cry, but she didn't know that men cried, too. It frightened her because it was strange, and because she was hungry, and because she liked the man who took her side, and because he didn't cry like anyone else she knew—eyes open, tears slipping down a still face.

Car doors slammed and Celestina heard the crunch of tires on gravel, just as her mother looked up from the table. Gina's own smile faded when she followed her daughter's gaze. Glancing in the direction of the two priests, Gina spoke to her sister-in-law in a low voice. Nodding, Carmella went to Don Vincenzo's side on her way to the kitchen with a stack of dishes. "The bedroom at the end of the hall, perhaps?" she suggested. "No one will disturb you there."

Celestina ducked out of the way as Don Vincenzo took the crying man by the arm, steering him through the loggia doorway and toward Carmella's room. "It was like that?" Celestina heard Don Vincenzo ask as they passed her. "They were amused when you struggled?"

Celestina followed them, embroidered anklets making whispers of her footsteps, and peeped through the little space where the door wasn't quite closed. The man with the machines was sitting in a chair in the corner. Don Vincenzo stood nearby, not saying anything, looking out the window toward Cece's pen. That's mean, Celestina thought. Don Vincenzo is mean! She hated it when she cried and no one paid attention because they said she was being silly.

The man saw her as she stepped into the bedroom, and he wiped his face on his sleeves. "What's the matter?" she asked, coming closer. "Why are you crying?"

Don Vincenzo started to say something, but the man shook his head and said, "It's nothing, *cara*. Only: I was remembering something—something bad that happened to me."

"What happened?"

"Some . . . men hurt me. It was a long time ago," he assured her as her eyes grew round, afraid the bad men were still in the house. "It was when you were very small, but sometimes I remember it."

"Did anyone kiss you?"

"*Mi scuzi?*" He blinked when she said it, and Don Vincenzo stood very straight for a moment.

"To make it better?" she said.

The man with the machines smiled with very soft eyes. "No, *cara*. No one kissed it better."

"I could."

"That would be very nice," he said in a serious voice. "I think I could use a kiss."

She leaned forward and kissed his cheek. Her cousin Roberto, who was nine, said kissing was stupid, but Celestina knew better. "This is a new dress," she told the man. "I got chocolate on it."

"It's still very pretty. So are you."

"Cece had babies. Want to see them?"

The man looked up at Don Vincenzo, who explained, "Cece is a guinea pig. Having babies is what guinea pigs do."

"Ah. *Si, cara.* I'd like that."

He stood, and she went to take his hand so she could bring him outside, but remembered about the machines. "What happened to your hands?" she asked, pulling him along by the sleeve.

"It was a sort of accident, *cara*. Don't worry. It can't happen to you."

"Does it hurt?" Vincenzo Giuliani heard the child ask, as she led Emilio Sandoz down the hall toward a door to the backyard.

"Sometimes," Sandoz said simply. "Not today."

Their voices were lost to him after he heard the back door bang shut. Vincenzo Giuliani stepped to the window, listening to the late afternoon buzz of cicadas, and watched Celestina drag Emilio to the guinea-pig pen. The child's lace-pantied bottom suddenly upended as she leaned over the wire enclosure to grab a baby for Emilio, who sat smiling on the ground, black-and-silver hair spilling forward over high Taino cheekbones as he admired the little animal Celestina dumped in his lap.

It had taken four priests eight months of relentless pressure to get Emilio Sandoz to reveal what Celestina had learned in two minutes. Evidently, the Father General observed wryly, the best man for the job can sometimes be a four-year-old girl.

And he wished that Edward Behr had stayed to see this.

BROTHER EDWARD WAS AT THAT MOMENT IN HIS ROOM IN THE JESUITS' Neapolitan retreat house some four kilometers away, still astounded that the Father General had chosen a baptism as the occasion for Emilio Sandoz's first venture out of seclusion.

"You're joking!" Edward had cried that morning. "A christening? Father General, the last thing in the world Emilio Sandoz needs right now is a christening!"

"This is family, Ed. No press, no pressure," Vincenzo Giuliani declared. "The party will be good for him! He's strong enough now—"

"Physically, yes," Edward conceded. "But emotionally, he is nowhere near ready for this. He needs time!" Edward insisted. "Time to be angry. Time to mourn! Father General, you can't rush—"

"Bring the car around front at ten, thank you, Edward," the Father General said, smiling mildly. And that was that.

Having dropped the two priests off at the church, Brother Edward spent the remainder of the day back at the Jesuit house, stewing. By three in the afternoon, he had convinced himself that he really ought to leave early to fetch them back from the party. It was only sensible to allow time for security checks, he told himself. Regardless of how well known the driver was, no vehicle got near Giuliani real estate or the retreat without being carefully and repeatedly considered by swarthy, suspicious men and large, thoughtful dogs trained to detect explosives and ill will. So Edward allowed forty-five minutes for a trip that might otherwise take ten, and was questioned and sniffed and inspected at every intersection of the road that paralleled the coast. It wasn't entirely wasted time, he noted, as the car's undercarriage was mirrored at the compound gate and his identification studied a fourth time. He had, for example, learned some remarkable things from several dogs about where weapons might theoretically be concealed on a tubby man's body.

However questionable the probity of the Father General's Neapolitan relatives, it was a comfort to know that Emilio Sandoz benefited from their thoroughness, and Edward was eventually allowed to pull into the driveway of the largest of the several houses visible from the front gate, its loggia festive with flowers and balloons. Emilio was nowhere to be seen, but before long, the Father General separated from a little crowd with a young blond woman. Giuliani raised a hand in acknowledgment to Behr and then spoke to someone in the house.

Emilio appeared moments later, looking stiff-backed and exhausted, a dark amalgam of Indian endurance and Spanish pride. There was a small girl in a very rumpled party dress at his side. "I knew it!" Edward muttered furiously. "This was too much!"

With as fortifyingly deep a breath as an asthmatic could manage, Brother Edward heaved his portly self out of the car and trundled around it, opening doors for the Father General and for Sandoz, while Giuliani made their good-byes to the hostess and the other guests. The little girl said something, and Edward groaned when Emilio knelt to receive her embrace and return the hug as best he could. Despite—no, because of the tenderness of that farewell, Brother Edward was not a bit surprised by the quiet conversation that was going on between the two priests as they made their way alone to the car.

"—if you ever do this to me again, you sonofabitch. Dammit, Ed, don't hover," Sandoz snapped, climbing into the back seat. "I can close the door myself."

"Yes, Father. Sorry, Father," Edward said, backing off, but actually rather pleased. Nothing like being right, he thought to himself.

"Jesus, Vince! Kids and babies!" Sandoz snarled as they pulled out of the Giuliani drive. "This was supposed to be good for me?"

"It was good for you," the Father General insisted. "Emilio, you were fine until the end—"

"The nightmares aren't bad enough? Now we're trying for flashbacks?"

"You said you wanted to live on your own," the Father General pointed out patiently. "Things like this are bound to come up. You've got to learn to deal with—"

"Who the fuck are you to tell me what I have to deal with? Shit, if this starts happening when I'm awake—"

Edward, wincing at the language, glanced into the rearview mirror when Emilio's voice broke. Cry, Edward thought. It's better than the headaches. Go ahead and cry. But Sandoz fell silent and stared out the window at the passing countryside, dry-eyed and furious.

"There are at present some six billion individuals under the age of fifteen in the world," the Father General resumed peaceably. "It's going to be difficult to avoid them all. If you can't manage in a controlled environment like Carmella's home—"

"*Quod erat demonstrandum*," Sandoz said bitterly.

"—then perhaps you should consider staying with us. As a linguist, if nothing else."

"You crafty old bastard." Sandoz laughed—a short, hard sound. "You did this to me deliberately."

"One doesn't become Father General of the Society of Jesus by being a dumb bastard," Vince Giuliani said mildly, and went on, straight-faced. "The dumb bastards become famous linguists and get themselves buggered on other planets."

"You're just jealous. When's the last time you got laid?"

Brother Edward turned left onto the coast road, seeing through Emilio's desperate bluff, marveling at the relationship between these two men. Born to wealth and unquestioned privilege, Vincenzo Giuliani was a historian and politician of international repute, still powerful in body and mind at the age of seventy-nine. Emilio Sandoz was the illegitimate child of a Puerto Rican woman who'd had an affair while her husband was jailed for trafficking in the very substances that had enriched an earlier generation of La Famiglia Giuliani. The two men had met over sixty years ago while studying for the priesthood. And yet, Sandoz was now only forty-six years old, give or take a bit. One of the many bizarre aspects of Emilio's situation was the fact that he'd spent thirty-four years traveling at a substantial percentage of the speed of light, to and from the Alpha Centauri system. For Sandoz, only about six years had gone by since he'd left Earth—difficult years, granted, but very few of them compared to those that had passed for Vince Giuliani, now decades Emilio's senior and his superior by several levels of Jesuit organization.

"Emilio, all I'm asking for now is that you work with us—" Giuliani was saying.

"All right. All right!" Emilio cried, too tired to argue. Which was, Brother Edward thought with narrowed eyes, undoubtedly the desired effect of the day's activities. "But on my terms, dammit."

"Which are?"

"A fully integrated sound-analysis system linked to processing. With voice control." Edward glanced into the mirror and saw Giuliani nod. "A private office," Emilio continued. "I can't use a keyboard anymore and I can't work when people can overhear me."

"And what else?" Giuliani prompted.

"Dump all the Rakhati song fragments to my system—everything the radio telescopes have intercepted since 2019, yes? Download everything the *Stella Maris* party radioed back from Rakhat." Again, agreement. "An assistant. A native speaker of Déné or Magyar. Or Euskara—Basque, yes? And fluent in Latin or English or Spanish. I don't care which."

"And what else?"

"I want to live by myself. Put a bed in the potting shed. Or the garage. I don't care. I'm not asking for the outside, Vince. Just someplace where I can be alone. No kids, no babies."

"And what else?"

"Publication. All of it—everything we sent back."

"Not the languages," Giuliani said. "The sociology, the biology, yes. The languages, no."

"Well, then, what is the point?" Emilio cried. "Why the hell am I doing the work?"

The Father General did not look at him. Scanning the Campano archipelago, he watched Camorra "fishing" boats patrol the Bay of Naples, grateful for their protection against media predators who'd do almost anything to question the small, thin man slumped beside him: the priest and whore and child killer, Emilio Sandoz.

"You are doing the work *ad majorem Dei gloriam*, as far as I am concerned," Giuliani said lightly. "If the greater glory of God no longer motivates you, you may consider that you are working out your room and board, provided gratis by the Society of Jesus, along with round-the-clock security, sound-analysis systems and research assistance. The engineering that went into those braces was not cheap, Emilio. We've paid out over a million six in hospital bills and medical fees alone. That's money we don't have anymore—the Society is all but bankrupt. I have tried to protect you from these concerns, but things have changed for the worse since you left."

"So why didn't you just kick my expensive ass out in the first place? I told you from the start, I'm a dead loss, Vince—"

"Nonsense," Giuliani snapped, eyes meeting Edward Behr's briefly in the rearview mirror. "You are an asset I intend to capitalize on."

"Oh, wonderful. And what are you buying with me?"

"Passage to Rakhat on a commercial vessel for four priests trained in K'San and Ruanja using the Sandoz-Mendes programs, which are the exclusive property of the Society of Jesus." Vincenzo Giuliani looked at Sandoz, whose own eyes were closed now against the light. "You are free to leave at any time, Emilio. But while you reside with us, at our expense, under our protection—"

"The Society has a monopoly on two Rakhati languages. You want me to train interpreters."

"Whom we will provide to business, academic or diplomatic interests until that monopoly is broken. This will help to recoup our expenses in underwriting the original mission to Rakhat and will allow us to continue the work begun there by your party, *requiescant in pace*. Pull over, please, Brother Edward."

Edward Behr stopped the car and reached toward the glove box for the injection canister, checking the dosage indicator before climbing out of the vehicle. By then Giuliani was kneeling next to Sandoz at the edge of the pavement, steadying Emilio as he vomited into the scrubby roadside weeds. Edward pressed the canister against Sandoz's neck. "Just a few minutes now, Father."

They were within sight of a pair of armed Camorristi. One of them approached, but the Father General shook his head and the man returned to his post. There was another bout of retching before Emilio sat back on his heels, disheveled and drained, eyes closed because the migraines distorted his vision. "What was her name, Vince?"

"Celestina."

"I won't go back." He was almost asleep. The drug always knocked him out when administered by injection. No one knew why; his physiological status was still not normal. "God," he mumbled, "don' do this to me again. Kids and babies. Don' do this to me again . . ."

Brother Edward's eyes met the Father General's. "That was prayer," he said firmly a few minutes later.

"Yes," Vincenzo Giuliani agreed. He beckoned now to the Camorristi and stood back as one of them gathered up the limbs and lifted the light, limp body, carrying Sandoz back to the car. "Yes," he admitted, "I'm afraid it was."

BROTHER EDWARD CALLED AHEAD TO APPRISE THE PORTER OF THE SITuation. There was a stretcher waiting for them when he pulled into the circular drive and parked at the front door of a large, sensible stone building, saved from austerity by the exuberant gardens that surrounded it.

"It's too soon," Brother Edward warned, as he and the Father General watched Emilio being carried up to bed. "He isn't ready for this. You're pushing him too hard."

"I push, he shoves back." Giuliani raised his hands to his head, smoothing back hair that hadn't been there in decades. "I'm running out of time, Ed. I'll hold them off as long as I can, but I want our people on that ship." His hands dropped and he looked at the hills to the west. "We can't afford another mission any other way."

Lips compressed, Edward shook his head, his lungs whistling slightly. The asthma was always worst in late summer. "It's a bad bargain, Father General."

For a time, Giuliani seemed to forget he was not alone. Then he straightened, outwardly calm, and regarded the fat, little man wheezing next to him in the dappled shade of an ancient olive tree. "Thank you, Brother Edward," the Father General said with parched precision, "for your opinion."

Edward Behr, put in his place, watched Giuliani stride away before getting back into the car to pull the vehicle into the garage. He plugged it in and locked up out of habit, although anyone who got past Camorra security would be interested in Emilio Sandoz, not in a car so outdated it needed recharging every night.

One of the cats appeared, purring and stretching, as Edward stood in the driveway staring up at a bedroom window where a curtain had just been drawn shut. Edward admired the beauty of cats, but had learned to think of them as lithe and lethal dander-delivery systems. "Go away," he told the animal, but the cat continued to rub against Edward's legs, as heedless of his concerns as the Father General seemed to be.

MINUTES LATER, VINCENZO GIULIANI ENTERED HIS OFFICE, AND though he pulled the door closed with a quiet, controlled click, he did not so much sit in his chair as collapse onto it. Elbows on the vast walnut desk's faultless, gleaming surface, he rested his head in his hands and kept his eyes closed, unwilling to look into his own reflection. Trade with Rakhat is inevitable, he told himself. Carlo is going, whether we help him or not. This way, we may be able to provide some sort of mitigating influence—

He lifted his head and reached for his computer tablet. Flipping it open with a snap of his wrist, he reread the letter he'd been trying to finish for the past three days. "Your Holiness," it began, but the Father General was not writing for the Pope alone. This letter would become part of the history of mankind's first contact with an intelligent alien species.

"Thank you," he had written, "for your kind inquiry regarding the health and status of Emilio Sandoz. During the year since returning to Earth from Rakhat in September 2059, Father Sandoz has recovered from scurvy and anemia, but remains frail and emotionally volatile. As you know from media reports leaked last year by personnel at the Salvator Mundi Hospital in Rome, the muscles between the bones of his palms were stripped away on Rakhat, doubling the length of his fingers and rendering them useless. Sandoz himself does not fully understand why he was deliberately maimed; it was not intended as torture, although that is certainly what it has amounted to. He believes that the procedure marked him as the dependent or, perhaps, the property of a man named Supaari VaGayjur, about whom more later. Father Sandoz has been fitted with external bioactive braces; he has worked very hard to achieve limited dexterity, and can now manage most self-care."

It's time to wean him from Ed Behr, the Father General decided, and made a mental note about reassigning Brother Edward. Perhaps to that new refugee camp in Gambia, he thought. May as well put Ed's experience in dealing with the aftermath of gang rape to work. . . . He sat up straighter and, shaking off distraction, returned to the letter.

"In the view of his mission superiors," it continued, "Emilio Sandoz was responsible for much of the early success of first contact. His extraordinary skill and stamina as an interpreter aided all the other members of the *Stella Maris* party in their research, and his personal charm won them many friends among the VaRakhati. Moreover, the evident beauty of his spiritual state during the early years of the mission restored the faith of at least one lay member of the crew, and enriched that of his brother priests.

"Nevertheless, Father Sandoz has been the object of virulent public condemnation for his alleged conduct on Rakhat. As you know, our ship was followed into space three years later by the *Magellan*, a vessel owned and operated by the Contact Consortium, whose interests were primarily commercial. Scandal sells; sensationalizing allegations against our people (and against Father Sandoz in particular) was to the Consortium's economic advantage, since their lurid reports were radioed back from Rakhat for sale to a worldwide audience on Earth. In fairness, the crew of the *Magellan* was utterly unfamiliar with Rakhat when they arrived, and there is reason to believe that they were misled by Supaari VaGayjur about many facts. The subsequent unexplained disappearance of the *Magellan* party suggests that they, too, fell prey to the near impossibility of avoiding fatal mistakes on Rakhat.

"Thus, of the eighteen people who traveled to Rakhat in two separate parties, only Emilio Sandoz has survived. Father Sandoz has cooperated with us to the best of his ability during months of intense questioning, often at the cost of great personal distress. I will provide Your Holiness with a complete set of the mission's scientific papers and supporting documents, as well as verbatim transcripts of the hearings; here, for your consideration, is a brief outline of salient points uncovered during the hearings just concluded.

"1. There are not one but two intelligent species on Rakhat.

"The *Stella Maris* party was initially welcomed as a 'foreign' trade delegation by the village of Kashan. The villagers identified themselves as Runa, which simply means 'People.' The Runa are large, vegetarian bipeds with stabilizing tails—rather like kangaroos; they have high mobile ears and remarkably beautiful double-irised eyes. Placid in disposition, they are intensely sociable and communitarian.

"Their hands are double-thumbed and their craftsmanship is superb, but some members of the Jesuit party suspected that the Runa in general were somewhat limited intellectually. Their material culture seemed too simple to account for the powerful transmissions first detected on Earth by radio telescope in 2019. Furthermore, the Runa were disturbed and frightened by music, which seemed anomalous, given that it was radio broadcasts of chorales that first alerted us to the existence of Rakhat. However, individual Runa seemed quite bright, and the tentative conclusion was that the village of Kashan was something of a backwater on the edge of a sophisticated civilization. Since there was so much to be learned in Kashan, the decision was made to remain there for a time.

"To the great surprise of our people, the Singers of Rakhat were in fact a second sentient species. The Jana'ata bear a striking but superficial physical resemblance to the Runa. They are carnivorous, with prehensile feet and three-fingered hands that are clawed and rather bearlike. For the first two years of the mission, the Jana'ata were represented by a single individual: Supaari VaGayjur, a merchant based in the city of Gayjur who acted as a middleman for a number of isolated Runa villages in southern Inbrokar, a state that occupies the central third of the largest continent of Rakhat.

"The Jesuit party had every reason to believe Supaari was a man of goodwill. If anything, their relationship with the Runa villagers was improved by Supaari's intervention and aid, and Sandoz attributes much of his own understanding of Rakhat's civilization to Supaari's patient explanations. Supaari's gross betrayal of Sandoz's trust remains one of the great puzzles of the mission.

"2. Humans make tools; the Jana'ata breed theirs.

"The Runa are the hands of the Jana'ata: the skilled trades, the domestic staffs and laborers, even the civil service. But the differences in status between the Jana'ata and Runa are not merely those of class, as our people believed. The Runa are essentially domesticated animals—the Jana'ata breed them, as we breed dogs.

"The Runa do not reproduce unless their diet reaches a critical level of richness that brings on a sort of estrus. This biological fact has become the basis of the Rakhati economy. The Runa 'earn' the right to have children by cooperating economically with the Jana'ata. When a village corporate account has reached a target figure, the Jana'ata make a sufficiency of extra calories available to the villagers to allow for a controlled production of young, without risk of environmental degradation by overpopulation.

"The core values of Jana'ata society are stewardship and stability, and in keeping with this, the Jana'ata also limit their own reproduction, maintaining their numbers at approximately 4 percent of the overall Runa population. Strict lines of inheritance rule a largely ceremonial life, and only the first two children of any breeding Jana'ata couple may themselves marry and reproduce. If later-born adults decline to be neutered, they are permitted to have sex with Runa concubines, since cross-species sex carries no risk of unsanctioned reproduction. Jana'ata thirds are most commonly involved in commerce, scholarship and, evidently, prostitution. In this context, it should be noted that Supaari VaGayjur was a third.

"Moreover, and most shockingly, the Jana'ata have bred the Runa not just for intelligence and trainability, but also for meat. We have paid in lives for this knowledge, Your Holiness."

It was there that Giuliani had stopped the night before, listening for a time to the sound of Sandoz's footsteps above him. Five steps, pause; five steps, pause. At least when Emilio was pacing, one could be certain that he had not yet added his own life to the toll taken by the mission to Rakhat. . . . Sighing, Giuliani now returned to his task.

"3. The Jana'ata do not keep the Runa in stockyards.

"When Runa adults have raised their own children to the age of reproduction, the parents voluntarily give themselves up to Jana'ata patrols, who periodically round up such older adults and any substandard infants, all of whom are then butchered.

"Your Holiness must understand that our people were completely unaware of the facts underlying the relationship of the Jana'ata and the Runa when they witnessed the arrival of a culling patrol that began killing VaKashani infants. The situation was complex, and I urge you to read the transcripts of Sandoz's testimony, but the *Stella Maris* party perceived this incident as an unprovoked attack on the VaKashani Runa. Led by Sofia Mendes, our people resisted, several of them dying in defense of innocent children. It was this act of selfless bravery that Supaari VaGayjur characterized as incitement to rebellion among the Runa, and that the Contact Consortium later publicized as reckless and culpable interference in Rakhati affairs. It must be admitted, however, that many Runa—inspired by the courage of Sofia Mendes to protect their own children—died as a result of their defiance."

The Father General sat back in his chair. And now, he thought, the worst of it.

"After the massacre at Kashan," Giuliani began again, "there were only two survivors from the *Stella Maris* party. Emilio Sandoz and Father Marc Robichaux were taken prisoner by the Jana'ata patrol and force-marched for weeks, during which time they both witnessed the deaths of many Runa. They were offered food each morning, and Sandoz did not realize for some time that he was eating the meat of Runa infants; when understanding dawned, he was starving, and continued to eat the meat. This is a source of continuing shame and distress to him.

"When Supaari VaGayjur learned of their arrest, he tracked the two priests down and evidently bribed the patrol's commander, thus obtaining custody of them. Once in Supaari's compound, Sandoz was asked if he and Robichaux were willing to 'accept *hasta'akala*.' Sandoz believed they were being offered hospitality and agreed. To his horror, his hands and those of Father Robichaux were promptly destroyed; Robichaux bled to death as a result. Approximately eight months later, Supaari VaGayjur sold Sandoz to a Jana'ata aristocrat named Hlavin Kitheri. I hope that Your Holiness cannot imagine the brutality of the treatment to which Sandoz was subject while in Kitheri's possession."

Shuddering, the Father General stood abruptly and turned away from what he had written. "What is a whore, but someone whose body is ruined for the pleasure of others?" Emilio had asked him once. "I am God's whore, and ruined." For a time, Giuliani moved sightlessly through his office—five steps, turn; five steps, turn—until he became aware that he had unknowingly matched the pacing he heard so many nights in the bedroom above his. Finish it, he told himself, and sat once more to write.

"Months later, when the *Magellan* arrived in orbit around Rakhat, members of the Contact Consortium boarded the derelict *Stella Maris* and accessed records of the first two years of our mission. The entire Jesuit party was missing and presumed dead. The *Magellan* party made landfall near the village of Kashan, and were greeted with hostility and fear, in stark contrast to the welcome the *Stella Maris* party had received. A young Runa female named Askama told them in English that Emilio Sandoz was still alive and residing with Supaari VaGayjur in the city of Gayjur. Hoping for guidance from Sandoz, the *Magellan* party was taken to that city by Askama, who was clearly devoted to Sandoz.

"When they arrived in Gayjur, Supaari admitted to the *Magellan* party that Sandoz had been a member of his household until recently. Sandoz was now living elsewhere at his own request, Supaari told them. Supaari also gave them to believe that many lives had been lost because of the foreigners' interference in local matters. Despite this, Supaari was helpful to the *Magellan* party and quite happy to do business with them, although he remained evasive on the subject of Sandoz's whereabouts.

"Several weeks later, Askama had located Sandoz herself, and took the ranking members of the *Magellan* party to him. He was found in Hlavin Kitheri's seraglio, naked except for a jeweled collar and perfumed ribbons, the bloody effects of sodomy visible. By his own admission, Sandoz had by that time reached a state of murderous desperation. Hoping to prove himself so dangerous that he would either be left alone or executed, he had that day made Jephthah's vow: that he would kill the next person he saw. He could not have anticipated that it would be Askama, a Runa child whom he had all but raised, and whom he loved deeply.

"When Sandoz looked up from Askama's corpse and saw the Consortium officials, he laughed. I think it was his laughter that convinced them of his depravity, and of course they had Supaari VaGayjur's later assurances that Sandoz had prostituted himself at his own request. I now believe that his laughter was evidence of hysteria and despair, but they had just witnessed a murder, and under the circumstances, the *Magellan* party was inclined to believe the worst."

As was I, Vincenzo Giuliani thought, standing once more and walking away from his desk.

It was absurd in hindsight—the very idea that a handful of humans might have been able to do everything right the first time. Even the closest of friends can misunderstand one another, he reminded himself. First contact—by definition—takes place in a state of radical ignorance, where nothing is known about the ecology, biology, languages, culture and economy of the Other. On Rakhat, that ignorance proved catastrophic.

You couldn't have known, Vincenzo Giuliani thought, hearing his own pacing, but remembering Emilio's. It wasn't your fault.

Tell that to the dead, Emilio would have answered.

2

Trucha Sai, Rakhat

2042, Earth-Relative

SOFIA MENDES HAD KNOWN FROM THE VERY START THAT THE MEMBERS of the Jesuit mission to Rakhat would be an endangered species on that planet.

The *Stella Maris* had begun with a crew of eight. Alan Pace died within weeks of landfall, and then they were seven. D. W. Yarbrough, the Jesuit superior, became ill a few months later and never recovered, although he survived an additional eighteen months, in declining health. Understandably, having no research facilities and no colleagues, the physician Anne Edwards was never able to understand either illness, although her care undoubtedly prolonged D.W.'s life. Later, Anne herself was killed, along with D.W., and their deaths were a staggering blow to the tiny band they left behind.

In the face of misfortune, the Jesuit party had rallied repeatedly. When a simple miscalculation in the aftermath of a serious accident resulted in the crew being marooned on Rakhat, they had adapted, establishing a garden to supply themselves with food, becoming part of the local economy by providing exotic trade goods. They were accepted by the villagers of Kashan, even to the point of being called by kinship terms by many families. And there were times of great joy, most notably Sofia's own wedding to Jimmy Quinn, and the announcement that they were awaiting a birth—just before it all went wrong.

Like so many Jewish children, Sofia Mendes had grown up with night-mare images of Egyptian slavemasters, of Babylonians and Assyrians and Romans, of Cossacks and inquisitors, and the SS coming to kill; she had vanquished a child's intense, impotent fear by imagining herself fighting back, repulsing would-be conquerors. So when the Jana'ata patrol had arrived at Kashan and burned the foreign garden and demanded that the VaKashani Runa bring their babies forward and then, systematically, began to kill the children, Sofia Mendes had acted without hesitation. "We are many. They are few," she called out to the VaKashani and lifted a Runa infant to breasts swollen with her own pregnancy.

"We," she said, and cast her fate with the Runa—with the untermen-schen of Rakhat.

Her gesture, briefly, turned the tide; her own fall, under the blud-geoning sweep of a Jana'ata arm, stiffened the resistance. Then, believ-ing that they could not win, Runa fathers fell over children to shield them with their bodies; Runa mothers sacrificed themselves to Jana'ata fury, absorbing the violence to save the rest. When it was over, there were scores of carcasses, heaped and bloody, most of which were quickly butchered.

When the patrol left, terror and the unprecedented exhilaration of mo-mentary triumph made consensus impossible. The village of Kashan had fissioned, in violation of the most basic Runa strategies for survival: stay together; circle to protect the greatest number; act in concert. Close to panic, individuals searched for anyone who shared some identifiable emo-tion, forming small, less vulnerable clusters as quickly as possible. Those whose families had been killed added sinuous scented ribbons to their arms and necks, too stunned to react. Most did little more than hope life would return to normal, now that all the foreigners except Sofia were gone and most of the illegal babies dead. Their impulse was to hand Sofia over to the Jana'ata government as proof that Kashan was once again within the law. "Spend one, buy many," they cried.

"But Fia didn't harm us! The *djanada* did this!" a girl named Djalao countered. Barely grown, she had no authority, but in the confusion, there were those so hungry for direction that they listened. "Warn as many other villages as possible. Tell them what happened in Kashan," Djalao told the runners in the aftermath of the massacre. "The *djanada* patrols are coming, but tell the people what Fia said: We are many. They are few."

Kanchay VaKashan was as confused as anyone, but it was his daughter Puska whom Sofia had saved, and he was grateful. So when a handful of men with surviving infants decided to wait until redlight and flee to the safety of the southern forest, he took Sofia as well.

Of their journey to sanctuary, Sofia herself remembered only the occasional thin keening of Runa infants; the swaying, fluid stride of Kanchay, who carried her on his back for days; the sounds of savannah changing to forest. At first, her face hurt so much she could not open her mouth, so Kanchay reduced food to a paste for her and mixed it with rainwater, drizzling this gruel through her clenched teeth. She took as much nourishment as she could that way. The child, she thought. The child needs it. Bled white, stupid with pain, she concentrated on her own baby, who was not yet lost to her like all the other people she had dared to love. She focused her life's blood on her center, where the child still lived, and felt each vague fetal movement as fear, each strong kick as hope.

She slept heavily in the beginning and even later dozed a great deal, warmed by three suns' light filtering through the forest canopy. When awake, she lay still, listening to the rhythmic, rasping slide of long, tough leaves the shape of samurai swords—bent and woven, bent and woven— as the Runa settled into a clearing made efficiently beautiful with sleeping platforms and windscreens. Nearby she heard the splash of creek water tumbling over smooth stones. Above, the booming groans of *w'ralia* trunks bending in the breeze. Everywhere, the soft, swooping vowels of Ruanja, the constant hum of Runa fathers loving babies who had not been meant to live.

When she was stronger, she asked where she was. "Trucha Sai," she was told. Forget Us. "The Runa come to Trucha Sai when the *djanada* smell too much blood," Kanchay explained, speaking simply as though to a child. "After a while, they forget. We-and-you-also will wait in the forest until then."

It was more than an explanation, she understood. Kanchay had chosen his words with intent. "There are two forms of first person plural," Emilio Sandoz had once told the other members of the *Stella Maris* party. "One is exclusive of the person addressed, yes? It means we-but-not-you. The other is we-and-you-also. If a Runao uses the inclusive we, you may be sure it is significant and you may rejoice in a friendship."

From all over the southern provinces of Inbrokar, Runa refugees joined the VaKashani in Trucha Sai. Each man carried a baby, each baby born to a Runa couple whose diets had been supplemented with plentiful food grown in gardens like that of the foreigners—couples who had come into season without Jana'ata supervision, who had mated without Jana'ata permission, who had circumvented Jana'ata stewardship with unthinking cheer, unintentional defiance. The Trucha Sai settlement slowly filled with men whose backs were raked with long, tripled, half-healed scars, gaily pink and waxy, that sliced through dense, buff-colored coats.

"*Sipaj*, Kanchay. It must have hurt you to carry this one here," Sofia had said one day, looking at those scars and remembering the journey to the forest. "Someone thanks you."

The Runao's ears dropped abruptly. "*Sipaj*, Fia! Someone's child lives because of you."

That's something, she'd thought bleakly, lying back again and listening to the forest symphony of calls and shrieks and rustling leaves dripping with misty rain. The Talmud taught that to save a single life is to save the whole world, in time. Maybe, she thought. Who knows?

NOW, A MONTH AFTER THE MASSACRE THAT HAD KILLED HALF THE RUNA village of Kashan, Sofia Mendes believed herself the last of her kind on Rakhat, the sole survivor of the Jesuit mission. Mistaking bloodless lethargy for calm, she believed as well that she felt no grief. With practice, she told herself, she had come to accept that tears were no remedy for death.

Her life had been blessedly unburdened by happiness. When some period of fleeting contentment ended, Sofia Mendes did not register it as outrageous, but merely noted a return to life's normal condition. So, as the first weeks after the massacre passed, she simply counted herself lucky to be among others who did not weep and wail for the dead.

"Rain falls on everyone; lightning strikes some," her friend Kanchay observed. "What cannot be changed is best forgotten," he advised, not with callousness, but with a certain quality of practical resignation that Sofia shared with the Runa villagers of Rakhat. "God made the world and He saw that it was good," Sofia's father had always told her when she complained of some injustice during her brief childhood. "Not fair. Not happy. Not perfect, Sofia. Good."

Good for whom? she had often wondered, first with juvenile petulance and later with the weariness of a woman of fourteen, working the streets of Istanbul in the midst of an incomprehensible civil war.

She had almost never cried. Child to woman, Sofia Mendes had never gotten anything by crying except a headache. From the time she was able to talk, her parents dismissed tears as the cowardly tactic of the weak-minded and schooled her in the Sephardic tradition of clear argument; she got her way not by sniveling, but by defending her position as logically and persuasively as she could, within the limits of her neurological development. When, barely pubescent and already hardened by the realities of urban combat, she had stood over her mother's mortar-mangled corpse, she was too shocked to cry. Neither did she cry for the father who simply failed to come home one day or ever again: there was no particular time to pass from anxiety to mourning. Nor did she sympathize with the other destitute young whores when they cried. She held herself together and did not spoil her looks with a puffy, blotched face, so she ate more regularly than the others and was strong enough to jam a knife between ribs if a client tried to cheat or kill her. She sold her body, and when the opportunity eventually presented itself, she sold her mind—for a much better price. She survived, and got out of Istanbul alive with her dignity intact, because she would not yield to emotion.

She might not have mourned at all, had it not been for a nightmare in her seventh month of pregnancy, when she dreamed that her baby had been born with blood pouring from its eyes. Waking horrified to the solid heaviness within her, she wept first with relief, realizing that she was still pregnant and a baby's eyes could not bleed that way. But the dike had crumbled, and she was at long last engulfed by an oceanic sadness. Drowning in a sea of loss, she wrapped her arms around her taut, round belly, and wept and wept, with no words, no logic, no intelligence to shield her, and understood that it was this—this terror, this pain—that she had fled from all her life, and with good reason.

As unfamiliar as she was with tears, it was a terrible thing to cry now, and feel only one side of her face wet—and with that realization, grief became hysteria. Alarmed by her sobbing, Kanchay asked anxiously, "*Sipaj*, Fia, have you dreamt of the ones who are gone?" But she could not answer or even lift her chin in assent, so Kanchay and his cousin Tinbar swayed and held her, and looked to the sky for the storm that would surely come now that someone had made a *fierno*. Others came to her as well, asking after her dead and donating ribbons for her arms, as she cried.

In the end, her own exhaustion saved her when no one else could. Never again, she vowed as she fell asleep, emptied of emotion at last. I will never let this happen to me again. Love is a debt, she thought. When the bill comes, you pay in grief.

The baby kicked, as if in protest.

SHE WOKE IN KANCHAY'S EMBRACE WITH TINBAR'S TAIL CURLED OVER her legs. Sweating, her face asymmetrically swollen, she disentangled herself from the others and rose awkwardly, lumbering big-bellied toward the creek with a dark *chaninchay*, newly made from the broad, shallow shell of a forest *pigar*. She stood for a few moments, then lowered herself carefully, reaching out into the stream to fill the bowl. Kneeling, she dipped her hands over and over into the cool pure water, sluicing it over her face. Then, filling the bowl once more, she waited for the black water to still before using it as a mirror.

I am not Runa! she thought, amazed.

This strange loss of self-image had happened to her before; several months into her first overseas AI contract in Kyoto, she was startled each morning to look into a bathroom mirror and discover that she was not Japanese like everyone around her. Now, here, her own human face seemed naked; her dark, snarled hair bizarre; her ears small and inadequate; her single-irised eye too simple and frighteningly direct. Only after she had come to grips with all this did the rest sink in: the slanting, three-tracked scar that sliced from forehead to jaw. The blind, cratered . . . place.

"Someone's head hurts," she told Kanchay, who had followed her to the creek and sat down beside her.

"Like Meelo," said Kanchay, who had witnessed Emilio Sandoz's migraines and considered headache a normal foreign response to grief. He settled back onto a thick-muscled, tapering tail and made a tripod with his upraised legs. "*Sipaj*, Fia, come and sit," he suggested, and she held out her hand so he could steady her as she moved to him.

He began to tidy her hair, combing through it section by section with his fingers, untangling knots with a Runao's sensitive touch. She gave herself up to this, and listened to the forest grow quiet in the midday heat. Occupying her own hands as little Askama always had while sitting in Emilio's lap, Sofia picked up the ends of three ribbons tied around her arm and began to plait them. Askama had often braided ribbons into Anne Edwards's hair and Sofia's, but none of the foreigners had ever been offered body ribbons to wear. "Probably because we wear clothes," Anne had thought, but it was just a guess.

"*Sipaj*, Kanchay, someone wonders about the ribbons," Sofia said, looking up at him, turning her head to see from her left side. She was a little shortsighted in that eye. A pity, she thought, that the Jana'ata who'd half-blinded her hadn't been right-handed—he'd have taken the bad eye instead.

"We gave you this one for Dee, and this is for Ha'an," Kanchay told her, lifting the ribbons, one by one, his breath perfumed with the heathery scent of the *njotao* greens that formed the bulk of their diet this week. "These, for Djordj and for Djimi. These, for Meelo and Marc."

Her throat closed as she listened to the names, but she was done with crying. It came back to her then that Askama had tried to tie two ribbons on Emilio after D.W. and Anne were killed, but he had been so sick. "Not for beauty, then," Sofia asked, "but to remember the ones who are gone?"

Kanchay chuffed, the breathy laughter kindly. "Not to remember! To fool them! If ghosts come back, they'll follow the scent, back into the air where they belong. *Sipaj*, Fia, if you dream of those ones again, you should tell someone," he warned her, for Kanchay VaKashan was a prudent man. Then he added, "Sometimes ribbons are just pretty. The *djanada* think they're only decoration. Sometimes that's true." He laughed again and confided, "The *djanada* are like ghosts. They can be fooled."

Anne would have followed up with questions about why ghosts come back, and when and how; Emilio and the other priests would have been delighted by the ideas of scent and spirit and congress with an unseen world. Sofia picked up the ribbons, running the satiny smoothness through her fingers. Anne's ribbon was silvery white. Like her hair, perhaps? But no—George's hair was also white, and his ribbon was bright red. Emilio's was green, and she wondered why. Her husband Jimmy's was a clear and lucent blue; she thought of his eyes and raised it to her face to breathe in its fragrance. It was like hay, grassy and astringent. Her breath caught, and she put the ribbon down. No, she thought. He's gone. I will not cry again.

"Why, Kanchay?" she demanded then, finding anger preferable to pain. "Why did the *djanada* patrol burn the gardens and kill the babies?"

"Someone thinks the gardens were wrong. The people are meant to walk to their food. It was wrong to bring the food home. The *djanada* know when it's the right time for us to have babies. Someone thinks the people were confused and had the babies at the wrong time."

It was rude to argue, but she was hot and tired, and irritated by the way he talked down to her because she was the size of a Runa eight-year-old. "*Sipaj*, Kanchay—what gives the Jana'ata the right to say who can have babies and when?"

"The law," he said, as though that answered her question. Then, warming to his topic, he told her, "Sometimes the wrong baby can get into a woman. Sometimes the baby should have been a *cranil*, for example. In the old times, the people would take that kind of little one to the river and call out to the *cranils*, Here is one of your children born to us by mistake. We'd hold the baby under the water, where the *cranils* live. It was hard." He was silent for a long time, concentrating on a knot in her hair, gently teasing it apart, strand by strand. "Now when the wrong child comes to us by mistake, the *djanada* do the hard things. And when the *djanada* say, This is a good child, then we know all will be well with it. A mother can travel again. A father's heart can be quiet."

"*Sipaj*, Kanchay, what do you tell your children? About giving themselves up to the Jana'ata to be eaten?"

His hands paused in their work and he gently brought her head to rest against his chest, his voice falling into the soft murmur of lullaby. "We tell them, In the old times, the people were alone in all the world. We traveled anywhere we liked without any danger, but we were lonely. When the *djanada* came, we were glad to see them and asked them, Have you eaten? They said, We're starving! So, we offered them food—you must always feed travelers, you know. But the *djanada* couldn't eat properly and they wouldn't take the food we offered. So the people talked and talked about what to do—it's wicked to let guests go hungry. While we were talking, the *djanada* began to eat the children. Our elders said, They're travelers, they're guests—we have to feed them, but we'll make rules. You must not eat just anyone, we told the *djanada*. You must eat only the old people who are no good anymore. That's how we tamed the *djanada*. Now all the good children are safe and only old, tired, sick people are taken away."

Sofia twisted around to look up at him. "Someone thinks: this is a pretty story for children, so they will sleep well and not make *fiernos* when the cullers come." He lifted his chin and began again to comb out her hair. "*Sipaj*, Kanchay, someone is small, but not a child who must be shielded from truth. The *djanada* kill the very old and the sick and the imperfect. Do they also kill the ones who make trouble?" she demanded. "*Sipaj*, Kanchay, why do you let them? What gives them the right?"

His hands stilled momentarily as he said with prosaic acceptance, "If we refuse to go with the cullers when it's time, others must take our places." Before she could reply, he reached down to stroke her belly as he would have his own wife's. "*Sipaj*, Fia, surely this baby is ripe by now!"

The subject was officially changed. "No," she said, "not yet. Perhaps sixty nights more."

"So long! Someone thinks you will pop like a *datinsa* pod."

"*Sipaj*, Kanchay," she said, with a nervous laugh, "maybe so."

Fear and hope, fear and hope, fear and hope, circling endlessly. Why am I so afraid? I am Mendes, she thought. Nothing is beyond me.

But she had also been—however briefly—joyously Quinn: happy for a single summer of nights and days, the unlikely wife of an absurdly tall and comically homely and wondrously loving Irish Catholic astronomer. And now, Jimmy was dead, killed by the *djanada*—

Feeling Kanchay's fingers working through her hair once more, she leaned back against him and looked across the clearing to the others of his kind: talking, cooking, laughing, tending babies. It could be worse, she thought then, remembering Jimmy's habitual good-natured response to crisis, and gasping at his baby's kick. I am Sofia Mendes Quinn, and things could be worse.

Naples

September 2060

SOMETIMES IF HE KEPT STILL, PEOPLE WOULD GO AWAY.

A lay chauffeur had lived here once. The room over the garage was only a few hundred meters from the retreat house, but that was distance enough most of the time, and Emilio Sandoz claimed it for his own with a fierce possessiveness that surprised him. He had added very little to the apartment—photonics, sound equipment, a desk—but it was his. Exposed rafters and plain white walls. Two chairs, a table, a narrow bed; a little kitchen; a shower stall and toilet behind a folding screen.

He accepted that there were things he could not control. The nightmares. The devastating spells of neuralgia, the damaged nerves of his hands sending strobelike bolts of pain up his arms. He'd stopped fighting the crying jags that came without warning; Ed Behr was right, it only made the headaches worse. Here, alone, he could try to roll with the punches—absorb the blows as they came, rest when things eased up. If everyone would just leave him alone—let him handle things at his own pace on his own terms—he'd be all right.

Eyes closed, hunched and rocking over his hands, he waited, straining to hear footsteps retreat from his door. The knocking came again. "Emilio!" It was the Father General's voice and there was a smile in it. "We have an unexpected visitor. Someone has come to meet you."

"Oh, Christ," Sandoz whispered, getting to his feet and tucking his hands under his armpits. He went down the creaking stairs to the side door below and stopped to gather himself, pulling in a ragged breath and letting it out slowly. With a short, sharp movement of his elbow, he flipped the hook out of its eye on the door frame. Waited, doubled over and silent. "All right," he said finally. "It's open."

There was a tall priest standing in the driveway with Giuliani. East African, Sandoz thought, barely glancing at him, his flat-eyed stare resting instead on the Father General's face. "It's not a good time, Vince."

"No," Giuliani said quietly, "evidently not." Emilio was leaning against the wall, holding himself badly, but what could one do? If Lopore had called ahead. . . . "I'm sorry, Emilio. A few minutes of your time. Allow me to—"

"You speak Swahili?" Sandoz asked the visitor abruptly, in a Sudanese-accented Arabic that came back to him out of nowhere. The question seemed to surprise the African, but he nodded. "What else?" Sandoz demanded. "Latin? English?"

"Both of those. A few others," the man said.

"Fine. Good enough. He'll do," Sandoz said to Giuliani. "You'll have to work by yourself for a while," he told the African. "Start with the Mendes AI program for Ruanja. Leave the K'San files alone for now. I didn't get very far with the formal analysis. Next time, call before you come." He glanced at Giuliani, who was clearly dismayed by the rudeness. "Explain about my hands, Vince," he muttered apologetically, as he started back up to his room. "It's both of them. I can't think." And it's your own damned fault for dropping in uninvited, he thought. But he was too close to tears to be defiant, and almost too tired to register what he heard next.

"I have been praying for you for fifty years," said Kalingemala Lopore in a voice full of wonder. "God has used you hard, but you have not changed so much that I cannot see who you were."

Sandoz stopped in his climb to the apartment and turned back. He remained hunched, arms crossed against his chest, but now looked closely at the priest standing next to the Father General. Sixtyish—maybe twenty years younger than Giuliani, and just as tall. Ebony and lean, with the strong bones and deep wide eyes that gave East African women beauty into old age and which made this man's face arresting. Fifty years, he thought. This guy would have been what? Ten, eleven?

Emilio glanced at Giuliani to see if he understood what was going on, but the Father General now seemed as much at a loss as Sandoz, and as startled by the visitor's words. "Did I know you?" Emilio asked.

The African seemed lit from within, the extraordinary eyes glowing. "There is no reason for you to remember me and I never knew your name. But you were known to God when you were still in your mother's womb—like Jeremiah, whom God also used cruelly." And he held out both hands.

Emilio hesitated before descending the stairs once more. In a gesture that felt, achingly, both familiar and alien, he placed his own fingers, scarred and impossibly long, into the pale, warm palms of the stranger.

All these years, Lopore was thinking, his own shock so great that he forgot the artificiality of the plurals he had forced himself to master. "I remember the magic tricks," he said, smiling, but then he looked down. "Such beauty and cleverness, destroyed," he said sadly and, bringing the hands to his lips, kissed one and then the other unselfconsciously. It was, Sandoz thought later, an alteration in blood pressure perhaps, some quirk of neuromuscular interaction that ended the bout of hallucinatory neuralgia at last, but the African looked up at that moment, and met Emilio's bewildered eyes. "The hands were the easy part, I think."

Sandoz nodded, mute, and frowning, searched the other man's face for some clue.

"Emilio," Vincenzo Giuliani said, breaking the eerie silence, "perhaps you will invite the Holy Father to come upstairs?"

For a hushed instant, Sandoz stared in blank astonishment and then blurted, "Jesus!" To which the Bishop of Rome replied, with unexpected humor, "No, only the Pope," at which the Father General laughed aloud, explaining dryly, "Father Sandoz has been a little out of touch the past few decades."

Dazed, Emilio nodded again and led the way up the staircase.

TO BE FAIR, THE POPE HAD COME ALONE AND UNANNOUNCED, DRESSED IN the simplest of clericals, having driven himself in an unremarkable Fiat to the Jesuit retreat north of Naples. The first African elected to the papacy since the fifth century and the first proselyte in modern history to hold that office, Kalingemala Lopore was now Gelasius III, entering the second year of a remarkable reign; he had brought to Rome both a convert's deeply felt conviction and a farsighted faith in the Church's universality, which did not confuse enduring truth with ingrained European custom. At dawn, ignoring politics and diplomatic rigidity, Lopore had decided he must meet this Emilio Sandoz, who had known God's other children, who had seen what God had wrought elsewhere. Having made that decision, there was no bureaucratic force in the Vatican capable of stopping him: Gelasius III was a man of formidable self-possession and unapologetic pragmatism. He was the only outsider ever to get past Sandoz's Camorra guards, and he had done so because he was willing to speak directly with the Father General's second cousin, Don Domenico Giuliani, the uncrowned king of southern Italy.

Sandoz's apartment was a mess, Lopore noted happily as he picked a discarded towel off the nearest chair and tossed it onto the unmade bed, and then sat without ceremony.

"I—I'm sorry about all this," Sandoz stammered, but the Pontiff waved his apology off.

"One of the reasons We insisted on having Our own car was the desire to visit people without setting off an explosion of maniacal preparation," Gelasius III remarked. Then he confided with specious formality, "We find We are thoroughly sick of fresh paint and new carpeting." He motioned for Emilio to take the other seat, across the table from him. "Please," he said, dropping the plurals deliberately, "sit with me." But he glanced at Giuliani, standing in the corner near the stairway, unwilling to intrude but loath to leave. Stay, the Holy Father's eyes said, and remember everything.

"My people are Dodoth. Herders, even now," the Pope told Sandoz, his Latin exotic with African place-names and the rhythmic, striding cadences of his childhood. "When the drought came, we went north to our cousins, the Toposa, in southern Sudan. It was a time of war and so, of famine. The Toposa drove us off—they had nothing. We asked, 'Where can we go?' A man on the road told us, 'There is a camp for Gikuyu east of here. They turn no one away.' It was a long journey and, as we walked, my youngest sister died in my mother's arms. You saw us coming. You walked out to my family. You took from my mother her daughter's body, as gently as if the baby were your own. You carried that dead child and found us a place to rest. You brought us water, and then food. While we ate, you dug a grave for my sister. Do you recall now?"

"No. There were so many babies. So many dead." Emilio looked up wearily. "I have dug a lot of graves, Your Holiness."

"There will be no more graves for you to dig," the Pope said, and Vincenzo Giuliani heard the voice of prophesy: ambiguous, elusive, sure. The moment passed and the Pontiff's conversation became ordinary again. "Every day of my life since that one, I have thought of you! What kind of man weeps for a daughter not of his making? The answer to that question led me to Christianity, to the priesthood, and now: here, to you!" He sat back in the chair, amazed that he should meet that unknown priest half a century later. He paused and then continued gently, a priest himself, whose office was to reconcile God and man. "You have wept for other children since those days in the Sudan."

"Hundreds. More. Thousands, I think, died because of me."

"You take a great deal on your shoulders. But there was one child in particular, We are told. Can you speak her name, so that We may remember her in prayer?"

He could, but only barely, almost without sound. "Askama, Your Holiness."

There was silence for a time and then Kalingemala Lopore reached across the small table, lifting Emilio's bowed head with blunt, strong fingers, and smoothing away the tears. Vincenzo Giuliani had always thought of Emilio as dark, but with those powerful brown hands cupping his face, he looked ghostly, and then Giuliani realized that Sandoz had nearly fainted. Emilio hated being touched, loathed unexpected contact. Lopore could not have known this and Giuliani took a step forward, about to explain, when he realized that the Pope was speaking.

Emilio listened, stone-faced, with the quick shallow movement of the chest that sometimes betrayed him. Giuliani could not hear their words, but he saw Sandoz freeze, and pull away, and stand and begin to pace. "I made a cloister of my body and a garden of my soul, Your Holiness. The stones of the cloister wall were my nights, and my days were the mortar," Emilio said in the soft, musical Latin that a young Vince Giuliani had admired and envied when they were in formation together. "Year after year, I built the walls. But in the center I made a garden that I left open to heaven, and I invited God to walk there. And God came to me." Sandoz turned away, trembling. "God filled me, and the rapture of those moments was so pure and so powerful that the cloister walls were leveled. I had no more need for walls, Your Holiness. God was my protection. I could look into the face of the wife I would never have, and love all wives. I could look into the face of the husband I would never be, and love all husbands. I could dance at weddings because I was in love with God, and all the children were mine."

Giuliani, stunned, felt his eyes fill. Yes, he thought. Yes.

But when Emilio turned again and faced Kalingemala Lopore, he was not weeping. He came back to the table and placed his ruined hands on its battered wood, face rigid with rage. "And now the garden is laid waste," he whispered. "The wives and the husbands and the children are all dead. And there is nothing left but ash and bone. Where was our Protector? Where was God, Your Holiness? Where is God now?"

The answer was immediate, certain. "In the ashes. In the bones. In the souls of the dead, and in the children who live because of you—"

"Nothing lives because of me!"

"You're wrong. I live. And there are others."

"I am a blight. I carried death to Rakhat like syphilis, and God laughed while I was raped."

"God wept for you. You have paid a terrible price for His plan, and God wept when He asked it of you—"

Sandoz cried out and backed away, shaking his head. "That is the most terrible lie of all! God does not ask. I gave no consent. The dead gave no consent. God is not innocent."

The blasphemy hung in the room like smoke, but it was joined seconds later by Jeremiah's. "He hath led me and brought me into darkness, and not into light. He hath set me in dark places as those who are dead forever. And when I cry and I entreat," Gelasius III recited, eyes knowing and full of compassion, "He hath shut out my prayer! He hath filled me with bitterness. He hath fed me ashes. He hath caused me disgrace and contempt."

Sandoz stood still and stared at nothing they could see. "I am damned," he said finally, tired to his soul, "and I don't know why."

Kalingemala Lopore sat back in his chair, the long, strong fingers folded loosely in his lap, his faith in hidden meaning, and in God's work in God's time, granitic. "You are beloved of God," he said. "And you will live to see what you have made possible when you return to Rakhat."

Sandoz's head snapped up. "I won't go back."

"And if you are asked to do so by your superior?" Lopore asked, brows up, glancing at Giuliani.

Vincenzo Giuliani, forgotten until now in his corner, found himself looking into Emilio Sandoz's eyes and was, for the first time in some fifty-five years, utterly cowed. He spread his hands and shook his head, beseeching Emilio to believe: I didn't put him up to this.

"*Non serviam*," Sandoz said, turning from Giuliani. "I won't be used again."

"Not even if We ask it?" the Pope pressed.

"No."

"So. Not for the Society. Not for Holy Mother Church. Nevertheless, for yourself and for God, you must go back," Gelasius III told Emilio Sandoz with a terrifying, joyful certainty. "God is waiting for you, in the ruins."

VINCENZO GIULIANI WAS A MAN OF MODERATION AND HABITUAL self-control. All his adult life, he had lived among other such men—intellectual, sophisticated, cosmopolitan. He had read and written of saints and prophets, but this. . . . I am in over my head, he thought, and he wanted to hide, to remove himself from whatever was happening in that room, to flee from the awful grace of God. "Let not the Lord speak to us, lest we die," Giuliani thought, and felt a sudden sympathy for the Israelites at Sinai, for Jeremiah used against his will, for Peter who tried to run from Christ. For Emilio.

And yet, one had to pull oneself together, to murmur brief, graceful explanations and soothing apologies, and to accompany the Holy Father down the stairs and out into the sunshine. Courtesy demanded that one offer His Holiness lunch before the drive back to Rome. Long experience allowed one to show the way to the refectory, chatting about the Naples retreat house and its Tristano architecture. One pointed out the artwork: an excellent Caravaggio here, a rather good Titian there. One was able to smile good-humoredly at Brother Cosimo, stupefied at finding the Supreme Pontiff in his kitchen, inquiring about the availability of a fish soup the Father General had recommended.

There was, in the event, *anguilla in umido* over toast, served with a memorably sulphurous '49 Lacryma Christi. The Father General of the Society of Jesus and the Holy Father of the Roman Catholic Church ate undisturbed at a simple wooden table in the kitchen and sat amicably over cappuccinos, toying with *sfogliatele*, each smiling inwardly at the unmentioned fact that they were both known as the Black Pope: one for his Jesuit soutane and the other for his equatorial skin. Neither did they mention Sandoz. Or Rakhat. They discussed instead the second excavation of Pompeii, about to be undertaken now that Vesuvius seemed satisfied that Naples had learned its latest lesson in geologic humility. They had mutual acquaintances and swapped stories of Vatican politicians and organizational chess matches. And Giuliani gained additional respect for a man who had come to the Holy See from the outside and was now deftly turning that ancient institution toward policies that struck the Father General as hopeful and wise, and very shrewd.

Afterward, they strolled out toward the Pope's Fiat, their long shadows rippling over uneven stone pavement. Settling into his vehicle, Kalingemala Lopore reached toward the starter, but the dark hand hovered and then dropped. He lowered the window and sat looking straight ahead for a few moments before he spoke. "It seems a pity," he said quietly, "that there has been a breach between the Vatican and a religious order with such a long and distinguished history of service to Our predecessors."

Giuliani became very still. "Yes, Your Holiness," he said evenly, heart hammering. It was for this, among other reasons, that he had sent Gelasius III transcripts of the Rakhat mission reports and his own rendering of Sandoz's story. For over five hundred years, allegiance to the papacy had been the pole around which the Jesuits' global service had revolved, but Ignatius of Loyola had aimed for a soldierly dialectic of obedience and initiative when he founded the Society of Jesus. Patience and prayer—and relentless pressure in the direction the Jesuits wished decisions to go— paid off time after time. Even so, from the beginning, the Jesuits had championed education and a social activism that sometimes verged on the revolutionary; clashes with the Vatican were not uncommon, some far more serious than others. "It seemed unavoidable at the time, but of course . . ."

"Things change." Gelasius spoke lightly, reasonably, with humor, one man of the world to another. "Diocesan clergy may now marry. Popes from Uganda are elected! Who but God knows the future?"

Giuliani's brows climbed toward where his hair had once been. "Prophets?" he suggested.

The Pope nodded judiciously, mouth pulled down at the corners. "The occasional stock market analyst, perhaps." Taken by surprise, Giuliani laughed and shook his head, and realized that he liked this man very much. "It is not the future, but the past that separates us," the Pontiff said to the Jesuit General, breaking years of silence about the wedge that had all but split the Church in two.

"Your Holiness, we are more than prepared to concede that overpopulation alone is not the sole cause of poverty and misery," Giuliani began.

"Fatuous oligarchies," Gelasius suggested. "Ethnic paranoia. Whimsical economic systems. An enduring habit of treating women like dogs . . ."

Giuliani took a breath and held it a moment before stating the position of the Society of Jesus, and his own. "There is no condom that prevents pigheadedness, no pill or injection that stops greed or vanity. But there are humane and sensible ways to alleviate some of the conditions that lead to misery."

"We ourselves have experienced the death of a sister, sacrificed on Malthus's altar," Gelasius III pointed out. "Unlike Our learned and saintly predecessors, We are unable to discern evidence of God's most holy will in population control carried out by the forces of war, starvation and disease. These seem to a simple man blind, and brutal."

"And inadequate to the task, for all that. As are human self-control and sexual restraint," Giuliani observed. "The Society merely asks that Holy Mother Church make allowances for human nature, as any loving mother does. Surely, the capacity to think and to plan is a divine gift that can be used responsibly. Surely, there is no evil in the desire that each child who is born be as welcomed and cherished as was Christ the Child."

"There can be no question of tolerating abortion—" Lopore said decisively.

"And yet," Giuliani pointed out, "St. Ignatius advised that 'we must never seek to establish a rule so rigid as to leave no room for exception.' "

"Neither can we abet systems of birth control as inflexible and cruel as the one Sandoz describes on Rakhat," Gelasius continued.

"The middle way is always the most difficult path to follow, Your Holiness."

"And extremism the simplest, but—. *Ecclesia semper reformanda!*" said Gelasius with sudden vigor. "We have studied the Jesuit proposals, and those of our Orthodox Christian brethren. There is good to be achieved! The question is how. . . . It will be a matter, We think, of redefining the domains of natural and artificial birth control. Sahlins—you have read Sahlins? Sahlins wrote that 'nature' is culturally defined, so what is artificial is also culturally defined." The hand moved, the starter hummed and the Pope made ready to leave. But then the dark-eyed gaze returned to Vincenzo Giuliani's face. "To think. To plan. And yet—what extraordinary children come to us unplanned, unwanted, despised! We are told that Emilio Sandoz is a slum-bred bastard."

"Harsh words, Your Holiness." Supplied no doubt by Vatican politicians who had moved smoothly behind the throne of Peter when that spot was vacated by exiled Jesuit antecedents. "But technically correct, I understand." Giuliani thought a moment. "Numbers 11:23 comes to mind. And Sarah's unlikely child, and Elizabeth's. Even Our Lady's! I suppose that if Almighty God wants an extraordinary child born, we may trust Him to arrange it?"

The gleaming brown eyes shone in a still face. "We have enjoyed this conversation. Perhaps you will visit Us in the future?"

"I'm sure my secretary can make the arrangements with your office, Your Holiness."

The Pope inclined his head, lifted his hand in blessing. Just before he blanked the Fiat's one-way windows to outside view and rolled out onto the ancient stone-paved road that led toward the autostrada to Rome, he said again, "Sandoz must go back."

4

Great Southern Forest, Rakhat

2042, Earth-Relative

SOFIA MENDES PULLED HERSELF TOGETHER DURING HER LAST MONTH of pregnancy, forcing the faces of the dead from her mind by concentrating on the unknown child within her. The turning point came several weeks after they arrived in Trucha Sai. "Someone thought: Fia is never without this," Kanchay said, handing a computer tablet to her one morning. "So someone brought it from Kashan."

Running her small hands over its smooth machined edges, feeling the well-known shape and heft, wiping off its photovoltaics, Sofia thanked Kanchay almost soundlessly and went off alone to sit against a downed *w'ralia* trunk, resting the tablet on her belly and drawn-up knees. After all the strangeness and fear, the confusion and sorrow, here was the ordinary, the familiar. Trembling, she called up the connect and gave a shouted gasp of relief when the *Stella Maris* library access appeared, patient and reliable as always.

She lost herself in the system, downloading data as she went. Childbirth, related terms: Childbirth at Home, Childbirth in Middle Age. Natural Childbirth. "My only option," she muttered. Then: "Underwater Childbirth!" she exclaimed aloud. Thoroughly mystified, she took a moment to pull the references up just to see what that could be about. Nonsense, she decided, and went on. Child Development—thousands of citations. She pulled out Infant Development—Normal, and, perhaps su-

perstitiously, bypassed references on Autism, Developmental Disable-
ment, and Failure to Thrive. Child-rearing—Maxims. Possibly useful, she
decided, having no grandmotherly source of advice. Oh, Anne! Oh,
Mama! she thought, but pushed them both away. Child-rearing—
Religious Aspects—Jewish. Yes, she thought, and brought the Torah down
as well. What will I do if it's a boy? she wondered then, and decided she'd
circumcise that problem if and when she came to it.

"There's an angel behind every blade of grass whispering, Grow, darling,
grow!" her mother told her when she was small and afraid of the dark. "Do
you think God would take all that trouble for a blade of grass and not
watch over you?"

Mama, I am a one-eyed pregnant Jewish widow, Sofia thought, and I am
very far from home. If this constitutes being watched over by God, I'd be
better off as a blade of grass. And yet. . . . A daughter, please, she prayed
swiftly. A little girl. A small healthy girl.

But Sofia had never relied on God, who tended to be terse even when
He was clearly on the job. Go to Pharaoh and free My people, He said, and
left the logistics to Moses as a lesson in self-reliance. So she spent the next
weeks reading and absorbing on-line books and articles, creating an AI
obstetrician: synthesizing, laying out sequences, finding branch points, re-
ducing as much as possible to "if (condition) then (action)" statements,
wherever the action was feasible on Rakhat, among the Runa. She refined
her explanations to simple sentences, graphic and plain; entered them in
Ruanja so that she might look up her own or her baby's distress and, without thinking, give instructions that might save them both. And in doing
all this, she lost some of her fear, if not any of her hope.

THE CULLS WENT ON, ACROSS SOUTHERN INBROKAR—ANYWHERE THE
gardens had been planted. Runa fathers in little groups of twos and threes
continued to arrive with infants, bringing news as well. Once women from
Kashan visited, led by the girl named Djalao, who was made much of by
the men who'd heeded her warning that the *djanada* patrols were coming.

Aware now that Djalao VaKashan had saved her life and the lives of
many others, Sofia took the girl aside to thank her during a brief lull in the
murmur of Ruanja that filled the redlit evenings, when fathers gathered to
talk children to sleep, arms over bellies, tails over legs, back against back.
Ears high, Djalao accepted Sofia's gratitude without embarrassment, and it

was this as much as anything that prompted Sofia to take the conversation further.

"*Sipaj*, Djalao, why must the Runa go back to the villages at all? Why not simply walk away from the Jana'ata? Why not show your tails to them and live here!"

Djalao looked around the forest settlement, and it was only then that her ears dropped. Distressed by the sight of Runa living like animals, she told Sofia, "Our homes are back there. We can't leave the villages and the cities. That's where we live and trade. We—" She stopped and shook her head, as though there were a *yuv'at* buzzing in one ear. "*Sipaj*, Fia: we made the cities. To come here—for a time—is acceptable. To walk away from the art of our hands and the places of our hearts is not—"

"Even so, you could stop cooperating with the *djanada*," said Sofia. Startled by the idea, Djalao huffed at her, but Sofia did not give up. "Are they children that you should carry them? *Sipaj*, Djalao: the Jana'ata have no right to breed you, no right to say who has babies, who lives and who dies. They have no right to slaughter you and eat your bodies! Kanchay says it's the law, but it's only the law because you agree to it. Change the law!" Seeing the doubt—the slight, anxious swaying from side to side—Sofia whispered, "Djalao: you don't need the *djanada*. They need you!"

The girl sat still, balanced and upright. "But what would the *djanada* eat?" she asked, ears cocked forward.

"Who cares? Let them eat *piyanot*!" Sofia cried, exasperated. "Rakhat is covered with animals that can be eaten by carnivores." She leaned forward and spoke with conviction and urgency, believing that at long last she had found someone who could see that the Runa need not collude in their own subjugation. "You are more than meat. You have the right to stand up and say, Never again! They have claws and custom on their side. You have numbers and—" Justice, she'd meant to say, but there was no word in Ruanja for justice, or for fairness, or equity. "You have the strength," Sofia said finally, "if you choose to use it. *Sipaj*, Djalao: you can make yourselves free of them."

Despite her youth and her species, Djalao VaKashan seemed not only able but willing to make up her own mind. Even so, when she spoke, her answer was merely, "Someone will consider your words."

It was a polite brush-off. Emilio Sandoz had always interpreted the formula "Someone will consider your words" to mean, "When pigs have wings, I'll tell you about my grandmother sometime."

Sofia sighed, giving up. I tried, she thought. And who knows? Seeds may have been sown.

THE VAKASHANI VISITORS LEFT THE NEXT MORNING, AND LIFE IN Trucha Sai settled back into the routine of caring for babies, gathering food and preparing it, eating—always eating. It was a tranquil life, if not a challenging one, and Sofia blessed each uneventful day that passed, resisting panic as cramps came and went. Low and deep within her, they were not strong enough to be of consequence, she thought, but she held herself still and willed her womb to quiet.

The Runa, who found so little in the world to be amazed by, nonetheless found Sofia's pregnancy remarkable for its duration and its effect on her. Bursting *datinsa* pods were mentioned once too often and, about four weeks before her due date, Sofia, whose back was aching and who was wretchedly uncomfortable in the steamy heat, proceeded at length to make it completely clear to everybody within a ten-square-kilometer area that she didn't want to hear another word about anyone or anything popping open, thank you all very much. This was hardly out of her mouth when a roaring storm, with terrifying winds that bent trees nearly double, broke loose.

The rain came down so hard during the worst of the tempest, she was afraid she'd have to name her child Noah, and she could hardly have been wetter if she'd stood in the ocean. Her water must have broken sometime during the storm; there was no warning when the contractions started in earnest a few hours later. "It's too soon," she cried to Kanchay and Tinbar and Sichu-Lan and a few others who crowded around her when she squatted, waiting for the contraction to let go.

"Maybe it will stop again," Kanchay offered, steadying her when the next wave came. But babies have their own agenda and their own logic, and this one was on its way, ready or not.

She had been through a great deal in her life, so the pain never overwhelmed her, but she was undersized and had not fully recovered from a nearly fatal injury only two months earlier. She paced a good deal of the time early in her labor because it made her more comfortable, but the walking wore her out; by sunrise the next day she was very, very tired and had stopped thinking about the baby. She just wanted to get through this, to be finished with it.

All the fathers had advice and opinions and observations and commentary. Before long, she found herself snarling at them to shut up and leave her alone. They didn't; they were Runa, after all, and saw no reason to shun or abandon her. So they went on talking and kept her company, their long-fingered hands busy and beautiful, reweaving windbreaks and sections of thatch for roofing damaged in the storm.

By midday, exhausted, she gave up trying to control what was going on and fell silent. When Kanchay carried her to a small waterfall near the camp, she did not argue, and sat with him under water that beat coolly down on her shoulders, drowning out the irritating voices of the others with its steady roar. To her own surprise, she relaxed, and this must have helped her dilate.

"*Sipaj*, Fia," Kanchay said after a time, watching her with calm eyes of Chartres blue, "put your hand down here." He guided her fingers to the crowning head and smiled as she felt the baby's wet and curling hair. There were three more crushing contractions and as the child emerged, she was swamped by the terror of a remembered nightmare. "*Sipaj*, Kanchay," she cried, before she knew if she had a daughter or a son. "Are the eyes all right? Do they bleed?"

"The eyes are small," said Kanchay honestly. "But that's normal for your kind," he added by way of reassurance.

"And there are two," his cousin Tinbar reported, thinking this might have worried her.

"They're blue!" their friend Sichu-Lan added, relieved because Fia's strange brown eyes had always been a source of vague unease to him.

There was a silence as she felt the infant's legs slip from her and she thought at first that it was born dead. No, she thought, it's all the other noise—the talking and the waterfall. Then, finally, she heard the baby squall—jolted into breathing by the chilly water that had been such a comfort to its mother at the end of this stiflingly hot and endless day.

Kanchay brought leaves to wipe it down and Sichu-Lan was laughing and pointing to its genitals, which were external. "Look," he cried, "someone thinks this child is in a hurry to be bred!"

A son, she knew then, and whispered, "We have a little boy, Jimmy!"

She burst into tears—not of grief or terror but of relief and gratitude—as strong warm hands lifted her from the cool water and the hot breeze dried her and the baby. With a shock, she felt again skin on human skin, and slept. Later, her son's lips closed for the first time around her nipple: a gentle, almost lazy suckling, as sweet as Jimmy's, as beautiful to feel, but feeble. There's something wrong, she thought, but she told herself, He's newborn, and premature. He'll get stronger.

Isaac, she decided then, whose father had, like Abraham, left his home to travel to a strange land; whose mother, like Sarah, had out of all expectation borne a single child and rejoiced in him.

Sofia held her infant to her breast and gazed down at the wise owl eyes in a tiny elfin face capped by dark red hair. She respected her son more than she loved him at that moment and thought, You made it. The *djanada* nearly killed us and you were born too soon and you've gotten a bad start, but you are alive, in spite of everything.

It could be worse, she thought as she drifted off to sleep again, with the baby close, the heat of Rakhat as enveloping as a neonatal incubator, the two of them surrounded by the arms and legs and tails of whispering Runa. I am Mendes, and my son is alive, she thought. And things could be worse.

5

City of Inbrokar, Rakhat

2046, Earth-Relative

"THE CHILD IS DEFECTIVE."

Ljaat-sa Kitheri, forty-seventh Paramount of the Most Noble Patrimony of Inbrokar, delivered this bald news to the infant's father without preface. Summoned by a Runa domestic to the Paramount's private chambers just after the rise of Rakhat's second and most golden sun, Supaari Va-Gayjur received the announcement in silence, and had not so much as blinked.

Shock or self-control? Kitheri wondered, as his daughter's preposterous husband moved to a window. The merchant stared out at the jumbled angles of Inbrokar City's canted, crowded rooftops for a time, but then turned and lowered himself in obeisance. "If one might know, Magnificence, defective in what way?"

"A foot turns in." Kitheri glanced at the door. "That will be all."

"Your pardon, Magnificence," the merchant persisted. "There is no chance that this was . . . malformation? Some slight insufficiency of gestational condition, perhaps?"

An outrageous remark but, considering the source, the Paramount ignored it. "No female in my lineage or my wife's has been at fault lately," Kitheri said dryly, pleased to see the merchant's ears flatten. "Lately," in this context and used by a Kitheri, implied a lineage older than any other on Rakhat.

Initially dismayed by his daughter's improbable marriage, Ljaat-sa Kitheri had become reconciled to the match simply because a third line of descendants presented a number of unusual political opportunities. Now, however, it was clear that the whole affair had been a travesty. Which was, the Paramount thought, only to be expected given Hlavin's involvement.

It was typical of Hlavin, who was himself a disgrace, that he would grant breeding rights to this Supaari person on a whim, simply to embarrass the rest of the family. From time immemorial, the legal power to create a new lineage had been entrusted to the Kitheri Reshtar, precisely because statutory sterility was the most notable aspect of his life. These hapless late-born males could normally be counted on to grant sparingly a privilege they themselves might never enjoy. But nothing about Hlavin had ever been normal, the Paramount thought with irritable distaste.

"Was it a son?" the merchant asked, interrupting the Paramount's thoughts.

Curious merely, his tone said. Already putting the child in the past. Admirable, under the circumstances. "No. It was female," the Paramount said.

Surprising, really—the outcome of the mating. When the merchant arrived in Inbrokar to cover Jholaa, the Paramount had been relieved to see that he was a goodly man with a fine phenotype. Ears well set on a broad head that sloped nicely to a strong muzzle. Intelligent eyes. Good breadth in the shoulders. Tall, and some real power in the hindquarters—traits the Kitheri line could benefit from, the Paramount admitted to himself. Of course, it was impossible to predict how an outcross with untested stock would go.

Leaning back on a tail thick-muscled and hard, the Paramount folded his arms over a massive chest, hooking his long curved claws around his elbows, and came to the point. "In cases like this, there is, you understand, a father's duty." Supaari lifted his chin, the long and handsome and surprisingly dignified face still. "There may be others," the Paramount offered, but they both knew Jholaa was almost unapproachable now. The merchant said nothing.

It was disconcerting, this silence. The Paramount sank onto a cushion, wishing now that he'd sent a protocol Runa to the merchant's chambers to deliver the news.

"So. The ceremony will be tomorrow morning, then, Magnificence?" Supaari asked at last.

My ancestors must have done this, the Paramount thought, moved in spite of himself. Sacrificing children to rid our line of recurring disease, wild traits, poor conformation to type. "It is necessary," he said aloud and with conviction. "Kill one insignificant child now, prevent generations of suffering in the future. We must bear in mind the greater good." Naturally, this peddler lacked both the breeding and the discipline that molded those meant from birth to rule. "Perhaps," Ljaat-sa Kitheri suggested with uncharacteristic delicacy, "you would prefer that I—"

The merchant stopped breathing for an instant and rose to full height. "No. Thank you, Magnificence," he said with soft finality, and slowly turned to stare. It was a finely calculated threat, the Paramount decided with some surprise, serving silent notice this man would no longer be insulted with impunity, but nicely offset by the deferential mildness of Supaari's voice when next he spoke. "This is, perhaps, the price one pays for attempting something new."

"Yes," Ljaat-sa Kitheri said. "My thoughts exactly, although the commercial phrasing is unfortunate. Tomorrow, then."

The merchant accepted this correction with grace, but left the Paramount's chambers without the prescribed farewell obeisance. It was his only lapse. And, the Paramount noted with the beginnings of respect, it might even have been deliberate.

I HAVE SANDOZ TO THANK FOR THIS, SUPAARI THOUGHT BITTERLY AS HE swept through twisted corridors to his quarters in the western pavilion of the Kitheri compound. Throat tight with the effort to hold back a howl, he fell onto his sleeping nest and lay there in stunned misery. How could it all have gone so wrong? he asked himself. Everything I had—wealth, home, business, friends—all for an infant with a twisted foot. But for Sandoz, none of this would have happened! he thought furiously. The whole thing was a bad bargain from start to finish.

And yet, until the Paramount announced this disastrous news, it had seemed to Supaari that he had behaved correctly at every step. He had been cautious and prudent; reconsidering three years of choices, he saw no alternatives to his decisions. The Runa of Kashan village were his clients: he was obligated to broker their trade, even when that required doing business with the tailless foreigners from H'earth. Who was the obvious buyer for their exotic goods? The Reshtar of Galatna Palace, Hlavin Kitheri, whose appetite for the unique was known throughout Rakhat. Should I have stayed with the foreigners in Kashan? he asked himself. Impossible! He had a business to run, responsibilities to other village corpo-rations.

Even when the foreigners taught the Runa how to cultivate food, and the authorities discovered the unsanctioned breeding in the south, and the riots broke out—even then, Supaari had regained control before Chaos could dance. The foreigners were strangers; they didn't know that what they'd done was wrong. Rather than let the two surviving humans be tried for sedition, Supaari had offered to make them *hasta'akala*. Admit-tedly, it was a bad sign when one of them died almost immediately. Per-haps I should have waited until I knew more about them before having their hands clipped, Supaari thought. But he was intent on establishing their legal status before the government could execute them. How could he have known that they would bleed so much?

When Sandoz recovered, Supaari did his best to incorporate the little interpreter into the life of the Gayjur trading company. He urged Sandoz to spend time in the warehouse and in the offices, encouraged him to deal with the dailiness of commerce, but the foreigner remained despondent. Finally, having done everything he could with courtesy, Supaari resorted to the rude expedient of asking Sandoz directly what was wrong.

"Your unworthy guest is alone, lord," Sandoz had said with a movement of the shoulders that seemed to signal resignation. Or acceptance, per-haps. Indifference, sometimes. It was hard to be certain what such gestures meant. But then the foreigner offered his neck, to remove the hint of crit-icism. "You are more than kind, lord, and your hospitality faultless. This useless one is exceedingly grateful."

He longs for others of his kind, Supaari realized, and wondered if the foreigners were more like Runa than like Jana'ata. Runa affections were genuine but elastic, encompassing anyone who was near, contracting smoothly when someone left. Even so, they needed a herd. Oh, the fe-males could tolerate some solitude and work with strangers, but males needed families, children. Isolated from kin and friends, some Runa men would simply stop eating and die. It was rare, but it happened.

"Sandoz, do you pine for a wife?" Supaari asked, blunt in his anxiety that this foreigner, too, would perish in his custody.

"Lord, your grateful guest is 'celibate,'" Sandoz told him, using a H'in-glish word, his eyes sliding away. Then he explained, in his charmingly awkward K'San, "Wives are not taken by such as this unworthy one."

"So! Your kind are like Jana'ata then, who permit only the first two children to marry and breed," Supaari said, relieved. "I too am this thing—celibate. You are third-born as I am?"

"No, lord. Second. But among such as your guest, any person may mate and have children, even fifth-born or sixth."

Five? Six! Litters? Supaari wondered then. How can they allow so many? He felt sometimes that he understood only one thing in twelve of what he learned about the foreigners. "If you are second, why did you not take a wife?"

"This unworthy one chose not to, lord. It is an unusual choice, among my species as among yours. Men such as your guest leave the families of their birth and do not form attachment to any single person nor make any children. Thus we are free to love without exclusion, and to serve many."

Supaari was shocked to learn this about the little foreigner, whom he had come to care for. "You yourself are a servant to many, then?"

"Yes, lord, this one was, when among his own kind."

But there are none of your kind to serve here, Supaari thought. Confounded, he fell back against the pile of dining cushions on which he had lingered as the leavings of his meal cooled, and thought wistfully of the days when his most perplexing problem was predicting next season's demand for *kirt*. "Sandoz," he said, reaching out to grip some kind of certainty, "what is your purpose? Why did you come here?"

"Lord: to study the gifts of the tongue—to learn the songs of your people."

"Ha'an told me this!" Supaari cried, making sense at last of something Anne Edwards had once said. "You came because you heard the songs of our poets and admired them." He stared at Sandoz: not an interpreter bred to trade, but a second-born who chose to make no children, and a poet who serves many! No wonder Sandoz had shown no interest in commerce! That was when everything fell into place—it seemed brilliant, at the time. "Would it please you to serve among the poets whose songs brought you here, Sandoz?"

For the first time in a full season, the foreigner seemed to brighten. "Yes, lord. This would honor your most unworthy guest. Truly."

So Supaari set out to make this possible. The negotiations were delicate, intricate, delicious. In the end, he achieved a subtle and beautifully balanced transaction: the crowning achievement of a remarkably successful mercantile career. The foreigner Sandoz would be provided with a life of service to Hlavin Kitheri, the Reshtar of Galatna, whose diminishing poetic power might once more be lifted to greatness by inspiring encounters with the foreigner. The Reshtar's younger sister, Jholaa, would be released from the enforced barrenness of her existence, as would Supaari himself, by their marriage and by the foundation of the new Darjan lineage with full breeding rights. Since Supaari VaGayjur's own wealth would endow the Darjan, the Most Noble Patrimony of Inbrokar gained a third sept without any hint of unseemly inconstancy: an ideal multiplication of descent lines with no division of inheritance.

Agreement reached, the transfer of custody took place. Sandoz appeared to settle into the Reshtar's household reasonably well after his placement in Galatna Palace. Supaari himself had overseen the foreigner's presentation to the Reshtar; he was, in fact, a little unnerved by the pathetic, trembling eagerness with which Sandoz invited Kitheri's attentions. But the merchant left Galatna Palace elated over his own good fortune, and believing that he had done right by Sandoz.

It wasn't long before Supaari realized that there might have been some kind of misunderstanding. "How does the foreigner?" he inquired some days after the transfer, hoping to hear that Sandoz was thriving.

"Well indeed," was the reply. Even after his initiation, the Reshtar's secretary reported, Sandoz was extraordinary: "Fights like a virgin every time." The Reshtar was pleased and had already produced a splendid song cycle. His best in years, everyone said. The puzzle, Supaari learned, was that the foreigner reacted to sex with violent sickness. This was disturbing but, Supaari thought, it was evidently normal for his kind. One of the other foreigners had been bred just before she was killed in the Kashan riot, and Sofia too had trouble with nausea.

In any case, the deal was done; there was no second-guessing it now. And the Reshtar's poetry was lovely. So was Supaari's new home, the city of Inbrokar; so was his new wife, the lady Jholaa.

But then the poetry took a very odd turn, and the Reshtar was silenced. And Inbrokar was maddeningly boring compared to the bustle of Gayjur. Jholaa, Supaari noted wryly, was not boring but she was, quite likely, mad. And Sandoz was gone now, sent back to wherever he came from by the second party from H'earth, which had itself disappeared. Returned to H'earth as well, most likely. Who knew?

In view of how the mating had turned out, Supaari was inclined to wish he'd never known any of them—Sandoz, the Reshtar, Jholaa. Fool: this is what comes of change, Supaari told himself. Move a pebble, risk a landslide.

It was then that Supaari realized with sickening certainty that if he was to sire another child to take this one's place, his second encounter with Jholaa would be even uglier than the first. At this level of society, bloodlines were guarded like treasure, and it occurred to him that Jholaa had probably never even seen Runa bred, which was the way most commoners got their first instruction in sex. Supaari had initially approached the lady with a certain untraditional anticipation of the staggering erotic beauty defined and promised by the Reshtar's poetry, but it had quickly become clear that Jholaa herself was unfamiliar with her famous brother's more recent literary output. The child Supaari would kill in the morning had, on the occasion of her conception, nearly cost her sire an eye; he'd have funked the job entirely if pheromones and the irresistible scent of blood hadn't taken over.

When the union was concluded, Supaari had retreated from it with relief, badly disillusioned. And he understood at last why so many Jana'ata aristocrats preferred to be serviced by Runa concubines—bred for enjoyment and trained to delight—the moment their dynastic duty had been accomplished.

SLEEPING NOW AND EXHAUSTED FROM THE STRUGGLE TO EXPEL HER husband's brat, the lady Jholaa Kitheri u Darjan had always been more of a dynastic idea than a person.

Like most females of her caste, Jholaa Kitheri had been kept catastrophically ignorant, but she was not stupid. Allowed to see nothing of genuine importance, she was keenly observant of emotional minutiae—astute enough to wonder, even as a girl, if it was malice or simply thoughtless cruelty when, at her father's whim, she was allowed beyond her chamber and permitted to recline silently on silken cushions in a dim corner of an awninged courtyard during some minor state gathering. But even on those rare occasions, no one came near or even glanced in her direction.

"I might as well be made of glass or wind or time," Jholaa had cried out at this indifference when she was only ten. "Srokan, I exist! Why does no one see me?"

"They do not see my most beautiful lady because she has the glory of the moons in her!" her Runa nursemaid said, hoping to distract the child. "Your people cannot look upon the moons, which live in truest night. Only Runa like your poor Srokan can see such things, and love them."

"Then I shall look upon what the others cannot," Jholaa declared that day, shaking off Srokan's embrace, and gave herself the task of staying awake past second sundown, and then past the setting of Rakhat's third and smallest sun, to see for herself these glorious moons.

There was no one to deny her this, no bar to her ambition except the powerful drowsiness of childhood and of species. It was as frightening as anything a Jana'ata could do, but Srokan was there in the courtyard with her, telling stories and sharing gossip, her fine hands stroking Jholaa: calming the girl as she lost sight first of blues and next of yellows, contrast fading to a gray lightlessness and then to a dense darkness as confining as an aristocratic woman's life. The only things that staved off blind panic were Srokan's voice and the comforting familiar scents of nursery bedding and incense, and the aroma of roasted meat lingering in the air.

Suddenly, Srokan gripped Jholaa's arms and lifted her to her feet. "There! The clouds have run away and there they are!" she whispered urgently, holding Jholaa's head so that the girl would look in the right direction—so she could see, like small cold suns, the glowing disks: moons in inky blackness, beautiful and remote as mountain snow.

"There are other things in the night sky," Srokan told her. "Daughters of the moons! Tiny sparkling babies." Jana'ata eyes were not made to see such things and Jholaa could only accept her nurse's word that this was so, and not some silly Runa story.

This was the only memorable event of her childhood.

For a time, Jholaa shared isolation with the Kitheri Reshtar, her third-born brother, Hlavin. His title meant "spare," and like Jholaa, Hlavin's purpose was simply to exist, ready to transmit the patrimony should either of their elder brothers come to nothing. Hlavin was the only one aside from Srokan who noticed Jholaa, telling her stories and amusing her with secret songs, even though he was beaten for singing when his tutor caught him at it. Who but Hlavin could have made her laugh as the wives of Dherai and Bhansaar filled nurseries with children who displaced Hlavin and Jholaa in the Kitheri succession? Who but Hlavin would have cried out for her, moved to keening by her story of the moons, and by her confession that as each new niece and nephew was born, Jholaa herself felt more and more like a moon child: invisible to her own people, sparkling, undreamt of, in the darkness.

Then Dherai's own Reshtar was born, and then Bhansaar's; the succession was deemed stable, and Hlavin was taken from her, exiled to the port of Gayjur to safeguard his nephews' lives from a young uncle's frustrated ambition. Even in exile, Hlavin found a way to sing to her, and sent Jho-laa a radio receiver so that she could hear her own words about the moons' daughters, riding on waves as invisible as stars, woven into a transcendent cantata sung during his first broadcast from Galatna Palace, which was al-lowed because he did not sing the traditional chants that belonged to those born first or second, but something new and wholly other.

The concert left Jholaa angry, somehow, as if her words had been stolen from her, not given as a gift. When the music ended, she swept the radio from its pedestal, as though it were to blame. "Where is Galatna?" she de-manded as Srokan bent to gather the wreckage.

"It is set like a jewel, on a mountain above the city of Gayjur, and that is by an ocean, my lady," Srokan told her. Srokan looked up, her blue eyes wide. "So much water, you can stand on its edge and look—look as far as you can, but there's no end to it!"

"You lie. There's no such thing as water like that. All Runa lie. You'd kill us if you could," Jholaa said with flat contempt, old enough, by then, to know a master's fear.

"Nonsense, little one!" Srokan cried with good-natured surprise. "Why, Jana'ata sleep away the red sun's time and true night, and no one harms you! This devoted one does not lie to her darling mistress. The moons were real, my lady. The ocean is real! Its water tastes of salt, and its air is of a scent no landsman knows!"

Resentment was, by then, the only leavening that could lift Jholaa from the torpor that immobilized her for days at a time. She had come to hate the luckless Runa domestics who were her only companions, despising their ability to go into the world, the shameless sluts, unveiled and un-guarded, to see oceans and breathe scents Jholaa would never know. Hold-ing an elegant claw to Srokan's ear, Jholaa began to peel it from the woman's head, relenting only when the Runao admitted she had not seen or tasted this ocean herself and had only heard stories from the kitchen help, who came from the south. Hlavin would have told her the truth of the ocean, but he was lost to her, so Jholaa allowed her nursemaid's shak-ing hands to stroke and soothe her, and breathed in the salt scent of blood, not ocean.

Later that night, as Jholaa lay blind in the dark, useless light of Rakhat's small, red sun, she decided to execute Srokan for thinking how she might murder Jana'ata in their sleep, and to have the woman's children killed as well, to clear the line.

Srokan was old anyway. Stew meat, Jholaa thought dismissively.

Which was why there was no one to warn Jholaa or to prepare her for what would happen after her wedding: her domestics were frightened of her and none had the courage to explain why they were dressing her for a state ceremony. But Jholaa was used to being displayed on such occasions, and was not surprised to find herself taken to a stateroom filled with dazzlingly decorated officials and all her male relatives, who continued to chant, as though she were not there.

She stood quietly through the endless ceremonial declamations; these events tended to go on for days, and she had long since given up listening carefully. But when she heard her own name sung, she began to pay attention, and then she recognized the melody that sealed a marriage, and realized that she'd just been legally bound to a man whose lineal name she'd never heard before. Eyes wide behind her jewel-encrusted veil of gold mesh, she turned to ask someone—anyone—if she were being sent to another country, but before she could speak, her father and brothers surrounded her and moved Jholaa to the center of the room.

Her Runa maids reappeared and, when they began to remove her robes, Jholaa spoke up, demanding to know what was happening, but the men only laughed. Furious now and frightened, she tried to cover herself, but then the man whose name she could not quite remember came so close she could smell him, and dropped his own robe off his shoulders and he—. He did not merely look at her, but moved behind her and gripped her ankles and—

She fought, but her screams and struggle were drowned by the wedding guests' roars of amusement and approval. Afterward, she heard her father comment with chuckling pride to the others, "A virgin! No one could deny it after all that!" To which her eldest brother replied, "Almost as much of a fighter as that outlandish foreigner Hlavin and his friends use . . ."

When it was over, she was taken through a courtyard made festive for the occasion to a small shuttered room where she sat, ripped and bewildered, and listened to poetry sung in honor of the fourth-born Jholaa Kitheri u Darjan: against all odds, bred to a third-born merchant who would never have sired a child at all but for the foreign servant Sandoz. And when at last Jholaa bore that child, its lineage was unquestionable; this was, she came to understand, the only reason for her own existence.

A similar fate, she believed, was all that awaited her daughter. The lady Jholaa never looked at her infant, after the first moments of its life, when she got a hand loose from the midwife's grip and tried to slash the child's throat, from pity and disgust. Later, when her brother Dherai appeared briefly in her room to tell her that the infant was deformed, Jholaa did not care.

"Kill it then," was all she said, and wished someone had done the same for her.

6

Naples

September 2060

IT HAD TAKEN HOURS TO CALM DOWN AFTER THE POPE'S VISIT, AND Emilio Sandoz had only just fallen asleep when the knocking startled him half out of his bed. "God! What now?" he cried, falling back against the pillow again. Prone and exhausted, he shut his eyes resolutely and shouted, "Go away!"

"I hope you're talking to God," a familiar voice called, "because I'm not going back to Chicago."

"John?" Sandoz bolted out of bed and pushed open the tall wooden shutters with his elbows. "Candotti!" he said, astonished, head stuck out the dormer window. "I thought they sent you home after the hearings!"

"They did. Now they've sent me back." Grinning up at him, John Candotti stood on the driveway, long bony arms wrapped around a paperplast box, Roman nose making a sundial of his half-bald head in the late afternoon light. "What is this? I gotta be the Pope to get invited in?"

Sandoz slumped over the windowsill, elbows on the wood, nerveless fingers dangling like stems of *sta'aka* ivy from his wrists. "Come on up," he sighed with theatrical resignation. "The door's open."

"So! El Cahuna Grande tells me you just interviewed the Holy Father for a research assistantship," John called, trudging up the stairs and ducking under a doorway that Emilio—head and shoulders shorter—had never noticed was low. "Nice play, Sandoz. Very slick."

"Thank you so much for pointing that out," Emilio said, his English suddenly more Long Island than Puerto Rico. He was bent over the little table, putting the braces on. "Now why don't you give me a nice paper cut and pour some lemon juice in it?"

"Billy Crystal. *Princess Bride,*" John said promptly, putting the box down in a corner. "You need some new material, man. Did you watch any of those comedies I suggested?"

"Yeah. I liked that Dutch one, *East of Edam,* best. *No Sign of Life* was good, too. I don't get the jokes in the newer stuff. Anyway," he cried, indignant now, "how was I supposed to know who the Pope was? Some old guy shows up at my doorstep—"

"If you'd taken my advice," John said with the thin patience of an exasperated seminary admonitor, "you would have gotten the jokes. And you would have recognized the effing Pope when he came to meet you!" Sandoz ignored him, as he had ignored the forty-year hole in his awareness of recent history, too sick to care at first and now simply refusing to acknowledge it. "Do you have any idea how important it was that Gelasius came to us? I told you—it's time for you to catch up on things! But do you ever listen to me? No!"

And you aren't listening now, John realized, watching him. Emilio had gotten better at putting the braces on by himself in the past two months, but the procedure still took a fair amount of concentration.

"—and Giuliani just stands there, letting me dig the hole!" Sandoz was muttering as he pulled each hand into an open brace and then rocked the atrophied forearms outward to toggle the switches. There was a quiet whirring noise as the flat straps and electronic hardware closed over his fingers, wrists and forearms. He straightened. "One of these days, John, I would really love to sandbag that sonofabitch."

"Good luck," John said. "Personally, I think the Cubs have a better chance at winning the World Series."

They sat at the table, Sandoz slouching into the chair nearest the kitchen and John taking the Pope's seat opposite him. Glancing around the room as they traded lines from *East of Edam* and *Back Streets* and a couple of old Mimi Jensen flicks, John took in the bed, the socks on the floor, the dishes in the sink, and then stared suspiciously at Emilio, rumpled and unshaven. Sandoz was ordinarily meticulous, the black-and-silver hair brushed, the conquistador beard closely trimmed, his clothes spotless. John had expected the apartment to be immaculate. "All spiritual enlightenment begins with a neatly made bed," Candotti intoned, waving broadly at the mess. He frowned at Emilio. "You look like shit. When's the last time you got any sleep?"

"About fifteen minutes ago. Then some pain-in-the-ass old friend came by and woke me up. You want coffee or something?" Emilio rose and went to the tiny kitchen, where he opened the cupboard and pulled out the beans, making himself busy with his back to Candotti.

"No. Sit down. Don't change the subject. When did you sleep before that?"

"Memory fails." Sandoz put the coffee back, banging the cupboard door, and sank into the chair across the table again. "Don't mother me, John. I hate it."

"Giuliani said your hands were giving you hell," John persisted. "I don't get this. They're healed!" he cried, gesturing at them accusingly. "Why do they still hurt?"

"Dead nerves, I am reliably informed, confuse the central nervous system," Sandoz said with a sudden acid vivacity. "My brain becomes alarmed because it hasn't heard from my hands in a long time. It thinks they might be in some kind of trouble so, like a pain-in-the-ass old friend, it calls attention to the situation by giving me a lot of crap!" Sandoz stared out the window for a moment, getting a grip on himself, and then glanced at John, who sat impassively, a veteran of these outbursts. "I'm sorry. The pain wears me out, okay? It comes and it goes, but sometimes . . ."

John waited a moment, and then finished the sentence for him. "Sometimes when it comes, you're afraid it will never go."

Emilio didn't agree, but he didn't deny it either. "The redemptive power of suffering is, in my experience at least, vastly overrated."

"Too Franciscan for me," John agreed. Emilio laughed, and John knew if you could get Sandoz to laugh, you were halfway home. "How long this time?" he asked.

Sandoz shrugged the question off, eyes sliding away. "It's better if I'm working. Concentrating on something usually helps." He glanced at John. "I'm okay now."

"But beat down to your feet. Right," John said, "I'll let you get some rest." He slapped his hands on his thighs and stood, but rather than leave, he went to the sound-analysis gear along the gable wall opposite the stairway. Curious, he looked it over and then spoke casually. "I just wanted to check in with my new boss—unless, of course, you already hired the Pope."

Sandoz closed his eyes and twisted in the chair so he could stare over his shoulder at John. "Excuse me?"

John turned, grinning, but his smile disappeared when he saw Emilio's face. "You said you wanted someone who spoke Magyar. And English or Latin or Spanish. My Latin is pretty feeble," John admitted, faltering under the chilly gaze. "Even so, I'm four for four. And I'm all yours. If you want me."

"You're joking," Emilio said flatly. "Don't fuck with me, John."

"Sixteen languages to choose from and that's the kind you use? Listen, I'm not a linguist, but I know my way around systems and I'm educable," John said defensively. "My mom's parents were from Budapest. Gramma Toth took care of me after school. My Magyar is actually nicer than my English. Gram was a poet in the old country and—"

Sandoz, by this time, was shaking his head, not sure whether to laugh or to cry. "John, John. You don't have to convince me. It's only—" Only that he had missed Candotti. Only that he needed help but hated asking for it, needed colleagues but dreaded breaking in someone new. Father John Candotti, whose great gift as a priest was to forgive, had heard everything—and still, somehow, failed to despise or pity him. Emilio's voice was mercifully steady when he found it. "It's only that I thought there had to be a catch. I haven't had much practice at receiving good news lately."

"No catch," John declared confidently, for his life had not taught him to brace for the unexpected blow. He headed toward the stairway down to the garage level. "When can I start?"

"Right away, as far as I'm concerned. But use the library system, okay? I am going to bed," Sandoz announced as firmly as he could around a huge yawn. "If I am still sleeping in October, as I devoutly hope I shall be, you have my permission to wake me up. In the meantime, you can begin with the instructional program for Ruanja—Giuliani's got the lock codes. But wait until I can help you with the K'San files. It's a bitch of a language, John." He put his left hand on the tabletop, rocking the arm outward to unhinge the braces, then froze, struck by a thought. "Jesus," he said. "Is Giuliani sending you out with the next bunch?"

There was a long silence. "Yeah," John said. "Looks like it."

"And you're willing to go?"

John nodded, eyes serious. "Yes. Yes, I am."

Breaking out of the paralysis, Emilio fell back against his chair and quoted Ignatius with brittle grandiosity. "Ready to move at a moment's notice, with your breastplate buckled."

"If I die on Rakhat," John said solemnly, "I ask only that my body be returned for burial in Chicago, where I can continue to participate—"

"—in Democratic party politics!" Emilio finished with him. He snorted a laugh, and shook his head. "Well, you know not to eat the meat. And you're big. You may have a fighting chance if some godforsaken Jana'ata takes a fancy to you."

"I guess that's what Giuliani thinks, too. If I bulk up a little, we've got the makings of a pretty decent NFL offense. The other guys are huge."

"So you've met them already?"

"Just the Jebs, not the civilians," John said, rejoining him at the table. "The father superior's a guy named Danny Iron Horse—"

"Lakota?" Sandoz asked.

"Partly—French and Swedish, too, he says, and he's kind of sensitive about it. Apparently, the Lakota side of the family's been off the rez for about four generations, and he's pretty tired of people expecting him to wear feathers and speak without contractions, you know?"

"Many moons go Choktaw . . ." Emilio intoned.

"Turns out, he grew up in the suburbs of Winnipeg, and he must have gotten his size from the Swedes. But he's got Black Hills written all over him, so he gets that shit all the time." John winced. "I pissed him off almost immediately, telling him about a guy I know out on Pine Ridge. He cut me off at the knees—'No braids, no shades, ace. I'm not a drunk, and I've never been in a sweat lodge.' "

Sandoz whistled, eyes wide. "Yep—that counts as sensitive. So, that's what he isn't. What is he?"

"One of the sharpest political scientists in the Society, from what I hear, and it's not like we're short of them. There's been talk about him winding up General one of these days, but when Giuliani offered him Rakhat, Danny left a full professorship at the Gregorian without a backward glance. He's pumped for this."

"What about the others?" Emilio asked.

"There's a chemist from Belfast—he's supposed to check out that nanoassembly stuff they do on Rakhat. I just met him last week, but Giuliani's had these guys in training for months! Who knew? Anyway, get this: his name is Sean Fein." Sandoz looked at him blankly. "Think about it," John advised.

"You're joking," Sandoz said after a moment.

"No, but his parents were. Daddy was—"

"Jewish," Sandoz supplied, straight-faced.

"Full marks. And his mother was political—"

"Sean Fein, Sinn Fein," Emilio said sympathetically. "Not just a joke, but a lame one at that."

"Yeah. I asked Sean if it helped at all to know that I went to high school with a kid named Jack Goff. 'Not a blind bit,' was all he said. The most morose Irishman I've ever met—younger than I am, but he carries himself like he's a hundred."

"Sounds like a fun group," Emilio commented dryly. "Giuliani said he was sending out four. Who's the other guy?"

"Oh, you'll love this—you asked for someone who spoke Basque, right?"

"Euskara," Sandoz corrected him. "I just wanted people who were used to dealing with really different grammatical structures—"

"Whatever." John shrugged. "Anyway, he walks in—this enormous guy with the thickest hair I've ever seen, and I'm thinking, Hah! So that's where all mine went! And then he says something absolutely incomprehensible, with way too many consonants. I didn't know whether to say hello or punch him! Here—he wrote it down for me." John dug a scrap of paper out of his pocket. "How the hell do you pronounce that?"

Emilio took the paper in his right hand, still braced, moving it back and forth at arm's length. "Playing air trombone! Can't see small print worth a damn anymore," he noted ruefully, but then he got a bead on it. "Joseba Gastainazatorre Urizarbarrena."

"Show-off," John muttered.

"They say the devil himself once tried to learn the Basques' language," Sandoz remarked informatively. "Satan gave up after only three months, having learned just two words of Euskara—both curses, which turned out to be Spanish anyway."

"So what should we poor mortals call him?" John asked.

"Joe Alphabet?" Emilio suggested, yawning as he unhinged the second brace. "The first name is just like José. It's easy: Ho-SAY-ba."

John tried it a couple of times and seemed satisfied that he could manage, as long as nobody expected him to go past the first three syllables. "Anyway, he's an ecologist. Seems to be a nice guy. Thank God for small mercies, huh? Jeez—sorry! I forgot how tired you are," John said, as Emilio yawned for the third time in as many minutes. "Okay, I'm going! Get some rest."

"I'll see you tomorrow," Emilio said, moving toward his bed. "And, John—I'm glad you're here."

Candotti nodded happily and stood to leave, but paused at the top of the stairs and looked back. Emilio, too whipped to undress, had already fallen onto his mattress in a heap. "Hey," John said, "aren't you going to ask me what's in the box?"

Emilio kept his eyes closed. "Say, John, what's in the box?" he asked dutifully before muttering, "Like I give a shit."

"Letters. And that's just the paper stuff. Why don't you ever check your messages?"

"Because everybody I know is dead." The eyes popped open. "So who the hell would write to me?" Sandoz asked the ceiling in rhetorical wonderment. There was a hoot of genuine amusement. "Oh, John, I'm probably getting mash notes from male convicts!"

Candotti snorted, startled by the idea, but Sandoz rose on his elbows, transfixed by the sheer delicious absurdity of it, his face vivid, all the tiredness draining away for a minute. "My dear Emilio," he started and, falling back on the bed, he began to improvise, obscenely and hilariously fluent, on the broad literary theme of prison romance in terms that rendered John breathless. Finally, when Sandoz had exhausted himself and his topic and John had wiped his eyes and caught his breath, Candotti cried, "You're so cynical! You have a lot of friends out there, Emilio."

"Indulge me, John. Cynicism and foul language are the only vices I'm presently capable of. Everything else takes energy or money."

Candotti laughed again and told Sandoz to say two rosaries for having spectacularly impure thoughts, and waved and started down the stairs. He was almost out the door when he heard Emilio call his name. Hand on the knob, still grinning, he looked back up toward Sandoz's room. "Yeah?"

"John, I . . . I need a favor."

"Sure. Anything."

"I—. There are going to be some papers I'll have to sign. I'm out, John. I'm leaving the Society." Sucker-punched, Candotti sagged against the doorjamb. A moment later, Sandoz's voice went on, quiet and hesitant. "Can you fix a pen so I can hold it? Like you did with that razor, yes?"

John ascended the stairs partway and then halted, as unwilling as Sandoz to carry out this awful conversation face to face. "Emilio. Look—. Okay, I understand, I guess—as much as anyone else can. But are you sure? I mean, it's—"

"I'm sure. I decided this afternoon." Candotti waited and then heard, "I'm carrying a lot of shit, John. I won't add fraud. Nobody can hate the way I do and claim to be a priest. It's not honest." John sat heavily on a stair tread and rubbed his face with his hands as Emilio said, "I think—

some kind of wedge-shaped thing that would hold the pen up at an angle, yes? The new braces are good, but I still haven't got much of a precision grip."

"Yeah. Okay. No problem. I'll figure something out for you."

John stood and headed back down the stairs, feeling ten years older than he'd been five minutes ago. As he shambled his loose-limbed way over to the main house, he heard Emilio's call drift out the dormer window: "Thanks, John." He waved a hand dispiritedly, without looking back, knowing Emilio couldn't see him. "Sure. You bet," John whispered, and felt a nasty crawling sensation on his face as wind off the Bay of Naples dried the tears.

7

City of Inbrokar

2046, Earth-Relative

THE ERROR, IF THAT'S WHAT IT WAS, LAY IN GOING TO SEE THE CHILD. Who knows what would have happened if Supaari VaGayjur had simply waited until the morning and, unsuspecting, freed his child's spirit to find a better fate?

But the midwife came to him, sure that he would want to see the baby, and he was rarely able to resist the uncomplicated friendship the Runa always seemed to offer him. So Supaari strode toward the nursery importantly: heavy embroidered robe rustling as softly as his slippered footsteps, eyes focused on the middle distance, ignoring the Runa midwife's chatter with his ears cocked forward, not deigning to reply to her pleasantries— all in conscious mimicry of an aristocratic Jana'ata crammed full of incorruptible civic virtue and monumental self-regard.

Who am I to sneer? Supaari asked himself. A jumped-up merchant prone to unfortunate commercial metaphors in conversation with his betters. A third-born son from a backwater town in the midlands who made a fortune brokering trade among the Runa. An outsider among outsiders, who'd literally stumbled onto a pack of impossible foreigners from somewhere beyond Rakhat's three suns, and parlayed that experience into this exacting facsimile of nobility that nobody but the Runa believed in.

He'd known from the moment the Reshtar agreed to his proposition that he would never be more than who he was. It didn't matter. Isolation felt normal to him. Supaari's life had always been an interstitial one, lived between the worlds of Runa and Jana'ata; he enjoyed the perspective, preferred observation to participation. He'd spent his first year among these exalted members of his own species studying the habits of the men around him as carefully as the hunter studies his prey. He came to savor the growing accuracy with which he predicted the snubs. He could anticipate who would refuse outright to attend a reception if he attended, and who would come for the sport of baiting him; who would fail to greet him entirely, and who would do so but with a gesture more properly due a second. Firsts preferred direct insult; seconds were more subtle. His eldest brother-in-law, Dherai, would push past Supaari through a door, but the second-born Bhansaar would merely stand as though Supaari were invisible and enter the room a moment later, as though it had just occurred to him to go inside.

In brokar society, taking its cue from the Kitheri princelings, ignored Supaari or gazed at him contemptuously from corners. Sometimes the word "peddler" would rise above the general conversation, sinking a moment later beneath gentle waves of well-bred amusement. Privately entertained, Supaari had borne all this with courteous detachment and genuine patience: for the sake of a son and a future.

The nursery was far into the interior of the compound. He had no idea where Jholaa was. The Runa midwife Paquarin had assured him of his wife's health but added, "She's worn to tatters, poor lady. It's not like that for us," the Runao said thankfully. "For us, the babies come out as easily as they get in—it's a mercy not to be a Jana'ata. And the Kitheri women are so small in the hips!" she complained. "Makes the job harder for a poor midwife." Paquarin admitted that Jholaa was upset by the birth, when Supaari asked. Naturally. Another reason for his wife to hate him: he'd gotten a deformity on her.

Busy with his thoughts, it was only when Supaari heard soft, huffing Runa laughter and cheerful, harmless Runa chatter drifting out of the kitchen with the smell of spices and frying vegetables that he realized Paquarin had led him through the nursery and past it. Passing through one last louvered door and entering a barren courtyard at the back of the compound, he noticed a small wooden box pushed into a corner of the yard. This was what he'd been brought to see, and he stopped in midstride.

No lavish embroidered nest net, no festive ribbons fluttering in the breeze to catch the child's eye and train attention to movement. Just a rag from the kitchen draped over the crate to shade her, to hide her shame—

and his own—from sight. It was not a new box, Supaari noted. It was ordinarily used for Runa infants, he supposed. A cradle for a cook's child.

Another man might have blamed the midwife, but not Supaari Va-Gayjur. Ah, Bhansaar, he thought. A hit. May your children become scavengers. May you live to see them eat carrion.

He had not expected this, not even after a year of affinal insult and effrontery. He accepted that his daughter was doomed. No one would marry a cripple. She was more hopeless than a third, first-born but fouled. Of all the things he had learned of the foreigners' customs, the most incomprehensible, the most unethical was the notion that anyone could breed, even those known to carry traits that would damage their offspring. What kind of people would inflict known disease on their own grandchildren? Well, not us! he'd thought. Not Jana'ata!

Even so, Dherai might have overridden Bhansaar's pettiness and allowed the child a decent nest in the nursery for her single night of life. Daughters who serve travelers, Supaari thought savagely. Cowards for sons, Dherai.

He strode to the cradle, snatching the cloth away with a hooked claw. "It's not the child's fault, lord," the midwife said hurriedly, frightened by the acrid smell of anger. "She's done no wrong, poor thing."

And who is to blame? he meant to demand. Who put her in this detestable little—. Who brought her to this wretched—

I did, he thought bleakly, gazing down.

Bathed, fed and sleeping, his daughter had the fragrance of rain in the first moments of a storm. He was dizzy with it, actually swayed before kneeling. Studying her tiny perfect face, he raised his hands to his mouth and bit hard, six times, severing each long claw at the quick, bewitched by the need to hold her and to do so without harming her. Almost at the same moment, he realized that he'd just committed a humiliating and irreversible gaffe. Clawless, he would have to let Ljaat-sa Kitheri carry out the father's duty after all. But his mind was not clear, and he lifted his child from the box, bringing her awkwardly to his chest.

"Those Kitheri eyes! She's a beauty, like her mother," the Runa midwife observed guilelessly, happy now that the Jana'ata had calmed himself. "But she has your nose, lord."

He laughed in spite of everything and, careless of his robes, shifted on the damp clay tiles that were still shining from the morning's drizzle, so that he could rest the baby in his lap. Aching, he ran a hand along the velvety softness of her cheek, his stubby fingertips feeling strangely naked, and as unprotected as his daughter's throat. I was not meant to breed, he thought. Her twisted foot is a sign. I have done everything wrong.

With all his considerable courage, his own throat tight, Supaari fumbled at the wrappings that concealed her, forcing himself to look at what had destined this child to die in infancy, taking all his hopes with her into darkness. What he saw pulled the breath from him.

"Paquarin," he said very carefully, in a voice he hoped would not alarm her. "Paquarin, who has seen the child, besides you and me?"

"The ranking uncles, lord. Then they told the Paramount, but he didn't come to inspect her. Such a pity! The lady tried to kill the little one already," Paquarin reported thoughtlessly. But hearing her own words, she realized she'd done wrong. Jholaa wanted the baby dead even before its deformity was discovered. The Runao began to sway from side to side, but stopped suddenly. "The lady Jholaa says, Better to die at birth than to live unmarriageable," she told Supaari then, and truthfully, although Jholaa had said it some years ago. Pleased with her own cleverness in stitching this into the present, Paquarin rattled on righteously, "So it must be done. No one will have a cripple. But it isn't right for the dam to do it. It's the sire's duty, lord. This helpful one saved the child for your honor."

Still stunned, only half-hearing Paquarin's chatter, Supaari looked at the midwife for a long while. Finally, making his face kindly and reassuring, he asked, "Paquarin, can you tell me, please—which foot is deformed? The right? Or the left?"

Embarrassed, she flattened her ears and she swayed again, more rapidly, and fell into her native Ruanja. "Someone isn't certain. Someone begs pardon. Runa don't know of such things. It's for the lords to decide."

"Thank you, Paquarin. You are good to save the child for me." He handed the infant to the midwife, each movement as controlled and careful as those he would have performed in the next morning's ritual. "It is best to say nothing to anyone else of my visit to the child," he told her. To be sure she understood, he said directly, in Ruanja, "*Sipaj*, Paquarin: someone desires your silence."

Eyes closed, ears folded back in terror, Paquarin offered her throat, expecting he would kill her to obtain it, but he smiled and reached out to calm her with a hand on her head, as a Runa father might, and assured her once again that she was good. "Will you stay with her tonight, Paquarin?" he suggested. He did not offer money, knowing that natural affection would keep her in the courtyard: this woman's line was bred to loyalty.

"Yes, lord. Someone thanks you. The poor mite shouldn't be alone on her only night. Someone's heart was sad for her."

"You are good, Paquarin," he told her again. "She shall have a short life, perhaps, but a proper and honorable one, shall she not?"

"Yes, lord."

He left Paquarin in midcurtsy and moved without unseemly haste through the nursery. Heard the laughter and scuffling of Ljaat-sa Kitheri's half-grown grandchildren, and decided that the boys' noisy wrestling was the only sign of genuine life in this dead and stifling place, and wished them luck in killing their fathers early. Walked down narrow corridors, past empty staterooms, hearing muffled snatches of conversation behind closed and curtained doors. Strode past placid Runa porters standing vigil at each doorway, well suited to their job, too phlegmatic to notice boredom. Nodded to them as they opened the inner gates and the outer portcullis and saluted his passing. Escaped, at last, onto the quiet street.

There was no sense of release, even beyond the compound. No feeling of being under the sky, inside the wind. Supaari glared up at the pierced-wood balconies and the overhanging eaves, seemingly designed to prevent the rain from ever washing the streets clean. Why does no one sweep here? he wondered irritably, ankle-deep in blown litter, outraged by the compacted, cluttered heaviness of the place. Inbrokar was chained and hobbled by every moment of its convoluted, incestuous history. Nothing is made here, he realized for the first time. It was a city of aristocrats and advisers, of agents and analysts, forever ranking and comparing, manuevering endlessly in feverish self-promotion and predatory competition. Madness, to believe he could ever have begun something here. Folly, to rage against this city's perpetual self-imposed darkness, its fibrous, matted preoccupation with position and degree.

Moving through a city he had once found beautiful, he was greeted here and there with counterfeit deference by various Kitheri friends, acquaintances, hangers-on. Their condolences came rather too soon, the child brought to light this very day and its birth unheralded, but they were as properly composed as their authors' faces. How long has this been planned? Supaari wondered. How many had been alerted to this delicious and elaborate joke, waiting out his wife's pregnancy, as anxious as he had been for the appearance of an infant he was meant to kill?

It occurred to him then that the luxurious thoroughness of the plot stank of the Reshtar's subtle sensibility. Who had spoken first of swapping Sandoz for Jholaa? he wondered, stumbling a little at the thought. Had

Hlavin Kitheri steered him toward the arrangement from the start? Staggered, Supaari leaned against a wall and tried to reconstruct the negotiations, carried out in language as ornate as the Reshtar's palace, in the company of poets and singers who shared Hlavin's voluptuous exile and who had seemed as eager to see the merchant elevated as Supaari himself was to be ennobled. Who gained? he asked himself, standing blindly in the street, oblivious to passersby. Who profited? Hlavin. His brothers. Their friends. Hlavin must have known Jholaa was too old, must have suggested to Dherai and Bhansaar how amusing it would be if the Darjan lineage were extinguished in its infancy, by its own deluded founder—

Lightheaded with humiliation, Supaari fought nausea and, dearly bought illusions gone, knew with a strange certainty that sickness was not normal for Sandoz's kind. Courteous and desiring to please, Supaari knew that he himself had invited Hlavin Kitheri's contempt as unknowingly as Sandoz had invited . . .

Who shall pay for this? he thought. And, fury rising to fill the place of shame, he told himself with ugly irony that this was an unfortunate commercial phrasing.

Seething, he turned back toward the Kitheri lair, his mind black with thoughts of bloody revenge, of challenges and ha'aran duels. But there was no recourse. Wait until the morning and, before witnesses, expose Kitheri duplicity—and listen to the laughter as the plot became merely a joke, played out publicly. Save the child's life now—and listen to the laughter again someday, when marriage contracts were made to be broken. Alive, beautiful and enchanting, the daughter would end as the mother had: a prop in an elaborate comedy, used to humiliate him for the amusement of the gentry.

It's not that personal, he thought, slowing down, in sight now of the Kitheri compound. It's not about me. It's simply my category that is to be kept in place. They need us where we are. Third-born merchants. The Runa. We feed and clothe and shelter them. We provide their needs and their wants and their whims and their desires. We are the foundation of their palace and they dare not let one stone shift, or the whole of it will fall around them.

He leaned against a neighbor's wall, staring at the palisaded enclosure of the family that had ruled Inbrokar for generations, and came finally to a cool familiar place in his heart, where decisions were made without anger or wishes.

From long experience, he knew the Pon river barge schedule out of Inbrokar's docks. Supaari VaGayjur considered the bargain he had made and fell back on a merchant's honor. He had kept his part of the agreement. He owed these people nothing.

I will take what is mine, he thought, and go.

"FRANKLY, HLAVIN, I EXPECTED MORE OF HIM," remarked Ira'il Vro to the Reshtar of Galatna. Alerted by informants, they had watched Supaari return to the Kitheri compound, moving to a corner tower to observe as the merchant spoke to the midwife in the back courtyard and then left with her and the child. Ira'il faced Hlavin Kitheri, only to confront an unnerving stare. "You must be so disappointed . . ." Ira'il said, voice trailing off uncertainly.

Confused, he inhaled guardedly to catch Kitheri's scent. There was no whiff of anger, but Ira'il turned back to the tower window to cover his unease. He could, by shifting his eyes a bit, pick out the treasury and provincial revenue offices, the state archives and libraries, the arena located only steps from the High Court. The baths, the embassies; the towering stone pillars, with their silvery cloisonné of radio transmission equipment, rising from the General Command. He knew all the landmarks now and admired the cityscape: a timeless celebration of stability and unchanging balance—

Balance! This was the very thing Ira'il lacked when dealing with the Kitheri Reshtar. Hlavin was third-born and Ira'il a first, but the Kitheri outranked every other family in the Principality of Inbrokar, so using the Reshtar's name in direct address or deciding who held right to the personal pronoun was a complicated and dangerous task. Without a Runa protocol specialist to advise him, Ira'il felt constantly on the verge of toppling into some unforgivable error.

To make matters worse, Ira'il had no idea why he'd been chosen to accompany the Reshtar from Gayjur to Inbrokar when Hlavin's exile was suspended for the birth of his sister's child. Granted, Ira'il had so admired the Reshtar's extraordinary poetry that he had defied his own family and renounced his right to transmit the Vro patrimony, in order to join the glittering society of Galatna Palace. But other men had done the same, and Ira'il himself was a poor singer who knew just enough about poetry to understand that his own verse would never rise above cliché. The only time he came to the Reshtar's attention was when he uttered some regrettably obvious praise for another man's lovely metaphor, or hit the wrong note in a chorus. So he had been content to sit at the edges of the Reshtar's court, feeling honored simply to be in the company of such artists. Someone, after all, had to be the audience.

Then, inexplicably, Hlavin Kitheri had reached out and pulled Ira'il Vro from obscurity, inviting him to attend the inauguration ceremonies of the extraordinary new Darjan lineage that the Reshtar had permitted to come into existence.

"Oh, but you must be there, Ira'il," the Reshtar had insisted when Ira'il had stammered a demurral, "to see the jest played out in full! I promise, you shall be the only one aside from me who will understand the whole of it."

Ira'il could only presume that the Reshtar enjoyed his company—a startling notion, but irresistibly flattering.

Everything about this excursion had been startling, really. Entering Inbrokar for the first time, Ira'il had been amazed by the Kitheri palace, here in the center of the capital. It was architecturally impressive but oddly quiet—very nearly empty, except for the family itself and its domestic staff. Ira'il had expected something more exciting, more alive at the very heart of his culture. . . . He turned away from the city and looked down at the kitchen yard and the Runa gate through which the merchant had just left. "One might have expected a glorious duel," he told the Reshtar then, hoping that Hlavin would forget the earlier use of dominant language. "The peddler could have taken Dherai. You'd have moved up to second."

"I think he did," the Reshtar said serenely.

"Apologies," Ira'il Vro said, flustered into another gaffe. "I'm not sure I follow—. Apologies! One doesn't understand—"

Of course not, you dolt, Hlavin Kitheri thought, gazing at the other man with something approaching affection, for he did enjoy Vro's company immensely—particularly the idiot's clumsy slights and graceless attempts at recovery. There were wondrously comic elements to this entire drama, and it had been fascinating to set it in motion. Supaari means to leave the city, the Reshtar had realized as his ludicrous brother-in-law stole away with his prize like a skulking scavenger, and the radiance that filled Hlavin Kitheri's soul rivaled those moments when the resolution of an improvised song came to him in midperformance. I could not have planned it more perfectly, he thought.

"I think the peddler killed my honored brother Dherai," the Reshtar said then, voice musical and clear, his limpid lavender eyes celestial. "And Bhansaar! And their brats. And then—in a delirium of bloodjoy, drunk on the dense, hot odor of vengeance—he killed Jholaa and my father, as well."

Ira'il opened his mouth to protest: No, he's just left.

"I think that is what happened," the Reshtar said again, placing a brotherly arm across the other man's shoulders and laying his tail cozily atop Vro's own. "Don't you?"

8

Inbrokar

During the Reign of Ljaat-sa Kitheri

THERE WERE QUESTIONS THAT COULD NOT BE ASKED, AND THE MOST powerful of these was, "Why?"

"What?" and "When?" were necessary, of course. "Where?" was usually safe. "How?" was permissible, although it often led to trouble. But "Why?" was so hazardous that Selikat beat him when he used the word. Even as a child, Hlavin had understood that this was her duty. She beat him for his own good: she feared for him, and did not want the best of her students to be made an example of. Better a tutor's whip than the slow and public extraction of instructive consequences, should any younger brother breathe treason.

"Am I a tailor's dummy then?" he had demanded at the age of twelve, still fearless and unsubtle. "If Bhansaar dies, they'll throw the cloak of office over me, and snap! I am Judgment! Is that how it works, Selikat?"

The tutor hesitated. It was a Reshtar's fate to observe his elders' ascendance, all the while knowing that if either proved out sterile or died before breeding, the extra son would step into the vacated position and be accorded the assumption of competence. Not tall but neat and agile, Hlavin was already physically as adept as Dherai, who was destined to be his nation's champion, should any challenge to the Patrimony be made. And even Jholaa was brighter than Bhansaar, who could remember all that he was taught and apply it, but rarely drew an inference or came to a conclusion on his own, and who would nevertheless preside one day over Inbrokar's highest court.

"The oldest songs explain it, sir," the Runao told him, her eyes closing and her voice taking on the rhythm if not the melody of the chants. "Ingwy, who loves order, spoke to the first brothers, Ch'horil and Srimat. 'When women gather, Chaos dances. Therefore, separate Pa'au and Ti-ha'ai, the fierce sisters you have married, and keep them apart and captive.' With trickery and cunning, Ch'horil and Srimat conspired with other men until all had subdued their wives and daughters. But when they themselves did the culling and the butchering, the men, too, became blood-drunk and fought. 'We cannot wall ourselves up,' they said. So Ingwy commanded, 'Let those who are wise decide who among you is too fierce to live, and let those who are strong kill the fierce ones condemned by the wise.' And because Ch'horil the Elder was strong and Srimat the Younger was wise, from that time on, the first-born males of each sept were charged with combat and ritual killing, the second-born with adjudication and decision."

"And do you believe that?" Hlavin asked her bluntly.

Her eyes opened. "It all happened long before the Runa were domesticated," Selikat replied, dropping her tail with a soft and possibly ironic thud. "In any case, of what importance is the belief of an insignificant tutor, my lord?"

"You are not insignificant. You are tutor to the Kitheri Reshtar. Tell me what you think," the child ordered, imperious even then, when it seemed that nothing more awaited him than an exile designed to distract him from futile resentment and dangerous questions.

Selikat drew herself up, a person of some dignity. "Stability and order have always been paid for with captivity and blood," the Runao told her charge, calm eyes steady. "The songs tell also of the Age of Constancy, when everything was as it should be and each man knew his place and his family's. There was respect for those above and courtesy from those below. All elements were in balance: Stewardship triumphant and Chaos contained—"

"Yes, yes: 'Ferocity controlled, like a woman in her chamber.' Or a Reshtar in exile," the boy said. She had beaten him regularly, but he was still impulsive, and perilously cynical. "Were things ever truly so neat, Selikat? Even when men keep their place, the ground can split, swallowing towns. What of balance then? Floods can drown half the population of a low-lying province. A city can lie under ash in less time than it takes to sleep off a meal!"

"True," Selikat conceded. "And worse: there are those who secretly nurture disputes, unleashing vendettas whenever circumstance favors them. Jealousy exists, and self-seeking; competition for its own sake. And aggression and anger: the blind, deaf rage to settle something, once and for all."

The Runao stopped, deferential, but the beneficiary of generations of selective breeding and absolute mistress of her field of knowledge. All her life, she had lived among people endowed with a predator species' anatomy, reflexes, instincts: the grasping feet, the slicing claws, the powerful limbs; the patience to stalk, the cleverness to ambush, the quickness to kill. Selikat had seen what was done to freethinkers, and she did not wish that fate for Hlavin.

"In opposition to all that ferocity," she resumed, "there have been great jurists, resourceful diplomats, men whose voices can restore calm and bring others to their senses. You, my lord, are named for the greatest of these: Hlavin Mra, whose wisdom is enshrined in the fundamental law of Inbrokar, whose oratorio 'Shall We Be as Women?' is sung by every breeding male when he comes of age and takes his place in society."

"And what if Hlavin Mra had been born third?" his namesake asked. "Or even first?"

Selikat was silent for a time. Then she beat him. "What if?" was more dangerous than "Why?"

BUT FOR SELIKAT'S INFLUENCE, HE MIGHT HAVE ENDED LIKE SO MANY other reshtari of his caste: seduced by the sumptuous pleasures of the third-born nobleman's indolent, easy life, and dead by middle age of obesity and boredom. There were nearly unlimited opportunities for consumption; Dherai and Bhansaar, fearing assassination, forestalling intrigue, were happy to provide Hlavin with anything he wanted, as long as he did not want what was theirs. Barred from breeding, banished to Galatna Palace with a harem of Runa concubines and neutered Jana'ata thirds, Hlavin had for his companions in exile the extra sons of the lesser nobility, who were allowed to travel more freely than their betters. Together, they filled the empty days with violent games that frequently ended with broken bones, or whiled the time away with monstrous banquets and increasingly debased sex.

"At least when she screamed, I knew someone was paying attention to me!" Hlavin shouted, drunk and adrift, when Selikat berated him for damaging a concubine so badly the girl had to be put down. "I am invisible! I might as well be Jholaa! Nothing is real here. Everything of importance is elsewhere."

A few reshtari embraced their own effacement and sought to lose themselves utterly in the chanting self-hypnosis of the Sti ritual. But Hlavin craved more, not less, of existence. Some reshtari were men of substance who had no taste for combat or for law and genuinely preferred scholarship; these continued their education beyond the training of their elders and from their ranks came architects, chemists, civil engineers, historians, mathematicians, geneticists, hydrologists. But Hlavin was no scholar.

Selikat's own training was thorough and she knew the warning signs of intelligence twisting. Without some way out of this trap, Hlavin would destroy himself, one way or another. There was one possibility. . . . She had resisted it for a long time, hoping that he would find some other scent to follow.

Selikat made her decision that evening, watching Hlavin from a little distance as he listened to the Gayjur civic choirs, the ancient chants filling the air as the second sun set. Put two Jana'ata within half a *cha'ar* of one another at this time of day and the chorusing would begin, inevitable as darkness. There was no part for thirds: all harmonies were based on two voices. She had never been able to beat the music out of Hlavin. He had no right to sing, but it was the only time he seemed content, and she could hear him when the breeze was right, taking the dominant melody or counterpoint as it pleased him, embellishing the original tones with chromatic elements that extended or defied the bass line. When the last notes faded with the dying sunlight, she went to him, and spoke, not caring who else heard.

"Do you recall, my lord, that once you asked: And what if Hlavin Mra had been born third?"

Staring at her, Hlavin lifted his head.

"Even so," Selikat said with quiet conviction, "he would have sung."

Why did she do it? he asked himself later. It was, of course, the Runa way to sacrifice themselves for their masters. And in any case, there was less than a season left to Selikat: she was nearly fifty, old even by the standards of court Runa. Perhaps she simply hated waste, and knew the end he'd come to if he could not release what was in him. It was even possible that she wished him happiness, and knew that without music, there would be none in his life. . . . Whatever the reason, the Runao who had raised Hlavin Kitheri chose to give him one last gift.

Startled by her words, they both fell silent. Listening carefully for the telltale sound of breath caught, they heard footsteps, both knowing the outcome. "He would have made his life song," Selikat called as she was taken away, "no matter what his life was made of!" These were her last words to him, and Hlavin Kitheri did his best to honor them.

ALMOST FROM THE BEGINNING, HE PUT HIMSELF AT RISK.

With the focused ferocity of his ancestors, Hlavin Kitheri dismissed the young fools his brothers had tried to stupefy him with, and called instead for physicists, mathematicians, musicians, bards, surrounding himself with anyone of any caste or age grade who could be induced to teach him. He devoured first the bones and meat of rhythm and harmony and imagery. Then, when the most desperate hunger was assuaged, he tasted the delicacies of solfège: pulse, meter, contour, ambitus; pitch, scale, microtones; vowel length and stress, the interplay of linguistic and musical structures.

Pleased to find so apt a student, his teachers thought him one of their own—a theoretician, who would expound on the traditional chants. Naturally, it was a shock when he sang aloud to check his understanding of a canto's phrasing, and they reported this to the paramountcy, but privately, they accepted it. And, they noted, the Reshtar had a remarkable voice: supple, true, with extraordinary range. A pity really, that it could not be heard more widely . . .

Soon, however, he dismissed the academics as well and, when he was rid of them, began to produce songs classical in form but unprecedented in content, a poetry without narrative but with a lyricism so compelling and powerful that no one who heard his songs could ever again be ignorant of the hidden treasures and unseen beauties of their world. The Va-Gayjuri firsts and seconds gathered at his gate to hear him. He permitted this, knowing that they might carry his songs away with them to Piya'ar, to Agardi, to Kirabai and the Outer Islands, to Mo'arl and finally to the capital itself. He wanted to be heard, needed to reach beyond his walls, and did not end his concerts even when he was warned that Bhansaar Kitheri had been dispatched to investigate this innovation.

When Bhansaar arrived, Hlavin welcomed him without fear, as though the visit were merely a courtesy call. Selikat had succeeded in beating obliquity into him and, choosing wisely from his seraglio, the Reshtar of

Galatna introduced his brother to several remarkable customs and, afterward, feted him with liqueurs and savories that Bhansaar had never tasted the like of. "Harmless novelties—charming really," Bhansaar decided. Somehow, in the midst of all the graceful, clever talk, with poetry that praised his own wisdom and discernment echoing in his mind as he fell asleep each night, it began to seem that there could be no legal reason to silence young Hlavin. Before he left Gayjur, Bhansaar even proposed—more or less on his own—that Hlavin's concerts be broadcast, like state oratorios.

"Indeed," Bhansaar ruled in his official finding, "that which is not forbidden must be permitted, for to find the opposite true implies that those who established the law were lacking in foresight."

And surely that was a more subversive notion than merely allowing the Reshtar of Galatna to sing his own songs! What more innocuous pursuit could a Reshtar indulge in than poetry, after all?

"He sings only of what can be had within Galatna: of scent, of storms, of sex," Bhansaar reported to his father and brother when he returned to Inbrokar. When they were amused, he insisted, "The poetry is superb. And it keeps him out of trouble."

Thus Hlavin Kitheri was permitted to sing, and in doing so he lured freedom to his prison. Hearing his concerts, staggered by his songs, even firsts and seconds were inspired to shake off the tyranny of genealogy and join him in sublime and scandalous exile, and Galatna Palace became the focus for the gathering of men who would never ordinarily have come together. With his poetry, the Reshtar of Galatna now redefined legal sterility as purity of mind; cleansing his life of the tainted past and forbidden future, he made it enviable. Others learned to live as he did—on the cusp of experience, existing entirely within moment after ephemeral moment of rarefied sexual artistry, unmuddied by considerations of dynasty. And among them were men who did not simply appreciate Kitheri's poetry but who were capable themselves of composing songs of startling beauty. These were the children of his soul.

He meant no more than this: to be content, to live in the eternal present, triumphant over time: all elements in balance, all things stable, the chaos within him contained and controlled, like a woman in her chamber.

And yet, when he had, at last, achieved that very desire, the music began to die in him. *Why?* he asked, but there was no one to answer him.

He tried at first to fill the void with objects. He had always prized rarity, singularity. Now he sought and collected the finest and oldest, commissioned the most costly, the most highly decorated, the most complex. Each new treasure bought a holiday from hollowness, as he studied its intricacies and pored over its nuances, tried to find in it some quality that would summon the light, the flashing brilliance. . . . But then he would put the thing aside, the savor gone, the scent dissipated, the silence unbroken. He passed the days pacing and waiting, but nothing would come—nothing ignited any spark of song. His life had begun to seem not a poem but an incoherent collection of words, as random as a Runa domestic's brainless chatter.

What he felt was beyond boredom. It was a dying of the soul. It was a conviction that there was nothing anywhere in his world that could cause him to breathe in a full measure of life again.

Into this night, like the gilding of first dawn, came a crystal flask of striking simplicity, containing seven small, brown kernels of extraordinary scent: sweetly camphoric, sugary, spiced—aldehydes and esters and pyrazines released in a sudden jolt of fragrance that rocked him as a volcano's eruption rocks the ground, which he breathed in, first gasping, then crying out like an infant newly born. With the fragrance filling his head and chest came the knowledge that the world held something new. Something wonderful. Something that drew him back toward life.

There was more: *syn'amon*, the merchant Supaari VaGayjur called the next consignment. *Klohv. Vanil'a. Yeest. Saydj. Ta'im. Koomen. Sohp.* And with each astonishing delivery, a promise of the unimaginable: sweat, oil, infinitesimal fragments of skin. Not Jana'ata. Not Runa. Something else. Something other. Something that could not be purchased except in its own coin: life for life.

Here then was the complex dance of unprecedented scent and sound and sensation, the superb moment of agonizing sexual tension, the astonishment of unparalleled release. All his life he had sought inspiration in the despised, the unnoticed, the unique, the fleeting; all his life he'd believed that each experience, each object, each poem could be self-sufficient, perfect and entire. And yet, eyes still closed in climax, finishing with the foreigner that first time, he realized, Comparison is the source of all significance.

How could he have been deaf to this for so long?

Consider pleasure, he thought, as the foreigner was taken away. With a Runa concubine or a captive Jana'ata female, there was inequality of a sort, certainly a basis for comparison, but it was obscured by the element of duty done. Consider power! To understand power, one had to observe powerlessness. Here, the foreigner was most instructive, even as the intoxicating scent of fear and blood began to dissipate. No claws, no tail, a laughable dentition, small, imprisoned. Defenseless. The foreigner was the most contemptible of conquests . . .

. . . the embodiment of Zero, the physical manifestation of the starting point of experience . . .

That night, Hlavin Kitheri lay still on his cushions, meditating on the absence of magnitude, on the cypher that separates positive from negative, on the nothing, on the No Thing. When such comparisons were made, orgasm became as inexhaustibly beautiful as mathematics, its gradations—its inequalities—sublimely arrayed for the highly trained aesthete to recognize and appreciate.

Art cannot exist without inequality, which is itself established by comparison, he realized.

He called for the foreigner again at first light. It was different the second time, and the third. He called together the best of the poets—the most talented, the most perceptive—and, using the foreigner to teach what he had learned, found that the experience was different for each of them. Now he listened with new understanding, and he was entranced by the variety and splendor of their songs. He was wrong about the possibility of pure experience—he knew that now! The individual was a lens through which the past looked on the moment, and changed the future. Even the foreigner was marked, changed, by each episode in a way that Runa concubines, that Jana'ata captives never had been.

In the heady days following that first encounter, Hlavin Kitheri produced a philosophy of beauty, a science of art and its creative sources, its forms and its effects. All life could be an epic poem, with each moment's meaning thrown into relief by the slanting light of past and future, of dusk and dawn. There must be no isolation, no random experience or any singularity! To raise life to Art, one must classify, compare, rank—appreciate the inequalities so that the superb, the ordinary and the inferior may be known by their contrast.

After seasons of silence, the transcendent music of Hlavin Kitheri was heard again in an outpouring of artistic energy that washed over his society like a tidal wave. Even those who had ignored him previously, made uncomfortable by his outrageous interests and extraordinary notions, were now transfixed by the glory he seemed to shine upon unchanging verities.

"How beautiful!" men cried. "How true! Our entire society, all our history, can be understood as a faultless poem sung generation after generation, with nothing lost and nothing added!"

In the midst of this ferment, more foreigners came to the gate of Galatna Palace, with a young Runa interpreter named Askama, who said these were members of the foreigner's family who had come to take him home.

Hlavin Kitheri had by that time nearly forgotten the small seed of this vast florescence, but when his secretary approached him, he thought, Let no one be mured up. Let no one be confined by another's wish or need. "The only prison is our own limitations!" the Reshtar sang out, laughing.

Swaying slightly from side to side, afraid to misunderstand, the secretary asked, "My lord: let the foreigner Sandoz go?"

"Yes! Yes—let the chamber be opened!" Kitheri cried. "Let Chaos dance!"

This, then, was the foreigner's last service. For Hlavin Kitheri had been born into a society that imprisoned the spirit of all its people, that perpetuated dullness and ineptitude and indolence among the rulers, that enforced passivity among the ruled. Hlavin understood now that the entire structure of Jana'ata society was based on rank, but this was an artificial inequality, propping up the worst and enervating the best.

"Imagine," the Reshtar urged his followers, "the spectrum of variation that might naturally be evident if all were released to battle for their place in an authentic hierarchy!"

"He's as mad as my mother," men began to say.

Perhaps he was. Unblinded by convention, freed from all restraint, having no stake in what was, Hlavin Kitheri conceived of a world where nothing—not ancestry, not birth, not custom—nothing but ability, tested and proven, would determine a man's place in life. And, briefly, he sang of this with a terrifying grandeur of imagination until his father and brothers realized what he was saying, and forbade the concerts.

Who would not have been unbalanced? To have dreamt of such liberty, to have imagined a world without walls—and then to be imprisoned again . . .

Hlavin Kitheri had true friends, genuine admirers among the poets, and some of them stayed on with him in this new and more awful exile. Prudent men, they hoped that he might find a way to be content once more within the small, exquisite territory of Galatna Palace. But when he began to kill the members of his harem one by one, and sat to watch the bodies rot, day after day, the best of them left him, unwilling to witness his descent.

Then, the flare of light in the darkness: news that Jholaa had been successfully bred and was now carrying, news that the Reshtar of Galatna would be released from his exile and allowed back to Inbrokar City for a short time, to attend the ceremonies marking the inauguration of the Darjan lineage, the naming of his sister's first child, and the ennobling of the Gayjur merchant who had brought him Sandoz.

Hlavin Kitheri had measured and compared and judged the mettle of those who ruled and knew himself unmatched, unfathomed. "Why?" had been answered. All that remained were "When?" and "How?" and, knowing this, the Reshtar of Galatna smiled in silent ambush, waiting for the moment to seize liberty. It came when his absurd brother-in-law Supaari VaGayjur left Inbrokar with a nameless infant. That afternoon—with the sudden, certain rapacity of a starved predator—Hlavin Kitheri brought down everyone who stood in his path to power.

He spent his final days as Reshtar in a series of death ceremonies for his murdered father and brothers, for his slaughtered nephews and nieces, for his defenseless sister, and the gallant but terribly unfortunate houseguest Ira'il Vro—all "foully attacked in the night by Runa domestics subverted by the renegade Supaari VaGayjur." Indeed, the entire domestic staff of the Kitheri compound was declared complicit and swiftly killed. Within hours, a writ of VaHaptaa status was laid on Hlavin Kitheri's fleeing brother-in-law, authorizing summary execution of Supaari VaGayjur and his child, and anyone who aided their escape.

Having swept aside obstacles like so many scythed flowers, Hlavin Kitheri began the elaborate ritual of investiture as forty-eighth Paramount of the Patrimony of Inbrokar, and prepared to set his people free.

9

Naples

October – November 2060

THE WEATHER THAT OCTOBER WAS DRY AND WARM, AND THIS ALONE was enough to make a difference to Emilio Sandoz. Even after a hard night, sunlight pouring through his windows was curative.

Using his hands gingerly because it was impossible to predict what would trigger the pain, he spent the earliest hours of each day neatening the apartment, determined to do as much as he could without anyone else's collaboration or permission. After such a long seige of invalidism, it was pure pleasure to make a bed and sweep a floor and put away clean dishes on his own. By nine o'clock, unless the dreams had been very bad, he was shaved, showered and dressed, and ready to move to the high, safe ground of solitary research.

In his work, he was the technical beneficiary of the nearly extinct American baby boom generation, whose senescence had created a huge market for equipment that aided the enfeebled and disabled. It took a week to train the system to recognize his speech patterns in the four languages he would use most often during this project, and then almost as long again to learn to subvocalize into the throat mike. Preferring the familiar, he also ordered a virtual keyboard and by the thirteenth of October, he had begun to pick up speed using handsets that allowed him to type with barely perceptible movement of the fingers.

Robolinguist, he thought that morning, settling in with headset, braces and keyboard gear. Absorbed by the search for hyponyms and collocations in data radioed back from Rakhat, he didn't notice the sound of knocking beyond the earphones, and so he was surprised by a woman's voice calling, "Don Emilio?" Pulling apparatus off his head and hands, he waited, not quite knowing what to do or say, until he heard, "He's not home, Celestina, but it was a lovely idea. We'll come back another time."

Deal with it now or deal with it later, he thought.

He reached the door just as the child's piping voice rose in insistence, and opened it to a woman in her thirties who looked harassed and tired, but who had Celestina's Renaissance angel looks: brown eyes in an ivory oval, wreathed by dark blond curls.

"I brought you a guinea pig," Celestina announced.

Sandoz, unamused, looked at her mother and waited for an explanation.

"I am sorry, Don Emilio, but Celestina has come to the conclusion that you require a pet," the woman apologized, gesturing impotence in the face of a juvenile onslaught that he surmised had been going on since the christening party. "My daughter is a woman of considerable moral stamina, once her mind is made up."

"I am familiar with the phenomenon, Signora Giuliani," he said with wry courtesy, remembering Askama—for once with simple affection and no jolt of pain.

"Please: Gina," Celestina's mother said, dry humor overcoming her discomfort with the situation. "As I am to be your mother-in-law, I feel we should be on a first-name basis. Don't you agree?"

The priest's eyes widened gratifyingly. "I beg your pardon?"

"Celestina didn't tell you?" Gina pulled a coiling strand of hair away from her mouth, blown there by the wind, and automatically did the same for Celestina, trying to make the squirming, resistant child look presentable. It was an uphill battle. "My daughter intends to marry you, Don Emilio."

"I'm going to wear my white dress with the names on it," Celestina informed him. "And then it's going to be mine forever. And you, too," she added as an afterthought. "Forever."

The mother's momentary distress registered, but Sandoz sat on the bottom step so he was eye to eye with Celestina, the curling halo around her face bright with the sunlight that fell just beyond his door. "Donna Celestina, I am honored by your proposal. However, I must point out that I am quite an elderly gentleman," he told her with ducal dignity. "I fear I am not a suitable match for a lady of your youth and beauty."

The child stared at him suspiciously. "What does that mean?"

"It means, *carissima*, that you are being turned down," said Gina wearily, having explained all this a hundred times, this morning alone.

"I am too old for you, *cara*," Sandoz confirmed regretfully.

"How old are you?"

"I am turning eighty soon," he said. Gina laughed and he glanced up at her, his face grave, eyes alight.

"How many fingers is that?" Celestina asked. Holding up four of her own, she said, "I'm this many."

Sandoz held up both hands and slowly opened and closed them eight times, counting for the child in tens as the braces whirred.

"That's a lot of fingers," said Celestina, impressed.

"It is indeed, *cara*. A multitude. A plethora. A whole bunch."

Celestina mulled this over, twisting a handful of hair around delicate fingers, small wrist braceleted with the last vestiges of baby fat. "You can still have the guinea pig," she decided finally.

He laughed with genuine warmth, but then looked up at Gina Giuliani, the reluctance plain on his face, and shook his head slightly.

"Oh, but you would be doing me a great favor, Don Emilio!" Gina pleaded, embarrassed but determined, for the Father General had encouraged Celestina's notion of giving Sandoz a pig on the grounds that caring for the animal would provide a certain amount of physical and emotional therapy. Besides. . . . "We have three others at home. The whole family has been mobbed by the creatures ever since my sister-in-law brought the first one home from the pet shop. Carmella didn't realize it was already pregnant."

"Truly, signora, I have no way to keep or feed a pet—" He stopped. A classic blunder! he thought, remembering George Edwards's advice to Jimmy Quinn at his wedding: Never give a woman reasons that can be argued with. Say no, or prepare for defeat.

"We brought a cage," said Celestina, who, at four, already understood the principle. "And food. And a water bottle."

"They are very nice pets," Gina Giuliani assured him earnestly, her hands on Celestina's shoulders, holding the child near. "No trouble at all, as long as they don't multiply beyond all reason. This one is quite young and innocent, but she won't remain that way long." Seeing Sandoz's resolve weaken, she pressed her attack with merciless melodrama. "If you don't take her, Don Emilio, she will surely be subject to unspeakable acts—by her own brothers!"

There was a silence one was tempted to call pregnant. "You, signora, are ruthless," Sandoz said at last, eyes narrow. "I am fortunate to escape having you as my mother-in-law."

Laughing and victorious, Gina led Sandoz to her car, Celestina skipping beside them. Opening the back door, Gina reached in and passed the priest a bag of kibble, heedless of his hands, which she had decided to ignore. He juggled the bag ineptly for a moment, but managed to get a secure grip on it as Celestina chattered about how to hold and feed and water the animal, and told him that its mother was Cleopatra.

"Named in a salute to the Egyptian custom of royal incest," Gina remarked very quietly, so Celestina wouldn't hear and demand an explanation. She lifted the cage out of the back seat.

"Ah," Sandoz said, equally quiet for the same reason, as they began the short walk back to his apartment. "Then this one shall be named Elizabeth, in the hope that she has followed in the footsteps of the Virgin Queen." Gina laughed, but he warned her, "If she is with child, signora, I shall not hesitate to have the entire dynasty returned to your doorstep."

They went upstairs and settled Elizabeth into her new home. The pig enclosure was a simple affair of lath and chicken wire, made to fit around a plastic orange crate. There was an overturned vegetable bin for the little animal to hide in. The cage was open at the top.

"Won't she climb out?" Sandoz asked, sitting down and peering at the pig: an oblong lump of golden hair, with a white saddle and blaze, the size and approximate shape of a cobblestone. Its front end, he observed, was distinguished from the back mainly by two wary eyes, bright as jet beads.

"You will find that guinea pigs are not a mountaineering race," Gina said as she knelt to attach a filled water bottle to the cage. She lifted the animal momentarily so he could inspect the absurd little legs that supported the pig's solid bulk and then she went to his kitchen for a dishcloth. "You will also find that a towel over your lap is a sensible precaution," she said, handing him the cloth.

"She'll make peepee on you," Celestina told him as he accepted the animal from her mother. "And she'll—"

"Thank you, *cara*. I'm sure Don Emilio can deduce the rest," Gina said smoothly, sitting in the other chair.

"It looks like little raisins," Celestina told him, relentless.

"And is quite inoffensive, unlike my daughter," Gina said. "Guinea pigs do enjoy being petted, but this one is still a little shy about being handled. Take her out for five or ten minutes now and then. Celestina is correct, if indelicate. Don't rely upon a guinea pig's continence. If you keep Elizabeth Regina in your lap for much longer than that, she is likely to take you for a Anglican convert and baptize you."

He looked down at the animal, which was instinctively trying to appear rocklike and decidedly inedible, in case an eagle flew overhead. There was a little V of black marking her forehead between silly folded-over ears the shape of scallop shells. "I've never had a pet," he said quietly. He retained feeling in the outer edges of his hands, where the nerves had not been severed, and now used an exposed section of his smallest finger to stroke the pig's back from blunt head to tailless behind, a short but silken distance. "All right. I will accept your gift, Celestina, on one condition," he said severely, looking at the mother. "I find, signora, that I require a purchasing agent."

"I understand," Gina said hurriedly. "I'll bring food and fresh bedding every week. At my own expense, naturally. I am very grateful that you'll take her, Don Emilio."

"Well, yes, that too. But also some other things. If it will not inconvenience you too much, I need some clothes. I have no established credit and there are certain . . . practicalities I cannot manage yet." He carefully lifted the pig from his lap and put her back into the enclosure on the floor. The animal shot under the vegetable bin and remained there, motionless. "I don't need you to pay for anything, signora," he said, straightening. "I have a small pension."

She looked surprised. "A disability pension? But you're still working," she said, gesturing at the sound equipment.

"A retirement pension, signora. I myself find the legalities of this situation mystifying," he admitted, "but I was informed last week that Loyola's Company is, in fact, operating in some regions as a multinational corporation these days, complete with health benefits and pension plans."

"And branch offices, instead of provinces!" Gina rolled her eyes, still amazed herself that the dispute had come to this. "The fault line was there for nearly a hundred years, of course, but it is remarkable how much damage can be done by two stubborn, uncompromising old men—both dead now, and not a moment too soon, in my opinion."

Sandoz grimaced. "Well, it's not the first time the Jesuits have gotten too far out in front of the Vatican. It's not even the first time the Society has been disbanded."

"But it was even messier this time," Gina told him. "About a third of the bishops declined to read the Bull of Suppression, and there are hundreds of civil suits over property still being litigated. I don't think anyone really understands the legal status of the Society of Jesus right now!"

He shook his head and shrugged. "Well, John Candotti tells me that negotiations have reopened. He thinks there is room for movement on both sides, and there may be some sort of settlement soon—"

Gina smiled, her eyes amused. "Don Emilio, anyone in Naples will tell you that there are very few political puzzles a Giuliani cannot either finesse or bludgeon into resolution. The new Pope is wonderful, and just as wily as Don Vincenzo. Be assured: those two will work it out."

"I hope so. In any case," Emilio said, coming back to the more immediate problem, "there is no provision in the articles of incorporation allowing for the contraction of time that occurs when someone travels near light speed. As I am nearly eighty by the calendar, I find that I am legally due a pension from what used to be the Antilles province." Johannes Voelker, the Father General's private secretary, had brought this to everyone's attention. The Father General was intensely annoyed by the reasoning but Voelker, a man of rigid principle, had insisted on Sandoz's right to the income. "So. Do they still make Levi's?"

"Of course," she said, a little distracted as Celestina left the guinea-pig cage and moved off toward the photonics. "Don't touch, *cara! Scuzi*, Don Emilio. You were saying? Levi's?"

"Yes. Two pair, if you please. Perhaps three shirts? It is a very small pension." He cleared his throat. "I have no idea what the fashions or prices are now and I will rely on your judgment, but I'd prefer you didn't select anything terribly—"

"I understand. Nothing extravagant." She was touched that he would ask her to do this for him, but kept her face businesslike, running her eyes over him with a tailorly efficiency, as though she did this kind of thing for priests all the time.

"One pullover sweater, I think—"

"No good," she said, shaking her head. "The braces will snag the knitting. But I know a man who makes wonderful suede jackets—" It was his turn to look doubtful, and she guessed at his objection. "Classic design in a durable material is never an extravagance," she told him firmly. "Besides, I can get you a good price. Anything else?" she asked. "I am a married woman, Don Emilio. I have purchased men's underwear before."

He coughed and flushed, eyes sliding away. "Not at the present time, thank you."

"I am a little confused," she said then. "Even retired, don't the Jesuits provide you with—"

"I am not just retiring from a corporation, signora. I am leaving the priesthood." There was an awkward pause. "The details have not been worked out. I will stay on here, as a contractor perhaps. I am a linguist by trade and there is work for me to do."

She knew a little of what he had been through; the Father General had prepared the family before bringing Sandoz to the christening. Still, she was surprised and saddened by the laying aside of vows, whatever the cause. "I sorry," she said. "I know how difficult a decision like that can be. Celestina!" she called, rising and gathering her daughter to her side. "Well," she said, smiling again, "we won't trouble you any longer, Don Emilio. We've interrupted your work long enough."

Celestina stood looking up at the two adults, dark and light, and thought of the paintings in the church, ignorant of the iconography that made them such a mismatch, thinking only that they looked pretty together. "Don Emilio isn't too old for you, Mammina," she observed with a child's rash acuity. "Why don't you marry him?"

"Hush, cara! What an idea. I am sorry, Don Emilio. Children!" Gina Giuliani cried, mortified. "Carlo—my husband—doesn't live with us any longer. Celestina, as you may have noticed, is a woman of action and—"

He held up a braced hand. "No explanations are necessary, signora," he assured her and, face unreadable, helped shepherd the child down the stairs and out the door.

They walked down the driveway together, the adults' silence decently covered by the little girl's prattle, until they reached the car. There, ciaos and grazies were exchanged as he opened doors for the ladies with the deliberate and stately dexterity the braces permitted and enforced. As they drove away, he yelled, "No black! Don't buy anything black, okay?" Gina laughed and waved an arm out the window, without looking back.

"You, madam, are married to a fool," he said softly, and turned toward the garage, where his work was waiting.

HE SETTLED INTO A ROUTINE AS THE MILD NEAPOLITAN AUTUMN SET IN and the rains became more frequent. As promised, Elizabeth was an undemanding companion who quickly took on the size and proportions of a hairy brick and greeted his morning stirring with cheerful whistling.

Never good company at dawn, he would call from his bed, "You're vermin. Your parents were vermin. If you have babies, they'll be vermin, too." But he took her out to eat a carrot on his lap while he drank his coffee and, after a while, hardly felt foolish at all when he talked to her.

Guinea pigs were, he discovered, crepuscular: quiet at night and during the day, active at dawn and dusk. The pattern suited him. He often worked nonstop from eight until past five, unwilling to pause until the pig whistled quitting time as the light diminished. He was aware, always, that his progress could be interrupted by the debilities he'd accumulated on Rakhat and in the months of malnutrition during the solitary voyage home. So he concentrated as long as he could and then made himself a supper of red beans and rice, which he ate with Elizabeth's beady eyes on him. Afterward, he would take her out and sit with her, numbed fingertips idly stroking her back as the little animal nestled down and slept the brief, uneasy sleep of prey.

And then he went back to work, often until past midnight, the overarching structure of K'San—the language of the Jana'ata—becoming plain to him now, and increasingly beautiful: no longer solely the instrument of terror and degradation. Hour after hour, the rhythm of search and comparison, the patient accretion of pattern pulled him along, its inherent fascination sufficient to defend against both memory and anticipation.

In late October, John tactfully informed him of the impending arrival of the other priests who were to be trained for the second Jesuit mission to Rakhat. They had all read the first mission's written reports and scientific papers, John said, and they'd already worked through Sofia Mendes's introductory AI language-instruction system and had begun studying Ruanja on their own. And each had been thoroughly briefed about Sandoz's experiences by the Father General, and by John himself. John didn't say it in so many words, but Emilio understood that the new men had been warned: Don't touch him, don't mother him, don't play therapist. Just follow his lead and get on with the work.

Emilio made little effort to get to know the new men, preferring to confer in cyberspace, buffered by machinery, or in the library, which he could leave when he needed to. But he broke his self-imposed solitude with trips to the kitchen to collect vegetable parings from Brother Cosimo for Elizabeth. And Gina Giuliani stopped by on Fridays, always with Celestina, to drop off pig supplies and sometimes other small items he could bring himself to ask for. She and John Candotti had a knack for helping him without making him feel helpless, and for this he was grateful beyond words. Heads together over lunch one Friday afternoon, the three of them had analyzed the apartment and Emilio's daily tasks. When Gina couldn't find ready-made items that suited his disabilities, John would make them: counterweights for things he needed to lift, utensils with broad handles, plumbing and door hardware that was simpler to operate, clothing that was easier to manage.

On November 5, 2060, which was—as far as he knew—more or less the occasion of his forty-seventh birthday, Emilio Sandoz poured himself a glass of Ronrico after his usual dinner of beans and rice. "Elizabeth," he announced, glass held high, "I am the absolute monarch of my domain, which stretches from that staircase to this desk."

He went back to work, his mind occupied with a K'San semantic field having to do with river systems that the Basque ecologist had suggested might be related to words used in reference to ranked political alliances. Like a series of tributaries! Emilio thought, and felt once more the strangely visceral thrill of trying to disprove a hypothesis he suspected was robust.

10

Pon River, Central Province, Inbrokar

2046, Earth-Relative

THE HEAT BROKE ON THE THIRD DAY SOUTH WITH A STORM THAT drenched the passengers on the river barge and sent sheetfloods a handsbreadth deep across the flats. Accustomed to the ways of the village Runa, Supaari VaGayjur stripped off his sodden city robes and, for the balance of the trip, went nearly as naked as his practical companions did. With his clothes, he stripped away the stink of Inbrokar, and felt real again.

It's over, Supaari thought, and there was no regret in him.

He had been close enough to his life's ambition to see what he was buying and to reckon the cost of living it out, snared in the twisted skein of aristocratic alliances, hatreds and resentments. With a merchant's certainty, he cut his losses, slicing through the tangle with a single word: "leave." So Supaari VaGayjur had walked away from the Kitheri compound without bothering to tell anyone he was going. He took only what was of value to him and to no one else—the child, who was at that moment being dangled over the edge of the barge, piss flying into the wake.

Paquarin had agreed to make the trip south with him as far as Kirabai, and she laughed now, swooping the baby through the water to clean her. She'll sleep now, he thought, smiling as the look of outraged startlement on the howling infant's face was replaced with drowsy contentment in Paquarin's lap, the Runao's fine hands stroking and soothing her.

Leaning against a transport basket of sweetleaf, drowsy himself, he watched the riverbanks slide by and wondered idly why the Jana'ata insisted on clothing bodies protected by dense coats of hair. Anne Edwards had asked him that once and he hadn't had a good answer for her, except to observe that the Jana'ata generally preferred elaborate to plain. Almost dozing as he dried in the breeze, it came to him that the purpose of clothing was neither protection nor decoration but distinction—to mark off military first from bureaucratic second and both of those from academic or commercial third, to keep everyone in his proper position so that greetings were correctly measured and deference appropriately apportioned.

And to put distance between the rulers and the ruled, he realized, so that no Jana'ata would be mistaken for a Runa domestic! Eyes closed, he smiled to himself, pleased to answer Ha'an at last.

Until the extraordinarily polymorphic foreigners pointed it out to him, Supaari himself had never wondered about the uncanny similarity between Jana'ata and Runa. Hadn't even noticed it, really—one might as well ask why rain is the same color as water—but it intrigued the foreigners. Once, while in residence with Supaari in Gayjur, Sandoz had suggested that in ancient times, the resemblance between the two species had been less, but the Runa had somehow caused the Jana'ata to become more like themselves. Predator mimicry, Sandoz called it. Supaari had been greatly offended by the notion that the most successful Jana'ata hunters preying on Runa herds might have been those who looked and smelled most like Runa—who could approach the herds without alarming them.

"Such hunters would be healthier and more likely to find a mate," Sandoz said. "Their children would be better fed and have more children. Over time, the resemblance to Runa would be more noticeable, more frequent among Jana'ata."

"Sandoz, that is foolishness," Supaari had told him. "We breed them, they don't breed us! More likely our ancestors ate the ugly ones, which left only the beautiful Runa—who looked like Jana'ata!"

Now Supaari admitted to himself that there might be some truth in what Sandoz had suggested. "We tamed the Jana'ata," his Runa secretary Awijan had told him once. At the time, Supaari had dismissed the remark as irony, but Jana'ata babies were raised by Runa nurses, and it was a sort of taming . . .

He slept then and, in his dream, stood at the entrance to a cave. In the way of dreams, he knew somehow that the passage before him led to caverns. He took a single step forward but lost his way immediately, and became more and more lost—and woke to the nuptial bellows of white-necked *cranil* lumbering in the shallows. Disturbed and anxious, he scrambled to his feet, and tried to shake off the unease by walking around the pilothouse to watch the animals roll together in titanic earnest, and to wish them good fortune, whatever that might be for *cranil*. When he looked back toward his daughter, sleeping curled next to Paquarin, he thought, I have taken a step into the cave, and I am carrying the child with me.

Not "the child." My child. My daughter, he thought.

There was no one to discuss her naming with. By custom, a first daughter would take an unused name from among the dead of the dam's lineage. Supaari had no wish to commemorate anyone from Jholaa's family, so he tried to remember names of his own mother's ancestors, and realized with dismay that he didn't know any. A third who, it was presumed, would never breed, Supaari had not been told the names of the old ones; or, if he had been told, he did not remember any. Having no fixed notion of what he would do next, beyond leaving Inbrokar with his child alive and intact, Supaari had decided to go home to Kirabai. He would ask his mother to choose a name, and hoped that his request would please her.

Filling his lungs with air that carried nothing of cities, he thought, Everything is different now.

And yet, the scents of home were the same. The horizon was blurred with redbush pollen, visible in the slanting light of second sundown—a haze of fragrance rising off the ground. Where the riverland flattened, and the water widened and slowed, lazy winds brought the familiar medicinal vapor of grass digested: the strangely clean smell of *piyanot* dung. And there was the peppery tang of green *melfruit* a few days before ripening, and the pungent smokiness of *datinsa* past its peak. All that welcomed him and his daughter, and he slept on deck that night, dreamless and content.

He roused on the fourth day south to a stirring among the passengers as the barge approached the Kirabai bridge; many would stop here overnight to trade. Supaari stood and told Paquarin to gather up their baggage and get ready to disembark, and began to brush himself down clumsily. Without his asking, a Runa trader stepped forward to join Paquarin in unpacking Supaari's best clothes and, chatting, helped with his laces and the overrobe buckles. Glad to be done with the forced hauteur of Inbrokar, Supaari thanked them both.

A small, strong excitement rose in him—optimism, pent-up energy, a gladness to be home. He turned to Paquarin and held out his own arms for the baby, careless of his finery. "Look, child," he said, as the barge passed under graceless limestone arches. "The keystone bears the emblem of your ninth-generation beforefather, who fought noticeably well in the second Pon tributary campaign. His descendants have held Kirabai since, as birthright." Her eyes widened, but only because the barge had moved from sunlight to the shadow beneath the bridge. Supaari lifted her to a shoulder and breathed in the musty infant sweetness of her. "I tell you truly, little one, we have to go back that far to find someone to be proud of," he whispered wryly. "We are hostelers, providing lodging four nights south of Inbrokar and three nights north of the seacoast. In return, we're due a stipend from the government, and one part in twelve of any trade carried out by VaKirabai Runa. Your father's family, I am afraid, is not illustrious."

But we don't murder children with deceit, he thought as the barge reemerged into the light.

"We will stop here only until the second dawn tomorrow, lord," the Runa barge owner called to him from the pilothouse. "Will you come with us downriver?"

"No," Supaari said, elated by the sight and smell and sound of Kirabai. "We are home."

Outwardly serene, he handed the baby back to Paquarin as the barge was poled to a halt, watching as huge braided tie lines were thrown over the pilings. He searched faces and tasted windborne scents among the carriers on the dock but found no kin to people he'd known as a boy, so he pressed past the Runa crowd declaring cargo and paying dock fees, and hired a Runao at random for the baggage, even though there was not much baggage and he did not have a great deal to spend on pride. He had been driven from Kirabai with almost nothing, but he'd built a trading company that generated money as the plains breed grass; he had known wealth and had thought sometimes, in the dark hours when sleep would not come, of returning home in luxury and triumph. Instead, he had surrendered all his assets to the state treasury when he took his place as Founder. Now he was arriving on a freight barge no better than the one he'd left on, with nothing to show for his striving but a nameless baby and six hundred *bahli*—all he had after selling his jewelry at the Inbrokar dock to hire Paquarin and buy her passage on the barge. So he had dressed in his best and hired a bearer, hoping to make a good first impression, and wished his claws were longer.

The child is worth the price, he thought, mercantile and unashamed. I can make money again.

The hostelry was visible from the docks, squatting astride an elongated hill that rose above the high-water mark of the river. Yesterday's storm had been stronger here than upriver and, as Supaari led his little entourage through the main gate and beyond the central plaza, up a mesh of narrow walkways lined by the limestone houses of the VaKirabai Runa, they had to step over roof tiles and broken *hlari* branches. The radio tower had blown over and, in the grove near the bridge, several big *marhlar* had tumbled into the river, their roots pulled loose from the banks. But storm damage aside, the town of Kirabai itself seemed almost untouched by the years of his absence . . .

Of course, he was used to the rushing energy of Gayjur and the cramped intrigue of Inbrokar—it was natural that Kirabai seemed lethargic to him. Still, this was a bridgehead for the eastern *rakar* fields, a reasonably important trading center for inland harvesters. And there were the Runa weaving cooperatives, and the *khaliat* factories. There is a lot I can do here, Supaari thought, refusing to be discouraged.

The doorkeeper at the hostelry compound was new, but the gate itself was not, and Supaari noted with some dismay that it still needed the upper hinge repaired. "Find your master!" he cried to the Runa porter, smiling in anticipation of his parents' surprise. "Tell him he has visitors from Inbrokar!"

Without a word, the Runao left them standing in the courtyard. A long silence ensued and when Paquarin looked at him inquiringly, Supaari dropped his tail in a gesture of ignorance. After a time, he called out a greeting and listened for voices, hoping to hear someone familiar. No one answered. Puzzled, Supaari began to look around. There was plenty of room for travelers' equipage in the courtyard, but evidently no one was in residence. Normal for the season, of course. Most Jana'ata traveled in early Fra'an before the heat set in—

"I won't have a bastard within my walls, so if that's what you want, you can leave now."

He whirled, too startled by his mother's voice to be wounded by her words.

"People send anonymous letters to Inbrokar about us, but my sons are useless," the old woman snarled, glaring at the baby, who was awake now and making small sounds as she rooted near Paquarin's neck. "I told them, Take the case to the Prefect! But the Gran'jori lineage has poisoned that bait. May as well howl at the rain. There's never any money for repairs. The Gran'jori want Kirabai and they're welcome to it—this place is nothing but bones. I was born to better, I can tell you! The Prefect pretends to settle things, but it suits him to have us claw at one another's guts. Don't stand there, idiot! Feed that brat or I'll have your ear," she snapped at Paquarin, as the baby began to keen. "The Prefect is supposed to investigate, but he believes what those scavengers upriver say, so where's the meat in trying? Nothing but bones. . . . My brother could have done something with this place! I was born to better, you know. A decent man would have left me in my sire's compound, but not your father!"

Speechless, Supaari followed his mother into the shade of the gallery along the riverward wall of the house, where the breeze was best. He asked her to sit, but she ignored him, sweeping from one end of the arcade to the other, veil askew, skirts gathering a cargo of dust and leaves and fallen *hlari* blossoms. Paquarin settled into a corner with the baby and got out the last of the pureed meat, methodically dipping a delicate finger into the paste and holding it to the child's lips. Supaari took a place on the cushions near the cool stone of the wall and watched his mother, grayed and shrunken, as she paced and ranted.

At last, his father appeared, coming around the back of the pumphouse with a Runa do-all, whom he dismissed with a grunt. "Nobody writes letters about us, wife. And the Prefect has better things to do than persecute hostelers." Enrai sighed, hardly glancing at Supaari and ignoring the baby entirely. "Go on, get back into the house where you belong, y'shameless old bitch. And send that girl out with some meat. I'm famished."

He collapsed onto a cushion at some distance from Supaari and stared out at the river, gleaming like gold foil in the brazen light of three suns. It was quiet, now that the old woman had gone into the house. "Your brothers are out butchering," Enrai said after a time. "These new Runa are worthless. I don't know how the Prefect expects us to train a whole new staff at once. The VaInbrokari rule, but they're as bad as your mother, dreaming up conspiracy and plots and tailless monsters with tiny eyes." He half-turned toward the kitchen and shouted again for meat before muttering, "She was a lovely thing once. You brats ruined her."

Waiting to be fed, the hosteler passed the time as his wife had, with a flow of democratic rancor that took in the living and the dead, the near and the distant, the known and the unknown alike. When Supaari's elder brothers appeared, they joined in with a complicated tale of feuds and rivalries, as intense as they were petty. In the midst of it all, an adolescent Runao appeared with a platter of meat, holding it at arm's length, moving sideways so it remained downwind.

Only Supaari looked at her. A VaKashani villager, he realized, but couldn't quite recall her family. He rose and took the platter from the girl, murmuring a greeting in Ruanja. She was about to speak when Enrai sneered, "If that's what you've learned in the city, Supaari, you can leave it off here. We don't coddle Runa in Kirabai." So she sank in an awkward curtsy, the movement still new to her, and hurried back into the kitchen.

Rigid, Supaari stood silently for a moment, then placed the platter on the low table as his brothers laughed. He returned to his place on the cushions, and it was a long while before his eldest brother noticed that Supaari had not eaten. "You can have a little of this," Laalraj said, waving the back of his hand toward the meal. But he added, "There's nothing extra here. Look around you."

"When will you be leaving?" his brother Vijar asked, chewing.

"Tomorrow at second dawn," Supaari said, and went to see that Paquarin had been settled in with the kitchen help.

HE SPENT THE ENDLESS TIME BETWEEN FIRST AND SECOND SUNDOWN with his brothers and a few neighbors summoned by runners. No one seemed interested in Gayjur or Inbrokar, nor did anyone ask why Supaari was in Kirabai or how he came to be traveling with an infant. Their conversation was salted with shouted demands for food from frightened, half-trained Runa, and was composed primarily of an exhaustive discussion of how a few judicious assassinations might shift genealogical and political status throughout the Pon drainage. Insufficiently to break the jam at the level of Kirabai was the consensus, reached with the spiritless resignation of men who knew themselves trapped by birth and history.

"The Triple Alliance has been a mistake from the start," a neighbor growled, head sunken on his chest. "We need combat like Runa need good fodder. We've all degenerated, waiting out these years. Idleness and decay . . ."

Leave, Supaari wanted to shout. Get out. Track a different scent.

But they could no more leave Kirabai than Runa could sing. It wasn't in them—or maybe it was, but they were too crippled by custom to try. Inheritance was all that counted, even when all the ancestors bequeathed was a list of whom to hate and whom to blame for every stroke of ill fortune in the past twelve generations. No fault is ever found within, Supaari thought, listening to them. None among us is dull or inept or shiftless. We are all powerful and triumphant, but for the ones above us.

The chants began as the light of second sundown burned away, voices raised in ancient harmonies as the neighbors left for home and his brothers prepared to sleep. Supaari's earliest memories were of hearing these songs at sunset, chest tight, his throat gripped by silence. The truest beauty he had known as the founder of a new lineage was joining the Inbrokar choirs at sunset; it was a joy surpassing even the announcement of Jholaa's pregnancy.

He now held legal right to take the part of Eldest, but on this evening, Supaari was as silent as the Runa domestics cowering in the kitchen. I will sing again, he promised himself. Not here, not among these benighted, spiteful fools. But somewhere, I will sing again.

HE BOARDED THE BARGE THE NEXT MORNING LIKE A MAN SNEAKING OUT of a city on the rumor of plague: fortunate to escape, but full of contemptuous pity for those left behind. Paquarin, distressed by the hostility around her, had begged him not to make her go further, so he'd endorsed her travel permit and left her with enough money to stay in Kirabai until the next northbound barge went by. With his last three hundred *bahli*, he bought the VaKashani Runao's labor from Enrai, promising the girl that he'd return her to Kashan if she'd take care of the baby for him until he found a permanent nursemaid.

"This one is called Kinsa, lord," she reminded Supaari after a few quiet hours on the barge, touching both hands to her forehead. "If it is pleasing to you, lord, may this useless one know the baby's name?"

Why am I so different? he had been thinking, blunted hands resting on the rail as he watched the river. All the world thinks one way and I think another. Who am I to judge it wrong? At the girl's words, he turned. "Kinsa—of course! Hartat's daughter." Her scent had changed since he'd met her last. "*Sipaj*, Kinsa," he said, "you've grown."

She brightened at the sound of her own language, and her natural cheerfulness reasserted itself. After all, Supaari VaGayjur was known to her from birth, had traded with her village for years; she trusted him. Lucky child, he thought for one wistful moment. Your people will be happy to touch you again.

"*Sipaj*, Supaari, what shall we call this little one?" Kinsa pressed.

Not knowing what to answer, he held out his arms and, unslinging the baby from her back, Kinsa handed the child to him. He smiled. Kinsa had been among the Jana'ata for so short a time, it still seemed normal for a father to carry his own infant. Holding the baby to his chest as shamelessly as a male Runao, Supaari began to walk the perimeter of the barge.

I don't know what I'm doing anymore, he told his daughter with his heart. I don't know what life I'm making for us. I don't know where we will live or whom you can marry. I don't even know what to call you.

Leaning back against a railing, he settled the child into the crook of his arm. For a time, his eyes left his daughter's face and came to rest on the far south, where river mist met rain, where there was no certain difference between sky and water, and felt again the dream's sensation of wandering. I am a foreigner in my own country, he thought, and so is my daughter.

Like Ha'an! he thought then, for of all the foreigners, Anne Edwards was most vivid to him. In K'San, the sound was good: Ha'anala. "Her name shall be Ha'anala," he said aloud. And he blessed his child: May you be like Ha'an, who was a foreigner here but who had no fear.

He was pleased with the name, happy to have the matter settled. The world seemed full of possibilities as he watched the riverbanks move past. He had contacts, knowledge. I won't sell to the Reshtar again, he thought, wanting nothing more to do with Hlavin Kitheri—no matter how well he paid. He remembered that he'd once considered opening a new office in Agardi. Yes, he thought. I'll try Agardi next. There are different cities. There can be new names.

And later on, quietly, so as not to alarm Kinsa or the others, he did what no Jana'ata father had ever done before: he sang the evening chant to his daughter. To Ha'anala.

11

Naples

October–December 2060

"I'M NOT ARGUING, FATHER GENERAL," DANIEL IRON HORSE ARGUED. "I'M just saying that I don't see how you're going to convince him to go back. We could bring laser cannon with us, and Sandoz'd still be scared spitless!"

"Sandoz is my problem," Vincenzo Giuliani told the father superior of the second mission to Rakhat. "You just take care of the rest of them."

The rest of the problems or the rest of the crew? Danny wondered as he left Giuliani's office that afternoon. Walking down the echoing stone hallway toward the library, he snorted: same thing.

Laying aside the question of Sandoz's participation for the time being, Danny was less than confident about any of the men he'd be risking his life with. They were all bright, and they were all big; that much was clear. For the past year, Daniel Beauvais Iron Horse, Sean Fein and Joseba Urizarbar-rena had worked to develop proficiencies that might prove critical on Rakhat: communications procedures, first aid, survival skills, dead reckoning, even VR flight training so that any of them could, in an emergency, pilot the mission lander. Each of them was thoroughly familiar with the first mission's daily reports and scientific papers. Having worked through Sofia Mendes's introductory AI language-instruction system, they had all studied Ruanja on their own, and had now converged on Naples to work directly with Sandoz on advanced Ruanja and basic K'San. Joseba was solid, and Danny understood why an ecologist had been assigned to the team, but no matter how much money the Company might be able to make by bringing back Rakhati nanotechnology, Sean Fein was a chronic pain in the ass, and Danny could think of a hundred other men who'd be better suited for the mission. John Candotti, by contrast, was a hell of a nice guy and very good with his hands, but he had no scientific expertise at all, and he was months behind the others in training.

The Father General, no doubt, had his reasons—usually at least three for every move he made, Danny had observed. "I must consider myself and conduct myself as a staff in an old man's hand," Danny would recite dutifully whenever he found himself thoroughly mystified, but he kept his eyes open, watching for clues as he and the others settled into an efficient working routine.

Mornings were devoted to language training, but afternoons and evenings were given over to further study of the first mission's records under Sandoz's direction, and it was during these sessions that Danny began to see why Giuliani remained adamant that Sandoz would be an asset. Danny himself had all but memorized the first mission's reports, but he was constantly startled by his own misinterpretations of events, and found Sandoz's memories and knowledge invaluable. Nevertheless, there were days at a time when the man was incapacitated for one reason or another, and Danny's own questions about the Jana'ata triggered the strongest reactions.

"Flashbacks, depression, headaches, nightmares—the symptoms are classic," Danny reported in late November. "And I sympathize, Father! But that doesn't change the fact that Sandoz is dangerously unfit for the mission, even if he could be convinced to go."

"He's coming around," Giuliani said carefully. "He's made real progress in the past few months, scientifically and emotionally. Eventually, he'll see the logic. He's the only one with any experience on the ground. He knows the languages, he knows the people, he knows the politics. If he goes, it maximizes the mission's chances of success."

"The people he knew will be dead by the time we get there. Politics change. We'll have the languages and we've got the data. We don't need him—"

"He will save lives, Danny," Giuliani insisted. "And there is no other way for him to come to grips with what happened," he added. "For his own good, he's got to go back."

·   ·   ·

"NOT IF YOU WENT DOWN ON YOUR KNEES AND BEGGED ME," EMILIO SAN-
doz repeated each time he was asked. "I'll train your people. I'll answer
their questions. I'll do what I can to help. I won't go back."

Nor had Sandoz reconsidered his decision to leave the Society of Jesus,
although this was not being made easy for him. His resignation was a private matter of conscience and should have been a straightforward admin-
istrative procedure, but when he signed the necessary papers "E. J. Sandoz"
and sent them to the Father General's Rome office in late September, they
were returned—weeks later—with a memo telling him that his full signature was required. Once more, he took up the pen that Gina had brought
him one Friday, its grip designed for stroke victims whose dexterity was as
impaired as his own, and spent his evenings in painful practice. Not surprisingly, another month passed without the new paperwork being for-
warded from Rome for signing.

He found Giuliani's delaying tactics first tiresome and then infuriating,
and ended them by sending a message to Johannes Voelker asking him to
inform the Father General that Dr. Sandoz planned to be too sick to work
until the papers arrived. The documents were hand-delivered the next
morning by Vincenzo Giuliani himself.

The meeting in the Father General's Naples office was brief and intense. Afterward, Sandoz strode to the library, stood still until he had the
attention of all four of his colleagues, and snapped, "My apartment. Ten
minutes."

"SOMEONE ELSE HELPED ME WITH THE PEN," SANDOZ TOLD CANDOTTI
tightly, tossing a small stack of papers down onto the wooden table where
John sat with Danny Iron Horse. At the bottom of each sheet, in unhandy
cursive, was a reasonably legible signature: Emilio José Sandoz. "If you
didn't want to be a party to this, you might have been honest enough to
tell me, John."

Sean Fein had been examining Sandoz's personal photonics rig, but now
he studied Candotti, as did Joseba Urizarbarrena, leaning against a half
wall that separated the apartment from the stairway to the garage. Danny
Iron Horse also glanced at John but said nothing, watching Sandoz move
from place to place in the bare room, angry and keyed up.

John's eyes dropped under the scrutiny. "I just couldn't—"

"Forget it," Sandoz snapped. "Gentlemen, I ceased to be a Jesuit at nine
o'clock this morning. I am informed that while I may resign from the So-

ciety or the corporation or whatever the hell it is now, I remain neverthe-less a priest in perpetuity. Outside of emergencies, I am not permitted to exercise priesthood unless I am incardinated by a bishop into a diocese. I shall not seek this," he said, eyes sweeping over them all. "Thus, I am de-clared *vagus*, a priest without delegation or authority."

"Technically, that's pretty much the situation for a lot of us since the suppression. Of course, sometimes we stretch the definition of 'emergency' pretty thin," Danny pointed out amiably. "So. What're your plans?"

The guinea pig, aroused by Emilio's pacing, began to whistle shrilly. He went to the kitchen and got a piece of carrot, hardly aware of what he was doing. "I shall remain here until my expenses are paid," he said, dropping the carrot into the cage.

Iron Horse smiled humorlessly. "Let me guess. Did the old man have an itemized list going back to your first day in formation? You aren't liable for that, ace."

"He can't make you pay for them fancy braces either," Sean added, around a thin-lipped smile. "The Company is a great one for insurance these days. You're covered."

Sandoz stood still and looked at Danny and then Sean for a moment. "Thank you. Johannes Voelker briefed me on my rights." John Candotti sat up straighter, hearing that, but before he could say anything, Sandoz continued. "There are, however, certain extraordinary debts for which I hold myself responsible. I intend to pay them off. It may take a while, but I retain my pension and I have negotiated a salary equal to that of a full professor of linguistics at Fordham for the duration of this project."

"So you're staying, for now at least. Good," Joseba remarked, satisfied. But he made no move to leave.

Danny Iron Horse, too, settled in, making himself comfortable some-how in the little wooden chair. "What about after the K'San project?" he asked Sandoz. "Can't hide forever, ace."

"No. I can't." There was a silence. "Perhaps when this job is done, I'll walk into Naples and call a news conference," Sandoz continued with airy bravado. "Admit everything. Announce that I ate babies! Maybe I'll get lucky and they'll lynch me."

"Emilio, please," John started, but Sandoz ignored him, pulling himself erect, the Spaniard in ascendance. "Gentlemen," he said, returning to the issue at hand, "I am not just leaving the active priesthood. I am apostate. If you do not wish to be associated with me under these conditions—"

Danny Iron Horse shrugged, unconcerned. "Doesn't make any difference to me. I'm here to learn the languages." He glanced, brows up, at the others, who nodded their agreement, then returned his gaze to Sandoz. There was a single uneven breath, a slight diminution of the rigidity. Sandoz stood still for another few moments and then sat on the edge of his bed, silent and staring.

"Nice duds," Danny observed after a time.

Taken by surprise, Sandoz gave a sort of gasping laugh and looked down: blue jeans, a white shirt with narrow blue stripes. Nothing black. "Signora Giuliani's selections," he told them self-consciously. "Everything seems big to me, but she says this is the style."

Glad of the change in subject, John said, "Yeah, they're wearing everything loose these days." Of course, almost anything would have looked big on Sandoz's fleshless frame, John realized with a start. Emilio had always been small, but now he looked wasted again—almost as bad as when he first got out of the hospital.

Apparently following the same line of thought, Iron Horse remarked, "You could stand to put a little weight on, ace."

"Don't start," Emilio said irritably, standing. "All right. Break's over. There's work to do."

He went to the wall of sound-analysis equipment, evidently dismissing them. Joseba stood and Sean moved toward the stairs. John rose as well, but Danny Iron Horse sat there like a pile of rocks, hands behind his head. "I got one leg weighs more than you, Sandoz," he said, looking Emilio over with canny black eyes, small in the pitted face. "You eating?"

John tried to wave Danny away from an injudicious display of solicitude, but Sandoz pivoted on a heel, and said with brittle clarity, "Yes. I eat. Father Iron Horse, you are here to learn Ruanja and K'San. I don't recall engaging you as a nurse."

"Well, good, because I'm not interested in the job," Danny said agreeably. "But if you're eating and you look like you do, what I'm wondering is if you've got whatever D. W. Yarbrough was dying of, on Rakhat. Anne Edwards never did figure out what he had, before they both got killed, eh?"

"Jesus, Danny!" Sean burst out, as Joseba stared and John cried, "For God's sake, Danny! What the hell are you trying to do?"

"I'm not trying to do anything! I'm just saying—"

"They kept me in isolation for months," Sandoz said, his color vanishing. "They wouldn't have released me if I was carrying something. Would they?"

"Of course not," John said, shooting a murderous glare at Danny. "You had every test known to science, Emilio. They wouldn't have let you out if there was any chance that you'd brought back anything dangerous."

Danny shrugged, getting to his feet, and waved the idea off as well. "No, Candotti's right. Couldn't be the same thing," he said. "Forget I mentioned it."

But it was too late. There was a thin gasp as the full weight of it hit Sandoz. "Oh, my God. Celestina and—. My God, John. If I brought something back, if she gets sick—"

"Oh, no," John moaned, and pleaded, "Emilio, nobody's sick! Please, don't do this to yourself!" But by the time he got across the room, Sandoz had already fallen apart and there was nothing anyone could do but wait it out: Joseba and Sean acutely uncomfortable, Iron Horse sitting hugely in the little wooden chair.

"I just . . . don't want . . . anyone else . . . to die because of me," Sandoz was sobbing. "John, if Celestina—"

"Don't talk like that," John snapped, kneeling next to him, unfriendly eyes on Iron Horse. "Don't even think like that. Okay. I know. Oh, God—I know! But nobody's dying! Let's calm down, okay? Listen to me. Emilio? Are you listening? If you were carrying anything, Ed Behr or I would have caught it by now, right? Or someone from the hospital when you first got home, right? Right? Emilio, nobody's sick!"

Sandoz held his breath, tried to slow himself down, tried to think. "There was a lot of diarrhea. For D.W., I mean. Very bad. Anne said it was like Bengali cholera. He said everything tasted like metal. There's been nothing like that for me."

"It's not the same thing," John insisted. "You aren't sick, Emilio! You're just skinny."

Joseba and Sean looked at each other, eyes wide, and then let out breath that had been trapped in their lungs for what felt like hours. Released from embarrassed immobility, Joseba found a glass and brought some water; Sean looked around for tissues and settled for handing Sandoz some toilet paper. With John still at his side, Emilio blew his nose awkwardly and sucked in a deep breath, getting shakily to his feet. Wrung out, he went to the table, sat abruptly in the chair opposite Danny and put his head down. For a while, the room was quiet, and John Candotti, for one, spent the time mentally composing a venomous letter of admonition to the Father General regarding his brother in Christ, Daniel Iron Horse, who seemed neither surprised nor notably remorseful about what he'd triggered, and who had observed Sandoz's collapse with the bland analytical interest of a civil engineer watching a bridge fail.

"Don't take this wrong, ace, but one breed to another?" Danny said to Sandoz. "I never saw an Indian turn that white before." John was appalled but, to his astonishment, Emilio laughed and sat up, shaking his head. "I'm sorry, Sandoz. I really am," Danny said quietly.

It even sounded sincere, John noted. But Emilio nodded, apparently accepting the apology. Relieved that the whole awful business seemed to be resolving itself and determined to pull some good out of it, John went to the kitchen cupboards and threw open the doors. "You just don't eat enough, that's your problem," John told him. "Look what you got in here—nothing but coffee, rice and red beans!"

Sandoz pulled himself straight, drawing tattered dignity around his shoulders like an ermine cloak. "I like beans and rice."

"For true," Sean remarked, "and y'don't have to cut up beans and rice, now, do you?"

"Hell," Danny said, "if you made anyone else exist on that diet, it'd be a human-rights violation, ace."

"The guinea pig eats better than you do," Joseba said, arms over his chest. "You aren't sick, I think. You're just living on your own miserable cooking."

"They were sure I wasn't carrying anything," Sandoz said, as much to himself as to the others.

"They were sure," Iron Horse confirmed softly. "You okay now? You want some more water?" Joseba took the glass from him and refilled it silently.

"Yes. No. I'm okay." Emilio wiped his face on his sleeves, still shaken but better. "Jesus. It's only that . . ."

"It's only that y'had yersalf all nerved up about resigning," Sean finished for him, looking at Iron Horse with hard blue eyes. "And Danny Boy comes up with this crap about being sick. Y'got scared for the little girl, that's all."

Iron Horse shrugged and with self-deprecating humor cheerfully declared himself "Big Chief Shit for Brains." John, who had watched this performance with increasing suspicion, folded his arms and stared. Shit for brains, John thought. Like hell.

"Candotti, you cook Italian?" Iron Horse asked, with a disarming smile.

John nodded, refusing to be charmed. "Yeah, I can cook."

"Well, then! Sandoz, if you can cook beans and rice, you can make spaghetti. You like macaroni and cheese? That'll put some weight on you. Macaroni and cheese was invented here in Naples. Pizza, too, eh? Did you know that?" Emilio shook his head. Iron Horse stood up decisively and moved toward the stairway. "You have never eaten until you've had real Neapolitan macaroni and cheese, right, Candotti? Tell you what. You guys start the water boiling and I'll go get some groceries from the refectory and we'll teach Sandoz here how to cook himself some decent food."

Then, with a big man's surprising quickness, he brushed past Joseba at the head of the stairs and was gone.

"SHATTERED LIKE A WHISKEY BOTTLE HITTING MAIN STREET IN FRONT of the Hotel Bell," Daniel Iron Horse said that evening. "I'm telling you: he'll be a liability out there. He will fall apart at the wrong time and somebody'll get killed! Let's just use him as a resource and then put the poor bastard out to pasture."

"Danny, we've been over this. We can't afford to waste him. What he knows cost us billions and three priests and four good laypeople, not to mention all the damage that was done to the Society because of the bad publicity."

"Hell, we were already in deep shit when that hit the fan. Point is, what'd it cost Sandoz?"

"Everything," Vincenzo Giuliani admitted with prompt precision, but he didn't turn from the window of his office. Staring into the darkness beyond the courtyard, or perhaps at his own reflection in the mullioned glass, he added, "I don't need you to remind me of that, Father Iron Horse." He left the window and moved behind the shining walnut desk, but did not sit. "For what it's worth, the Holy Father insists that Sandoz is meant to return to Rakhat," Giuliani said in a tone that left his own opinion of this matter strictly out of the discussion. "His Holiness points out that six ships have attempted to reach Rakhat in the past forty years, and only the two directly concerned with Sandoz have made it. Gelasius III sees Providence in this."

Booted feet stretched far in front of him, a heavy-bottomed crystal tumbler in one large languorous hand, Iron Horse watched the Father General circle the room, moving soundlessly over priceless antique Orientals. "So what does His Holiness propose?" Danny asked, amused. "We prop Sandoz up on the dashboard of our spaceship like a plastic Jesus and use him to ward off collisions with interstellar debris? Bundle up his little bones with some bird feathers in a medicine pouch and hope the hull doesn't crack apart?"

"Are you finished?" Giuliani asked lightly, pausing in his circuit. Iron Horse nodded, unabashed and unrepentant. "The Pope believes Sandoz must return to Rakhat to learn why he was sent there in the first place. He believes Emilio Sandoz is beloved of God."

Danny pursed his lips judiciously. "Like Saint Teresa said: If that's how God treats His friends, it's no wonder He's got so few of them." Iron Horse lifted his glass to eye level and contemplated the contents before taking a last sip of single malt—leaving, as he always did, precisely one finger's worth of alcohol at the bottom of the glass before setting it aside. "This is prime liquor. I admire your taste," he remarked, but his next words were uncompromising. "Sandoz is medically fragile, emotionally unstable and mentally unreliable. The mission doesn't require him and I don't want him on it."

"He is the toughest man I've ever known, Danny. If you had seen what he was like a year ago, even a few months ago. If you knew what he's—" He stopped, astounded that he was arguing. "He will be on that ship, Father Iron Horse. *Causa finita.* The matter is closed."

Giuliani moved to leave, but Iron Horse remained where he was, immobile as the Grand Tetons. "Do you hate him that much?" Danny asked curiously as Giuliani's hand touched the door. "Or does he just scare you so bad, you don't even want to share a planet with him?"

The Father General, mouth open slightly, was too amazed to walk out.

"No. That's not it." Iron Horse paused, the speculative look on his unlovely face replaced by serene certainty. "Taking Sandoz back to Rakhat is the price of getting the Suppression lifted, isn't it. All we have to do is humor the Pope! Put one poor, old, broken-down ex-Jeb on the next ship out, and win, lose or draw—the prodigals shall be welcomed back to the bosom of Peter, with Vatican bells ringing and a glory of angels shouting hosannah." There was a low appreciative chuckle. "The Dominicans will be furious. It's a beautiful deal, Father General," Danny Iron Horse said, smiling with all the warmth and good humor of a timber wolf at the end of a bad winter. "Why, this time, *you'll* be the one making history."

There had been a fad for a while, Giuliani recalled while standing at the door, for housing domestic photonics in folksy-looking pine cabinetry with iron-work hinges, all cozy and warm on the outside and pure high-speed calculation on the inside. "You are a first-class sonofabitch, Danny,"

Giuliani said pleasantly, as he walked out the door. "I'm counting on that."

Daniel Iron Horse sat still as the old man's footsteps receded. He stood then and retrieved his glass from the heavy silver service tray, for once in his life draining the contents, while Vincenzo Giuliani's ambiguous laughter echoed down the stone-paved hallway.

12

Village of Kashan

2046, Earth-Relative

"SUPAARI HAS BROUGHT SOMEONE HOME!" KINSA CALLED JOYFULLY AS the barge tied up briefly at the Kashan dock.

The cliffside village was not quite one day's travel south from Kirabai, and Supaari had been content to spend that time drowsing on the sunwarmed boards of the barge deck with the Runa passengers, planning no plans, thinking no thoughts, holding the baby Ha'anala, and chatting with Kinsa and the others. Off-loading his own baggage, he glanced up as the Runa poured out of their cut-stone dwellings and smiled as they cascaded like a spring torrent down the rocky paths toward the riverside.

"*Sipaj*, Kinsa: they were worried about you," he told the girl, before acknowledging the shouted farewell of the barge pilot as the vessel disappeared around the southern branch of the river.

But it was Supaari himself whom the VaKashani crowded around—all of them swaying, the children keening. "*Sipaj*, Supaari," was the most common refrain, "you are not safe here."

With an effort, he restored some kind of order to the gathering, speaking loudly over the chaotic Runa babble, persuading them finally to go back up to their largest meeting room, where he could listen to them properly. "*Sipaj*, people," he assured them, "everything will be peaceful. There is nothing worth making such a *fierno* about."

He was wrong, on both counts.

The proclamation had reached his hometown of Kirabai only hours after he'd left, received when the storm-downed radio tower was repaired. The Inbrokari government had declared him renegade. Hlavin Kitheri, now Paramount Presumptive, had called Supaari's life forfeit for the murder of the entire Kitheri family and of some man named Ira'il Vro, whom Supaari had never heard of. Already, a bounty hunter had come here to Kashan. "*Sipaj*, Supaari," one of the elders told him, "the midwife Paquarin sent us word. She used your money to send a runner." "So we knew why the hunter came," another woman said, and then the others began again to talk all at once. "*Sipaj*, Supaari. Paquarin is gone now too."

Of course, he thought, eyes closing. She knew I didn't do it—not that Runa testimony would have made a breath of difference.

"A hunter took her," someone said. "But her runner saw, and came to us." And the cry went up again, "You are not safe here!"

"*Sipaj*, people! Someone must think!" Supaari pleaded, ears folded flat against the uproar. Ha'anala was hungry and rooted near Kinsa's neck, but the frightened girl was swaying witlessly. "Kinsa," he said, laying a still-blunt hand on her head, "take the baby outside and feed her, child. There're provisions in the luggage." Turning back to the elders, he asked, "The hunter who came here—where is he now?"

The sudden silence was startling. A young woman broke it. "Someone killed him," said Djalao VaKashan.

If she had burst into song, he could not have been more dumbfounded. Supaari looked from face to face, saw the shuffling, swaying confirmation in their bodies and thought, The world's gone mad.

"The *djanada* say there must be balance," said Djalao, ears high. She was perhaps seventeen. Taller than Supaari himself, and as powerful. But clawless. How had she . . . ? "Birth by birth," Djalao was saying. "Life by life. Death by death. Someone made a balance for Paquarin."

He fell back against his tail like a random-bred drunk. He had heard the stories—there were other Runa like this, who had dared to kill Jana'ata, even after most of the rebels had been culled. But here? In Kashan, of all places!

Sinking onto the stone floor, he began to think the business through. He was known to have traded with Kashan and Lanjeri. None of the southern towns would be safe. He had been seen on the barge, so the river-ports would be watched. Pieces of his bedding would be distributed to all the checkpoints: his scent would be known wherever he fled.

"*Sipaj*, Supaari," he heard someone say. Manuzhai, he realized, looking up and seeing him for the first time since the death of the man's daughter, Askama, almost three years earlier. "Can you not become *hasta'akala*?"

"*Sipaj*, Manuzhai," Supaari said quietly. "Someone is sorry for your loss." The VaKashani's ears dropped listlessly. Supaari turned back to the others, as the impossible idea of making him *hasta'akala* rippled through the crowd. "No one will take this one for *hasta'akala*," he told them. "When someone was made Founder, he gave everything he had to endow the new lineage. Now there is no property to compensate the sponsor."

"Then we will sponsor you," somebody cried, and this idea was taken up with enthusiasm.

They meant well. A man in trouble could barter his property and titles for immunity to prosecution if he could find someone to take him on as a dependent and keep him off the public stipend rolls. In return for lodging and provision, the *hasta'akala* yielded everything he possessed to the sponsor and had his hands clipped—a lifelong guarantee against his becoming a VaHaptaa poacher. Supaari stood so they could all see him clearly. "Someone will explain. The sponsor must be able to feed the one taken *hasta'akala*. You would not be able to feed this one," he said as gently as he could.

They understood then. Runa had no access to state meat allowances, and obviously no right to hunt. There was a soft thudding of tails, raised and dropped to the ground in gestures of dismay and pity, as the talk fell off to an unhappy silence.

"*Sipaj*, Supaari," Manuzhai said then, "we could feed you ourselves. Someone is ready. Someone's wife and child are gone. Someone would rather be yours than a stranger's."

Other voices joined Manuzhai's: "*Sipaj*, Supaari, we can make you *hasta'akala*." "The VaKashani could sponsor you." "This one, too, is ready to go." "We can feed you."

To the end of his days, Supaari would remember the sensation of the ground moving under his feet, as though there had been a minor earthquake. For an instant, it felt so real that he looked around at the Runa in astonishment, and wondered why they did not flee to open ground, to escape the rockfall sure to follow.

Why not? he thought then. Runa had been bred since beyond remembering to serve Jana'ata in life and to sustain them in death. Manuzhai was clearly pining away from loneliness; if the Runao didn't want to live—. Again, Supaari felt the sensation of movement. Even now, he would have eaten the supply of food he'd brought with him from Kirabai without a thought! But that wasn't . . . people like these. He had never taken meat from his own villages or household compound. Indeed, he had never killed his own prey. He was a city man! He collected his meat already butchered, never thinking—. There was nothing wrong with it; it was perfectly natural. Everything dies. It would be a waste if . . .

People like these.

Walking out to the edge of the meeting hall's terrace, where the rockface dropped away steeply to the river below, Supaari stared into the distance and would have keened like a child if he had been alone. No, he thought, looking back at the VaKashani, seeing them all with new eyes. Better to starve. Thinking this, he realized at long last why Sandoz, whom Supaari knew to be carnivorous, had obstinately insisted on eating like a Runao while in Gayjur. Well, I cannot eat like a Runao, he thought angrily. And I will not scavenge!

Which left one honorable course open to him and his child. The dream cave, he thought, and saw himself, lost, with his daughter in his arms.

When he spoke, it was firmly. "*Sipaj*, people, this one cannot accept your offer."

"Why not?" the cry went up. He shrugged: a movement of the shoulders that he had learned from Sandoz, a foreigner trapped in a situation he could not escape and hardly understood. The Runa were a practical folk, and so Supaari fell back upon plain facts.

"As *hasta'akala*, someone's hands would be clipped. This one would not be able to . . . take the meat, even when it is offered with such generosity of heart."

It was Manuzhai who said, "*Sipaj*, Supaari, we can make you *hasta'akala* and Djalao can take the meat for you. She knows how. The rest of us could learn!"

Again there was a burst of cheerful agreement, the VaKashani pressing forward to pat his back, pledging him their support, delighted by their solution to his troubles, happy to help this Jana'ata merchant who'd always been kind and decent. It was nearly impossible to resist them, but then he met the eyes of Djalao, standing apart from the others.

"Better to die for a good reason," said Djalao, holding his gaze like a hunter, but it seemed that she was offering death to Supaari himself, not to Manuzhai.

The others took up the notion happily; no VaRakhati—neither Runa nor Jana'ata—had ever yet said, "Better to live."

Supaari turned his head away, unable to bear Djalao's stare. He agreed to consider their offer, and promised a decision in the morning.

RUNA BLADES WERE OF VOLCANIC GLASS, SHARPER THAN ANY STEEL, with a knapped edge so fine that Supaari would hardly feel its work. There would be a few quick, neat strokes through the fleshless webbing between his fingers, and the short, thick-muscled digits would fall free almost bloodlessly. In some ways, he had already adapted to the reduction in function, having severed his own claws days before. He expected that his hands would be clumsier than ever, but he had always had Runa to take care of his clothes, to write for him and open doors and groom his coat and prepare his food.

To be his food.

Physically, the *hasta'akala* was a trivial procedure, but the permanance of it! The irrevocable change in status! Always before, Supaari had met adversity with the conviction that he could turn it to advantage somehow, but if he accepted the *hasta'akala*, he conceded guilt. He was marked forever as a dependent—of Runa! And though he now admitted to himself that he had always been dependent on Runa—even so, it was bitter.

Apart from Sandoz, Supaari had never known a *hasta'akala*. Once accepted by a sponsor, such men were of no further interest to the government and there was nothing to prevent them from traveling abroad except shame. Now Supaari understood why Jana'ata who submitted to the procedure most often withdrew from society, sequestering themselves like women, loath to be seen. He himself could hardly stand to be with the elated Runa villagers who continued to talk blithely through the evening of their plans to care for him, discussing the order in which Djalao could slaughter the elders . . .

Sometime that night, during the endless blind misery that sleep did not curtail, he realized that their scheme was well meant, but it couldn't work. If the village corporation fed Supaari and Ha'anala, it wouldn't make its quota to the state. It was unprecedented, that a Runa corporation would take on the sponsorship of a *hasta'akala*. A Runao culling another Runao—it might be illegal. There was no telling what a court would make of it. The arrangement probably wouldn't hold up under legal scrutiny and, even if it did, Hlavin Kitheri could annul the *hasta'akala* contract by decree.

By first sunrise, he had resolved to walk into the wilderness and die there with his child. "*Sipaj*, people," he called out, when the Runa roused and his vision sharpened. "You are not safe if someone stays here. This one can only be a danger to Kashan and all who live here. Someone will take Ha'anala and leave, to keep you safe."

They would not simply let him go; they were Runa, and nothing could be done without consensus. The discussion seemed to him interminable and he was frantic to leave, truly frightened now by what could happen if he were discovered here.

In the end, it was Djalao who dropped a tail and said without emotion, "Take him to Trucha Sai."

Naples

December 2060 – June 2061

"WHY NOT?" CELESTINA ASKED.

"Because he has asked us not to come, *cara*," Gina Giuliani said very clearly, beginning to lose patience on the fourth time through this particular line of interrogation. It was hard enough to manage her own disappointment without dealing with Celestina's over and over. The story of my life these days, Gina thought, and tried not to sigh as she drained the pasta.

"But why can't we?" Celestina whined. She leaned on the kitchen table with her elbows and rocked her little behind back and forth. "What will Lizabet eat?" she asked slyly: a sudden inspiration.

Gina looked up. Good, she thought judiciously. Very good. But she said aloud, "I'm sure Brother Cosimo has plenty of vegetables for Elizabeth." She stared at Celestina. "This is, by actual count, the seven hundred and thirty-first serving of macaroni and cheese I have made for you. This year alone."

"That's a lot of fingers," Celestina said, and giggled when her mamma laughed. "Can we go tomorrow?"

Gina closed her eyes for a moment. "*Cara*. Please. No!" she said loudly, stirring in the cheese.

"But why not!" Celestina yelled.

"I told you: I don't know!" Gina yelled back, plunking a bowl onto the table. She took a breath and lowered her voice. "Sit down and eat, *cara*. Don Emilio's voice sounded a little husky—"

"What's 'husky'?" Celestina asked, chewing.

"Swallow before you speak. Husky means hoarse. Like when you had your cold last week. Remember how your voice sounded funny? I think perhaps he's caught your cold and doesn't feel well."

"Can we go tomorrow?" Celestina asked again, spooning in another mouthful.

Gina sighed and sat down across from her daughter. "Relentless. You are absolutely relentless. Look. We'll wait until next week and see how he feels. Shall we ask Pia's mamma if Pia can come over to play after lunch?" Gina suggested brightly, and thanked God when the diversion worked.

This morning had marked the first time Emilio Sandoz had ever rung Gina Giuliani up, but her pleasure was quickly dampened by his tone when he asked if he might cancel their usual Friday visit. She agreed, naturally, and asked him if anything was wrong. Before he could answer, she made sense of the unusual roughness in his voice and asked, a little anxiously, if he were sick. There was a stony silence and then she heard his cool comment, "I hope not."

"I'm sorry," she said, a little huffily. "You're right, of course. I should have realized it wasn't good judgment to bring Celestina."

"Perhaps we have both made an error in judgment, signora," he said, the chill becoming glacial.

Offended, she snapped, "I didn't realize she was coming down with anything. It's not a very bad cold. She was over it in a few days. I'm sure you'll survive."

When he spoke again, she could tell something was working on him but couldn't imagine what it was.

"*Mi scuzi, signora*. There has been a misunderstanding. The fault is not in any way yours or your daughter's." The Viceroy, she thought irritably, and wished he'd allowed a visual for the call—not that his face gave much away when he was like this. "If you will be so kind, I find that for now it is not . . . convenient that you should come." He paused, groping, which surprised her. His Italian was ordinarily excellent. " 'Convenient' is not the correct word. *Mi scuzi*. I have no wish to offend you, signora."

Confused and disappointed, she assured him that no offense had been taken, which was a lie but one that she was determined to make true. So she told him that a change of scene would do him a world of good and prescribed an evening in Naples, which would be crowded and merry with shoppers. She was sure he'd be over the cold by mid-December. "No one does Christmas like the Neapolitans," she declared. "You have to see it—"

"No," he said. "This is impossible."

It was difficult not to be insulted, but she'd begun to know him and correctly interpreted his rigidity as fear. "Don't worry! We'll go at night! No one will recognize you—wear gloves and a hat and dark glasses," she suggested, laughing. "My father-in-law always sends guards with me and Celestina anyway. We'll be perfectly safe!"

When this failed to move him, she took a step back and assured him, with a generous measure of irony, that she had no designs on his virtue and promised that Celestina would be their chaperone. This backfired rather decisively. There was another round of stiff apologies. She was astounded, when the call was over, by how very much she wanted to cry.

The flowers arrived that afternoon.

A week later, Gina pitched them onto a compost pile with a resolute lack of sentimentality. She did keep the card. There was no signature on it, of course—only a note in a shopgirl's handwriting: "I need some time." Which, she supposed, was the exact if unenlightening truth. So, for Christmas, Gina Giuliani gave Emilio Sandoz time.

ADVENT THAT YEAR WAS DIFFICULT. GINA SPENT IT WITH FAMILY AND old friends, trying not to think of where Carlo was, or with whom, or of what the flowers from Emilio might have meant. Gina Giuliani was not good at not thinking about things. December seemed as endless to her as it did to Celestina, who was dying for the month to be over so it would be time for the big Epiphany party at Carmella's. That was when all the children would learn if they'd gotten coal or gifts from La Befana—the Bitch, who had rudely driven the Wise Men away when they stopped in Italy on their way to see the Christ Child.

Everyone tried to prevent Celestina's holiday from being spoiled by spoiling her with presents instead. Gina's in-laws were particularly lavish in their giving. They liked Gina, who was also the mother of a beloved granddaughter, and made sure that Carmella included her at all the parties. But despite Don Domenico's regular denunciations of his son, Carlo was family, and blood counts.

Only Carlo's aunt Rosa, seventy-four and not inclined to subtlety, addressed the situation at Carmella's party. Trying to escape the crush of friends and relatives and the mind-boggling noise produced by dozens of children whipped into a froth of sugar, excitement and greed, she and Gina took refuge in the library.

"Carlo's a prick," Rosa said flatly, as the two women settled into butter-soft leather chairs and put their feet up on a stylishly low table. "A gorgeous man, Gina, I see why you fell for him. But he's never been any good! He's my own brother's son but I'm telling you, he'll screw anything with a pulse—"

"Rosa!"

"Boys, dogs, whores," Rosa went on, as relentless as Celestina. "They think I don't know, but I hear things. I'd shoot the bastard right in the balls if I were you." Her cloudy eyes full of conspiracy and violence, the skinny old woman leaned over to grip Gina's arm with surprising strength. "You want me to shoot him for you?" she asked. Gina laughed, delighted by the idea. "I'll do it!" Rosa assured her, sitting back comfortably. "I'd get away with it, too. Who's going to prosecute an old broad like me? I'll be dead before the appeals are done."

"It's a tempting offer, Rosa," Gina said, loving her, "but I knew he was a rat when I married him."

Rosa shrugged, agreeing reluctantly. Carlo had, after all, left his first wife for Gina. Worse, Gina Damiano had met the gorgeous Carlo Giuliani at an ob-gyn clinic; she was the nurse who took care of Carlo's mistress in post-op after an ugly second-trimester abortion. Gina could still remember the sense of detached amazement at her own stupidity when, mesmerized by his looks, she heard herself accepting Carlo's irresistibly charming offer of dinner that first night.

She shouldn't have been surprised when she caught him with the next lover, but Gina was pregnant with Celestina at the time and made the mistake of being outraged. The first beating was such a shock, she could hardly believe it had happened. Later, she remembered the mistress's bruises, and Carlo's explanations. The signs were all there—it was her own fault for ignoring them. She filed for divorce; believed his promises; filed again . . .

"Your marriage never would have worked anyway," Rosa said, breaking into Gina's thoughts. "I didn't want to say anything before the wedding—you always hope for the best. But Carlo's gone so much—all that space shit. Even if he wasn't a prick, he's never home." Rosa leaned forward, voice low. "In my opinion," she offered, "it's mostly my brother's fault. Carlo takes after my sister-in-law's side, you know? Even when they were first married, Domenico was screwing around so much, he couldn't imagine that his own wife wasn't. Never believed Carlo was his. Poisoned everything. Then my sister-in-law spoiled Carlo rotten, to make up for it. You know why Carmella turned out so well?"

Gina shook her head, brows up.

"Her parents ignored her. Best thing that could have happened! They were so busy fighting over Carlo, they never got around to making a mess of their daughter. Now look at her! A good mother, a wonderful cook, beautiful home—and she's a very smart businesswoman, Gina! It's no wonder Carmella's running everything now!"

Gina laughed. "Now there's a novel approach to parenting! Have two kids, and concentrate on ruining one."

"At least you won't have to take care of Carlo when he's old," Rosa resumed philosophically. "I thought Nunzio would never die!" A bluff, Gina knew. Rosa had been devoted to Nunzio and missed him very much, but unlike most Neapolitans, she refused to give in to operatic bathos. It was a characteristic that bound the two women together, across the generations. "Men are shits," Rosa declared. "Find yourself a twelve-year-old and train him right," the old lady advised. "It's the only way."

Before Gina could reply, Celestina—extravagant compensation for a brief marriage to a gorgeous rat—burst into the room. Wailing, she delivered herself of a wide-ranging indictment, charging her cousins Stefano and Roberto with several atrocities having to do with her new bride doll and a space freighter. "It's hopeless," Aunt Rosa said, throwing up her hands. "Even the little ones are shits." Shaking her head, Gina went off to set up some kind of demilitarized zone in the playroom.

THAT WINTER, GINA WOULD SOMETIMES TAKE THE FLORIST'S CARD OUT of her bureau drawer and look at it. Holding up an unbraced hand, she would say aloud, with Sandoz's own antique formality, "No explanations are necessary." Nor were any likely to be offered, she realized as the weeks became months. Every Friday, she left guinea-pig chow and a bag of fresh litter at the refectory with Cosimo. After the first two visits, she made a point of doing this while Celestina was at kindergarten. It was bad enough trying to explain Carlo's absences and inconsistencies to the child without attempting to explain Emilio Sandoz as well. Once, in early spring, she worked herself into a rage and considered banging on Sandoz's door to tell him he could ignore her but not Celestina, but she identified this almost immediately as displaced emotion, more properly aimed at Carlo Giuliani than at an ex-priest she barely knew.

She understood that a good portion of what she felt and thought about Emilio Sandoz was concocted of equal parts romantic idiocy, hurt pride and sexual fantasy. Gina, she would tell herself, Carlo is a prick but you are a fool. On the other hand, she thought prosaically, fantasies about a dark, brooding man with a tragic past are more interesting than blubbering over getting dumped by a jerk for a teenaged boy.

And Emilio had sent her flowers. Flowers and four words: "I need some time." That implied something, didn't it? It wasn't all in her head. She had the note.

She might have wished for some golden mean between Carlo's endlessly inventive eloquence and the strict, unexpansive silence of Emilio Sandoz. But in the end, she decided to play by Emilio's rules, even if she didn't know quite what they were. There didn't seem to be any other choice, apart from forgetting him altogether. And that, Gina found, was evidently not an option.

WHAT COULD HE HAVE SAID? "SIGNORA, I MAY HAVE EXPOSED YOU AND your child to a fatal disease. Let's hope I'm wrong. It will be months before we know." There was no point in scaring her—he was frightened enough for both of them. So Emilio Sandoz took himself hostage until he could prove to his own satisfaction that he was not a danger to others. It was an act of will, and it required of him a complete strategic reversal in his war with the past.

Living alone had allowed him to withdraw with honor from the battlefield his body represented. Once a source of satisfaction, it had become an unwanted burden, to be punished for its frailties and vulnerability with indifference and contempt. He fueled it when hunger interfered with his work, rested it when he was tired enough to sleep through nightmares, despised it when it failed him: when the headaches almost blinded him, when his hands hurt so much that he sat laughing in the dark, the pain comic in its intensity.

He had never before felt so entirely disconnected from himself.

He was not a virgin. Neither was he an ascetic; while studying for the priesthood, he had come to the conclusion that he would not be able to live as a celibate by denying or ignoring his physical needs. This is my body, he told his silent God, this is what I am. He provided himself with sexual release and knew this was as necessary to him as food and rest, as lacking in sin as the desire to run, to field a baseball, to dance.

And yet, he was aware that he had taken inordinate pride in his ability to govern himself and that this, in part, accounted for his reaction to the rapes. When he began to understand that resistance made it worse for him and more gratifying for those who used him, he tried to submit passively, to deny them as much as he could. It was beyond him: intolerable, impossible. And when he could not endure being used again, when he decided to kill or die rather than submit once more, it had cost Askama's life. Was rape his punishment for pride? An ugly lesson in humility, but one he might have been able to learn, had Askama not died for his sins.

None of it made sense.

Why had God not left him in Puerto Rico? He had never sought or expected spiritual grandeur. For years he was, without complaint, *solo cum Solus*—alone with the Alone, hearing nothing of God, feeling nothing of God, expecting nothing of God. He lived in the world without being part of it, lived in the unfathomable without being part of it. He was grateful to be what he had become: an ex-academic, a parish priest working in the slum of his childhood.

But then, on Rakhat, when Emilio Sandoz had made a place in his soul large enough and open enough, he had, against all expectation, been filled with God—not filled but inundated! He felt himself flooded, drowned in light, deafened by the power of it. He had not sought this! He had never taken pride in it, never understood it as recompense for what he had offered God. What filled him was incommensurate, measureless, unearned, unimagined. It was God's grace, freely given. Or so he'd thought.

Was it arrogance and not faith, to have believed that the mission to Rakhat was part of some plan? Until the very moment that the Jana'ata patrol began to slaughter children, there was no warning, no hint that they were making a fatal mistake. Why had God abandoned them all, human and Runa alike? Why this silent, brutal indifference after so much apparent intervention?

"You seduced me, Lord, and I let You," he read in Jeremiah, weeping, when Kalingemala Lopore left. "You raped me, and I have become the object of derision."

Outraged that anyone's faith should be tested as his had been, and profoundly ashamed that he had failed that test, Emilio Sandoz knew only that he could not accept the unacceptable and thank God for it. So he had abandoned his body, abandoned his soul—surrendered them unconditionally to whatever force had beaten him, tried to live only in a mind over which he retained sovereignty. And for a time, he found not peace but at least a kind of uneasy ceasefire.

Daniel Iron Horse put an end to that; whatever had happened on Rakhat, whoever was to blame, Emilio Sandoz was alive and his life touched other lives. So, he told himself, face it.

He ate decent meals three times a day, as though the food were medicine. He began again to run, circling the dormant retreat house gardens, working up to four eight-minute miles every morning, rain or shine. Twice a day, he forced himself to break off work and carefully picked up a set of handweights, methodically exercising arm muscles that now did double duty, indirectly controlling his fingers through the brace mechanisms. By April, he was approaching welterweight, and the shirts he wore no longer looked as though they were still on hangers.

The headaches persisted. The nightmares continued. But he won back lost ground with infantry doggedness and, this time, he was determined to hold it.

IT WAS AN UNUSUALLY CHILLY MORNING IN EARLY MAY AND CELESTINA was at kindergarten when Gina Giuliani glanced out the kitchen window and noticed a man on foot talking to the guard at the end of the drive. She recognized the gray suede jacket she'd bought for him before she recognized Sandoz himself and briefly considered doing something about her hair, but changed her mind. Pulling on a cardigan, she walked out the back door to meet him.

"Don Emilio!" she said smiling broadly as he approached. "You look well."

"I am well," he said without a trace of irony, responding to the automatic pleasantry as the literal truth that it was. "I was not certain before, but I am now. I have come to beg pardon, signora. I believed it was better to be rude than to worry you uselessly."

."*Mi scuzi?*" she said, frowning.

"Signora, two members of the *Stella Maris* party became ill on Rakhat. One died overnight. The other was sick for many months and was near death before he was killed," he told her with expressionless calm. "We were never able to determine the cause of either illness, but one of them was a wasting disease. Ah, I was correct not to say anything of this earlier," he said when her hand went to her lips. "Perhaps then you will forgive me.

In December, it was brought to my attention that I might have carried that illness back with me." He held his arms out slightly from his body, presenting it to her as the irrefutable evidence he had required himself to produce. "As you see, I was suffering from cowardice, not from any pathogen."

She was speechless for a time. "So, you put yourself in quarantine," she said finally, "until you were sure you were healthy."

"Yes."

"I don't quite see where cowardice fits in," Gina said.

The gulls were screaming and he let her wonder if the wind had carried her words away. "The men I spoke to on my way here tell me this stretch of coast is under guard at all times," he said. "This is true?"

"Yes." She pulled the hair away from her face and the cardigan tighter around her.

"He says 'Mafia' is the wrong term. It is the Camorra in Naples."

"Yes. Are you shocked?"

He shrugged and looked away. "I should have realized. There were indications. I have been preoccupied." He stared at the view of the sea that she had from her bedroom window. "It's very beautiful here."

She watched him, profiled, and wondered what to do next. "Celestina will be home from school in a little while," she told him. "She'll be sorry if she misses you. Would you care to wait? We could have a coffee."

"How much do you know about me?" he asked bluntly, turning toward her.

She straightened, startled by the question. I know that you treat my daughter like a little duchess, she thought. I know that I can make you laugh. I know that you. . . . She found the directness of his gaze sobering. "I know you are in mourning for dear friends, and for a child you loved. I know you believe yourself responsible for many deaths," she said. "I know that you were raped."

He did not look away. "I wish there to be no misunderstanding. If my Italian is not clear, you must tell me, yes?" She nodded. "You have offered me . . . friendship. Signora Giuliani, I am not naive. I am aware of the emotions of others. I wish you to understand that—"

She felt sick. Ashamed of her own transparent schoolgirl crush, she began to pray for a major tectonic event—something that would cause, say, the entire Italian peninsula to sink into the Mediterranean. "No explanations are necessary, Don Emilio. I'm terribly sorry that I've embarrassed you—"

"No! Please. Let me—. Signora Giuliani, I wish that we had met before—or maybe a long time from now. I am not clear," he said, looking to the sky, impatient with himself. "There is . . . a habit of thought in Christianity, yes? That the soul is different from and higher than the physical self—that the life of the mind exists separate from the life of the body. It took me a long time to understand this idea. The body, the mind, the soul—these are all one thing to me." He turned his head, letting the wind take the hair out of his eyes, which rested on the horizon where the brightness of the Mediterranean met the sky in a knifeblade of light. "I now believe that I chose celibacy as a path to God because it was a discipline in which the body and the mind and the soul were all one thing."

He stood silent for a moment, gathering himself. "When—. You must understand that there was not one rape but many, yes?" He glanced at her, but looked away again. "There were seventeen men, and the assaults went on for months. During that time, and afterward, I tried to separate what happened to me physically from what it . . . did to me. I tried to believe, It is only my body. This cannot touch what I am. It was . . . not possible for me to think in this way. Forgive me, signora. I have no right to ask you to hear this."

He stopped then, nearly defeated. "I'm listening," she said.

Coward, he thought savagely, and forced himself to speak. "Signora, I wish there to be no misunderstanding between us. Whatever the legalities, I am not a priest. My vows are a nullity. If we had met at another time, I would wish for us perhaps more than friendship. But what I once gave to God freely is now enforced by—" Nausea. Fear. Rage. He looked into her eyes and knew that he owed her as much truth as he could bear. "By aversion," he said finally. "I am not whole. Can it be acceptable to you that what I offer in return for your friendship will be something less?"

My body is healed, he was asking her to understand; my soul is still bleeding. It's all one thing to me.

The wind, constant this close to the coast, sounded loud in her ears and carried the scent of seaweed and fish. She looked, as he had, toward the bay, its water sequined with sunlight. "Don Emilio, you offer me honesty," she said, serious for once. "This, I think, is not less than friendship."

For a time, there was no sound but the call of gulls. In the distance, down the driveway, a guard coughed and threw a cigarette on the ground, crushing it out with his shoe. She waited, but it was clear that Sandoz had done all he could. "Well," she said finally, remembering Celestina and the guinea pig, "you can still have the coffee."

There was a sort of gasping laugh that gave some measure of the strain, and the braced hands went to his head, as though to run his fingers through his hair, but then returned to his sides. "I think I'd rather have a beer," he said with artless candor, "but it's only ten o'clock."

"Travel is so broadening," she remarked equably. "Have you ever had a Croatian breakfast?" He shook his head. "A shot of plum brandy," she explained, "followed by espresso."

"That," he said, rallying a little, "would do nicely." Then he became very still.

She was held in the tension just before movement, about to walk back toward the house. Later she would think, If I had turned away, I'd have missed the moment he fell in love.

He would not remember it that way. What he experienced was not so much the beginning of love as a cessation of pain. It felt to him as physical and as unexpected as the moment when his hands finally stopped hurting after some awful bout of phantom neuralgia—when the pain was simply gone, as suddenly and as inexplicably as it had come. All his life, he had understood the power of silence. What had eluded him was the ability to speak of what was inside him, except sometimes to Anne. And now, he found: to Gina.

"I missed you," he told her, discovering it as he said the words.

"Good," she said, her eyes holding his, knowing more than he did himself. She started off for the kitchen. "How's Elizabeth?" she called over her shoulder.

"Fine! She's a good pet. I really enjoy having her around," Emilio said, jogging a few steps to catch up with her. "John Candotti made her an amazing cage—three compartments and a tunnel. Pig Land, we call it." He reached past Gina to open the door, closing his hand over the knob without thinking of the movement at all. "Would you and Celestina like to come for lunch some time? I have learned to cook," he told her grandly, holding the door for her. "Real food. Not just packaged stuff."

She hesitated before stepping through. "We'd love to, but I'm afraid Celestina eats very little aside from macaroni and cheese."

"Kismet!" he cried, with a smile like sunrise that warmed them both. "Macaroni and cheese, signora, happens to be my speciality."

AS THE DAYS LENGTHENED, THERE WERE LUNCHES, BRIEF VISITS, SHORT calls, messages left three and four times a day. Emilio was at the house when the papers came in the mail, finalizing the divorce, and Gina cried anyway. She learned early on that he could not eat meat; eventually, he was able to explain why, and she wept again, this time for him. When he admired Celestina's drawings, the little girl went into mass production, and soon the bare walls of his apartment were brightly decorated with crayoned renderings of fairly mysterious objects in very nice colors. Pleased by the effect, Gina brought brilliant red geraniums for his windows one day, and this was an unexpected turning point for him. He had forgotten how much he'd enjoyed his turns taking care of the Wolverton-tube plants on the *Stella Maris*, and began finally to remember the good times and to find some inner balance.

They took Celestina for walks, sweating in the glorious light of the *mezzogiorno*—a violet sea to the west, shimmering sunlit crags to the east, the acrid-sweet scent of dust and flowers and asphalt sharp in their throats. Strolling along, they argued over stupid things, and enjoyed it, and went home to fresh bread fried in oil from olive trees eight hundred years old, and zucchini with *provolone dolce*, and almonds in honey. Lingering after supper, Emilio would put Celestina to bed, and Gina would listen, shaking her head, as the two of them made up a long, complicated story with many episodes, about a princess with curly hair who was allowed to eat nothing but treats even though her bones would get bendy, and a dog named Franco Grossi, who went on trips with the princess to America and the moon and Milan and Australia. By June, Emilio had admitted to the migraines, and Gina brought several new medications for him to try, one of which was a remarkable improvement over the Prograine.

There was, as the weeks passed, an unspoken understanding that he needed time, but perhaps not as much as he'd once thought.

Gina taught him to play *scopa* one night; once he got the hang of the game, she was amused by the ferocity with which he played, though distressed by how difficult it was for him to hold the cards. When she asked about this, he changed the subject and she dropped it for the time being. Then, on midsummer's eve, perhaps to prove that his hands were fine, he and Celestina set themselves the goal of tying their own shoelaces, something both of them had given up on in the past.

"We can do it," Emilio insisted. "This time for sure! Even if it takes us all day, it's okay because this is the longest day of the year."

All morning, they commiserated over how easy this was for other people, but conquered frustration together, and ultimately shared a radiant self-satisfaction in the accomplishment. Happy for them both, Gina suggested a celebratory picnic down on the beach, pointing out that this plan would afford many opportunities to take off and put on shoes with unnecessary frequency and great flourish. And so the long midsummer evening was passed in quiet contentment, Emilio and Gina ambling along the seashore behind Celestina, watching her chase seagulls and grub for treasures and heave stones into the water until she wore herself out. As the darkness began at last to deepen, they climbed the cliffside stairway—Gina's pockets and hands full of shells and pretty rocks, Emilio's arms full of sleeping child—and murmured greetings as they passed the Camorra guards, who smiled with complicity.

When they got to the house, Gina held the back door open for him but did not turn on the lights; knowing the way, he carried Celestina through the quiet house to her doll-crammed room and waited while Gina cleared a nest in the bed full of stuffed animals. He could lift Celestina's small weight if he was careful when he picked her up, but could not set her down again without damaging the braces, so Gina gathered her baby from his arms and lay the child in bed, and stood awhile, gazing down at her daughter.

Celestina, she thought. Who never stopped moving, who never stopped talking, who exhausted her mother before breakfast, who would have driven the Holy Mother herself to consider hiring a hit man. Whose face in sleep still showed the profile of a newborn, whose small fingers still held her mother rapt, whose knotted navel still traveled the coiled route to another belly in spirit. Who had quickly learned not to mention Papa's new friends to Mamma.

Gina sighed and turned, and saw Emilio leaning against the door frame, watching her with a still face and eyes that hid nothing. He held his arms slightly away from his body, as he did for Celestina's hugs, to keep from scratching the child with the hardware of his braces when she came to him for an embrace. So Gina came to him.

The edge of her lower lip was as fine as the rim of a chalice, and the thought almost stopped him, but then her mouth rose to meet his and there was no turning back, nor any wanting to. After all the years, the effort, the anguish—it was, he found, all very simple.

She removed his braces and helped him with his clothes, and then took off her own, feeling as familiar with him as if they had always been together. But she did not know what to expect and so she braced herself for a failure of nerve, or for brutal urgency, or for weeping. There was instead laughter, and she too found that it was simple. When the time came, she took him into her and smiled over his shoulder at the small sound he made, and nearly wept herself. Naturally, he came too soon—what could you expect? It didn't matter to her, but a few moments later she heard his muffled chagrin next to her ear. "I don't think I did that quite right."

She laughed as well, and told the air above him, "It takes practice."

He went motionless and she was afraid then that she'd hurt his feelings, but he rose on his elbows and looked down at her, face amazed, eyes merry. "Practice! You mean we get to do that more than once?"

She giggled as he collapsed on her again. "Get off me," she whispered after a while, still smiling, hands drifting along his back.

"I don't think so."

"Get off me! You weigh a ton," she lied, kissing the side of his neck. "All that macaroni and cheese!"

"No. I like it here," he told the pillow under her head.

She put a finger into his armpit. He exploded and rolled away as she laughed and shushed him and whispered, "Celestina!"

"Soy cosquilloso!" he said, astonished. "I don't know what that is in Italian. What do you call it when there's a reaction to touch like that?"

"Ticklish," she told him and listened, amused, as he guessed at the verb and quickly conjugated it. "You sound surprised."

He looked over at her, chest quiet now. "I didn't know. How would I find that out? People don't tickle Jesuits!" She looked at him, massively skeptical in the dark. "Well, some people tickle some Jesuits," he admitted indignantly, "but I assure you, madam, that no one tickled me."

"Not even your parents? You weren't always a priest."

"No," he said curtly.

Oh, God, she thought, realizing she'd wandered into some new minefield, but he rose up on one elbow and draped an arm over her belly. "I hate macaroni and cheese," he confessed. "There were no dragons to slay for my beloved, but I ate macaroni and cheese for you. I want credit."

She smiled up at him, wholly content. "Wait," she said as he went to kiss her. "Go back to that part about 'beloved.' " But his lips dropped once more onto her mouth, and this time he did better.

They were discreet, for Celestina's sake, and he was gone before dawn. It was as difficult as anything he'd ever done, to say good-bye to her and leave. But there were other days at the beach that wore Celestina out early, and other nights that wore them both out late, and as that summer passed, she made him whole again. There was no memory of bestiality that she did not efface with beauty and gentleness, no humiliation that was not eclipsed by her warmth. And sometimes, when the dreams came, she was with him: salvation in the night. Before the summer was over, while the days were still far too long and the nights all too short, when the fragrance of lemon trees and oranges had deepened and drifted each night through her bedroom window to scent the sheets and her hair, he began to give back to her some of what she had given him.

He had a sense, sometimes, of flawless peace. The words of Donne seemed perfect: "For I am every dead thing / In whom love wrought new Alchemie." Attacked by hope, he could no longer resist belief in the goodness of having a future, and felt the past's grip loosen. It's over, he would think now and then. It's finally over.

14

Trucha Sai

2042–2046, Earth-Relative

SOFIA MENDES DID NOT LACK COMPANIONSHIP IN TRUCHA SAI. THE VIL-
lage population stabilized at about 350, and there were other settlements
nearby; visits were common and festive. She shared chores and meals with
many people, and soon it felt natural to pass the time weaving the sword-
like leaves of *diuso* trees into mats, windbreaks, umbrellas, cooking packets for steaming roots, baskets for collecting fruit. She participated in the
seasonal round of ripening, and learned the location and identification of
useful plants, the ways to avoid dangers, and how to find one's way in what
had first appeared impenetrable jungle.

She was becoming a competent Runa adult—a knowledgeable field
botanist, a useful member of the community—and found a certain satisfaction in that. But during the early months of her exile, the orbiting *Stella
Maris* library system was the nearest thing she had to an intellectual companion. She could not reach the ship physically, but she spent much of her
day in radio contact with the library. After she had polished and edited
them, she poured her observations of Runa life and her private thoughts
into its memory, rather than leave them logged only on her own computer
tablet. This habit made her feel less isolated, as though she were sending
messages, not making entries in a diary. Someday her words would reach
Earth, and she could believe herself a solitary scientist, contributing to her
own society with her research. Still human. Still sane.

Then, when Isaac was only fifteen months old, the morning came when she called up the access routines and was greeted by an unyielding silence. Staring at the laconic error message on her screen, she felt the physical jolt of a ship whose mooring rope has suddenly given way. Had the onboard systems become corrupted somehow? Perhaps the ship's orbit had degraded and the *Stella Maris* itself had burned up in the atmosphere or fallen into the Rakhati sea. There were endless possibilities. The only thing she did not consider was what had actually occurred: a second party from Earth, traveling under the auspices of the United Nations, had in fact arrived on Rakhat. Some twelve weeks after landfall, the Contact Consortium had located Emilio Sandoz. Believing him the sole survivor of the Jesuit mission, they had sent the *Stella Maris* on its automated way back to Earth, navigated by Sofia's own artificial-intelligence programs, carrying Emilio Sandoz home alone to infamy.

There were many kinds of loneliness, she discovered. There was the loneliness that came from understanding but not being understood. There was the loneliness of having no one to banter or argue with, no one to be challenged by. Loneliness at night was different from the daylight loneliness that sometimes overwhelmed her in the midst of a crowd. She became a connoisseur of loneliness, and the worst kind of all, she discovered, came after a night when she dreamed of Isaac laughing.

A tiny infant, long and fatless, he had slept away his early weeks with a heavy unresponsiveness that frightened her. She recognized that sleep was his way of concentrating his meager resources on survival, so she fought the desire to rouse him, knowing it to be a sign of her own need for reassurance. But even when he was awake, he could not meet her eye for more than a moment or two without going gray under his papery skin, and though he suckled more strongly as the weeks passed, he often vomited her milk. No matter what she told herself about a preemie's undeveloped digestive system, it was difficult not to feel this as a heartbreaking rejection.

At six months, Isaac remained birdlike and remote, always looking into the distance, intent on some far-off mystery of leaves and light and shadow. By his first birthday, he had an otherworldly dignity, a tiny quiet unsmiling boy with deep-set elvish eyes, who spent a great deal of his time examining the kaleidoscope of his own fingers, entranced by the patterns they made. She began to hope that his silence had its roots in deafness, for he did not babble, did not turn toward her when she called his name, seemed not to hear the Runa children around him as they squabbled and played and teased and huffed in breathy laughter. But one day, he said, "*Sipaj*," and repeated it endlessly until the word for "Hear me!" became as meaningless as a mantra for all who listened. Then the silence closed in again.

As his second birthday approached, he seemed to have achieved a state of unassailable self-containment: a precocious Zen master without needs, without desires. He would nurse when Sofia placed her nipple in his mouth; later, he would eat when food was placed on his tongue, drink if water were brought to his lips. He would allow himself to be picked up and held, but he never raised his arms to anyone. Carried about by his Runa playmates as though he were a doll, he would wait unmoving and un-moved for the interruption of his reverie to cease; put down, he would re-turn to his meditation as though the incident had not occurred.

Inside his invisible citadel, it seemed, there was a perfection from which the outside world could not distract or tempt him. He sat for hours, still and well balanced as a Yogi, his face sometimes transformed by a smile of shattering beauty, as though privately pleased by some secret, sacred thought.

Sofia did not have to ask what would have been done with a Runa baby so abnormal. Like a Spartan exposing his deformed infant on a wolf-prowled hillside, a Runa father would have given a defective child up to the *djanada*—veal for Jana'ata aristocrats. Perhaps the Runa did not real-ize there was anything wrong with Isaac, or perhaps they didn't care; Isaac was not Runa and so the rules for him were different. As far as Sofia could tell, they simply accepted Isaac's solitary silence as they accepted his lack of tail and his hairless body, as they accepted nearly everything in their world: with placid good humor and unruffled calm.

So Sofia, too, tried to accept her son as he was, but it was not easy to watch her child stare for hours at his hands or sit patting the ground with a quiet unchanging tattoo as he listened to some inner melody. As beau-tiful and inhuman as an angel, Isaac would have been difficult for any mother to love, and Sofia Mendes's life had provided little opportunity to practice loving.

In the most hidden region of her soul, she felt an unspeakable relief that her son desired so little of her. For years, the only measure she had of how deeply she felt the loss of her parents was the unreasoning terror that swept through her at the mere thought of dying young and orphaning a child of her own. There were some compensations for Isaac's condition, she told herself. If she died, he'd hardly notice.

She would realize later how close she'd come to madness. She'd looked over the edge of it, dizzy and careless at the brink, by the time Isaac was four years old. It was then that Supaari and his infant daughter arrived in Trucha Sai, brought there by Djalao and several other VaKashani women. The forest Runa showed no amazement at his unexpected appearance in a haven they had always kept a secret from their Jana'ata masters; it was their nature to accept things without much questioning, and Supaari Va-Gayjur had always been different from other *djanada*. But if the Runa were as calm as ever, Sofia Mendes was rocked by the strength of her emotions. Supaari was Jana'ata and yet, when she first saw him, she did not think of riot or death, of oppression or exploitation or cruelty, but only of friendship and an end to loneliness.

It was the first time since Isaac's birth that she had found something to thank God for.

"THEY TOLD ME YOU WERE DEAD," SUPAARI SAID IN H'INGLISH, STARING at the tiny foreigner. Horrified, he spun away and walked a few paces and then returned to her, like a scavenger returning to a carcass. He reached down toward Sofia's face, disfigured by the tripled scar, and felt even more ashamed when she seemed to flinch away from his touch. "I would have looked for you," he said, pleading for understanding. "The VaKashani told me you were dead!"

Because he expected it, he saw hatred and blame in her face. Exhausted from his journey and all that had gone before it, staggered by the sheer majestic variety of ways he had managed to be wrong about things, the Jana'ata sank by degrees, weight shifting from feet to tail to knees to haunches until at last he slumped on the ground, head down between hands sunken into the forest humus. Her wordless reproach—her very existence—seemed to him a killing blow and he was fervently wishing for some quick death when he felt her small hands on each side of his head, lifting it.

"*Sipaj*, Supaari," she said, kneeling so that she could look into his eyes, "someone's heart is very glad you have come here."

Bleakly he thought, She didn't understand me. She has forgotten her own language. "Someone thought you were gone," he whispered. "Someone would have tried to find you."

He rolled heavily into a sitting position, knees akimbo, and looked around: sleeping shelters, with their graceful sloping thatched roofs, creaking and flexing in the breeze; woven windbreaks decorated with flowers and ribbons; raised sitting platforms paved with beautifully made cushions. Runa, going about their lives, untouched by Jana'ata law or custom. Apart from the awful disfigurement, the little foreigner appeared well.

"*Sipaj*, Sofia," he said finally, "someone has a great talent for error. Perhaps it was better for you to be free of his help."

She said nothing and he tried to read the expression on her face, to make sense of her scent, her posture. It was unnerving, this inability to be sure of what anything meant, knowing now how little he had understood Sandoz, wondering if he had even been wrong to believe that Ha'an had cared for him. "I think," he said slowly in K'San, for Ruanja did not have what he needed and he believed Sofia had forgotten H'inglish, "I think that you will hate me when you know what I have done. Do you understand this word, 'hate'?"

"Apologies." She joined him on the ground, sitting cross-legged on the low grassy herbage that covered the clearing. "Someone has forgotten your language. Someone knew only a little." She could see how tired he was and the long, handsome face seemed thin to her, its elegant bones more prominent than she remembered. "*Sipaj*, Supaari, such a long journey you have made," she began, the Ruanja formula as natural to her now as if she had lived with it all her life. "Surely, you are hungry. Will you—"

He stopped her with a single stubby claw pressed gently against her lips. "Please," he said in a tone that Anne Edwards had interpreted as wry. "Please, don't offer." He threw his head up and away from her. "How can I eat?" he asked the sky in K'San. "How can I eat!"

From out of the crowd surrounding Supaari's VaKashani escort, Djalao came forward, having heard his cry. She was carrying the sturdy basket she had packed with provisions for him and his child and dumped it abruptly on the ground. "Eat as you always have," she said quietly, but with a hardness that Sofia had never before heard in a Runao's voice.

Some kind of unspoken understanding passed between Djalao and Supaari then, but it was beyond Sofia's ability to read from their body language. The children—scampering and chasing one another, excited by the visitors and the break in routine—became louder and more unruly by the minute, and before Sofia could call out a warning, Kanchay's daughter Puska took advantage of her father's absorption in adult talk to leap onto his back, instantly pushing off it with an arching joy-jump that tipped Supaari's basket over. Unruffled, Kanchay separated himself from the adults' conversation, repacking the basket's contents quickly before the children could catch the scent, and then tore off, bent over and arms flung wide, gently barreling into the little mob of youngsters, sweeping them into a delighted, squirming heap.

Smiling, Sofia looked around for Isaac, concerned that he had wandered off while everyone was preoccupied. But there he was: lying on his back, watching winged seeds spiral down toward his face from the *w'ralia* above him. Sofia sighed and returned her gaze to Supaari, sitting dazed on the ground.

"*Sipaj*, Fia. Everything has changed," he said. He glanced up at Djalao VaKashan, and his ears flattened. "Someone didn't understand!" he cried. "Someone knew but didn't understand. Everything has changed."

"*Sipaj*, Supaari," Djalao said, standing above him. "Eat. Everything remains as it was."

Not *what*—*who* is in the basket? Sofia thought, realizing now that Kanchay had repacked it quickly to protect the children from an early understanding. Chilled, staring at Supaari, she thought, He eats Runa. He is *djanada*.

It was a long time before any of them could speak. "*Sipaj*, Supaari, we are what we are," Sofia said at last with the simple Runa logic that was, for the time being, all she could muster. Standing, she grasped the Jana'ata's arm in a token effort to lift him to his feet. He looked up at her, distracted. "Come and eat. Life goes on," she said, tugging on his arm a little. "We-and-you-also will think of problems later."

SUPAARI GOT UP AND TRIED TO CARRY THE BASKET AWAY FROM THE clearing so he could eat downwind and beyond the lines of Runa sight. He must always have known what he was doing at some level; even before, it had seemed unconscionable to eat meat in the presence of Runa. Snarling softly, he struggled with the basket—the handles of which were, after all, suitable only for a Runao to carry—and felt even worse when Kanchay climbed out of the tangle of children to help him.

The girl Kinsa, neither adult nor child herself, had sat murmuring to Ha'anala all this time, not quite sure where she belonged. Seeing Supaari move off, she decided to follow along, carrying the baby on her back. Sofia, walking beside her, reached out and put a finger under the infant's tiny curved claws. "Supaari!" she cried. "Yours? But how? Someone thought—"

"It is a long song," he said, as Sofia took Ha'anala in her arms and Kanchay calmly unpacked a portion of meat. "When someone arrived in Kashan after the riot—" He paused, looking again at her terrible scarred face. "You understand this word, 'riot'?" Sofia looked up from the baby cradled in her lap and lifted her chin in affirmation. He went on, "The VaKashani were in a great confusion. So many were gone and among them, most of the Elders. There was no one to tell it clearly and there was everywhere *fierno*, even days after the culling. Your 'lander' was still there, but the VaKashani said that all the foreigners were gone. The carcasses were eaten, they said."

She had been thinking what a joy it was to have an infant meet her eye, but hearing this. . . . Of course, she thought. Meat is meat. But even after what happened to Anne and D.W., it had never occurred to her that the others had been—. Oh, Jimmy! she thought, throat closing spasmodically.

Mouth dry, Supaari put his meal aside. "Later, when it was nearly dark, Askama came forward. She was only a child, but she knew you foreigners well, so someone listened to her words. She used H'inglish because Ruanja is confusing for this. She said: Meelo is not dead—" He stopped when Sofia changed color abruptly. He could see the pulse racing at her throat, understood now the full tragedy of what he had to tell her. "You didn't know?"

"Where is Meelo now?" she asked. "My God. My God, if he's alive it changes everything—"

"He is gone!" Supaari cried. "Someone is so sorry! Do you understand? Someone would have looked for you, but the VaKashani said you were all gone and 'gone' can mean two things! Askama said only Meelo is not dead, that he was with the Jana'ata patrol. She said nothing of the foreigner Marc or of you—"

"Marc!" Sofia cried. "Marc is alive, too?"

"No! He is gone!" Supaari doubled over in frustration. "Sandoz is gone also, but a different way!" Tired as he was, he got to his feet and began to pace. "Ruanja is impossible for this! Can you remember any H'inglish?" he demanded, swinging around to look at her.

"Yes," she said. Supaari's baby began to keen. Kinsa, too, was becoming upset by the intensity of the emotion and seemed about to cry herself. Handing the infant to Kanchay, Sofia stood as well and stopped Supaari's agitated prowling with a hand on his arm. "Yes. I remember English," she said again. "Supaari, where is Marc? Where is Sandoz now? Are they dead, or not where we can see them?"

"Marc is dead. It is my fault. I meant no harm!" Inexplicably, he held up his hands, but she was too distracted to see any point in the gesture. "The *hasta'akala* doesn't make us bleed—"

"Supaari, for God's sake, where is Sandoz?"

"The others sent him home—"

"What others?" she cried, frantic now. "What do you mean, home? To Kashan?"

"No, not Kashan. There were other foreigners who came—"

"Other foreigners! Supaari, do you mean people from another river valley or people like—"

"Foreigners like you. With no tails. From H'earth."

She was swaying and he caught her before she fell, pressing his hands against her shoulders. "I'm all right," she told him, but he could see that she wasn't. She sat on the ground and put her head in her hands. Kanchay gave the wailing baby to Kinsa and told the girl to go back to the clearing and stay with the others. He came and sat behind Sofia, arms around her shoulders protectively, and she leaned back to let him know she appreciated his gesture, but spoke again to Supaari, as calmly as she could. "Tell me," she said. "Tell me everything."

IT TOOK A LONG TIME, AND THREE LANGUAGES. HE TOLD HER HOW HE had tracked down Sandoz and found that Marc was alive as well but only just; told about bribing the patrol commander, and about the *hasta'akala* and how he'd meant only to protect Marc and Sandoz from being tried for inciting the Runa to riot. "You see?" he asked her, showing his hands again to display the thin, tough webbing between his fingers. "It is nothing for us—it only weakens the hands if the webs are clipped. But for the foreigners, there was so much blood and Marc died." And then there was the season in Gayjur with Sandoz, and Supaari's own fear that Emilio would perish of loneliness.

That much, God help her, Sofia understood. "But others came," she reminded Supaari. "Where are the other foreigners now?" When he didn't answer, she leaned forward to clutch at his arm and cried, "Supaari, did they all leave? Oh, my God. Don't tell me they're gone! Did they all go back to Earth?"

"I don't know." He turned away, ears down. "They sent Sandoz away first. The others sojourned with me awhile in Gayjur." He stopped speaking abruptly.

"They're gone, aren't they," she said dully. "Are they dead, or did they go back to Earth?"

"I don't know!" he insisted, but she could sense that he was concealing something. Finally, he spoke again, very quietly. "I don't know, but I think . . . I may have created a market for . . ." There was a long silence. "Sofia, what is this word: 'celibate'?"

She looked up, amazed that he should ask this now. But it wasn't like him to evade. . . . How could she explain? "It means abstention from sex." Supaari looked blank; English was no good. She tried again in Ruanja. "To make a child begin, there is an action—" He lifted his chin. "Among us, this action is also done for pleasure. Do you understand? For enjoyment." Again, the chin went up but slower this time, and he was staring at her intently. "A celibate is one who never . . . behaves this action—not to begin children or for pleasure. Do you understand?"

"Even if they are first- or second-born?"

"Birth rank makes no difference among us—"

"A celibate is VaHaptaa, then. A criminal without rights?"

"No!" she said, startled. "*Sipaj*, Supaari, even this one finds celibacy hard to understand." She paused, unsure how to put this, which language to use, how much to tell him. "Men such as Sandoz and Marc and Dee set themselves apart. They choose not to behave this action for children or for pleasure. They are celibates so that they may serve God more completely."

"Who are 'god'?"

She took shelter in grammar. "Who is, not who are. There is only one God." She said this without thinking, but before she could even attempt to explain monotheism, Supaari cut her off.

"Sandoz said he was celibate—he said he took no wife so that he could serve many!" the Jana'ata cried indignantly, standing once more and walking away from her. He spun and glared, ears cocked forward, on the attack. "He said he was celibate. Celibates serve god. God must be many."

Q.E.D., she thought, sighing. Where were the Jesuits when you needed them? "God is one. His children are many. We are all his children. Sandoz served God by serving His children." Supaari sat down abruptly and rubbed the sides of his head. "*Sipaj*, Supaari," she said sympathetically, reaching out to touch the lean-cheeked, wolfish face. "Does your head hurt, too?"

"Yes. You make no sense!" He stopped himself, and changed his mind and then his language, going back to H'inglish. "Maybe you make sense to you. I don't understand."

Sofia smiled slightly. "Anne said that's the beginning of wisdom." He looked at her, mouth open. "Wisdom: true knowing," she explained. "Anne said wisdom begins when you discover the difference between 'That doesn't make sense' and 'I don't understand.'"

"Then I must be very wisdom. I don't understand anything." His eyes closed. When he opened them, he looked as though he might be sick, but soldiered on in the jumbled creole that was all they had to work with. "*Sipaj*, Fia. What means in H'inglish 'serve'? Can service mean the behavior for—for having pleasure?"

"It can," she said finally, confused. "But not for Marc and Dee and Meelo. For them, to serve meant to give help freely to others. To give food to the hungry, to make lodgings for. . . . Wait—serves many? Oh, my God. You created a market? Supaari, what happened to Emilio!"

IN THE ROSY LIGHT THAT FOLLOWED SECOND SUNDOWN, SOFIA SAT AND watched Supaari sleep, too worn out to feel much more than resignation. It took hours to get the whole story straight and toward the end, Supaari seemed to invite her contempt. "I was proud of my cleverness! I made myself stupid with my wish for children, but I thought, This Supaari, he is a fine, clever man. I should have understood!" he cried, exhausted and distraught. "These were Jana'ata. My own people. I made great harm to Sandoz. Perhaps now the other foreigners also have been harmed the same way. And now, you shall hate me."

We meant well, she thought, looking up at a sky piled with cumulus clouds turning amethyst and indigo above the clearing. No one was deliberately evil. We all did the best we could. Even so, what a mess we made of everything . . .

Sitting with her back against Kanchay's, she reached out to stroke her sleeping son's auburn curls, and thought of D. W. Yarbrough, the father superior of the Jesuit mission to Rakhat, now almost five years gone, buried near Kashan with Anne Edwards, his companion in sudden death.

Sofia Mendes and D. W. Yarbrough had worked together closely during the long months of preparation for the Jesuit mission to the planet of the Singers. Many who watched their partnership develop and deepen thought them proof that opposites attract, for D. W. Yarbrough, with his cast eye and his meandering nose and that unruly mob of anarchic teeth, was as outlandishly ill-favored as Sofia Mendes was startlingly, classically beautiful. A few understood the sanctuary of uncomplicated friendship Sofia and D.W. could offer one another, and those few were privately pleased that these two souls had been brought together.

It was not long before the Sephardic Jew and the Jesuit priest established a working routine; within weeks, it was their habit to end each long, difficult day of compilation, analysis, argument and decision with dinner and a couple of Lone Star beers at a quiet bar near D.W.'s provincial residence in New Orleans. The talk sometimes went late into the night, turning to religion more often than not. Sofia was defensive at first, still clinging to a certain amount of historical hostility to Catholicism, but embarrassed by how little she knew of Judaism. Yarbrough was aware of how abruptly and how badly her childhood had ended; an admirer of Judaism on its own terms and not merely as a precursor to his own religion, he became both a goad and a guide in her rediscovery of the tradition she was born to.

"There's a fine fierceness to Jews that I like a whole lot," the Texan told her one night, during a discussion of the Virginal intercessions and saintly go-betweens, of the baroque hierarchy of priests and monsignors and bishops and archbishops and cardinals and pope that lay between God and the Catholic soul, which Sofia found pointless and mystifying. "Most people, now, they don't like to go straight to the top, not really. They need to sidle up to a proposition, come at the thing a little off-center. They feel better with a chain of command," D.W. said, an old Marine squadron commander whose years in the Jesuit order had done nothing to diminish his tendency to think in military terms. "Got a problem, you ask the sergeant. Sergeant might go to a captain he knows. Most folks would have a hell of a time getting up the nerve to bang on the general's office door, even if he was the nicest fella in the world. Catholicism makes allowances for that in human beings." He'd smiled then, teeth and eyes askew, the ugliest and most beautiful man she'd ever met. "But the children of Abraham? They look God straight in the face. Praise. Argue! Dicker, complain. Takes a lot of guts to deal with the Almighty like that." And she had warmed to him, feeling it the highest accolade he could have given her and her people.

They agreed on many things during those midnight conversations.

There was, they decided, no such thing as an ex-Jew or an ex-Catholic or an ex-Marine. "Now why is that?" D.W. asked one night, after noting that ex-Texans were hard to come by, too. It was, he thought, crucial to get at your recruits when they were young and impressionable. Pride in tradition was part of it as well, Sofia pointed out. But most important, D.W. said, was the fact that all these groups based their philosophies on the same principle.

"Talk is cheap. We believe in action," Yarbrough said. "Fight for justice. Feed the hungry. Take the beach. We none of us sit around hopin' for some big damn miracle to fix things."

But for all his emphasis on action, D. W. Yarbrough was a highly educated and conscientious man who was well aware of the cultural and spiritual damage missionaries could do, and he had laid out strict rules of engagement for the Jesuit mission to Rakhat. "We don't preach. We listen," he insisted. "These're God's children, too, and this time we're gonna learn what they got to teach us 'fore we go around returnin' the favor."

Of all the members of the *Stella Maris* crew, Sofia Mendes had been the most relieved by that clear-eyed humility and reluctance to proselytize. It was superbly ironic, then, that this afternoon, against all probability, it had fallen to Sofia Mendes herself to speak of God to a VaRakhati.

"Who are 'god'?" Supaari had asked.

I don't know, she thought.

Not even D.W. was willing to make a statement of full faith. He was tolerant of skepticism and doubt, at home with ambivalence and ambiguity. "Maybe God is only the most powerful poetic idea we humans're capable of thinkin'," he said one night, after a few drinks. "Maybe God has no reality outside our minds and exists only in the paradox of Perfect Compassion and Perfect Justice. Or maybe," he suggested, slouching back in his chair and favoring her with a lopsided, wily grin, "maybe God is exactly as advertised in the Torah. Maybe, along with all its other truths and beauties, Judaism preserves for each generation of us the reality of the God of Abraham, of Isaac, of Jacob, of Moses—the God of Jesus."

A cranky, uncanny God, D.W. called Him. "A God with quirky, unfathomable rules, a God who gets fed up with us and pissed off! But quick to forgive, Sofia, and generous," D.W. said, his voice softening, eyes full of light, "always, always in love with humanity. Always there, waiting for us—generation after generation—to return His passion. Ah, Sofia, darlin'! On my best days, I believe in Him with all my heart."

"And on your worst days?" she had asked that night.

"Even if it's only poetry, it's poetry to live by, Sofia—poetry to die for," he told her with quiet conviction. He slouched in his chair for a time, thinking. "Maybe poetry is the only way we can get near the truth of God. . . . And when the metaphors fail, we think it's God who's failed us!" he cried, grinning crookedly. "Now there's an idea that buys some useful theological wiggle room!"

D. W. Yarbrough had taught her that she was the heir to an ancient human wisdom, its laws and ethics tested and retested in a hundred cultures in every conceivable moral climate—a code of conduct as sound as any her species had to offer. She longed to tell Supaari of the wisdom of Hillel who taught, a century before Jesus, "That which is hateful to you, do not do unto others." If you would not live as the Runa must, stop breeding them, stop exploiting them, stop eating them! Find some other way to live. Love mercy, the prophets taught. Do justice. There was so much to share! And yet, the history of her home planet was one of almost continual warfare, and with tragic frequency, war's taproot was set deep in fervent religion and unquestioning belief. She longed to ask D.W., If it was right for us to learn from the VaRakhati, isn't it right for them to learn from us?

I don't know what to do, she thought. Even the laws of physics resolve to probabilities. How can I know what to do?

"God who has begun this will bring it to perfection," Marc Robichaux always said. Emilio Sandoz told her once, "We are here because God has brought us here, step by step." Nothing happens by chance, the Jewish sages taught. Perhaps, she thought, it was to bring this wisdom to Rakhat that I have been left here. Perhaps this was why I was the only one of us to survive on Rakhat . . .

And perhaps I have lost my mind, she thought then, startled to be taking such a notion seriously.

It had been a grueling day. She didn't dare think about what might have been, if only Supaari had realized she was alive. Be glad for what you have, she told herself, settling down near Kanchay, in sight of her strange son's sleeping face; near Supaari and his tiny, beautiful Ha'anala; surrounded by Sichu-Lan and Tinbar and all the others who had made her welcome.

It was dawn the next morning when Supaari's words came back to her. "The others—" She sat up, breathing unevenly, and stared into the darkness. Others. Other people had come.

"*Sipaj*, Fia! What are you doing?" Kanchay asked sleepily. He too sat as she rose onto her knees and began to feel around the edge of the shelter. "What do you seek?"

"The computer tablet," she said and hissed as she cut herself on a knife left carelessly in a pile of platters.

"Agh, Fia! Stop that!" Kanchay cried disgustedly, as she cursed and sucked the thin, salty line of pain on her hand. There was a general outcry of dismay from the others, awakened by the sudden spurt of blood scent that roused them as a shout might have roused humans, but Sofia continued to rummage through the storage area around the perimeter of the shelter.

"Emilio was sent home on the *Stella Maris*," she muttered. "That's why the signal went dead three years ago." Her hand touched the edge of the tablet and she clutched it to her chest, picking her way through the huddled mass of bodies and moving outside, where the sky was half golden, half aquamarine. They must have gotten here the same way we did, she thought. They had a mother ship and they had a lander. Supaari wasn't sure if anyone but Sandoz had actually left Rakhat. The other ship might still be up there. Their lander might still be somewhere on the planet. There would be fuel. "If they haven't left . . ." she said aloud. "Oh, God, oh, please . . ."

The satellite network put in place over eight years earlier by the *Stella Maris* crew was still functional. Working rapidly, she reprogrammed the radio relays to carry out a systematic broadband search for any active transponder currently in orbit around Rakhat. Once the software was altered, the search took only minutes: 9.735 gigahertz. "Yes!" she shouted, weeping and laughing, but then fell silent again, ignoring the Runa who now pressed around her, their questions falling on her ears as meaninglessly as rain.

There was no answer to her hail, but there were standardized navigation routines, interfaces established by the U.N. Space Agency when near-Earth traffic had become dense enough to be hazardous. Like a harbor pilot taking over a freighter, Sofia took control of the *Magellan*'s computer system and then hacked her way into its logs. There was no record of the ground party's return to the ship. There had been no transmissions for nearly three years. Their lander must be somewhere on Rakhat, maybe near Kashan.

She began to broadcast a repeating message on the *Magellan* downlink to all land-based nodes, asking any respondent to reply through the *Magellan* return path. She listened, heart hammering, waiting for some response, any indication that she and Isaac were not the only human beings on Rakhat.

It was well past second dawn when she was able to sit back and think. The lack of reply was not proof that the others were dead. They might be separated from their transponders. Supaari believed they might still be alive but in captivity, as Emilio had been. Six months, she decided, her eye burning from the intensity of the work she'd just done. She owed the others that much. She would not abandon her own kind here without a serious attempt to find them.

Six months.

But then, by the God whose poetry was forgotten now, she would steal their lander and their ship. Then, by God, Sofia Mendes would take her son and go home.

15

Naples

July 2061

THERE WAS NO FORMAL PROPOSAL. SITTING ON THE HUGE STONE OUT-
cropping near the beach that had been his sanctuary when churches held
out no hope to him, Emilio was watching Celestina play on the shore,
talking to Gina about nothing in particular when he asked, after a com-
panionable silence, "Would you object to a civil ceremony?"

"That would certainly be nicer than shouting abuse at one another,"
Gina replied, straight-faced, which, along with a settling into the hollow
of his outstretched arm, served as an assent. "When?"

"You and Celestina are going to the mountains with your parents at the
end of August, yes? So: first weekend in September."

Gina nodded agreeably. "Maybe late in the afternoon?" she suggested
after a few minutes, smiling toward the sea. "That way, if the marriage
doesn't work out, we won't have wasted the whole day."

"Ten o'clock," Emilio said. "Ten in the morning. September third, the
Saturday after you get home."

The means to this end had been buried like treasure in the boxful of letters collected by Johannes Voelker in Rome and delivered to Sandoz by
John Candotti.

Although hardcopy was routinely scanned for bombs and biologicals,
all mail could conceal words with the power to inflict more pain. Emilio
knew himself defenseless against this, and had refused to look at any of it,

but Gina loved him, and believed that others must share her opinion of him. So one day in early July, while Emilio worked at the other end of the room and Celestina played house with Elizabeth and a stuffed dog named Franco Grossi, Gina sat on the swept wooden floor of his apartment, separating the messages into four piles: hateful, sweet, funny and interesting. When she finished the first pass through the box, she and Celestina took a walk over to see Brother Cosimo in the kitchen and watched him burn the hateful ones in the bread oven. Cosimo, who was among those who approved of the couple, sent the ladies back with three hazelnut gelati and a plate of leftover salad greens for Elizabeth.

"Sweet" was composed mainly of letters from Emilio's students, the earliest of whom had been boys of fifteen when he'd taught them Latin I and were now men in their mid-sixties with enduring and fond memories of his classroom. Several—jurists, attorneys—offered to file suit on Sandoz's behalf against the Contact Consortium for slander and defamation. Gina was cheered by their loyalty, but Emilio still believed himself guilty of some of what he'd been charged with in absentia. So she put the letters aside, thinking, Someday perhaps.

"Funny" included several from women whose grasp of reproductive biology was less firm than their grip on the basics of blackmail, and who attributed the paternity of their children to a celibate who wasn't even on the planet at the time of conception. Emilio read one of these, but he found it less amusing than Gina had, so that pile too was consigned to the bread oven.

Which left "Interesting."

Most of these, she believed, would be rejected out of hand: requests for interviews, book contracts, and so on. There was, however, a letter from a legal firm in Cleveland, Ohio, written in English, and this envelope included a copy of a handwritten note dated July 19, 2021, signed with a name Gina recognized: Anne Edwards, the physician who had gone, along with her husband, the engineer George Edwards, to Rakhat as part of the first Jesuit mission. Emilio had spoken of Anne, briefly and with difficulty, so Gina hesitated before reopening this wound. But concerned that this was a matter of legal importance, she brought the letter to Emilio and saw his color vanish as he read.

"*Caro*, what's wrong? What does it say?"

"I don't know what to do with this," he said, shaking his head, throwing the papers down on his desk. He stood and walked away, clearly upset. "No. I don't want it."

"What? What is it?" Celestina asked, sitting on the floor. Alarmed, she looked from one grown-up's face to the other's, and dissolved into tears. "Is it another divorce paper, Mamma?"

"Oh, my God," Emilio said and went to the child, kneeling to offer her his arms. "No, no, no, *cara mia*. Nothing like that, Celestina! Nothing bad." He looked up at Gina, who shrugged unhappily: what can we do? "It's just something about money," Emilio told the child then. "Nothing important, *cara*—just money. Maybe it's good, okay? I have to think about this. I'm not used to having other people to think of. Maybe it's good."

The note from Anne was short, written on a sunlit day during the excitement of the preparations for the first mission to Rakhat, with mortality only a vague theoretical notion. "It can't buy happiness, darlings. It can't buy health. But a little cash never hurts. Enjoy." She and George had set up trust funds for each member of the Jesuit party and, with over forty years to accumulate, the law firm informed him, the individual portfolios had done handsomely. In addition, Emilio Sandoz had been named a beneficiary of the Edwardses' personal estate, along with Sofia Mendes and James Quinn. In the judgment of the law firm, Sandoz was also legally due one-third of that estate. The terms of the will stipulated that while Sandoz remained a member of the Society of Jesus, he would be invited to serve on the board of trustees to help oversee distribution of the funds to charities benefiting education and medicine. However, if he decided for any reason to leave the active priesthood, the money was his to use as he saw fit.

Frightened by the bequest, ignorant of its management, he lost sleep over it that first night. But in the morning, he contacted Brother Edward Behr, who'd been a stockbroker before joining the Society, and mulled Ed's advice over, gradually getting used to the fact that he was now a remarkably wealthy man. The decision came a week or so after first reading Anne's note. Getting out of bed, he accessed listings for antique furniture dealers in the Rome and Naples region, eventually logging a request for estimates on availability and price for one item. That done, he went back to bed. He fell asleep the moment his head touched the pillow, and took that for a good omen.

Entering his Neapolitan office during one of his periodic visits several days later, Vincenzo Giuliani was startled to find in it a superb seventeenth-century table, its highly polished and intricately inlaid surface gleaming in the sunlight that poured through tall, mullioned windows. The table was not, the Father General noted, an exact match for the one Emilio Sandoz had wrecked eleven months earlier, but it was close enough. On it was an envelope containing a paper confirmation of the transfer to the Society of Jesus of a breathtaking sum of money, drawn on the private account of E. J. Sandoz. All of which elicited from the Father General a lengthy and meditative curse.

Debts paid, in possession of more than sufficient funds to shelter himself and to hire his own bodyguards and support a family, Emilio Sandoz was at forty-seven an independent man, ghosts laid to rest, guilt fading, God renounced.

It's not too late to live, he thought. So it was decided: a civil ceremony, on the morning of September 3, with a few friends in attendance.

THAT SUMMER, DETAILED REPORTS OF WHAT GINA GIULIANI AND Emilio Sandoz had every right to believe was a purely private matter rose along the lines of hierarchy in three ancient organizations, reaching at various velocities the Father General of the Society of Jesus, the Supreme Pontiff of the Roman Catholic Church and the Neapolitan Capo di Tutti Capi, each of whom was interested for different but dovetailing reasons. In the face of this unfortunate new circumstance, their collective decision was to accelerate preparations for the latest attempt to reach Rakhat.

The ship chosen for this voyage was now fully configured for interstellar travel. Carlo Giuliani had christened it the *Giordano Bruno,* after a Florentine priest burned at the stake in 1600 for suggesting that the stars were like Sol, and might be orbited by other planets where life could exist. The *Bruno* was highly automated; her crew was small but competent and experienced. Her Jesuit passengers' training was nearing completion. Food, trade goods, medical supplies and communications and survival gear were already being ferried to the *Bruno,* now in low Earth orbit. Navigation programs were locked in for launch in mid-September of 2061.

There was no need to convey any urgency to Sandoz. Indeed, the Jesuits assigned to the mission were very nearly exhausted by the pace he set, for he meant to finish the K'San analysis by August 31 if it killed them all, and threw himself into the project with astonishing energy.

Bedridden less than two years earlier, the linguist's first word to John Candotti had been a bewildered question: "English?" Now Emilio was in nearly constant motion, pacing the length of the library, explaining, reasoning, arguing, gesturing, shifting with lightning suddenness from K'San to Latin to Ruanja to English; then, he was suddenly still, thinking, dark hair falling over his eyes and tossed back with a jerk of the head as the answer to some puzzle came to him, and the pacing began again.

Gina, fuel for this engine, came each evening at eight to pry him out of the library, and in some ways the other men welcomed her arrival as much as Emilio did. Without her intervention, Sandoz would have gone on hours more, and the bigger men were usually famished by the day's end and looked forward, in spite of themselves, to hearing Celestina's piping voice call to Don Emilio and her small footsteps clattering down the long hallway from the front door.

"Christ! Look at them. Gabriel and Lucifer, with a wee cherub in attendance," Sean Fein muttered one night, watching the three of them leave. He turned from the window, face sour, his features a collection of short horizontal lines: a small, lipless mouth, deep-set eyes, a snub nose. "Whoredom," he quoted lugubriously, "is better than wedlock in a priest."

"St. Thomas More could hardly have had Emilio's situation in mind," Vincenzo Giuliani commented dryly, walking into the library unexpectedly. "Please—sit down," he said, when the others got to their feet. "The old orders have retained our vow of celibacy, but diocesan priests may marry now," he pointed out reasonably to Sean. "Do you disapprove of Emilio's decisions, Father Fein?"

"The parish men may marry because ordainin' women was the only alternative to changin' the rule," said Sean with luxurious cynicism. "Hardly a ringin' endorsement of familial love, now, was it?"

Giuliani bought himself time by strolling through the library, lifting reports from desks, smiling a greeting to John Candotti, nodding to Daniel Iron Horse and Joseba Urizarbarrena. As troubled by the situation as he was personally, Giuliani decided it was time to address the issue.

"Even when I was young, more men left the Society than stayed," he told the others lightly, sitting with a window at his back so that he could see their faces clearly in the waning light, while his own was obscured. "It is better for everyone if only those who feel truly called to this life remain in it. But there was a time, long ago, when we treated a resignation as though it were a suicide—a death in the family, and a shameful one at that—particularly if a man left to marry. Friendships that had endured decades would rupture. There were often feelings of betrayal and abandonment, on both sides."

He paused, and looked around as the younger men shifted uncomfortably in their chairs. "How does it make you feel, to see Emilio and Gina together, I wonder?" the Father General asked, brows up with mild curiosity.

The Father General was looking at Daniel Iron Horse as he said this, but it was Sean Fein who threw his head back and closed his eyes with schoolboy earnestness. "Persistence in celibacy requires a firm sense of its value in making us perpetually available for God's good use of us," he recited in a loud monotone, "as well as a desire to uphold an ancient and honorable tradition, and the sincere hope of drawing on a source of divine grace that enables us to love the presence of God in others, without exclusion. Otherwise, it is pointless self-denial." Having delivered himself of this statement, Sean looked around with theatrical melancholy. "Then again, pointless self-denial was half the fun of Catholicism in the old days," he reminded them, "and I, for one, regret its passing."

Giuliani sighed. It was time, he decided, to unmask the chemist. "I have it on good authority, gentlemen, that Father Fein is a man capable of describing the hydrogen bond as being, and I quote: 'like the arms of Christ crucified, flung wide, holding all life in an embrace.' I am assured by Sean's Provincial that when you know poetry lurks in his soul, it is somewhat easier to put up with his bullshit." Noting with aesthetic pleasure the way Sean's pink flush was set off by his blue eyes, Giuliani returned to the task at hand without missing a beat. "You do not shun Emilio Sandoz, and none of you begrudges him this happiness. And yet it must raise questions for you, and it should. Which of us is doing the right thing? Has he thrown away his soul or have I thrown away my life? What if I'm wrong about everything?"

It was Joseba Urizarbarrena who put the problem in its starkest terms. "How," the ecologist asked quietly, "in the face of that man's joy, can I go on alone?"

John Candotti's eyes dropped, and Sean snorted, looking away, but the Father General's gaze remained on the mission's father superior. "The stakes are enormous: life, posterity, eternity," Giuliani said, looking directly at Daniel Iron Horse. "And each of us must discern the answers for himself."

For a long time, the quiet was unbroken by any sound elsewhere in the house. Then the silence was ripped by the the abrasive squeal of wooden chair legs grating against the stone floor. Danny stood looking at Vincenzo Giuliani for a few moments, his small, black eyes hard in the broad, pitted face. "I need some air," he said, throwing down a stylus, and left.

"If you will excuse us, gentlemen?" Giuliani said mildly, and followed Iron Horse out of the room.

DANNY WAS WAITING FOR HIM IN THE GARDEN: CONSCIENCE INCARNATE, a massive presence in the deepening darkness. "Allow me," the Father General said placidly, when it became obvious that Iron Horse would not give him the satisfaction of speaking first. "You find me contemptible."

"That'll do for a start."

Giuliani sat on one of the garden benches and gazed upward, picking out the few bright constellations visible at twilight. "Ignatius once said that his greatest consolation was to contemplate the night sky and its stars," he said. "Since Galileo, space has been the domain of telescopes and of prayer. . . . Of course, Loyola and Galileo didn't have to deal with light pollution from Naples. The sky must be astonishing on Rakhat. Perhaps the Jana'ata are right not to permit the artificial extension of daylight." He looked at Danny. "You wish to ask me how, in the face of that man's joy, can the mission go forward as planned?"

"It is dishonest," Danny said with clipped exactitude. "It is arrogant. It is cruel."

"The Holy Father—"

"Stop hiding behind his skirts," Danny sneered.

"You are scrupulous," Giuliani observed. "There is a way out, Father Iron Horse—"

"And cede the Society to your kind?"

"Ah. My kind," the Father General said, almost smiling. The evening seemed oddly still. In his childhood, Vince Giuliani had loved the sound of swamp peepers, trilling in every low spot, filling the summer dusk with wordless song. Here in Italy, he heard only the treble rasp of crickets, and the night seemed poorer for it. "You are young, Father Iron Horse, and you have a young man's vices. Certainty. Shortsightedness. Contempt for pragmatism." He leaned back, hands clasped and untrembling in his lap. "I only wish that I could live long enough to see what kind you turn out to be."

"That could be arranged. Would you care to exchange positions? Spend a year in transit to Rakhat. When you get back, I'll be eighty."

"The proposal has a certain appeal, I assure you. Unfortunately, it is not an option. We are each alone before God, and cannot exchange lives. Shall I hang one of those ubiquitous Italian signs on the Gesù?" Giuliani offered, brows climbing. His light ironic tone was infuriating, and he knew it. "*Chiuso per restauro:* closed, until Daniel Iron Horse returns, for restoration."

"I hope to Christ that your job is harder than it looks, old man," Daniel Iron Horse hissed, before he turned on his heel to walk away. "Otherwise, there's no excuse for you."

"It is. It is *very* hard," Vincenzo Giuliani said with a sudden ferocity that stopped Danny in his tracks and forced him to turn back. "Shall I confess to you, Father Iron Horse? I doubt. In my old age, I doubt." He stood and began to pace. "I am afraid that I have been a fool to live as I have lived and to believe as I have believed all these years. I am afraid that I have misunderstood everything. And do you know why? Because Emilio Sandoz is not an atheist. Danny, we have among us one of our own, whose life has been touched by God as mine has never been touched, and who believes that his soul has been laid waste in a spiritual rape—his sacrifice mocked, his devotion rejected, his love desecrated."

He stopped, coming to rest in front of the younger man, and spoke very softly. "I envied him once, Danny. Emilio Sandoz was everything I ever hoped to be as a priest, and then—this! I have tried to imagine how I would feel, were I Sandoz and had I experienced what he has." He looked away into the darkness and said, "Danny, I don't know what to do with what happened to him—and all I had to do was listen to the story!"

And then he was moving again, the pacing an outward sign of the inward argument that had drowned out prayer and faith and peace for nearly a year. "In the darkness of my soul, I have wondered if God enjoys watching despair, the way voyeurs watch sex. That would explain a great deal of human history! My faith in the meaning of Jesus's life and in Christian doctrine has been shaken to its core," he said, his voice betraying the tears that glistened now in the moonlight. "Danny, if I am to sustain my belief in a good and loving deity, in a God who is not arbitrary and capricious and vicious, I must believe that some higher purpose is served by all this. And I must believe that the greatest service I can do Emilio Sandoz is to make it possible for him to discover what that purpose may have been."

Giuliani stopped and, in the shadowed, shifting night, he searched the other man's face for understanding, and knew that he had been heard, that his words had registered.

"Post hoc reasoning," Danny said, backing away. "Self-serving horseshit. You've made up your mind and you're trying to justify the unjustifiable."

"And for my penance?" Giuliani asked with a desolate amusement that mocked them both.

"Live, old man," Danny said. "Live with what you're doing."

"Even Judas had a role in our salvation," Giuliani said, almost to himself, but then he spoke at last with the authority it was his duty to exercise. "It is my decision, Father Iron Horse, that the Society of Jesus will once again serve the papacy, as it was meant to—by its founder and by Our Lord. This tragedy of rupture will end. We will once again accept the authority of the Pope to send us on whatever mission he deems desirable for the good of souls. Once again, 'all our strength must be bent to the acquisition of that virtue we call obedience, due first to the Pope and next to the Superior of the Order—' "

" 'In everything that is not sin!' " Danny cried.

"Yes. Precisely: in everything that is not sin," Vincenzo Giuliani agreed. "So I cannot and I will not order you to do what you find unacceptable, Danny. Your soul is your own—but others' souls are at risk as well! Act in accordance with your conscience," he called as Danny strode away into the darkness. "But, Danny—remember the stakes!"

MOMENTS LATER, DANIEL IRON HORSE FOUND HIMSELF LOOKING UP AT the brightly lit dormer windows. He hesitated, half-turned, and then went back to the garage door and knocked. There were light, quick footsteps on the stairway and he heard the metallic snick of the hook being flicked out of its eye. Sandoz appeared and the two men stood silently for a time, adjusting their reactions, each having thought Gina might be on the other side of the door.

"Father Iron Horse," Emilio said at last, "you look like a man with something to confess." Danny blinked, startled. "I was a priest for a long time, Danny. I recognize the signs. Come upstairs."

Sandoz had been halfway to bed, but he put the braces back on and went to his cupboard for two glasses and a bottle of Ronrico, carefully pouring out a measure for each of them, his bioengineered dexterity now strangely graceful. He sat across the table from Iron Horse and inclined his head, willing to listen.

"I came to apologize," Danny told him. "For that crap I pulled on you last winter—when I said you might have brought back whatever Yarbrough died of. I knew that wasn't so. I did it to see how you'd react. It was dishonest and arrogant and cruel. And I am ashamed."

Sandoz sat still. "Thank you," he said finally. "I accept your apology." He closed his hand around the glass and tossed the contents back. "That couldn't have been easy to say," he observed, pouring himself another shot. "The end justifies the means, I suppose. You got me to pull myself together. I'm better off because of what you did."

"Do you believe that?" Danny asked with an odd intentness. "The end justifies the means?"

"Sometimes. It depends, obviously. How important is the end? How nasty are the means?"

Iron Horse sat hunched over his untouched drink, his elbows almost reaching both corners of his side of the table. "Sandoz," he asked after a little while, "is there anything that would persuade you to go back with us to Rakhat?"

Emilio snorted, and picked up his glass, taking a sip. "I honestly don't think I could get drunk enough for that to seem like a good idea," he murmured, "but I suppose we could give it a try."

"Giuliani and the Pope both believe it's God's will that you go back," Danny persisted. "D. W. Yarbrough said that you were once wedded to God—"

"Nietzsche, of course, would argue that I am a widower," Emilio said crisply, cutting him off. "I consider that I am divorced. The separation was not amicable."

"Sandoz," Danny said carefully, "even Jesus thought that God had forsaken Him."

Emilio leaned back in his chair and stared now with the stony contempt of a boxer about to level an inadequate opponent. "You don't want to try that with me," he advised, but Iron Horse would not drop his gaze. Sandoz shrugged: I gave fair warning. "It was all over for Jesus in three hours," he said softly, and Danny blinked. "I'm done with God, Danny. I want no more part of Him. If hell is the absence of God, then I shall be content in hell."

"My brother Walter's daughter drowned," Danny said, reaching for the glass of rum and putting it at arm's length. "Four years old. About six months after the funeral, Walt filed for divorce. It wasn't my sister-in-law's fault, but Walt needed someone to blame. He spent the next ten years trying to drink himself to death, and finally managed it. Rolled his car one night." Having made his point, he said, with no little compassion, "You must be very lonely."

"I was," Sandoz said. "Not anymore."

"Change your mind," Danny implored, leaning forward. "Please. Come with us."

Incredulous, Emilio gasped a laugh. "Danny, I'm getting married in twenty-five days!" He glanced at a clock. "And thirteen hours. And eleven minutes. But who's counting, right?" His smile faded as he looked at Iron Horse; it was strangely affecting to see that big and unemotional man on the verge of tears. "Why is it so important to you?" Emilio asked. "Are you afraid? Danny, you and the others have so much more to go on than we had! Yes, you'll make mistakes, but at least they won't be the same ones we made." Iron Horse looked away, his eyes glittering. "Danny," Emilio ventured, "is there something else . . . ?"

"Yes. No—. I don't know," Danny said finally. "I—I need to think about this. . . . But—. Just don't trust any of the Giulianis, Sandoz."

Confused, Emilio frowned. Danny seemed to think he was revealing some great secret, but everybody knew that the Father General's family was Camorra. At a loss, and looking for a way out, Emilio could only change the subject. "Listen, John was asking me about some Ruanja syntax—I put together some notes for him this evening, but I know I was working on something similar just before—before the massacre. I told Giuliani to dump everything we sent back to my system, but I can't find that file. Is there any chance that some of my stuff is stored separately?"

Danny seemed distracted, but dragged himself back to what Sandoz was saying. "It was at the end of the transmissions?"

"Yes. The last thing I relayed to the ship."

Danny shrugged. "Might still be in the queue waiting to be sent."

"What? Still on the ship? Why wouldn't it have been transmitted?"

"The data went out in packets. The onboard computers were programmed to store your reports and send them in groups. If the Rakhati suns or Sol were positioned badly, the system would just queue everything until the transmissions could get through without being degraded by stellar interference."

"News to me. I thought everything went out as we logged it," Sandoz said, surprised. He'd paid almost no attention to technical considerations like that. "So it just sat in memory for over a year, until the *Magellan* party sent me back? Would there have been that much time between packets?"

"Maybe. I don't know too much about the celestial mechanics involved myself. There were four stars the system had to work around. Wait—the people from the *Magellan* boarded the *Stella Maris*, didn't they? Maybe when they were accessing the ship's records, they disabled the transmission code." The more he thought about it, the likelier it seemed. "The last packet is probably still sitting in memory. I can pull it out for you if you want."

"It can wait until morning."

"No. You've got me curious now," Danny said, glad of something concrete to do. "It should only take a few minutes. I don't know why no one checked earlier."

Together, the two men moved to the wall of photonics and Iron Horse worked his way into the *Stella Maris* library storage system. "Sure enough, ace," he said minutes later. "Look. It's still coded and compressed." He reset the system to expand the data and they waited.

"Wow. There's a lot of it," Sandoz remarked, watching the screen. "Some more stuff by Marc. Joseba will be pleased. Yes! There's mine. I knew I'd done that work already." He stood silently a while longer, looking over Danny's shoulder. "There's something for you," Sandoz said as a new file scrolled by. "Sofia was working on trade networks . . ." His voice trailed off. "Wait. Wait, wait, wait. Go back! Can you stop it?"

"No. It's going to decompress all of it. . . . There. It's done," Iron Horse said.

Sandoz had spun away, breathing hard. "Not for the Society. Not for the Church," he whispered. "No. No. No. I saw her dead."

Danny twisted in his chair. "What are you talking about, ace?"

"Get out of the way," Sandoz said abruptly.

Danny vacated the desk chair and Sandoz sat down in front of the display. He seemed to settle himself, as though to take a blow, and then carefully spoke the ID and date stamp again, bringing up the last set of files held in the queue, which were logged, impossibly, months after his own final transmission, now some eighteen years in the past on Rakhat.

"Sandoz, what? What did you see? I don't understand—" Frightened by the other man's pallor, Danny leaned over Sandoz's shoulder and looked at the file on the display. "Oh, my God," he said blankly.

During the past months, as he had studied the mission reports and the scientific papers sent back by the *Stella Maris* party, Daniel Iron Horse had sometimes, with a strange feeling of unfocused guilt, called up images of the artificial-intelligence analyst Sofia Mendes: digitized and radio-transmitted watercolors painted by Father Marc Robichaux, the naturalist on the first mission. The earliest of these was done on Rakhat, during Sofia's wedding to the astronomer Jimmy Quinn; others were painted later, as pregnancy softened the classical lines of her face. When Danny

had first seen these portraits, he thought that Robichaux must have ideal-
ized her, for Sofia Mendes was as beautiful as a Byzantine Annunciation in
the last painting, done only days before her death in the Kashan massacre.
But when, for comparison, Danny had pulled up one of the few archived
photos of Sofia, he could only acknowledge the scientific accuracy of Robichaux's draftsmanship. Brains and beauty and guts, everyone agreed. An
extraordinary woman . . .

"Oh, my God," Daniel Iron Horse repeated, staring at the screen.

"Not even for her," Sandoz whispered, trembling. "I won't go back."

16

Trucha Sai

2047, Earth-Relative

"SUPAARI, DO YOU UNDERSTAND WHAT YOU'RE ASKING?" SAID SOFIA. "I can't promise that anyone will ever bring you home—"

"You home," said Isaac.

"I will not wish to come back! There is no reason to come back! I am nothing here. I am less than nothing—"

"Than nothing," said Isaac.

"Then think of Ha'anala!" Sofia urged, the child in question then only a season old and asleep in her arms, a curled ball of fur and latent energy. "What kind of future can she have among my people?"

"Mong my people," said Isaac.

Sofia glanced down, the rare error in pronunciation catching her attention. There had been a time when the sound of Isaac's voice had flooded her with joy and relief; now she knew this was merely echolalia—compulsive, toneless parroting—meaningless, and intensely irritating.

"I do think of Ha'anala," Supaari cried. "She is all I think of!"

"Think of."

Supaari rose abruptly from their leafy asylum and walked away, only to face Sofia again, his heavy tail sweeping a circular swath in the ground litter. He seemed completely unaware of the gesture, but Sofia had seen it often enough in the past few months to know that it was a mime of staking out territory. He meant to hold his ground in this argument. "No one will marry the child of a VaHaptaa, Sofia. And if we stay here among the Runa, Ha'anala is as dead. I am as dead—worse than dead! We are all four trapped here among people who are not our own—"

Supaari stopped and inhaled, checking for scent.

"Our own," said Isaac.

Sofia watched tensely as Supaari sampled the air. They listened, alert for the sounds of their Runa patrons waking up after the midday siesta, but there was nothing beyond the normal noise of biomass and the fecundity that enveloped the embowered hut where Sofia sheltered a few days a month, when her scent became temporarily obnoxious to the Runa. Sometimes she and Supaari came here simply to get away for a while; even in seclusion, they used English as a private language, the way Sofia's parents had used Hebrew when she was a child in Istanbul.

Only Isaac had followed them here today. It was the closest he came to expressing a desire to be near others—this willingness to walk along behind his mother and her friend, never looking at them, but matching their direction and speed, stopping when they did, sitting quietly until they moved again. He seemed oblivious to their existence, but Sofia was increasingly convinced that Isaac took in a great deal more than he let on, and this could be infuriating. It was as though he were refusing to speak, as though he wouldn't give her the satisfaction of speaking because she wanted it so desperately—

"Sandoz told me you have stupid meat on Earth," Supaari said, breaking into her thoughts. "Meat of not-people—"

("Not-people.")

"Supaari, this place is rich with meat! You could eat *piyanot*. Or *cranil*—"

(*"Cranil."*)

"And how shall I catch them?" Supaari demanded coldly. "*Piyanot* are too fast and *cranil* too big—they'd roll and crush a hunter who tried to take them! We have always only eaten Runa, who can be caught—" He shot a prehensile foot out and gripped Isaac's ankle. "Do you see this?" Supaari snarled, in anger and in anguish. "We are made only for prey so slow as this child! If the Runa did not come to us to be killed, the cities would starve in less than a season. This is why we have to breed them. We need them—"

"Supaari, let Isaac go."

The child's habitual stillness had become utter immobility, but he did not cry out or weep in fear. Supaari released the boy instantly, his ears dropping in apology. There was no visible response from Isaac, but Sofia let out a breath and looked up at the Jana'ata looming over her. "Come back here and sit down," she said evenly, and when Supaari did, she told him, "There are other ways to hunt! The Runa can build deadfalls for you. Or traps."

"Traps," said Isaac, as tonelessly as before.

"Take us back to your H'earth, and my daughter and I can eat without shame," Supaari insisted. Kneeling, he stared at the baby lying in her arms, but then lifted his eyes. "Sofia, I can never go back to my people. I can never be as I was. But I don't think I can stand to stay with the Runa," he said with soft desperation. "They are good. They are honorable people, but . . ."

"But." They both noticed Isaac's word this time, and it hung in the air with everything it implied left unsaid.

She reached out to run the back of her hand along a lupine cheek. "I know, Supaari. I understand."

("Understand.")

"I think I can live with your people. Ha'an. You. Your Djimi. Djorj. You were friends to me and I believe I could—" He stopped again, gathering courage, throwing his head back to look at her from the distance of his pride. "I wish also to find Sandoz and offer my neck to him." She tried to say something, but he went on resolutely, before Isaac could mimic his words. "If he does not kill me, then Ha'anala and I will live with you and learn your songs."

"Learn your songs," said Isaac. He glanced at the adults then: a momentary flicker of direct attention so fleeting that neither noticed it.

"Whither thou goest, there go I, and thy ways shall be my ways," Sofia was murmuring in rueful Hebrew. Mama, she thought, I know he has a tail, but I think he wants to convert.

How could she say no? She had waited out these six endless, fruitless months on the bare chance that her radio beacon might bring a response from unknown humans. Right here, so close she could feel the heat from his body, was a man she knew and cared for, and was beginning to understand. Less alien to her than her own son, more like her than she could have imagined a few years earlier, just as ashamed to discover that his gratitude to the Runa was insufficient to overcome a gnawing need to think a single thought uninterrupted by endless talk, to make a single gesture disregarded and uncommented on, to be able to take a walk without incurring the gentle, insistent Runa dismay that followed any temporary escape from the group.

"All right," she said at last. "If this is truly what you think is best for Ha'anala. If you wish this—"

("Wish this.")

"Yes. I wish it."

("Wish it.")

They sat a while longer, each sunk in thought. "We should get back to the village," Sofia said after a time. "It'll be redlight soon."

("Redlight soon. Supaari sings.")

She almost missed it, so nearly immune was she to her son's toneless voice.

Supaari sings.

She had to replay the sound in her head to be certain. My God, she thought. Isaac said, Supaari sings.

She did not engulf her son in an embrace or scream or weep or even move, but only glanced at Supaari, as surprised as she and as immobile. She had seen too often the way Isaac drained himself away—became Not There in some mysterious fashion when he was touched. "Yes, Isaac," Sofia said in an ordinary voice, as though this was a normal child who had simply made a comment for his mother to confirm. "Supaari sings at second sundown. For Ha'anala."

"Supaari sings at second sundown." They waited, breathless in the heat. "For Isaac."

Supaari blinked, mouth open, so human in his reaction Sofia nearly laughed. His daughter in her arms, Sofia lifted her chin: For Isaac, Supaari.

He stood then and went nearer to Isaac, alert to the smooth, small muscles, to the barely perceptible quiver that would precede flight. By some instinct never before exercised in such a manner, he knew that he should not face the boy, so Supaari knelt at Isaac's side and sang to the child, softly and unseen.

Sofia held her breath as the first notes of the evening chant floated out to join the forest choir of cries and hoots, of buzzing rasps and fluting whistles. Listened as Supaari's bass—melodic and fluid—was joined by a child's soprano, unerringly on pitch, word-perfect, but in miraculous harmony. Gazed with her one myopic, tear-blurred eye at her son's face, incandescent in the roseate light: transfigured, alive—truly *alive* for the first time. And blessed the God of her ancestors, for granting them life, for sustaining them, for allowing them to reach this new season.

When the chant drew to a close, she filled her lungs with air that seemed perfumed with music. Voice steady, face wet on one side,

Sofia Mendes asked her son, "Isaac, would you like to learn another song?"

He did not look at her but, standing with the uncanny steadiness and balance that had attended his earliest attempt to walk, he came closer. Head averted, her elfin son lifted a small hand and placed on her lips a single finger, delicate as a damselfly's wing. Yes, please, he was saying in the only way he could. Another song.

"This is what our people sing at dawn and sundown," she told him, and lifted her voice in the ancient call, "Sh'ma Yisrael! Adonai Eloheynu, Adonai Echad." Hear O Israel! The Lord is our God, the Lord is One. When she was finished, the small finger brushed her lips again, and so she sang once more, and this time her son's voice joined hers: word-perfect, and in harmony.

When it was over, Sofia blew her nose on a handful of balled-up leaves and wiped one side of her face against a shoulder clad in one of Jimmy's remaining T-shirts. For a few moments, she fingered the soft, worn fabric, grateful for some contact with Isaac's father. Then she stood. "Let's go home," she said.

SHE HAD LONG SINCE LOCATED THE MAGELLAN'S LANDER, USING THE OR-biting ship's transponder to activate its beacon to the global positioning subroutines of the orbiting satellites, which relayed its coordinates to her computer tablet. The abandoned plane was only a few kilometers outside Kashan. As far as she could tell, tapping its onboard systems, it had been locked down properly, was sufficiently fueled to return to orbit, and seemed potentially operational. Activating communications now, she zeroed a time-date stamp, set the transponder for infinite repeat, and recorded a new message. "This is Sofia Mendes, of the *Stella Maris* party. Today is March 5, 2047, Earth-relative. I have waited 165 days local time for a response to my call from any human on Rakhat. This message serves notice that I am planning to leave this planet in fifteen days Rakhat-relative, using the *Magellan's* lander to get to the mother ship. If you can't get to the lander by that time, you will be marooned here. I regret this, but I cannot wait any longer."

She had found it difficult to tell Kanchay and the others of her plan to leave Rakhat but, to her relief, there was no great distress among the Runa. "Someone was wondering when you would go home," Kanchay said. "You'll need to bring goods back to your people, or they'll think your journey was a failure." The Runa, she was thus reminded, had always assumed that the Jesuit party from Earth had come simply to trade. Supaari's sudden decision to go with her, they thought, was a sensible plan to do business abroad, where he was not under a death warrant.

So this is what the Jesuit mission had come to, and Sofia was content with that; she was, after all, a practical woman and the daughter of an economist. Commerce was perhaps the oldest motive for exploration, and it now seemed entirely sufficient to her. Her grandiose thoughts of a higher purpose seemed revealed for what they were: a reaction to isolation, a desire for significance. Delusional but adaptive, she thought, a way to cope with the fear of dying here, alone and forgotten.

Energized by the process of analysis and organization, Sofia had spent the months of waiting in thorough preparation for the journey home. In consultation with Supaari, she had drawn up lists of the light, compact trade goods and scientific specimens she thought most likely to be of financial or academic value at home: precious stones that were biological in origin, like pearls and amber, but unique to Rakhat; small and ordinary but exquisitely crafted bowls and platters carved from native shells and wood; soil samples, seeds, tubers. Textiles of dazzling complexity; polychrome ceramics of charm and wit. A plant extract that numbed wounds and seemed to speed healing, even for Sofia's skin. Jewelry. Perfume samples. Vacuum-packed specimens of coatings that seemed impervious to weather; technical manuals from chemists, and formulas, and drawings that illustrated several manufacturing processes that Sofia thought unique to Rakhat. Enough to ensure financial independence, she believed, if there were still patent law and licensing agreements by the time they got to Earth.

She and Supaari would also be able to sell intellectual property—knowledge of Runa and Jana'ata culture, interpretive skills, unique understanding and perspectives that could be added to the uncounted gigabytes of geological, meteorological and ecological data collected continuously and automatically by the *Magellan* and relayed home all these years. But Sofia was no fool and her own experience of her home planet did not inspire Panglossian optimism. They might be killed on sight, out of fear of disease and xenophobia. Their cargo might be confiscated and Supaari seized for exhibit in zoos. Her son might be institutionalized and she herself held incommunicado by whatever government they might first encounter.

Or perhaps, God who has begun this will bring it to perfection, she thought, remembering Marc Robichaux. Perhaps there will be Jesuits to meet us at spacedock. Perhaps Sandoz—

She stopped, stunned by what it would mean for her to see Emilio again, and for him to meet Supaari. Perhaps, she thought, he'll have forgiven Supaari by then. Christians are supposed to forgive. It occurred to her that when her reports were transmitted and finally heard at home, Emilio might simply turn around and come back for her as soon as a new ship could be configured. It was just the sort of Quixotic gesture he was capable of. Unnecessary, of course, but typical. We might pass each other! she realized, shivering at the thought.

No, she decided finally, God couldn't be that cruel. And she forced herself to think of other things.

Naples

August 2061

"WHAT'S WRONG?" EMILIO ASKED AS GINA STOOD TO CLEAR THE PLATES after a meal that was pleasant enough but oddly charged.

"Nothing," she said, fussing at the sink.

"Which means that something is. Even an ex-priest knows that!" Emilio said with a smile that melted away when she didn't answer.

Considering how short a time they'd been together, the two of them had already managed to have some remarkably good arguments. They had fought over the proper way to cook rice, the correct strength of coffee and various means of brewing it, and whether artichokes were edible, Gina taking the position that they were evidence of divine beneficence while Emilio declared tree bark more appealing. His favorite thus far was a memorable and still unresolved debate that had initially ended in incredulous shouting, succeeded by outraged silence, over which was more stupefyingly boring, World Cup soccer or World Series baseball. "Baseball uniforms are ugly, too," Gina declared a week later, which started that one all over again. And then there was a really wonderful fight about the cut and color of the suit that he was to wear at their wedding. Eventually Emilio gave in on the lapels Gina liked so he could get the gray silk he preferred to the black she insisted he looked fabulous in, but only because she'd made an aesthetic concession on the baseball uniforms.

It was fun. They were both products of cultures that considered marital dispute a performance art, and they encouraged Celestina to join in for the sheer pleasure of having her yell exuberantly along with whichever adult was currently her favorite—a status, Emilio had observed, that ordinarily accrued to whoever had thwarted her second to last. But nothing had been in earnest until today, when he'd walked over for lunch, intending to help them pack for the trip to the mountains with Gina's parents.

Emilio frowned at Gina's back, and then glanced at the kitchen clock. A great deal had changed in the years of his absence, but little kids still loved animation. "Celestina," he said evenly, "it's time for *I Bambini*." He waited until Celestina had rocketed off to her bedroom to play the day's installment of her favorite interactive. "Let's try this again," he suggested quietly when he and Gina were alone. "What's wrong?"

She spun around, head up, eyes brimming, and declared in a voice as firm as her chin wasn't, "You should go back to find Sofia!"

Stunned, Emilio gaped at her for a moment, then closed his eyes and breathed in slowly, hands resting on the tabletop. When he looked at Gina next, it was with the obsidian stare that had frightened people far better equipped to withstand his anger than she was. "Who told you?" he asked very softly.

"Don't look at me like that," she said.

"Who told you?" he repeated even more quietly, each word separate.

"What difference does it make who told me? She's alive. That poor woman—she's all alone!" Gina exclaimed, starting to cry, but determined now to confront him on the very points of honor she feared he would defend. "You should go back to rescue her. She needs you. You loved her."

He might have turned to stone. "One," he said at last. "It makes a difference because I intend to kill whoever told you. Two. All we know for certain is that she was alive in 2047. Three. The *Giordano Bruno* won't reach Rakhat for another seventeen years. The probability of finding her alive, having survived alone on Rakhat to the age of seventy-one, approaches zero. Four—"

"I hate it when you're like this!"

"Four!" he said, standing now, his voice rising. "Sofia Mendes was the single most competent person I have ever met. I assure you that she would find laughable the concept of needing me, of all people, to rescue her! Five. Yes. I loved her! I also loved Anne, and D.W., and Askama. I didn't marry any of them. Gina, look at me!" he shouted, stung that she doubted him, enraged that someone had tried to drive this wedge between them. "If Sofia Mendes miraculously walked in that door at this moment, alive, well and in the bloom of her youth, it would change nothing between you and me. Nothing!"

Gina only cried harder, glaring in wet defiance. Exasperated, he turned abruptly and walked to the kitchen desk, rummaging through the clutter for a code written on a scrap of paper.

"Who are you calling?" she asked, eyes streaming, as he activated the phone.

"The magistrate. I want him here. Now. We are getting married this afternoon. Then I am going to call the tailor and cancel the order for that damned suit. And then I am going to murder Vincenzo Giuliani and probably Daniel Iron Horse as well—"

"Why is Mamma crying?" Celestina demanded, standing in the kitchen doorway, little hands fisted, scowling at him.

Gina hastily wiped her eyes. "It's nothing, cara—"

"It's not nothing! It's important and she deserves to understand," Emilio snapped, having understood very little of his own mangled childhood. He canceled the call and got a grip on himself. "Your mamma is afraid that I might leave her, Celestina. She thinks I could love someone else more than I love her, cara."

"But you do." Celestina looked nonplussed. "You love me best."

Gina laughed a little and turned to Emilio. "Go ahead," she said in bleary-eyed challenge, sniffing mightily. "Handle this one."

He threw her a look worthy of a pool shark calling a bank shot to the corner pocket. "You," he told Celestina with perfect aplomb, "are my very best little girl and your mamma is my very best wife." Brows up, he turned back to Gina expectantly and received a nod of ungrudging if somewhat damp commendation. Satisfied, he went back to the mess on the desk, muttering, "Which is to say, she *will* be my very best wife as soon as I can get the magistrate out here—"

"No," said Gina, stopping him with a hand on his arm. She leaned her head against his shoulder. "It's all right. I needed to hear it, I guess. We can wait until September." She laughed again and lifted her head, tucking her hair behind her ears and wiping her eyes. "And don't you dare cancel that suit!"

Wedding jitters, he thought, looking at her. She'd been uncharacteristically emotional lately and this business about Sofia had capped it all off. Cursing his hands and the braces, he took her shoulders and gingerly held her at arm's length. "I am not Carlo, Gina. I will never leave you," he whispered, watching to see if she could believe it. He pulled her to him and sighed, thinking, It's not like either of us is coming to this with a clean slate. Then he looked at Celestina over her mother's shoulder and raised his voice so they could both hear him. "I love you, and I love Celestina, and I am yours forever."

"Well," said Celestina, almost six, in the ringing tones of a grande dame of seventy, "I'm certainly pleased we've straightened that out!"

Gina and Emilio stared at each other open-mouthed as the little girl flounced out of the kitchen and went back to her cartoons. "I never said that. Do you say that? Where does she get this stuff?" Gina asked, astounded.

Emilio was laughing. "That was really good! Don't you recognize it? Valeria Golina—La Contessa!" he cried. "No—wait, you fell asleep on the sofa, but Celestina and I watched it last Sunday." He shook his head, extravagantly pleased that Celestina was picking up one of his own habits. "She was doing Valeria Golina. That was really good!"

IT IS DIFFICULT TO SUSTAIN HIGH DRAMA IN A HOUSEHOLD WITH CHIL-dren, particularly those who have learned to do creditable Golina impressions. They spent the afternoon arguing with Celestina over the minimum number of stuffed animals (four) and maximum number of party dresses (one) necessary for a two-week holiday in the mountains. Emilio helped mainly by keeping Celestina out of Gina's hair until Celestina's best friend, Pia, came over to play, at which time he announced that he intended to fold all the clothes that had been laid out on the bed for packing.

"You're very good at that," Gina observed, glancing over her shoulder at his handiwork as she rooted in a bureau drawer for underwear her mother would not be disgusted by.

"Dazzling," he agreed and added, "I used to work in the house laundry. Would you like me to come with you to the mountains?"

She straightened slowly, astonished. "And if you're recognized?"

"I'll wear dark glasses and a hat and gloves," he said, looking up from the suitcase.

"And a trenchcoat?" she suggested dryly. "*Caro*, it's August."

"All right, what about a veil?" he asked airily, going back to the clothes.

"Nothing flashy—not an embroidered silk veil hung with gold coins. Something tasteful!" There was a pause. "Silver coins, perhaps." He blew it off, laying blouses in her bag. "If I'm recognized, I'm recognized! I'll deal with it."

They could hear the two little girls' shrieking laughter out in the yard. The house itself seemed very still. Gina walked to the bed and sat down, watching his face. Finally, he sat next to her. "Okay," he admitted, the cockiness gone, "maybe it's not such a great idea."

"You've got to finish the K'San project for the Jesuits. They're leaving soon," she pointed out. "Maybe next year for the mountains?"

Head down, hair over his eyes, he probed the hurt places, judging himself. "The Society is going to release the scientific papers in October," he said, serious now. "I have been thinking that perhaps the best way to handle it really is to call a news conference. Spend a whole day, if necessary. As long as it takes. Be done with it. Answer every damned question they throw at me—"

"And then come home to your family." She reached over and took his face in her hands and looked into the dark eyes, watching the doubt and the fear recede.

"Do people still dance?" he asked suddenly. "Someday, I would like to take you dancing."

"Yes, caro," she assured him. "People still dance."

"Good," he said, and leaned forward to kiss her, but then just closed his eyes in resignation and rested his forehead against hers as the kitchen door crashed open and a tidal wave of noise rolled down the hallway toward them.

Celestina skidded to a halt at the bedroom door, hair wild and face rosy with the heat. "We're starving!" she cried dramatically and demonstrated this by collapsing semi-gracefully into a pitiable heap at their feet.

"Note, if you will," Emilio pointed out to the dying swan's mother, "that she made sure to fall onto the bedroom carpet, rather than the tiled floor of the hall." Celestina giggled, eyes closed.

"Will you make us macaroni and cheese again?" Pia begged Emilio, hopping up and down, hands pressed together in supplication. "Just like last time? Please, please, please. Extra soupy? With lots of milk?"

Gina smiled at her lap, shaking her head, as Emilio was borne off to the kitchen by two boisterous little girls. "Pia, call your mother," she could hear him say in his very best papa voice. "And ask if you may stay for supper. Celestina, you set the table. Lots of milk, the lady says! Why is it you can never find a cow when you need one . . ."

FINALLY, THE TIME CAME TO PUT CELESTINA TO BED AND, AS GINA touched off the light and tucked the child in, Emilio cleared a space to sit amid the doll-and-stuffed-animal populace. From out of nowhere, he produced a small silver box that one of the Camorra guards had purchased for him in Naples and held it up for Celestina's perusal.

"Is it for me?" she asked, her yearning naked.

"Who else?" he asked, smiling at Gina, enjoying her obvious perplexity. "This is a magic box, you know," Emilio confided then, face grave, eyes alight, as Celestina examined the tiny, perfect flowers that decorated its lid. "You can keep words in it."

The child looked up at him, massively skeptical in the dark, and he smiled at her remarkable resemblance to her mother. "Take the top off for me, if you please," he said. He had planned to do this himself, but small precise movements were sometimes excruciatingly hard. No matter, he thought, I can adapt the act. "Now. Get ready because you have to put the top back on very quickly after I say the words." Caught up in the game, Celestina tensed and held the box to his lips. Eyes on Gina, he whispered, "*Ti amo, cara,*" and then cried, "Quick! Get that top on!" Squealing, Celestina clamped the lid down as quickly as she could. "Whew! That was close. Now," he said, taking the box from her, "tap the top and count to ten."

"Why?"

"Why, why, why! We don't beat this child enough," he complained to Gina, who was smiling broadly. "In my day, kids did as they were told, no questions asked."

Celestina was not impressed. "Why?" she insisted on knowing.

"To let the words know they're supposed to stay inside," he told her in an exasperated tone: any silly would know that! "Do as you're told. Tap the top and count to ten!" he repeated, holding the box out in what was left of a palm, balancing it on the brace strap. She no longer saw his hands, he realized. Even Pia was used to them now.

Celestina, mollified, tapped and counted. He handed the box to her. "Now, open it, and put it right next to your ear."

Small fingers pried the lid off and her oval face, the mirror of her mother's, became still as she thrust the box into blond tangles near a golden ear sprinkled with summer freckles. "I don't hear anything!" Celestina declared, skepticism confirmed. "I think you're goofing me."

Emilio looked indignant. "Try it again," he said, but he added, "This time, listen with your heart."

In the magical silence of a little girl's bedroom, they all three heard his words: *Ti amo, cara.*

BEFORE IT WAS OVER, CELESTINA HAD ASKED FOR A DRINK OF WATER AND reminded her mother about the night-light and told Emilio she was going to keep the box under her pillow and asked for one last trip to the toilet, and then tried to initiate a discussion of monster-under-the-bed behavior that had the potential for delaying "Good night" five more minutes, but didn't work.

Finally, pulling the door almost closed, they left Celestina with "Sweet dreams," and Gina caught her breath, feeling vacuumed of energy but happy. "You are going to be the greatest papa in world history," she said with quiet conviction, putting her arms around Emilio.

"Depend on it," he told her, but she could tell something was wrong. He made no move toward their bedroom and finally told her wryly, "You could save me a lot of embarrassment if you had a headache tonight."

She stepped back. "Your hands?" There was a small shrug and he looked away. He started to apologize, but she stopped him with a finger on his lips. "*Caro,* we have our whole lives for it." And to tell the truth, she'd felt faintly queasy all day anyway, so she changed the subject as they headed for the kitchen table. "Don Vincenzo told me they found another surgeon for you last May, but you wouldn't see him. Why not, *caro?*" Emilio slumped into a chair opposite her, face stony, his breathing shallow. "You heal well enough now. They can do amazing things, Emilio. Reglove the hands with artificial skin, reposition some tendons to take advantage of the nerves that weren't cut. You'd have much better function afterward."

"I'm used to the braces." He sat up, half defiant. "Look. I've had enough, okay? I don't want to start all over learning how to use my hands."

That much he had told the Father General. She waited, giving him time to say the rest himself. When he didn't, she answered the unspoken objection, and knew she'd guessed correctly when his eyes slid away.

"The phantom neuralgia won't be any worse afterward—it might even be better."

There was no answer for a time. "I'll think about it," he said, blinking. "Not right away. I need some time."

"Maybe after New Year's," she suggested gently.

"Maybe," he said. "I don't know. Maybe."

There was no rush, apart from her own desire to see him made whole, so Gina let it go. He'd had scurvy when he first came home and, for a long time, his connective tissue had simply been too fragile to permit surgery; the longer he waited, the healthier he would be and the faster he would heal. The damage to his hands was already three years old. Another six months would make no difference clinically.

The last thing they talked about before he walked back to his apartment was the arrangement he'd made with the law firm in Cleveland and the bank in Zurich, giving Gina free access to all his accounts.

"Don't you want to wait until after the wedding?" she asked, standing in the doorway.

"Why? Are you going to run away with the money?" he replied. She could barely see him in the dark. "No, I just want you to take your parents out for dinner a few times. Someplace nice, yes? And tell them it was my idea! I want credit. A son-in-law has to think about this kind of thing."

She laughed and watched until he disappeared into the moonless night.

THEY WERE IN TOUCH DAILY WHILE GINA WAS GONE, ALTHOUGH TO-ward the end of the second week, Emilio was swamped, wrapping up the final details of the K'San programs, trying to meet his own self-imposed deadline at the end of the month. By the time she and Celestina got back to Naples, it had been a couple of days since they'd spoken. She called the minute she walked in her door, but the number was disconnected. She tried again to be sure she hadn't touched the wrong code, then drove over to his apartment as soon as she'd brought the luggage in from the car and taken care of Celestina's immediate needs for a toilet and lunch, telling herself all the while that what she knew must be wrong.

The main retreat house was not deserted, as she had irrationally feared, but no one she knew was in residence. The lay brother who'd taken Cosimo's place in the refectory was Vietnamese and she couldn't make out a word of his Italian. The door to Emilio's apartment over the garage was locked, and the geraniums were gone from his unshuttered windows. She demanded explanations, wept, screamed, accused, and everywhere met *omertà*—the silence of the South. Her second daughter was nearly ten years old before Gina understood the whole of it.

Giordano Bruno

2061–2062 Earth-Relative

"REALLY, SANDOZ, I WOULD HAVE THOUGHT THAT SULKING WAS BE-neath your dignity," Carlo Giuliani remarked with cool amusement, watching as Nico d'Angeli checked the blood chemistry readouts before adjusting the IV line running into Sandoz's arm. "It's your own fault, you know. You were given every opportunity to volunteer. This attitude will get you nothing but bedsores and a bladder infection."

Leaning with elegant composure against the soundproofed bulkhead of the *Giordano Bruno*'s sick bay, Carlo studied the still, dark face. He saw nothing of coma's slackness or sleep's easing. This was sheer obstinance.

"Do you enjoy opera, Sandoz?" Carlo asked curiously when Nico, humming "Nessun dorma," started the sponge bath. "Most Neapolitans are mad for opera. We love the passions, the conflict—life lived on a grand scale." He waited for a moment, watching the man's closed eyes as Nico lifted the unresisting limbs, wiping down the armpits and groin with gentle efficiency. "Gina never cared for opera," Carlo recalled. "Grandiose nonsense, she called it. A thoroughly boring little housewife, Gina. You should thank me, Sandoz. I have saved you from a stifling fate! You would not have been content for long to sit at home with her, eating pasta together and getting fat. You and I were meant for greater things."

Finished with the bath, Nico set aside the washcloth and covered Sandoz with the sheet for a few minutes, to let the dampness subside before reapplying the electrodes. In no hurry, Carlo waited until the heart monitor had begun its steady ping before speaking again. "We have a great deal in common, you know—even apart from our use of Gina," he suggested, and smiled with satisfaction at the raggedly quickened tempo of the pinging. "We were both despised by our fathers, for example. Papa used to call me Cio-Cio-San. The allusion is to *Madama Butterfly*, of course. To call me Cio-Cio-San was to accuse me of flitting from one thing to another, do you see? Since the day of my birth, I have been a bitter disappointment to my father. Like yours, my father saw in my face only evidence of his wife's infidelity. There, perhaps, our experience differs: my mother was falsely accused. But it has always been easier for Papa to assume that I am not his than to accept that I am not he."

Unable to work without singing, and partial to Bellini, Nico went on to *Norma*: "Me protegge, me difende . . ."

"I have always been good at anything I put my hand to," Carlo reported without false modesty. "Every teacher I studied with took an interest in me. Each assumed I'd be a protégé—an engineer or biologist or pilot. When I refused to follow in their footsteps, they blamed my inconstancy and disloyalty, rather than recognize their own disappointed desire for acolytes. But I am no one's disciple. My life is my own, and I follow no one else's path."

Nico moved to the foot of the bed to change the urine bag. It was a tight fit in the cramped space at that end of the medical bay, but he was a methodical and careful person who did one thing at a time, in a set order, and he had learned how to accomplish this maneuver with a minimum of disturbance.

"I know what you're thinking, Sandoz: delusions of grandeur," Carlo continued soberly. "Men like you and my father excel in a narrow field of endeavor. You are intent from your youth on one thing, and achieve a great deal early in your lives, and you scorn those who are not similarly focused. My father, for example, took over Naples before he was thirty—it was quite a remarkable rise to power," Carlo admitted. "By the time he was forty, he controlled businesses accounting for eighteen percent of Italy's gross national product, with an annual income greater than Fiat. At forty-two, only a year older than I am now, Domenico Giuliani was the head of an empire with tentacles reaching into the whole of Europe, South Africa, the Middle East, the Caribbean and the Americas. An empire larger than

Alexander's—my father would remind me of this at breakfast, nearly every morning."

Carlo fell silent for a time. Then he drew himself up and shrugged. "But true greatness is in part a matching of the man and the times, Sandoz. Versatility can be a virtue! I'd have done well in the Renaissance, for example. A merchant prince! Someone who could write a song and wage war and build a catapult and dance well. Even my father had to admit that launching this venture required talent in many fields. Politics, finance, engineering . . ."

Finished with his chores and two arias, Nico looked to his padrone. "Well done," Carlo said, on cue. "You may go now, Nico." He waited for Nico to leave before standing and moving to the bedside. "You see, Sandoz? Knowing your frailties as well as your strengths, I have even provided you with a very fine nurse. Not one as delightfully accommodating as Gina, perhaps, but quite adequate to his task."

He glanced at the readouts, but this time Gina's name provoked no change in the life-sign data now flowing to the monitors. "An extraordinary situation, is it not?" said Carlo Giuliani, looking down at the man who'd very nearly married his own ex-wife. "Unforeseen and unfortunate. You may believe that I have taken you away from Gina out of some romantic Neapolitan fury but I assure you, I was finished with her. The simple fact is that I need you more than she does." He opened the sick-bay door, standing there for a time without leaving. "Don't worry about Gina, Sandoz. She'll find someone new, now that you're gone."

It was not until the sick-bay hatch was shut and locked from the outside that the readouts changed.

CARLO HAD SENT THREE OF THEM FOR HIM. THEY KNEW HE'D BEEN A priest and were, perhaps, complacent in that knowledge. They could see that he was small. They were told he had been sick and that his hands were essentially useless. What they did not know was that he was a veteran of a hundred emetic nightmare reenactments of this very experience. Over and over, he relived it and what came afterward. This time, there was no hesitation, no foolish hope, and he did damage before, inevitably, they overpowered him. For weeks afterward, he would remember with satisfaction the feel of a cheekbone giving way under his heel when a face came within striking distance, would recall with pleasure the nasal cry of the man whose nose he broke when he got an elbow loose.

He marked them. This time, he made himself felt.

He had been beaten before and there was no novelty in it. He rolled with as much as he could, kept tensed and braced for as long as possible, and finally took a savage satisfaction in the silence that would become his principal weapon against them. Unconscious during the trip to the launch site, he was kept under sedation for a time, even after they were on board the *Giordano Bruno*.

But he had sampled product when he was a kid; familiar with the doped drift between dream and waking, it did not frighten him. Slack and boneless whenever anyone was near, he let them think the dose was enough to put him under, and waited. A chance came while the crew was occupied with the final preparations for leaving high Earth orbit. Ripping the IV line out of his arm with his teeth, he lay motionless until his head cleared a little, watching his blood mix with the saline and glucose and medication from the pumpwell, dispersing evenly throughout the compartment in a pale iridescent haze that suddenly sank to the floor as the engines fired and the ship began to accelerate. He struggled out of the zero-G moorings that had held him in place; stood, wobbling slightly; made his way with the careful balance of a self-conscious drunk to the system access panel in the sick bay. What he could not stop, he could sabotage. A minute error in navigation would be enough to throw them years off course and he meant to change a single number in the navigation calculations.

He was caught, and there was another beating, fueled this time by fear of what he'd almost done. There was blood in his urine a few days afterward, and they did not find it necessary to restrain him that week.

It occurred to him that if he had taken this kind of abuse a year ago, it would have killed him. Timing, he thought bitterly, is everything.

Throughout the days that followed, he lay still, hating in silence. Sometimes, for a moment, when the sick-bay door opened, he would hear voices. Some were well known. Others were new to him, most notably that of a tenor: unschooled and a little nasal, with a slightly sanded quality that took the brilliance off his top notes, but true and often lovely. He hated them all, without reservation and without exception, with a pure and incandescent outrage that sustained him and replaced the food he would not take. And he resolved to die rather than be used again.

THERE WERE, OF COURSE, MANY WAYS TO OBTAIN COOPERATION. CARLO had, at one time, considered having Gina and Celestina killed, to loosen

Sandoz's ties to Earth, but had rejected the idea. Sandoz was more likely to commit suicide under those circumstances than to work out his grief in space. Studying his quarry, Carlo settled on a judicious combination of direct force, modern chemistry and traditional threat.

"I will come straight to the point," Carlo said briskly, entering the medical bay one morning, after Nico had reported that Sandoz was dressed and calm, and prepared now to discuss the situation rationally. "I would like you to consider working for me."

"You have interpreters."

"Yes," Carlo conceded readily, "but without your breadth of experience. It will take the others years to develop the knowledge of Rakhat that you carry—consciously and unconsciously. I have waited a long while to come into my own, Sandoz. Decades will pass on Earth while we make this journey. I have no intention of wasting additional time."

Sandoz looked faintly amused. "So. What deal am I offered?"

His speech was a little slurred. Carlo made a mental note to reduce the dosage. "I am a reasonable man, Sandoz. For a mere cessation of hostility to the mission, you will be allowed to send a message back to Gina and my daughter. If, however, you attempt to undermine my plans or harm me in any way, now or in the future," Carlo Giuliani warned regretfully, "I'm afraid John Candotti will die."

"Iron Horse, I presume, suggested that particular carrot and stick."

"Only indirectly," Carlo confided. "Interesting man, Iron Horse. I don't envy him. He was placed in a difficult position. Isn't that what they used to say about the Jesuits? They stood between the world and the Church, and got shot at by both sides. Speaking of difficult positions, by the way, Candotti is in the lander hangar now. If I don't countermand my instructions within ten minutes, my people will vent it to vacuum."

There was no reaction but, after a time, Sandoz asked, "And for active cooperation?"

Carlo leaned toward a mirrored medicine cabinet for a moment of contemplation, his long-nosed, high-boned face serious under a cap of golden hair, cropped but curling: Apollo come to life. "There will be money, of course, but—" He shrugged an acknowledgment of the paltriness of such a motive; in any case, Sandoz had money. "And a place in history! But you have that as well. So," he continued, turning back to Sandoz, "for active cooperation, I am prepared to offer you an opportunity for revenge. Or justice, depending on how you look at it."

Sandoz sat for a time, staring at his hands. Carlo watched with uncon-cealed interest as the man straightened the fingers and then let them drop, their fall from his wrist bones almost beautiful, the ribboning scars faded to ivory. "The nerves to the flexors were destroyed, for the most part. As you see, the extensor muscles are still fairly well innervated," Sandoz pointed out with clinical accuracy: he had cross-trained as a medic for the first mission, and was quite knowledgeable about hand anatomy now. Over and over, the fingers straightened and dropped. "Perhaps it's a sign," he said. "I can't grasp anything. All I can do is let things go."

How very Zen, Carlo thought, but he didn't say it. Not that Sandoz would have been angered—nothing could anger him now, although Carlo had taken the precaution of stationing Nico just outside the door.

"Cooperation in what?" Sandoz asked, coming back to the point.

"Simply stated, my goal is to establish trade with the VaRakhati," Carlo said. "The cargo Supaari VaGayjur sent back with you on the *Stella Maris* was remarkable in many ways, not least of which was the price that even the most insignificant item of Runa manufacture brought from museums and private collectors. Imagine what could be accomplished if the cargo were chosen with its intended market in mind, rather than according to the tastes of a Jana'ata merchant. I expect this enterprise to make me im-mensely wealthy, and completely independent of the opinions of others."

"And what do you bring in trade, Don Carlo?"

Carlo shrugged. "Most of it is quite innocuous, I assure you. Pearls, per-fumes. Coffee, of course. Botanicals with distinctive scents—cinnamon, oregano. Belgian ribbon- and lace-manufacturing equipment that can produce multiple colors, patterns, varying weaves. Given the Runa taste for novelty, I should do quite well." Carlo smiled disarmingly and waited for the obvious question, Then why do you need me?

The maimed hands quieted and basilisk eyes lifted to meet Carlo's own. "You mentioned revenge."

"You prefer that term to justice? Perhaps we can do business after all," Carlo cried good-humoredly. Sitting in the sickbay chair, he rested an ankle on his knee, watching his man carefully. "I have studied the rela-tionship between predators and prey, Sandoz. It interests me. I would argue that the human species came into its own when it stopped being prey, when it turned on its predators and made itself master of its own fate. There are no wolves in the streets of Moscow or Rome," he pointed out. "There are no pumas in Madrid or Los Angeles. No tigers in Delhi, no lions in Jerusalem. Why should there be Jana'ata in Gayjur?" He stopped, his gray eyes unreadable. "I know what it is to be prey, Sandoz. As do you. Be honest: when you watched the Jana'ata slaughter and eat Runa infants, it wasn't like watching bear eat salmon, was it?"

"No. It wasn't."

"Even before you left Rakhat, some Runa had already begun to fight back. The Contact Consortium reported that there were minor rebellions all over southern Inbrokar after your party demonstrated that tyranny could be resisted." He paused, genuinely puzzled. "The Jesuits seem ashamed of this! I cannot imagine why. Your own Pedro Arrupe said that injustice is atheism in action! No human society has ever wrested liberty from its oppressors without violence. Those in power rarely give up privilege voluntarily. What was it you said at the hearings? 'If the Runa were to rise against their Jana'ata masters, their only weapon would be their numbers.' We can change that, Sandoz."

"Command-and-control communications equipment?" Sandoz suggested. "Weaponry adapted to Runa requirements, and manufactured on site."

"I am certainly prepared to provide such technical support," said Carlo. "What is more important, I would not hesitate to suggest the ideology necessary to wrest liberty, equality and justice from their Jana'ata overlords."

"You wish to rule."

"As a transitional figure only. 'For all things fade and quickly become legend, soon to be lost in utter forgetting,'" Carlo recited, quoting Aurelius grandly. "There is, nevertheless, a certain appeal to the notion of being immortalized in Runa mythology—as their Moses, perhaps! With you as my Aaron, speaking to Pharaoh."

"So. Not just southern Italy," Sandoz observed. "Not just Europe, an old whore, corrupted long ago, but a whole virgin planet. Your father will never know, Carlo. He'll be dead before you return."

"Now there's a cheerful thought," Carlo remarked comfortably. "Almost makes one glad for hell. I'll tell him all about it when I arrive. Do you believe in hell, Sandoz, or are ex-Jesuits too sophisticated for that kind of melodrama?"

"'Why this is hell, nor am I out of it: Think'st thou that I who saw the face of God am not tormented with ten thousand hells?'"

"Mephistopheles!" Carlo cried, amused. "My role in the drama, surely, although you look the part. You know, I've always thought it was a tactical mistake for God to love us in the aggregate, when Satan is willing to make a special effort to seduce each of us separately." Carlo smiled, Apollonian beauty transformed by what he knew to be a devastating little-boy grin. "An inspiration!" he announced joyfully. "Shall we amuse ourselves? Shall we plumb our depths? Surely, even on a journey such as this, the greatest adventure is the exploration of the human soul. I offer you a bargain: you may decide whether or not we liberate the Runa! We shall pit my thirst for operatic grandeur against your moral strength. An interesting contest, do you agree?"

Sandoz lifted his head away from the bulkhead and gazed at Carlo from a drug-mediated distance. "John must be anxious," he said. "I should like a little time to consider your proposal in full. For now, I give my word not to interfere with your business arrangements. I agree to nothing further, but perhaps that will do as earnest money on what's left of my soul?"

"Nicely," Carlo said, smiling benignly. "Very nicely indeed."

THEY LEFT THE SICK BAY, AND EMILIO FOLLOWED CARLO ALONG A CURVing hallway and up the spiral of a ship's ladder. He had the impression of a hexagonal plan, the chambers fitting together like the space-efficient cells of a remarkably luxurious beehive: carpeted, quiet, beautifully appointed. There were at least three levels, stacked up, and undoubtedly storage bays he couldn't see.

Making a turn around a final bulkhead before coming to the central commons room, he glanced into a bridge, off to one side, and saw a bank of photonics glowing with graphics and text. He could hear the thrumming of fans and filter motors and the musical splash of fish-tank aeration and the faint grinding sound of mining robots shunting slag to the mass drivers, which provided acceleration and gravity simultaneously. Like the *Stella Maris*, this ship was based on a partially mined asteroid and much of its fundamental equipment was recognizable. The air-and-waste system included a Wolverton plant tube in the central cell. Full marks to God, Emilio thought. Plants still do a better job of making air than anything humans have invented.

It was only after taking in the general layout of the room that he looked at the six men who now stood or sat staring back at him.

"You knew," Sandoz said to Danny Iron Horse. Joseba Urizarbarrena turned, open-mouthed, toward Danny. Sean Fein's expression was already beginning to harden into censure. "A sin of omission," Sandoz commented, but Danny said nothing.

"Your braces are in storage, Sandoz," Carlo said. "Would you like them now?"

"After I get John, thank you. Where is the hangar hatch, please?"

"Nico!" said Carlo, "show Don Emilio the way."

Nico stepped forward and led Sandoz through a corridor. "Two landers, Sandoz!" Carlo called out while the air pressures between the crew quarters and the cavernous hangar were being equalized. "Both with fuel efficiency and range vastly improved over the lander that failed you in the first mission. And one of mine is a drone that can be operated remotely. I have learned from my predecessors' mistakes! The crew of the *Giordano Bruno* shall not be marooned on the surface of Rakhat!"

There was a sighing hush as Nico unlocked the hatch. *"Per favore,"* Sandoz asked, *"un momento solo, si?"*

Nico looked back down the passageway to Carlo for permission. This was granted with a regal nod. Stepping out of the way, Nico held the hatch open for Sandoz.

He stepped through, the heavy steel door closing behind him with a metallic clang that would have been terrifying if he weren't doped to the gills. Working his way around the landers, he stopped to check the tiedowns and the cargo doors. Everything was secure. Even the engines' bell housings were clean. Then he spotted John. Candotti was sitting on the uneven surface of the floor, his back against the roughly sealed bulkhead, just behind the drone.

Gray as the stone guts of the asteroid that formed the *Bruno*'s hull, John looked up as Emilio ducked under the lander fuselage and stood above him. "Oh, my God," John moaned miserably. "Just when I thought things couldn't get worse."

"Take it from a man who knows," Emilio said, voice slightly blurred. "Things can always get worse."

"Emilio, I swear, I didn't know!" John said, starting to cry again. "I knew Carlo had somebody in the sick bay, but I didn't know who or why—. I should have tried—. Oh, Jesus . . ."

"It's okay, John. There was nothing you could have done." Even drugged, Emilio knew how to go through the motions: what to do and what to say. "That's better," he said, kneeling next to Candotti, using his wrists to pull the larger man's head to his chest. "It's better to cry," he said, but he didn't feel anything, not really. Odd, he thought numbly, as John sobbed. This is what I wished for, all those months before Gina . . .

"I couldn't pray," John said in a small voice.

"It's okay, John."

"I sat here by the door so I wouldn't make a mess and foul up the landing gear," John said, sucking in snot and trying to get a grip on himself. "Carlo told Nico that if he didn't come back in ten minutes, vent the bay! I couldn't pray. All I could think about was raspberry jam." He made a sound like an explosion and grinned wetly, eyes raw. "Too many space vids."

"I know. It's okay." His hands were bad, but he let John cling to him in spite of that, and realized with detached interest that the pain was easier to tolerate because he couldn't seem to worry that it would be permanent this time. A useful lesson, he thought, looking over John's head at the exterior hangar doors. They were free of dust and had been cycled recently. "Come on," he said. "Let's go inside. Can you stand?"

"Yeah. Sure." John got to his feet on his own and wiped his face, but flopped against the sealed rock wall, looking even more loosely strung together than usual. "Okay," he said after a time.

When they got to the hatch that led back into the living quarters of the ship, Emilio motioned for John to bang on it, not wanting to jar his own hands. "Don't give 'em anything, John," he said as they waited for the door to be reopened. John looked blank at first, but then nodded and stood straighter.

"Words to live by," Emilio Sandoz said quietly, not seeing John anymore. "Don't give the bastards a goddamned thing." '

IT WAS NOT NICO BUT SEAN FEIN, LOOKING LIKE THE WRATH OF GOD, WHO reopened the door for them and silently took charge of John, shepherding him around a bulkhead toward the upper-deck cabins. Carlo was nowhere to be seen and Iron Horse was gone as well, but Joseba's voice, demanding and insistent, could be heard indistinctly from somewhere below the commons.

The braces were waiting on the table, where Nico was eating lunch with a square and fleshy person whose gross bulk made a remarkable contrast to his flowery Impressionist coloring: jonquil-yellow hair falling lankly over skin of rosebud pink and eyes of hyacinth blue.

Sandoz sat down and dragged the braces closer, drawing his hands into them, one by one.

"Frans Vanderhelst," the fat man said, by way of introduction. "Pilot."

"Emilio Sandoz," his table companion replied. "Conscript." Hands in his lap, he regarded the huge young man who sat next to Frans. "And you are Nico," Sandoz acknowledged, "but we have not been formally introduced."

"Emilio Sandoz: Niccolo d'Angeli," said Frans obligingly, around a mouthful of food. "He doesn't say much, but—*chizz è un brav' scugnizz'*—you're a good boy, aren't you, Nico? *Si un brav' scugnizz'*, eh, Nico?"

Nico dabbed at his mouth with a napkin before speaking, careful of his nose, which was faintly discolored. "*Brav scugnizz*," he affirmed obediently, liquid brown eyes serious in a skull that was a little small for a man of his size.

"How's your nose, Nico?" Sandoz asked without a hint of malice. "Still sore?" Nico seemed to be thinking hard about something else, so Sandoz turned to Frans. "Last time we met, you were helping Nico kick the shit out of me, as I recall."

"You were fucking with the navigation programs," Frans pointed out reasonably, taking another bite. "Nico and I were only doing our jobs. No hard feelings?"

"No feelings at all, as far as I can tell," Sandoz reported amiably. "I presume from your accent that you are from . . . Johannesburg, yes?" Frans inclined his head: very good! "And from your name, that you are not a Catholic."

Vanderhelst swallowed and made an offended face. "Dutch Reformed agnostic—very different from a Catholic agnostic, mind you."

Sandoz nodded, accepting the observation without comment. He leaned back in his chair and looked around.

"The best of everything," Frans pointed out, following Sandoz's gaze. Every fixture, every piece of equipment was shining, dustless and neatly stowed or properly in use, Frans noted with pride. The *Giordano Bruno* was a well-run ship. And a hospitable one—Frans raised his nearly invisible yellow eyebrows, along with a bottle of pinot grigio. Sandoz shrugged: Why not? "Glasses're stowed on the second shelf above the sink," Frans told him, going back to his meal. "You can get yourself something to eat if you're hungry. Plenty to choose from. The boss sets a nice table."

Sandoz stood and moved to the galley. Frans listened to him unlocking pot lids and opening food storage compartments to look over the possibilities, which were dazzling. A few minutes later, Sandoz returned with a glass in one robot hand and a plate of chicken cacciatore in the other. "You do pretty well with those things," Frans said, motioning at the braces with his fork.

"Yes. Takes practice," Sandoz said without emotion. He poured himself some wine and took a sip before starting on the stew. "This is excellent," he said after a time.

"Nico made it," Frans told him. "Nico is a man of many talents."

Nico beamed. "I like to cook," he said. "*Bucatini al dente*, grilled *scamorza, pizza Margherita*, eggplant fritatas . . ."

"I thought you didn't eat meat," said Frans, as Sandoz chewed chicken.

Sandoz looked down at his plate. "I'll be damned," he remarked mildly. "And my hands are killing me, but I don't seem to care about that either. What am I on?"

"It's a variant of Quell," said Danny Iron Horse, just behind him. He moved noiselessly around the table and stood behind Nico, across from Sandoz. Frans, feeling very happy, looked from one face to the other like a spectator at Wimbledon. "It's generally used to control prison riots," Iron Horse said. "Leaves cognition intact. Emotion is flattened."

"Your idea?" Sandoz asked.

"Carlo's, but I didn't try to talk him out of it." Danny might have been doped on Quell himself for all the emotion he showed; Frans began to be disappointed.

"Interesting drug," Sandoz commented. He picked up a knife, examining its edge idly, and then glanced at his plate. "The smell of meat has nauseated me ever since the massacres, but now . . ." He shrugged, raising his eyes from the blade to Iron Horse. "I believe I could cut out your heart and eat it," he said, sounding vaguely surprised, "if I thought it would buy me ten minutes with my family."

Iron Horse remained impassive. "But it wouldn't," he said. Frans was smiling again.

"No. So I may as well make the best of things as they are."

"I was hoping you'd see it that way," said Iron Horse, and he turned to leave.

"Danny?" Sandoz called, as Iron Horse was about to disappear.

If the bulkheads hadn't been treated with a polymer that made them resistant to rupture, the knife would have sunk a good way in; instead, it bounced off the wall next to Danny's face and clattered to the floor.

"Amazing how old skills come back when you need them." Sandoz smiled, cold-eyed. "I would like to have seen *one child* grow up," he said in that awful, ordinary voice. "How long have we been under way, Mr. Vanderhelst?"

Frans realized that he'd stopped breathing and shifted his bulk in the chair. "Almost four weeks."

"I was never able to understand why time contracts this way. Kids change so quickly, especially when their daddies are traveling at relativistic speeds. Why, Danny? The means are very nasty indeed. May I know the ends that justify them?"

"Tell him," Sean Fein snapped wearily, entering the commons after having seen Candotti safely into his cabin. "God knows what day it is on this forsaken tub, but it must be Yom Kippur on some calendar or other. A rabbi would tell you it isn't enough t'beg God's forgiveness, Danny. You must ask pardon of the man y'wronged." When Danny remained silent, he snapped, "Tell him, dammit, for Jesus' sake and the good of your miserable soul."

Back stiff against the bulkhead, Daniel Iron Horse spoke, the hollowness of his voice matching that of his rationales. "The reversal of the Suppression of the Society of Jesus, with all suits and countersuits dropped or settled out of court. A position of influence from which programs of birth control and political action on behalf of the poor will be implemented throughout the sphere of Church authority. The transfer from the Camorra to the Vatican of evidence establishing the identity of priests corrupted by organized crime, as well as those who are known to be incorruptible, so that the Church can be purged of elements that have undermined the moral authority of Rome. The means for the Society of Jesus to return to Rakhat and to continue God's work there." He paused, and then gave the only reason that mattered. "The salvation of one soul."

"Mine?" Sandoz asked with amused detachment. "Well, I admire your ambition, if not your methods, Father Iron Horse."

"They wouldn't have hurt John," Danny said. "That was a bluff."

"Really?" Sandoz shrugged, mouth pulled down in thought. "I've been kidnapped and beaten senseless twice in a month," he pointed out. "I'm afraid I'm inclined to take Carlo's threats seriously."

Wretched, Danny said, "I am sorry, Sandoz."

"Your sorrow is of no interest to me," Sandoz said softly. "If you want absolution, go to a priest."

Disgusted, Sean went to the galley. When he returned to the table with a glass and a bottle of Jameson's, Danny was still standing there, bleak eyes locked on Sandoz. "And what about Candotti?" Sean snapped at Iron Horse. Danny drew in a breath and turned to leave, but not before picking up the knife and laying it down in front of Sandoz.

Which, in Frans's opinion, must have taken a fair bit of nerve. The Puerto Rican was unsteady from weeks of confinement to bed and, of course, his hands were crippled, so it was hard to distinguish inaccuracy from intent, but Frans had the impression that Sandoz could have nailed Danny to the wall if he'd felt like it. Carlo had Candotti for insurance, but the Chief was on his own . . .

"Well, now, like it or not, here we all are," Sean said, pouring himself a drink. He tossed it off before looking at Sandoz with humorless blue eyes. "It's just a guess, but I'm willin' t'bet nothin' in God's wide universe would make that man feel worse than your forgiveness. It'd be coals on his head, Sandoz."

"Well, now," Sandoz said dryly, mimicking Sean's accent, "that's worth considerin'."

Frans was hugely entertained. "You play cards?" he asked Sandoz.

"I wouldn't want to take unfair advantage," Sandoz demurred, unruffled by the drama. He stood and carried his dishes back to the galley. "I have always heard that the Dutch Reformed aren't much for cards."

"We aren't much for liquor either," Frans pointed out, pouring another round for everyone but Nico, who didn't drink because the sisters had told him not to.

"This is true," Sandoz said, returning to the table. "Poker?"

"It'll make a change from that bloody *scopa*," said Sean.

"How about you, Nico?" Frans asked, reaching for a worn deck that was always on the table.

"I'll just watch," Nico said courteously.

"I know, Nico," Frans said patiently. "I was only being polite. It's okay, Nico. You don't have to play."

"I'd like to send a message home first, if it wouldn't be too much trouble," Sandoz said.

"Radio's right through that hatch, to your left," Frans told him. "It's all set up. Just record the message and hit 'send.' Yell if you need help."

"Not bloody likely," Sean muttered as Sandoz left the commons.

He sat down in front of the communications equipment and considered for a while what he would say: "Fucked again," came to mind, but the message would arrive when Celestina was still very young, and he rejected the remark as too vulgar.

He settled on eleven words. "Taken by force," he said. "I think of you. Listen with your hearts."

City of Inbrokar

2047, Earth-Relative

"I WON'T HAVE IT," THE AMBASSADOR FUMED, CLAWS CLICKING AS HE paced from one end of the embassy's innermost courtyard to the other. Ma Gurah Vaadai came to rest in front of his wife, his ears cocked, and defied her to argue. "I'll resign before I give my daughter to that beast. How dare he ask for a child of mine!"

"My lord, Hlavin Kitheri hasn't asked for our Sakinja," soothed the lady Suukmel Chirot u Vaadai as she lifted a graceful hand and with a gesture of melting beauty, pulled a simple silken headpiece back into place as though she were wrapping her soul in calm. "His invitation was simply—"

"He is a coward," Ma snarled, swinging away from her. "He assassinated his whole family—"

"Almost certainly," Suukmel purred as he stalked away, "but unproven."

"—and then lied about it! As though anyone would believe that vaporous nonsense about a merchant—a midlands peddler!—bringing down the whole of a lineage like the Kitheri. And now he dares to ask for my daughter!" Face twisted with disgust, Ma turned to his wife. "Suukmel, he buggers animals—and *sings* about it!"

"Admittedly." She did not object to her husband's vulgarity. It was an ambassador's daily burden to speak always with forbearance and tact; Suukmel was happy to afford Ma this small relief. "Hlavin Kitheri is, as my lord husband points out, many remarkable things," she continued with pacific confidence, "but he is also a man of admirable breadth of view, a great poet—"

"That rubbish!" the ambassador muttered, glaring past her in the direction of the Kitheri palace, dominating the center of Inbrokar. "He's mad, Suukmel—"

"Ah, forgive your poor wife, my gracious lord, but 'madness' is a word used imprecisely, and too often. A careful person might say discontented or desperate or extraordinary instead," Suukmel suggested. "Have pity on anyone whose nature is not well suited to a role decreed by birth, for it is a difficult life." She rearranged her gown and settled into a new posture, more graceful but subtly more commanding as well. "Hlavin Kitheri has acceded to his Patrimony, my lord. Whatever his past, whatever the circumstances of his rise, whatever your private reservations about his character, it is your public duty as Mala Njer's ambassador to treat the forty-eighth Paramount as the legitimate ruler of Inbrokar."

Her husband growled at that, but she continued thoughtfully. "Kitheri is a man worth studying, my lord. Even apart from the poetry, his years of exile in Galatna Palace do not appear to have been wasted. He has, shall we say, intimate contacts all over his territory?" Ma grunted, amused, and she continued smilingly, voice light. "Men of ability and energy, men who now bring to Kitheri information and insight. Ideas. Perspective. Already, in the first season of his reign, he has created new and unprecedented offices and appointed such men to them, even thirds, and he has done this almost without opposition from those who cherish tradition."

Ma Gurah Vaadai's prowling ceased and he turned to stare at his wife. Her eyes dropped becomingly only to return to his with a gaze that seemed both direct and curious. "It is interesting, is it not? How has he managed this?" she asked in a voice full of wonder. "Perhaps my dear lord will discover something of value in your observation of him at court?" she suggested. "In any case, Kitheri is no longer looking for a wife."

"Of course not. He's probably looking for more tailless monsters to couple with—" Then the news sank in. "What have you heard?"

"He is affianced, my lord husband. A VaPalkirn child. The regent's eldest."

"Elli'nal? She's hardly out of swaddling!"

"Precisely." Ears falling, her husband gaped at her. "It is a masterly stroke, don't you agree?" she instructed him. "Inbrokar is the central state of the Triple Alliance, with Mala Njer to the west and Palkirn to the east. A marriage contract with Elli'nal leaves the Palkirn government quiet at Kitheri's back while the child grows. Then he may deal with his western neighbor, Mala Njer, on pragmatic grounds." A moment passed, but he understood. "Mala Njer can be many things to Inbrokar, my lord husband. Protector. Partner. Prey. Perhaps Kitheri wishes to reconsider the terms of our alliance."

"I have not been informed of this Palkirn marriage," Ma said.

"Nevertheless . . ."

He followed her glance to Taksayu, her Runa maid, sitting in a corner: the very model of silent, deferential attention to her mistress. Who could be trusted to make friends among others of her kind. Who spoke K'San well; who heard things and reported them. Who had the intelligence required to appear stupid when it was useful.

"Well, then!" Ma burst out, flummoxed. "What does Kitheri want with my daughter?"

"Nothing at all, my own dear master," said Suukmel sweetly. "It is not your daughter whom Hlavin Kitheri wishes to meet but your wife."

Ma threw his head back and roared. "You can't be serious," he cried.

"Quite serious, my lord. Furthermore, I should like to meet him."

It was hard to say which was more shocking: a woman's use of the word "I" or the notion that her husband would permit her to meet any unrelated male, let alone one of Kitheri's revolting nature. "Impossible," Ma said at last.

"Nevertheless," she said, eyes steady.

It was common knowledge that more than half of the uxorious Ma Gurah Vaadai's considerable success as a diplomat, and nearly all his satisfaction in life, was his wife's doing. Hidden away, gathering information, judging, measuring, working twice removed—after sixteen years of marriage, the lady Suukmel Chirot u Vaadai continued to surprise her husband, to horrify and challenge him. Not beautiful but knowing, adroit, desirable. Not mad, he thought, and yet what she proposed certainly was . . .

"Impossible," he repeated.

Nevertheless.

TWO DAYS LATER, MA GURAH VAADAI, AMBASSADOR OF THE MALA NJERI Territorial Government to the Patrimony of Inbrokar, went to the Kitheri compound to present his personal credentials to the forty-eighth Paramount: to this shameless poet, this bald assassin, this perverted prince who wished to meet Suukmel.

The encounter was to be purely ceremonial, yet another tedious example of Inbrokari protocol, as convoluted and nonsensical as the Kitheri compound itself with its mismatched towers, its palisades and balconies connected by swooping ramps, soaring archways, by fretted and carved galleries. Generations of Kitheris had lived here, each new paramount honoring his dead father with a newly winged roofline, a pointless martello, a spiraling turret, a stratum of carving, another tier of covered walkways. The entire palace was physical demonstration of the folly of novelty. It was, Ma Gurah Vadaai thought, typical of the Kitheri dynasty to preach invariance and practice innovation. Bred and trained for combat, Ma hated the place, as he hated hypocrisy and pretense, even though his duty now was to practice hypocrisy and preserve pretense. Only Suukmel's enjoyment of subtlety made this fatuous game tolerable.

Both the Paramount and the ambassador could sing in High K'San, though Inbrokari custom demanded that they pretend that this was not so, the better to slow and complicate the ritual. But the Paramount's responsum to Ma's opening oratorio was beautifully sung, and one had to admit that the Runa interpreters and protocol experts were excellent. Ma's own women had no reason to correct anything said on his behalf by the Inbrokari Runao assigned to translate his Malanja for the Paramount, nor were there any errors in the translation of the Paramount's lyrics. And as much as the Runa ordinarily hated music, the Paramount's staff never so much as flicked an ear during the ceremony. Far more familiar with the procedure than either Jana'ata, they actually seemed to enjoy it, and discreetly led the solemn way through stately exchanges of elaborate greetings, elaborate presents and elaborate promises.

Just as Ma Gurah Vaadai began to wonder if he would sink back against his tail and fall asleep standing in the stifling heat of this princely oven, there was a final exchange of elaborate farewells and he woke up sufficiently to sing, as required, in close harmony with the Paramount. This done, Ma was preparing, with relief, to make his escape when Hlavin Kitheri rose from his pillowed, padded, gilt and jeweled daybed and approached the Mala Njeri ambassador with amused eyes.

"Dreadful, isn't it?" the Paramount remarked, glancing at the cramped and airless stateroom and displaying a dismay not unlike Vaadai's own, carefully concealed. "I have begun to hope for a fire. At times, the solution to a maze is to reduce it to embers and walk straight through the ashes." He smiled at Ma's surprise and continued, "In the meantime, I have caused a summer encampment to be established in the mountains, Excellency. Perhaps you will join me there and we may come to know one another in comfort?"

The formal invitation arrived at the ambassador's residence the next morning and, six days later, Ma Gurah Vaadai was taken upriver in an embassy barge, accompanied by his official interpreter, his personal interpreter, his secretary, his cook, his body valet, his dresser and his wife's maid, Taksayu.

He'd assumed that the Paramount was simply indulging in Inbrokari understatement when he referred to his "encampment." Ma expected the place to be as extravagant and awful as the Kitheri palaces but, to his surprise, the camp was a simple series of pavilions, scattered throughout a high valley cooled by mountain breezes. Apart from the fact that the tents were of gold tissue, supported by silvered poles and upholstered with divans of the softest and most finely woven fabric Vaadai had ever felt, the site was as austere as a military bivouac.

"More to a Mala Njeri soldier's taste, I dare say," Kitheri called out, approaching the dock without an escort as the barge was made fast. Kitheri smiled at the ambassador's evident surprise and held out an arm to steady Ma as he climbed out of the barge. "Have you eaten?"

It was not the last time that Ma Gurah Vaadai would be thrown off balance by this man. At rest, in informal conversation, the odious Hlavin Kitheri was a person of dignity and presence. The other guests at the encampment were intelligent and interesting as well, and the opening banquet was unusually tasty, its presentation exquisite.

"You are kind to say so," Kitheri murmured, when the ambassador complimented the meal. "I am pleased you have enjoyed it. The result of a new pastime. Or rather, the revival of an old skill. I have established a hunting reserve here in the hills."

"The meat is wild-caught," one of the other guests confided. "Good exercise and excellent eating afterward."

"Perhaps the ambassador will join us in the morning?" Kitheri suggested, his face gilded by sunlight filtering through woven gold, the extraordinary amethyst eyes transmuted to topaz. "I hope you shall not be shocked by our customs here—"

"We stalk naked as the Heroes," one of the younger men told Ma eagerly.

"My young friend has a poetic nature," Kitheri remarked, reaching out to grip the young man's ankle affectionately. His gaze returned to Ambassador Vaadai, who was trying not to shudder. "As naked as our prey, a practical man might say."

"This herd is aware of us, naturally," an older man commented, "but my lord Kitheri hopes to backbreed to more naive stock."

"To recapture the experiences of our forefathers," Kitheri explained. "One day, the best of our sons will come here to bring to life their heritage, so that they may earn the old strengths in the old ways." But then, surprisingly, he looked directly at the maid, Taksayu, silent in the corner all this time, sitting among the ceremonial interpreters who attended every gathering, needed or not. "The game program would involve utility Runa only. Specialists, I believe, we have bred to a point of intellectual maturity that will allow emancipation soon. But perhaps the Mala Njeri ambassador disagrees?" he said, returning serene eyes to a dumbfounded Ma Gurah Vaadai.

"Fascinating legal problems," one of the others offered before Ma could speak, and the discussion quickly became scholarly and intense.

The evening chorale was glorious. Kitheri, Ma was informed, had studied such things during his exile at Galatna and believed that the melodies were best stripped of accumulated embellishment so that the supple lines of the original harmony could be appreciated, pure and plain, and as clean as the days when men hunted with their brothers and friends simply to provide for their wives and young ones.

Ma Gurah Vaadai went to his tent that night disarmed and slightly dazed, but emerged from it hungry and sharp-minded at first light. Wearing neither robe nor badge of position, he was secretly pleased by the opportunity to reveal that he had maintained himself well during the soft years of peace. Unclothed, one's character was exposed and, observing the Paramount, Ma was impressed to see that what might have been merely an impression given by superb tailoring was, in fact, genuine. Most reshtars ran to fat in their middle years, but Hlavin Kitheri had remained taut and strong in maturity.

The hunt was exhilarating from the start. Several times Ma found himself paired off with Kitheri, who had a short reach but powerful pedal grasp and a formidably efficient kill. Perhaps more remarkable, Kitheri was generous in his strategy, noting Ma's position and passing the prey on to him without hesitation, setting up and helping to execute several exhausting but quite wonderful snares, and Ma Gurah Vaadai's spirits rose with the suns, doubts dimming in their glare.

Kitheri is right, Ma thought. This is what we need.

To match a Runao, stride by stride, heartbeat by heartbeat, was to transcend the self, to lose all consciousness of separation until you were one with the prey. And then: to reach out from behind, to grip a doe's ankle and bring her down into a headlock, to lift the jaw and expose the throat, slicing through it with a single clean action—to do all this and to eat the meat in the end—was to survive your own death: to die with the prey and yet to live again.

He had almost forgotten what it was like.

As far as Ma Gurah Vaadai was concerned, the day could have been improved upon only if Suukmel had been there waiting in a tent for him to heave a carcass at her feet as he sang an ancient song of triumph. Kitheri confessed himself a trifle disappointed: some of the Runa had spoiled the hunt by offering themselves. His breeders had ear-notched each lineage and marked the children of these docile females for ordinary butchering later, he told the others. The more sporting individuals, those who dodged away successfully or fought briefly and then eluded pursuit, were also noted. These would be bred to the males who had been most protective of the young, in the center of the herd.

That night, muscles satisfyingly sore, mind empty of compressed court intrigue and rigid international politics, it occurred to Ma that Kitheri's agility and strength and capacity for plan were all of a piece with what he had done to his entire family. Suukmel was right, Ma thought, eyes opening in the dark. This is not madness but ambition.

He resolved to remain on guard, not to be seduced again, but the next morning, as well-trained and beautifully liveried domestics collected the equipment and struck the pavilions and organized the return to Inbrokar, the ambassador found himself inviting the Paramount to join him in the embassy barge as an honored guest of the Mala Njer Territory. The day downriver passed agreeably and as they approached the docks of the capital, it began to seem both prudent and pleasant to invite the Paramount to the embassy for the upcoming Mala Njeri Festival of Suns.

And, yes, the ambassador told the Paramount in answer to a casual question, the lady Suukmel would be in residence.

•   •   •

LIKE A HUNTER STRIPPED TO STALK, HLAVIN KITHERI ARRIVED A WEEK later at the embassy of the territory of Mala Njer wearing the simple robes of a scholar, one powerful shoulder becomingly bared, his jewels superb but chastely set. He had told the flattered ambassador that he admired the forthright informality of Mala Njer, which did not waste effort on point-less ceremony, so the call-and-response chorale in his honor was brief. Thus, the forty-eighth Paramount of Inbrokar was left free to stroll un-hobbled by protocol through the embassy gathering, greeting dignitaries and acquaintances with graceful ease, commenting on the festival's long history, allowing himself to be drawn into a discussion of Mala Njeri chant harmonics.

With an unerring instinct for danger, he identified the men most hos-tile to him—men whose dedication to stability and law was most honor-able and unimpeachable. In brief, private moments, he sought their advice on one question or another, listened gravely to their opinions, was cir-cumspect in his own. Now and then, he would mention matters that such men might turn to their families' advantage. And as the day passed, he saw wariness and suspicion become alloyed with a willingness to suspend judg-ment.

He did not yet know how to bring about the transformation he hun-gered for. The very language of his thoughts hampered consideration of the problem: there was no word in K'San for the kind of cleansing, puri-fying revolution that danced in Hlavin Kitheri's mind. Combat, battle, struggle, yes; warrior, champion, duelist, adversary, enemy—the K'San lexicon was lavish in its vocabulary for such things. There were words as well for rebellion and revolt, but these implied impieties, not political up-heaval.

Sohraa, Hlavin Kitheri thought. *Sohraa*.

To a poet's ear, *sohraa* had a lovely sound—like the breath of wind on a hot still day, whispering of coming rain. Yet nearly all the words based on *sohraa* were associated with disasters, with degradation and degeneration. It was the stem word for change, and he had heard it often these days—from military men called back from inspection tours of the outer provinces, from bureaucrats currying favor with the new regime, from trib-utary nobility coming to pledge fealty, from foreign embassy personnel siz-ing up this new embodiment of Inbrokari strength. The ruling castes of Rakhat felt vaguely diminished and disturbed by the stink of change on the wind, but it was dangerous to point out that Hlavin Kitheri's own po-etry had destabilized society to an alarming degree. Safer blame fell on the insidious foreign influence, which had affected simpleminded Runa villagers along the Masna'a Tafa'i coast. The campaign to clean out rebel villages was typical of the south—corrupt, inefficient and insufficient. Anxiety flowed beneath Jana'ata society like an underground river of unease, murmuring *sohraa, sohraa, sohraa.*

Now Kitheri bided his time, for pursuit can drive the quarry away. When the attention of the festive embassy crowd had shifted to the banquet table, he contrived to drift toward the large central wind tower: a hollow pillar of unaesthetic proportion, its louvers replaced with decorative grillwork that slightly but tellingly decreased the column's capacity to move air into the compound's main courtyard. The stonework was nearly seamless.

His tension did not surprise him; a future lay in hazard. "He sings now to architecture!" they would say, should any notice him, and he risked undoing all his careful work of the past season by reawakening the rumor of madness. Nevertheless, he thought. And sang, in a voice pitched low but resonant and pure, of the night-bred chrysalis, cool and concealed, warmed by the suns at last; of Chaos emerging to dance in daylight; of veils parting, blown by the hot winds of day; of Glory flaring in sunlight.

The sounds of the large room, humming with conversation and with eating, did not alter. Resting a negligent shoulder against the pillar's cool and polished stone, near the fretted window of her lair, he asked, "And what does my lady Suukmel hear as she listens?"

"*Sohraa,*" the response came, soft as the breeze that heralds rain. "*Sohraa, sohraa, sohraa.*"

IN THE BEGINNING, HE SENT HER JEWELS OF UNMATCHED BRILLIANCE AND clarity, lengths of shimmering fabric heavy with gold thread, anklets and rings for her feet, tiny silver ornaments to be fastened to her talons. Bronze chimes of extraordinary length, their tone so low as to resonate in her very heart, and sweet-sounding bells to hang from her headdress. Silken awnings, embroidered and bejeweled, finely wrought enameled casks. Perfumes that brought mountain, plain and ocean to her chamber.

All this was refused—returned, untouched.

And so: Runa weavers, whose skills were unrivaled by any on the continent. A superb cook whose pâtés and roulades were of greatest savor and delicacy. A masseuse, storytellers, acrobats. All these were invited into the lady's chamber. All were spoken to with interest and courtesy, but sent away with polite regrets. And all were questioned closely by Hlavin Kitheri himself, when they returned to his palace.

The Paramount sent next a single fragile egg of the mountain *ilna*, nestled in a bed of fragrant moss. Then a meteorite that had flashed down from the suns' realm, and a simple crystal flask containing a lavish length of umber *syn'amon* from beyond those suns. One perfectly formed *k'na* blossom. A breeding pair of tiny *hlori'ai* whose breathy courtship song had provided melody for the oldest of Mala Njeri's sunset hymns. These, too, were refused—except for the *hlori'ai,* which she'd kept for one night, enchanted by their beauty. In the morning, Suukmel herself had opened their cage and released them.

The next day Taksayu appeared at the front gate of the Kitheri compound and announced to the porter that she wished to be taken into the presence of the Paramount. To the astonishment of his horrified household, Hlavin Kitheri relayed instructions that this Runa maid be allowed in by that entrance and escorted with courtesy to his own chamber.

"My lady Suukmel wishes this most humble one to speak plainly to the most noble Paramount," Taksayu said, but the humble one stood before the ruler of Inbrokar in her mistress's stead, and so was calm and dignified. "My lady Suukmel asks the Paramount: Am I a child to be corrupted by gifts?"

At her words, the celestial violet eyes snapped into focus, but Taksayu's ears did not drop. "He will not kill you," Suukmel had assured her. "He wants what he cannot take—what must be given freely or not at all." For if Hlavin Kitheri had desired Suukmel's bloodlines merely, he could easily have arranged the death of her husband. He could have taken her by force and gotten children on her the same way, even if it meant a war with Mala Njer. And so, the lady Suukmel had concluded, what he wanted from Suukmel Chirot u Vaadai was not her progeny but her self.

Surviving the moment, Taksayu continued. "My lady asks: What might a man accomplish whose allies were his by force of love and loyalty? Far more, my lady believes, than men alone in the world, whose fathers are obstacles and brothers are rivals, whose sons only yearn for their deaths; whose sisters and daughters are used to bind subordinates or buy rank or placate enemies." She paused. "My lady asks: Shall I continue?"

Silently, the Paramount drew breath, and then lifted his chin.

"Thus my lady Suukmel counsels the Paramount: First, may he take wisdom and skill from anyone of intelligence and talent, but especially from those ill matched to the station of their ancestors, for in these persons, the

Paramount may inspire such loyalty as my lady Suukmel freely gives to her good husband, who has afforded her as much liberty as could be desired by a woman of honor. Further, she counsels: May the Paramount revive a custom of the earliest Paramounts of Inbrokar, old as the oldest songs, and take to himself a harem of third-born women to bear him children to be neutered and raised without inheritance. Their status would not distress the future children of his infant VaPalkirn bride, thus preserving the advantages of that alliance with the east. My lady asks: Shall I continue?"

He was no longer looking at her, but said, "Go on."

"If it pleases the Paramount, my lady Suukmel says: The freeborn children of the harem might one day dance in daylight and glory in the suns, furthering their father's desire for change better than even he can imagine. My lady says: May the Paramount consider who among his children might be taught to sing new songs. Send that child to the lady Suukmel for fostering, for in this she would be your partner, and such a child may be a bridge between what is and what can be. My lady asks: Shall I continue?"

"Yes," the Paramount said, but he heard very little of what the Runao said after that. Instead, Hlavin Kitheri felt in his mind the hot breeze of a courtyard, saw in thought the way soft wind would seek the edges of a silken tent and lift the translucent fabric a handsbreadth from the stones, unveiling soles as soft as dawn's air. Envisioned the ankles briefly revealed—strong-boned, well-formed, ringed and jeweled. Imagined what it would be, to take then whatever he desired and not merely what she offered . . .

Candor. Alliance. A mind the equal of his own. Not all that he had wished but all, he understood, that she would give him.

"Tell your lady that she is everything rumor whispers of," Hlavin Kitheri said, when the Runao fell silent. "Tell her that . . ." He stood and looked directly at Taksayu. "Tell her . . . that I am grateful for her counsel."

Giordano Bruno

2063, Earth-Relative

"I WANTED TO BE A TERRORIST WHEN I WAS A LITTLE BOY," JOSEBA Urizarbarrena said. "It was a family tradition—both my grandmothers were ETA. We called ourselves freedom fighters, of course. Better?"

"Yes," Sandoz gasped.

"Good. Let me try the other." Sandoz held out his other hand and let the Basque steady the forearm against his raised knee. "This doesn't always work," Joseba warned, probing with his thumbs along the space between the two long bones until he reached the place where muscle refined to tendon. "My uncle lost most of his right hand when I was about eight. Do you know what they call it when a bomb goes off too soon? Premature disassembly."

Sandoz barked a laugh and Joseba was pleased. Even drugged, Sandoz found wordplay funny, although other forms of humor escaped him. "My aunt used to think he was lying about the pain to get sympathy," Joseba said, pressing hard now. "Dead dogs don't bite, she used to say. The hand's not there anymore. How can something that's not there hurt? My uncle used to tell her, Pain is as real as God. Invisible, unmeasurable, powerful—"

"And a bitch to live with," Sandoz whispered, voice shaking. "Just like your aunt."

"You're right about that," Joseba said fervently, bent over the arm. He adjusted the location of his thumbs and increased the pressure, a little astonished to find himself in this position. Clad only in his underwear, he'd gotten up at two in the morning with a full bladder, and found Sandoz pacing the commons room like an animal crazed by caging. "What's wrong?" Joseba had asked and was initially snarled at for his trouble. Sandoz was not an easy man to help, but those were the kind who needed it most, in Joseba's experience.

Afraid he'd simply leave a bruise and dying now for a pee, Joseba was about to give up when he heard a single explosive sob. "Yes?" Joseba asked, to be sure before easing off.

Sandoz didn't move, eyes closed, face tight, not breathing. Joseba sat quietly, familiar with this suspense; it always took his uncle a few moments to believe the pain had really ended. Finally Sandoz let out a breath and his eyes opened. He seemed dazed, but said, "Thank you." Then, blinking, he sat straighter and moved back in his chair, out of contact.

"I don't know why that works," Joseba admitted.

"Maybe direct pressure on the nerves higher in the limb disrupts stray signals?" Sandoz suggested, his voice still a little ragged.

"Maybe." And even if it's only the power of suggestion, Joseba thought, what works, works. "If you'd told me about this before, I could have helped," he scolded.

"How was I to know you had inept bombers in your family?" Sandoz asked reasonably, his breathing steadier now.

"My uncle used to cry. Just sit there and cry," Joseba remarked. "You pace."

"Sometimes." Sandoz shrugged and looked away. "Work used to be best."

"You don't work now," Joseba observed.

"Can't seem to care about working," Sandoz said. "The Quell usually helps—about half of pain is fear. But it got bad this time."

Interested but at the outer limit of bladder control, Joseba stood. "Has it ever occurred to you," he asked, pausing before he resumed his trip to the toilet, "that Matins was instituted by old monks with prostate trouble? Had to get up anyway, might as well pray, right?"

With that, Joseba padded off like a bear, but when he returned through the commons, much relieved, Sandoz was still sitting in the dark. He'd have gone back to his cabin if he didn't want company, Joseba thought. Taking a chance, he said, "I have been reading the Book of Job. 'Hast thou seen the doors of deepest darkness? Canst thou bind the chains of the

Pleiades, or loose the cords of Orion?'" Leaning against a bulkhead, the Basque gestured toward the enigmatic dark that surrounded them. "Man's answer now would be: Almost. We have entered the springs of the sea and walked the recesses of its depths. We have comprehended the expanse of the Earth and stretched a line upon it. 'Canst thou send lightnings? Hast thou commanded the morning?' Here we are, between stars!"

Joseba shook his head, genuinely amazed. Then he said, "The music changed, you know. After you were on Rakhat."

"I prefer Wolfer's translation of Job myself," Sandoz commented. "So. Why did terrorism lose its charm for you?"

"Ah. The subject is changed," Joseba observed equably. "It didn't, not for a long time, anyway. Then Spain and France finally decided, To hell with the Basques—who needs them? So we fought among ourselves for a while. Gets to be a habit." He stopped and looked at Sandoz. "Did you know Hlavin Kitheri's voice was heard for less than a year after you left Rakhat, and then never again?"

"Perhaps he died," Sandoz suggested blandly, "of something unpleasant and prolonged. What did you do after terrorism ceased to be a viable career option?"

"A lot of hunting, actually. We still hunt in the little corner of the world where I come from. I was outdoors all the time, surrounded by what's left of nature in Europe. A hunter—a good one—often identifies very strongly with the prey. One thing led to another. I studied ecology at university."

"And how from there to the priesthood? You fell in love, perhaps, with God's complex and beautiful creation?" The light, soft voice was curiously flat and uninflected in the gloom, all its music drained away, the empty face barely illuminated by the yellow and green readouts shining dimly from the bridge.

"No," Joseba said frankly. "It is difficult to see the complex beauty of creation these days, on Earth at least. Things got a lot worse while you were gone, my friend. Ecology has become a study of degradation. We mainly work backward now, trying to reconstruct systems thrown out of balance and wrecked. For each step forward, we are forced two steps back by the press of population. It's not a cheerful discipline."

The Basque moved in the darkness across the commons and took a seat a little distance from Sandoz, the molded polymer chair creaking under his substantial weight. "When you see a system disturbed, it is a great joy to discover a single cause—the cure then seems simple. As an undergraduate, I would look at satellite images of the planet at night, and the connected concentrations of city lights looked to me like streptococcus taking over a petri dish. I became convinced that *Homo sapiens* was a disease that was ravaging its hostess, Gaia. The Earth would be well rid of us, I thought. I was nineteen, and the population had already gone from seven to fourteen billion in my lifetime. I began to hate this species that called itself wise. I wanted to cure Gaia of the sickness our species inflicted on her. I began to consider seriously how I might exterminate very large numbers of humans, preferably without being caught. I believed myself heroic and selfless—a solitary worker for the planetary good. I switched college majors at that time. Virology began to seem very useful to me."

Sandoz was staring at him. A good sign, Joseba thought. Even drugged, he is capable of moral judgment on some level.

"As I said," Joseba continued dryly, "terrorism did not lose its charm. I was living with a girl at the time. I broke it off. She wanted children, and I loathed children. Disease vectors, I called them. I used to look at people like Nico and think, There's a botched abortion. One more useless human to consume the planet, capable only of eating and making more of himself."

Somewhere in the ship a compressor kicked in and its hum joined the soft splashing of the fish-tank aerators and the constant hush of filtered fans. Sandoz did not move.

"The last thing my girlfriend told me when we parted was that it was wicked to wish death on people whose only crime was to be born at a time when there are so many of us." He sat for a while, trying to remember her face, wondering what she might look like now—a woman in her late forties, given the relativity effects. "She opened my eyes, although we never spoke again. It took a while, but eventually I began to search for a reason to believe that humans are more than bacteria. One of my professors was a Jesuit."

"And now you are going to a world where the sentient species do not degrade their environment. To see what it costs them?"

"Penance for my sins, I suppose." Joseba stood and moved toward the bridge, where he could stare out the observation port toward hard stars and unplumbed blackness. "I think sometimes of the girl I did not marry." He looked back at Sandoz, but there was no reaction he could see. "I read somewhere an interesting suggestion. The nations of the world that most vigorously foul the planetary nest and those in possession of the most destructive arsenals ought to be governed only by young women with small kids. More than anyone else, such mothers must live in the future, and they also face each day the realities of raw human nature. This gives them a special insight."

Joseba stood up straight then, stretching and yawning, and disappeared around the bulkhead into the passageway to his cabin, calling, "Good night," as he went. Emilio Sandoz sat alone in the commons for a long time, and then went to bed as well.

"I'M NOT ARGUING. I'M JUST CONFUSED," JOHN CANDOTTI HAD SAID TO the Father General, a few months before the mission was launched. "I mean, everybody else is some kind of scientist. My forte is more along the lines of weddings and baptisms. Funerals. School plays? Bailing guys out?" The question in his voice invited the Father General to jump in any time, but Vincenzo Giuliani simply looked at him, and other people's silence tended to make John talk more and faster. "Writing the church bulletin? Reffing fights between the choir director and the liturgist? None of that is likely to come up, right? Except maybe funerals." John cleared his throat. "Look, it's not that I don't want to go, it's just that I know guys who would give a kidney to be on this mission and I don't get why you're sending me."

The Father General's eyes left John's face and rested on the olive trees and the stony hills that surrounded the retreat house. After a time, he seemed to forget Candotti was there and started to walk away. Then he hesitated and turned back to the younger priest. "They're going to need someone who is good at forgiveness," was all he said.

So, John now supposed, it was his job to forgive Danny Iron Horse.

Back in Chicago, John Candotti had been a notoriously easy mark in a confessional, the kind of priest who didn't make a penitent feel like a three-year-old who'd had a potty accident. "We all screw up," he would remind people. A lot of what people confessed to him had its origin in thoughtlessness, lack of empathy, indifference to others. Or idolatry—mistaking money or power or achievement or sex for God. John knew from experience how you could let yourself get swept up in something you'd regret, kidding yourself that you could handle some potentially harmful situation and weren't about to step knee-deep into a pool of shit. He was skilled at helping people work through what they'd done and why, so they could make good—literally, make good out of bad.

But Daniel Iron Horse hadn't just screwed up. This wasn't a mistake—it wasn't even self-deception. It was deliberate, knowing collusion in an act that was illegal, unethical and immoral. Realizing later that Vincenzo

Giuliani and Gelasius III must have been complicit only deepened John's outrage, but those two weren't available to be vilified. Danny Iron Horse was here, every day, every night, and his silence seemed to acknowledge John's assessment: that he was an arrogant man, corrupted by ambition.

For the first time in his life, the Mass failed John. He had always counted on the celebration of the Eucharist to be a time of renewal and rededication, especially among men who had given their lives over to be entirely at the disposal of God. Now, on the *Giordano Bruno*, the Mass was a daily reminder of division and hostility; the very word "Communion" seemed to mock him.

John wanted desperately to talk to Emilio, but Sandoz treated him as he did all the crew members: with a distant, drugged courtesy. "I have given my word that I will not obstruct Carlo's plans," was all he would say.

Joseba Urizarbarrena's policy seemed to be one of strict nonengagement—staying in his quarters as much as possible, carrying food in, plates out, picking odd hours to come and go, so as to avoid the others, Jesuit and lay. "It's hard to imagine how this could be justified," Joseba admitted when John cornered the Basque in the galley one night. "But remember the name of the pirate who took Francis Xavier to Japan? Avan o Ladrao—Avan the Thief. I think perhaps God uses the tools He's got, even the ones that are bent or broken."

When John's protests persisted, Joseba advised, "Talk to Sean." But when John asked directly for some kind of guidance, the Irishman told him with curt irritability, "Mind yer own business." For Sean, John realized, the matter was now under the seal of confession.

Never one to back off from a fight, John decided in the end to go straight to Iron Horse. "My sins are my affair, ace," Danny told him flatly. "You know the facts, so decide. Are the Pope and the Father General frauds? Or do you understand less than you think?"

His way blocked, the dilemma tossed back in his face, his need to talk all this through becoming more pressing, John considered the others. He couldn't quite decide if Nico was retarded, but the big man with the small head was unlikely to have much in the way of ethical insight, in John's opinion. Carlo Giuliani was fond of quoting Marcus Aurelius, but the Caesar that John thought of was Caligula—all honeyed gorgeousness and self-deception: dangerous in more ways than John cared to count.

Which left Fat Frans.

"You're asking me?" the South African cried, as John laid out his problem one morning when there was no one else in the commons except

Nico, whom everyone mostly ignored. "Well, Johnny, you could do worse. I read philosophy at Bloemfontein—"

"Philos—! How the hell did you end up piloting rocks for the Camorra?" John asked, astounded.

Frans shrugged ponderously. "Philosophy, I discovered, is now more of an attitude than a career path—the job market has fallen off somewhat, since the Enlightenment. The Camorra, on the other hand, offers a competitive salary, excellent retirement benefits and very good health insurance," Frans said. "Unless you turn state's evidence—then they provide a very nice funeral."

John snorted, but went back to gnawing on one of the fingernails that constituted a substantial portion of his diet these days.

"Now then," Frans said amiably, in the clipped lilt of Johannesburg, "your problem is an interesting one. Personally, I have no firm opinion about God, but I must tell you that I do consider the entire Catholic Church a fraud, along with all its imps and elves, which would subsume the Black Popes, as specific cases of the general proposition."

"Fuck you, too," John said pleasantly, and went back to his nail.

"A gentleman and a scholar," Frans observed, raising an espresso in salute. "Well, then, perhaps we should look for an axiom upon which we can agree." He studied the ceiling for a while. "You feel the need to discern some kind of hidden meaning here, am I correct? Something that will redeem the sorry mess you find yourself in."

John grunted, working on an index finger.

"But that shouldn't be hard," Frans declared encouragingly. "If your perspective is broad enough, or your sense of history deep enough, or if you are sufficiently imaginative, you can find some kind of deeper meaning in almost anything. Take dreams. Ever hear of the *Libro della Smorfia?*" John shook his head. "Neapolitans, even educated ones, sleep with a book of dreams next to their beds. First thing every morning, even before they take a leak, they look up their dreams. Long journeys, dark strangers, dreams of flying—everything means something."

"Superstition," John said dismissively. "Tea leaves and tarot cards."

"Don't be rude, Johnny. Call it psychology," Frans suggested, grinning, dewlaps swagged around his mouth. "It is a scholar's task to find patterns in nature or cycles in history. Initially, it's no different from finding portraits of animals and heroes in the stars. The question is, Have you discovered a preexisting truth? Or have you imposed an arbitrary meaning on whatever it is you're considering?"

"Yes. Maybe yes, to both," John said. "I don't know." He stopped chewing and realized one of his fingers was bleeding.

"Ah. I don't know: a truth we can rally to." Frans smiled beatifically, small teeth ivory in the pastel face. He adored conversations like this, and years of chauffeuring thugs and stiffs around the solar system had afforded very few of them. "This is delightful. I am playing devil's advocate for a Jesuit! Perhaps," he suggested slyly, "Abraham invented God because he needed to impose meaning on a chaotic, primitive world. We preserve this invented god and insist he loves us because we fear a large and indifferent universe."

John stared at him and then examined his own response, but before he could say anything, the forgotten Nico surprised them both by remarking, "Maybe when you're frightened, you can hear God better because you're listening harder."

Which was an interesting notion, except that it certainly hadn't worked that way for John Candotti, waiting in the lander bay to be blown into space with nothing but bloody death on his mind. "I don't know," he repeated finally.

"The human condition." Frans sighed dramatically. "How we suffer in our anxiety and ignorance!" He brightened. "Which is why food and sex are so nice. Have you eaten?" he asked and, with that, got up and lumbered into the galley, leaving John to suck blood from a mangled nail bed.

CANDOTTI WAS GONE WHEN FRANS CAME BACK TO THE TABLE WITH HIS lunch. Frans smiled at Nico, sitting serenely in his corner, humming "Questa o quella" from *Rigoletto*—the only opera Frans really liked.

"Nico," Frans announced as he sat down to eat, "I have spent the past few weeks in careful observation of our little band of travelers, and in marked contrast to Candotti's existential angst, I myself have reached an inescapable conclusion. Would you like to hear it?" Nico stopped humming and looked at him: not expectant but polite. Nico was always polite. "Here is my conclusion, Nico: it'll be a fucking miracle if anyone comes back from this run alive," Frans told him around a mouthful of *paglio fieno* that he washed down with a swallow of *moscato d'Asti*. "You know what a Runao is, Nico?"

"A kind of old car?"

Frans took another bite. "No, Nico, that's a Renault. A Runao is one of the Runa—the people who live on Rakhat, where we're going." Nico nodded and Frans continued. "A Runao is, for all practical purposes, a cow with an opinion." He chewed for a while and swallowed. "His magnificence, Don Carlo, is a megalomaniac whose grand ambition is to rule over a nation of talking cows. To carry out this glorious mission, he has gathered together a circus freak, a dimwit, four priests and a goddamn cripple you had to beat half to death to get onto this ship." Frans shook his head in amazement but stopped, still disgusted by the way his jowls and chins moved out of phase with his skull. "The priests think they're going to Rakhat to do God's work but do you know why you and I are here, Nico?" Frans asked rhetorically. "Because I am now so fucking fat I will never get laid again in my life anyway, so what the hell? And you are too dumb to say no. Carlo couldn't get anybody else to come."

"That's not true," Nico said with bland conviction. "Don Carlo decided to go because he found out his sister Carmella was going to be boss."

Frans blinked. "You knew about that?"

"Everybody knew, even the Yakuza in Japan," Nico confided. "Don Carlo was very embarrassed."

"You're right," Frans admitted. Besides, there was no sense in stirring up trouble. Carlo was the padrone and Nico was devoted to him—he'd damned near killed a guy who'd given Giuliani a hard time over a bar bill. "And I apologize for saying you were dumb, Nico."

"You should take it back about the Runa, too, Frans."

"I take it back about the Runa," said Frans promptly.

"Because the Runa aren't cows. They're the good ones," Nico informed him. "Those Jana people are the bad ones."

"I was only trying to be funny, Nico." Years of experience to the contrary, Frans still hadn't given up hope that Nico would learn to recognize irony and sarcasm. Which just goes to show who's dumb, Frans thought, scooping up another forkful of pasta. "Are you a praying man, Nico?" he asked, changing the subject.

"In the morning, and before I sleep. Hail Marys," Nico told him.

"Like the sisters taught you in the home, eh?"

Nico nodded. "My name is Niccolo d'Angeli. 'D'Angeli' means from the angels," he recited. "That's where I came from, before the home. The angels left me. I say my prayers in the morning and before I sleep. Hail Marys."

"*Brav' scugnizz'*, Nico. You're a good boy," Frans said aloud, but he was thinking, The angels who dropped you off must have been short a few last names in their genealogy, my friend. "You believe in God, then, do you, Nico?"

"Yes, I do," Nico affirmed solemnly. "The sisters told me."

Frans chewed for a while. "I have a little hypothesis about God, Nico," he said, swallowing. "Want to hear my hypothesis?"

"What's a hy . . . ?"

"Hy-po-the-sis," Frans said slowly. "An idea. A testable guess about the way something works. You understand, Nico?" The little skull nodded uncertainly. "Now here's my idea. There's an old story about a man and a cat—"

"I like cats."

Why do I try? Frans asked himself, but soldiered on. "The man was a famous physicist named Schrödinger—don't worry, Nico, you don't have to remember his name. Schrödinger said that a thing isn't true unless there's someone to observe that it's true. He said that observing actually makes an event turn into being true."

Nico looked miserable.

"Don't be worried, Nico. I'll make it easy for you. Schrödinger said that if you put a cat in a box with—okay, let's say with a plate of good food and a plate of poison food, and then you close the box—"

"That's mean," Nico observed, glad to be back on concrete.

"So is beating the crap out of ex-priests, Nico," Frans told him, taking another bite. "Don't interrupt. Now: the cat's in the box, and he may have eaten the good food or the bad food. So he might be alive or he might be dead. But Schrödinger said that the cat isn't actually alive or dead unless and until the man outside opens the box to see that the cat is alive or dead."

Nico thought that over. "You could listen to hear if it's purring."

Frans stopped chewing for a moment and pointed at Nico with a fork. "That's why you're a thug, and not a physicist or a philosopher." He swallowed and went on. "Now here's my idea about God. I think we're like the cat. I think that God is like the man outside the box. I think that if the cat believes in the man, the man is there. And if the cat is an atheist, there is no man."

"Maybe there's a lady," Nico suggested helpfully.

Frans choked on a piece of pasta and coughed for a while. "Maybe so, Nico. But here's what I think. I think because you believe in God, maybe there's going to be a God for you, when you get out of the box." Nico opened his mouth and then closed it again, and appeared about to cry. "Don't worry about it, Nico. You're a good boy, and I'm sure God is there for good boys."

Frans got up and waddled back to the galley for something sweet. "That's why I need you to pray for something," he called as he rummaged through the bins. "Because God is there for you, but He might not be there for people who aren't sure if they believe in Him." He came back to the table with a generous portion of Black Forest cake. "I want you to pray for a miracle. Okay, Nico?"

"Okay," Nico agreed with utter sincerity.

"Good. Now here's my problem. Do you know why I'm so fat, Nico?"

"You eat all the time."

"I'm an Afrikaner, Nico," Frans said wearily. "Eating is our national sport. But I ate all the time before, remember? And I wasn't like this two years ago! Sometimes when you're out in space, your DNA—the instructions that make your body work, understand? Your DNA gets nicked by a few atoms of cosmic dust. That's what happened to me, Nico—a random speck of shit just passing through on its way to the rim of the universe hits some critical piece of biological machinery and all hell breaks loose . . ."

Suddenly, whatever he ate was used and used and used, every last erg of energy torn from each molecule of hydrogen, oxygen, carbon and nitrogen, and stored away in miserly, paranoiac fat cells waiting for a famine of mythic proportions to call upon them for heroic rescue of the body they were slowly, inexorably suffocating. "I fought it, Nico. In the beginning, I fought it. Exercised like a maniac. Starved myself. Spent all my time Earth-side going from doctor to doctor," Frans told him.

He had taken any drug anyone would prescribe or sell, looking for a cure or even just some hope, and became grosser and grosser, more and more a stranger to himself, scared shitless by the prospect of congestive heart and kidney failure.

There was a sort of poetic justice in it, he supposed, and Frans Vanderhelst was nothing if not philosophical about such things. For years, he himself had profited from other people's pathetic belief in a miracle cure. Carlo had run the scam for almost a decade before the insurance companies caught on. He preyed like a wolf on the weak—selecting only the richest and sickest, the most desperate and suggestible marks, assuring his hopeful, hopeless half-dead passengers that if they went fast enough, time would slow down for them and when they got back, medical advances on Earth would have caught up with their diseases and they'd go home to be cured. Convincingly sympathetic to their plight, Carlo explained how they would pay nothing now, that it was only necessary to list the Angels of Mercy Limited as the beneficiary to their life insurance policies.

It was bullshit, of course. Frans just took them up and ran the engines at quarter-power for a few weeks, far from the unblinking gaze of medical ethics boards and police surveillance. The marks themselves never knew the difference. Most of them died on their own; Carlo's drunken, defrocked doctors made sure of the rest.

But now, Carlo had parlayed a scam into something real and Frans Vanderhelst actually was on his way to Rakhat—accelerating at an increasing percentage of the speed of light. And this time Frans himself was the poor, dumb fuck who hoped that during the four decades of his projected absence from Earth, someone would figure out how to make his body right again. Because, underneath an ever-thickening pad of adipose, behind now piggish eyes peering over puffed and pasty cheeks, Frans Vanderhelst was only thirty-six, a man in his prime. And Frans wanted very much to live.

"So, here's the miracle you should pray for, okay, Nico?" Frans said, laying down his fork. "Pray that we get back to Earth alive and pray that when we get there, someone will be able to fix it for me, so I can eat and still be normal? You got that, Nico?"

Nico nodded. "Pray so we get back alive and you're normal."

"Good, Nico. That's good. I appreciate it," said Frans as Nico went back to Verdi, picking up the Duke of Mantua's aria where he'd left off a few minutes earlier.

Frans sat for a time, thinking about Pascal's wager. It was then that he realized he really did appreciate Nico's prayers. After all, he thought, the one thing an agnostic knows for sure is: you never know.

21

N'Jarr Valley, Northern Rakhat

2078 – 2085, Earth-Relative

DURING THE FINAL DAYS OF HIS LIFE, DANIEL IRON HORSE WOULD watch the tripled shadows on the walls of his stone house in the N'Jarr valley and think about the past. He was lucid until the end, but his mind would constantly take him back to the awful months spent on the *Giordano Bruno*. It would seem to him that he had existed then in a kind of silent limbo, aching for the end of his punishment, while the years rushed by on Rakhat.

His penance had begun at the moment he gave his assent to the abduction, and it was the very one he had laid on Vincenzo Giuliani—to live with what he had done. His own was the lighter sentence. There was, for Daniel Iron Horse, some hope that he might live long enough to know the answer to a question Giuliani would carry to his grave: What if I am wrong about everything?

Danny had asked himself that question over and over, as the weeks in Naples crawled by in the presence of the man they intended to harm irreversibly and, perhaps, for no good reason. He lived with that question for months on the *Bruno* in the company of men who could hardly stand the sight of him. He accepted their judgment. Pride was his sin, the worm at the core—a surefooted drive, powered by a lifelong and quite possibly deluded sense of having been prepared by God to do something extraordinary.

As far as his father's family had come from the squalor and debasement of the reservations, as much as he himself publicly rejected the stereotypes and romance of his Lakota heritage, Daniel Iron Horse had taken secret satisfaction in it. From childhood, he had known himself to be the scion of men who rode with Crazy Horse and Little Big Man of the Oglalas, with Black Shield and Lame Deer of the Miniconjous, with Spotted Eagle and Red Bear of the Sans Arcs, with Black Moccasin and Ice of the Cheyennes, and with Sitting Bull of the Hunkpapas—heroes who led the finest light cavalry in history in defense of their families and their land, who had fought to preserve a way of life that valued, above all else, courage, fortitude, generosity and transcendent spiritual vision.

Just as strong a tradition: his family's long association with the Black Robes, whose own beliefs upheld those same values. His five-times great-grandmother was among the first of the Lakota to be converted to Christianity by Pierre-Jean De Smet, a Jesuit of legendary charm and grace, whose utter fearlessness had afforded him unrivaled credibility among the tribes of the American West. The Lakota believed that all peoples, if not all persons, seek the divine; the Christian God's call to universal peace was proclaimed as well by the White Buffalo Calf Woman. Blood sacrifice to the Wakan Tanka—the Great Mystery—was familiar as well. Even the crucifix was resonant: Jesus's body, arms outstretched, pierced and hung from a cross, so like the pierced and suspended bodies of the Sun Dancers, visionaries who knew what it was to offer their own flesh and blood to God on behalf of their people—in thanks, in supplication, in terrible joy. At Masses celebrated by Jesuit friends, many Lakota had worshiped the sacred and incomprehensible power that watched over all, that listened to the prayers of those who offered sacrifice, not their own flesh and blood any longer—for Jesus changed all that—but bread and wine, consecrated in memory of ultimate sacrifice.

Surely, this was apprenticeship: the mixed nature of his making, the manner of his education, the talent and energy and insight that Daniel Iron Horse brought to maturity. It was all preparation for the day when he first opened the Rakhat mission reports and read the accounts of what the *Stella Maris* party had seen and learned. He came to believe, with a conviction that grew stronger and more unshakable as he read, that he was meant to go to Rakhat, for of all those who might have been sent, only Daniel Iron Horse would truly understand the fragile beauty of Jana'ata culture.

He feared for them.

The people of the plains, too, had depended utterly on a single species of prey and they, too, had been been thought by outsiders to be a dangerous people who loved war. Danny knew that was true, but only a small crooked part of the truth. And he came to believe that if he went to Rakhat, he might somehow redeem the heartbreaking losses that had befallen the Lakota by helping the Jana'ata find a new way of life—one that would preserve the highest virtues of the warrior, and of the hunter, and of the Jesuit: courage and fortitude, generosity and vision.

Sometimes on the *Bruno,* late at night, the filter fans humming, the subaural rumble of the *Bruno*'s engines more felt than heard, Danny would recall the thought that had come to him as he read the Rakhat reports: I would do *anything* to go. He had meant it only as a figure of speech but God held him to a Faustian bargain.

"We are closer to the old ways, you and I," Gelasius III had said to Daniel Iron Horse, in private audience. "We understand the need for sacrifice, to make our belief in God concrete, to offer God our faith entire: that if we align ourselves with His will, all will be well. Now you and I are called upon to offer a sacrifice that will test our faith, almost as Abraham's was tested. It is harder than to offer our own bodies. You and I must offer Sandoz, bound like Abraham's son Isaac. We must do what seems cruel and incomprehensible and, in doing so, prove that we trust in God's plan and act as His instruments. We serve a Father Who did not flinch from Abraham's sacrifice, Who required and permitted the crucifixion of His own Son! And Who sometimes requires that we also sacrifice that which we hold dearest, in service to His will. This I believe. Can you also believe this?"

What made him nod his unspoken acquiescence to an act he found abhorrent? Was it truly ambition? Danny had examined himself with fierce scrutiny, and the answer was no, no matter what the others believed. Was it the majesty of the Vatican, the moral weight of two millennia of authority? Yes, partly. The strength of the Pope himself? The compassion and beauty of those lustrous, knowing eyes?

Yes. Yes, all of that.

Did the Holy Father and the Father General have more than one reason for sending Sandoz back to Rakhat? Unquestionably. There would be desirable political, diplomatic, practical outcomes of this decision. Did those other motives outweigh the Holy Father's uncanny certainty and the Father General's almost desperate hope that Sandoz was meant by God to return to the place of his spiritual and physical violation?

Daniel Iron Horse did not think so.

He didn't know what he thought, what he believed anymore. He was sure of only one thing: it was beyond him to look into the eyes of Gelasius III and listen to his words and then to sneer, "Self-serving horseshit." For Jesuits are taught to find God in all things, and Danny could not walk away from the moral and ethical problem he had been set: if you believe in God's sovereignty and if you believe in God's goodness, then what happened to Sandoz must be part of a larger plan; and if that is so, you can help this one soul and serve God by returning with him to Rakhat.

And so, for the betrayal of his ethics and the sacrifice of his integrity, Daniel Iron Horse could only watch what he had helped make possible: to live with what he had done, and try to find God in it—to hope that the ends would someday justify the means.

ON THE *BRUNO*, TIME SEEMED A SENTENCE TO BE SERVED, BUT THAT WOULD change as Daniel Iron Horse grew old on the planet of Rakhat.

"In the beginning," Scripture taught, "there was the Word," and Danny would come to believe that the two great gifts his God had given to the species He loved were time, which divides experience, and language, which binds the past to the future. Eventually all the priests who remained on Rakhat would devote themselves to buying time and working toward an understanding of the events that took place there during the years between the first and second Jesuit missions. For Daniel Iron Horse, this was not merely research but constant prayer.

The lady Suukmel Chirot u Vaadai was to become his partner in this task. By the time Danny met her, she was not the wife but the widow of the Mala Njeri ambassador to the court of Hlavin Kitheri, a woman bereft of status but not of respect, and well past middle age. Danny was enthralled by her from the start, but Suukmel was wary and inclined, herself, to delay trust in the man she knew as Dani Hi'r-norse.

Even so, as Danny's hair grayed and Suukmel's face whitened, there came a day when she and the foreigner could meet for pleasure and not only for policy. He believed, as she did, that the past was not dead but alive, and important by virtue of the very invisibility of its influence. When she discovered this, their friendship began in earnest.

It became their custom to walk together every morning, their path following the foothills encircling the N'Jarr valley, and to speak as they walked of what Suukmel now understood and wished Danny to understand as well. Danny would often begin these talks with a proverb, inviting her to respond. "On Earth, there is a saying: The past is another country," he told her once, and Suukmel found this a useful notion, for she did indeed feel a foreigner in the present. But even when she disagreed with Danny's maxims, the exercise was interesting.

"Power corrupts," he suggested one day, as they started up the slope to the ring path on one of their earliest walks. "And absolute power corrupts absolutely."

"Fear corrupts, not power," she countered. "Powerlessness debases. Power can be used to good effect or ill, but no one is improved by weakness," she told him. "The powerful can more easily cultivate longsightedness. They can be patient—even generous—in the face of opposition, knowing that they will prevail eventually. They do not feel that their lives are futile, because they have reason to believe that their plans will become reality."

"Do you speak of yourself, my lady Suukmel?" Danny asked, smiling. "Or of Hlavin Kitheri?"

She paused to consider him. "There were certain harmonies of soul," she said carefully before resuming her ascent. Then she continued, "It was when Hlavin Kitheri was merely Reshtar that his life was corrupt. He was desperate, and he had the vices of desperation. This changed when he took power."

The path became steep and treacherous with scree, and for a time they climbed in silence. A little winded near the top, Suukmel sat on a fallen *tupa*'s smooth, substantial trunk, and gazed across the N'Jarr toward mountains rising from the ground like colossal projectiles shot from the center of Rakhat. "Of course, power can come to inadequate people," she admitted, when her breath again came easily. "Dull minds, small hearts, impoverished souls could once inherit power. Now such people can grasp it, or buy it, or stumble into power by chance." Her voice hardened. "Power does not necessarily ennoble." She said this looking south, and rose once more to her feet. "Tell me, Dani, why do you spend so much time with old women?" she asked with a sidelong glance as they resumed their walk.

He offered his strange naked hand to help her around an eroded ditch that thwarted the trail. "When I was very young," he told her, "my father's beforemother came to live with us. She would tell us tales of the old times, which she herself had learned from her own beforemothers. Everything had changed, during those few generations. Everything."

"Do you remember her stories?" Suukmel asked him. "Perhaps," she suggested lightly, "knowledge of earlier times was of no use to you."

"I remember them." Danny stopped, and Suukmel turned back to see him looking at her—shyly, she thought. "But I was a scholar in my own land. So I tested the truth of the tales that came to me from five generations removed against the research of many other scholars."

"And did your beforemothers remember truly?" she asked.

"Yes. The tales proved themselves not stories but history. Why else would I spend so much time with old ladies now?" he teased, and she laughed.

"Change can be good," Suukmel said then, walking once more. "Many Jana'ata still believe as we all did in ages past: that change is dangerous and wrong. They believe everything my lord Kitheri did was error—that he was wicked to change a way of life bequeathed from one generation to the next without degradation or fallacy. Can you understand this? Have you such perfection on your H'earth, Dani?"

Danny fought a smile. "Oh, yes. I myself am a member of a 'church' that is believed by many to be an infallible repository of timeless truth."

"My lord Kitheri and I considered this problem very carefully," Suukmel told him. "It was our belief that any institution considering itself the guardian of truth will value constancy, for change by definition introduces error. Such institutions always have powerful mechanisms to shore up invariance and defend against change."

"Appeal to tradition," he said, "and to authority. And to divinity."

"Yes, all those," she said serenely. "Nevertheless, change can be desirable or necessary, or both at once! How then does a wise prince introduce change when the generations have enshrined a practice or a prohibition that now harms or cripples?"

She stopped to look at him directly, no longer startled by the clarity of near vision she now enjoyed, with no veil to film her eyes. "Tell me, Dani, do you tire of an old woman?" Suukmel asked, head tilted in speculation. "Or shall I tell you of those first days of Kitheri's reign?" Even now, knowing what would come, her eyes still glowed with the excitement of those times.

"Please," he said. "Everything you can remember." And so she began.

THE FIRST OF KITHERI'S DECREES MET WITH NO RESISTANCE, FOR HE merely revived the tournaments that had fallen out of practice: the dance duels, the massed voices of choir battles. "Not change," Suukmel murmured in conspiratorial remembrance. "Simply a return to earlier ways—which were, as he said, purer and closer to the old truth."

Soon, Kitheri established national competitions in poetry, architecture, engineering, mathematics, optics, chemistry. Having sworn during his investiture as Paramount to uphold the immutable Inbrokari order, he had to leave the ancient lines of inheritance untouched, and so prizes in such competitions were of no intrinsic value. "Tokens, merely," Suukmel said dismissively. "A single *traja'anron* blossom, or a pennant, or a rhyming triplet composed by the Paramount himself." But it was not long before there were acceptable ways for warriors with a scholarly bent or third-born merchants of athletic talent to hone their knowledge or skills: to be recognized for what they had within, and not merely for what they had been born to.

"Parallel hierarchies, based on competence," Danny observed. "Open to all, and bleeding off discontent. Your idea, my lady?"

Not since Hlavin had she enjoyed a man's company so well. "Yes," she said, eyes downcast but pleased. "These competitions allowed my lord Kitheri to identify men of talent, wit, imagination, energy."

Drawing on a lifetime of well-used confinement, Suukmel Chirot u Vaadai had learned that almost any event or condition could be turned to advantage. "Locally strong government or evidence of incompetence could be equally favorable to the Paramount's purpose, since both engendered resentment in the ranks below," she told Danny during another stroll. "My lord Kitheri was third-born, and trained therefore in law as well as combat. He could nearly always find legal precedent for deposing uncomfortably powerful or egregiously stupid nobles when younger brothers were better men, more attuned to the new regime. Where legal means were lacking," she said dryly, "accidents were encouraged to occur." Ears cocked forward, she invited him to comment.

"With the Paramount's complicity?" Danny asked. Suukmel did not deny it. "So those who acceded under these conditions did so knowing whose influence made their own rise possible. Their claims to power and position would have been every bit as questionable as Hlavin Kitheri's." He thought a moment. "Such men would have formed a reliable cadre of supporters, I think. Their fate was bound up with his."

"Precisely." She had become very frank with him as their time together lengthened. Danny was a wily listener, who appreciated careful phrasing, and his admiration perfumed her hours with him. "We found many ways to extend the Paramount's reach," she said. "For example, when a lord died, the interregnum between new and old could be prolonged by delaying investiture ceremonies. The Paramount, whose presence was indispensable, was simply unable to attend—often," Suukmel said with limpid innocence, "for many seasons."

Nephews or brothers-in-law or third-born uncles could be placed in regency while revenue ledgers and tax records were confiscated for inspection by merchant thirds and Runa bookkeepers from a far-removed province. "Sometimes it was merely a matter of putting the territory on a sound accounting basis," Suukmel recalled. "Regional revenues often increased dramatically, and this was much to the advantage of the family in question."

"But the Paramount would then have an inventory of all sources of wealth filed," Danny said.

"At which time, he would, at last, become available for the necessary ceremonies," Suukmel said. "When control of the patrimony was transferred, everyone knew now exactly how much could and would be extracted in taxes. Displaced regents, if they showed promise, could then be incorporated into the new chancery."

"And these men, too, were added to the growing corps of Kitheri supporters," Danny observed.

"Naturally."

Danny looked at her with sly delight. "And, if I might know, my lady: to whom did the chancery report?"

"I was, by that time, a person of some modest influence," Suukmel murmured, and remained carefully composed even while he laughed and shook his head. "If gross irregularities in territorial affairs were discovered," Suukmel continued, "two paths were open. The day before his investiture, a new lord could be made aware of his ancestors' dishonor in a private meeting with the Paramount. This man was given to understand that the Paramount had chosen to allow him to remain in office, and expected gratitude."

"And cooperation, no doubt," said Danny. "But if the lineage was unalterably opposed to changes favored by the Paramount?"

"If the lineage was unyielding," Suukmel said carefully, "then news of its crimes would be broadcast, and these unworthy men were declared Va-Haptaa—outlaws, their patrimonies forfeit."

"And to enforce such judgments?"

"There was a small troop of martial tournament champions, equipped and fielded with monies brought in by the new taxes." She looked across the valley. "There was also the war in the south," she said. "My lord Kitheri could make it seem both honorable and necessary to the more . . . traditional men that they defend Jana'ata territory and our way of life."

"Leaving northern land and titles open, when they were killed." Suukmel's chin lifted, acknowledging the inference. "Two birds with one stone," said Danny, but left that untranslated.

"YOU WILL DOUBT THIS," SUUKMEL WARNED DANNY ON ANOTHER DAY, "but it is true. Hlavin had support among the Runa. He had learned to value their capabilities and made them a part of his plans. One of his earliest decrees regarding the Runa was that their urban specialists send delegations to the Inbrokar court. Their advice was sought in all that concerned them, and he did this despite opposition from the lesser nobility."

At Suukmel's suggestion and under the direction of her former maid, the discreetly emancipated Taksayu, a tapestry of Runa informants was woven during Kitheri's first years as Paramount. Reports soon filtered back from cooks and valets, secretaries and masseurs; from groundskeepers, research assistants; from scullery maids and sexual servants. "Before long," Suukmel said, "my lord Kitheri knew each great household's disputes and discontents, their secret alliances and petty jealousies—"

"And knowledge is power," Danny interjected.

Suukmel chuckled, a low and throaty sound. "Now that is a wise proverb," she granted.

"And how were the Runa compensated for their contribution to Kitheri's plans?"

"Naturally, the informants themselves had to be left in place, but their children were allowed to express an opinion about their area of work. And when the time came, about a preferred mate. These were my friend Taksayu's suggestions," she told him, pausing a moment to mourn the dead. "She was a Runao, but my lord Kitheri took wisdom where he found it. He even established pensions for Runa informants who had reached the age of slaughter—"

"Who could feed him information—a commodity more valuable than meat," Danny pointed out coldly.

Not catching his tone, Suukmel went on, anxious to explain. "This was a radical change, in reality, but it was considered a harmless eccentricity of the Paramount by those whose domestics were pensioned. Who would object to an old retainer living off the Kitheri largesse?" she asked rhetorically. "Meat, after all, could be had from villagers backbred to doorkeepers and fan-pullers and draft Runa—"

She fell silent, stopped by his stare.

"It was the only way we knew," she said, tired all at once. "Dani, you must understand it was not only the Runa who were born to their fate— we all were! Birth rank, the rank of one's family—even for a man, those determined every detail of life! The length of his claws, which door he was permitted to pass through. Whom he could marry, what his work would be. The number of earrings he could wear, the grade of perfumes he could buy! And yes—what portion of a Runa carcass his meat would come from. Dani, Hlavin meant to change all that!"

"But change takes time," Danny said. "Another proverb."

Suukmel raised her tail slightly and let it drop: as you say. "I think perhaps that it is not change but resistance to change that takes time."

"But surely, my lady, the Paramount did not pension those elderly Runa purely to reward their usefulness with kindness," Danny pointed out, more aggressive now that he knew her better. "The accumulated knowledge of Runa from all over Inbrokar was made directly available to Kitheri's chancery, to Kitheri's private police and to Kitheri himself."

"Yes! Of course! Can you build a wall with a single stone?" she asked. "The sign of a good decision is the multiplicity of reasons for it. If more than one goal is served, then a decision is more likely to be wise—"

To her surprise, Danny began to speak, fell silent and turned away. She understood that he was distressed by what she had just said, and felt compelled to make her words clearer for him.

"Dani, when we change things, we are like the little gods: we act, and from each act falls a cascade of consequence—some things expected and desired, some surprising and regrettable. But we are not like your God who sees everything! We cannot know the future, so we anticipate as much as we can, and judge by the outcome if we have done rightly." His back was stiff, his breathing odd. She had never seen him react this way. "Dani, have I offended you?" she asked, astonished.

He spun, his face slack with dismay. "My lady: never!" He pulled in a long breath and let it out slowly. "You are the instrument of my conscience," he said lightly. He tried to smile, but it was not convincing, not even to Suukmel, who still found foreign faces difficult to interpret. Seeing her confusion, he performed an obeisance. "My lady, it was once my belief that when a multiplicity of reasons is sought, the rightness of an act is suspect, that one is trying to justify the unjustifiable. Long ago, I made a decision for which I sought a multitude of reasons. That decision brought me here to you, but I will not know if it was right until I am judged by my God."

She considered him for a long time, to understand his face in such moments, to memorize the scent of shame, to learn the sound of scruple in his voice. Then she turned toward the N'Jarr valley, where low stone walls glowed like gold in morning's slanting light. "Look," she commanded, her arm describing a graceful arc, sweeping from west to east. "And listen," she said, for all the children, Runa and Jana'ata, were singing. "How can you doubt?"

He did not reply, but only looked at her with his small, black eyes held wide. That day they walked home in silence, and did not speak of this again.

"WHAT YOU HAVE TOLD ME EXPLAINS POLITICAL POWER, MY LADY," Danny said later that year, "but there was more to Kitheri than that, I think. Men followed him, but not for a single *traja'anron* blossom or a pennant or a rhyming triplet. And not, I think, for wealth or power or even breeding rights."

"They followed him out of love, and out of loyalty," Suukmel said serenely. "Hlavin Kitheri began to seem the embodiment of their own greatness. They loved him for what he and they had become, and they would have done anything for him."

"So when the Paramount let it be known that he desired that such men should be bound closer to him, they forgot or forgave Kitheri's reputation for—" He stopped, unwilling to offend her.

"Sexual . . . sophistication, perhaps?" she suggested, amused at his delicacy. "Yes. These men willingly gave their third-born sisters or daughters to his harem."

"Even knowing that the children of those matings would have no appointed place in the hierarchy?"

"Yes, knowing that the lives of those born to Kitheri's house would not be decreed by birth or governed by death. So be it, such men said. Let the future carve out its course, like a river in flood. Neither did they falter at Hlavin's lifting of the breeding bans on certain merchant thirds. Can you understand how 'revolutionary' this was?" she asked, using the H'inglish word. "We had always been careful stewards of our inheritance. Our honor was to pass down, undegraded, whatever legacy we ourselves had received. To bequeath more was dishonor: this implied theft. To bequeath less was dishonor: this implied profligacy. But Hlavin showed us all that there could be creation! Something, out of nothing! Poetry, wealth, music, ideas, dance: out of nothing! Stewardship could encompass increase! Everyone began to see this, and we all wondered—even I wondered— what had we been frightened of all these years?"

LIKE AN ANCIENT HUNTER DROPPING MEAT AT HIS WIFE'S FEET, HLAVIN Kitheri had laid all he accomplished at the exquisite feet of the lady Suukmel Chirot u Vaadai. It was to please her that he took the final step, opening the last door, letting both Chaos and Wisdom free.

From all over Inbrokar, his young consorts had come, veiled and guarded and ignorant. For Suukmel's sake, and perhaps in guilty memory of his late sister Jholaa, Hlavin Kitheri brought the wonders of land and sea and air into his seraglio; filled his palace with Runa tutors, storytellers, talking books, with Jana'ata politicians and scientists, bards and engineers. At first, his girls were separated from the men with a pierced wooden screen; later, with heavy curtains only. Still later, it began to seem quite ordinary and acceptable that the ladies should hear the debates, now and then comment audibly on them, and finally participating fully in the colloquia from behind the merest suggestion of a gauzy wall: transparent, diaphanous, floating.

These girls bore Kitheri children. The first was a son he called Rukuei, neutered as an infant and given to Suukmel to be fostered at the Mala Njeri embassy. But there were many other children as the years passed, and one of these was a daughter who did not know it was forbidden for females to sing. When Hlavin Kitheri heard that small, high, pure voice, his heart's very rhythm paused, made motionless by beauty.

Except for the evening chants, Hlavin himself had not sung in years. Now, with a relief more profound than the consummation of any physical yearning, he found his way back to poetry and music. He brought in musicians and choirmasters, and let the women and children sing, depending on the shimmering loveliness of their voices to drown his society's lingering ability to find scandal in the new. Once again, he created a torrent of cantatas, chorales, anthems: for his consorts and his young.

By the twelfth year of Hlavin Kitheri's reign, the Principality of Inbrokar was the most powerful political entity in the history of Rakhat—

wealthier than Mala Njer, as populous as Palkirn—and Hlavin Kitheri held undisputed sovereignty over the central kingdom of the Triple Alliance. Already, he had made close allies among his Chirot and Vaadai contacts in Mala Njer. In a year or two more, it would have been time at last to take the Palkirn girl as his wife and establish a legitimate succession, now that he had brought about the revolution he had no word for.

"WHEN DID YOU FIRST REALIZE WHAT WAS HAPPENING IN THE SOUTH?" Daniel Iron Horse asked, many years after Kitheri's death.

"Almost from the beginning, there were signs," Suukmel recalled. "Less than a season after Hlavin acceded to the paramountcy, the first of the refugees appeared at the gates of Inbrokar." Stunned and terrified as refugees everywhere always are, with stories of fire, of betrayal and death in the night, their lives had been spared by Runa whose loyalty and love these few Jana'ata had earned, and whose warnings these few had heeded. "My lord Kitheri appreciated the irony, Dani. He himself once said, 'I fathered the destruction of the new world at the moment of its conception.' "

"There are limits, of course, to anyone's breadth of view," Danny pointed out. They sat silently for a time, listening to a midday chain chorus, the sound of which spread from compound to compound across the valley. "It seems to me, my lady, that if things had been only a little different—" Danny hesitated. "Perhaps Supaari VaGayjur might have become the first and most useful of Kitheri's supporters."

"Perhaps," Suukmel said after a long time. "What made him contemptible in the old regime were the very traits that would become most admirable in my lord Kitheri's paramountcy." She paused, thinking. "The merchant would have made an excellent chancellor, for example. Or he might have headed a Ministry of Runa Affairs . . ." Chest tight, she looked at Danny, who was her equal in height, and in many other things. "Perhaps," she said steadily, "it all might have been avoided, but at the time? There seemed no other way . . ."

22

Southern Province, Inbrokar

2047, Earth-Relative

> Just like Jesuits — pushing
> forward even tho may be
> dangerous

"SOMEONE HAS ASSEMBLED THE TRADE GOODS YOU SPECIFIED. THEY'RE cached near the lander site," Djalao VaKashan informed Sofia and Supaari when she finally showed up in Trucha Sai. She was days late. "There are *djanada* patrols everywhere out there."

"Cullers?" Supaari suggested warily. "Or inspection teams, perhaps, just taking census for the new paramountcy?"

"Someone thinks neither," Djalao said, ignoring the other Runa who crowded around them, and who were beginning to sway uneasily. "At Kirabai, the people say these are men from the north, from Inbrokar City. They have foreign Runa with them—from Mala Njer, someone thinks. The elders at Kirabai had to call on interpreters whose lineages are very old, to understand them."

Djalao was not visibly frightened, but she was concerned. All the village councils were talking about what this meant, what was changing. "The patrols ask always about Supaari," she told them quietly. "They ask also about foreigners."

"Is it safe for us to travel?" Sofia asked, stomach tightening. "Perhaps we-but-not-you must wait until this trouble is over."

"Someone thinks, we-and-you-also can travel, but in redlight only. It might be best for you to go without delay." Djalao looked at Supaari and switched to K'San. "Lord, will you permit one of us to lead you?"

There was a noticeable silence and Sofia made a half turn to be able to look at Supaari. He was standing very straight, staring at Djalao. "Am I a lord," he asked, "who can permit or forbid?" Then, ears dropping, he brought himself to acceptance. Eyes on the middle distance, somewhere to Djalao's left, he lifted his chin. "Apologies," he said finally. "Someone will be grateful for your guidance."

Everyone shuffled, embarrassed. Sofia could see that it cost Supaari something to say this and understood that Djalao intimidated him in a way no other Runao did; the subtleties were lost on her, as were the details of the interminable discussion that followed, encompassing as it did political and geographic considerations about their route to the *Magellan* lander. She had done all she could during the six months of preparation for the voyage home. Now there was no choice but to trust that Supaari and Djalao would make the right decisions.

Drowsy with the heat, already halfway to Earth in spirit, Sofia leaned against a shelter pole, one knee up, the other leg dangling over the platform, and let her mind drift as she watched the Runa children play with Ha'anala who was just beginning to walk and pounce, unaware of her differences from her only companions. Isaac, at Sofia's side constantly these days, more than made up for his mother's quiet, ceaselessly producing a monotone stream of phrases in both Ruanja and English, his pronunciation perfect. Mostly it was mimicry but, on occasion, genuine speech would emerge—most often after he had sung the Sh'ma with her and the evening chant with Supaari. They always retreated into the quiet of the forest to sing, far from the hubbub of the Runa, for whom song was threatening—the instrument of *djanada* control. Perhaps, Sofia thought, it was that temporary silence that allowed Isaac to get beyond echoing. "Isaac hears you," he told Sofia once. And another time, in observation, "Ha'anala fell."

But there was a price to pay. To speak, Isaac had broken through some inner wall, and that tiny breach in his fortress now allowed the awful chaos around him to invade his private world. Shadows, his delight since infancy, suddenly seemed alive: unpredictable and menacing. The color red, never significant before, now horrified him, evoking banshee shrieks that upset everyone. The normal noise of Runa children playing would sometimes drive him to a screaming, spinning frenzy.

He'll be better off on the ship, Sofia thought, barely listening to his monologue or the Runa debate going on around her. It will be difficult for him in the beginning, but we can keep to a routine and he'll adapt. No surprises—everything the way he wants it. Nothing red. I can cover the read-outs with something. And there can be music all day long, on board. That alone would improve Isaac's life, she thought. That alone was worth the risks they were taking.

At peace, she lay back against a cushion and let the sounds of the village lull her to sleep, and woke hours later to Supaari's touch and to the quiet that signaled consensus, when all that needed to be considered had been said; with a decision reached, the council had dispersed.

"Tomorrow, at second dawn," Supaari told her, distilling hours of debate. "We'll stay in the forest as long as possible—it's a little farther to walk, but it will be safer than taking the shortest route across the savannah. When we have to cross open country, we'll travel at night."

Sofia sat up, looking around the village. The last meal of the day was being prepared. Everyone was settling in for the evening.

"Shall you be sad to leave, Fia?" Supaari asked, hunkering down next to her.

She listened to the whispering of the fathers, the cooing and giggles of the children. "They have been so kind—so good to us," she said, missing them already, all the irritation and impatience swept away by a flood of gratitude. "If only there were some way to repay them . . ."

"Yes," Supaari agreed. "But I think the best course is to leave. The patrols are looking for us, Sofia. We can only be a danger to the Runa now."

THE BEGINNING OF THE JOURNEY WAS NO DIFFERENT FROM A HUN-dred other foraging expeditions Sofia had participated in, strange only in that the specially woven backbasket she wore was not empty at the start of the trip. Kanchay and Tinbar and Sichu-Lan had come along with Djalao, to help carry the children and the burdens of travel; the conversation was lighthearted, the Runa men looking forward to seeing friends and relatives in Kashan for the first time in years. For a time, there was only the metronome beat of their legs, and Sofia hardly heard the talk that went on around her, content to have Isaac march along at her side, his taut, little body wiry and beautiful. He's going to be tall, she realized, like his father.

The highlands began to flatten on the third day and they came at last to a place where the light brightened noticeably and the woodland grew drier, rains balked by mountains to the west. The canopy was still intact overhead, but here the trees were more widely spaced, and at the edge of the woods, Sofia could just make out a subsidence smoothing onto a savannah that stretched all the way to Kashan.

"We'll wait here," Djalao said, so they put their baskets down, fed Isaac and Ha'anala, and had a meal themselves.

As the light began to change, and second sundown approached, Isaac insisted as always that the songs be sung. The three male Runa went off some distance and clamped their ears shut and swayed. Djalao remained nearby, listening to Supaari impassively, ears high, as though she were putting herself to a sort of test of strength, Sofia thought. When the chants were done, Djalao's immobility broke and she dug into one of the packs, handing around a jar of strong-smelling ointment that the Runa began to smear into their groins and armpits and along their legs and arms.

"Stinks like a pack of *benhunjaran*," Supaari growled, his face twisted with distaste as Djalao rubbed the grease into his fur. Watching Sofia dip a tiny hand into the jar, he explained, "Even if a Jana'ata patrol catches the scent during redlight, they'll move upwind and as far away as possible the next morning." He studied the four Runa with ears cocked forward. "Someone wonders, how long have the people been getting away with this trick?"

Kanchay laughed his soft, huffing chuckle, and looked at Sofia. She smiled back, wishing she had a tail to drop as she said, "The *djanada* are like ghosts. They can be fooled." Supaari grunted, refusing to be baited.

They waited, the adults' silence underscored by Ha'anala's purring and Isaac's monotone mutter, until Supaari declared himself blind as dirt, which meant that any other Jana'ata would be equally sightless. Then they moved out, the Jana'ata stumbling and self-conscious, but gamely allowing himself to be guided toward the forest edge, his nose and ears working constantly to pull in as much information as he could from scent and sound.

They had planned for stealth: they would move unseen in redlight, their true scents undetectable beneath the stench of Djalao's ointment. They had forgotten about the vast incendiary sky of Rakhat's smallest sun. But as the little party stepped away from the familiar blue-green canopy of the forest, Isaac Mendes Quinn saw not the heavens but the vault of a red hell.

BRILLIANT STREAMERS OF VIOLENT, CRIMSON CLOUD, ABOUT TO fall on him—a whole huge landscape, bloody red and purple, about to crush him—the plain's panorama just beyond his hands—small, inadequate shields thrown up to parry the impact. He screamed once and then screamed again, and then screamed and screamed, as the woods exploded with wings and raucous calls and the crash of vegetation giving way to fleeing wildlife. Arms tried to eat him alive! Noise everywhere—Ha'anala howling, the Runa keening, Supaari, frantic, shouting over and over, "What has happened? What is it?" Red—the ground, the air, behind his hands, behind his eyes, squeezed shut—

It was his mother's voice that found him under the monstrous sky. Somehow in the chaos, he heard the low, grainy notes of the Sh'ma: soft, soft in his ear, soft, over and over, not insistent but consistent. Not the meaningless babble of words but the ordered, predictable, sacred haven of music: safety to move toward, a way out of the wilderness.

He could not get there for a long time but, as he exhausted himself, the screaming slowed and quieted to long, sucking sobs. At last, kneeling on the damp ground with his arms wrapped around his head, his narrow little hips thrust in the air, Isaac rocked in rhythm to his mother's voice, and found his way to the music: to salvation.

He slept then, limp, and did not know that the adults would not sleep for hours, their plans in ruins.

"ALL RIGHT," SOFIA SAID WEARILY, WHEN SUPAARI WOKE AT DAWN. "WE are going to leave the children here for now. You and Sichu-Lan and Tin-bar can stay with them. Kanchay, Djalao and I will go on alone to the lander. I've checked the fuel levels and I can make a flight back here to collect you and the children and the trade goods without risking the return to the mother ship. We can carry Isaac into the plane while he's asleep. By the time he wakes up, we'll be on board the *Magellan*. Do you understand?"

"I'm coming with you."

"Oh, God, Supaari, we argued all night. It's been decided—"

"I'm coming with you," he insisted.

Already the male Runa were swaying. Sofia glanced at Djalao, who was visibly tired but as determined as Sofia to keep the men from falling apart. "*Sipaj*, Supaari. You are a hazard," Sofia told him firmly. "You will slow us down—"

"We will travel in full daylight. We can make the journey in half the time that way, and we won't have to do it reeking of *benhunjaran*—"

"*Sipaj*, Supaari, are you mad?" She turned to Djalao, silently pleading for help. "If a patrol sees us—"

"There is a bounty for me and for any foreigner," Supaari reminded her in English. He turned to Djalao. "Someone thinks these Runa are delivering outlaws to the authorities."

"And when such a patrol finds us-and-you-also? They will take custody," Djalao said, her bloodshot eyes calm.

"Then we-and-you-also will kill them in their sleep."

"Supaari!" Sofia gasped, but Djalao said, "So be it," without waiting for the others to express an opinion. "We'll rest until second sunrise. Then we'll go."

THE PLAINS WERE EMPTY, AND FOR A TIME IT APPEARED THAT THE worry and precautions were unjustified. For two days, they seemed to be the highest things on the horizon. No one challenged or greeted them, and Supaari should have been reassured, but he wasn't. There's something wrong with the sky, he thought, lowering his backbasket and sitting on the ground while the Runa foraged. The light was subtly dimmed in a way he couldn't define. A volcano? he wondered.

"Supaari?"

He turned and saw Sofia, who was gnawing on a *betrin* root. She looked so brown! Was there something wrong with his eyes or had she changed color? Unsure of his own perceptions, Supaari gestured toward the sky. "Does that look right to you?" he asked.

She frowned. "It does look . . . odd somehow. The suns are out, but it seems a little dark," she said. Almost five years in a forest, she thought, remembering sunlight shattered by shifting leaves. "I'm not sure I remember what the sky is supposed to look like!"

"*Sipaj*, Djalao," Supaari called softly. She straightened from the *melfruit* bush she was stripping. "There's something wrong with the sky."

Sofia snorted. "You sound like Isaac," she told Supaari as Djalao walked over, but sobered when she saw the Runao's face.

"The color is wrong," Djalao agreed uneasily.

Supaari stood and faced into the wind, clearing his lungs through his mouth, then inhaled a long breath through his nostrils; the breeze was too stiff for a coherent plume, but he hoped at least to snatch a hint from the air. Djalao watched him intently. "No sulfur," he told her. "Not a volcano."

"This is trouble," Djalao whispered, not wanting to alarm Kanchay, who was ambling over with an armload of *trijat* leaf.

Sofia asked, "What's wrong?"

"Nothing," said Djalao, glancing significantly at Kanchay, who'd had enough to cope with the past few days.

But Supaari told Sofia quietly, "We'll know in the morning."

IN THE STILL AIR, LIT BY THE LOW LIGHT OF FIRST DAWN, THE PALL OF smoke became visible, its multiple columns rising and coalescing in the sky like the stems of a *hampiy* tree rising to meet in its crown. That day, as they moved downwind of the closest villages, even Sofia could detect the smell of char, which penetrated the stench of *benhunjaran* ointment lingering in their hair.

"Kashan will be all right," Kanchay said over and over, as they walked. "The *djanada* burned our garden a long time ago." And the VaKashani had been compliant and virtuous by Jana'ata standards ever since.

But he was alone in his hope, and as they approached the wreckage of the *Magellan's* lander, the bodies became visible in the distance: some butchered, some scavenged, most twisted and blackened by fire.

Sofia left the VaRakhati staring across the plain toward the corpses, and climbed into the remains of the *Magellan* lander emptied by vandals. Someone's crying, she thought, and wondered Who, as the sound of sobbing reverberated hollowly against the hull. She paid no attention— hardly heard it, really. Things could be worse, she thought, wiping her face and picking through the wreckage. She found odds and ends of useful technology, the best of which was a spare computer tablet stowed in a locker that had been overlooked in the pillaging. Careful not to cut herself on the jagged metal where the cargo-bay door had been forced open, she reemerged into the smoky sunlight and joined the others. Sitting cross-legged on the ground, she flipped the new tablet open and accessed the *Magellan's* system, concentrating on finding the past week's meteorological imaging logs.

"They must have hit every village that ever had a garden," she told Supaari without emotion, recognizing the diffusion pathways that Anne Edwards had identified years earlier.

"But there are no more gardens," Kanchay said plaintively, looking back toward his vanished village. "We never planted food again."

"Every place we foreigners and you touched," Sofia said, looking up at Supaari. "Gone."

"All my villages," he whispered. "Kashan, Lanjeri, Rialner. All those people . . ."

"Who can wear so many ribbons?" Kanchay asked, dazed. "Why would they do this? What gives them the right?"

"The new Paramount's legitimacy is in question," Djalao explained, her voice as empty as Sofia's. "The lords say he is not suitable for his office. He must be seen to restore balance, to remove all foreign and criminal influence from his territories."

"But he said the south was restored to order!" Kanchay cried. "The radio reports all said—" Kanchay turned and looked at Sofia and Djalao. "What gives them the right?" he asked, and when no one responded, Kanchay took three long steps toward Supaari, and shoved the Jana'ata hard. "What gives you the right?" he demanded.

"Kanchay!" Sofia cried, startled out of her own numbness.

"What gives you the right?" Kanchay shouted, but before the Jana'ata could stammer an answer, the Runao's anger erupted like molten rock and he was roaring now—"What gives you the right?"—over and over, each word punctuated with a blow and a burst of blood from the face of a man who staggered back but did nothing to counter the attack.

Her face white with terror, Sofia scrambled up and threw her arms around Kanchay. He flung her off like a rag doll, not even pausing in his assault. "Kanchay!" Sofia screamed, astonished, and tried again to push between the two men, only to be knocked away once more. "Djalao!" she shouted from the ground, her own face spattered with gore. "Do something! He's going to kill Supaari!"

For an eternity, Djalao stood gaping, too stunned to move. Then finally, she dragged Kanchay off the bleeding Jana'ata.

Shocked senseless, all of them stood or knelt or lay where they were, until the sound of Kanchay's gasping grief subsided. It was only then that Supaari got to his feet, and spat blood, and wiped his mouth with the back of his hand. He wheeled slowly, looking all around him, as though searching for something he would never find again; leaned back against his tail, winded and lost.

Then, without a word, he walked away from the ruins of Kashan, empty-handed and empty-souled.

THE OTHERS FOLLOWED. HE DIDN'T CARE. HE DID NOT EAT; COULD NOT, in truth. Regret sickened him as much as the cloying smoke of burnt meat that remained in his fur despite two drenching rains on the journey back to the forest. Not even the scent of his infant daughter could drive off the stink of death; when they were reunited at the woodland's edge, he refused to hold Ha'anala. He did not want to contaminate his child with what her people—what his people—

What *he* had done.

When at last they arrived at Trucha Sai, he was too far gone in guilt to hear what anyone said. He sat at the edge of the clearing, allowing no one to touch him, not even to scrub the stink from his coat. What gives us the right? he asked himself when the sky's darkness matched his heart's. What gives us the right?

He did not sleep that first night back among the Runa; when dawn lightened the sky enough for him to see, he left before they roused. No Runao could track him, and he believed that death would find him in the forest if he simply waited long enough. For uncounted days in a black absence of thought, he wandered aimlessly while it was light, lay down wherever he was when fatigue and hunger overcame him. On that last night, with his gut cramped against its hollowness, he sank blindly to the ground near a recently abandoned *tinper* nest. It was crawling with vicious little *khimali* and, while he slept, they burrowed through his fur and fastened onto his skin, making a meal of his blood. He awoke once in the middle of the night to physical misery, bleeding from thousands of small wounds, but did not move or try to pick the parasites from his body.

Close now, he thought with vague relief. He did not so much fall asleep as lose consciousness. It rained that night. He didn't hear the thunder.

It was full morning when the bright golden glare of the middle sun found his face through a small space in the shifting leaves. Sodden, curled on the forest floor, he opened his eyes without lifting his head and dully watched the *khimali* at close range as they trundled through the miniature forest of fine fur that covered his wrist.

They don't take enough to kill their host, Supaari thought, sorry to have lived through the night, and disgusted by the jointed carapaces, the scuttling gait of the bloated little beasts. They suck blood and give back nothing. That is the way of parasites. They . . .

He sat up, and blinked—

He was dizzy and near starvation, but his mind felt at that moment perfectly translucent. The sensation, he would tell Sofia later, was not serenity—although he knew even then that serenity would be his reward, when his part in the plan was fulfilled. What he felt was joy. It seemed to him that perfection was revealed all around him, that he and the forest and the *khimali* were all one thing, all part of a strange brilliance. Sunlight shafted the small clearing, and this too seemed a revelation. His own confusion and wretchedness had parted, like clouds, and allowed this . . . illumination to penetrate. He could envision everything before him: the steps he would take, the path he would travel, the end. He had only to see it through.

Everything was clear to him now.

This joy lasted only a little while, but he knew he would never be the same. When it passed, he staggered to his feet, unaware of his own light-headedness. A strong odor caught his attention; something had died that morning somewhere in the understory. Without thinking, he crouched and spun slowly, tail sweeping low through the vegetation, arms flung outward for balance, sampling the air until he located the source of the scent: a good-sized bush *wa'ile*, wasted with age. Supaari ate it raw, ripping its belly open with his teeth and claws. Better a scavenger, he thought, than a parasite.

He knew, even then, that he would eat Runa again. The difference was that he meant now to transform their sacrifice. He would return it to them: life for life.

"SIPAJ, SUPAARI!" THE RUNA CRIED WHEN THEY FIRST SAW HIM STANDing at the edge of the settlement. "We thought you were gone!"

"Keep distance—someone must stay apart," he said, and he held out his arms to display the sores in his armpits, the blotched red stains that spoiled his coat.

Sofia approached despite his warning and said, "Someone will groom you. Someone is so—"

"Stay back," he said. Her offer touched him to his heart, but he could not permit this, not yet. Looking past Sofia toward the Runa, he gazed at the village, neat, well cared for and well run; gazed at the Runa themselves, who had lived in Trucha Sai for years without Jana'ata interference or exploitation. "What causes these sores?" he asked them loudly. There was a mutter of response and a tendril of their anxiety began to reach him. He was worrying them and he regretted that. But it was necessary—this confusion before clarity. "What causes them?" he asked again.

"*Khimali*," Djalao said shortly, coming forward, standing next to Sofia. She wanted to stop this odd behavior, he knew. Wanted to draw Supaari away to a place where she could pick through his coat, wanted to crush the revolting little creatures between her fingers and be done with this. "They are dangerous," she snapped. "They're making you sick. Please, allow this one—"

But Supaari called, "And what are *khimali?*"

"Parasites!" Djalao answered, exasperated, staring at him now. "*Sipaj,* Supaari, why do you—?"

"And what are parasites," he asked, still looking past her to the others, "but those who take their sustenance without benefit to the host? Those who draw their lives from the lives of others and give nothing back?" Most of the Runa looked around uncertainly, shifting from foot to foot. But Djalao straightened, and met his eyes. She knows, he thought. She understands.

"And what," he asked her softly, "must we do to rid ourselves of parasites?"

"Kill them," she said as softly and as certainly. "Kill them, one by one— until they trouble us no longer."

23

Giordano Bruno

2064, Earth-Relative

"JOHN, I'M SORRY, BUT I DON'T SEE A LOT OF ALTERNATIVES HERE," Emilio Sandoz remarked mildly. "What are you suggesting? Mutiny on the *Bruno?*"

"Don't patronize me, Emilio! I'm serious—"

"No, I'm not certain that you *are* serious," Emilio said, pouring reconstituted scrambled eggs into a pan. Quell seemed to improve his appetite, and he'd awakened at five in the morning, ship's time, ravenous. When he went to the galley to fix himself something to eat, John Candotti had been lying in wait, all cranked up with plans to take over the ship and go home. "You want some of this? I could make enough for two."

"No! Listen to me! The longer we wait, the farther we are from home—"

"So what are you going to do? Cut Carlo's throat while he's asleep?"

"No!" John whispered urgently. "But we could lock him in his cabin—"

"Oh, please!" Emilio sighed, rolling his eyes as he stirred his eggs. "Get me some juice, will you?"

"Emilio, he's only one man! There are seven of us—"

"Have you talked to any of the others about this, Mistah Christian?" he asked, relying on Charles Laughton to make his attitude clear.

John flushed at the mockery. He opened a storage cabinet and got out a mug for the juice, but went on resolutely. "I came to you first, but I'm sure—"

"Don't be," Emilio said flatly. Without the distracting noise of emotion, political realities were obvious, and he understood why rioting prisoners would give up a losing battle when Quell was fired like tear gas into a lockup. "The count is seven to one, but you're the one, John."

Dumping the eggs onto a plate, Sandoz carried it to the table and sat with his back to the galley. John followed him, lips compressed, plunking the mug of orange juice down belligerently and sitting across the table from him. Emilio ate under his friend's withering glare for a time before pushing his plate aside.

"Look. John. Face facts," he advised finally. "No matter what you think of him or his motives, Danny Iron Horse has already staked his soul on this mission, yes?" He stared, level-eyed, until John nodded reluctantly. "Joseba has his own reasons for wanting to go on to Rakhat, regardless of anyone else's. Sean—I don't understand Sean, but he seems to think that cynicism about human nature is an adequate response to sin. He won't take a stand."

John's eyes hadn't dropped, but it was beginning to sink in. "As for Nico," Emilio said, "don't underestimate him. He is not as dim as he looks, and he has been thoroughly inculcated with the notion of loyalty to his padrone. Attack Carlo, and you will have Nico to deal with, and I warn you: he is very good at his job." Emilio shrugged. "But let's say Sean stood out of this, and you could co-opt Danny and Joseba, and overcome Carlo and Nico somehow. You'd still need Fat Frans to pilot the ship back to Earth—"

"Right, and Frans is a shameless mercenary! So we buy him off! And anyway, he thinks Carlo is crazy—"

"Frans has a wonderful gift for colorful exaggeration." Emilio sat up and rested his arms on the table. "John, Carlo is cold and unscrupulous and completely selfish, but he is a long way from crazy. Even if he were barking mad, I wouldn't count on Frans's cooperation with your plan, such as it is." John bristled, but Emilio continued, "The Camorra has a long reach and a longer memory. Frans would be running a great risk to buck Carlo—"

"An excellent analysis, Sandoz!" cried Carlo as he walked into the room. "Positively Machiavellian. Really, Candotti," Carlo said dryly when John jumped at the sound of his voice, "secrecy is the first principle of conspiracy! The commons room is hardly the place for this sort of thing." He turned his merry gray eyes from John's now roseate face to Sandoz's, lined and still. "And you, Sandoz? Have you no wish to return to Gina and my daughter?"

"What I wish is irrelevant. The fact is, I was a part of their lives for only a few months." John gasped, and Emilio turned to him. "Years are passing at home, John. Even if we were to come about and return now, I could hardly expect to drop back in on them as though I'd been away on a business trip."

John looked stricken, but Carlo beamed. "I may assume then that you have reached a decision regarding my proposals—"

They would remember later that the impact sounded like a rifle shot.

There was a single unresonant bang, followed by an instant of utter silence in total darkness, and then the shouts and cries throughout the ship of men tumbling blindly when the engines cut out and they lost the gravity provided by acceleration.

The emergency lighting came on almost immediately, but with restored vision came the screaming of klaxons signaling a hull breach and then the high-pitched whine of compartment doors rolling shut and locking themselves down, endeavoring with mechanical efficiency to isolate regions of atmospheric pressure loss. A moment later, the spin imparted by the collision took over and every loose object in the ship was now flung away from the ship's center of mass. John was thrown into the table's edge, the breath driven from his lungs. Emilio, knocked sideways when the ship lurched, was now pinned against a bulkhead, the outline of an air intake square against his back. Ears ringing from the blow when his head hit the wall, he watched the Wolverton tube with wide-eyed fascination, as plants and soilmix ripped loose and whirled, propelled by a tornado within the transparent cylinder that had been a vertical garden moments before.

"That's the axis . . . in the tube!" Carlo yelled. He was spread-eagled, back against the bulkhead opposite Sandoz. The sensation was like that of an amusement park ride that had thrilled him when he was a child—a large padded cylinder that spun faster and faster until centrifugal force held people against the walls and the floor dropped out from under them. It was hard to breathe against a force that wanted to flatten him, so he kept his phrases short but calm. "Sandoz, there is a . . . red control button . . . to your left—. Yes. Be so kind . . . as to press that, please?"

Carlo tensed in sympathy while Sandoz struggled to inch a leg toward its target, and tried to move his own leg, just to see what it was like: very difficult indeed, with these G forces. There wasn't enough strength in Sandoz's ankle alone; working with his whole body, he arched away from the wall to bring the edge of his foot down on the button. The klaxon was silenced. "Well done," Carlo said, with an involuntary sigh of relief echoed by Candotti.

But now they could hear more ominous sounds: the creaking of the ship's stony substance, the sound of water gushing from some pipe, the cyclonic hissing whistle of escaping air and the moan of stressed metal, like the mournful song of humpback whales.

"Intercom: all transceivers on," Carlo said, in a normal tone of voice, activating the ship's internal communications system. One by one, he called the names of the men he could not see. One by one, Frans, Nico, Sean, Joseba and Danny reported in. Above and below the center deck, the spin had pinned each man to an unaccustomed surface, and they were now sealed in their cabins by AI emergency programs that turned each compartment of the ship into a lifepod.

"This is like . . . our drills," Nico's voice gasped cheerfully. "We're . . . going to be fine."

Face pulled toward the tabletop, John's eyes bulged sightlessly at that sanguine pronouncement, but from somewhere in the ship came Frans's voice, crying, *"Brav' scugnizz', Nico!"*

Carlo, too, continued to sound serene. "Gentlemen," he called, knowing he could be heard throughout the ship, "I believe . . . the *Giordano Bruno* must have struck a micrometeorite. Since . . . we have not been reduced to . . . mineral dust and a haze of organic . . . molecules, we may deduce that whatever we hit . . . was very small. But we are . . . moving very quickly, which accounts for . . . the result of that impact." He began to find his rhythm, his breathing easier now. "Ah! You see, Sandoz?" Carlo asked, gray eyes moving in his immobilized head, "the vacuum is sucking dirt from . . . the Wolverton tube . . . through the channel . . . drilled by the particle. It has now been clogged with plant debris . . . and sealed itself off."

The hissing stopped, and the tornado inside the transparent tube was suddenly replaced by an apparently solid mass of soilmix, flung with a thud against the walls of the cylinder, just as Sandoz and Carlo were themselves pinned against the outer walls of the common room.

Rolling his eyes wildly, John could just glimpse Carlo at the edge of his field of vision. "You mean . . . all that's between . . . us and space is . . . dirt?" John gasped frantically.

"That, and the . . . love o' God," came Sean Fein's strained voice over the intercom.

Carlo somehow managed to laugh delightedly. "If there is anyone among our passengers . . . who is so inclined, you might consider . . . praying to the soul of James . . . Lovell, patron saint of hard-luck spacefarers! He . . . was surely watching over us this morning, my friends. Listen!" he ordered, hearing the photonics systems powering on and resetting themselves. "Get ready to fall. If all goes well, the inertial guidance system will . . . begin firing the attitude rockets soon—"

There were short, heartfelt prayers and curses—both consisting entirely of the name of Jesus—and more cries of fear, startlement and pain as the AI guidance system began firing its jets, which automatically registered their own effects on the stability of the ship and readjusted the *Bruno*'s pitch and roll and yaw with brief thrusts. In the commons, globules of orange juice formed up in momentary spells of weightlessness, and the carnival ride gave way to a nauseating kaleidoscope of scrambled eggs and dust, with Emilio's fork spinning crazily near a floating plate. In the cabins, anything left loose—computer tablets, razors, socks, bedding, rosaries—danced with men's bodies to the erratic forces of the ship's motion, which changed instant by instant. Everywhere, boluses of spit and vomit and tears—briefly held together by surface tension—were now added to the mess, shattering as they splashed against surfaces or collided with some other object or were struck by the frantic movement of a man's arms and legs seeking purchase.

Within endless minutes, the spin stabilized and they were pulled back toward the ship's periphery but now with far less force. "Do you feel that, Don Gianni?" Nico called, apparently concerned by the fear he'd heard in John Candotti's voice. "Feel it? It's starting to slow down—"

"All right," Carlo said, cool as ever, "start moving toward the floor as the centrifugal force decreases."

"Do you understand, Don Gianni?" Nico asked helpfully, without a trace of irony. "The ship is going to let us go now."

"When the engines fire," Carlo warned, "we're going to have full power—"

Which meant full, normal gravity. Floors abruptly reestablished their claim on Down, and anyone who had not made it to the bottom of his wall while the guidance system slowed and stopped the spin acquired a few more bruises for his tardiness.

"Well!" Carlo cried cheerfully, picking himself up with the almost magical self-satisfaction that handsome Italian males acquire in middle age. "That went about as well as could be expected. Will everyone please report to the commons?"

AGAINST ODDS, THE MEN OF THE *GIORDANO BRUNO* WERE ALL CAPABLE of staggering out of their compartments when the emergency lockdown was released, and presented themselves one by one, naked or in undershorts. Frans, amply padded and phlegmatic, had come through without injury, and Nico's inability to imagine how much danger they'd just been in had served him well. Joseba was silent and breathing hard, but otherwise intact. Sean was visibly shaken, but Danny Iron Horse was focused and alert. Carlo himself knew exactly where each Newtonian law of motion had been demonstrated on his body, but was fully functional. John, too, insisted he was okay and was already at work; having located a galley water pipe that had burst under torsion, he had cut off the main valve and was going through the plumbing supplies with Nico, looking for what he needed to fix it. Sandoz was calm, of course, saying only, "One of my braces is damaged. It looks repairable."

Apart from cuts and bruises, there were no injuries, perhaps because most of them had been in bed. Allowing no time for anyone to give way to post-traumatic panic, Carlo handed out assignments with a brisk, businesslike dispatch. "I want everyone in pressure suits until we are certain the ship is stabilized. Nico, after you have your suit on, you'll be cleaning up for us. Start in the galley. Make a list of what needs to be repaired for Don Gianni. Sean, help Sandoz get into his suit, then put on your own—"

"My hands are useless in a suit," Sandoz objected. "I can't . . ."

"Just until we're certain we've got the ship stabilized," Carlo said. Sandoz shrugged: resigned or indifferent. "Frans, as soon as you're ready, take Sandoz with you to the bridge. Sandoz, you'll be helping with a complete review of the photonics—check the ship's status, system by system. That can be done with voice control, and as soon as the emergency passes, we can dispense with the pressure suits. Candotti," he called, "leave the swabbing for Nico—check out the plumbing on the other levels. There may be damage elsewhere and we don't need anything shorting out. Sean! Wake up! Help Sandoz into his pressure suit."

When the others had gone, Carlo spoke to Joseba and Danny. "After the ship is sound, the priority will be to reactivate the biological air and waste systems." It was only then that Joseba and Danny looked at the Wolverton tube in the center of the commons and stared, horrified, at the battered and torn plants that had been ripped from their moorings. "This is not fatal, gentlemen," Carlo insisted. "We can maintain air quality with scrubbers and we have backup oxygen generators, but I don't like to lose redundancy in any system, so we need to salvage as many plants as we can—that's your job," he told Joseba. "Even if they're all dead, we're carrying seeds on board, and we can reestablish the tube in a couple of months. When Sean is capable, put him to work on the fish tanks, Joseba. They're sealed, but have him check for leaks and cracks. I imagine the tilapia survived the ride, but the tanks and filters themselves will need to be checked over and thoroughly cleaned at the very least."

Joseba stood there dumbly for a moment, but finally moved off toward his cabin to suit up, and to make sure Sean and Sandoz were doing the same.

"Hail, Caesar!" Danny Iron Horse said to Carlo when they were alone. "Very cool, ace."

One hand raised, palm inward, the other laid gracefully upon his chest, Carlo struck a pose implying an invisible toga. "I am not cold, unscrupulous and selfish," he declared, brows raised imperiously. "I am a philosopher-king, and the embodiment of Stoic detachment!"

"In a pig's eye," Danny said affably. "You Giulianis are stone-hearted bastards to a man."

"So my father tells me," Carlo said, unruffled. "My mother denied everything and demanded DNA tests. Suit up. You're coming with me. We need to check out the hull and see how bad the damage to the landers is. I think we'll all sleep better if we seal those pinholes with something a bit more reliable than clumps of dirt."

"Duct tape?" Danny suggested as they walked toward the spiral stairs that led to their cabins below. Carlo laughed, but before he could go through the hatch, Iron Horse put out an imposing arm, blocking his way.

"Just how close was that?" Danny asked curiously, black eyes steady.

"I won't know for certain until I inspect the hull," Carlo said, but Danny wouldn't let him pass so Carlo took a step back and stood quietly, hands behind his beautiful back, classical head cocked, gray eyes speculative. His contemporaries found him surprisingly fastidious: Carlo Giuliani rarely used vulgarities unless the situation genuinely seemed to demand them. "So fucking close," he said very gently and very distinctly, "that the only reason we can possibly be alive is that the Pope and Don Vincenzo were right—God wants Sandoz on Rakhat."

They looked at each other for a long time. Dropping his arm, Danny nodded and started down the stairs.

ENCASED IN PRESSURE SUITS FIFTEEN MINUTES LATER, DANNY AND Carlo met again in the passageway beyond their cabins and moved from room to room, surveying the damage. Carlo's orders to keep every loose item stowed and secure had been fairly well complied with, even in private spaces, and this had undoubtedly decreased the severity of the injuries sustained. Mostly they saw a jumbled mess but ignored that, pushing bedding and clothing aside to inspect the walls, floors and ceilings of each room.

The surfaces were coated with a stress-crackle polymer on which the effects of twisting were evident. It was most severe on the outer walls, but research and experience had shown that in-line collisions were the only survivable scenario, so Carlo had chosen an asteroid and configured it with that in mind. Cracks in the outer shell were still a possibility—it would take sonar soundings to discover those. But the life-supporting central cylinder of the *Bruno*, it seemed, was in no immediate danger of splitting apart.

Passing through the commons on the way to the lander bay, Carlo noted that Nico was already done with the galley. Food and equipment had been kept tightly packed and locked in storage bins. Nothing but Sandoz's frying pan had been left out. Satisfied, Carlo stopped at the bridge, where Frans and Sandoz were already running diagnostics.

"Where's your suit, Frans?" Carlo said. His voice through the throat mike was thin and uninflected; even so, it was clear that there had better be good reason for insubordination.

"I'm a growing boy. It doesn't fit anymore," Frans said shortly. He grinned then at Danny Iron Horse, impassive behind his suit's face shield. "Pray that we don't suck any serious vacuum, Chief. If I explode, you'll be scrubbing fat out of the instrumentation for the rest of the trip."

"Or resting in the bosom of Jesus," Danny said dryly.

"What have you found so far?" Carlo asked Frans.

"We're blind in one eye," Frans informed him, serious again. "When you go forward, look near the starboard sensor panel."

Lucky, Carlo thought. Very lucky indeed. But he said, "All right. Iron Horse: go check on Sean and Joseba—see how the biologicals came through. Then take a look at the landers yourself. I'm going forward to see what the hull looks like. Frans: monitor me."

"THE CHIEF SOURCE OF ALL EVILS TO MAN," WROTE THE STOIC EPICTETUS, "as well as of baseness and cowardice, is not death but fear of death."

Carlo Giuliani had read those words at the age of thirteen, a week after one of the many funerals he attended as a child. A cousin had been blown to bits by a car bomb; there was nothing much to put in the coffin, but two hundred vehicles had followed the nearly empty box as the cortege wound its way through Naples. Carlo had not personally witnessed that particular demise, but he had been spattered with blood and gobbets of brain at the age of seven—an uncle that time—and so had contemplated mortality from an early age.

Another boy might have gone into the priesthood; certainly, there was ample precedent for that in the family—there was even a fourteenth-century stigmatic surnamed Giuliani. But there were far too many martyrs in Christian hagiography to suit Carlo. With an adolescent's romantic sense of self-importance, he focused not on Jesus Christ but on Marcus Aurelius. It took the greatest of the caesars, a hero of monumental self-control and fearlessness, to shore up the fragile courage of a boy who would be fair game soon, should a rival *famiglia* need to target a low-risk victim for a revenge execution.

Aurelius proved a difficult role model. Carlo strove for a Stoic's rationality and courage, only to be dragged down into the strange Neapolitan mire of pre-Christian superstition and rococo Catholicism. He had grown up both cosseted and reviled, outrageously overindulged and viciously undermined. He remained in some ways his mother's disastrously spoiled son, enraged by the slightest opposition; like his father, he could be all but blind to the desires of others, except insofar as they meshed with his own. Nevertheless, he knew these characteristics to be flaws and fought them. "The noblest kind of retribution," wrote Marcus Aurelius, "is not to become like your enemy."

"I have learned from my predecessors' mistakes," Carlo had told Emilio Sandoz. This was no idle boast but the touchstone of his life, and the *Giordano Bruno* was proof that his struggles had not been without consequence. The ship was configured within a large, solid, unusually symmetrical rock—virgin mineral, with no prior mining to weaken its structure. Its interior cylinder was carefully assayed, sounded, and drilled out by mining robots. Top-of-the-line crew quarters were sealed into the center, well shielded from cosmic radiation. The entire outer surface of the asteroid was pressure-treated with resilient self-healing foam. All photonics, life-support and guidance systems were triply redundant, controlled by exhaustively tested artificial intelligences programmed to respond to any unscheduled interruption of function with automatic power-on sequences and stabilization procedures, even if the crew was incapacitated.

It had cost a fortune. Carlo had made his arguments to his father in commercial terms and his sister Carmella had backed him up, of course—the project would remove him as a potential rival while the bitch consolidated power. But, as his sister pointed out, money spent up front to increase the chances of a successful voyage would pay a satisfying return on a long-term financial investment. That this might also result in the return of Domenico Giuliani's son was, that estranged son suspected, an acceptable risk, given that Domenico would not be around to deal with it personally.

Rot in hell, old man, Carlo thought, his own breathing loud in his ears as he climbed through the central access core of the ship to find out precisely how close he had come to joining his father there, two hours earlier.

There was a fine coating of black dust everywhere inside the ship's forward utility bay, where the remote sensing equipment was housed. Following the fanlike spray of dirt to its origin in the floor, he brushed at a miniature Vesuvius with a booted foot and then bent to clear the rest of the fine dust with his glove. He found a hole. Straightening, he stepped back and looked now to the ceiling, which was the ship's bow when it was under power, and found the entry wound, also plugged with sieved soilmix sucked into the breach by the vacuum of space and held there by friction. He knew without looking that there would be identical exit holes at the other end of the ship.

Trusting in physics for the time being, he left the plug alone and mentally charted the collision. A particle of matter—a speck of iron perhaps—got in their way and drilled a narrow column from bow to stern . . .

It was not a good moment. If the drill hole had been a bit more off-center, the spin would have been more violent and the ship would have gone to pieces; even if it held together, its passengers might have been pulped. If the micrometeorite had been much larger, the ship would have been destroyed. If the collision had occurred at their maximum velocity, an impact like this would have vaporized them before they knew anything had happened, and the *Giordano Bruno* would have joined the list of ships mysteriously lost en route to Rakhat.

He almost giggled, giddy at last, when he heard himself thinking, A novena for the Virgin when I get home. . . . No—a whole church, filled with treasures from Rakhat! Rationality, he was finding, took a poor second to religion after a morning like this.

He roused himself, and looked at the sensor box just to starboard of the drill hole. Careful not to disturb the dirt that stood between him and the void, Carlo pulled the box out of its housing and gently shook out a diaphanous shower of fine particles—it was fouled by soilmix. There were two more sensor packs stored below. He would replace this box, but decided to put Candotti to work reconditioning the one in his hands.

We may yet need this one as a backup, Carlo thought. "The safest course," Seneca taught, "is to tempt fortune rarely." Which probably ruled out relying on miracles more than once a week.

24

Trucha Sai

2047–2061, Earth-Relative

FOR YEARS AFTER SHE WAS MAROONED THE SECOND TIME, SOFIA MENDES dreamed of home. She hated this, and ended her transmissions to Earth, believing that to sever this last tie would end the dreams, but they continued.

Most often, she was in an airport, waiting for her flight's departure to be announced, or in some train terminal; in these dreams, she believed that Jimmy was waiting for her somewhere. Sometimes she would be walking on a once-familiar city street in Tokyo or Warsaw. More often, she was in some chimerical dream-place that merely stood for Earth. She was nearly always alone in her dreams but, once, she was sitting in a coffee shop, listening to conversations around her, when Sandoz walked in—late, as usual. "Where were we?" he asked, and sat across from her in the booth. "We were in love," she answered, and startled herself awake by saying in dream what had never been spoken in daylight.

She lay in the rustling, dripping noise of the forest that night, eyes open, sorting out the shards of reality from which this was constructed. The coffee shop was in Cleveland, of course. How long ago had she first met Sandoz there? she asked herself. Then, with more urgency, she wondered, How old am I? Nearly fifty, she realized with a jolt. Seventeen years here, she thought. Longer than I lived in Istanbul. Longer than I've lived anywhere.

"*Sipaj*, Fia," Supaari's daughter, Ha'anala, had asked her once, "are you not sad that your people left you here alone?"

"Everything happens for a reason," Sofia told the girl. "The Runa are my people now, and your people as well."

She said this with fierce, unfeigned conviction, for she had long since sunk her private, paltry sadness to the bottom of a pure and selfless outrage at the Runa's bondage. She had discovered the purpose for her life on Rakhat. She had come here to teach a single word to the VaRakhati: justice.

All over Rakhat's largest continent, inarticulate resentment had been given voice by Supaari VaGayjur and Djalao VaKashan and their followers. The ordinary weapons of the powerless—the specious compliance and counterfeit ignorance, the pilfering and petty obstructions, the foot-dragging and pretense of vacuous misunderstanding—all these were laid aside in favor of an astonishing and exhilarating strength. Like sleepers awakening from a dream of impotence, the Runa awoke to their own power and unleashed a force whose potential was previously understood only by the Jana'ata, who had rightly feared it.

After the first convulsion of revolt, after Gayjur and Agardi were liberated, fear and suspicion did a great deal of the work for them. A Jana'ata patriarch would wake in the morning to find his household deserted by its Runa staff, and a knife lying on the sleeping nest next to his throat. If he had any sense at all, he'd take his family and flee north. Oh, there was resistance. There were forays and challenges, even in the beginning. But knowledge is power, and with Sofia Mendes's help, the Runa had become very knowledgeable indeed.

She had provided schematics of advanced communications and data-processing equipment, and, more important, Sofia provided the awareness that such things could be manufactured: given the seed of an idea, the Runa were capable of elaborating on it quickly and creatively. Radio equipment, made by Runa hands, had once served Jana'ata governments; now it was modified to make use of the orbiting satellites put in place by the crew of the *Stella Maris*, allowing the entire army to communicate instantly. After a time, all young officers learned English—as unbreakable a code as Navajo had been in Earth's second global war.

With the *Magellan*'s remote sensing and imaging capabilities, Sofia herself could survey the continent for nearly forty degrees of latitude on either side of the equator—only the southern ocean and land north of the Garnu mountains remained out of range. Hidden in Trucha Sai, she provided weather reports and river transport times; tracked the small, mobile detachments of Jana'ata troopers, who could be picked off when they entered terrain that suited Runa women, unhampered by any tradition of formal combat. As the Jana'ata pulled back on three fronts to more defensible territory, Sofia could locate the new enclosures where domestic and draft Runa were herded together. These could be targeted and stormed in redlight, at a stroke freeing captives and starving the *djanada* out, driving them further north.

"But do you not wish for others of your kind?" Ha'anala asked.

"I have you and your father. I have Isaac and the Runa," Sofia told her. "I have what I need."

"Truly, mother?"

"Truly!" Sofia cried. "I am grateful for what I have, Ha'anala."

She might also have said, Wishing for more is asking for disappointment. But Sofia Mendes had banished such thoughts long ago.

AND THERE WERE COMPENSATIONS FOR HER SITUATION, SOFIA WOULD remind herself. On Earth, her son would have been a tragedy, but here in the forest, protected by the watchful gaze of a hundred fathers, all the children were safe, damaged or whole, quick or halt. No one was discarded as too broken or too odd. Imperfection was permitted in Trucha Sai, the only place on Rakhat where this was so. The Runa asked nothing of Isaac. They did not judge him and find him wanting, did not care when he learned to control his bowels or that he went naked.

And if Isaac was deaf to the emotions of others, he was alive to this habitat of things. There were vines to swing on, downed *w'ralia* limbs to scramble over and climb, to march along with his strange perfection of balance. There was mud to pat and throw, to ooze between fingers or toes. Water to fling, to fall backward onto, to float in. Huge river-polished rocks to scoot down, over and over and over, flapping his hands in private delight; a smooth wealth of riverbed stones to collect and lay out, row by row, in strict straight lines that Sofia realized with a start were grouped by prime numbers: 1, 3, 5, 7, 11, 13, on and on. Here in Trucha Sai, the trees whispered to Isaac, the brook bubbled for him. Rain washed him clean. Animals sometimes came to him because he could be so still, so long.

"*Sipaj*, Fia: when can we go to a city?" Ha'anala would ask. "Do people there all have five fingers, or do some have only three?"

"It's too dangerous for you in the cities," Sofia would tell her.

"The other girls go to the cities!"

"They're soldiers. You'll understand when you're older."

"That's what you said last time. Someone is older now! When will you explain?"

"*Sipaj*, Ha'anala, don't make a *fierno*. Listen to that thunder!"

"You said people can't really make the weather change!"

"And what does make the weather change?" Sofia asked, glad of the diversion.

IN THE MIDST OF WAR, SOFIA MENDES LEARNED THAT SHE MIGHT HAVE been a teacher, had her own childhood not taken such an ugly turn. Her clarity of mind and habit of organization, her ability to break any process down and present it to a novice step by step—all the skills that had once made her a superb AI analyst now served her many and disparate students.

The Runa children did best with the mnemonics that she created to help them remember the names of the suns and rivers and cities, chemical elements, multiplication tables. She let them teach her the botany their fathers taught by example and then, with the children, she created new taxonomies of use and of structure and of location, and watched with pleasure when they began to classify animals and sounds and words and stones, to make logical connections and find clever solutions to the problems they set themselves.

These Runa were noticeably quicker than the VaKashani children she had first known. In the beginning, she took credit as their teacher, but as time passed, she understood that their intelligence was due in part to the fact that they were all adequately fed—not kept on short rations by Jana'ata breeders who wished to control their reproductive status and their labor and their lives—

The *djanada* must have known, must have understood that this would stunt Runa minds as well, she realized. It was when such abominations were revealed to her that she would remember the poetry of the doomed Warsaw ghetto uprising: "The meat defiant, the meat insurgent, the meat fighting! The meat in full cry . . ." This time, she thought, the meat will triumph. We will loose the bonds of injustice and break every yoke, and let the oppressed go free! We are doing the right thing. We are.

And then, with renewed conviction, she would return to the task of teaching Runa children the lessons they would need to live well in the liberty their mothers fought for.

Even Isaac could be taught, she discovered. Or rather, he would learn if she was careful not to invade his world. She let the computer tablet carry her messages to him, across the secret barriers and invisible walls that shut him off from others; it was her surest way of reaching him aside from song. He liked the keyboard's ordered ranks, and when she first showed him how to use it, he was wild with joy at the way it made the letters and symbols march across the screen in perfect, infinite rectilinearity. The Runa would complain in kind, tactful ways when Isaac flapped his hands and shrieked his bliss at this parade of letters; she learned that if she sat at his side and snatched the tablet away from him at the moment the *fierno* began, he quickly quieted. Within days, he was able to control the disruptive behavior that he understood would rob him of his treasure.

Each night, Sofia would add some tiny element to her son's virtual world: sound that gave a letter's name when it appeared, over and over; then whole words, written and spoken, to match pictures. He taught himself to read that way, to her astonishment. It was, she thought, more like learning Chinese ideographs than like reading phonetically, but it worked for him somehow. Sofia showed him the file that displayed Marc Robichaux's detailed and beautiful drawings of Rakhati plants and animals, and for these she supplied names in Ruanja. She wept the day he appeared at her side with a real leaf to match one on the screen, but she did not embrace him. Love for Isaac had to be on his terms. On his own or by obliquely watching Sofia with Ha'anala, he learned to call up the *Magellan* library and find his bookmarked nodes. He learned where the music was kept and would take the tablet off to a quiet corner to listen. The rapt look that came over him then reminded Sofia forcefully of her own mother's face when she lost herself in a nocturne at the piano. When he listened, Isaac seemed not merely normal but transcendent, transfixed.

In this creeping, incremental way, she came to know that some of what she valued in herself and admired in Isaac's father had been passed on: intellect and a love of music. Isaac was, she realized, very bright, or would have been if—

No, she decided, he is bright, but in his own way: a truly alien intelligence.

"He is like an angel," Sofia had mused when Ha'anala was only seven. They clung together watching Isaac stand, long-boned and slender, at the edge of the river, oblivious to anything but the water. Or perhaps a rock in the water. Or perhaps simply oblivious. "An angel, pure and beautiful and remote."

"*Sipaj*, Fia," Ha'anala had asked. "What is an angel?"

Sofia came to herself. "A messenger. A messenger from God."

"What is Isaac's message?"

"He can't tell us," Sofia said, and turned away, dry-eyed.

EVENTUALLY THE TIME CAME FOR THE OLDEST OF THE TRUCHA SAI girls to leave. Sofia asked that the brightest of them be allowed to stay in the forest, to become teachers in other villages like Trucha Sai—filling with young Runa as the front lines expanded and fathers fell back to raise their children far from the *fierno* of war. The answer was almost always, "No. Boys can teach. It is the women's way to die for children."

Sofia understood this, and did not weep when girls were judged ready to join the struggle, and left the forest to be devoured not by *djanada* but by revolution. It was, she realized, just as well that she could love the Runa as a people, but rarely mourned them as individuals.

Her mistake, if that was what it was, lay in loving Ha'anala.

HA'ANALA: HER FATHER'S DAUGHTER—QUICK AND DECENT AND FULL of energy, who repaid with intellectual interest all that Sofia Mendes could offer a child, who wanted more of an answer to "Why should I be good?" than "Making a *fierno* brings thunderstorms." Ha'anala, who could hold in her mind both science and song, fact and fable; who could, as young as nine, move easily from the Big Bang to "Let there be light."

I am making a Jew of her, Sofia thought one day, alarmed. But then she asked herself, Why not? Ha'anala loved the stories that Sofia told to satisfy the child's hunger for authoritative answers. So Sofia freely drew upon ancient parables to teach enduring morals, with slight emendations to allow for local conditions. The story of the Garden was a favorite because it seemed so like the forest in which they lived. Following Isaac on his solitary wanderings through the trees, it was easy to believe that they were all alone, with no one but God and each other for companions.

But Ha'anala was her own person and drew her own conclusions and one day, she stopped in her tracks and said, "*Sipaj*, Fia: God lied."

Startled, Sofia stopped as well and looked back at her, her eye moving nervously between Isaac, who continued on his way, and Ha'anala, who stood her ground.

"The wife and husband didn't die, and they knew good and evil," Ha'anala said in English, looking up at Sofia with her head cocked back, the image of her father about to issue a declaration. "God lied. The longneck told the truth."

"I never thought of that," Sofia said after a moment. "Well, they did die eventually, but not that day. So, both God and the longneck told part of the truth, I suppose. They had different reasons for what they did." Which led, as they began to walk again, to a long, delicious discussion of complete honesty, partial truth, tact, and deliberate deception for personal gain.

Sofia would report all this to Supaari in their daily radio contacts, sharing stories of his daughter's insights, of her cleverness and creativity, her mischief and essential goodness. His reaction told Sofia a great deal. If he had been behind Runa lines for a time, he would soften and laugh and ask questions. But if he had been in a city, among the Jana'ata, steeped in Runa scent, dressed as a Runao, silently accepting humiliation and unthinking slights as he spied on fortifications and the strength of a garrison, then stories of his daughter's squandered splendor would fuel his anger.

"They wanted her dead," he would say, with a cold fury that Sofia understood and shared. "They wanted such a child dead!"

And yet, he hardly ever visited Ha'anala. Sofia understood this, too. He could not let himself be weakened. He needed to focus on war's clean and uncomplicated emotions. It was necessary that his daily companion be not a child of bright promise with no future but a Runao whose reputation for ferocity of devotion to the making of a new world matched his own— Djalao VaKashan.

It seemed quite likely that they were lovers. Sofia knew that this was both possible and accepted, among VaRakhati of both species. Djalao had taken no husband. "The people are my children," she said. Sofia understood as well what Djalao represented to Supaari: respect earned and acceptance given, recognition that this one *djanada* was worthy to be called one of the People. Supaari shared danger with Djalao, Sofia told herself, and dreams and work. Why not share respite as well? She did not begrudge them that small comfort.

Another woman might have been jealous, but not Sofia Mendes. She had, after all, survived a great deal by blocking out emotion—her own and others'. And love was a debt, best left unincurred.

City of Gayjur
2082, Earth-Relative

"WHEN DID ISAAC FIRST BECOME INTERESTED IN GENETICS?" DANIEL IRON Horse would ask Sofia, near the end of her life.

She was all but blind by then, one eye clouded by a cataract, the other gone; bent nearly in half by a lifetime without the calcium her bones had needed. A crone, she thought. A ruin. But she said aloud, "It was when we were all still living in Trucha Sai, Isaac and Ha'anala and I. Isaac was twenty, I think. Perhaps twenty-five, by your count—the years are longer here. It was just before he left." She sat for a time remembering. "He became, I think, increasingly unsuited to life among the Runa. The constant talk—. Well, you get used to it. You learn to tune it out. But Isaac couldn't do that, and the noise seemed almost painful to him. When he was younger, he would press his fingers into his ears and moan—just make his own noise to drown the talk out. But he simply couldn't stand it as he got older. He spent more and more time by himself, and one day he disappeared."

"And Ha'anala followed him?"

"Yes."

The priests were always so patient with her when she stopped speaking. Sometimes she simply forgot what they had asked and got lost in her own thoughts, but not this time. This was simply difficult to face, and she found it necessary to approach it from a distance. "You see, the Runa children had questions about the weather and the suns and moons, and about plants," she told Danny. "Where does rain come from? they wanted to know. Why do the moons change shape? Where do the suns go at night? How do little seeds make giant *w'ralia* trees? Good questions. I had to work hard to answer them, to keep up with those children. They kept my mind alive. But they never asked about human differences, about differences among the species." She paused, still struck by this. "It was Ha'anala who asked those questions. Why don't you and Isaac have tails? What happened to your fur? She wanted to know, Why do I have only three fingers, not five like everyone else?"

"What did you tell her?" Danny asked gently.

Such a quiet man, Sofia thought. So careful with her, so loath to judge. When she was very young, Sofia had thought of priests as condemning and punitive. Whatever made me believe that? she wondered. Not knowing any priests, perhaps. That was the root of so much fear and hatred, she realized. Not knowing any . . .

You're drifting, Mendes, she told herself, and came back to his question. "Well, at first, I told her what Marc Robichaux always used to say about things like that: Because that's the way God likes it." She reached out, to feel Danny's face, to see if he was smiling. The beardless skin was so smooth. . . . Keep to the point, Mendes, she scolded. "Ha'anala understood the difference between God and science, that there were different ways—parallel ways—to think about the world. So. There were very good AI genetics tutorials in the *Magellan* library, of course. We downloaded those. There were graphics of the DNA helices for humans, and my own tablet's memory had the work on VaRakhati genetics that Anne Edwards and Marc Robichaux did. So I showed her those data as well."

"And Isaac? Did you show him? DNA sequences for all three species?"

"Not directly. Isaac was often nearby when I taught Ha'anala. I had the impression he was listening sometimes. He must have been, I guess. I didn't realize how closely he was paying attention. Or perhaps he went back to the tutorials on his own. Autistics of normal or superior intelligence sometimes read very deeply on one subject at a time." It must have seemed to him to be the perfect reduction of life's chaos and noise to its constituent elements, she thought. Simple, neat, explanatory. Adenine, cytosine, guanine, thymine—that was all you needed.

There was a long silence. Maybe Danny's mind wandered as well, Sofia thought. "Mrs. Quinn," he said after a time, and she smiled sightlessly. How quaint, to be called that now, here, after so many years . . . "Did you ever suspect, about Isaac? Was there anything that made you think that he might be . . . ?"

No one could say the word. It was too frightening. "No," she said. "Not until I heard the music. I had no idea. But I knew from the beginning that Ha'anala was something special. Once, when I was trying to explain to her about the war, I told her the story of the Exodus. I meant for her to learn about the liberation of the Hebrew slaves, so that she could understand why the Runa were fighting, but she couldn't get over the VR displays of Egypt, and the hundreds of gods of Egypt. A few days later, Ha'anala said, 'The Egyptians could see their gods. If you wanted to talk to the god of the river, you dressed well, made yourself ready and went to him. He saw you only at your best. The God of Israel can't be seen, but he sees us—when we are ready, when we are not ready, when we are at our best or at our worst or paying no attention. Nothing can be hidden from such a God. That's why people fear Him.' "

"A remarkable insight," Danny Iron Horse observed.

"Yes. She was an extraordinary child—" Sofia stopped, struck by a thought. Perhaps Ha'anala wasn't extraordinary. Perhaps she was just what others of her kind could have been, but Sofia hadn't known any others. Except Supaari. And now. . . . So many dead, she thought, her small, arthritic hands curled on her thighs. So many dead . . .

That was when the other priest spoke up. Sean Fein. "And what did y'tell her about the God of Israel?" he asked.

How long has he been listening? Sofia wondered irritably. John Candotti always tells me when he's here. Why don't people speak up? Then she thought, Maybe Sean did, and I forgot. "I told her, That is why my people fear God, but also why we love Him, because He sees all we do, knows all we are, and still loves us."

As was so often the case these days, she drifted away then, to spend her time with people who were long gone, who were more real to her than these new ones. "Even if it's only poetry, it's poetry to live by, Sofia—poetry to die for," D. W. Yarbrough had told her—when? Fifty years ago? Sixty? And she herself was so old, so old. She didn't know if there was an afterlife, but she had begun to hope so, not because she feared oblivion, but simply because she wanted to know if she had done the right thing.

It might have been a minute, or an hour, or a day later when she spoke again. "Once I told Ha'anala about the cities of Sodom and Gomorrah," she said, and waited for some response.

"I'm right here, Sofia," John told her.

"I told her how Abraham bargained with God for the lives of ten righteous men who might have lived there. She said to me, 'Abraham should have taken the babies from the cities. The babies were innocent.' " Sofia turned her face toward John's voice. "I wasn't wrong to tell her the stories," she said. "I don't believe that I was wrong."

"You did the right thing," John Candotti told her. "I'm sure of it."

She slept then. John's faith was enough.

25

Giordano Bruno

2065, Earth-Relative

"WHAT? WHAT IS IT?" SANDOZ ASKED, SHIELDING HIS EYES AGAINST THE sudden light with an arm thrown across his face.

"You were screaming again," John told him.

Emilio sat up in his bunk, puzzled, but not distressed. He squinted at John, who was standing half-naked in the cabin doorway. "Sorry," Emilio said blandly. "Didn't mean to wake you up."

"Emilio, this can't go on," John said tightly. "You've got to make Carlo take you off this drug."

"I don't see why, John. It helps with my hands, and I've been over-amped so long, it's kind of nice not to give a damn about anything."

John gaped at him. "You're screaming damned near every night!"

"Yeah, well, the nightmares have been bad for years. At least now I don't remember them when I wake up." Moving back to lean against the bulkhead, he studied John with an infuriatingly tolerant amusement. "If the noise bothers you, I could move back into the sick bay—that room's soundproofed."

"Jesus, Emilio—it's not *my* sleep I'm worried about!" John cried. "I looked this Quell shit up, okay? You are going into debt, man. You don't feel anything directly, but the bill is coming due! Look at how you're breathing! Pay attention! Your heart is racing, right?" Sandoz frowned, and then nodded, but shrugged. "Quell's only supposed to be used for a couple of days at a time. You've been on it for almost two months! You've got to come back to reality some time, and the sooner the better—"

"Jeez, John, relax, will you? Maybe you should try this stuff—"

John stared at him, openmouthed. "You're not thinking straight," he said flatly, and with that, he touched off the light and left, closing the cabin door behind him.

EMILIO SANDOZ SAT FOR A TIME PROPPED AGAINST THE BULKHEAD, ruined hands limp and nerveless in his lap, as his body cooled. He tried to reconstruct the nightmare that had jarred John awake, but was content when it stayed just beyond his mind's reach.

Nocturnal amnesia was quite possibly the best part about being doped, he decided.

He had always paid attention to dreams. Early in formation, he'd made a habit of thinking about the last one of the night, probing for anxieties and hidden concerns that hadn't yet surfaced in his waking life. But for the past three years, his dreams had rarely required interpretation. Terrifying in their unadorned verisimilitude, his ordinary nightmares were plain and simple reenactments of incidents during his last year on Rakhat. Even now, drugged and placid, he could see it all: the slaughter, the poets. Not needing to dream, he could hear the sounds of massacre and of violation. Taste the meat of infants. Feel the unbreakable grip, the hot breath on the back of his neck. Watch from a distance as he shouted God's name and heard nothing but his own sobbing and a rapist's labored groan of satisfaction . . .

Night after night, he'd awakened from such dreams nauseated to the point of vomiting. The screaming was new. Had the nightmares themselves changed? he wondered, and answered himself: Who cares? Screaming beats the hell out of throwing up.

John was probably right—he'd have to return to reality sometime, he supposed. But reality didn't have a great deal to recommend it these days, and Emilio was quite willing to exchange whatever message was embedded in these new dreams for the artificial tranquility of Quell.

Chemical Zen, he thought, as he slid back down under the covers of his bunk, submerging again in the drug's quietude. Cops're probably handing this crap out on the street corners like candy.

Just before he dozed off, he wondered idly, Christ—what kind of dream would it take, to make *me* scream? But, like Pius IX after the Mortara boy's kidnapping, *ipse vero dormiebat*: he slept well after that.

NO ONE ELSE DID.

John Candotti went directly from Sandoz's cabin to his own, where he activated the intercom codes needed to speak to everyone but Emilio. "Commons. Five minutes," he said, in a voice that left no doubt that he would personally drag each of them out of bed if they didn't come voluntarily.

There was a certain amount of grumbling, but no one could pretend they hadn't been startled awake again by the screams, so, one by one, they appeared as summoned. John waited silently, arms over his chest, until Carlo finally strolled in, fresh-looking and beautifully dressed, as always, with Nico in his wake.

"Okay," John said with tight and quiet courtesy, looking at each of them in turn, "you've all got your reasons. But he's no good to anybody if he's psychotic, and that's where this is heading!"

Sean nodded, rubbing his prematurely drooping jowls with both hands. "Candotti's right. Y' can't fack with the man's neurochemistry forever," he told Carlo. "This'll get worse."

"I have to agree," Joseba said, raking fingers through the snarled mess of his hair and studying Iron Horse. He stretched and yawned. "Whatever the motive for drugging him in the beginning, it's time to deal with the consequences."

"I imagine he's over his sulk by now," said Carlo, shrugging ersatz indifference, for his own dreams lately had been of falling alone through black places that appeared under his feet and had no bottom. It was difficult not to be unnerved by Sandoz's nightmares. "Your call, Iron Horse," he said lightly, quite willing to let Danny take the rap.

"It's not just the Quell," John warned, glaring at Danny. "It's having his life wrecked—again. It's being screwed over—again, and this time by people he should have been able to trust. There's a lot to answer for."

"Lock up the knives," Frans Vanderhelst advised cheerfully, his pale belly lunar in the dim light of a shipboard night, "or the Chief is going to get it in the back."

Nico shook his head. "There will be no fighting on the *Bruno*," he said firmly, pleased when Don Carlo nodded his approval.

"I'll speak to him, then, Danny, shall I?" Sean Fein asked.

Iron Horse nodded and left the commons, without having said a word.

"FOR YOU, CHEMISTRY IS HOLY ORDER AND SACRED BEAUTY," VINCENZO Giuliani had remarked on the day he'd assigned Sean to the Rakhat mission. "Humans simply fuck things up, don't they, Father Fein."

And there was no point in denying the observation.

Sean Fein was only nine when he received his first imperishable lesson in human folly. The movement that made an orphan of him had gotten its start in the Philippines in 2024, the year he was born, but by the time it reached its peak in 2033, he was old enough to be concerned. It had seemed that Belfast, for once, would not get caught up in the craziness; having concentrated venomous attention on the hairsbreadth of difference between its Catholic and Protestant citizens, the town seemed not to notice the odd Jew here and there in its brick mazes. And yet there had been great expectation that the second millennium since the Crucifixion would end with the Second Coming of Christ. When Jesus failed to materialize on the millennialists' timetable, the rumor began that it was the Jews' fault because they didn't believe.

"Don't worry," his father told Sean the night before the firebomb. "It's nothin' to do with us."

Bitterness was the backbone of Belfast, but Maura Fein was a philosophical woman who took her widowhood in stride. Sean had asked her once why she had not converted to Judaism when she married. "The great appeal of Jesus, Sean, is the willingness of God to walk among the benighted creatures He just can't seem to give up on," she told him. "There is a glorious looniness to it—the magnificent eternal gesture of salvation, in the face of perennial, thickheaded human inanity! I like that in a deity."

Sean had not inherited his mother's basic cheer, but he did share her jaundiced enjoyment of divine lunacy. He had followed the banner of the Lord, heedless of the personal consequences, and accepted that it was now leading him to another planet, with not one but two sentient species to bollix up creation.

Hand out free will, he'd think gazing at a crucifix, and look where it gets You! Bored with physics, were You? Plants too predictable, I suppose? Not enough drama in big fish eatin' the littlies, eh? What on Earth were Y' thinkin' of! Or what on Rakhat, for that matter . . .

Sean had been born into a world that took the existence of other sentient species for granted. He was fourteen when the first mission reports had come back from Rakhat; seventeen when they ended mysteriously. Twenty-two when he heard of the scandals and tragedies that surrounded Emilio Sandoz. He had merely shrugged, unsurprised. Humans and their ilk were God's problem, as far as Sean Fein was concerned, and the Almighty was more than welcome to them.

But if Sean Fein, chemist and priest, rarely found reason to approve the results of his God's whimsical decision to bestow sentience on the odd species here and there, he could nevertheless admire the mechanics that ran the show. Iron and manganese, pried by rain from stone, swirled with calcium and magnesium in ancient milky seas. Small, nimble molecules—nitrogen, oxygen, water, argon, carbon dioxide—dancing in the atmosphere, spinning, glancing off one another, "the feeble force of gravity gathering them in a thin vapor around the planet," wrote chemistry's psalmist Bill Green, "like some invisible shepherd, drawing together his invisible flock." Cyanobacteria—the clever little buggers—learning to break the double bonds that bind oxygen in carbon dioxide; using the carbon and a few other oceanic bits and pieces to produce peptides, polypeptides, polysaccharides; throwing off oxygen as waste, setting it free. Genesis for Sean was literal: Let there be sunlight to power the system, and the whole biosphere comes alive. God's chemistry, Green called it, with its swimming, dancing, fornicating ions, its tangled, profligate undergrowth of plant lignins and cellulose, the matlike hemes and porphyrins, the helical proteins winding and unwinding.

"Steep yourself in the sea of matter," the French Jesuit Teilhard de Chardin advised. "Bathe in its fiery waters, for it is the source of your life." This was a glory Sean Fein could appreciate, this was a glimpse of Divine Intelligence that he could adore unreservedly.

"The people you feel sorriest for are the fools who hope for justice and sense, and not just in the world to come," the Father General told him. "But God instilled in us a capacity to value mercy and justice, and it's only human to hope for them, here and now. Maybe it's foolish, but we do. This mission is going to teach you something, Sean. Compassion for fools? Perhaps even respect? Learn the lesson, Sean, and pass it on."

"THIS INGWY, SHE'S A HIGH GODDESS, IS SHE?" SEAN ASKED SANDOZ when the others had cleared out of the commons after a quiet breakfast.

Emilio set his coffee mug on the table, brace servos humming. There was still a fault in one of the electroelastic actuators, but he had learned to work around it. "I don't think so. I had the impression she might be a personification of foresight or prophesy—just from context. Supaari was not a believer, but her name came up now and then." It was interesting, the way the drug took him. He felt almost like an AI construct, able to respond to requests for information, even to solve problems at times. On the other hand, it seemed impossible to learn anything new. No desire for mastery, he guessed. "There are others," he told Sean. "Wisdom—or Cunning, perhaps, also feminine. It wasn't clear what the translation should be. He also mentioned a goddess of Chaos once. She is one of the Calamities."

"Female deities," Sean said, frowning. "Odd, wouldn't y'say? In a society dominated by males?"

"There is perhaps an older belief system underlying the present culture. Religion is generally conservative."

"True. True for you." Sean looked away, quiet for a time. "Did y'ever wonder then why Orthodox Jews count lineage through the mother's ancestry?" Sean asked. "Strange, isn't it? The entire Old Testament, filled with *begats*. Twelve tribes for the twelve sons of Jacob. But Jacob had a daughter, too. Remember? Dina. The one who was raped." There was no reaction from Sandoz. "And yet, there's no Tribe of Dina. Patrilineage, all through the Torah! Religion is conservative, as y'say. So why? When was it declared that a Jew is the child of a Jewish mother?"

"I have always hated the Socratic method," Sandoz said without heat, but he answered dutifully. "During the pogroms, to legitimize the Cossacks' bastards."

"Yes, so none of the children would be stigmatized as half-Jew or no Jew a-tall. And good for the rabbis, I say." Sean had spent a childhood being asked, "What are y'then?" Whatever he answered, the buggers'd laugh. "So. To legitimize the children of rape, when rape was so common the rabbis had to overturn twenty-five hundred years of tradition to cope with it. Good girls and bad. Virgins and whores. Young and old alike. Devout and indifferent and apostate. All done." He gazed at Sandoz with steady blue eyes. "And not a one of 'em ever got an apology from God, nor from the fackin' basturd who done her."

Sandoz didn't even blink. "Your point is taken. I am neither the first nor the only person to be worked over."

"So what?" Sean demanded. "Does it help to know that?"

"Not a blind bit," Sandoz said in Sean's own voice. He sounded irritable. It might have been the mimicry.

"Nor should it," Sean snapped. "Sufferin' may be banal and predictable, but it doesn't hurt any less for all that. And it's despicable to take comfort in knowin' that others have suffered as well." He was watching Sandoz carefully now. "I'm told y'blame God for what happened on Rakhat. Why not blame Satan? Do y'believe in the devil, then, Sandoz?"

"But that is irrelevant," Sandoz said lightly. "Satan ruins people by tempting them to take an easy or pleasurable path." He was on his feet, taking his mug and plate to the galley.

"Spoken like a good Jesuit," Sean called to him. "And there was nothin' easy nor pleasurable in what happened to you."

Sandoz reappeared, empty-handed. "No. Nothing," he said, voice soft, eyes hard. " 'As fish are caught in a net and as birds are trapped, so are the children of men entrapped—this I experienced under the sun, and it seemed a great evil to me.' "

"Ecclesiasticus. *Omnia vanitas:* All is vanity and chasing after the wind. The wicked prosper and the righteous get rooted up the hole, and is that all y'learned in a quarter of a century in the Company of Jesus?"

"Fuck off, Sean," Sandoz said and moved toward the doorway that led to the cabins.

Suddenly, Sean was out of his chair and, cutting him off, blocked the way out of the room. "Nowhere t'run now, Sandoz. Nowhere t'hide," Sean said, and he did not waver under the murderous glare he got for his trouble. "You were a priest for decades," Sean said with quiet insistence, "and a good one. Think like a priest, Sandoz. Think like a Jesuit! What did Jesus add to the canon, man? If the Jews deserved one thing, it was a better answer to sufferin' than the piss-poor one Job got. If pain and injustice and undeserved misery are part of the package, and God knows they are, then surely the life of Christ is God's own answer to Ecclesiasticus! Redeem the suffering. Embrace it. Make it *mean* something."

There was no response except that stony stare, but the shaking was visible.

"Yer feelin' it now, aren't you. Carlo stopped the Quell aerosol he's been pumpin' into yer room while y'slept," Sean informed him. "There's no way past the next forty-eight hours except through them. Y'watched a thousand babies die, slaughtered like lambs. Y'saw the bloody corpses of everyone y'loved. You were gang-raped for months and when you were rescued, we all assumed you'd prostituted yersalf. Well, the dead are dead. You'll never be unraped. And you'll never live out yer life with sweet Gina and her wee daughter. And yer feelin' it."

Sandoz closed his eyes, but Sean's voice went on, with its hard r's and the flat, unmusical poetry of Belfast. "Pity the poor, wee souls who live a life of watered milk—all blandness and pleasantry—and die nicely asleep in ripe old age. Water and milk, Sandoz. They live half a life and never know the strength they might have had. Show God what yer made of, man. Pucker up and kiss the cross. Make it your own. Make all this mean something. Redeem it."

Sean noticed only then that Daniel Iron Horse was standing silently behind a bulkhead just beyond the commons. Danny came forward and stood now in plain sight. For a moment, Sean frowned, unsure of Danny's intention, but then it came clear to him. "Here's one thing y'can do to redeem the next two days, Sandoz. Y'can let this man witness them. Will y' permit it?"

Sandoz would look at neither of them, and remained silent. But he didn't say no, and so Sean left and Danny stayed.

SANDOZ SEEMED STUNNED IN THE BEGINNING BUT, BEFORE LONG, withdrawal began to work on him physically. Too tense to stay still, he needed to walk the pain out, and Danny followed him into the chilling silence of the lander bay, which was nearly thirty meters long and afforded him room to move, and privacy.

For the first hours, Sandoz said nothing, but Danny knew the anger was coming and tried to brace himself for it. He believed that there was nothing Sandoz could say to him that he had not said to himself, but he was wrong. When Sandoz spoke at last, brutal mockery quickly escalated beyond rage to a pure moral fury, its expression informed by decades of Jesuit study. Tears, Daniel Iron Horse discovered that first morning, felt cold against skin flushed with shame.

Then the silence settled in again.

Danny left only twice on the first day, to go to the head. Sandoz paced and paced, and after a time, stripped off his shirt, sodden with sweat that leached the moisture from his body even in the numbing cold of the lander bay. A while later, he took off the braces as well and then sat down as far away from Danny as possible, near the exterior hangar-bay door, his back against the sealed stone walls, head resting on arms wrapped around raised knees, the nearly dead fingers twitching sometimes.

In spite of himself and his intentions, Danny fell asleep as the hours passed. He woke once and saw Sandoz standing at the bay door, staring into the darkness through the small porthole. Danny dropped off once again, only to hear the words *"Aqui estoy"* sometime during the night. He was not sure of the language, but he remembered the words and, later on, asked the other priests if any of them understood. Both Joseba and John recognized the Spanish: Here I am. It was Sean who said, "That's what Abraham answered when God called his name." But Sandoz had said it with a kind of beaten resignation, and Danny thought it might only have signaled the man's recognition that he was stuck on the *Bruno*, with nowhere to go but forward.

Or perhaps it was the resignation of Jonah realizing that God would find him and use him no matter where he was, even in the belly of a whale.

There was no dawn to wake Danny in the morning, but the noise and movement inside the commons room came muffled through the lander-bay hatch. He sat up and then stood, stiff and miserable. Sandoz had not moved. Danny left again for a few minutes, but came back without eating, determined to take no food or drink while Sandoz went without. As the hours of the second full day crawled by, Sandoz remained motionless and silent, eyes fixed on distances no other man had seen. Vision quest, Danny thought, when the soul opened to whatever could be conveyed by the Great Mystery, Whose thoughts were not the thoughts of man, Whose ways were not the ways of man . . .

He had not wanted to sleep. Danny had resolved to witness it all from start to finish, and so he woke on the third morning with a start, only to find himself looking into the obsidian eyes of Emilio Sandoz, sitting cross-legged on the lander deck, where he had waited for Iron Horse to wake up.

"It must have been hard," Sandoz said after a time, his voice soft and unresonant in the echoing space of the bay.

Danny wasn't sure what he meant but, lately, nothing had been easy, so he nodded.

"If you stare into the abyss," Sandoz reported, "it stares back."

"Nietzsche," Danny said almost inaudibly, identifying the quote.

"Two points." Waxen and exhausted, Sandoz got slowly to his feet and stood blankly for a while. "God uses us all, I suppose," he said, and walked to the hatch, banging on it with an elbow.

In an instant, the sounds of pressure equalizers and locking mechanisms echoed emptily against the stone walls of the hull. When the door opened, Danny realized that John Candotti, too, had stood vigil during these three days. But the rest of the crew was there now as well, waiting.

"He did what he had to," Sandoz told them, and stepped through the hatch without another word.

For the first time since his mother died when he was sixteen years old, Daniel Iron Horse broke down and sobbed. The others stood and listened until John Candotti said, "Leave him alone," and the little crowd dispersed.

After a decent interval, John ducked into the bay. He looked around and then retrieved Sandoz's discarded shirt, offering it to Danny to blow his nose on. Danny accepted it, but reared away when he brought it closer to his face.

"It's pretty funky," John admitted. "If that's the odor of sanctity, God help us all."

Danny managed a small laugh and pulled up his own shirt, wiping his nose on the inside of the collar.

"My mom always hated it when I did that," John said, sliding down the wall next to Danny until his bony legs stuck straight out in front of him.

Danny wiped his eyes and cleared his throat. "Mine, too," he said almost soundlessly.

They both sat staring at the far end of the bay for a while. "Well, hell," John said finally, "if it's okay with Emilio, it's okay with me, I guess. Pax?"

Danny nodded. "I'm not sure it's all that okay with him. But thanks," he said.

John got to his feet and offered the other man a hand up. Danny, red-eyed and wrung dry, shook it gratefully, but he said, "I think I'll just sit here awhile, ace. I need some time."

"Sure," John said, and left Danny alone.

Great Southern Forest

2061, Earth-Relative

"—was ripe two nights ago—" "—pon River. But someone thinks—" "—no market anymore for—" "—stern campaign is undersupplied and if—" ("Uunnhh.") "—omeone is hungry! Who ha—" "—*rakar* fields are north of the—" "Sipaj, Panar! Someone heard—" "—oo early. It ripens af—" "—focus instead on consolidating the—" ("Uuuunnhh.") "—*nitarl* pickers at Kran port—" "Sipaj, Djalao, surely you are hungr—" "We found more by the riv—" "—paari will be there soon—" ("Uuuuuuuuunnhh.") "—weavers can't use so—" "—ut if we go after the *rakari* are—" "—someone that bundle of *ree*—" "—nala, get Isaac to stop—" "Scratch just there. No, lower! Ye—" ("Uuuuuuuuuuuuuuunnhh—")

"*Sipaj*, Isaac! Stop!" Ha'anala shouted.

Isaac sank to the ground, dizzy but satisfied. Spinning could transform the incomprehensible into a uniform blur, and if he made his own sound, he could sometimes drown the racket out, but best of all was when one voice cut through all the rest and made everyone quiet.

"*Sipaj*, Isaac," Ha'anala said slowly, her voice pitched low. "Let's go to the shelter." She waited the right amount of time before adding, "We'll listen to music."

Ha'anala had clarity.

Isaac stood, clutching the computer tablet to his bare, bony chest, feeling its cool, flat, unblemished perfection. All around him: inconstancy, unpredictability, irrationality. His own body could not be trusted. Feet became more distant, arms wrapped further around the torso. Hair appeared in places where none had been before. Stones, smooth and faultless one time, might be covered by a leaf or flawed by the presence of a bug the next time he looked. Ears and eyes and mouths and limbs moved endlessly. Bodies sat and slept in different places. How could they expect him to understand what they were saying while he was still trying to figure out who they were? Plants sprang up and changed size and disappeared. Buds, flowers and withered things came and went. He could sit and stare for hours—days! But he couldn't see this happen. He fell asleep and, in the morning, the old thing was gone and a new one was there and sometimes it acted the same way as before and sometimes it didn't. There was no clarity.

The computer held a world that was precisely the same every morning, except for his mother's daily message—he knew now that she made small changes because she showed him how to do this. He complained, so she put all her messages in a separate file and that was all right because it didn't change anything else in his other directories; Isaac was the only one who changed those. The computer was better than spinning—

"*Sipaj*, Isaac. Come with me," Ha'anala said, each word distinct. She picked up his cloth—a silken blue square that could cover him from head to waist. His prayer shawl, Sofia called it with dispirited irony. "We'll listen to music," Ha'anala repeated, tugging at his ankle with her foot.

Isaac jerked away and muttered, "Now someone has to start over."

Ha'anala lifted her chin and sat down to wait. Isaac couldn't bear to have a thought interrupted and he had to begin at the beginning. If anyone disturbed him as he spoke, he would repeat the entire speech word by word until the end of what he'd meant to say. That's why he spoke so little, she supposed. It was nearly impossible to complete a thought or a statement to his satisfaction when there were Runa around. Even at the risk of a *fierno*, the people couldn't seem to remain silent long enough to suit him.

When Isaac was finished, he stood up straighter: his signal that he could move again. Ha'anala rolled to her feet and walked off toward the edge of the village clearing. Isaac tracked her tangentially, head up and tilted crazily, relying on peripheral vision, so he wouldn't have to see her legs move. The people were already talking again. "—adio control of the—" "—pay, Hatna! Don't make—" "—over two hundred *bahli* now!" "—new windbreaks for th—" "—is nice combined with *k'ta*—" "—torm coming in—"

The conversation receded, only to be replaced by the patternless noise of the forest: squawking, buzzing, dripping. Shrieks and whistled arpeggios; snuffling, rustling. Nearly as bad as the village. The forest, at least, had no baffling jumble of talk and intonation, no half-grasped meaning shrouded by the next words.

Impasto, Isaac thought. This is worse than red. The village is an impasto of words. The forest is an impasto of sounds. There is no clarity!

He had found the word "impasto" in one of Marc Robichaux's files. He looked it up in the dictionary and saw a naked hand with five fingers applying dabs of molten color in many layers, each one almost concealing the others beneath it. For a long time now, "clarity" had been his best word, but he liked "impasto" very much. He appreciated the nicety of its meaning, how neatly it fit his desire to label a perception. When he could focus on one word at a time, the meaning of things could come clear for him, like a high note rising out of a choir, and there was joy in that. But there was no clarity in the village and it was difficult to make the distractions go away long enough—

Ha'anala stopped and sat just outside his little rectangular shelter. Isaac, too, stopped and rethought his thought about impasto from beginning to end. Then he handed Ha'anala his tablet without meeting her eyes and said, "Be careful with it." He told her that every time, just as Sofia had told him that over and over, when she first let him have the computer. For a while, he thought becarefulwithit was the name of the computer. There were very few of these tablets in the world, he found out eventually, although the people had made other things they sloppily labeled computer even though such things were clearly different from his tablet and couldn't be carried around; so this one was still precious, and not only to Isaac.

He waited until Ha'anala said, "Someone will be careful," and then he smiled, face lifted to the suns. She said that every time. Ha'anala had clarity. "The rule is: No Runa," he said loudly.

"Except Imantat," Ha'anala replied dutifully. Imantat was a relatively quiet Runao who kept the rainroof thatched. Ha'anala herself stayed out of Isaac's line of sight as he went to work removing all the detritus that had blown or fallen or grown into his little fortress since his last visit. It took some time. When everything was properly squared up, all the curves and mess done away with, he held out his hand and the tablet appeared in it without anyone having to say anything.

It weighed less than before. Once it had taken all his thin-boned, six-year-old strength to heft it, but now it was so light he could grasp it easily with one hand. This gradual loss of weight was a sly betrayal that Isaac had not overlooked; he always inspected the tablet minutely, vigilant for other changes. Satisfied, he placed the computer tablet on a flat rock he'd brought here from the river, to keep the tablet out of the mud. Rain was no threat, but his mother had always told him to keep the tablet clean. With a special stick he kept for this purpose, he measured off the distance from each edge of the tablet to the shelter's walls, so that it was perfectly centered.

He held out his hand and this time the blue cloth appeared. Pulling this over his head, he sat down on the western side of the shelter and draped the shawl over the tablet as well. Oblivious now to the slanting shafts of three-toned light filtering through the canopy's breeze-driven movement, he began to relax. Then: the feel of the latch against his thumb, the soft snick of the mechanism, the lovely arc of hinged movement describing in a single sweep—acute to obtuse—the unchanging geometry of the cover. The simultaneous whirr of power-on, the brightening of the screen, the familiar keyboard with its serried ranks.

"*Sipaj*, Isaac," Ha'anala said. "What shall we listen to?"

She knew how long to wait before asking this question, and she always asked the same way, and he always chose the same piece: Supaari's voice, the evening chant. First Isaac listened silently. Then again, singing harmony. Then again, with his own harmony and with Ha'anala joining in to double Supaari's part. He followed the same pattern with the Sh'ma, Sofia's voice solo, replayed so he could harmonize, and a third time with Ha'anala doubling Sofia.

Finally he could move on, choosing from the *Magellan*'s stored collection of songs, symphonies, cantatas and chants; the quartets and trios, the concertos and rondos; Gaelic jigs and Viennese waltzes; the lush four-part harmonies of a cappella Brooklyn doo-wop and the whining dissonance of Chinese opera; the modal and rhythmic shifts of an Arabic *taqasim*. Music entered Isaac's heart directly and effortlessly. It slipped into his soul like a leaf settling into clear, still water, sinking silkily beneath the shining surface.

Having purged the noise and confusion of the village and the forest, Isaac's mind became as orderly and precise as the keyboard. He could begin again to explore the *Magellan*'s vast on-line library, reading steadily with emotionless concentration every item found in the *Magellan* catalog on whatever subject had snared his interest.

"Clarity," he sighed, and began to study.

· · ·

THE WHOLE VILLAGE WAS HAPPY TO SEE HA'ANALA LEAD ISAAC OFF when he became disruptive; they praised her for being so kind to him, for watching over him. "Ha'anala is a good father," the people said, smiling a little at that. Even Sofia was grateful. But it was no sacrifice to accompany Isaac to this refuge, for if her brother craved clarity, Ha'anala was starved for privacy. It amounted to the same thing, she supposed.

For years, Isaac had mostly echoed others and even Sofia had come to believe that he was all but incapable of direct speech. Then one day, wearied by the village noise, feeling fragmented and exasperated herself, Ha'anala had simply acted on an impulse. She was younger than Isaac, but far stronger if not taller, so when he began to spin and hum, she simply grabbed his ankle and marched him off to a place in the forest where it was quiet. She had expected silence from him, or at worst some meaningless phrase repeated over and over until it meant even less. Only later did Ha'anala realize that her own exhausted, petulant silence had permitted Isaac to complete a thought and then to repeat it aloud. And such a thought!

"How can you hear your soul if everyone is *talking?*"

He said nothing more that day, but Ha'anala spent hours considering his words. A soul, she decided, was the most real part of a person, and to discover what is real requires privacy.

In the village, every act, every word, every decision or desire was examined and commented on and compared, debated, evaluated and reconsidered—participated in! How could she tell who she was, when everything she did acquired a council of 150 people? If she so much as hid her eyes behind her hands or clamped her ears shut for a moment, a solicitous Runao would approach and inquire, "*Sipaj*, Ha'anala, are you not well?" And then everyone would discuss her recent meals, her stools, the condition of her coat, whether her eyes were hurting her, and if that might be because there had lately been more sunlight and less rain than usual, and if that meant the *dji'll* harvest would be late this year, and how would that affect the market for *k'jip*, which was always combined with *dji'll* . . .

So Ha'anala thanked God that Isaac's ability to tolerate the village commotion was even more limited than her own. She had never told Sofia about the things Isaac said during their times alone. This was a source of guilt. Ha'anala sometimes felt as though she had stolen something from Sofia, who wanted so much for Isaac to speak to her.

Once, when Ha'anala heard Isaac yawn underneath his head covering, and knew that he was done reading and could tolerate a question, she had asked, "*Sipaj*, Isaac, why do you not speak to our mother?"

"She wants too much," he said tonelessly. "She rips away the veil."

Isaac had twice typed a message on the tablet to Sofia. "Leave this alone," was the first. Their mother had wept at it: his only words to her a rebuff. But later, during the period of intense frustration and fear that occurred when he came to the end of some line of obsessive research, he had asked, "Will I run out of things to learn?" "No," Sofia had typed back. "Never." He seemed glad, but that single reassurance was all he wanted from her.

Ha'anala sighed, saddened by the memory, and settled back against a sun-warmed boulder, closing her eyes. Midday heat and boredom joined with an adolescent carnivore's physiology to conspire against consciousness, but her drowsiness that day was compounded by Isaac's latest craze. He had set himself the task of memorizing every base pair in human DNA, having assigned a musical note to represent each of the four bases—adenine, cytosine, guanine and thymine. He would listen to the monotonous four-note sequences for hours.

"*Sipaj*, Isaac," she'd asked when this jag started, "what are you doing?"

"Remembering," he said, and this struck Ha'anala as unusually pointless, even for Isaac.

Even Sofia had become more distant in the past few years, often doing several things at once, listening to the Runa discussions while working through reports or preparing weather data for dissemination to the officers or coordinating the delivery of supplies to a salient. Over and over, Ha'anala tried to help, distressed by Sofia's isolation, wanting to be her partner even while she resented her mother's patent, unspoken needs. "It has nothing to do with you," Sofia would say, closing Ha'anala out as effectively as Isaac could. Sofia seemed to come fully alive only when she spoke of justice, but as the years went by, even that topic elicited silence. None of the people welcomed Ha'anala's interest in the war, and her questions were adroitly deflected—

They are ashamed, Ha'anala realized. They wish me not to know, but I do. I will be the last of my kind. They have begun something that can end only one way. Sofia and Isaac might be right, she thought, drowsing. Stay distant, keep your heart hidden, don't want what you can't have . . .

She had been asleep for some time when she heard Isaac's blaring, toneless voice announce, "This is worse than red. Someone is leaving."

"All right," she murmured, without really rousing. "Someone will meet you back at the village."

• • •

"SIPAJ, PEOPLE," SOFIA CALLED OUT HOURS LATER. "IT'S ALMOST RED-light! Has anyone seen Isaac and Ha'anala?"

Puska VaTrucha-Sai separated from the knot of girls chattering about their assignments, and looked around curiously. "They left this morning for Isaac's hut," she reminded Fia.

"*Sipaj*, Puska," her father, Kanchay, called, "you will please us if you go out and bring them back."

"Oh, eat me," Puska muttered, to the scandalized laughter of the other girls. Puska didn't care. A year in the army was more than enough to coarsen a woman's attitudes and language, and she had chosen the mildest of the vulgarities that came to mind—these recruits would learn the others soon enough. Puska smiled at the girls and said, "A good soldier is responsible," with the exaggerated sincerity that covers rock-hard cynicism, and loped off to find Fia's children.

It took her perhaps twice-twelve paces to get beyond the shelters and storage huts, and again that many to pass out of earshot of the village noise. Puska had dreamed of home nearly every night of her first month in the city of Mo'arl; yearning for the forest's peace and security, she'd sought refuge there in sleep when daylight was filled with shock and outrage and sadness. For a time, she'd envied Ha'anala, safe forever in the village. Now, Trucha Sai seemed cramped and limited, and Puska could understand why Ha'anala was so often bad-tempered and restless.

The roofline of Isaac's shelter came into view, a *cha'ar* past the settlement's edge. Imantat's work was not as sturdy as that of his father, who was a master thatcher, but the boy showed promise: the shelter had held up well during the last storm. Someone will need a husband soon, Puska thought, and made a mental note to bring this up with the council, for she had seen enough of war to know that babies should not be postponed, and the people would need a child to replace her if she fell in battle.

"*Sipaj*, Ha'anala," Puska called as she approached the hut, "everyone's waiting for you! It's almost redlight!" There was no response—the shelter was empty. "Stew," she swore under her breath. Ha'anala couldn't see in redlight and Isaac could see too well. He needed to get under the sleeping shelters, where he couldn't see the red in the sky, or there'd be trouble. "Ha'anala! Someone will have to carry you back!" Puska teased loudly. "And Isaac will make a *fierno*!"

"Over here!" Ha'anala yelled from a distance.

"Where's Isaac?" Puska shouted back, cocking her ears toward the sound, relieved to hear Ha'anala's voice at last.

Already losing contrast, hands out in front of her, Ha'anala moved uncertainly toward Isaac's hut. "He's not here," she cried, lifting a foot to rub the opposite shin where she'd crashed into a fallen log a moment earlier. "Isaac left!"

Puska's ears came up. "Left? No—someone would have seen him. He's not in the village and he wasn't on the path home—"

Stumbling over a root, Ha'anala snarled in frustration. "*Sipaj*, Puska: he's left! Out into the forest! Can't you smell it? He said he was leaving, but someone was sleepy—"

Puska strode decisively to Ha'anala's side and began to smooth the younger girl's face, running her hands along the sides of Ha'anala's long, thin cheeks. "Make your heart quiet," she crooned, falling back into the habits of childhood. "A *fierno* won't help," Puska warned. "Bad weather will frighten everyone."

And it would wipe out Isaac's scent, Ha'anala realized, before she could dispute the meteorological effects of emotional distress. She stood at full height. "We have to find him. Right away, Puska. His scent trail is very clear now, but if it rains, someone will lose him. He'll be gone. Fia will—"

"But you can't see—" Puska started to protest.

"Not with eyes," Ha'anala said carefully. Evidence of Isaac's passage fairly glowed for her: his footprints bright with scent, the leaves he'd brushed past powdered with shed skin cells and misted with his expelled breath. "It's like firespore—remember? Like small points of light, along the path he took. *Sipaj*, Puska, someone can follow him if you will help. But we have to leave now, or the trail might stop glowing."

Puska swayed from side to side as she considered this. On the left foot: Isaac might be lost. On the right foot: she should go back to the village and get permission. On the left foot: it smelled like rain. On the right—

"*Sipaj*, Puska," Ha'anala pleaded, "someone's heart will stop if she has to tell Fia that Isaac is gone! Someone thinks she can follow him, and when we two catch up with him, we shall be three, and we'll be back before full night."

Which settled it for Puska. One person made a puzzle. Two people made a discussion. Three made a plan.

· · ·

"THE PEOPLE WILL BELIEVE THAT THE DJANADA GOT US," PUSKA POINTED out, worried from the moment she awoke the next morning. She looked up at Ha'anala, who was a little distance away, poised on a tail and one leg. "Someone should have gone back to tell the others."

Ha'anala didn't respond, afraid she'd alarm her breakfast, which was about to move within reach, directly beneath her suspended foot. Patience . . . patience . . . "Got it!" she cried, grasping a small, scaly *lonat*. "We don't need help," she told Puska firmly, pinching the animal's neck between a pedal thumb and forefinger. "If we go back now, someone will lose the scent."

Puska's face contorted, watching the *lonat*'s twitches subside into limp stillness. "Are you really going to eat that?"

"Consider the alternative," Ha'anala said, shooting a foot out to grip Puska's ankle. "Oh, Puska! Someone was joking!" she cried when Puska jumped and wrenched her leg free.

"Well, don't. Don't ever joke like that!" Puska shuddered. "If you'd seen what *I've* seen in Mo'arl—" Ha'anala's mouth dropped open and Puska stopped, embarrassed by her own self-referential crudity. I really have gotten bad, she thought. "Sorry," she apologized and held out a hand for the *lonat*, holding her breath as she scraped the scales from its legs. "Someone thinks such jokes are in very poor taste."

"Someone thinks *lonati* are in very poor taste," Ha'anala muttered, biting off a nasty little haunch when Puska handed the thing back to her. The main virtue of *lonati* was that they were easy to catch. Both Ha'anala and her father were used to the small, poor prey they could sometimes capture to supplement offerings of "traditional meat," as it was delicately referred to, but eating was always a hurried, furtive task.

"What's it like in the cities?" Ha'anala asked, trying to divert Puska's horrified fascination with the tiny carcass.

"You don't want to know," Puska told her with evident disgust, and left to find herself some rainberries for breakfast.

THEY PRESSED ON, PUSKA INCREASINGLY EXASPERATED, HA'ANALA ALmost as irritable. Traces of Isaac's passing had been trampled by forest things—sweating, panting, defecating in the humid heat—and she lost the scent repeatedly as his path veered unexpectedly toward patches of fruiting bush. Even when she caught his course again, it was mingled with clouds of *vraloj* pollen and the stench of rotting plants, and difficult to follow. By their fourth day on the trail, Puska was complaining bitterly and continuously, and stopped to forage with resentful thoroughness while Ha'anala fumed and clawed under logs for bitter grubs, silent and ravenous and more determined with every passing moment to run Isaac to ground and haul him back by his ankle.

"One more day," Puska warned that night. "Then we're going back. You are too hungry—"

"Isaac will be even hungrier," Ha'anala insisted, for she had never seen Isaac feed himself and had begun to hope that he would weaken so that they could overtake him.

But his dung told her otherwise. In the absence of those who had cared for him since infancy, Isaac was managing rather well, Ha'anala realized. His bowels could stand a Runao's diet and he had probably watched Runa foraging, attentively if obliquely; he understood what was edible and knew how to find it. So now he feeds himself, Ha'anala thought, remembering the stories about how Isaac had begun to walk one day and to sing one day and to type one day. He evidently rehearsed each new skill in his mind until he was certain he could do it, and then simply did.

Has he been planning to leave? Ha'anala wondered that night as she drifted off to sleep. What does he think he'll find? But then she thought, He's not searching. He's escaping.

THEY SLEPT BADLY THAT NIGHT, AND AWOKE TO A THUNDERING DOWN-pour that made travel impossible. Still unwilling to admit defeat, Ha'anala sat at the edge of the woods, staring disconsolately at a limitless plain, her nostrils flaring with the effort to retain Isaac's scent even as it dissolved into the dirt, churned by fat drops and mixed with the scent trails of prairie herds. Even Puska was quiet.

"Gone," Ha'anala whispered that evening, as the wet, gray light dwindled. "Someone has lost him."

"He lost himself. You tried to find him," Puska said softly. She put an arm around Ha'anala and rested her head on the Jana'ata's shoulder. "Tomorrow we will go home."

"How can I tell Sofia?" Ha'anala asked the darkness. "Isaac is gone."

27

Giordano Bruno

2066–2069, Earth-Relative

"YOU'RE JOKING," JOHN INSISTED.

Fat Frans looked up balefully from his plate. "Is suicide still considered a sin?"

"It depends—. Why?"

"Well, for the sake of your theoretically immortal soul, I'll give you some advice," said Frans. "Never get into a plane piloted by Emilio Sandoz."

Colorful exaggeration, John thought, and pushed his own plate aside. "He can't be that bad!"

"I'm telling you, Johnny, I've never seen anyone with less natural ability," said Frans, somewhat belatedly swallowing a mouthful of tilapia and rice. "Nico, tell Don Gianni how long it took you to learn to fly the lander."

"Three weeks," said Nico from his seat in the corner. "Don Carlo says the landers practically fly themselves, but I had a hard time with the navigation programs."

John winced. Emilio had been working on this for a month.

"His brain must be completely crammed with languages. As far as I can tell," said Frans, adding some salt to the rice, "there is not one spare synapse available for flight training. Look, I admire perseverance as much as the next man, but this is pointless. Even D. W. Yarbrough gave up on him. Know what it says in the first mission's records?" Frans paused, chewing, and then recited, " 'As a pilot, Father Sandoz is one hell of a linguist and a pretty fair medic. So I am taking him off flight training and assigning him to permanent passenger status, to avoid getting anybody killed.' " Frans shook his head. "I thought I had a better chance with him because the new landers are almost entirely automated, but Sandoz is so terrible, it's eerie." He scooped up another forkful of fish and peered over mounded cheeks at John. "Do something, Johnny. Talk to him."

John snorted. "What makes you think he'll pay any attention to what I say? Apart from reaming me out for some damned mistake in Ruanja subjunctive, Emilio hasn't said two words to me in the past eight weeks." It was hard not to be hurt, actually. Drugged or sober, Sandoz would let no one near him. "Where is he now?" John asked Frans.

"He practices in his cabin. I can't even monitor him anymore—it's too awful to watch."

"All right," said John. "I'll see what I can do."

THERE WAS NO ANSWER TO THE FIRST KNOCK, SO JOHN BANGED HARDER.

"Shit!" Emilio yelled without opening the door. "What!"

"It's me—John. Lemme in, okay?"

There was a pause, and the sound of the door latch rattling. "Shit," Sandoz said again. "Open it yourself." When John did, Sandoz was standing with the full-coverage VR visor shoved back on his forehead like a conquistador's helmet.

John slumped at the sight of him. He was encrusted with equipment, the VR gloves overlaying his braces, the skin under his eyes purplish with chronic fatigue. "Oh, for God's sake," John said, tact forgotten. "Emilio, this is stupid—"

"It's not stupid!" Emilio snapped. "Did Frans send you? I don't give a damn what he thinks. I have to learn this! If I just didn't have all this crap on my hands—"

"But you *do* have all that crap on your hands, and I still can't get that left brace to work right, and the controls in the lander are even harder than the VR sims! Why can't you just let—"

"Because," Emilio said, cutting him off with soft precision, "I'd rather not depend on anyone else to get me off the planet."

John blinked. "Okay," he said finally, "I get it."

"Thank you," Emilio said sarcastically. "You may recall that the last time I was on Rakhat, the cavalry was a little late riding to the rescue."

John nodded, conceding the point, but still in the mood to argue. "You look awful," he said, picking a fight. "Has it occurred to you that maybe if you got some rest, you might do better? When the hell do you sleep?"

"If I don't sleep, I can't dream," Emilio told him curtly, and shoved his door closed, leaving John alone in the passageway, staring at its blank metal surface.

"Get some rest, dammit," John yelled.

"Go to hell!" Emilio yelled back.

John sighed and walked away, shaking his head and talking to himself.

WITHIN DAYS OF WITHDRAWING FROM QUELL, SANDOZ HAD BROKEN THE Jesuit monopoly on both Rakhati languages, insisting that Carlo, Frans and Nico become competent in basic Ruanja and K'San, even though Frans would remain on the ship for the duration of the mission. Soon he demanded that they all begin working together in increasingly rigorous classes. Day after day, night after night, he ordered them to interpret what he was saying in K'San or Ruanja, throwing his questions at them like bombs, criticizing their answers on every level: grammar, logic, psychology, philosophy, theology.

"Prepare to be wrong. Assume that whenever you find something simple or obvious, you are wrong," Sandoz advised. "Everything we thought we understood, all the most basic things we shared with them—sex, food, music, families—those were the things we were most wrong about."

There were midnight exercises involving the drone lander, details of simulated Rakhati geography, a theoretical but statistically likely cyclone, and not one but two surface rendezvous sites. He would permit them two or three hours of sleep and then the klaxons would go off again, and he'd badger them in K'San or Ruanja to explain who they were, why they had come, what they wanted, dissecting each man's answers publicly and without anesthesia, exposing weaknesses, blind spots, assumptions, stupidities, laying them open like frogs on a tin plate. It was brutal and insulting and very nearly intolerable, but when Sean dared to protest the ill treatment, Sandoz reduced him to tears.

And yet, even as the others trudged off to stuporous sleep after some grueling drill or interrogation, Sandoz himself would put in a few more kilometers on the treadmill. No matter how ferocious his program of training became for the rest of them, they had to admit its rigor was always exceeded by that of his own, despite the fact that he was the smallest man among them and nearly twenty years older than the youngest of them.

He even ate standing up. Nothing stopped the dreams.

"SANDOZ!" CARLO SHOUTED, SHAKING HIM. THERE WAS NO RESPONSE, so he shook the man harder, until the bruised eyes focused.

"¡Jesús!" Emilio cried, pulling violently away. "¡Déjame—"

Carlo released Sandoz's shoulders abruptly, letting him drop against the bulkhead. "I assure you that my intentions were strictly honorable, Don Emilio," he said with specious courtesy, sitting down on the end of the bunk. "You were screaming again."

Still breathing hard, Sandoz looked around his cabin blearily, trying to get his bearings. "Fuck," he said after a while.

"Now there's a thought," said Carlo, eyes half-closed in speculation. "Versatility can be a virtue, you know." Sandoz stared at him. "It doesn't have to hurt," Carlo suggested silkily.

"You come near me," Sandoz assured him wearily, "I'll find a way to kill you."

"Just a suggestion," Carlo said, unruffled. He stood and moved to the desk, where he'd laid the paraphernalia out. "So, barring a more interesting avenue to relief and rest, what shall it be tonight? Quick oblivion, I hope. Perhaps I should have Nico move the treadmill into the sick bay so the rest of us don't have to listen to you pounding away all night." He picked up the injection canister and turned, brows raised in inquiry. "You're building up a tolerance to this, by the way. I've doubled the dosage over the past two weeks."

Sandoz, who had obviously been too tired even to undress before falling into bed, got out of his bunk, put on his braces and left the room, brushing past Nico, who always rose when Don Carlo did.

"Treadmill it is, then," Carlo observed. Sighing, he sat alone for a few minutes, waiting for the relentless sound of footfalls to begin. He could tell from the tempo that Sandoz had set the pace for a thirty-seven-minute ten-kilometer run, hoping to exhaust himself, wearing out the rest of the ship's company in the bargain.

Determined to have things out, Carlo rose and walked to the small gym, moving to the front of the treadmill, where he stood with his hands behind his back, head cocked in contemplation. "Sandoz," he said, "it has come to my attention that you have commandeered the *Giordano Bruno*. The situation suits my purposes, although frankly I find your command style lacking in finesse." Amused black eyes returned his stare; Sandoz was back in control now, deigning to be entertained. "In the beginning," Carlo went on, "I thought, This is revenge—he's getting his own back. Later I thought, This is an ex-Jesuit who has taken orders all his life. Now he gives them. He is drunk with power. Now, however—"

"Shall I tell you why you allowed me to take over your ship?" Sandoz offered, cutting him off. "Your father was right about you, Cio-Cio-San. If you ever finished anything, you could be judged, and found wanting. So you find a reason to quit and tell yourself lies about Renaissance princes. Then you move on to the next thing before you can demonstrate inadequacy. My coup d'état suits your purposes because now you have someone you can blame when this venture fails."

Carlo continued as though the other man had not spoken. "It is not power or revenge that drives you, Sandoz. It is fear. You are afraid, all day, every day. And the closer we get to Rakhat, the more frightened you become."

In superb physical condition now, sweat coming easily, Sandoz decreased the pace until the treadmill stopped. He stood still, his breathing hardly affected by the exertion; then he simply let the mask drop.

Carlo blinked, startled by the unexpected nakedness of Sandoz's face. "You are afraid," Carlo repeated quietly, "and with good reason."

"Don Emilio," Nico said, coming into the room, "what do you see in your dreams?"

Carlo had asked this very question many times, in the hours before what would have been dawn, awakened night after night by the unnerving wail, with its burden of hopeless refusal, the cries of "No!" rising in intensity from denial to defiance to despair. By the time Carlo or John got to his cabin, Sandoz would be sitting up, jammed into the corner of his bed, back against the bulkhead, eyes wide open, but still asleep. "What do you see?" Carlo would demand when he'd shaken the man awake.

Always before, Sandoz had refused to talk. This time, he told Nico, "A necropolis. A city of the dead."

"Always the same city?" Nico asked.

"Yes."

"Can you see the dead clearly?"

"Yes."

"Who are they?"

"Everyone I ever loved," said Sandoz. "Gina is there," he said, looking at Carlo, "but not Celestina—not yet. And there are others, whom I do not love."

"Who?" Carlo demanded.

There was an ugly laugh. "Not you, Carlo," Sandoz said with cheerful contempt. "And not you, Nico. The others are VaRakhati. Whole cities of them," he said lightly. "The bodies change. I've seen them rot. I can smell them in my sleep. There's a time, while the carcasses are decomposing, when I can't tell what they were—Jana'ata or Runa. They all look alike then. But later, when it's just the bones, I can see the teeth. Sometimes I find my own body among them. Sometimes not. It's better when I do because then, it's over. Those are the nights I *don't* scream."

"Do you know how to use a sidearm?" Carlo asked after a silence.

Sandoz nodded in the Rakhati fashion—a short jerk of the chin upward—but held his hands out slightly, inviting Carlo to think it through. "I could probably get a burst off . . ."

"But the recoil would damage the brace mechanisms," Carlo observed, "and you'd be worse off than before. You will, of course, be under my protection, and that of Nico."

The derisive eyes were almost kindly. "And you believe you will succeed, where God has failed me?"

Carlo stood his ground, head back. "God may only be a fable, whereas I have an investment to watch over. In any case, my family has generally found bullets rather more reliable than prayer."

"All right," Sandoz said, smiling briefly and broadly. "All right. Why not? My experience with illusions has not been happy, but who knows? Perhaps—short-term—yours will help us both."

Satisfied with what he had learned, Carlo nodded to Nico. He turned to leave the exercise bay and saw John Candotti standing in the doorway. "Worried, Gianni?" Carlo asked blithely, as he brushed past him. John glared and Carlo backed away in mock alarm, raising both hands. "I swear: I didn't touch him."

"Screw you, Carlo."

"Any time," Carlo purred as he and Nico retreated down the curving passageway.

Emilio was already back on the treadmill.

"Why?" John demanded, facing him.

"I told you, John—"

"No! Not that! Not just trying to pilot the lander! I mean, all of it. Why have anything to do with Carlo? Why are you helping him? Why are you teaching them the languages? Why are you willing to go back—"

" 'Night and day lie open the gates of death's dark kingdom,' " Sandoz recited, hiding behind Virgil, amused but by whom it was not clear. " 'To find the way back to daylight: that is work, that is labor—' "

"Don't. Don't shut me out like this!" John hit the treadmill power toggle so abruptly Sandoz stumbled. "Dammit, Emilio, you owe me something—an explanation, at least! I just want to *understand*—" He stopped himself, startled by the reaction. Shout at me, John thought, going cold, but don't look at me like that.

Finally Sandoz willed the trembling to stop, and when he spoke, his eyes were so hard and his voice so soft that his words seemed to John a vicious insult. "Were your parents married?" he asked.

"Yes," John hissed.

"To each other?" Sandoz pressed, just as quietly.

"I don't have to take this shit," John muttered, but before he could leave, Emilio turned and kicked the door shut.

"Mine weren't," he said.

John froze, and Emilio looked at him for a long time. "One of my earliest memories is of my mother's husband yelling at me for calling him Papi. I remember wondering, Maybe I should call him Papa. Or maybe Padre? Perhaps that's when I became a linguist—I thought there was another word I was supposed to use! I would try saying it a different way, but he'd get even madder and knock me across the room for being a smart-ass. Usually he'd end up beating the crap out of my mother—and I knew it was my fault somehow, but I didn't know what I'd done wrong! I kept trying to find the right way to say things. Nothing worked." He paused and looked away. "And there was my older brother. It seemed like he was permanently pissed off at me—nothing I did was right or good enough. And there was the way everyone would stop talking when my mother and I walked into a store or passed people in the street." Emilio's eyes returned to John's. "You know what *puta* means?"

John nodded slightly. Whore.

"I'd hear that when my mother and I were out together. From kids, yes? You know—just kids, trying to be real witty and bold. I didn't get it, of course. Shit, I was what? Three, four years old? All I knew was there was something going on and I didn't understand it. So I kept looking for an explanation." He stared at John for a time and then asked, "Ever been to Puerto Rico?" John shook his head. "Puerto Rico is really mixed. Spanish, African, Dutch, English, Chinese, you name it. People are all different colors. For a long time it didn't strike me as odd that my mother and her husband and my older brother were all light-haired and fair-skinned, and here I was, this little Indio, like a cowbird in a warbler's nest, yes? But one day, when I was about eleven, I slipped and called my mother's husband Papa. Not to his face—I just said something like, When did Papa come home? He always got ugly when he was drunk, but that time—Jesus! He really took me apart. And he kept yelling, Don't call me that! You're *nothing* to me, you little bastard! Don't *ever* call me that!"

John closed his eyes, but then opened them and looked at Emilio. "So you got your explanation."

Emilio shrugged. "It still took me a while—Christ, what a dumb kid! Anyway, afterward, when they were putting the cast on my arm, I was thinking, How can a son be nothing to a father? Then it hit me, so to speak." There was a brief bleak smile. "I thought, Well, he's been telling me I was a bastard all along. I was just too stupid to realize he meant it."

"Emilio, I didn't mean to—"

"No! You said you wanted to understand. I'm trying to explain, okay? So just shut up and listen!" Emilio sank onto the edge of the treadmill. "Sit down, will you?" he said wearily, neck craned. "Everybody on this goddamned ship is so fucking big," he muttered, blinking spasmodically. "I feel like a dwarf. I *hate* that."

For an instant John could see a skinny little kid, huddled up and waiting for the beating to be over; a small man in a stone cell, waiting for a rape to end. . . . Jesus, John thought, sitting on the floor across from Sandoz. "I'm listening," he said.

Emilio took a deep breath, and started again. "See, the thing about all this is, when I finally worked it out, I wasn't angry, okay? I wasn't ashamed. I wasn't hurt. Well, I was hurt—I mean, the guy put me in the hospital, right? But I swear: my feelings weren't hurt." He watched John carefully. "I was relieved. Can you believe that? I was just so fucking *relieved*."

"Because things finally made sense," said John.

Emilio inclined his head. "Yes. Things finally made sense. They still sucked, but at least they made sense."

"And that's why you want to go back now. To Rakhat. To find out if things make sense?"

"*Want* to go back? Want to?" Emilio cried. The bitterness was sharp but short-lived, replaced by simple tiredness. He looked down at the floor of the exercise bay, and then shook his head, the bone-straight hair, more silver than black now, falling over eyes almost bloody with fatigue. "I keep thinking of that line: if you are asked to go a mile, go two. Maybe this is the extra mile. Maybe I've got to give it all another chance," Emilio said quietly. "I can tolerate a great deal if I just understand *why*. . . . And there's only one place I can find that out."

He was silent for a long time. "John, when you arrive on Rakhat, all you will have are the knowledge and skills you and your companions can bring to bear on problems you cannot imagine or anticipate—problems you cannot pray or buy or bluff or even shoot your way out of. If I withhold information from Carlo and his people and if something happens because of their ignorance, I will be responsible. I'm not willing to take that chance."

He pulled in a breath and held it before asking "Did you hear what Carlo said? Before? That I'm frightened?" John nodded. "John, I'm not just scared, I'm probably fucked up for life," he said, laughing at how awful it was, the glittering black eyes held wide with the effort to contain the tears that had not yet spilled. "Even with Gina—. I don't know, maybe it would have gotten better, but I still had nightmares, even with her. And now—Jesus! They're worse than ever! Sometimes I think, maybe it's better this way. The screaming would have scared Celestina, you know? What kind of life is that for a little kid, growing up with her stepfather screaming every night?" he asked, the sound wrung from his voice. "Maybe it's better for her, this way."

"Maybe," John said doubtfully, "but that's not much of a silver lining, is it?"

"No, it's not," Emilio agreed. "I'll take what I can get, I guess." He glanced at John, infinitely grateful that there had been no platitudes, no half-assed attempt to make him feel okay. He filled his lungs shudderingly, and got a grip on himself. "John, I—. Listen, you've been—"

"Forget it," John said, and thought, That's what I'm here for.

SANDOZ STOOD UP AND STEPPED BACK ONTO THE TREADMILL. AFTER A time, John got to his feet as well and went to his cabin, where he flopped onto his bunk in a loose-limbed heap and put his hands over his eyes. He thought of all the ways of coping with undeserved pain. Offer it up. Remember Jesus on the cross. The bromides: God never gives us a burden we cannot bear. Everything happens for a reason. John Candotti knew for a fact that the old sayings worked for some people. But as a parish priest, he had often observed that trust in God could impose an additional burden on good people slammed to their knees by some senseless tragedy. An atheist might be no less staggered by such an event, but nonbelievers often experienced a kind of calm acceptance: shit happens, and this particular shit had happened to them. It could be more difficult for a person of faith to get to his feet precisely because he had to reconcile God's love and care with the stupid, brutal fact that something irreversibly terrible had happened.

"Faith is supposed to be a comfort, Father!" a bereaved mother had once cried to him, weeping over her child's grave. "How could God let this happen? All those prayers, all that hope—it was just howling into the wind."

He was so young. A few weeks past ordination, all dewy and optimistic. It was his first funeral, and he thought he'd handled it pretty well, not stumbling over the prayers, alive to the grief of the mourners, ready to comfort them. "The disciples, and Mary herself, must have felt the same way you do now, when they stood at the foot of the cross," he'd said, impressed by his own gentle voice, his own loving concern.

"So fucking what?" the mother snapped, eyes like coals. "My kid is dead, and she's not coming back in three days, and I don't give a shit about the resurrection at the end of the goddamn world because I want her back *now*—" The weeping ceased, replaced by pure steely anger. "God's got a lot to answer for," she snarled. "That's all I can tell you, Father. God's got a lot to answer for."

A father and a brother, he thought. Was that how it had started for Emilio? A Father he could count on, a Brother he could look up to. How long had he resisted the Spirit? John wondered. How long did he protect himself from the fear that God was just a bullshit story, that religion was just a load of crap? What kind of courage had it taken—summoning the trust that faith requires? And where the hell was Emilio finding the strength now to hope again that maybe it would all make sense? That if he could just bring himself to listen, maybe God would explain.

What if God did explain, and it turned out that what had happened was all Emilio's fault? John wondered. Not the gardens—everyone on the *Stella Maris* crew had agreed to grow the gardens, and no one could have anticipated what happened because of them. But later—what if it was something Emilio said or did that was misunderstood on Rakhat?

Listen, John prayed, I'm not telling You what to do, but if Emilio brought the rapes on himself somehow, and then Askama died because of that, it's better if he never understands, okay? In my opinion. You know what people can take, but I think You're cutting it pretty close here. Or maybe—help him make it mean something. Help him. That's what I'm asking. Just help him. He's doing his damnedest. Help him.

And help me, John thought then. He reached for his rosary, and tried to empty his mind of everything but the rhythm of familiar prayers. He heard instead the rhythmic pounding on the treadmill: the sound of a small, scared, aging man, going the extra mile.

28

Central Inbrokar

2061, Earth-Relative

IT WAS PAST SECOND DAWN WHEN HA'ANALA WOKE TO DAYLIGHT IN HER eyes. She turned her face away from the glare and stared at Puska, still lax with sleep.

How can I tell Sofia? she asked herself miserably—her first thought on this new day identical to her last of the previous one. Sitting up, she looked at herself and grimaced: her fur was matted and muddy, and her teeth felt as thick as her head. Oh, Isaac, she thought hopelessly, getting up slowly, stretching each stiff limb. Her mind as blank as the flatlands that stretched out before her, she stared east over an immense plain, the lavender of its shortgrass blossoms pale in the bleached light of full day.

"*Sipaj*, Puska," she said. "Wake up!" She felt around with her tail and slapped Puska's hip. Puska brushed her away. "Puska!" she cried, more urgently, not daring to move her head for fear of losing the plume. "He's alive! I can smell him."

That brought the Runao to her feet in a swift roll. Puska stared in the same direction that Ha'anala was looking, but saw only emptiness. "*Sipaj*, Ha'anala," she said wearily, "there's no one there."

"Isaac's out there," Ha'anala insisted, making a quick attempt to brush dried mud from her coat. "It depends on the wind, but someone thinks he's moving northeast."

Puska couldn't detect a useful thing herself, except for some *sintaron* setting fruit nearby and a little patch of sweetleaf that might make a decent breakfast. "*Sipaj*, Ha'anala, it's time to go home."

"We just have to catch up with him—"

"No," said Puska.

Shocked, Ha'anala glanced over her shoulder and saw equal parts of skepticism and regret in Puska's face. "Don't be frightened," she started.

"I'm not frightened," Puska said bluntly, too tired for courtesy. "I don't believe you, Ha'anala." There was an awkward pause. "*Sipaj*, Ha'anala, someone thinks you have been wrong about all of this. He's not out there."

They looked at each other for a long time: all but sisters, almost strangers. It was Ha'anala who broke the silence. "All right," she said evenly. "Someone will go on alone. Tell Fia that someone will find Isaac even if she must follow him all the way to the sea."

AS THE SOUNDS OF PUSKA'S RETREAT RECEDED, HA'ANALA CLOSED HER eyes and formed an image of the plume: diffuse and broad at its top, narrowing at the base toward a point she could not detect, but could infer from the taper. Not caring that Puska had given up, she said, "He's out there," and followed the pillar of his scent into the wilderness.

In the first few hours, the wind played with the plume and she was twice forced to double back so she could arc across the trail to find the line strongest with his passing on the ground. But as the suns climbed and the wind stilled, her skill strengthened, and she had only to shift her head from side to side to gauge the gradient.

The plain was not empty, as it had seemed, but creased and furrowed with narrow streams swollen from the previous day's rain. Many of the creeks were bordered by bushes bearing purplish fruits that Isaac had eaten, she noted, examining his spoor. Ha'anala herself was hungry a great deal of the time, but stayed alert for burrows along the banks where small prey whose name she did not know could be dug out or snagged on a claw when she thrust an arm deep into a den. Once, hot and dirty, she waded into a creek and sat on its stony bottom, hoping to be scrubbed clean and cooled by the rain-quickened current; to her astonishment, as she leaned back against her tail, some kind of swimmer blundered into the weir of her spread legs. "Manna!" she cried, and laughed into the sunlight.

The land was full of wonders. She could see from one side of the world to the other, and on her sixth day of travel she had watched suns both rise and set, and understood at last why the colors of the sky changed. Her own body was an astonishment. Confined by dense vegetation throughout her childhood, she had never before felt the rightness of her natural gait. The rhythm of her steady stride sang to her: a poetry of walking, of silent space, of purpose. Leaning into a floating canter, tail level with the ground, she knew for the first time balance and speed, precision and grace, but she felt no need to hurry. She was gaining on Isaac, knew that he was alive and well. She was certain that he was happy, as she herself was.

She allowed herself a day of rest by a gullied stream, where she discovered hundreds of mud nests filled with infant somethings whose foolish parents had left them unguarded, and she fell asleep that evening with a full belly, secure in the belief that Isaac was not far ahead and that she could follow him even after a rain, and awoke the next morning, stiff-muscled but joyous.

She caught up to him at midday. He was standing on the edge of an escarpment where the plain fractured, its eastern half lower than the west by the height of a mature *w'ralia* tree. Isaac said nothing, but when she came to a halt some sixty paces away, he flung his arms wide as though to embrace all the empty fullness around him—not spinning to blur the world, but turning with ecstatic slowness to see it all. When he had come full circle, his eyes met her own. "Clarity!" he cried.

"Yes," she called, elated, for a moment knowing everything hidden in his strange, secret heart. "Clarity!"

He swayed slightly: naked, tall and tailless. Ha'anala followed his gaze to the vast sky. "Red is harmless," he declared with fragile bravery, not knowing himself how wrong he was. After a time, blinking, and beginning to shiver, he said, "I won't go back."

"I know, Isaac," Ha'anala replied as she walked toward him—Sofia and the Runa forgotten, all her life before now lost to view. "I understand."

He fell silent, which was no surprise, but as Ha'anala drew close her own quiet became speechlessness. Isaac was the color of blood, his poor pale skin blistered and swollen. What could have done this to him? she wondered, ears flattened. He sat abruptly next to his two possessions, the computer tablet and his fraying blue shawl, but did not draw the cloth over his head and shoulders as was his custom even in the forest, where the canopy had shielded him from the suns' power. "Tha's all," she heard him say, the muttered words slurred.

Not knowing what else to do, she felt compelled to ask, "*Sipaj*, Isaac, are you not hungry?" And cursed herself for uselessness.

"Listen," he said, trembling, the tension in his narrow, nearly hairless body visible. "Music." She didn't move, paralyzed by the oozing sores, the smell of corruption. . . . "Listen!" he insisted.

Thus commanded, she went motionless, ears high and open. Above her, she heard the slow beat of some large thing's wings as it climbed to meet a thermal that would lift it out over the rim of the escarpment. Below, at the base of the cliff, the crash of water and alarming bellows that diminished into comic squeals or a ponderous trill of grunts. Westward, the fluting whistles of some kind of herd keeping itself gathered as its long-necked members grazed, heads to the ground. Nearby, tiny scratchings, wind hissing in grass. A soft popping noise that drew her eye: seedpods cracking open as some critical shift in temperature or humidity swelled or shrank their cells.

"God's music," she breathed, her own heartbeat loud in her ears.

"No," said Isaac. "Listen. There are others who sing."

Others! she thought then, hearing the notes of the evening chant, thin and distant, coming in fragments with the fitful wind. Others who sing. *Djanada*—Jana'ata!

Isaac thrust his thin arms out to support the treacherous weight of his head and shoulders, which seemed to him to have become heavier just now, and leaned at the edge of the precipice. Seeing him rapt and heedless of his wounded skin, Ha'anala crept nearer the brink, listening to a well-known melody sung uncertainly by two voices, their harmony unfamiliar but beautiful. A mixed multitude, Ha'anala thought, looking down on them. Jana'ata and Runa, but a puzzling collection of ages and sexes. *Djanada* babies riding the backs not of their own fathers but of female Runa, who were huddled together, ears clamped against the song. A few veiled and robed persons. Then she spotted the singers—a man wearing metal clothing, and a boy a little younger than Ha'anala herself.

Momentary mourning came like a cloudburst: she wanted to be here alone with Isaac, to be as solitary as two stones, side by side. She wanted to ask him one question each day, and to take the whole of the world's turning to think about his answer. She wanted to know what he had heard as he walked. Was there a kind of poetry in his legs too? Did the wind roar wordlessly in his small ears?

Not yet! she thought, anguished. I don't want any others!

• • •

WHICH WAS THE VERY THOUGHT PRESENTLY PASSING THROUGH THE mind of Shetri Laaks, who had caught the scent of a female, and looked up just in time to catch a glimpse of yet another refugee peering down at him from the escarpment that divided the grasslands.

No more! he thought, appealing to any deity who'd listen. I don't want any others!

As if in accordance with his prayer, the girl's unveiled head disappeared. Even so, Shetri Laaks was thrown sufficiently off balance by her unwelcome appearance to stumble over the evening chant's concluding verse, thus earning another of his nephew Athaansi's insolent smirks. I never wanted any of this, you superior young stud, Shetri wanted to snarl at Athaansi. Take the damned armor and my obstinate sister and the wretched chants and just go on by yourselves, and may Sti dance on your bones!

To date, Shetri Laaks had sung the evening chant all of ten times. This was, not coincidentally, the exact number of days he had been taking his little mob of women and children north.

No matter what his resentful young nephew thought, Shetri Laaks had never aspired to anything but the quiet life of an apothecary specializing in the Sti canon. Indeed, until informed by a novice that his second-born sister, Ta'ana Laaks u Erat, and her entire household had just appeared at the gate, Shetri Laaks had been only vaguely aware of the revolt in the south, and had certainly never expected to be affected by it—only draft Runa were allowed anywhere nearby. Adepts like Shetri lived simply, their provisions periodically supplied by their natal families, occasionally supplemented by the offerings of those hoping to have ailments declared uninheritable or injuries deemed minor enough to be treated without iniquity. Now and then, widows bought the right to prepare for a serene death by witnessing the water ritual. Otherwise, the adepts were left alone, and that had suited Shetri admirably.

"Our brother Nra'il has been killed in combat," Ta'ana had informed him without preamble when he presented himself to her in the visitors' shelter ten days earlier. "All his people are murdered. My husband, as well."

Shetri had stared dumbly for a time, still hoping that his sister and her entourage would prove an unusually convincing hallucination. Why are you telling me this? he thought. Go away.

"I cannot travel alone," Ta'ana had insisted then, despite the fact that she had come this far unaccompanied by an adult male relative. "The north is defensible. It is your duty to take us there."

"Not possible," he'd muttered, barely able to speak. He held up his claws, stained with pigment from the spoiled rite Ta'ana had called him away from. He had only recently mastered the full body of the canon, and hadn't built tolerance to the inhalants used during the water ritual. "The drugs will be in effect for days," he told her, blinking. She smelled of smoke and was wearing a smudged veil that fell to her feet; it was shot through with silver threads and its hem was embroidered with a lattice pattern that seemed to Shetri to be crawling. "There are visual disturbances," he reported.

"It is your duty," she repeated.

"And what of the duty of your husband's brother?"

"Dead," she said, not burdening him with superfluous detail or herself with the telling of it: her calm was brittle. "You are my son's regent now. There is no one else. The armor is yours until Athaansi is trained."

"I'm old enough," Athaansi had snarled with a fifteen-year-old's reflexive ferocity. "This is insult. I will fight you, Uncle!"

Ta'ana whirled and cuffed the boy violently, stunning the three of them—mother, son and uncle. Athaansi broke the silence with a shuddering gasp and began to sob. "Control yourself," Ta'ana ordered, finding her own voice. "If you give way, the others will too. Go sit with your sister." Then she'd further scandalized the adepts, who were watching from a barely polite distance, by gathering up her veil and raising it with both hands so she could stare unimpeded at her surviving brother. "Focus!" she snapped. "Would I have left my walls if there was anyone alive to defend my honor? You are regent, Shetri," she said in a tone that he was obliged to consider persuasive. "The armor is in the wagon."

So he had pulled off and laid aside his plain gray robe and called upon skills indifferently learned during his days of training as a young reshtar of barely respectable rank. Whether it was the drug or genuine forgetfulness, he couldn't picture how to put on the armor. Athaansi, red-eyed and humiliated, found solace in contempt, turning the shin plates right side up for his hapless uncle, to the silent amusement of the Runa valet who fastened the buckles.

"We must walk. Wear boots," Ta'ana had told him as he struggled with the breastplate. The navigable rivers south of Mo'arl were now wholly controlled by Runa rebels. "And bring ointments for burns."

He was too befuddled to argue that his feet were used to the ground—he walked every day, collecting psychotropic herbs and the minerals that could be ground for pigment; he did not think to ask who was burned.

With brilliant color still pulsating around every solid object, Shetri Laaks had begun the trek north, nominally in command of his sister's household while following the directions of a Runa maid, who was actually leading the way. Farce, he'd thought with every step of his first day's travel. This is farce.

But by the end of the second full day on the road, Shetri had seen enough to recognize his elder sister's laconic courage, for he had learned why the ointments were needed. Ta'ana had remained in her burning compound until the last moment, gathering her dependents and organizing an orderly retreat by firelight with an audacity born of desperation. The entire town had been fired—even the quarters of Runa domestics, whose goodwill and affection Ta'ana had nurtured and won, anticipating a day when war would find her. She and her children were alive only because their household Runa had smuggled them out of the burning Laaks compound in a false-bottomed wagon—prepared long ago in expectation of such a night—apparently loaded with loot, but actually packed with food and the family's valuables, including Nra'il's dented, blackened armor.

The half-marked path the housemaid knew passed within sight of several other smoldering towns. No male Jana'ata over the age of sixteen breathed; here and there, a wailing child or a bewildered woman was found wandering. Some were too badly burned to save; to these Shetri gave quietus, using the embers of their own compounds to light pitiably ineffective pyres. The rest he treated for burns as he had his sister, and Ta'ana made every one of them part of her migrant household, without regard to lineage or birthrank.

"We can't feed any more," Shetri would declare as each new refugee joined their band.

"We won't starve," Ta'ana insisted. "Hunger is not the worst thing."

But their progress was slowed, and they had gathered more people than could be fed with the provisions packed in the wagon. Nights were always broken by someone's dream of flames; in the mornings, exhaustion fought fear to determine their pace. By the fifth day, Shetri was thinking clearly enough to realize that he could slaughter one of the draft Runa. By the ninth, they had left the wagon behind. Everyone, master and domestic, carried a child or food or a bundle of essentials.

Now, after days of flight and still far from safety, the numbers of Jana'ata and Runa in their little party were dangerously unbalanced. The more refugees Ta'ana took on, the slower they traveled and the sooner they had to butcher; two more Runa domestics had snuck off the previous night.

At this rate, we'll never get to Inbrokar City, Shetri thought, looking up at the cliff edge where the newest girl was hiding. He turned to his sister, hoping that she hadn't noticed the latest refugee, but Ta'ana was standing, veil off, ears cocked forward.

"Get her," Ta'ana said.

"It'll be dark soon!"

"Then you'd best go now."

"Come down, girl!" he yelled, turning cliffward. There was no response. Shetri glanced at his sister, who stared uncompromisingly back. "Oh, all right," he muttered, flicking an ear at the valet, who came to unburden him of the armor. Ta'ana had earned obedience; Shetri, not much in the habit of leadership anyway, gave it to her.

Free of the armor's weight, he picked his way carefully across the rocky riverbed, trying not to attract the attention of a pair of *cranil* snuffling and squealing in the shallows upstream, and then stood looking upward toward where this inconvenient girl had last showed herself. The escarpment was not a sheer drop. Blocks of stone had fallen toward the water, and these presented a fair approximation of a stairway for the first two-thirds of the distance before giving way to an increasingly uncongenial verticality. Mere expectation of a ludicrous death yielded twice to near certainty, so Shetri Laaks was in a thoroughly unhappy frame of mind—and in the midst of a wide-ranging and almost sincere curse calling down plague, deformity, insult, diarrhea and mange on every living creature east and west of the Pon River and all its tributaries—when he came face to face with what simply had to be a lingering effect of the Sti drugs.

"Don't fall," the girl advised as he crested the cliff, his lungs and feet straining for air and purchase respectively.

For a time, he gazed dumbfounded at a young woman who was not merely unveiled but completely naked. Embarrassed beyond description, he finally averted his eyes from this spectacle, only to behold the noseless, tailless, oozing figment sitting woozily on the ground next to her.

"Someone's brother is ill," the girl said.

Shetri gaped at her, ears drifting sideways, and belatedly realized that his pedal grip was beginning to give way. Scrambling with sudden undignified zeal, he established a graceless momentary balance on the stem of a scrubby bush growing horizontally from a crack in the rock, and heaved himself over the edge of the escarpment without further delay. "My lady," he gasped, in breathless, abbreviated greeting when he arrived belly-down. "Your *brother*?" The girl looked blank. "Your brother?" he repeated, in kitchen Ruanja. She lifted her chin.

Slumped over, legs crossed, its skeletal arms thrust out like buttresses, the "brother" had evidently been flayed alive by some remarkably ineffi-cient hunter. There was a tiny nose, Shetri saw now that he was closer, but like much of the rest of this monster, it was blistered and raw.

"He's too far gone," Shetri told the girl, getting up wearily. "Someone will grant him peace."

"No!" the girl cried, as Shetri moved into position behind the poor beast and lifted its little jaw to open its throat. Shetri froze. She was not large, but she looked quite capable of biting through a man's neck. Shetri himself had not so much as wrestled with anyone in years. "Go away," she ordered. "Leave us alone!"

What has happened to all the women in the world? Shetri asked him-self. He held his position for a moment and then, with great care, removed his hands from the beast's neck and backed off. "My lady: one can think of nothing more inexpressibly agreeable than to obey your command," he said with an elaborate obeisance to the naked little bitch, "but whatever this thing is, the wretch is dying. Would you have your 'brother' suffer?"

Her glare remained undimmed. Shetri was beginning to realize that she didn't have any idea what he was saying. Summoning a Ruanja half-remembered from the nursery, he repeated the burden of his question as best he could.

"Someone would not have him suffer. Someone would have him *live*," the girl declared with a vehemence that seemed to Shetri unnecessarily threatening.

Well, choose! Shetri wanted to say. You can select one condition or the other. He looked around experimentally and noted with some satisfaction that there was still a vague pulsing aura around anything blue, which in-cluded the "brother's" bizarre little eyes. This was exceedingly if tem-porarily reassuring. Maybe the brother wasn't real! Perhaps the girl wasn't either . . .

Except that Ta'ana had seen her as well. Sighing, Shetri straightened and moved cautiously from behind the poor, skinned thing. He leaned out over the cliff to look at his sister.

"What's going on?" Ta'ana called up to him.

"Why not come and see for yourself?" Shetri suggested cheerfully, no longer maintaining even a pretense of command.

Ta'ana arrived at the top of the cliff a short time later, stripped to a chemise for the climb. Shetri himself was, by then, sitting serenely a little space away from the girl and what she insisted was her brother, quietly singing a verse or two for Sti. To his beatific gratification, his sister's face went as slack as his own must have earlier.

Ta'ana assessed the situation with the admirable alacrity of a middle-rank householder used to coping with unexpected visitors. "Honored guests," she said, getting to her feet and addressing the two newcomers as she had each of the refugees they'd taken on during the trek north. The girl looked at her warily. "If it pleases you, be welcomed into my household and sojourn under my lord brother's protection." Turning to Shetri, Ta'ana added, low-voiced, "Make sure the monster lives."

IT WAS AN UNREASONABLE DEMAND BUT, BY THE DYING LIGHT OF Rakhat's second sun, Shetri Laaks did what he could.

Which was little enough. Calling down to Ta'ana's maid, he instructed her to bring the cleanest sleeping sheet she could find and to get a chemise from one of the other refugees. "No," he corrected himself, disturbed by the new girl's exposure, "bring two chemises, not one. But rinse one in the stream before you come up. Keep everything as clean as you can! And bring me all the ointments!"

While he waited, he examined the monster carefully, but did not touch him. He and Ta'ana were nearly blind when the Runao arrived, but by that time, Shetri had formed a plan of treatment. "Put that . . . *person* on the sheet, and be careful of its skin," he told the maid, not giving her time to panic. "Then examine every part of it and pick out any dirt or debris you find. Be gentle." He waited, expecting to hear the pathetic beast cry out, but there was no sound. "Does he live?" he asked the darkness, reluctant to deplete his precious stock of medicine on a corpse.

"He lives," the maid's voice informed him.

"What are you doing?" the new girl demanded. "Tell this one what you're doing to him!"

The maid kept silent, not sure who was in charge now. "Tell her, child," Shetri said wearily, and waited for the chatter to pause. "All right," he said to the Runao then, "unwrap the convex silver spatula carefully—don't get your hands on the end! Use the spatula to spread the ointment over his entire body—a very thin layer, understand? Rounded surface toward the patient—keep the edges of the instrument away from the skin. When the skin is covered with ointment, spread the wet chemise over him, child. Tonight, you will keep the covering damp with fresh water, do you understand?"

Having done all that was possible, Shetri Laaks gave up on the long day, and went to sleep that night hoping that when he awoke, he would spend the morning chuckling about the absurdity of the dreams Sti had provided.

WHEN ISAAC OPENED HIS EYES, THE DAWN CHANT WAS NEARLY OVER and the smell of roasting meat incensed the air. "They've killed a Runao," Ha'anala whispered. "They're eating her."

"Everyone eats," Isaac said, granting emotionless absolution. He closed his eyes again.

But she insisted, "No, it's wrong. There are other things to eat."

Isaac listened carefully to the chant. Then he slept.

"TRY THIS," HA'ANALA SAID WHEN NEXT HE WOKE. SHE SAT AT HIS SIDE, out of his line of sight, but her hand motioned toward a small cup of broth that was sitting nearby. He turned his head away. "Everyone eats," she reminded him. "Shetri says meat will make you stronger. Someone caught this herself. It isn't Runa."

He sat up. Everything had changed. They were at the bottom, not the top. They were under an awning made of fabric with silver thread. He liked the color. It was quiet here. The Runa kept their distance and spoke in low tones. There was a damp thing draped over him. His skin shone with something slippery. Because no one was talking, he could consider all this. The slippery stuff felt cool.

"Tablet?" he asked Ha'anala.

"Someone was careful with it." He saw her gesture at the edge of his field of vision. The tablet was set on a flagstone nearby.

Isaac drank the broth and lay down again. "We'll stay with these people," he said.

There was an uncertain pause. "Until you are strong again," Ha'anala said.

"They sing," Isaac said, and fell asleep.

"HOW CAN YOU KNOW THAT?" ATHAANSI ERAT DEMANDED, CERTAIN that his mother's notion was preposterous.

"You were too young to remember—the Paramount once passed through our compound on an inspection tour. A horrible man! But when he looked at me—a god's eyes! She has the same," Ta'ana Laaks u Erat insisted, out of the hearing of their Runa and the other refugees. "That girl is a Kitheri."

"Wandering out here alone, with a monster like that?" Shetri cried. "Speaking only Ruanja? Naked?" He preferred his own initial conviction that he was hallucinating again, a hope he still found difficult to relinquish entirely.

"The traitor had a daughter out of Jholaa Kitheri. That was sixteen years ago," Ta'ana said emphatically. "Don't you see? She's been brought up in the south, by Runa. The tailless monster has to be one of the foreigners." Athaansi opened his mouth to ask again how she knew. Cutting him off, Ta'ana said, "I listened to the Paramount's concerts! I know about—" She hesitated, both embarrassed and aroused by the memory of that particular poetic theme. "I know about those things."

If her son was tempted to lecture her on propriety, the set of her ears changed his mind. "Well, then," Athaansi said, "we should execute them and bring their scent glands to Inbrokar. There are standing orders for the nameless one's death and for his whole sept. And for all foreigners as well!"

To his surprise, his mother did not agree at once. "Haste in a moment, regrets forever," she said after a time, looking at her son speculatively. "It occurs to me that you need a wife, Athaansi."

Shetri Laaks was certain that he was now beyond being amazed by his sister, but Athaansi Erat, he noted delightedly, was still capable of astonishment. "Her?" the boy squawked. "She's VaHaptaa! She's under writ of execution! Her children would be—"

"Born in a time when nothing can be predicted," his mother finished for him. "She is collateral to Hlavin Kitheri's lineage, for which succession is not yet established. Who knows what compromises may become necessary? Kitheri has changed everything else, and she wouldn't be the first niece to transmit an open patrimony," Ta'ana pointed out. "The girl is small, but of good conformation, and she's the right age—"

Athaansi's protests became vigorous at this point. His uncle enjoyed the drama for a time, glad to be forgotten, but his relief was short-lived.

"It seems that Athaansi is too fastidious to cover a VaHaptaa of ancient lineage," said Ta'ana Laaks u Erat, undismayed, and turned her attention from son to brother with dispassionate pragmatism. "Perhaps you would like to make a start on reestablishing the Laaks lineage, now that our brother and his family are dead?" Ears high, Ta'ana invited comment.

There was none, Shetri Laaks being occupied with a silent reassessment of his capacity for astonishment.

Ta'ana rose then, glancing over at the two newcomers, sheltered under the awning she had caused to be made for them out of her own silvered veil. "As for the foreign monster," Ta'ana continued, "he may be useful as a hostage, if things go badly in the south." Which effectively concluded the discussion.

"SOMEONE THINKS YOUR BROTHER SINGS WELL," SHETRI LAAKS TOLD the girl as they walked together the next morning. He did not tell her that her voice was beautiful as well. He was still surprised that she dared to sing the chants, though Ta'ana said that this was now considered permissible among members of Kitheri's court. So much had changed while he himself had studied changeless ritual. "He has a pleasing, clear voice, and his harmonies are . . ."

"Otherworldly," Ha'anala supplied, smiling as Shetri considered the construction and then blinked at the word's meaning. "Isaac loves music, as he can love nothing else."

"What is it that you sing with him, after the chants?"

"The Sh'ma: a song of our mother's people."

Shetri had given up trying to work out Ha'anala's notions of kinship. Music, on the other hand, was something he appreciated. "It's beautiful."

"As are your own songs." She was silent for a time. "Someone thanks you for singing to Isaac. The Sti chants make the heart quiet. Someone wishes she understood the words, but the melody is enough."

Shetri paused in their procession, willing now to ask a question that made him uneasy. "How is it possible for Isaac to know the whole of an epic, hearing it but once? Someone studied years . . ." He looked away, embarrassed. "Is he a memory specialist or is such a feat normal for your . . . mother's kind?"

"Our mother says that Isaac's mind is made differently from anyone else's anywhere. Isaac would not be like anyone else, even if he were among his own people."

"A genetic freak," Shetri suggested, but she didn't understand. She knew the evening chants but very little modern K'San, and he couldn't summon any similar idea in Ruanja. Falling silent, he set himself to study the low-growing foliage around them, noting the herbs that grew here, and leaned over to slice a stem of feverbalm, inhaling its fragrance. He was glad of the distraction, gladder still that the girl was not contemptuous of a man who cared about plants.

Until Ta'ana had proposed a match, Shetri had never in his life considered taking a mate, not even privately, not even after he had first learned of the deaths of Nra'il and his heirs. Ha'anala was young, he knew, but he himself felt newborn in the world. He wondered if Ta'ana had spoken to the girl already. He had no idea how these things were arranged; he was a third, and had never expected to care. "Ha'anala. It's a strange name," he said.

"Someone was named for a person her father admired."

It seemed to him that she neither revealed nor concealed her identity. Perhaps she thought it obvious—and indeed, it had been to Ta'ana. Or perhaps she had told Shetri himself, but he had understood her Ruanja imperfectly and missed some subtlety. Her soul seemed to him like colored glass: translucent but not transparent.

He was embarrassed to find that he was staring at her again; she would not submit to being gowned, let alone to veiling, and her scent was intoxicating. Shetri gazed back toward his sister's encampment in the distance, makeshift and muddy with the night's rain. Very soon he would have to ask his sister to choose between nakedness and hunger. The valet was the most expendable Runao now; given Ta'ana's abandonment of her veil, he suspected that the dresser's time was coming. "We must move on to Inbrokar City. Ta'ana is concerned that they may not let us in if too many others have already taken shelter there," he told Ha'anala as they walked again. "What will you do, when Isaac's wounds are healed?"

She did not seem to answer directly. "It's wrong to eat Runa," she said. She stopped walking and met his eyes. "*Sipaj*, Shetri, otherwise, we would stay with you."

He had to listen to her words in his mind again, to be certain: she had used a form of address that meant him personally, not him as a part of his

sister's household. Before meeting Ha'anala, he had rarely spoken to a female not of his own family, but the meaning of Ha'anala's scent was now
unmistakable, and her eyes were the color of amethyst, and she looked at
him with what he imagined might be the unfrightened gaze of a Runa
courtesan. "Someone is . . ." His voice faded away. Then, recalling himself
regent and determined to be honorable, he began again, "Someone's
nephew Athaansi—"

"Is of no interest," Ha'anala finished decisively. "Your sister will find another wife for him. Perhaps two." Shetri reared back, shocked. "*Sipaj,*
Shetri, everything will change soon. There will no longer be any 'sires' to
waste," she told him, using the K'San term she'd learned from Ta'ana.

She had thought hard about what she must do. On the right foot, there
was love for and obligation to Sofia, and a desire to ameliorate unavoidable sorrow. On the left, a need for refuge, for survival on her own terms.
Ha'anala could not, would not turn against the Runa, whom she loved and
understood; neither could she idly witness the destruction of her own
kind. The solution had come as she watched Ta'ana and her maid working together with a practical equality as they organized the little band of
refugees for the next leg of the journey.

The people themselves will choose from among us, Ha'anala thought.
And we *djanada* will begin again, having been chosen.

Raised by Runa, Ha'anala had no wish to alarm a male, but she had confirmed Ta'ana's own worst fears about the war. There would be no more
talk of Isaac as hostage—he was to have full status as a brother-in-law.

"*Sipaj,* Shetri," Ha'anala said then, "someone has discussed this matter
with Ta'ana, and we-but-not-you are agreed. Isaac wishes to remain with
people who sing, and someone wishes you for a husband. Your sister
agrees." She looked at Shetri until his own eyes dropped; he had begun to
tremble, and she herself was hardly less driven by the need to fill an emptiness she had never felt so physically. "It remains for your consent," she
said, her voice not quite as steady as she might have wished.

It was all he could do to order his thoughts in K'San and when he was
as ready as he could be, he translated them into Ruanja for her. "Someone," he said quietly in a language ill-suited to his tongue and task, "has
no experience. Someone studied the Sti epics all his life. There is—there
was a small estate, ten day's travel south of here, but now someone's sister
says there is nothing. Everything is gone. Someone can promise nothing—not even food—to . . ."

She waited for him to find his words, familiar with Isaac's need for silence in which to think. After a time, she said, "To study poetry seems an enviable life."

She turned away then and looked south, toward the broad, flat plains she'd traveled over, and thought of all that had happened since leaving Trucha Sai. She thought again of the people, and how much she loved them; of their engulfing affection and their never-ending concern; of their beautiful, terrible need to touch, to speak, to watch, to care. She closed her eyes, asking herself what she wanted.

This, she thought. I want to live among people who sing, who are quiet enough to let Isaac think. I want to be with this shy and awkward man, who is kind to Isaac and who will be a good father. I want to belong with someone. I want to feel at the center of something, and not the edge. I want children and grandchildren. I don't want to grow to be old and die, knowing that when I die, there will be no more like me.

"I won't go back," Shetri heard her say, but in a language he did not recognize.

She spoke again, and this time he understood. "Someone's father once told her that it was better to die than to live wrongly. I say: better to live rightly." Once again, he was confused by the mix of languages she needed to think this way. So she said, "Someone can feed herself and her brother. And you, until you learn." He knew this to be so. She had brought back wild game; roasted, it was tough and fibrous, but the remaining domestics were convinced they could make such meat palatable, given time to learn its preparation. "Someone requires a promise: you will not eat Runa."

It seemed a small thing, somehow, almost reasonable, very nearly sensible, to throw aside the very basis of Jana'ata civilization, merely because this extraordinary girl asked it of him. "As you wish," he said, wondering if this conversation too were some drugged illusion, knowing suddenly that it was not the power of the Sti inhalants but her fragrance, her nearness—

He should not have been surprised. If Ha'anala was who his sister said she was, then she had grown up with Runa and mating was no mystery to her. Even so, that morning, under a wide sky, with three suns' witness, and no wedding guests but wind and herbs, Shetri Laaks found that it was once again necessary to reassess his capacity for astonishment.

"*Sipaj*, Shetri: it is not safe to go to the city of Inbrokar," she said, later, when she believed that he could hear again. "We-and-you-also must go beyond the Garnu mountains. Ta'ana agrees. There are places in the far north that will be safe."

Wordless, enveloped, emptied, felled: if she had told him to take up residence on a sun, he'd have climbed through cloud and fallen into fire for her.

"Do you know who we are?" she asked him. "This one and her brother?"

"Yes," he said.

She pulled away, leaving him chilled by her withdrawal, and faced him. "I am a teacher," she said. "My brother is a messenger."

He understood little more than the Ruanja word, messenger. "And what is his message?" he asked, seeing he was meant to.

"Walk away," she said. "And live."

"WE MUST TELL OUR MOTHER," HA'ANALA TOLD ISAAC THAT AFTERNOON. "Someone needs the tablet."

Isaac lifted his chin: permission.

They would be able to monitor any radio transmission on Rakhat, via the *Magellan*, and tap all its resources, but they themselves could not be located. The *Magellan*'s systems would record only that their tablet's signals had passed by way of one of the satellite relays positioned over the continent. Sofia would know that much: they were still on the continent.

Ha'anala sat thinking for a long time, trying to find the words to tell Sofia that there were Jana'ata who were good and decent, that justice could become tainted with revenge. But she knew what the people thought of those who collaborated with the *djanada*; no matter how nuanced, her words would be understood as treachery.

Throat tight, Ha'anala opened the connection to the *Magellan*. The enormity of her decision made speech impossible; she pecked out a short message with a single claw. "Sofia, my dear mother," she wrote, "we have left the garden."

29

Giordano Bruno

2070–2073, Earth-Relative

"I FAIL T'SEE THE PROBLEM HERE," SAID SEAN FEIN, SERVING HIMSELF some stew from the pot in the center of the table. "Put it on the speakers. Crank up the volume. It's not as though the wee man can take himself out for a little walk, now, is it?"

"It's not a matter of simply hearing the songs. It will require study and analysis," Danny Iron Horse insisted. "Half the words are a mystery to me, but what I did understand is—. Look, I've done all I can with them! Sandoz has to help."

"I told him once that the music changed after he was there. He had no interest in this," Joseba informed them, bringing his plate to the table. "He was averse to listening to these songs even before we left."

"That was when it was Hlavin Kitheri's voice," John pointed out, chewing thoughtfully. "Or one of the others he recognized. These are so different!"

"But it's unquestionably Kitheri's style," Carlo commented, pouring himself a little Ferreghini red.

"Yes," Danny agreed, "and if this is what Kitheri is writing now, then the whole structure of that society—"

Sandoz appeared in the doorway to the commons, VR visor tucked under an arm. The room fell silent, as it generally did whenever he first walked in and his mood was unclear. "Gentlemen, Geryon is tamed," he announced. "I have successfully completed a simulated lander flight from the *Bruno* to the surface of Rakhat and back again."

"I'll be damned," Frans Vanderhelst breathed.

"Quite likely," Sandoz replied, and bowed with mock modesty when cheers and whistles and applause erupted.

"I really don't understand why you had so much trouble with it," said John, as he and Nico came to Emilio's side, like attendants at a prize fight, to remove the VR gloves and take the visor from him. "I mean, how much harder could it be than fielding a baseball?"

"Just couldn't seem to picture what I had to do. I'm almost blind, mentally," Sandoz told him, taking his place at the table. "I didn't even know other people could see things in their heads until I was in college." He nodded to Carlo when a celebratory glass of wine was offered. "And I can't read maps for shit—if somebody gave me instructions on how to get someplace, I used to write it all out in prose." He sat back in his chair, looking relaxed if tired, and smiled up at Nico, who'd brought him a bowl from the galley. "I should still probably be dead last on the flight schedule—"

"So to speak," John murmured sitting across the table from him, inordinately pleased with himself when Emilio laughed. "Now maybe you'll cut everybody a little slack!"

There was a round of grunted agreement with that sentiment, and for the first time since the voyage had begun, a sort of communal contentment took hold as they ate and drank and the talk became general. They were all aware of the fragile sense of being on the same team, but no one dared comment on it, until the end of the meal when Nico said, "I like it better this way."

A small silence settled in then, as it will at any dinner party, but it was broken by Danny Iron Horse saying, "Listen, Sandoz, there's a new Rakhati song I've been working on—"

"Come on, Danny!" John protested. "No shop talk, okay?"

But Emilio hadn't frowned and Danny took this as permission to continue. "Just this one piece," he insisted. "It's extraordinary, Sandoz. I honestly think it's important from a political standpoint that we understand what these lyrics imply, but I've done as much as I can with them."

"Danny—" John started again.

"John, when I want a spokesman, I'll let you know," Emilio warned. John shrugged: I wash my hands of it. Emilio went on, "All right, Danny. Let's hear it."

The music itself was as recognizable as Mozart's, as powerful in its play on the emotions as Beethoven's. Except for a chanted baritone bass line, the voices were unlike anything previously heard: creamy, sumptuous altos, shimmering, brilliant trebles, the whole woven into harmonies that left them breathing raggedly. Then a single voice: rising, rising, pulling them helplessly—

"That word," Danny said emphatically as the soprano sank into the chorus, like a spent wave into the ocean. "That's the key. It has to be. Do you know it?"

Sandoz shook his head, and held up a hand, listening to the entire piece before speaking. "Again, please," he said when it was finished. And then: "Once more," listening the third time before breaking his silence. "Get my tablet, please, Nico," he said, when it was over. "When did this arrive, Danny?"

"Last week."

"Let me see if I understand the process by which we received this transmission," Sandoz said dryly as Nico trudged off for the computer. "When these songs were first broadcast on Rakhat, they were automatically collected by the *Magellan*, encoded, compressed and packeted, yes? Held in memory, and not sent out until the stars were right. Picked up at home by radio telescopes over four years after the *Magellan* sent them. Sold by the Contact Consortium to the Jesuits, no doubt after a period of negotiation over price. Studied, packeted again. Shot off to us, after what? Two years, perhaps? And we're now moving at maximum velocity?" he asked, looking at Fat Frans for confirmation. "So more years have gone by since the packet caught up with us last week, because of the relativity effects. I have no idea what that adds up to, but it's old news, Danny—. Ah, *grazie*, Nico."

For a time, they simply watched the process they were all familiar with, as Sandoz checked through his files, looking for similar roots, to confirm or disprove whatever hypothesis was forming in his mind.

"The word is related, I think, to a stem word for change: *sohraa*," he said at last. "The first syllable is an intensifier, of course. The term is, I think, a poetic neologism, but I am not familiar with this construction. It could be archaic rather than new, yes? It combines *sohraa* with a stem that implies a breaking out or breaking free: *hramaut*. The only time I heard that was when Supaari took me to his courtyard to show me a small animal that was emerging from a kind of chrysalis." His eyes rose to meet Danny's. "If I must guess, I would say the force of the word is emancipation, perhaps. The theme of the entire piece is perhaps joy at the breaking of bonds."

Daniel Iron Horse closed his eyes briefly, perhaps in prayer. There was a burst of talk, but Danny spoke above it. "You agree that this is Kitheri's composition? His style, both in lyric and musical form?" Sandoz nodded: unquestionably. "The voices?" Danny pressed. "Who is singing? Not who. I mean, what species?"

"The basses, of course, are male Jana'ata. The others are of a much higher register," Sandoz observed calmly.

"*Scuzi,*" Nico said politely. "What does emanci—. What is that word?"

" 'Emancipation.' It means, to set free," Emilio told him. "When slaves are legally freed, it is called emancipation."

"Runa have much higher voices, don't they?" Nico suggested. "Maybe they're singing because they're happy they're free."

Iron Horse's eyes were steady on Emilio's. "Sandoz, what if Kitheri's emancipated the Runa?"

It was the first time he'd dared to say this aloud. Around the room, the men sat straighter, blinking, and reconsidered what they'd just heard.

"My God, Emilio," John cried, "if the Runa are singing—. If emancipation is the theme of that song . . ."

"That would change everything," Sean whispered, as Carlo sighed theatrically, "I'm too late!" and Frans Vanderhelst cried, "Congratulations, Johnny! There is your hidden meaning!"

"Sandoz," Danny said carefully, "maybe this is why you were meant to go back—"

Sandoz cut the rising noise of speculation off, staring at Danny. "Even if you are correct, and I doubt that for a number of reasons—linguistic, political and theological—it would hardly have required my presence on Rakhat to learn of this." He glanced at the Earth-relative time-date readout. "I could have heard this music when the transmission reached Earth. Years ago, yes? About the time Gina and I celebrated our eighth anniversary, perhaps?" he said, glancing cold-eyed at Carlo.

There was an uneasy quiet.

"I am sorry to disappoint Nico and the more romantic among you," Sandoz continued, "but the voices don't sound to me like those of Runa. Also, the song is in High K'San, which does not disprove Danny's hypothesis, but hardly supports it. The altos consistently use personal pronoun forms I've never heard. I was never spoken to by any Jana'ata woman, not even when I was a member of Kitheri's harem, so my guess is that the pronoun is feminine and that these voices are adult females. Perhaps the highest voices are those of children, but it seems likely to me that these are Jana'ata children, not Runa."

"But even if it's Jana'ata women he's liberated—" Danny started.

"Father Iron Horse, I detect a certain indulgence in wishful thinking," Sandoz said with the acid courtesy they all had come to dread. "Why do you credit Kitheri with precipitating such an event, instead of merely observing it, for example? Is it possible that you are imposing your own desire for self-justification on a situation and a man you can know nothing about?" Danny absorbed that like the slap in the face it was meant to be. "If," Sandoz continued, "Hlavin Kitheri were somehow responsible for a change in the status of such members of his own species—and I can't imagine how he could be—I would be happy for them. I forgive him nothing."

"But a small change can perturb a system," Joseba remarked, still taken by the idea. "What if something you said or did influenced Kitheri or one of the other Jana'ata? That would make what happened—" He stopped when Sandoz rose abruptly and walked to the other side of the room.

"What, Joseba? Forgivable?" Sandoz asked. "Tolerable? Okay? All better?"

"It would redeem what happened to you," Sean Fein suggested quietly. He nearly recanted under the sear of the black-eyed stare, but forced himself to go on. "Look, y'never know, Sandoz!" he cried. "What if that bloody Austrian admissions committee had accepted young Mr. Hitler for art school? He was pretty decent with landscapes and architecture. Maybe if he'd gotten his wretched arts degree, everything would have been different!"

"A few words, Emilio!" said John with urgency. "An act of kindness, or love, or courage—"

Sandoz stood still, his head turned down and away from them. "All right," he said reasonably, looking up. "For the sake of argument, let's assume that unintended consequences can be for good as well as ill. The trouble with your proposition, as applied to my case, is that there was never any opportunity for me to give Hlavin Kitheri or his associates a stirring sermon on liberty or the value of souls—Jana'ata, Runa or human." He stopped, waited, eyes closed. He was tired, naturally. That was part of it. "I don't recall being allowed to say a single word, actually. I did scream quite a bit—fairly incoherently, I'm afraid." He stopped again and took in an uneven breath, letting it out slowly before lifting his eyes to their faces.

"And I fought like a sonofabitch to keep those fuckers off me, but I doubt even the most charitable of observers would have called that a display of courage. 'An amusing exercise in futility' may have come to mind."

He paused again, breathing carefully. "So you see," he resumed calmly, "I don't think there is a shred of hope that anyone abstracted any edifying lessons about the sanctity of life or the political virtues of freedom during my . . . *ministry* to the Jana'ata. And I suggest, gentlemen, we drop this subject for the duration of our journey together."

THE OTHERS WATCHED, BLINKING IN THE AFTERMATH, AS SANDOZ LEFT the room under his own power. No one noticed when Nico, standing unobserved in the corner, left the commons as well and went to his cabin.

Opening the storage cabinet on the wall over his desk, Nico rummaged through his small collection of personal treasures and located two hard cylinders of unequal length: one and a half Genoa salamis he had hoarded away. Laying them on his desk, he sat down and breathed in the fragrance of garlic while giving serious thought to the issue of salami. He considered how much he had left, and how long it would be before he could buy more, and how Don Emilio felt when he had a bad headache. It would be a waste to give salami to a person who was only going to throw it up. Still, Nico thought, a present could make a person feel better, and Don Emilio could save it for later when the headache was gone.

People often laughed at Nico for taking things too seriously. They would say something seriously, and he would take it seriously, and then be embarrassed when it turned out that they were only joking. He could rarely tell the difference between that kind of joking and sensible talk.

"It's called irony, Nico," Don Emilio had explained to him one night. "Irony is often saying the opposite of what is meant. To get the joke, you must be surprised and then amused by the difference between what you believe the person thinks and what he actually says."

"So it would be irony if Frans said, Nico, you're a smart boy."

"Well, perhaps, but it would also be making fun of you," Sandoz said honestly. "Irony would be if you yourself made a joke by saying, I'm a smart boy, because you believe you're stupid and most other people believe this of you as well. But you're not stupid, Nico. You learn slowly but thoroughly. When you learn something, you have learned it well and don't forget it."

Don Emilio was always serious, so Nico could relax and not try to find hidden jokes. He never made fun of Nico and he took extra time to teach him and made it easy to remember the foreign words.

All that, Nico decided, was definitely worth half a salami.

THE LAST THING EMILIO SANDOZ WANTED WAS A VISITOR, BUT WHEN HE responded to the knock on his door with a parsimonious "Piss off!" there were no footsteps and he could tell that whoever it was intended to stay there as long as necessary. Sighing, he opened the door and was not surprised to find Nico d'Angeli waiting expectantly in the curving hall.

"*Buon giorno*, Nico," he said patiently. "I am afraid I would rather not have any company right now."

"*Buon giorno*, Don Emilio," Nico responded pleasantly. "I am afraid this is very important."

Emilio took a deep breath, and almost gagged on the smell of garlic, but he stepped away from the door, inviting Nico in. As was his habit, he moved to the farthest corner of his small room and sat on his bed, back against the bulkhead. Nico perched on the edge of the desk chair and then leaned forward to place half a salami on the foot of the bunk. "I wish to make you a gift of this, Don Emilio," he said without further explanation.

Gravely, and breathing shallowly, Emilio said, "Thank you, Nico. This is very thoughtful, but I don't eat meat anymore—"

"I know, Don Emilio. Don Gianni told me: because you still feel bad about eating the Runa babies. This salami was just a pig," Nico pointed out.

Smiling in spite of everything, Emilio said, "You're right, Nico. This was just a pig. Thank you."

"Is your headache better now?" Nico asked anxiously. "You can save this for later, if you're going to throw up."

"Thank you, Nico. I took some medicine, and my headache is gone, so I won't throw up." He sounded more certain than he was: the garlic was staggering. But this was clearly a present of significance from Nico, so he slid down the bed and picked up the salami with both hands, to signify his wholehearted acceptance of it. "It would please me to share this with you," he said. "Do you have a knife?"

Nico nodded and pulled out a pocketknife and then smiled at him shyly: a rare occurrence and one that was remarkably cheering. Dutifully, Emilio unwrapped the salami, a process that went fairly easily because his hands were okay today. Nico took it from him. Drawing his blade toward his thumb with great care, he cut two round, slender wafers from the end. Emilio found himself accepting one of these with the kind of dignity he'd once reserved for a consecrated Host. It's only a pig, he reminded himself, and managed to swallow after a while.

Nico, chewing, beamed greasily around his slice, but then remembered something he'd been meaning to say for some time now. "Don Emilio," he began, "I wish you to absolve me—"

Sandoz shook his head. "Nico, you must go to one of the priests to confess. I cannot hear confessions anymore."

"No," Nico said, "not a priest. You yourself must absolve me. Don Emilio, I am sorry that I beat you up."

Relieved, Emilio said, "You were only doing your job."

"It was a bad job," Nico insisted. "I'm sorry I did it."

No excuses about following Carlo's orders. No hedges. No self-serving justifications. "Nico," Emilio said with the quiet formality the occasion required, "I accept your apology. I forgive you for beating me up."

Cautious, Nico pressed, "Both times?"

"Both times," Emilio confirmed.

Nico looked solemnly glad to hear this. "I took your guinea pig to the sisters. The children promised to take good care of her."

"That's good, Nico," Emilio said after a time, astonished by how much it helped to know this. "Thank you for doing that, and for telling me."

Heartened, Nico asked, "Don Emilio, do you think we are going to do a bad job on that planet?"

"I'm not cert   " Emilio admitted. "The first time I was there, we wanted very m   e good people and to do the right things, but it all went wrong. This time, our motives for going to Rakhat are not . . . pure. But who knows? Maybe things will turn out well in spite of us."

"That would be irony," Nico observed.

Emilio's face softened and he gazed at the big man with real affection. "Yes, indeed. That would be irony." He was glad Nico had stopped by, he realized. "And you, Nico. What do you think? Will it be a bad job down there?"

"I'm not certain, Don Emilio," Nico said seriously, mimicking Sandoz's own tone and words as he often did now. "I think we should wait until we get there and see what's going on. That's my advice."

Emilio nodded. "You're very sensible, Nico."

But Nico went on, "I think that the man who did bad things to you—

that Kitheri? He might be sorry, like I am. I think his music is wonderful—better than Verdi, even. Someone who makes such good music can't be all bad. That's what I think."

Which was a great deal harder to accept, but might have some germ of truth. . . . Emilio stood then, to signal the end of the visit, and Nico rose as well, but did not move to the door. Instead he reached down and gently lifted Sandoz's right hand and bent low over it, to kiss it. Embarrassed, Emilio tried to draw back, to refuse this homage, but Nico's gentle grip seemed unbreakable.

"Don Emilio," Nico said, "I would kill or die for you."

Emilio, who understood this code, looked away and tried to imagine how he could respond to such a display of undeserved devotion. There seemed only one reply possible and, eyes closed, he examined himself to see if he could say this with the honesty such a man deserved. "Thank you, Nico," he said finally. "I love you, too."

He hardly noticed when Nico left.

City of Gayjur
2080, Earth-Relative

MANY YEARS LATER, JOSEBA URIZARBARRENA WOULD REMEMBER THE children's chorale—and the K'San word for emancipation—during a conversation with the daughter of Kanchay VaKashan. Puska VaTrucha-Sai was a respected parliamentary elder in Gayjur when Joseba first met her, and he often found her viewpoint illuminating as he and the other priests pieced together the history of the Runa revolution.

"There had been sporadic fighting for years," Puska told him, "but in the beginning, Fia advocated 'passive resistance.' There were general strikes in several cities. Many of the urban Runa just walked away, refusing to give themselves up to the cullers."

"How did the government respond?" Joseba Urizarbarrena asked.

"By wiping out villages that gave shelter to the city Runa. Before long, they were burning out natural *rakar* fields in the midlands—to starve us into submission." She stopped, remembering, reassessing. "What tipped the balance was when Fia believed they had begun to use biologicals against us. When she was a child, Fia had seen diseases used against a people called the Kurds. When the plagues began, we thought that Runa behind *djanada* lines were made ill and then smuggled south and left to infect all who came in contact with them."

"But that sickness might also be explained by the sudden mixing of Runa populations during the rebellion," Joseba suggested. "The sharing of disease reservoirs, the exposure to unfamiliar environments? Swamp harvesters working with city specialists—people exposed to local illnesses they had no immunity to, and spreading them?"

"Yes," Puska said after a time. "Some of our scientists said so. It was not a consensus view at the time . . ." She sat as straight as possible, her ears high. "The *djanada* appeared to leave us no alternative but to strike back with overwhelming force. The people were dying. Thousands and thousands died of plague. We were fighting for our lives." She looked to the north, and forced herself to be just. "So were they, I suppose."

"*Sipaj*, Puska, someone wonders if the Jana'ata themselves changed or if the Runa idea of the Jana'ata changed."

Puska considered this for a while, and then began to use English pronouns, as many Runa did now, to signify a strictly personal comment. "My idea of the *djanada* changed when I left Trucha Sai." She paused for a time, eyes on the middle distance. "When we first went to Mo'arl—. *Sipaj*, Hozei: the things we saw! I keened every night for a season. There were roads paved with our bones, crushed and mixed with limestone, levees along the rivers—three times the height of a woman—all bone. Boots from the skins of our dead—even Runa wore them in the cities! There were shops—" She looked now directly at Joseba. "Platters of tongues, platters of hearts. Legs, shoulders, feet, fillets and chops! Rump and tail and elbows and knees—all beautifully displayed. Runa domestics would come and pick out the cut of meat to serve to their masters. How could they stand it?" she demanded. "How could the *djanada* have asked it of them?"

"Someone is unsure," Joseba said honestly. "Sometimes, there's no choice. Sometimes the choices aren't thought of. People can get used to anything." Puska lifted her chin, and then let her tail drop, unable to imagine how that vanished world had functioned. "Yet," Joseba pointed out, "there were some Runa who remained with the Jana'ata—"

"*Sipaj*, Hozei: those people were traitors," Puska told him with flat conviction. "You must understand that. They became very wealthy, selling the corpses of dead soldiers to the *djanada*, who would pay anything for even small scraps of meat. But those Runa paid in kind for their treachery: eventually the *djanada* ate them, too."

"*Sipaj*, Puska, someone is sorry to keep asking—"

"There is no need for apology. Someone is content to answer."

"There were Runa who stayed with the *djanada*, even after the war. Even now." He watched her carefully as he asked this, but Puska did not sway. "They have said to us that they loved the Jana'ata."

"That is sometimes so. The Runa are a noble people," she said. "We repay kindness with kindness."

"Do you believe those Runa wrong to live with the Jana'ata? Are they traitors, like the black marketeers?"

"Not traitors. Dupes. In the end, they'll be eaten. The *djanada* can't help it. It's the way they are. The *djanada* are guilty in their genes, in their whole way of life," she told him calmly.

It was then that he recalled the chorale. "*Sipaj*, Puska, someone wishes to understand this clearly. You are patient and someone is grateful. It is said in the north that Hlavin Kitheri had begun to emancipate the Runa—"

For the first time, Puska became upset, rising and beginning to pace. "Emancipation! Emancipation meant, We'll eat you when you're older! The *djanada* told us we were stupid! Here is stupidity: Hlavin Kitheri walking out alone to do battle with an army of two hundred thousand. Refusing to negotiate with us was stupid! We offered them terms, Hozei! Just free the captives and we'll leave the north to you. Hlavin Kitheri chose combat. He was crazy—and so were all the others who believed in him."

She was looking directly into his eyes now. "*Sipaj*, Hozei, the Runa did everything for the *djanada*. They kept us enslaved and fed us only enough to make us good slaves. Until your people came and showed us that we could feed ourselves as much as we needed, our minds were kept small and slow so that we'd accept our slavery. Hear me, Hozei! Never again. Those times are gone forever. We will never be slaves again. Never."

He stood his ground, but it was not easy: a Runao risen up in righteous anger was a formidable menace. "*Sipaj*, Puska," he said when she had brought herself to quietness, "you grew up with Ha'anala. Did you ever wonder about her? Was she crazy, too?"

There was a silence before Puska said, "Someone thought of Ha'anala. She was not crazy. But she left the people to go with the crazy ones! So someone's heart was confused. Supaari was one of the people, but Ha'anala never came home."

"Did you know where she went, after she left Trucha Sai?"

"She went north." There was an uncomfortable silence before Puska admitted, "Someone thought she might be in Inbrokar."

"During the siege?" he asked. Puska raised her chin in affirmation. "Puska, what did you hope for Ha'anala?"

"That she would come home," Puska said firmly.

"And when she didn't?"

The swaying began at last, and when Puska spoke, it was not to answer his question but her own conscience. "The *djanada* changed first. They gave us no choice! The *djanada* made us fierce." Not looking at him, she added, "To be hungry is a terrible thing. Someone hoped that Ha'anala would die quickly."

"And when Inbrokar fell, how many died quickly?"

She looked away, but Puska VaTrucha-Sai was a woman of courage and, once again, she left the safety of the herd. "They were as grass to me," she said. "I did not count them."

30

City of Inbrokar

2072, Earth-Relative

"THEY'RE OUTSIDE THE NEW WALLS NOW," TAKSAYU REPORTED, HER
words echoing hollowly down the stone throat of the wind tower in the
embassy courtyard.

"And my lord husband?" Suukmel Chirot u Vaadai called from below,
looking up at Taksayu's gown and slippered feet. "And the Paramount?
Can you see them?"

"There!" Taksayu said, after a time, arm extended southward, toward a
flash of armor. "The Paramount wears a gold ventral plate and caudal
guard. And—yes, silver arm and thigh plates. The ambassador is to his
left, all in silver. They are at the head of the war party, with the nobles behind them."

"And the others?" Suukmel asked, looking up at her Runa—what? she
wondered. Not maid, any longer. Companion, often. Ally, perhaps? There
was no word in K'San for Taksayu now. "How many are there?"

So many, Taksayu was thinking, with an illicit thrill. We are so *many*!
How could she describe this to a woman who'd never seen beyond the curtains of her conveyance or the walls of her compound? All her life, the
lady Suukmel had held in her mind the subtle structure of power and relationship, the delicate web of Jana'ata politics, but this was not abstrac-
tion. It was physical might. "The rebels are as the hairs of a body," Taksayu
ventured. "As the leaves of a *marhlar*, Mistress: too many to count."

"I'm coming up," Suukmel declared. The city was ruled by rumor now that the power grid for the radio system had failed, and Suukmel was starved for information. Ignoring Taksayu's protests, she forced herself to climb the internal spiral of the wind tower to see the gathered multitude herself, but when she arrived at Taksayu's side and lifted her veil, she was staggered.

"Are you ill?" Taksayu cried, gripping Suukmel's arms, afraid the reeling woman would fall.

"No! Yes! I'm not—" Suukmel dropped her veil, and closed her eyes behind it. Beyond the distance of a hallway or the length of a banquet room, all the colors seemed to blur. "Explain this," Suukmel said, steadying. She lifted her veil again. "Tell me what I am seeing. Everything is confused."

Taksayu did her best, pointing out landmarks Suukmel knew by reputation and familiar objects. Buildings looked like toys, and a'aja trees like those that shaded Suukmel's own courtyard seemed to be twigs or seedlings, or could not be picked out at all in the nonsense of shapes. The Runa were nothing but dots of color, like knots in a patternless carpet. Enraged and nauseated by the senseless jumble, Suukmel gave up and retreated down the ramp to her refuge at its base.

It was her last bastion of privacy, this small stone room; the embassy was packed with refugees. Following Hlavin Kitheri's example, Ma Gurah Vaadai had done his best to take in as many people as could be fed, but it was Suukmel who had to live with the consequences. Nonessential Runa had been slaughtered to stave off starvation; there were very few domestics left in the city, and those few were so overworked that one could understand why so many left to join the rebels. Not even the Paramount's reforms had prepared Jana'ata women for life in close quarters among strangers. No one knew who held rank anymore. Snarling squabbles were as constant as the rain, and all too often escalated to slashed faces and bleeding bellies—

"That must be the foreigner Fia!" Taksayu cried, her arm flung out over the tower's stone edge.

"Truly?" Suukmel breathed, moving back to the tower ramp and looking up, throat stretched. "What does it look like?"

"Very small—like a child! How can it breathe? It has no nose! And no tail." Taksayu shuddered. "It must be deformed. Hair only on part of its head." Taksayu was briefly distracted by the idea of the Paramount mounting such a freak. "A monster," she confirmed, "as our lord the ambassador has always said."

"Can you see the other one?" Suukmel called. No one spoke the traitor's name any longer. Supaari VaGayjur's existence was being expunged from memory; his entire clan had been executed long ago. Today he will die at the hands of Hlavin Kitheri, Suukmel thought. The Runa say his daughter is already gone, which leaves only the foreigner, Fia, who cannot live forever. Then, Suukmel thought, we will let the rebels have the south and leave them to their fate. The Paramount will build new cities and get these strangers out of our compounds. We will be poor, perhaps, and hungry, surely, but the time will come again for beauty and civility, for learning and song . . .

"There! The nameless one is coming forward now." There was a cautious pause. "He is without armor," Taksayu reported, voice pitched low so it would not carry this news beyond the tower to those who should not hear such things. It was a terrible insult to the Paramount, to appear on the field without armor: I have no need of defense, the challenger was saying.

The battle hymn began, a roaring chorus of men preparing for death or victory—ranked duelists, readying themselves to step forward one by one, taking on an opposing champion until one side or the other yielded. Today, this preparation was merely ceremonial. There was only one warrior who could champion the Runa, so this would be a battle of two men only—of the Paramount and the nameless one: single combat agreed to by all, witnessed by all, its outcome affirmed by all.

"And then this will be over," Suukmel whispered, leaning against the cool stone of her tower. And she tried not to hear the desperation in her words.

"SUPAARI, HE'S WEARING ARMOR," SAID SOFIA, ACROSS THE VALLEY, IN sight of Suukmel's tower.

"But I have none, so he will remove his," Supaari told her, eyes calm as gray-blue stones under a still lake. "It's cowardice to meet a challenger with more than the opponent brings to the field. Kitheri cannot be seen to be a coward."

"It will make no difference," Djalao said, standing next to Sofia, her contempt for this dumb show plain. "Armored or naked, the outcome will be the same."

"If they would just let their Runa go, we wouldn't have to do this!" cried Puska, at Djalao's side. "They can't win. Why don't they let their Runa go?"

Without another word or gesture, obeying some inner sense of time, Supaari left them then, walking alone down the hill toward the battlefield. Voice shaking with anger, Djalao shouted, "You throw yourself away!"

Puska keened at the sight of his back, but Sofia snapped, "Don't weaken him." And watched Supaari go, her halved vision blurred only by myopia.

THIS WOULD BE THE FIRST STATE-LEVEL COMBAT IN FOUR GENERATIONS and it had taken the combined memories of all the remaining protocol Runa in Inbrokar to stage it. They had outdone themselves this time, and felt it was a fitting way to conclude their lives.

From childhood, such women had taken pleasure in seeing their masters properly dressed, properly adorned, tiny pleats lying neatly on a broad shoulder, jewels sparkling in the proper settings. It was a protocol specialist's satisfaction to know that she had prepared her lord for each new encounter so that no offense would be given or taken, without intent. Before the war, each had been consulted, sometimes hourly, and her advice taken. The living repositories of Jana'ata genealogy, such women knew the historic deeds and present importance of each sept, and were clever in their suggestions for defusing useless conflict or for heightening disputes that could be turned to their masters' advantage. They often lived longer than the norm for Runa because it took so long to train their successors, but they willingly suffered the griefs and debilities of old age, even knowing that their toughened, stringy meat would be eaten by the lower ranks when the time came. Their work was the foundation upon which Rakhati civilization rested.

In the crowded streets and jammed compounds of the last few cities, their advice was now more crucial than ever—there were so many strangers, so many people thrown together! Starving and confused, Jana'ata would lash out in anger and fear, tearing without warning at the throat of any Runa porter who refused them entry. Protocol Runa took over at the gates, listening to stories of old alliances, deciding whom to admit. They chose only the best of the Jana'ata, the highest, those of the oldest septs to defend Inbrokar; sent the others on, farther north, to survive as they might.

Now, looking out across the valley at the gathered host of their own kind, they busied themselves with the floating ensigns and the flashing armor, with the ordering of the Jana'ata warriors in riverine ranks, and prepared themselves to witness, with their masters, the combat. But when it was time for the challengers' response, the rebels did not sing, their distant high cries of derision spoiling the lords' harmonies with a dissonant, droning sameness.

The protocol Runa ignored the screaming taunts flung at them by their conspecifics on the hill. They had devoted their lives to the stately ballet of rank and respect. Their profession was about to become extinct, but these women would leave the realm of light and movement knowing that they had done their duty to the last.

INSIDE THE WALLS, MORE PRAGMATIC PEOPLE HAD PREPARED DIFFERently for this day, years in the making, and were preparing even now. Loyalty ran as deep in some Runa as their very veins, and when this loyalty had been repaid with kindness or even simple decency, such Runa saw no reason to abandon their families.

So they looked to the north, and wondered if the snow in the high mountains was melted by now, and packed hoarded food, and shared desperate rumors.

"There is a safe place in the mountains."

"They have their own foreigner there."

"They turn no one away."

THICK-MUSCLED ARMS HELD AWAY FROM A TAUT BODY, HLAVIN KITHERI felt the weight of his overgarments—stiff with gold embroidery and glittering with jewels—taken from his shoulders. He was not large nor was he young, but he had hunted for food and wrestled for sport frequently throughout his middle years, and now he breathed with ease and confidence as his armor was unbuckled and laid neatly on the ground nearby. He paid no heed to his attendants. Instead, he concentrated on the walk, the build, the scent of the man who approached him now from the south, armed only with the weapons phylogeny had provided them both: grasping feet and bludgeoning arms with slicing claws; heavy, powerful tails; jaws capable of ripping a throat away from its spinal column.

They had not seen each other in many years, but Supaari's face was still familiar. He had the advantage of height and reach, but he'd aged poorly, Kitheri observed. The muzzle was flecked with gray, the cheeks were hollow—he was, undoubtedly, missing teeth. And thin: ribs showing, tail badly filled out. Stiffness in the right knee, and—yes, a hesitation in movement at the hip. Chest muscles weakened by long raking scars that scored the left shoulder.

This will be not a contest but an execution, Hlavin Kitheri thought. A pity, for we are two of a kind. We have both tried to change the world from rock to cloud, and our lives from bone to pelt. I battle for the future, for the lives of children unborn. He, too, battles for the lives of children, but he fights for the past—to exact revenge, to balance old wrongs, to wipe from the world reminders of old shames. Neither of us will live to see what we have made, but an element of tragedy always makes for good poetry, Kitheri thought, smiling. And he wondered who would sing it.

Rain before long, he thought, looking at the thunderheads building in the west as the battle hymns drew to their climax. The wind shifted then, bringing Runa taunts from the distance, and the quiet near sound of his adversary's steps. Will he speak? Kitheri wondered urgently as Supaari came to a halt a little distance away. What will such a man say at such a moment?

Nothing, evidently: this was a practical person, not a poet. Without a word, Supaari sank into a bent-kneed crouch with a slight hitch in the movement that shouted news of his bad right leg. So, equally silent, Hlavin Kitheri stepped forward with conscious grace, ready to engage.

The instant the Paramount came within reach, Supaari threw his weight back on his left leg and tail; gripping Kitheri's ankle, he heaved himself backward and pulled the other man to the ground in a startling move that brought the Paramount's throat within reach. Kitheri twisted free and, in a single sweeping motion, he uncoiled from the ground and whirled head downward, bringing his own tail to bear. Half-standing, Supaari jerked away, but was not fast enough and took a staggering blow just below his ear—insufficient to bring him down but a solid hit—and he backed off for a few moments to recover.

Both more cautious now, the two men circled, arms bent and wide, their own loud breathing deafening them to shrieks and distant roaring. Without warning, Supaari pivoted on his stronger leg, but rather than a caudal attack to bash breath from the Paramount's chest, he used the momentum to send his right heel down hard on the back of Kitheri's knee. An excellent move and one that might have worked, had he kept his balance. He lost advantage when they both went down, grunting at the impact with the ground.

Grinning now, pleased that the fight was not such a mismatch as he had feared, the Paramount rolled upright, celestial violet eyes steady, body obedient to his will. "You're better than I expected," he told his dead sister's widower, without a whiff of irony. "It won't be good enough, but you will die well."

There was no answer except the sharp, instructive smell of rage, and the next attack was more effective. The Paramount worked to break the tail-launched pedal grip that pinned both his arms, but he failed, so he pushed hard with all the strength of his lower body, and they went down together, muscles violently strained, lungs bursting. The fall broke Supaari's hold on him and Kitheri took that chance to twist, locking his arms around the other man's body.

The delicate arteries of Supaari's eyes could be seen with utter clarity, the short fine hairs of the muzzle coming into view as he threw his head back to get a grip on the Paramount's throat. Enthralled, Hlavin Kitheri did not strain away from the teeth that sank into the thick skin at the base of his own neck, but rather closed his eyes, savoring with all his being this one last wholly experienced instant. He could smell Supaari's panting breath now, knew subliminally what this man had eaten and drunk on his last day of life. Listening to the thudding of tails thrashing against the ground in search of leverage, Kitheri heard with a rapist's intimacy the small, whining sounds of another's body in extremity.

He bent then into a crescent. Jamming his feet against Supaari's chest, Kitheri straightened like a bow with a scream of release. He hardly noticed the pain as Supaari's teeth ripped from his throat, but he was gallant enough to declare, gasping, as he struggled to his feet, "First blood to the challenger!"

The soft-footed circling resumed, and there were three more near encounters that left their chests heaving with a noisy, exhausted hunt for air; neither was young, and this match had been harder fought and longer than either had expected. Breaking the rhythm of the bout, close to the end of his own strength, Kitheri took the offense at last, turning his own shorter reach to advantage with the feint of a low turn. When this drew Supaari into a parry for a blow to his legs, Kitheri converted the motion into a lunge, throwing his shoulder into Supaari's chest, past arms bent for defense. There was an instantaneous, reflexive response: Supaari locked his arms around the Paramount's back—the fatal error.

Their eyes met once more in that lethal embrace; then, with a swift upward rip, Kitheri ended it, and stepped away. Arms flung wide in ecstasy, he sang out to the multitude on the hillside before him: "Behold the art of dying!"

SUPAARI DID NOT FALL IMMEDIATELY, NOR DID HE LOOK DOWN TO SEE what had happened to him. He simply turned away and took a few steps as his guts roiled out of the rent in his belly onto the spoiled ground. For one terrible moment, it seemed to Sofia that he would trip over them, but then his knees buckled. For uncounted seconds, she did not breathe, reluctant to fill her own lungs and allow life to go on, without him.

"He will kill me, Fia," he'd told her, his voice as cool as a breeze that carried the pure, transparent fragrance of mountain snow, and the promise of storms. "Kitheri has trained from childhood as a warrior, and he will kill me."

Supaari had sat across from Sofia on the ground that morning, surrounded by the Runa army they had helped Djalao to create, a force now swollen by VaInbrokari Runa who had seized their freedom and joined their people outside the walls. Sofia did not protest what he said, concentrating instead on feeling nothing at all. It was an old skill, one that had allowed her to survive the war that ended her childhood, and second nature now that war had become her whole world again. In some ways, Supaari had already left her. They had not seen each other much in the past years, fighting on different fronts. Once the children had gone, there was so little to speak of, except the war.

There was a strange sacred hollowness to Supaari, as though each advance for the Runa had carved out some new space in his own soul, each success and competence driving home to him the utter irrelevance of his own kind. "They don't need us anymore," he'd said once, with a kind of ethereal joy. "Perhaps they never did."

So when Supaari announced that he would die, Sofia simply rose onto her knees and held out her arms to him. He leaned forward and rested his forehead against her body. "He will kill me," he said again, his voice so low that she could feel the sound in her own small chest, "but I will do the people honor."

Alone now, staring at his gutted body in the distance, Sofia said, "You fought well." Lifting a still face to the mountainous clouds, she heard the splat and spatter of the storm's first drops, and then only felt them as their quiet song was drowned by the shrill screams of Runa soldiers giving voice to frustration and boredom, to grief, and to their rage at these stubborn *djanada* holdouts who still dared to defy Runa authority and power and justice.

Armored infantry thundered down the slope like a cataract, parting around Sofia as a river flows around a rock, flooding the Jana'ata field before smashing through the main gate. The meat defiant, the meat insurgent, the meat fighting, Sofia thought. The meat in full cry.

She stood a long time watching, but then began her own progress across the trodden, sloping ground, aware of the sharp fragrance of crushed vegetation broken by the charge; aware of intermittent explosions and shrieks of terror and triumph; aware of the wind's roar, augmented now by the roaring of a fire too fierce to be rained out.

Supaari's corpse and the Paramount's were nearest to her, for their combat had taken place in the center of the field, in view of each side. Both bodies had been equally trampled and tumbled in the rush toward the gate: united in death.

She was too small to straighten Supaari's limbs and could not bring herself to gather his belly's contents, so she ignored all that. Sitting by his head, she ran her hand along the fine soft fur of his cheek, over and over, while his body cooled and she paid the awful debt of love.

"LET ME DIE," SUUKMEL SAID, DULLY INSISTENT, AS TAKSAYU PULLED HER along. "Let me die."

"No," her Runa friend told her, as often as she said this. "There are the children to think of."

"Better to die," Suukmel said.

But Taksayu and the other Runa harried and tormented her, each of them carrying a Jana'ata infant or dragging a child or pushing a woman along, cruel in their desire to get these few to safety. So Suukmel kept on, one step following the other like heartbeats that would not cease, until the light and her own unhardened body began to fail, and she crumpled to the ground. The respite was brief. A child's soft slippers, shredded and bloody after hours of forced marching over increasingly rocky ground, stepped under her eyes. Dazed by exhaustion, Suukmel looked up and saw the stony face of her foster son, Rukuei, the Paramount's first-born, who had been, only hours ago, a boy of twelve.

Rukuei: whose hard violet eyes had seen the forty-eighth Paramount of Inbrokar dismembered by a mob, whose mind would always carry the vision of a burning city and of a battlefield humped and soaked by Jana'ata dead, black with blood. Teachers and poets and storytellers; engineers, geographers, naturalists; athletes of balance and beauty, whose very walk was artistry. Philosophers and archivists; financiers and specialists in law. Men of state and men of music; men of youth and of maturity and of gray age. All left to decay in the rain.

"My father honored you," Rukuei told his foster mother pitilessly. "Be worthy of him, woman. Stand up and live."

So she got to her feet, and walked on northward, leaving scarlet footprints on the stones, next to those of a man of twelve.

IT WAS WELL PAST FIRST SUNDOWN LONG DAYS LATER WHEN THEY SAW the monster. Perched on two bony legs, it was naked, and hairless but for a beard and mane and mystifying patches of fur here and there, and it held a parasol made of frayed blue fabric high over its head. Beyond surprise even at a sight so bizarre, none of the refugees spoke. Neither did the monster. It simply stood in their way.

Without warning, a Jana'ata appeared. Many Runa broke free of paralysis then, and moved to place their bodies between their charges and this stranger. When they realized the Jana'ata was unarmored, with a small child riding his back, they looked at each other in confusion, no longer knowing who was a danger and who could be trusted.

"I am Shetri Laaks," the man called out. "You are all here because Runa have chosen to preserve the lives of Jana'ata. Therefore, my wife, Ha'anala, and I offer you food and shelter until you are strong enough to make your next decisions. This is my brother-in-law, Isaac. As you see, he is a foreigner, but one who is no danger to you. My wife will explain the rules of our settlement. If you care to abide by them, you are all, Runa and Jana'ata, welcome to remain with us, as others have."

From somewhere in the little knot of weary bewildered women, a voice cried out in irritable protest, "Your brother-in-law! Are you married to a foreigner then—?"

But before Shetri could answer, Rukuei came forward. "I see the face of a coward, who lives while warriors rot," he shouted. "I smell the stink of one fit only to eat dung!"

"Ah, but dead men have such small appetites, even for dung," Shetri replied, not unkindly, but with no intention of being drawn into combat with an exhausted youth. He had seen this aggressive terror in so many boys: still reeling from the deaths of fathers, uncles, brothers, and ashamed to be alive. "I am afraid, sir, that I'd have proved a warrior of indifferent conviction and less skill. Instead, I have contrived to live at the expense of no person's life," he said, glancing at Taksayu and the other Runa before returning his eyes to the boy's and adding, "not even my own. If my company displeases you after you've eaten and rested in my compound, you may relieve yourself of its inconvenience by leaving."

Befuddled by the soft response, the boy was speechless. He was also swaying with fatigue and his feet were torn to tatters, Shetri noted. But it would be an insult to offer him any aid, so Shetri simply said, "Allow me to show the way."

It was then that a woman of middle years came toward him and rested her hand briefly on his arm. "What a lovely child," she said, trying not to let her voice quaver as she gazed up at the baby on Shetri's back. "Such beautiful eyes."

"Yes," Shetri agreed neutrally, knowing that she was working through the genealogical possibilities.

She drew in a small breath as she drew also the inevitable conclusion. "A family trait, coming down from the dam's lineage perhaps?" she asked from behind a finely woven veil, torn now and unraveling from one edge.

"Yes," Shetri said again, preparing to be attacked, if not injured.

But the woman merely spoke to the boy who had challenged Shetri. "Rukuei," she said, finding some reserve of stateliness within, "it seems that you have arrived by the gods' decision among . . . family. This man's wife will be, I think, a near cousin, through your father's line." She turned back to Shetri Laaks and straightened. "I am Suukmel Chirot u Vaadai, and this is my foster son, Rukuei Kitheri." Shetri's visible astonishment allowed her a moment of restored superiority, but Suukmel was a realist. "Your invitation is a great kindness. We are in your debt. My foster son and I—. No," she corrected herself, holding out her other hand to Taksayu, "we would all be grateful to accept your hospitality, on whatever terms you shall be pleased to dictate."

"There will be no debt, my lady, nor even terms," said Shetri, tearing his eyes away from the boy he now recognized as a young, male version of his wife. "An agreement rather, if you are pleased to stay with us."

"Do they sing?" Isaac asked then in the flat, toneless speaking voice so eerily at odds with the high purity of his singing.

Suukmel, uneasy, looked to Shetri. "My brother-in-law loves music,"

Shetri explained minimally, knowing she was too tired to take in more.

But Suukmel answered Isaac. "Rukuei knows many songs. He has the makings of a poet," she said. "And of a warrior," she added for his pride's sake.

Isaac did not look at anyone. "He'll stay," was all he said.

N'Jarr Valley

2072, Earth-Relative

IT WAS NOT COWARDICE OR WEAKNESS THAT UNDERMINED RUKUEI'S bright, fierce resolve to return to the south and fight on. It was the unanswerable question he heard in his dead father's voice, melodic with irony: "And whom shall you challenge? Some Runa horde?"

Had his mother been of first rank, or even second, Rukuei would now be Paramount Presumptive, but she was only a third. Was a concubine's child entitled to fight as his people's champion? There were no ranked half-brothers to inherit in their own right, nor any uncles to serve as regent while he was trained, if the law held the patrimony his. Who then is Paramount? Rukuei asked himself, no longer seeing the exhausted women and children around him, or the stranger with the baby or the freakish foreigner, or the eroded hills and gorges revealed as he and the others followed Shetri Laaks through a labyrinth of ravines.

Blackened stones, whitened bones: color is gone from the world, Rukuei thought, oblivious to the tilted, fractured strata—ocher and jade and cobalt in the late light of second sundown. Dance is gone, and beauty, and law and music, he thought. Smoke remains, and hunger.

Beyond fatigue, Rukuei found one certainty to grip. He was now the eldest male of his sept, and the responsibility for decision was his. Suukmel and the other women and children could go no farther. We will remain with these people until the lady Suukmel is ready to travel again, he thought as his little band trudged the last *cha'ar* to the strangers' encampment.

It was beyond thinking where they would go then—just as the place they were led to was now beyond seeing. Already blind, he let himself be guided by strong, gentle hands to a place that smelled of unfamiliar bodies. Too tired to eat, he plunged into a sleep so deep it was all but unconsciousness, and did not awaken for many hours.

WHEN HE DID, IT WAS IN SLOW SEQUENCE, EYES LAST: TO THROBBING PAIN in his feet, to the scent of ointment bound to them by clean dressings, to a gabble of languages, to bright daylight filtering through the dirty fabric of a ragged tent.

Lying still, he listened to the conversations just outside—a revolting mix of K'San and Ruanja with random elements of commercial Malanja and snatches of court Palkirn'al. The appalling grammar and sloppy diction instantly put him into a foul humor made worse by the frantic morning hunger of a young male who was only beginning to put on the height and muscle of manhood.

Already on edge, he was startled by a slight motion to his left and came upright, ready to fight—whom he had no idea, why he could only guess. The world was full of enemies and everything good was gone. But the movement was only a woman's hand pushing a crudely carved bowl toward him. He stared at it, repulsed by the jellied mess it contained, and then followed the hand to the arm to the face, and blinked when he saw his father's eyes, alive and amused.

The woman was young and visibly pregnant, naked and unveiled. "You look like my daughter," she said, and sat back comfortably, at ease on the ground, and unconcerned to be alone in a tent with him. She gave the bowl another little push.

He turned his head away, mouth twisting with revulsion, but heard the woman's voice again. "The life you knew is over. You must live in a new way," she said. "Before, everything was decided. Now you must make choices." She spoke in K'San but its precision was polluted by Ruanja's slurred vowels—a rural domestic's grating accent. "You may choose to hate the necessity of choosing, or you may value it. Each choice has consequences, so you must choose wisely."

He stared at her and, infuriatingly, she smiled. "For the present, of course, you need only choose between eating this awful-looking stuff or remaining very, very hungry."

He sat up straighter and reached for the bowl, as she knew he would. He was, after all, a normal boy, constantly hungry under the best of circumstances and starving now. He lifted the bowl to his mouth, but reared back from the unfamiliar smell; then tipped it down his throat in ravenous, almost sobbing gulps.

"Good," she said, pleased as she watched him.

"It's not as bad as I thought it would be," he said, wiping his mouth with the back of his hand.

"Think hard about what you just said," she advised. "My experience is that many things are not as bad as I thought they would be." The smell of anger filled the tent, but she did not retract her use of the dominant pronoun in his presence. "Here, each of us makes choices, so each of us must learn to be a sovereign soul: I think, I decide. This is no insult to you or anyone else." She gestured again toward the emptied bowl. "It's better with salt," she informed him prosaically, "but we don't have any salt right now."

"What was it?"

"Are you sure that you choose to know?" she asked, ears wide, his father's eyes entertained. He hesitated, but lifted his chin. "*Kha'ani* embryos," she told him.

Horrified, his own ears flattened and he nearly vomited, but then he glanced back into those eyes and swallowed hard.

"Good," she said again. "Do you understand? Everything is a choice, even what you eat. Especially what you eat!" She stood and looked down at him, her face a slender version of his own—the Kitheri bloodline visibly governing this generation as it had the last. "Here Jana'ata eat no Runa. In this settlement, we do not repay life with death. So. Choose. Will you live at the expense of others or will you do what you must to live another way?" And permitting him to think for himself, she turned and left the tent.

HE WAS YOUNG AND SOUND, AND HIS FEET HEALED MORE QUICKLY THAN the women's. Within a day or two, he was able to leave the tent and hobble a little distance up the nearest foothill to a vantage from which he could see the shards and remnants of a civilization. For a few days, solitary and silent, he watched the people in this high, chilly valley. Burning with disgrace, writhing at their debasement, he sought out his foster mother, and raged and raged. She listened without comment until he was done, and then gestured for him to sit by her.

"Do you know what I miss most?" Suukmel Chirot u Vaadai asked serenely. "Table manners." Rukuei pulled away from her embrace to gape at her. Suukmel smiled, and drew him close again. "No one knows how to eat this stuff properly. I've spilled *kha'ani* egglings on myself three times already. How can one maintain any dignity with albumin all over one's fur? No wonder Ha'anala goes naked!"

Suukmel said this to amuse Rukuei and the absurdity worked, but Taksayu was unbending. "That person goes about naked because she doesn't know any better," the Runao sniffed from a nest in the corner. "Raised in the wilderness by foreigners and feral Runa!"

Rukuei hardly knew what to think about that extraordinary statement, which didn't prevent him from having an opinion. "It is unendurable that a Jana'ata woman should go about utterly unclothed," he declared, "no matter how degraded her upbringing."

"She says that we Jana'ata must learn to live only by our own devices. It may be necessary for us to become completely independent of the Runa, although she herself hopes this shall not come to pass, and does what she can to prevent it," Suukmel informed them. Rukuei and Taksayu both stared. "She's trying to learn to weave with a foot loom, but she hasn't managed it yet, and until then, she goes naked as she was born—"

"Can you imagine!" Taksayu cried. "Jana'ata weaving!"

"Also, she says she simply doesn't like clothes," Suukmel continued. "But she knows it upsets the rest of us, and she doesn't like to make a *fierno.*"

"What is a *fierno?*" Rukuei demanded irritably, the Ruanja word suddenly infuriating him. Of all the differences he had to face among these strangers, the bastardization of language was the most distressing. How can anything make sense if the words you think with are disordered and imprecise? he cried inwardly.

"I asked her that," Suukmel said comfortably. "*Fierno* means 'a thunderhead' but the phrase implies being the cause of a big storm. Making a fuss." Rukuei grunted. "It is a nice image," Suukmel offered, knowing Rukuei well. "I like the phrase. It reminds me of my lord husband, prowling the courtyard after some tedious meeting, working himself into a *fierno*—"

She stopped abruptly, rain falling into her heart. The tent suddenly felt cramped and confining, too filled with people, even though she had only Taksayu and Rukuei with her.

"Perhaps," she said, "walking would be good for me." Taksayu's ears dropped, and Rukuei looked dubious. "Yes," Suukmel said then, certain because they doubted both her wisdom and her propriety. "Yes, I should like to try a walk."

"HOW CAN THIS HA'ANALA BE MY COUSIN?" RUKUEI ASKED SUUKMEL SEVeral mornings later, as they broke their fast with a strange but not unpleasant pâté provided by the Laaks household. "My father had no brother or sister. And how can that foreigner be Shetri's brother-in-law?"

There was a momentary stiffening. "Isaac is certainly unusual, but he sings beautifully, don't you agree?"

The change of subject did not go unnoticed. "Is it so awkward, what I have asked?"

"Awkward?" Suukmel repeated.

She had known this day would come, but had never anticipated that it would be in such circumstances. Pride of lineage was moderated among the unranked children of Hlavin's harem, but Rukuei knew who his father was, if not what Hlavin had done to reach the paramountcy. Whose disgrace to reveal first? she asked herself. The father's or the uncle's? There are no innocents in this except the children of dead men: Ha'anala and Rukuei.

"I wonder if you would take me to your place on the hillside this morning?" she asked lightly, rising from a badly made cushion that was nonetheless fragrant with mountain moss. She moved to the tent opening, letting her eyes become accustomed to the light, looking up at the colorful shapes that she had initially taken for unusually designed city walls ringing the valley.

Rukuei stared up at her. "Is it worse than awkward?" he asked, getting to his feet as well.

"I believe with practice I shall learn to see things at a distance, instead of merely imagining them," she said, confirming his suspicions. "Shetri tells me those are not ramparts but mountains! He says it takes some six day's constant climbing to reach the peaks. How far is it to the place you go to?"

"Far enough for privacy," Rukuei told her.

They left the tent and began the ascent, taking care with the loose rocks that made the climb a scramble. Suukmel coped with the disorientation by keeping her eyes down, not in submission but to focus on the relatively solid ground nearby. Glancing up every few moments, she tried to estimate the size of things, but she was constantly surprised when she found some "tree" was only a shrub much nearer than she had thought, or when a bright color she believed to be some far-off person's cloak suddenly took flight and darted into the thin air.

"Things are not always what they seem," she said aloud, as Rukuei showed her how to sit on a fallen *tupa*'s trunk. As she caught her breath, she looked out over the valley, trying to reconcile what her eyes told her with what she knew was there. "The tents look lovely in this light, don't they? Like jewels in the sun. Which is real, I wonder? The beauty of the tents at a distance or—"

"The wretchedness they conceal," Rukuei finished for her, and settled himself. "Tell me what is so terrible that it must be heard up here, my lady."

It seemed at first some epic poem of heroes and monsters, of prisons and escapes, of triumph and tragedy. She told of the crushing sameness of unvarying tradition, of a world in which nothing mattered but what had been decided uncounted generations earlier. And she tried to explain the despair of knowing that nothing could change, the fear that something would: the terror of the unknown and the secret wish for it, in so many hearts.

Caught up in this romance, it was a long time before Rukuei realized that the nameless one was Supaari VaGayjur; that this traitor was his own uncle by marriage, having sired a daughter out of Jholaa Kitheri; that this daughter was now grown and pregnant with her second child by Shetri Laaks; that Ha'anala's eyes were like his own because they shared a grandsire. It was even longer before he could take in what Suukmel told of how Hlavin Kitheri had seized the paramountcy—

"Are you saying that my father *killed* them?" Rukuei cried. "Killed them all? His own kin?" He stood and strode away, not tall but gangling. So young, Suukmel thought. So young. . . . "I don't believe you!" he insisted, sweeping out a circle of defense. "This is impossible. He would never have—"

"He did. He did, beloved! Try to understand!" she cried, as desperate as he. "Your father was like lightning in the night—beautiful and dangerous and sudden. They forced it on him! *They* were killing *him*! They had shut him up behind walls greater than those mountains," she said, waving her arm at the huge stone crags she only half understood. "They had silenced him, and he was dying, Rukuei! He was dying of the silence! Think of the music he wrote for you and the other children! Hear it in your heart! Know that it would have died in him if he hadn't—"

Rukuei sank to the ground like the child he was. The constant wind sweeping the valley was loud in their ears, and brought the shrieking laughter of small children chasing one another through the village of tents, the calls of women, the songs of men, the ordinary bustle of a village going about the tasks of everyday life. Deaf to this cheerful noise, he saw in the distance what Suukmel was blind to: destitution, bare subsistence, naked poverty, the words for which did not yet exist in any Rakhati language because such conditions had never before existed on Rakhat.

"How?" he cried. "How could it have come to *this*?" Suukmel went to him and knelt at his side. He wrenched away, ashamed and angry, and stood again on feet still swollen and sore, and left his foster mother without a glance, for he was his father's son and felt the charge build within him and looked now only for someone to strike. Striding down the shattered stone of the hillside, heedless of the falls he took and the cuts he added to his battered young body, he followed the sound of his cousin's voice to a small crowd of Runa and Jana'ata, her odd accent notable among the gabble as she helped build a barrier—who knew why—across a small swift river that cut through the valley center.

"No, don't try to pick them up! Just kick the stones along!" Rukuei heard her call merrily to her husband, Shetri, who was staggering clumsily with a small boulder in his arms. "Look at Sofi'ala! Roll them!" Their firstborn daughter was doing just this with a little rock, the child bent comically in half, short tail in the air, tiny face stiff with concentration. "See how my darling is working!" Ha'anala cried, naked and grunting like a stevedore. "Good girl, helping others!"

Outraged, Rukuei strode up behind Ha'anala and gripped her ankle, hauling her around, pulling her off balance. "You are Kitheri!" he screamed at her, at his father, at himself. "How can you degrade yourself this way? You drag your own child down! How dare you—"

In the space of a breath, the indifferent soldier Shetri Laaks was on top of the boy, and would have torn his throat out, had not Ha'anala stopped him with a shouted warning. She took her husband's shoulders and moved him aside and knelt down to look questioningly at Rukuei with eyes she had no right to—eyes that should be dead.

"We are close kin," Rukuei snarled, glaring at her from the stony ground where he had stumbled under Shetri's weight. "Your dam was my sire's sister!" Her face brightened, confused but happy. He wanted nothing more in all the world than to smash that happiness. "My father killed yours," he told her with blunt brutality, "twice-twelve days past."

He was delighted by the silence his words imposed, glad to make someone else gasp with loss, joyful to see her face go slack with pain. "Your father did not die alone. The plain of Inbrokar is heaped with dead, and when I last saw him, my father lay next to yours. Killed by such as these!" he howled, arm flung wide with indictment, at all the Runa who surrounded them. "You speak of choices. So choose, woman! Who shall die to restore the honor of the dead?"

There was no sound but their own breath, and the wind, and the far, thin bugling of some mountain animal heedless of the moment, and the high wail of Isaac, spinning and spinning on the edge of the crowd.

Ha'anala rested a hand on her belly and got to her feet, and he saw here in full daylight that she was not sleek with her pregnancy, but raw-boned and tired. Wearily, she looked around at the Jana'ata who had chosen to remain in the N'Jarr valley.

"My choices are the same as yours," she told them. "Survival or revenge. I choose to live." She stared down at Rukuei, and pointed to a stony trail that led east, to a pass between two mountains. "There are others like you, who choose death. Three days' walk that way. Ask for my husband's nephew, Athaansi Erat. They eat well in his camp," she said, raising her voice so all could hear her. "Or should I say, they eat plenty. Everything they choose is death. They avenge their losses and pay death with death, and they will die bloody but with full stomachs. You will be welcomed there, cousin. I shall honor the dead by living, and by teaching those who will listen that there is valor in this choice."

Isaac's wail fell off to a moaning that was joined by the keening of a bereft Jana'ata man-child. Sitting at his side, Ha'anala rested her head against Rukuei's, putting a thin arm around his shoulders and holding him near. "Our fathers are dead," she whispered as the boy wept. "We are not. Live with me, cousin. Live . . ."

Mesmerized by the drama, the villagers stood swaying or staring until Shetri shepherded them away. Finally, there was no one left but the two cousins, and Isaac, whose spinning gradually slowed.

Older now and steadier, less vulnerable to turmoil if it was quickly brought under control, Isaac did not understand or even notice the emotions at work on his sister and her cousin. But he did what he could to bring clarity.

"I have something to say," he announced in a loud, flat voice. He would not look at Rukuei, and certainly would not approach someone so demonstrably unpredictable, but Isaac told him, "Your work is to learn songs." He waited a moment and then added, "And to teach them."

The quiet persisted, so Isaac was able to finish. "I'll teach you one someday," he told the boy. "It's not ready yet. You can leave for a while, but come back."

Giordano Bruno
2084, Earth-Relative

"I STAYED WITH HA'ANALA AND MY FOSTER MOTHER, SUUKMEL, UNTIL I was fourteen," Rukuei Kitheri would tell Emilio Sandoz years later. "I learned to sing with Isaac, and sometimes he would say the most extraordinary things. I came to trust his . . . judgment. He was very strange, but he was right: I was born to learn songs and to teach them. I spent nearly five years wandering through the Garnu mountains—I needed to hear and remember the story of each Jana'ata who had lived through those last days. I hungered for the lullabies and the literature. I wanted to understand the laws and the politics, and the poetry, to preserve some small portion of the intellect and art of a world that had died before my eyes."

"But eventually you went back to the valley," Sandoz said. "To Ha'anala and Isaac?"

"Yes."

"And by then, Isaac was ready to let you hear the music he found."

"Yes."

Isaac had met Rukuei at the mouth of the pass. Naked as ever, the ragged parasol high over his head, he did not look at Rukuei or greet him, or ask about his travels. He simply stood in the way.

"I know why you're here," Isaac told him finally. "You came back to learn the song." A pause. "I found the music." Another pause. "It doesn't have words yet."

There was no emotion in his voice, but driven by some inner dismay in the face of unresolved disorder, Isaac began to spin, and hum, and flap his hands.

"What's wrong, Isaac?" Rukuei asked, schooled by then in others' pain.

The spinning stopped abruptly, and Isaac swayed, dizzy. "The music can't be sung unless it has words," he said at last. "Songs have words."

Rukuei, who had learned to care for his cousin's bizarre brother before he'd left on his own journey, felt moved to comfort him. "I'll find the words, Isaac," he promised.

It was a vow made in youth and ignorance, to be lived out in maturity and full understanding. Rukuei Kitheri would never regret it.

32

Giordano Bruno

October 2078, Earth-Relative

"LOOK AT WHAT THEY'VE DONE," JOSEBA URIZARBARRENA BREATHED,
first with awe and then in mourning, as the images began to pour in. "Look
at what they've done!"

"My God," John Candotti whispered, "it's so beautiful . . ."

"Beautiful!" Joseba cried. "How much has died to make this happen?"
he demanded, gesturing angrily at the display. He stopped, stricken, afraid
that Sandoz had heard and would take this accusation personally, but the
linguist was absorbed in his own work at the far end of the bridge, monitoring the radio transmissions they could now listen to directly.

"Joseba, what are you talking about!" John sputtered. "It's gorgeous!
It's—it's—"

"It's a catastrophe!" Joseba whispered fiercely, shaking with helpless
outrage. "Don't you see? They've totally disrupted the ecology. Everything
has been changed!" He stood and turned away from the displays, despairing. "Agriculture!" he moaned, face in his hands. "Another planet, gone
to hell—"

"I think it's pretty," Nico remarked politely to Sean Fein, who was also
leaning against the bridge bulkhead, watching as the system updated and
repainted multiple displays, scan by scan.

"So it is, Nico," said Sean. "So it is."

First blurred, then emerging from the mist of atmosphere and the fitful concealment of cloud, becoming clean-edged and brilliant with color, composite images of Rakhat had revealed upon the arrival of the *Giordano Bruno* in lowering orbit a world transformed: raw Paradise made formal garden. The change was most extensive in the midlatitudes of the northern hemisphere, where the largest continent's southern cities—first identified by Jimmy Quinn and George Edwards and Marc Robichaux forty years earlier—embraced coast and river. Superimposing old and new images, it was still possible to discern the outlines of urban centers. But now, where untouched savannah or jungle or fen or montane forest once lay, there was instead an exquisite lacework of plantation—colossal parterres laid out in interlocking knotted designs like Celtic jewelry: husbandry, geometry, artistry on a grand scale.

"Look keenly at it," Sean Fein recited quietly, remembering a twelfth-century scholar's description of the *Book of Kells*, "and you will penetrate to the very shrine of art. You will make out intricacies, so delicate and subtle, so full of knots and links, with colors so fresh and vivid, that you might say all this was the work of angels and not of men."

"They must be using satellite images to plan the layouts," Frans Vanderhelst said prosaically. "I don't think you could do that without seeing it all from above."

"Perhaps," said Carlo. "But you can do a lot with ropes and stakes. Simple surveying tools . . ." He leaned forward over Frans's vast shoulder and traced a curving line of mountain that formed a template for exuberant terracing. "Some of the design is coming directly from the geology." He turned to Sandoz, tucked into a corner of the bridge, oblivious to the visuals, concentrating on the radio chatter. Carlo waved to draw his attention. "Take a look at this new survey, Sandoz. What do you think?" Carlo asked him when he'd pulled the earphones off.

Sandoz stood with a groaning stretch before joining Danny, Sean and Nico against the wall, where they could take in the bank of screens. "Jesus," he said, stunned. "The Jana'ata must have decided gardening was a good idea for the Runa after all." He stared for a time, watching as sequential images added resolution and brought out finer detail in composite frames. "How does the infrared look?"

Joseba went to a false color display. "Even worse! Look at the heat signature in these cities." He brought up an overlay with comparison data from the *Stella Maris* library. "My God. This has got to be, what? Thirty-five percent population growth, in two generations!"

"Don't exaggerate," said Danny, doing the estimate in his head. "I make that heat increase closer to twenty-nine percent, overall. And you can't be sure it's from population growth. Could be changes in the industrial base—"

"But look here," Carlo said. "There are new settlements along the rivers. More roads than before." Following the terrain, he noticed. Not like the Romans' roads—ramming straight through from point A to point B—but roads nonetheless. Good for business, he thought. "Anything new from the radio data?" he asked Sandoz.

Emilio shook his head. "Trade quotes, market analysis. Weather reports, crop yields, shipping schedules. Endless announcements of meetings! All in Ruanja," he said with a shuddering yawn. "I've got to take a break. This is putting me to sleep."

"Still no music?" Danny Iron Horse asked.

"Not a note," Emilio confirmed as he left the bridge.

He was doing nearly all the translation work now, but Danny had the more difficult task. There were decades of transmissions relayed from Rakhat to the *Magellan* to Earth, samples of which were routed back to the *Bruno*; those had to be reconciled with what the *Bruno* had intercepted from the *Magellan* while in transit and what they could hear directly now. Emilio's mind went white amid the tangle of time sequences, but Danny seemed able to cope with it. There were big shifts in content signaled by vocabulary that Emilio had never heard and could only guess at—and, of course, they were only getting scraps and partials. Even so, for a time the samples had featured a heartening mixture of languages, song and news, and he had begun to think that perhaps something really had changed for the better.

He didn't know what to make of the absence of K'San now, any more than he understood what the acceptance of agriculture implied, so he left Joseba and Danny's growing argument about industrial development behind, and headed to the galley for coffee. He was pouring it when, behind him, John cleared his throat in warning.

"Thanks," Emilio said, glancing over his shoulder. "It's not as bad as it used to be, John."

"Yeah. I've noticed that. But I'd rather not startle you if I can help it." John didn't come into the cramped room, but stood in the doorway. "No response to the hails, I guess. You'd have mentioned it, right?"

"Of course." Emilio turned around, holding the cup with both hands.

When he spoke next, it was in Sean's voice. "The fine thing about expectin' the worst is, when it happens, y'have the satisfaction of bein' right."

"She might not be listening, you know," John said. "I mean, she's not expecting visitors, right? She could still be alive."

"It's possible." Maybe her computer tablet had deteriorated. Or it might have been lost or stolen. Or she might have simply given up using it. Face it, Emilio told himself. She's dead. "The odds against Sofia's survival were pretty bad," he said aloud, carrying his coffee out to the table, where he sank into a chair.

John followed and sat across from him. "She'd have been over seventy by now, I figure."

Emilio nodded. "Which is about thirty years younger than I feel." He yawned again and rubbed his eyes against his shoulders. "Jesus, I'm tired. This was a long way to come just to listen to crop reports."

"It's strange, isn't it," John said. "We might not have come the first time if we'd heard that stuff instead of the music."

Emilio slid down until his head rested against the chair's back and his chin rested on his chest. "Nah, we'd have come," he said, smiling at John's unconscious use of the Jesuit "we." "I probably would have talked myself into believing that the shipping schedules were a litany of the saints." Emilio rolled his eyes. "Religion—the wishful thinking of an ape that talks! You know what I think?" he asked rhetorically, trying to distract himself from yet another death. "Random shit happens, and we turn it into stories and call it sacred scripture—"

John was very still. Emilio glanced up and saw his face. "Oh, God. I'm sorry," he said, sitting up wearily. "Emilio Sandoz, the human toxin! Don't listen to me, John. I'm just tired and foul-tempered and—"

"I know," John said, taking a deep breath. "And I am willing to concede that you've got a black belt in pain and suffering, okay? But you're not the only one who's tired, and you're not the only one who's foul-tempered, and you're not the only one who wanted Sofia to be alive! Try remembering that."

"John, listen! I'm sorry, okay?" Emilio called as Candotti left the room. "Christ," he whispered bleakly, alone in the commons. Elbows on the table, braced hands on either side of his cup, he stared down into the mug. What year is it? he wondered irrelevantly. How the hell old am I now? Forty-eight, maybe? Ninety-eight? Two hundred? After a while he realized that he could see his own reflection in the black, still surface of the coffee:

a thin face etched by bad years, the evidence of their passing pain. Nothing he could say would shake John's faith—he knew that, but he slumped back in the chair, cringing anyway. "Nice play, ace," he sighed.

Hating himself, and John, and Sofia, and everyone else he could think of, he went back to work mentally, to escape. It came to him that he should probably give up listening directly to the monitored radio signals—just scan for changes in language at a higher playback speed. Why didn't I think of that before? he wondered. Not exactly operating at peak efficiency . . .

A moment later, the drop of his head woke him, and he roused himself, opening his eyes and seeing the coffee mug in front of him on the table. His arms felt leaden, too heavy to reach for it. I'm way past caffeine anyway, he thought, sitting up a little. Time for some of Carlo's magic pills.

This wasn't the first time he'd forced himself to live this way; he'd discovered long ago that he could function fairly well on three or four hours of sleep a night. He felt like hell all the time, but that was nothing new. You ignore it, he told himself. You get used to the way your eyes burn, the constant dull headache. It isn't that you forget the tiredness or the fear or the grief or the anger, he observed, or that anything is better or easier. But the fact is, you can work in spite of it. You just stay on your feet, keep moving . . .

Because if you sit down for a moment, he thought, waking again, if you let yourself rest. . . . Well, you don't. You keep working, because the alternative is to enter the city of the dead, the necropolis inside your head. So many dead . . .

. . . he was trying to straighten them, to lay the corpses out. It was night, but there was moonlight from every direction, and the bodies were almost beautiful. Anne's hair, silver in the lunar glow. The ebony limbs of a Dodoth boy's small sister—delicate and fragile—her perfect little skeleton revealed and lovely, but so sad, so sad. . . . Except that her suffering was over, and she was with God.

That was the worst, he knew in his dream. If God is the enemy, then even the dead are in danger. All the ones you loved might be with Him, and He was not to be trusted, not to be loved. "All that lives dies," Supaari was telling him. "It would be a waste not to eat them." But the city was burning again, the smell of charred meat was everywhere and it wasn't moonlight, it was fire and there were Jana'ata everywhere and they were all dead, all dead, so many dead—

Someone was shaking him. He woke with a gasp, the stench still in his nostrils. "What? What is it?" He sat up, disoriented, terror still alive in him. "What! Shit! I wasn't dreaming!" he lied, not even knowing why. "Is there—"

"Emilio! Wake up!" John Candotti stood above him grinning, face lit up like a Halloween pumpkin's. "Ask me what's new!"

"Oh, Christ, John," Emilio moaned, falling back against the chair. "Jesus! Don't fuck with me—"

"She's alive," John said. Emilio stared at him. "Sofia. Frans finally raised her on the radio about ten minutes ago—"

Sandoz was up and moving, pushing past John and headed for the bridge. "Wait, wait, wait!" John cried, grabbing his arm as Emilio went by. "Relax! She's broken the connection. It's okay!" he said, his face shining, their brief estrangement forgotten. "We told her you were asleep. She laughed and said, 'Typical!' She said that she's been waiting for almost forty years to hear from you and she can wait a few more hours, so we shouldn't wake you up. But I knew you'd kill me if I didn't, so I did."

"She's all right, then?" Emilio asked.

"Evidently. She sounds fine."

Emilio sagged back against a bulkhead for a moment, eyes closed. Then he headed for the radio, leaving John Candotti smiling beatifically in his wake.

BY THE TIME SANDOZ GOT TO THE BRIDGE, EVERYONE WAS CROWDED around the entry as Frans put through the connection a second time.

"What language is she speaking?" Emilio asked.

"English, mostly," Frans reported and got ponderously out of the way, ceding the console to Sandoz. "Some Ruanja."

"Sandoz?" he heard as he sat. The sound of her voice jolted through him: lower and grainier than he remembered, but beautiful.

"Mendes!" he cried.

"Sandoz!" she said again, her voice breaking on his name. "I thought—I never—"

Dammed emotion crashed through barriers they had both believed insuperable until that moment, but the sobbing was soon leavened with laughter and chagrined apologies and finally with what was clearly joy, and they began to argue, as though no time had gone by, over who had started crying first. "Anyway," Emilio said, deciding to let her win, "what the hell are you doing alive! I said Kaddish for you!"

"Well, I'm very sorry, but I'm afraid you wasted a prayer for the dead—"

"It didn't count anyway," he said dismissively. "No minyan."

"Minyan—don't tell me you speak Aramaic now, too! What's the count?"

"I'm up to seventeen, I think. I've picked up some Euskara, and I've learned how to be rude to Afrikaners." There was some static, but not much. Not too much for him to feel as though they were somehow, madly, just two old friends, talking on the phone. "But no Aramaic, I'm afraid. I just memorized the prayer."

"Cheater!" she said, with the familiar husky laugh now free of tears. He closed his eyes and tried not to thank God that her laugh had not changed. "So, Quixote," she was saying, "have you come to rescue me?"

"Of course not," he replied indignantly, astounded at how well she sounded. How elated. . . . "I just stopped by for a coffee. Why? Do you need rescuing?"

"No, I most certainly do not. But I could really use some coffee," she admitted. "It's been a long time between buzzes."

"Well, we brought plenty, but I'm afraid it's decaf." There was an appalled silence. "Sorry," he said unhappily. "Nobody cleared the cargo manifest with me." The silence was now broken by little horrified noises. "It was a clerical error," he told her with earnest distress. "I'm really sorry. I'll have everyone involved executed. We'll put their heads on pointy sticks—"

She started to laugh. "Oh, Sandoz, I think I've always loved you."

"No, you didn't," he said huffily. "You hated me on sight."

"Did I? Well, I must have been a fool. That was a joke about the decaf, wasn't it?" she asked warily.

"Would I joke about a thing like that?"

"Only if you thought I'd fall for it." There was a small space, and when she spoke again, it was with the kind of calm dignity that he had always admired in her. "I am glad I've lived to speak to you again. Everything is different. The Runa are free now. You were right, Sandoz. You were right all along. God meant for us to come here."

Behind him, there were the sounds of the others reacting to what she had said, and he felt John grip his shoulders and whisper fiercely, "Did you hear that, you shithead? Did you *hear* it?" But his own vision seemed to lose focus, and he found that he couldn't breathe well, and lost the thread of what she was saying until he heard his name again. "And Isaac?" he asked.

The silence was so abrupt and went so long, he twisted in the seat to look at Frans. "Connection's still open," Vanderhelst told him quietly.

"Sofia?" he said. "The last we heard, Isaac was very young. I didn't mean to—"

"He left me a long time ago. Isaac was—. He went off on his own years ago. Ha'anala followed him and we had hoped—. But neither of them ever came back. We tried and tried to find them, but the war went on so long—"

"War?" Danny asked, but Sandoz was saying, "It's all right. It's all right, Sofia. Whatever happened—"

"No one expected it to go on so long! Ha'anala was—. Oh, Sandoz, it's too complicated. When can you come down? I'll explain everything when you get to Galatna—"

It felt like a blow to the stomach. "Galatna?" he asked almost inaudibly.

"Sandoz, are you there? Oh, my God," she said, realizing. "I—I know what happened to you here. But everything is different! Hlavin Kitheri is dead. They've both—. Kitheri's been dead for . . . years," she said, voice trailing away. But then she spoke firmly. "The palace is a museum now. I live here, too—just another piece of history!"

She stopped, and he tried to think, but nothing would come. "Sandoz?" he heard her say. "Don't be afraid. There are no *djanada* south of the Garnu mountains. We-and-you-also are safe here. Truly. Sandoz, are you there?"

"Yes," he said, getting a grip. "I'm here."

"How soon can you come down? How many of you are there?"

Brows up, he turned to Carlo and asked, "A week perhaps?" Carlo nodded. "A week, Sofia." He cleared his throat, tried to put more strength behind his voice. "We are eight here, but the ship's pilot will stay on board. There'll be four Jesuits and two . . . businessmen. And me."

She missed the implication. "You'll have to land southeast of Inbrokar City to get beyond the gardens. Have you seen them? We call them robichauxs! There are competitions for the most beautiful and productive designs, but there are no prizes, so no one gets *porai*. I'll send an escort for you. It's safe, but I don't get around too well anymore and finding your way through the garden mazes is impossible unless you're a Runao—. Listen to me! I've lived with the Runa too long! *Sipaj*, Meelo! Did someone always chatter like this?" she asked, laughing. She paused, took a breath, slowed down. "Emilio, don't expect who I was. I'm an old woman now. I'm a ruin—"

"Aren't we all?" he said, getting his bearings. "And if you are a ruin," he said softly, "you will be a splendid one—Mendes, you will be the Parthenon! All that matters is that you are alive and safe and well."

He found that he meant it. At that moment, it was truly all that mattered.

33

Rakhat

October 2078, Earth-Relative

THERE WAS MORE: TALK OF TRADE GOODS WITH THE SMOOTH ITALIAN voice, discussion of coordinates and flight paths with the pilot. Tentative plans were made for landfall near the Pon river, as were agreements to check in daily, to question and confirm, to reconsider and adjust. An awkward good-bye to Sandoz, and then . . . she was back on Rakhat, by herself again, in a quiet room, hidden away with her memories, apart from the bustle and talk.

There were no mirrors now in Galatna Palace. Without any reminder of the reality Sandoz would see, Sofia Mendes could, for a time, believe herself thirty-five: straight-backed and strong-minded, clear-eyed and full of hope. The hope at least had remained—. No, had been fulfilled. There are wars worth fighting, she thought. Deaths redeemed. It was all for a reason. . . . Oh, Sandoz, she thought. You came back. I knew all along that you'd come back—

(Come back.)

Isaac, she thought, going still. Ha'anala.

She sat for a long time, summoning everything she had in her soul. Was it courage, she wondered, or stupidity, to expose her heart to chill air, and wait once more through silent days for hope to wither?

How can I not try? she asked herself. And so, she did.

• • •

"READ THIS," ISAAC SAID.

It was waiting for him, as other pleas had waited over the years. He always checked his mother's file first thing in the morning because checking was what he did, but he never responded. He had nothing to say.

Another man, in somewhat similar circumstances, might have spared his sister the heartache of these messages begging beloved children to come home, or simply to reassure their mother that they were both alive. Isaac didn't understand heartache. Or regret or longing or divided loyalties. Or anger or shattered trust or betrayal. Such things had no clarity. They involved expectations of another's behavior, and Isaac had no such expectations.

Sofia's messages were always addressed to both of them, in spite of everything that had happened during the long years since they'd left the forest. After she'd read the latest, Ha'anala closed the tablet carefully. "Isaac? Do you want to go back?"

"No." He didn't ask, Back where? It didn't matter.

"Our mother wishes it." There was a pause. "She is old, Isaac. She will die someday soon."

This was of no interest. He held his hands close to his eyes and began to make patterns with his fingers. But he could see Ha'anala looking at him, even through his fingers. "I won't go back," he said, dropping his hands. "They don't sing."

"Isaac, hear me. Our mother sings. Your people sing." She paused, and then continued, "There are others of your kind, Isaac. They have come here again—"

This interested him. "The music I found is right," he said, not with triumph or wonder but flatly: clouds rain, night follows day, the music was right.

"They may not stay, Isaac. Our mother may go back with them." A pause. "Back to where your species comes from." A longer pause, to let him hear this. "Isaac, if our mother decides to return to H'earth, we will never see her again."

He tapped his fingers against his cheeks, on the smooth place where the hair didn't happen, and began to hum.

"You should say good-bye to her at least," Ha'anala pressed.

"Should" had no clarity. He'd looked "should" up, but he found only noise about responsibility to others, obligations. He did not understand emotion that required two or more persons. His emotions took cognizance of his own state. He could be frustrated, but not frustrated by. He felt anger, but not anger at. He experienced delight, but not delight in. He lacked prepositions. Singing broke this pattern. He understood harmony: to sing with. That was how Ha'anala had explained her marriage to Shetri: "We are in harmony."

Isaac cranked his head back on his neck to look up at the tent fabric, studying the sunlight that made each tiny pixel between warp and weft glow. He had refused a new stone house because the tent was familiar and he liked the color. It moved, but not like leaves. He glanced down and saw that Ha'anala had not left, so he held out his hand and waited for the weight of the tablet to settle into his palm. The tent was a veil that no one pulled away. The tent kept dust and leaves out, unless there was a big storm. Even so, he got his sticks to check the rectangle, to be certain it still had the correct proportions.

Then: the feel of the latch against his thumb, the soft snick of the mechanism, the unchanging geometry of the cover. The whirr of power-on, the brightening of the screen, the keyboard with its serried ranks. A few keystrokes and a few words, there it was again, precisely as he'd left it, each note perfect and precise. He thought, I was born to find this.

He was, in his own way, pleased.

THE WIDOW SUUKMEL CHIROT U VAADAI NO LONGER HAD A FIRM OPIN-ion about which god ruled her life.

In her youth, she had been inclined toward the more traditional deities: old, fussy goddesses who took pains to keep the suns in their proper paths, the rivers in their banks, the rhythms of daily life reliable. After her marriage, she had become rather fond of Ingwy, who ruled fate, for Suukmel knew the evils of lucklessness and was grateful to have been vouchsafed a husband who valued her. Many godlings took up residence in her untroubled household: Security, Luxury, Purpose, Balance. It was a rewarding life. Suukmel had seen daughters well married to husbands who met her private requirements, as well as those dictated by their lineal position and contemporary politics. She herself had scope for quiet accomplishment, and genuine contentment.

Then, in her middle years, Chaos ruled her. Chaos, dancing. Chaos, singing. Not a goddess but a man who had sent her treasure: life lived with an intensity that often frightened her, but from which she would not, could not turn away. Power came to her. Influence. She tasted the exhilaration of the forbidden, the unpredictable. Chaos demanded not the death of Virtue in her life but the birth of Passion. Joy. Creation. Transformation.

And now? Who rules me now? Suukmel wondered idly, watching as Ha'anala abruptly left her strange brother's tent. A light breeze carried information confirming observation: Ha'anala was furious. Sweeping sightlessly past Suukmel, she strode beyond the confines of the settlement without a word to anyone, pausing only to snatch up the straps of a huge basket with one short hooked claw and sling it over her shoulder.

For a time, Suukmel simply gazed at the younger woman as she climbed jumbled glacial scree, and held her breath, hoping Ha'anala would not fall, balance thrown off and strength sapped by her fourth pregnancy. Sighing, Suukmel rose to follow, picking up her own basket and a tough old tarpaulin, heavy with wax and dirt and recent rain. Ha'anala seemed to welcome the attacks of the *kha'ani* when she was in this mood; Suukmel preferred to do her maurauding under the protection of a tarp.

There were a multitude of rocky outcrops in the mountains that surrounded the N'Jarr valley, and these crags were the favored nesting sites of the settlement's most abundant source of permissible food. At the end of Partan, when the rain's power diminished, the *kha'ani* bred early and often, in staggering numbers. Adults, darting and dodging, could rarely be caught, but during the dry season, their eggsaks were easy prey—leathery oval bags of protein with generous lashings of fat; that which nourished *kha'ani* embryos could also sustain Jana'ata if eaten in sufficient quantity. It was a monotonous diet and rather tasteless, but adequate and reliable, and it was varied now and then by other prey more worthy of the term, but also far more dangerous.

"Be warned," Ha'anala called, sensing Suukmel's approach. "I am not fit company."

"When have I required you to be convivial?" Suukmel asked, coming close. "Besides, I'm here to harass *kha'ani*, not you." Suukmel hooked her claws into the tarp and gave it a vigorous flap, driving some startled adult *kha'ani* off, and then slipped under it herself, quickly rolling sak after sak into her basket in the yellowish filtered light of the fabric, humming as she worked.

"What am I to do?" Ha'anala demanded, her voice mixing with the *kha'ani* shrieks, and coming muffled to Suukmel under her protective covering. "What does she expect? Am I to walk into Gayjur with Isaac? Do you know what she said? *All will be forgiven. She* forgives *me*! They forgive! How dare she—"

"You're right. You aren't fit company," Suukmel observed, sweeping another nestful of saks into her basket. "Whom are you vilifying, if I may know?"

"My mother!"

"Ah."

"Three times we've opened negotiations, and three times our emissaries were killed on sight over six hundred *cha'ari* outside of Gayjur," Ha'anala fumed, flinging another sak into her basket, ignoring the shrieks and nips of the *kha'ani* who swarmed around her. "She speaks of trust! She speaks of forgiveness!"

"You're going to burst the saks at the bottom if you fill that basket much more," Suukmel pointed out, emerging from her tarp. An outraged *kha'an* launched a flying counterattack and Suukmel took a swipe at it before shouldering her basket and hurrying a few paces away to a patch of grass. *The little brutes were vigilantly territorial, but couldn't see very well. We all have our weaknesses,* Suukmel thought, commiserating with her prey's parents.

She sat in the rare sunshine, warming herself, and took out a few eggsaks. "Come and eat with me, child," she called to Ha'anala.

Ha'anala stood for a time, making an easy target for the *kha'ani,* but finally lugged her basket over and dropped it next to Suukmel, who serenely kneaded an eggsak until its contents were well mixed. It had taken her some time, but she had worked out a way to manage these things neatly. *You had to be deft. Compress the tough, fibrous outer covering in one hand to make the sak taut, and force a claw from the other hand into one end. Then suck out the contents quickly while being careful not to put too much pressure on the sak. Squeeze too hard and you'd have albumin all over your face.*

"Sit and eat!" she ordered more firmly this time, and handed a sak to Ha'anala before starting her own breakfast.

"Suukmel, I have tried to understand her," Ha'anala insisted, as though her older friend had argued. "I have tried to believe that she did not know what was happening to us—"

"Sofia was at Inbrokar," Suukmel pointed out.

"So she herself saw that slaughter." Ha'anala downed the eggsak's contents, oblivious to its taste. "She knows now—even if she didn't plan it herself from the beginning. She knows how few we are!"

"Unquestionably," Suukmel agreed.

Ha'anala lowered herself to the ground, making a tripod of her legs and tail, belly swelling out before her. "And yet she expects me to forget all this, to leave my people, and come to her!" Ha'anala cried. "We have paid in lives for every attempt to find some kind of understanding or to make some kind of agreement!" Suukmel put out a hand and gently pulled Ha'anala over until she lay down, head in Suukmel's lap, wrapping her tail around herself like an infant. "Maybe Shetri's nephew Athaansi is right. We're fools to keep on hoping . . ."

"Perhaps," Suukmel allowed.

"But it's Athaansi's raids that feed their fear! Every time his men bring down a Runao for his settlement, they eat their fill for a few hours and Athaansi is a hero—"

"And for every Runao who is killed, there is a whole village freshly convinced that the only way to live safely is to begin the war again," Suukmel pointed out.

"Exactly! The imaging satellites are too far south on the horizon to see us, and the Runa can't track us, but they are not stupid! One day Athaansi, or someone like him, will lead them back to the valleys! I'm sure of it, Suukmel. If they ever find us, they'll finish us! I have tried and tried to make Athaansi see that he multiplies our enemies faster than we can make children—"

"Athaansi is trapped in his own politics, child. He can't rule without the VaPalkirn faction, and they will defend tradition at any price." Suukmel's legs were cramping and she took Ha'anala firmly by the shoulders, lifting her to a sitting position, noting as she did so the narrowness of Ha'anala's hips so late in pregnancy, the thinness of her tail, the dullness of her coat. "It must be admitted that the mothers of Athaansi's valley are well fed," Suukmel said gently, "and they bear healthy children regularly."

Ha'anala glared down at the N'Jarr, where lean women bore fewer children every year, no matter whom they mated with. "If any wish to leave here, they may go!" she declared recklessly. "Athaansi will welcome the numbers."

"Undoubtedly," Suukmel said, watching Ha'anala's gallantry fade. There had been no births during the past year, and few before that. Sofi'ala was a sturdy child who looked likely to survive childhood, but Ha'anala had lost a spindly toddler to the lung blight Shetri's herbs could not stave off, and had borne another son dead.

"Maybe Athaansi is right," Ha'anala said, almost soundlessly.

"Possibly. And yet," Suukmel pointed out with wonderment, "we stay with you, and there are Runa who stay with us."

"Why?" Ha'anala cried. "What if I'm wrong? What if it's all a mistake?"

"Eat this," Suukmel said, handing Ha'anala another eggsak. "Be glad for abundance and sunshine when they come." But Ha'anala simply let her hand fall listlessly, too distracted and dismayed to be heartened by a day when dense northern clouds parted around thin, silvery light. "Once, long ago," Suukmel told her, "my lord husband asked Hlavin Kitheri if he never worried that it might have been a mistake to do as he had done. The Paramount answered, 'Perhaps, but it was a magnificent mistake.'"

Ha'anala stood and walked to the edge of the rocks, the breeze riffling through her fur. Suukmel stood then herself and walked to Ha'anala's side. "I have heard the songs of many gods, child. Silly gods, powerful gods, and capricious gods, and biddable gods, and dull. Long ago, when you first welcomed us to your household, and fed us and gave us shelter, and invited us to stay, I listened to you say that we are all—Jana'ata and Runa and H'u-man—children of a God so high that our ranks and our differences are as nothing in his far sight."

Suukmel looked out over the sweep of the valley, dotted now with small stone houses and filled with the sound of voices high and low, home to Runa and to Jana'ata and to the single outlandish being whom Ha'anala called brother. "I thought then that this was merely a song sung by a foreigner to a foolish girl who believed nonsense. But Taksayu was dear to me, and Isaac was dear to you. I was willing to hear this song, because I had once yearned for a world in which lives would be governed not by lineage and lust and moribund law, but by love and loyalty. In this one valley, such lives are possible," she said. "If it is a mistake to hope for such a world, then it is a magnificent mistake."

Ha'anala dropped to her knees and put her hands to the rock, to hold herself up. The keening was soft at first, but they were alone on this hillside, far from those whose faith could be undermined by a leader's failure of nerve. Now was as good a time as any to give in to tiredness and worry; to hunger and responsibility; to yearning for lost parents and mourning for lost children, and for all that might have been and wasn't.

"Rukuei came home," Ha'anala said finally in a tiny voice, face pressed now into Suukmel's belly. "That's something. He's seen everything, and been everywhere. He came back here. And he has stayed . . ."

"Go back down the mountain, my heart," Suukmel advised serenely. "Listen to Isaac's music again. Remember what you thought when you first heard it. Know that if we are children of one God, we can make ourselves one family in time."

"And if God is just a song?" Ha'anala asked, alone and frightened.

Suukmel did not answer for a while. Finally she said, "Our task is the same."

"LISTEN TO THEM!" TIYAT VA'AGARDI WHISPERED, AMAZED. "WOULD YOU have guessed that *djanada* were capable of arguing like that?"

"Just like the old days," Kajpin VaMasna agreed, "except now it's them and not us." She listened to the wrangling for a while and then lay back to watch the clouds roll over the valley. It had been a long time since Kajpin herself had required agreement before making a decision—a character flaw she was no longer embarrassed by. She looked over at Tiyat. "I say we give them until second sunrise, and then we go."

Tiyat gazed affectionately at her companion. A former soldier, sickened by killing, Kajpin VaMasna had come north by herself, and since then had helped to ease the lives of VaN'Jarri of both species by raiding Runa trade caravans. Tiyat was just a domestic in the old days. She'd held a position of trust and responsibility even then, but she still sometimes hid in the middle of the herd, and admired Kajpin, who did not abase herself but still got along with everybody.

When the news about the new foreigners spread through the community, it was Kajpin who suggested that she and Tiyat should go south and bring a human back to the N'Jarr, touching off the *fierno* that was still raging. Most of the Runa had gotten bored and gone off to find something to eat, but the Jana'ata showed no signs of consensus.

"Ha'anala," Rukuei was saying, "I've studied all the records! Yes, there is a great deal I don't understand. Too many words and ideas I can't make clear to myself," he admitted. "But the foreigners first came here because of our music, and now they've come back. We have to know them—"

"And if all this talk of God's music is nonsense?" Ha'anala demanded, trying to ignore Isaac's humming, which was getting louder and more insistent by the moment. "If we are wrong—"

Tiyat spoke up for the first time. "It's not nonsense! Someone thinks—" She stopped, shy but ashamed of taking cover, especially on this point. Tiyat loved the music Isaac had found; it was the only kind of music she had ever been able to listen to, and it had changed her. "I say we should let the other foreigners hear it. They're part of this!"

"And there may be ways they can be useful to us—as honest brokers, for example," Suukmel pointed out, with the practicality that had once served two governments. "They could go back to the south and open negotiations on our behalf—"

("Uuuunnhh")

"Why would they agree to come here in the first place, let alone help us?" Ha'anala objected. "Sofia has poisoned their minds against us! They will believe us nothing more than murderers and thieves and—"

"They don't have to agree," Shetri said, glancing at his collection of narcotics.

Ears toppling, Ha'anala cried, "Abduction is hardly the way to make allies!"

("Uuuuuuuuunnhh")

"I have been everywhere but to the south," Rukuei said over Isaac's noise. "I need to see the others in their own place. If I am to understand, I must hear their words spoken freely—"

"Besides," Shetri said, with a slight edge to his voice, "Rukuei has had plenty of practice at deception. Who lies more convincingly than a poet who makes songs out of hunger and death?"

Ha'anala looked up sharply, but refused to be sidetracked. "This is crazy, Shetri," she said flatly. "It's uselessly dangerous for you and Rukuei. Let Tiyat and Kajpin do this—"

("Uuuuuuuuuuuuunnhh—")

"For solving problems, two kinds of mind are better than one," Tiyat pointed out, mild eyes sweeping around the gathering. "If two kinds are good," she said again, "then three are better yet, so we should go get a foreigner."

("Uuuuuuuuuuuuunnnnnnhh—")

Yellow light now flared in the southeast, but the chill hardly lessened, even as the second of Rakhat's suns rose. Kajpin stood and yawned, stretching her legs and shaking off boredom. "Just keep your mouths shut and your boots on and your hands in your sleeves," she advised Shetri and Rukuei. "If you're exposed, then Tiyat and I are constables bringing in a couple of VaHaptaa."

"Kajpin can lie as well as a poet," Tiyat noted solemnly, and got slapped with her friend's tail for her trouble.

"What goes wrong can be turned to advantage," Suukmel said. She looked down at the Runa toddler squirming in her lap—Tiyat's son, who resembled his mother: good-tempered, but resolute when thwarted. This child would never question his right to say "I" to any person he met. He would always feel himself the equal of any soul: something all the VaN'-Jarri wished for their children. "Let them go, Ha'anala. It will be well. Let them go."

Ha'anala, holding Sofi'ala close, said nothing. A contest, she was thinking, between Ingwy and Adonai. Fate against Providence, in a place where Fate had ruled so long . . .

She realized then that Isaac had stopped humming. He was naked as always, but never seemed to feel the cold. Or perhaps he did, but had no interest in it. For a flashing moment, he looked into Rukuei's eyes.

"Bring back someone who sings," was all he said.

N'Jarr Valley
2085, Earth-Relative

"SHETRI, I THINK, MIGHT HAVE MANAGED TO MAINTAIN HIS ANONYMITY, but there was something unmistakably Jana'ata about my foster son," Suukmel told Sean Fein many years later, recalling Rukuei's account of that journey. "So they fell back on Kajpin's story: that Rukuei was a follower of Athaansi Erat, captured while attempting to prey on a village. They claimed Shetri was a bounty hunter—a man who traded his tracking abilities to the police in exchange for meat from executed Runa felons. They were bringing Rukuei to Gayjur to be questioned about the location of the northern raiders."

Some Runa the party encountered took the opportunity to fling stones at a safely vanquished enemy, or to shout abuse. Still others let fly random kicks that Tiyat and Kajpin fended off with casual efficiency but no great emotional heat that would give the deception away. Before they reached the northernmost navigable tributary of the Pon river and had taken a short-term lease on a private powerboat, Rukuei had tasted the salt of his own blood from a broken tooth. But there was an old man, a Runao, who followed the four of them for a long time. Curious, they decided to wait for him one morning.

"He told them that he had never known he could get so old," Suukmel remembered. "Rukuei was very moved by this."

"Someone's bones hurt," the old man had said. "Someone's children went off to the cities. Let the *djanada* take this one!" this Runao begged Tiyat. "Someone is tired of being alone, and of hurting."

Tiyat looked at Kajpin, and they both turned to Rukuei, who had not eaten Runa for years. Kajpin's hand shot out and pushed Rukuei theatrically forward along the road. "Right," Tiyat agreed loudly, dismissing the old one. "Let the *djanada* starve." But Rukuei felt it would uncover no lie if he called out to the old man, "Thank you. Thank you for offering—" and stumbled again as Shetri cuffed him.

"There were genuine allies in some places," Suukmel told Sean. "Now and then, people offered a night's shelter, or hid them in a shed and told Rukuei and Shetri of some long dead Jana'ata who had been kind. But there were few, very few of these. Mostly there was indifference. Vague curiosity occasionally, but commonly a bland inattention. My foster son was very impressed by this: the Runa were living their lives as though we had never existed."

"The people of the third Beatitude have well and truly inherited the world, my lady, and they acquired a grand, high opinion of themselves while they were at it. You Jana'ata spoil the illusion," Sean told her. "So they pretend that you were never important to them."

The Jana'ata are alone, Sean thought then, like godlings whose believers had become atheists. In his own soul, he knew with sudden certainty that it was not rebellion or doubt or even sin that broke God's heart; it was indifference.

"Don't expect gratitude," he warned Suukmel. "Don't even expect acknowledgment! They're never going to need you again, not like they did before. A hundred years from now, you may be nothing but a memory. The very thought of you will fill most of them with shame and loathing."

"Then we shall truly be gone," Suukmel whispered.

"Perhaps," this hard man said. "Perhaps."

"If you have no hope for us, why have you stayed?" she demanded. "To watch us die?"

Perhaps, he almost said. But then Sean remembered his father, eyes shining with the unadulterated glee that Maura Fein had loved and shared, shaking his head at some ignominious example of the human capacity for boneheaded, self-inflicted calamity. "Ah, Sean, lad," David Fein would say to his son, "it takes an Irish Jew to appreciate a cock-up this grand!"

Sean Fein gazed for a time at the pale northern sky, and thought of the place where his own ancestors had lived. He was a Jesuit and celibate, an only child: the last of his line. Looking at Suukmel's drawn, gray face, he felt at long last compassion for the fools who expected fairness and sense—in this world, not the next.

"My father was the son of ancient priests, my mother the daughter of petty kings long gone," he told Suukmel. "A thousand times, their people might have died out. A thousand times, they nearly killed themselves off with political bickering and moral certainty and a lethal distaste for compromise. A thousand times they might have become nothing but a memory in the mind of God."

"And yet they live?" she asked.

"Last time I looked," he said. "I can't swear to more than that."

"And so might we," Suukmel replied, with frail conviction.

"Shit, yes, y'might at that," Sean muttered in English, remembering Disraeli's wee couplet: How odd of God / to choose the Jews. "My very much esteemed lady Suukmel," he said then in his strangely accented K'San, "one thing I can say for certain. There's just no telling whom God will take a liking to."

34

Rakhat: Landfall

October 2078, Earth-Relative

EVEN IF SEAN FEIN HAD HARBORED ANY ILLUSIONS ABOUT THINGS MAK-
ing sense on Rakhat, he'd have lost them all to the near oblivion he
achieved during the hours before the *Giordano Bruno* party made landfall.

As beautiful as he found the laws and workings of chemistry, the physics
of flying defeated him, and Sean always expected his innate pessimism to
be rewarded by the flaming crash of whatever aircraft he was on. So he had
hoarded his last bottle of Jameson's for this occasion, and spent his final
hours on the *Bruno* preparing himself spiritually to meet his Lord and Sav-
ior with an apology for the whiskey on his dying breath.

Weightlessness and chill dominated the first stage of the descent from
the vacuum of space. There was a brief, blessed interval of low gravity and
growing warmth, but that was followed by perceptible acceleration. As
they entered the atmosphere, the lander began to vibrate, and then to
buck like a small boat in a dirty sea.

Alcohol failed him. Nauseated and cotton-mouthed, Sean spent the
balance of the flight alternately invoking the Virgin's intercession and
chanting, "Fack, fack, fack," like a litany, with his eyes closed and his
palms stinking. Just when it seemed it couldn't get any worse, they hit a
wall of bad air left over from the last tropical storm to move through the
region, and as the entry heat grew in ferocity, his body fought crazily with

its own autonomic nervous system: ice-cold with terror and sweating to stave off fever.

Which is why the first man from the *Giordano Bruno* to set foot on Rakhat was not Daniel Iron Horse, who was the mission's superior, or Joseba Urizarbarrena, an ecologist aching for his first glimpse of this new world; not Emilio Sandoz, who knew the place and would react most quickly to danger, or John Candotti, determined to be at his side, in case disaster struck again; nor was it the would-be conquistador Carlo Giuliani or his bodyguard Niccolo d'Angeli. It was Father Sean Fein, of the Society of Jesus, who pushed his way to the front of the queue and exited the lander the moment the hatch opened, stumbling forward a few steps and falling gracelessly to his knees, where he threw up for a good two minutes.

They might have hoped for a more auspicious beginning to their stay. Sean at least managed to arrange for the first words spoken by a member of their mission to be a kind of prayer. "Dear God," he gasped, when things slowed down, "that was a shameful waste of good liquor."

IT WAS ONLY WHEN SEAN SAT BACK ON HIS HEELS AND HAWKED AND SPAT and caught his breath that any of them looked beyond his distress to the high plateau south of Inbrokar City, which Sofia Mendes had recommended as their landing site.

"I had forgotten," Emilio Sandoz whispered, walking as they all did now away from the lander's ticking-hot hull, away from the stench of burnt fuel and vomit, into the redolent wind. "I had forgotten."

They'd meant to come earlier, just after the first of Rakhat's suns had risen, before the steaming heat of full day, but the weather was more than usually unstable this time of year and storms had delayed landfall twice. Finally, Frans had identified a break in the rains and Carlo had decided to go down, even though it would be close to second sunset when they landed.

So they had by accident arrived on Rakhat at the most beautiful time of day, when the late afternoon chorale of wildlife announced its existence to an unheeding world intoxicated with its own luxuriance. To the east, the far landscape was veiled by sheets of gray rain, but there were two suns low behind them, just above the white limestone escarpment that helped contain the Pon river, and these lit up the near country brilliantly, making an immoderate world sparkle like a pirate's jewel box: all diamond raindrops and golden clouds, its wanton foliage amethyst and aquamarine and emerald, its extravagant blossom citrine and ruby and sapphire and topaz. The very sky flared like opal: yellow and pink and mauve, and the azure of the Virgin's robes.

"What is that scent?" John asked Emilio, standing next to him.

"Which one?" Joseba cried, agriculture's depredations forgotten in the languorous panorama of lavender savannah. There was a lifetime's work within a few paces of where he stood. The soil alive with tiny vertebrate fauna, the air teeming with flying things, membranous wings flashing as they wheeled in the sunlight. Overwhelmed by the sheer volume of data, Joseba could hardly keep himself from staking out a square meter and beginning the research that very moment; he needed to contain it somehow—divide it, tame it, know it.

"It's like a perfume shop!" said Nico.

"But there's one scent, especially," said John, searching for words. "Like cinnamon, except—more flowery."

"Yes, exquisite," Carlo agreed. "I recognize it—there were ribbons with that scent in the shipment the Contact Consortium stowed on board the *Stella Maris* when they sent Sandoz back."

Emilio looked around and then walked to a patch of low-growing bushes a few paces away. He picked a trumpet-shaped blossom, its petals the hallucinatory scarlet of a poppy, and held it out to John, who leaned forward to inhale. "Yeah, that's what I'm smelling. What's it called?" John asked, offering the blossom to Sean, who backed away, still feeling rocky.

"*Yasapa*," said Emilio. "And *yasapa* means?"

John pulled the pieces apart. *Ya s ap a* . . . "You can make tea with it!" he translated triumphantly.

Pleased with his pupil, the linguist nodded as Carlo reached for the flower, carrying it with both hands to his face and inhaling deeply. "The Runa fill a glass jar with the blossoms, cover them with water and set it in the sun—too sugary for my taste," Emilio said, "but they add sweetleaf to the tea as well. If you leave it long enough, it ferments. You can distill that for a kind of brandy."

"Just as I predicted!" Carlo crowed triumphantly. "We've been here less than half an hour and you have already paid for this entire expedition," he told Sandoz, looking at the blossom. "Beautiful color—" He paused, and then sneezed violently.

"*Crisce sant'*," Nico intoned.

Carlo nodded, and tried again, "Is the brandy th—" He stopped, mouth open, eyes closing, and this time there was a series of sneezes, with Nico blessing each small detonation. "Thank you, Nico, I think I'm sufficiently sanctified," Carlo said. "Is the brandy this color?" he finally managed to ask before sneezing again. "God," he cried, "I can't be coming down with a cold!"

"It's that damned flower," said Sean, lip curled at the cloying odor.

"Or the lander fumes," Danny suggested.

Carlo shook his head in amazement, and managed to continue his thought. "Is the brandy this color as well? The demand would be huge—"

"Just don't let the Jebs in on the deal," Danny warned as Carlo abandoned himself to an artillery barrage of sneezing. "The only time we ever tried to run a winery, we lost money on it. On the other hand, it might be fun to give the Benedictines a little unhealthy competition—"

Carlo was now staggering backward, as though jet-propelled. "*Possa sa' l'ultima!*" he gasped with his hands over his mouth, which felt bizarrely numb. His eyes were starting to itch and water. "Drop the flower," he heard Sean say. "Get it away from your face!" Sandoz ordered. And Carlo did so, but the sneezing continued unabated, and his eyes were swelling shut . . .

"This is the last time I go on a package tour with you guys," John was griping. "Sean throws up, Carlo's allergic to flowers—"

"Padrone, is something wrong?" Nico asked. When there was no answer, Nico turned to Emilio and asked again, "Is there something wrong?"

Everything began happening at once: Emilio yelling, "Get the anaphylaxis kit! *Run*, for crissakes! He's going down!" Carlo hitting the ground, each breath a separate struggle to suck air past a rapidly constricting pharynx. Danny dashing back to the lander for the ana kit. Emilio barking at John, "Get him on his back! Start CPR!" Then Carlo turned blue and Nico's fright turned to sobs. Sean tried to calm him, but Emilio turned away from the grief, arms across his chest, and paced for a few moments before glancing back to see Joseba take over the rhythmic effort to restart Carlo's heart when John began to flag. "Danny—come *on!*" Emilio yelled as Iron Horse skidded to a halt and dropped to his knees next to Carlo's lifeless body. "The red syringe," Emilio said, his voice low and tense as he watched Iron Horse dig through the kit. "Yes! That's it. Right into the heart. We're losing him—"

But even as he spoke, Carlo's color pinked and the gasping breaths started to come again without Joseba's aid. Suspended in time, they all watched silently as the hit of epinephrine took hold. "Jesus," John whispered. "He was dead."

"All right," Emilio said, coming to life himself, "get him into the lander and lock it down—he's still exposed out here."

"Nico," Sean said evenly, "be a good boy and clear a space for Don Carlo on the deck, please."

Bleary-eyed and scared but always ready to obey a direct order, Nico ran ahead to open the cargo-bay door while John, Sean and Joseba carried Carlo to shelter. "If he stabilizes, that may be all he needs," Emilio was telling Danny as they dogtrotted behind the others. "But if he goes under again, try aminophylline, yes?"

By the time they had the lander systems reactivated and the filters began cleaning the interior air, Carlo was coming around. "—ole atmosphere must be drenched in pollens and danders and God knows what else," he could hear Joseba point out. But Sandoz said, "No, it must be *yasapa*. Anaphylaxis takes at least two exposures, and he recognized the scent—" Throat still constricted and eyes puffed shut, Carlo struggled to sit up; someone took him under the arms and pulled him to his feet, maneuvering him into a flight seat. Drained and disoriented, he whispered, "That was certainly exciting."

"Yes, indeed," he heard Sandoz agree. He could not see the man, but Carlo could picture the head shaking in wonder, silver hair falling over black eyes. "Of all the lives on two planets that I might have chosen to save," Sandoz told him, "yours, Don Carlo, would have been at the very bottom of my list. How do you feel?"

"Inglorious but better, thank you." Carlo tried to smile and was startled by how odd his swollen face felt. I must look like Frans, he thought as his vision cleared and breathing became easier. Then it struck him: "Your dream, Sandoz! You said I wasn't in the city of the dead—"

"Yes, and I am afraid you won't be going to the city of Gayjur either," said Sandoz dryly. "I'm sending you back to the *Bruno*. Danny is going along as medic, in case you crash again. John will pilot—"

"Sandoz, I didn't come all this way—"

"To die of anaphylaxis," Emilio finished for him, "which is exactly what you did a short while ago. *Yasapa* blooms year-round. You can try the surface again later, if you like—maybe John can reconfigure a pressure suit for you. For now, I recommend that you return to the mother ship. The decision is yours, of course."

"Right," said Carlo, not one to argue with facts for very long. "Radio the change of plans to Signora Mendes and put Frans on remote as backup pilot. Do you suppose *yasapa* brandy would affect people as the blossom did me?" he asked. "We'll have to put warning labels on anything we export—drink at your own risk. That will probably increase the appeal! An element of danger—"

"You'll still get sued, ace," Danny told him. "I'm going to move you to the cockpit. We need to reopen the cargo bay, but you should be okay if you're sealed off, up front. As soon as we get the gear unloaded, you're going back to the *Bruno*."

NOT FAR TO THE NORTHWEST, IN THE SHADOW OF A LIMESTONE ESCARP-ment, a small mixed party of awestruck travelers listened for the second time to a shrieking roar that reached them from the darkening flatlands. This time the wedge-shaped mechanical object rose slowly into their sightline on gouts of flame, its blackened carapace absorbing the dying light of the second sun. They watched, mute, as the lander reached an altitude that allowed for straightforward propulsion and readjusted the attitude of its engine bells, shooting forward and upward, then banking and climbing. Soon there was no sound but the slap of the water against the hull of their boat as they stared at the rapidly dwindling sight.

"Sti's feet dancing," Shetri Laaks swore in the gloom, as a blast of burnt fuel reached them. "What a *stench*! Those people must be dead in the nose."

"Why did they go back so soon?" Kajpin wondered. "I thought their plans were to wait here for the escort from Gayjur."

"Now what shall we do?" Tiyat asked. "Go back to—"

"Quiet!" Rukuei whispered, ears cocked toward the landing site. "Listen!" At first there was only the usual tumult of the prairie reasserting itself, now that the reek and noise of the foreign machine was gone: the stridulation and whining buzz of the grasslands once again undisturbed. "There! Hear it?" Rukuei asked. "They haven't all gone!"

"They sing!" Tiyat whispered. "Isaac will be pleased."

"*Sipaj*, Kajpin, tie off," Shetri said urgently. "We're upwind! Rukuei, can they taste scent at all?"

"Not so well as we, but they're not oblivious. Perhaps we should circle around to get downwind of them." He couldn't see a thing anymore. "Or wait until morning."

There was a splash and a rocking shudder as Kajpin began pulling the shallow-drafted boat onto the sloping east bank, not waiting for anyone else's opinion. "The water's warm down here!" Tiyat exclaimed when she hopped out to help Kajpin haul the boat close enough to a *marhlar* stump to make it fast.

"You two monitor the radio," Kajpin told Rukuei and Shetri. "We'll go up and see what we can find out."

A few scrambling moments later, they heard Tiyat call quietly, "There are three of them!"

"Go sit in the boat!" Kajpin sneered good-humoredly, lying on her belly next to Tiyat. "There're four! See? There's a child sitting by that shelter."

"A translator?" Shetri speculated, face turned up toward their voices.

"No, they don't bring children to learn to be interpreters," Rukuei informed the others. "At least, they didn't last time. Some of their adults are small." He turned his attention to the radio monitor, but was distracted when a few notes of song reached him. "That's the one for Isaac. Can you see who's singing?"

Another small dispute broke out. "*Sipaj*, Kajpin, did your grandmother screw *djanada*? You're the one who's blind!" Tiyat teased. "It's the one doing the cooking. Watch the mouths! The others are just jabbering. The cook—do you see? His mouth stays open longer, while the song comes out." There was the sound of sliding as the Runa skidded down the bank, still arguing. Rukuei, listening to the radio, motioned for silence.

"One of their party got sick, so they took him back up," he reported, when the transmission ended. "The others are still waiting for an escort to Gayjur."

"So. There are three adults and one child—or whatever that little one is," Kajpin said, brushing debris from her knees and climbing back into the boat. "There's black rain east of here, but the VaGayjuri could show up any time, once the weather clears. I say we wait for the foreigners to fall asleep tonight, take the singer for Isaac, and go home."

"The others will wake up!" Tiyat objected. "Isaac can see at night, you know. They're not like *djanada*."

"Then grab all four! They don't look like much for a fight—"

"No," Rukuei said firmly. "Ha'anala was right—you don't make allies by sneaking up and grabbing people."

"Just invite them to breakfast!" Shetri insisted again. "*Sipaj*, foreigners, such a long journey you've had!" he whispered in a piping Runa falsetto that made Tiyat smother a laugh. "Won't you join us?" This had been

Shetri's plan from the start, and he was convinced it would work. "Roast some *betrin* root—Isaac likes *betrin*," he'd argued back in the valley. "Mix a few grains of *othrat* into the seasoning, and they'll sleep all the way to the N'Jarr!"

"Listen to that song," Rukuei breathed. The wind was shifting as the smallest sun dropped below the horizon, and "Che gelida manina" floated toward them on the breeze. "*Sipaj*, Tiyat, what do you think?" Rukuei asked. "Any ideas?"

"I say wait until morning, so you can see them, too," Tiyat declared. "Two kinds of mind are better than one for making plans."

Which was true, but nothing went as planned.

"SIGNORA," CARLO INSISTED THREE DAYS LATER, "I ASSURE YOU, THEY are at the rendezvous coordinates you gave us—"

"They're not *there*," Sofia repeated, cutting Carlo off. Her voice was clear and hard, despite the huge storm system over Gayjur, which made her transmission pop and hiss. "The escort reports they have located the site. Signor Giuliani, my people say that the camp smells strongly of blood, but there are no bodies."

"Oh, my God," John Candotti whispered, hugging himself and pacing along the bridge bulkhead. "I knew we should have gone back down!"

"Let's not panic, ace," said Danny, but like everyone else, he was reconsidering the facts. Three days of terrible weather, with short reports from the ground crew: "We're fine." But no details . . .

"Signora, our entire party has subcutaneous GPS implants," Carlo said, having taken this step to avoid the fate of the lost Contact Consortium party. He watched as Frans Vanderhelst brought up the readouts from the global positioning system. "We are checking the position data as I speak, but there is no reason to believe—"

"What the hell . . . ?" Frans said.

Carlo swore briefly. "Signora, we show three GPS transmitters at the coordinates of the rendezvous. But the implants haven't moved for sixty-eight hours—. That doesn't make sense. We heard from the ground party last night. Wait. There is a fourth trace showing a position approximately two hundred and forty kilometers northeast of the landing site."

"Whose trace is still active?" Sofia asked tightly.

"That's Sandoz," Frans reported.

There was a moan from John and something near a growl from Sofia Mendes. Carlo cut in, still studying the GPS data. "Yes. Definitely. Sandoz started moving north almost three days ago."

"He's been taken hostage. The others are dead—or worse!"

"Signora! Please! They—"

"Why didn't you cross-reference the GPS locale with the origin of the radio transmissions?" Sofia demanded. "You should have realized days ago that something was wrong!"

"Never occurred to me," Frans said defensively. He was already pulling up the transcripts to see if there was something he missed, some clue . . . "Everyone sounded fine!"

"Signora, please! You are assuming your conclusions," Carlo cried. He was hardly one to dither, but Mendes seemed to leap out ahead of everything that was said. "The ground party checked in last night!"

"Have you spoken to all four of them?"

"Yes, at one time or another."

"Then obviously they have been reporting under duress," Sofia snapped, furiously impatient with their slowness. "The GPS implants have been ripped out—"

"Signora, how would anyone know—"

"—which is why there's been no movement for three days. Someone has managed to take Sandoz's with them and they're—"

"One of my men is still down there," Carlo said, trying to slow her down. "Nico has orders to protect Sandoz in particular. If Sandoz were in danger, Nico would have told me."

"There was blood at the campsite," Sofia reminded him. "Signor Giuliani, they've been taken hostage. There are renegades in the northern mountains. We've never been able to root them out, but now—. This *ends*," she said almost to herself, her anger like the thunderheads in Gayjur's sky, whose lightning made the radio crackle and spit. "This ends. The raiding, the theft, the lies. The kidnapping, the murders—it all ends now. I will get our people back and, by God, I will put a stop to this. Signor Giuliani, I am going north with troops to intercept them. I'll want a continuous monitor of your GPS trace and all radio contacts with the ground party, is that understood? We are going to track those *djanada* bastards to their lair and *finish* this, once and for all."

35

Pon River Drainage

October 2078, Earth-Relative

EMILIO SANDOZ WAS THE FIRST TO NOTICE THE TRAVELERS APPROACH-ing the campsite on foot from the west. All four VaRakhati wore the robes and boots of urban Runa traders, and he had no reason to doubt their identity. "Visitors," he announced, and walked out to meet the newcomers, Nico at his side, Sean and Joseba behind him. He was not afraid. Sofia had assured him repeatedly that there were no *djanada* south of the Garnu mountains, and Nico was armed.

He held out both his hands, palms upward in the Runa manner, and readied himself for the once-familiar warmth of the long Runa fingers that would rest in his own, then remembered the braces and lowered his arms. "Someone's hands are not fit for touch, but someone greets you with goodwill," he explained. Glancing at Nico, he urged, "Say hello," and watched, pleased, as Nico's grave and correct greeting—"*Challalla khaeri*"—was acknowledged and returned by the two Runa who came forward.

Turning to Sean and Joseba, he smiled at their dumbstruck immobility. "The two in front are women," Emilio told them. "The ones hanging back may be males. Sometimes they prefer to let the ladies do the honors. Say hello." When the greetings had been exchanged, he continued as though he had never been away, "Such a long journey you have had! We would be pleased to share our meal with you."

He saw the two people in the back look at each other, and it was then that he stopped breathing, and stared at the smaller of them. Not a Runao, but someone Emilio Sandoz had seen in all too many nightmares: a man of medium stature, with violet eyes of surpassing beauty that met and held his own with a gaze so direct and searching that it took all his strength to stare back, and give no ground.

It can't be, he thought. This cannot be the same man.

"You are—you must be the son of Emilio Sandoz?" he heard the man ask. The voice was different. Resonant, and beautiful, but different. "I've seen your father's image. In the records . . ."

At the sound of the K'San language and the sight of the Jana'ata's carnassial teeth, revealed as Rukuei had spoken, Sean backed away. Nico drew his weapon, but Joseba stepped up swiftly and said, "Give it to me." He flicked off the safety and with a Basque hunter's reactions, turned and fired at something snuffling piglike in the bushes nearby.

The gunshot and death squeal set off an explosion of reaction among the wildlife, and the VaRakhati staggered back, eyes wide and ears clamped shut. Joseba handed the pistol back to Nico, who trained it on the Jana'ata who'd spoken, but kept an eye on all of them—now frozen and visibly frightened. Walking to the carcass in the ensuing silence, Joseba bent and lifted the body by one leg, letting its blood drip educationally. "We have no ill will toward you," he said firmly. "Neither will we permit you to harm us."

"Well put," said Emilio. He was breathing hard, but Carlo was right: bullets worked. "I am no one's father," he said, staring at Rukuei. "Rather, I am the one you have named: Emilio Sandoz. At my word, this man Nico kills anyone who threatens us. Is that understood?"

There were gestures of assent from all four VaRakhati. Dazed, Rukuei said vaguely, "My father knew you . . ."

"In a manner of speaking," Sandoz said coldly. "How are you to be addressed?" he demanded in High K'San, assuming the belligerent tone of a ranking aristocrat. "Are you first-born or second?"

The Jana'ata's ears folded back slightly and there was an embarrassed shuffling among the others as he said, "I am freeborn. My mother was not a woman of standing. If you please: Rukuei Kitheri."

"Christ Almighty," Sean Fein gasped. "Kitheri?"

"You are son to Hlavin Kitheri?" Sandoz asked, but there was no doubt in his mind. The stamp of the father was clear, and the son's chin lifted in confirmation. "You lie. Or you are a bastard," Sandoz snapped. The challenge was deliberate—a testing of response, a probing for flashpoint, knowing that Nico was at his side. "That Kitheri was Reshtar, and had no right to breed."

Too stunned by the actuality of the encounter to react as he might have otherwise, Rukuei merely dropped his tail, but then the fourth person came forward and revealed himself to be Jana'ata as well.

"I am Shetri Laaks." With the instructively dead *froyil* still dripping blood in one foreigner's grip, Shetri kept his voice mild, but nevertheless used the dominant pronoun to invite dispute, if the foreigners were inclined to offer combat. "Rukuei is my wife's cousin and I must not tolerate offense to my affinal kin. He has not lied, nor is he a bastard, but the song of his birth would take long to sing. I believe our purposes will be better served if none of us indulges in further insult."

There was an uneasy silence as both parties waited for Sandoz to respond. "I grant parity," he said finally, and the tension relaxed fractionally. "You speak of purpose," he said, addressing Shetri.

But it was Rukuei who answered him. "I know why you came here," he said, and noted the reaction: a quickening of breath, an intentness. "You came to learn our songs."

"This is true," the small foreigner allowed. "Rather, it was once true." He stopped and drew himself up, throwing his head back to glare at them from a distance with small eyes, black and alien—not like Isaac's, which were small but blue as normal eyes should be, and which had never stared like this. "We came because we believed you sang of truth, and of the Mind behind truth. We wished to learn what beauties this True Mind had revealed to you. But you sang of nothing beautiful," he said with insulting softness. "Your songs were of the pleasure to be found in unmerciful power, the satisfaction of crushing opposition, the enjoyment of irresistible force."

"Everything is changed from those days," a Runao said. "This one is Kajpin," she told them, raising both hands to her forehead. "Now it is the southern Runa who enjoy such power. We VaN'Jarri are different."

"We have one among us who has learned the music you sought—" Rukuei started.

"If you want to hear it, you'll have to come with us," Tiyat added quickly. "Isaac wishes you to—"

There was a small convulsion among the humans. "Isaac," Sandoz repeated. "Isaac is a foreign name. Is the person you speak of one of us?"

"Yes," said Shetri. "He is of your species, but he is not like his mother, nor like his sister—"

"His sister!" Sandoz cried.

"His sister, my wife, whose name is Ha'anala and whose foster mother was Sofia Mendes u Ku'in," Shetri continued, despite the uproar this provoked.

"You knew my cousin's sire," Rukuei said then, hoping to reassure Sandoz and the other foreigners, who were clearly upset. "Ha'anala is the daughter of my father's sister and of Supaari whose landname was Va-Gayjur—"

"This whole thing stinks to high heaven," Sean was muttering. "Why didn't Isaac come here with you then?" he demanded in K'San. "Why hasn't he contacted his mother? Does he live still, or do you merely use his name?"

Not waiting for the answer, Joseba said in English, "What if they're holding him hostage? Sandoz, what if they're using him—"

"Hostage!" Kajpin cried, startling them with her knowledge of English. "That's Athaansi's game!"

"We do not hold hostages," Rukuei began.

"Nico," Sandoz said quietly, "take that man down."

Before anyone else could move, Rukuei Kitheri had been slammed to the ground and was choking wide-eyed on the gun that Nico had jammed into his mouth with professional efficiency.

"Hear me, Kitheri: if you are tired of life, lie to me now," Sandoz suggested, dropping to his knees to whisper his threat. "How many are there in your party today? Nico, let him talk."

"Four," Rukuei said, the taste of steel in his mouth. "Truly. Only those you see."

"If there are more, I will have you and them killed—you last. Do you believe me?" Rukuei lifted his chin, the gorgeous eyes wide with a satisfying fear. "I say you hold the foreigner Isaac against his will. I say you use him as your father used me."

"These people are crazy!" Tiyat cried above him.

Without taking his eyes off Rukuei, Sandoz shouted, "I will hear *this* man's words! Speak, Kitheri: is the foreigner Isaac alive?"

"Yes! Isaac is a person of honor among the VaN'Jarri," said Rukuei, swallowing uselessly, dry-mouthed and confused. "He left the southern Runa many years ago of his own volition. He is free to go or stay. He chooses to stay among us. He likes our songs—"

"*Sipaj*, Sandoz, we could have taken you hostage last night as you slept!" Kajpin pointed out, too exasperated by this inexplicable hostility to sway.

"It was Rukuei's idea to be honest with you! The escort from Gayjur will be here soon—"

"How do you know that?" Sean demanded, but Kajpin went on, "It is we-but-not-you who are in danger! We are no threat to you. We need you, and we have something to offer in return, but if we're captured, we'll be executed!"

Emboldened by the small foreigner's stillness, Shetri knelt at Sandoz's side, and spoke with quiet urgency. "The last three times the VaN'Jarri tried to make contact with the government in Gayjur, our delegates were killed on sight. Please. Listen to me. We wish an agreement with the southerners, but the VaGayjuri will not negotiate with us because my nephew Athaansi keeps raiding Runa villages, and we are *all* held responsible!" He stopped, and calmed himself. "Hear me, Sandoz. I will stand surety. If we lie, if we deceive you in any way, then have me killed as that *froyil* was killed. I will be your hostage."

"We as well," Kajpin said, standing with Tiyat.

"I also offer you my neck," said Rukuei Kitheri, from the ground. "But you will have to go to Isaac, for he will not come to you. We can take you to him, but you have to trust us. Some of us believe that Isaac has learned the music of the True Mind, which you sought, but he will not come to you to teach it."

"Lies," Sandoz said at last. "You say what we wish to hear—"

"How could *we* know what you wish to hear?" Tiyat cried.

With a sudden short gasp, Sandoz staggered to his feet and walked a few paces away, his back to them all. "Let him up, Nico," he snapped, but did not turn, unable to sustain the pose any longer. He felt sick, and he needed time to think. "Watch them," he flung back over his shoulder, and strode away.

IT WAS HARD TO SAY WHICH GROUP WAS MORE RELIEVED TO SEE SANDOZ go, but with his intimidating presence removed from their midst, there was a distinct lessening of strain all around.

"It would be a shame to let that *froyil* go to waste," Shetri commented to Joseba Urizarbarrena once Sandoz was out of hearing, and the hunter in Joseba agreed. So a fire was prepared, and the *froyil* gutted and hung on a spit, and other provisions brought from the boat by Tiyat, under guard. As meat and vegetables roasted, Sean and Joseba and even Nico questioned hard, and listened hard, and considered at some length what they had been told: whether it was accurate, and what it might imply. In the end, they went to Sandoz.

He was a few hundred meters away, sitting hunched and haggard on the ground. "Nico, why aren't you watching them, as you were told?" he demanded, hiding behind as much severity as he could still muster.

"They don't want to run away. They're waiting for us to go with them," Nico said mildly. "Don Emilio, I had a thought: if we find out where Isaac lives, Signora Sofia will be pleased." The pistol was still in his hand and he kept an eye on his charges, just in case. "Don Carlo will know where we are," he said, glancing at the small lump on his forearm where the GPS transmitter capsule was lodged. "We have guns, and they don't."

"We're not going anywhere with them. We're waiting here for Sofia's escort," Sandoz said, not moving from the ground.

Joseba looked at Sean and then said, "Nico, would you please get Don Emilio some water? Perhaps a little something very plain to eat?" Nico nodded and trudged off toward the camp as Joseba sat down across from Emilio. "Sandoz, do you have any idea what the population of the Jana'ata was, when you were here before?" he asked.

Sandoz shrugged, eyes dull, not really caring that it was starting to rain again. "No. I don't know. Except that it was about three or four percent of the prey population. Maybe six hundred thousand? That's just a guess." He looked at Joseba. "Why do you ask?"

Sean and Joseba exchanged glances, and Sean sat down as well. "Listen, Sandoz, the buggers may be lying, but that Rukuei says there're only about fifteen hundred Jana'ata left now." Sandoz looked up sharply and Sean went on. "The Runa've rousted them all off the land. They're scattered, but there're two main groups of several hundred apiece, plus some pockets of survivors too scared t'go near anyone else. The VaN'Jarri live in a valley on their own. They've got barely three hundred Jana'ata among them, with about six hundred Runa in the same settlement."

Joseba leaned forward. "Carnivores generally need at least two thousand individuals, with two hundred and fifty breeding pairs, just to keep the population genetically healthy. Even if Rukuei is underestimating the total, the Jana'ata are very close to extinction," he whispered, as though to speak aloud of this prediction would make it come true. "If he's overestimating it, they're probably doomed." He sat for a while, working it through. "It makes sense, Sandoz. From what we've seen and what Shetri says, the Jana'ata must be living at the absolute margins of their ecological range. Even without the collapse of civilization, this species would be on the edge."

"There's more," Sean said, a little loudly now that the rain had begun in earnest. "There's something goin' on up in the north. I had t'ask twice t'be sure of what I was hearin', but when we asked about them eatin' that *froyil*, one of them—that Shetri—told us the VaN'Jarri Jana'ata are near t'starvin'. They won't eat Runa." Sandoz looked at him, narrow-eyed. "Brace yersalf: the phrase he used was, The meat's not kosher." Sandoz reared back, and Sean raised a hand. "I swear that's what he said. Apparently this man Shetri's wife, Hanala or whatever her name is, was raised by Sofia Mendes in the south, among the Runa."

Joseba said, "Obviously, there has been a certain amount of cultural exchange. Shetri says his wife is a teacher, but Sandoz—the title he used was 'rabbi'. It's possible that these men are simply lying about not eating Runa, but *look* at them! They're thin, their coats are dull, they're missing teeth—"

"And they're travelin' with two fine, fat Runa, who don't seem a bit concerned about becomin' anybody's breakfast." Sean hesitated before going on. "And, Sandoz," he said, "listenin' t'this Kitheri? Well, it seems to me that Hanala may be a sort of . . . I don't know, but I ask myself, What if Moses had been an Egyptian, raised among the Hebrews?"

Sandoz sat open-mouthed, trying to take this in. "You're serious?" he asked, and when Sean nodded, Sandoz cried, "Oh, for God's sake!"

"Precisely," Joseba agreed, and watched without moving as Sandoz stood, soaked to the skin.

"You're hearing what you want to hear!" Sandoz accused. "You're imposing your own folklore on this culture!"

"Perhaps we are," Joseba agreed, from his seat in the mud, "but I came here as both an ecologist and a priest. I want to know about this. I am going north with them, Sandoz. Sean wants to go, too. You can stay here with Nico and wait for Sofia's people to arrive. All we ask is that you don't give them away. We'll take our chances with them—"

With Nico's approach, they fell silent and watched as Sandoz drank water from the canteen and got a little food into himself, refusing to discuss this nonsense further.

But Nico, ordinarily the quietest of them, had something on his mind. "Don Emilio, one of those Jana people has a bad dream like yours," he said, wiping his wet hair back out of his eyes. Sandoz stared at him, and Nico continued, "He dreams of a city burning. He told me. It's from when he was a little boy, he says, but he's seen you there. In the city. In his dream. I think you should ask him about it."

WHICH IS WHY, AFTER CONSIDERABLE ADDITIONAL INTERROGATION AND discussion, eight people of three species finally went north together in secrecy and foul weather. They did not tell Carlo Giuliani of their decision, concerned that the radio was being monitored by the Gayjur government. Knowing now the danger the VaN'Jarri were in, it was Joseba's suggestion that they remove their GPS implants—a small cut each, nothing to be concerned about.

They intended to travel as quickly and inconspicuously as they could, but if anyone questioned them, their story would be simple. The foreigners were friends to Fia. Shetri and Rukuei were VaHaptaa mercenaries who were leading these Runa and the foreigners to the last stronghold of the predators who'd preyed on the Runa since time began. When the place was known, the army could come and clean the last of the *djanada* out, and then they would be gone, forever.

The VaN'Jarri believed that this was all merely a convincing lie. In fact, it was very nearly the precise truth.

Nico d'Angeli had not really understood what Joseba said about minimum breeding population and species collapse, nor had he followed much of the talk of revolution or religion. But Nico understood very well what Frans had told him before landfall. "I can't find you if you take the GPS implant out, Nico. The people on the *Magellan* were all lost—no one knows what happened to them, *capisce?* Never remove this, Nico. As long as you have a transmitter with you, I can find you."

So while the others were loading the boat and making ready to leave, Nico slowly came to the conclusion that it was best for Don Carlo and Frans to know where they were going, even if the others didn't think so. That was why he retrieved one of the discarded implants and put it in his pocket.

He meant no harm.

Gonna Start War

36

Central Inbrokar

October 2078, Earth-Relative

THEY WENT BY RIVER AT FIRST, JANA'ATA AND HUMANS CROWDED INTO
the cargo hold, their Runa conspirators topside, calling out greetings to
sodden barge passengers and crew as their wakes crossed. The powerboat's
batteries were as silent as sail and its passengers almost as quiet, even when
there was no one to hear them. One human or another would think of
some objection to what he had been told, and would say what was on his
mind, and have his doubts assuaged. The VaN'Jarri, too, would venture a
question now and then, but the one most eaten by desire to know about
the foreigners was also the one most frightened of Sandoz, who had barely
spoken since agreeing to go as far as Inbrokar City with them. So Rukuei
kept quiet as well.

Not wanting to compromise their safe houses by duplicating their route
south, they left the river behind on their second day. Tiyat and Kajpin let
the others off near a cave a few *cha'ari* short of the Tolal bridgehead, and
then went on alone, returning the powerboat to the livery, where Tiyat
made a show of disputing the damage done to the hull when they'd run the
boat aground. Finally Kajpin waved the extra charge off and said expan-
sively, "It's only money! Pay the woman—we'll make it up on that *rakar*
deal." Which led to comfortable small talk about the new *rakar* planta-
tions, and then to amiable farewells, called loudly over the pounding rain
as Tiyat and Kajpin moved off toward town.

"It's only money," Tiyat echoed irritably, as they stopped in the Tolal market district and spent their last few *bahli* on salt.

"Don't worry," Kajpin told her when they were out of earshot, heading out of town on a road that went northeast. "We can jump a caravan next season!" When they were sure no one was behind them, they veered overland and doubled back toward the south at a trot.

Reunited at the cave without further incident, the party left roads and rivers behind and traveled instead through an endless rolling landscape. Stopping periodically to listen and watch and stand nose to the wind, the VaN'Jarri became increasingly confident that they'd escaped detection. Indeed, there was little left in this monstrous, lovely, depopulated land that bore the imprint of mortal mind or hand. For hours, walking without haste but without rest, they saw nothing but low-growing clumps of lavender-leaved plants with bell-shaped blooms that nodded on wiry stems, battered by rain as warm as blood, and heard nothing but the drumming of rain and the squelching of footsteps, and the lilt of Nico's singing.

"You don't mind?" Sandoz asked the Runa as they walked. "Someone could ask Nico to stop singing."

"I don't mind," Kajpin said.

"It's not as beautiful as Isaac's music," said Tiyat, "but it's nice."

The foreigners carried communications gear, and answered periodic status calls from the *Giordano Bruno* with laconic reports that sounded bored.

"It's rainin' here like the third ring of hell," Sean said once. "What's the weather look like for tomorrow?"

"Clearing up," Frans told him.

"Thank God for that," was the heartfelt reply. And Sean closed the connection.

THEIR SLEEP WAS BROKEN EARLY NOT BY THUNDER BUT BY THE RADIO transponder's whistle, clear and musical in the scrubbed morning air. It was Frans Vanderhelst, hailing anyone from the *Giordano Bruno*. Sean answered, yawning, and heard Frans say, "Is everything okay down there?"

"Shit, yes," Sean answered irritably. He nodded agreement as Joseba, bleary-eyed, leaned over to put the transmission on conference so everyone could listen to both sides of the conversation.

"We've lost live traces from three of the four GPS implants. What's going on?"

That brought them fully awake. They had expected questions about the implants eventually, but not this one. "Three of the four?" Sean looked at his companions and saw the story on Nico's face, rosy in the cloudless dawn. Joseba moaned and put his head in his hands. The VaN'Jarri roused as well and began to ask questions, but Sandoz hissed a warning as Sean raised a hand for silence.

"We have three GPS signals at the rendezvous showing no movement for three days," Carlo was saying. "There's another one two hundred and forty kilometers northeast of the site. Are you all right?"

"Yes! We're fine, dammit, except y'woke us all up! Can we talk later? I was havin' a very fine dream—"

"So what's going on with the implants?" John cut in. "Why can't Sofia's escort find you guys? They said the campsite smells of blood. For a minute there, we thought you were dead and eaten! We just talked to Sofia and she's convinced Emilio's been kidnapped by renegade Jana'ata—she's ready to come after you with an army! What's going on?"

Kajpin's ears folded back at the word "army," and the other VaN'Jarri began to show signs of stress. Sean yawned theatrically, and looked around with large, desperate eyes while sputtering, "Christ! Is that you now, Candotti? One question at a time! We're fine, I tell you! The blood was—" Sandoz, struggling to get a brace on, glared a warning at him. "Hang on, now. Sandoz wants to speak to you," Sean said, and handed the transceiver to him with some relief.

"John, this is Emilio. Tell Sofia she watched too many old Westerns with me," Sandoz suggested with a very nice imitation of amusement. "We don't need the U.S. Cavalry riding to the rescue! Wait—have Frans put me through, yes? I'll talk to her directly."

They all waited, tense and silent, as Sandoz walked a little distance away and stood with his back to them. Even so, they could hear his side of the conversation clearly in the still morning air. "Mendes? No, listen to me! We're all right—. Oh, God. Don't cry, Sofia! I'm fine. Truly. . . . Yes. Everything is fine. . . . Calm down, okay?" He looked at the others and winced, shaking his head slightly: never tell a woman to calm down. "No, Sofia, listen! That was just a *froyil* that Joseba shot! Yes—we barbecued it! I decided we should move camp so the blood wouldn't put the escort off. We're not far away."

"Relative to Earth," Joseba muttered.

"I don't know what to tell you about that signal north of the rendezvous site," Emilio said then.

"Not one lie so far," Sean whispered, impressed.

"Maybe the implants are defective?" Sandoz suggested, pacing now. "Or the software's no good?" A pause. "Well, it doesn't matter, because we're fine, okay? Listen, Mendes, we were up kind of late last night and everybody's pretty tired, so we'd like to get a little more rest before we—. Sure! Yes, have them wait right there for us! That's perfect!" he cried, standing still, eyes wide with relief. "You, too. Go back to bed—. Then have breakfast!" he said, smiling now. "Are you all right? Sure? Don't worry about us! We'll be in touch."

"Christ," Sean breathed as Sandoz returned to their circle and sank to the ground. "Remind me never to play poker with you again."

BACK ON THE SHIP, DANNY SHRUGGED. "D. W. YARBROUGH ALWAYS SAID Sofia Mendes could think too damned quick for her own good."

But Frans Vanderhelst was looking at Carlo. "There's nothing wrong with those implants."

"Oh, yeah?" said John. "Look at the screen."

The fourth trace had just gone dead.

"I'M SORRY, DON EMILIO," NICO REPEATED AS JOSEBA POUNDED THE GPS transponder to pieces between two rocks. "Frans said—"

"It's all right, Nico, I understand. You meant well," Emilio muttered, "for all the difference that ever makes."

"The army is coming," Kajpin said. "They think we've taken you hostage—"

"And they know where we are right now," Joseba told them.

"But Sandoz bought us some time," Sean pointed out. "They think we're safe and camped somewhere near the rendezvous site—" Then his face fell further than it normally hung, and he stared balefully at the remains of the GPS implant. "Fack."

Joseba, rock still in hand, went motionless and then closed his eyes, realizing the deception had just been revealed. Only Sandoz had a clue as to what he said for the next few moments, but the burden of his speech was clear even to the VaN'Jarri. "Apologies," he said finally, his face flushed with shame. "I acted in haste."

"Go on without us," Sean urged the VaN'Jarri then. "We'll go back and meet the escort. It's us they're concerned about. Soon as they know we're all right, they'll relax. We can figure out how to get to the N'Jarr later—"

"How much farther is it to Inbrokar?" Sandoz asked Rukuei quietly.

"We could be there by second sunrise today, if we move fast."

"It takes time to mobilize troops," Sandoz said. "We're three days away from the rendezvous site, and it will be farther for them, because they'll have to come overland the whole way, won't they?"

"No, they can use troop barges, but that's slow, too," Kajpin said.

Tiyat began to sway. "They don't need the troops—there'll be militia alerted all over the country. We're cooked."

"I'm sorry," Nico said again. "But—what if we told Signora Sofia that we'll bring back her son? We tell her, Don't follow us. If you do, the deal is off. You cooperate, your boy comes back to you, no harm done." He looked around, hopeful that he had redeemed himself.

"It might work," Sandoz said after a time. He started to laugh, but then sobered and lifted his chin thoughtfully, grew somehow heavier and older before their eyes, and when he spoke it was in the hoarse tones of Marlon Brando, resurrected in the Rakhati sunlight. "We make her an offer she can't refuse."

Joseba looked at Sean, who shrugged, and then put the call through to the *Bruno*. Emilio took the transceiver and cut off John's demands to know what the hell just happened to that fourth implant. "Don't ask, okay? Just don't ask. I'm going the extra mile, John. I can't tell you more than that. Have Frans put me through to Sofia."

The others watched while he waited, still grinning, for Sofia's connection, but the sense of fun died almost immediately. Reluctant to threaten, he began with an appeal to friendship and trust, but met an icy wall of objection.

"You're right, Sofia," he said. "Absolutely. But we are not under duress—. Listen to me!"

Instead he listened, letting her warn him, plead with him, threaten him, condemn his judgment. "Sofia," he cut in finally, "I have to do this. There is something I have to see for myself. All I'm asking is that you give me some time to work this through—a couple of weeks, maybe. Please. I never asked you for anything before, Sofia. Just this one thing, okay? Give me a chance to see for myself . . ."

There was no reasoning with her; there never had been. He turned to look at the VaN'Jarri—their faces tight with anxiety, pinched with hunger—and listened to the uncompromising words of a woman he had known long ago.

"Sofia, you leave me no choice," he said finally, hating himself. "I believe I can locate Isaac and bring him back to you, but only on the condition that we are not followed. That's the deal, Mendes. Back off, and I'll do what I can to bring your son home to you."

He closed his eyes as he listened to her tell him what she believed he had become. He didn't argue. Mostly, she was right.

AT MIDDAY THEY CRESTED A LOW RISE THAT GAVE OUT ONTO A FIELD rank with weed, and from that vantage the ruins of Inbrokar could be seen in the milky haze of prairie heat. For a time, Emilio gazed silently at the blackened rubble. It was not the city of his dreams, but the charred gates seemed familiar, and if he closed his eyes, he could almost picture the chiseled stone walls that had once given an illusion of safety.

"Can you smell it?" Rukuei asked him.

"No," Emilio said. "Not yet." Then—a faint sweetness: corruption's ghost. "Yes. I smell it now," he said, and turned to meet Kitheri's eyes: beautiful, haunted, and as weary as his own. "Wait here," Sandoz told the others, and walked with Rukuei down the sloping hill onto the battlefield.

"I was twelve," Rukuei said, measuring his stride to the pace of the small person beside him. "The war was as old as I was. Thirty thousand men died here in a single day, and then a city full of refugees. Within another year or two—a civilization."

Weather and the work of scavengers had made dust or dung of all but the densest elements of bone, but of these, there were many. " 'Their blood has been shed like water, round about Jerusalem, and there was none to bury them,' " Sandoz murmured. Here and there, the glint of fragile rusted metal caught the eye as they walked. Bending to examine a helmet, Sandoz saw a single tooth, flat-crowned and broad. "Runa," he remarked, with some surprise. "When did they start wearing armor?"

"Toward the end of the war," Rukuei said.

"I've heard it said: Choose your enemies wisely, for you will become them," Sandoz told him, and was moved to apologize for frightening the young man so badly at their first meeting, but fell silent when he saw Rukuei stiffen.

"My father wore silver and gold," the Jana'ata said quietly, walking toward a gleaming scrap of metal. A finely wrought fastener, ripped loose, trampled into the mud, concealed from gleaners for years, weathering out again sometime during the last rainy season. Rukuei bent to pick it up, but stayed his hand when he noticed something white nearby. The tough, compact bone of an opposable toe, perhaps. And there, a fragment of the heavy nuchal crest from the base of a skull. "We—we cremate our dead," Rukuei said, straightening, looking at the ruins now to escape the sight of scrappy remnants lying on the ground. "So, in some ways, it seemed acceptable that so many died in the fires, after the battle."

But this, he thought. This . . .

The mechanical whirr of the foreigner's hands brought him back to the present, and Rukuei saw in flesh what had once been merely dream—Emilio Sandoz, on the battlefield of Inbrokar. Stooped over, reaching for the bits of bone and teeth. Carefully picking each small piece up, gathering the remains methodically: Runa and Jana'ata, mingled in death.

Without speaking, Rukuei joined him in this task, and then the others came to help—Kajpin and Tiyat, Sean Fein and Joseba Urizarbarrena, and Shetri Laaks, silently bringing the anonymous dead together. Nico removed his shirt, spreading it out to collect the relics, and soon the quiet was broken by the plaintive melody of "Una furtiva lagrima." As fragmentary as the remains were, there was too much scattered across too broad a field to do right by it all, so when the makeshift shroud was filled, they counted themselves done, and carried what they had gathered to a place inside the ruins, where the smell of weathered char was stronger. They added to it with a smoky pyre built of half-burnt wood pried from what had once been a storage building near the Embassy of Mala Njer.

"What I remember most clearly is my small sister's voice," Rukuei told them as the fire crackled. "All the Paramount's freeborn children were in the embassy—he must have known how it would end, but hoped that there would be perhaps some respect for diplomats." Rukuei laughed—a short, hard sound—at his father's naïveté. "My sister was somewhere in the fire. As we ran from the city, I could hear her call my name. A silver wire of sound: Ru-ku-eiiiii . . ."

That evening, as the light died, he sang for them a poetry of wounds, of loss and of regret and of yearning; of the concentration and intensification of such hurts with each new injury to the soul; of the slackening and rarefaction of pain and sorrow in the dance of life and in the presence of children. In the midst of this, Shetri Laaks stood and stumbled blindly away, hoping to escape the songs' pain, but when he came to rest a good distance

[handwritten marginal note: "Like a funeral"]

from the pyre, he heard a foreigner's footsteps behind him, and knew from the scent that it was Sandoz.

"Tell me," Sandoz said, and his silence was a void that Shetri felt compelled to fill.

"He doesn't mean to hurt me," Shetri whispered. "How can he know? Rukuei thinks children are hope, but they're not! They're terror. A child is a limb that can be torn from you—" Shetri stopped, and tried to slow his breathing, to force it into an even rhythm.

"Tell me," Sandoz said again.

Shetri turned toward the foreigner's voice. "My wife is pregnant, and I fear for her. The Kitheris are small, and Ha'anala nearly died during the last birth—the baby was large in the hindquarters, like a Laaks. Ha'anala hides a great deal. This pregnancy has been very hard. I fear for her, and for the baby. And for myself," he admitted. "Sandoz, shall I tell you what my daughter Sofi'ala asked me when she learned her mother was pregnant again? She asked, Will this baby die, too? She has lost two younger brothers. She expects babies to die. So do I."

He sat down where he stood, heedless of the mud and ash. "I was once an adept of Sti," said Shetri. "I was third-born, and content. Sometimes I long for the time when there was nothing in my life but still water, and the chants. But six must sing together, and I think the others are all dead now, and there is no one who can be spared to learn the ritual. I once believed myself fortunate to become a father but now—. It is an awful thing to love so much. When my first son died . . ."

"I am sorry for your losses," Sandoz said, sitting down next to him. "When is the new baby due?"

"In a few days, perhaps. Who can tell with women? Maybe it's come already. Maybe it's over." He hesitated. "My first son died of a disease of the lungs." He tapped his chest, so the foreigner understood. "But the second—" He fell silent.

"Tell me," said the foreigner softly.

"The priests of Sti are known—were known for our medicines, our knowledge of how to heal wounds and help the body overcome illness when it was fitting to do so. I could not stand to watch Ha'anala die, so I tried to help her. There are drugs to ease pain . . ." It was a long while before he could finish. "It was my fault that the child was stillborn," he said at last. "I only wanted to help Ha'anala."

"I, too, watched a child dear to me die. I killed her," Sandoz told him plainly. "It was, I suppose, an accident, but I was responsible."

There was lightning to the east; for a moment Shetri could see the foreigner's face. "So," Shetri said with a soft grunt of commiseration. "I grant parity."

They listened for a time, waiting for the low rumble of thunder to reach them. When the foreigner spoke again, his voice was soft but clear in the darkness. "Shetri, you risked a great deal to come south. What did you expect us to do? We are but four men, and foreigners! What do you want from us?"

"Help. I don't know. Just—some new idea, some way to make them listen! We've tried everything we can think of, but. . . . Sandoz, we are no danger to anyone anymore," Shetri cried, too desperate to be ashamed. "We wanted you to see that, to tell them that! We're not asking them for anything. Just leave us alone! Let us live. And—if we could just move a little farther south, where the *cranil* and *piyanot* are, I think we could feed ourselves decently. We've learned ways to take wild meat—we can support ourselves without taking any Runa. We could even teach Athaansi's people, and then they'd stop the raiding! If we could just get someplace warmer—if we could keep the women better fed! The mountains are killing us!"

Nico was singing now: "Un bel dì," the notes lifting on the night breeze.

"Shetri, hear me. The Runa love their children, as you do," Sandoz said. "This war began with the slaughter of Runa infants by Jana'ata militia. How do you answer this?"

"I answer: even so, our children are innocent."

There was a long silence. "All right," Sandoz said at last. "I'll do what I can. It probably won't be enough, Shetri, but I'll try."

"GOOD MORNING, FRANS," EMILIO SAID THE NEXT DAY, AS THOUGH nothing much had occurred since his last transmission. "I'd like to speak to John and Danny, if you don't mind."

There was a slight delay before John's voice was heard. "Emilio! Are you safe? Where the hell have you—?"

"Listen, John, about that extra mile I was prepared to walk," Emilio said lightly. "If you and Danny don't mind coming down here to give my friends and me a lift, I think I'd rather fly."

"Not without an explanation, ace," said Danny Iron Horse.

"Good morning, Danny. I'll explain in a moment—"

Carlo cut in. "Sandoz, I've had quite enough of this. Mendes will give us almost no information and I'm certain she's lying when she does!"

"Ah, Don Carlo! I trust you slept better than I did last night," Sandoz said, ignoring the sounds of irritation. "I find that I must ask you for the loan of a lander. There's no money in this venture, I'm afraid, but I can get a very good poet to write an epic about you, if you like. I don't want the drone. I want the manned lander—with Danny and John—and I want it empty, except for a case of cartridges and Joseba's hunting rifle."

"What's the ammunition for?" Danny asked suspiciously.

"First principles, Danny: we intend to feed the hungry. The situation on the ground is not as we expected. If our information is correct, there remain only a few small enclaves of Jana'ata, and some of them are presently starving. Joseba believes the entire species may be on the brink of extinction." He waited for the clamor on the *Giordano Bruno* to die down. "He and Sean are determined to find the truth, as am I. I want Danny and John down here as neutral witnesses. I'm afraid Sean and Joseba and I are not generating much in the way of objectivity anymore."

Frans said, "Sandoz, I've got a fix on your transmission site near what looks—"

"You needn't mention the coordinates, Frans. We may be overheard," Emilio cautioned. "I need an answer, gentlemen. There's not a lot of time to waste."

"An epic, you say?" Carlo asked, self-mockery plain. "Well, perhaps I can work out something more lucrative later. I'll send the lander, Sandoz. You can pay me back when we get home."

"Don't tempt me," Emilio warned him with a small laugh, and they made arrangements for the landing.

37

N'Jarr Valley

October 2078, Earth-Relative

HA'ANALA HAD TWO DREAMS THAT NIGHT. HER THIRD CHILD—THE unnamed stillbirth—appeared at the doorway, small and fetal but cheerful, his face full of mischief. "Where have you been?" Ha'anala cried when she saw him. "It's nearly redlight! You shouldn't stay out so long!" she scolded affectionately, and the baby answered, "You shouldn't worry about me!"

She roused briefly, with a sensation of tightness across her belly, but the visit from her dream son was reassuring and she drifted back to the heavy sleep that had characterized this pregnancy. The second dream was also of a dead child but, this time, she relived the last few minutes of Urkinal's life and awoke with a start, the hiss and rattle of his tiny lungs in her ears.

Suukmel, who had moved in with her while Shetri was gone, came awake in an instant. "Is it time?" she asked quietly in the thin light of dawn.

"No," Ha'anala whispered. "I had a dream." She sat up with a graceless lurch but as carefully as she could, not wanting to wake Sofi'ala, sleeping in the nest beside her. Another gray day, she noted, peering out through cracks in the stonework. There was no sound yet from the other houses. "The children came to visit again last night."

"Someone should tie ribbons on your arms," Suukmel said, smiling at the superstition.

But Ha'anala shuddered, as much from the chill of the sunless morning as from the memory of a small rattling chest. "I wish Shetri hadn't gone. Was Ma with you when your daughters were born?"

"Oh, no," Suukmel said, getting to her feet and beginning the morning chores. "Ma would never have come near a birth—very unseemly. The women of my caste were always alone—well, not alone. We had Runa. Men generally had nothing to do with women and birth, apart from providing the impetus for the event. And I can't say that I'd have welcomed an audience."

"I don't want an audience, I want company!" Ha'anala shifted her position and rested her back against her husband's rolled-up sleeping nest. She felt vaguely uneasy, despite the fact that they'd received good news directly from Shetri, via the *Bruno*. He and the others were well and would be arriving today, with the foreigners, in an extraordinary craft that could bring them home quickly and without detection. "Even if Shetri can't stand to be here when the baby's born, I'll be glad—"

She stopped, face still. At last! she thought, welcoming the wave of cramp, rolling from top to bottom. When she raised her eyes, Suukmel was watching knowingly. "Don't tell anyone else yet," Ha'anala said, glancing significantly at Sofi'ala, who was beginning to stir. "I want company, not a *fierno*."

"I'm hungry!" Sofi'ala whined, eyes still closed. It was the inevitable morning greeting, this time of year.

"Your father's bringing wonderful things to eat," Suukmel told the child gaily, and smiled a little sadly when the child's glorious lavender eyes snapped open at that news. They could hear other households awakening nearby, and the first wisps of smoke from Runa dung fires were beginning to reach them. "He'll be here soon, but why don't you go to Biao-Tol's hearth and see what's cooking there?"

"Wait—" Ha'anala called as Sofi'ala ran out to join the other children, who spent their mornings dashing around the village, peering into pots, hunting for the most abundant or tastiest meal available. "*Sipaj*, Sofi'ala! Don't be a nuisance!" Suukmel chuckled at that, but Ha'anala insisted, "She is! She is a nuisance! And I hate the way she orders the other children around."

"You see yourself in her," Suukmel told her. "Don't be hard on the girl. It's natural for her to try to dominate them."

"It's also natural to defecate whenever and wherever the urge arises," said Ha'anala in riposte. "That doesn't make it acceptable behavior."

"But even the Runa children resist her! It's good training," Suukmel parried. "They all gain strength."

They spent the morning jousting like this, enjoying the mental combat, but the tempo and strength of the contractions were constantly on their minds. "They should be quicker now, and stronger," Ha'anala said, when all three suns were up, the brightest a flat, white disk burning through the cloud cover overhead.

"Soon enough," Suukmel said, but she, too, was concerned, watching with some dismay as Ha'anala curled up in her nest and fell silent.

By that time, Ha'anala's daughter had worked out what was going on, and Suukmel turned her attention to reassuring the child and greeting the guests who began to gather, alerted by Sofi'ala's anxious wail. Though the Jana'ata considerately withdrew after conveying their good wishes, the house was soon crowded with Runa, who brought enthusiasm and encouragement and food for the assemblage, along with the warmth of their bodies and of their affection. Like the Runa, Ha'anala believed a birth was an occasion for festivity and seemed happy for the distraction, so Suukmel did not drive the visitors off.

If the contractions did not quicken, they did at least increase in intensity and Ha'anala welcomed that, despite the pain. In the midst of an endless discussion of what might hurry the labor along, a boy ran in with news of the lander and soon they all heard its horrifying noise, the room emptying abruptly as the crowd moved off to witness this astonishing arrival.

"Go on—see what it's like!" Ha'anala told Suukmel. "Tell me about it when you come back! I'll be fine, but send Shetri!"

"Orders, orders, orders," Suukmel teased as she left for the landing site at the edge of the valley. "You sound like Sofi'ala!"

Alone at last, Ha'anala rested as best she could, surprised by how tired she was so early in this labor. She listened as the roar of the engines abruptly ceased, heard the buzz of conversation indistinct in the distance. Days seemed to pass before Shetri came to her; despite all she wanted to ask him, the only words she spoke aloud were, "Someone is cold."

Shetri went to the door and shouted for help. Soon Ha'anala was lifted to her feet and, though she stopped and squatted now and then, hit by another contraction, she was able to walk slowly to a place where game in miraculous quantity was spitted and roasting over smoky fires. Smiling at the spontaneous carnival that had erupted, her eyes sought out the foreigners in the crowd. One was close in size to Sofia, the others as tall as Isaac, but with none of his wandlike slenderness. Dark and light; bearded and hairless and maned, And the languages! High K'San and peasant Ru-anja and H'inglish—as hilariously mixed in the confusion of the cooking and greetings and stories as Ha'anala's own speech had been when she'd first met Shetri.

"They are so different!" she cried, to no one in particular. "This is won-derful. Wonderful!"

Cheered by warmth and the prospect of rapprochement with the south, Ha'anala knelt heavily, bearing down with a will, certain that this was the moment when the new child should be brought into light and laughter. She felt instead a tearing pain that made her scream and silenced the oth-ers, so that only the hiss of fire and the distant warbling of a *p'rkra* could be heard. When she could breathe again, she laughed a little and assured everyone wryly, "I won't try *that* again!"

Slowly the merriment and conversation resumed, but she could smell Shetri's anxiety and this worried her. "Tell me about your journey!" she commanded affectionately, but he was frightened and made an excuse to help the foreigners distribute meat, sending Rukuei to sit behind her like a Runa husband. Suukmel came as well, and Tiyat, with her youngest rid-ing her back. Content to have her cousin's arms around her shoulders, Ha'anala leaned back against his belly, his legs drawn up around her own, his cheek resting near hers, and listened as Rukuei sang of his adventure in a spontaneous poem with the rocking rhythm of a steady walk. She was genuinely interested in the story, and drifted along, buoyed by the tale, laughing when Rukuei made comedy out of the fright he had been given by the little foreigner Sandoz.

"Small individuals can be surprisingly powerful," Ha'anala observed breathlessly, leaning over to press her lively belly between her chest and legs, glad that she could summon up a little humor even now.

Hearing his name, Sandoz had joined them, making an obeisance rather than offering his hands. When the introductions were over, he sat where he too could watch the party: silent, hunched and rocking slightly, his arms crossed over his chest. His posture very nearly mimicked her own during a contraction, and Ha'anala's first words to him were, "Funny, you don't look pregnant."

He stared and then hooted, startled by the remark but apparently amused. "If I am, we're definitely going to have to start a new religion," he replied, and if she didn't understand all of his words, she liked his smile. He had eyes like Sofia's—brown and small—but warm, not stony. "My lady, what language best pleases you?" he asked.

"Ruanja for affection. English for science—"

"And jokes," he observed.

"K'San for politics and poetry," Ha'anala continued, pausing as the wave crested and then receded. "Hebrew for prayer."

For a time, the five of them watched Runa tending fires and roasting sticks of root vegetables now that the Jana'ata had been able to eat their fill. "We have dreamed of this," Suukmel said, smiling at Tiyat and then reaching out to grasp first Rukuei's ankle and then Ha'anala's.

"Dreamed of what?" Sandoz asked. "Eating well?"

Suukmel considered him for a time and decided he was being ironic. "Yes," she agreed easily, then swept an arm across the panorama. "But also of this: all of us together."

"Someone's eyes feel good to see it," said Tiyat. She looked down at her sleeping son, and then at the people surrounding Ha'anala. "Three kinds are better than one!"

"Sandoz, tell me about each of your companions," Ha'anala said, in the language of politics.

He motioned toward the one with the bare skull first and answered her in the language of affection. "Djon has clever hands, like a Runa, and a generous heart. Look now at his face, and you will learn how a human appears when he enjoys something. Someone thinks: to help others is Djon's greatest pleasure. He has a talent for friendship." He paused, and switched to K'San. "I believe he is incapable of lying."

"The one next to him?" Ha'anala asked, glancing at Suukmel, who was also listening carefully.

The answer was in Hebrew. "He is called Shaan. He sees very clearly, without sentiment." Sandoz paused, looking at the others, and realized that only Ha'anala spoke Hebrew. In K'San he said, "Sometimes it is necessary to hear hard truths. Shaan is fierce, like a Jana'ata, and unsparing. But what he says is important." He gestured then toward Joseba, and simplified the name. "Hozei also sees clearly, but he is subtle. When Hozei speaks, I listen carefully."

"And the black-haired one?" Suukmel asked, when Ha'anala was silenced by another contraction.

Sandoz drew in a chestful of air and let it out slowly. "Dani," he said, and they waited to hear which language he selected. "He may be of use to you," he said in K'San. "He knows from his own people's experience what the Jana'ata face, and he wants very much to be of aid to you. But he is a man of ideals, and has sometimes chosen them over ethics."

"Which makes him dangerous," Suukmel remarked.

"Yes," Sandoz agreed.

"The one who is singing?" Ha'anala asked. "He, too, is like a Jana'ata, I think. Is he a poet?"

Sandoz smiled and continued in Ruanja. "No, not a poet, but Nico appreciates the work of poets, and his voice graces it." He glanced at Tiyat and chose his words carefully. "Nico is more like a village Runao, who can be led easily by anyone who is forceful." He paused as the three Jana'ata exchanged looks. "Nico can be a danger, but I trust him now. In any case, he won't stay with you," Sandoz told them. "He is a member of a trading party that will only be here long enough to do business in the south. The others wish to remain here, to be of use and to learn from you, if you will permit it."

"And you, Sandoz?" Rukuei asked. "Will you stay or go?"

He did not answer because Ha'anala closed her eyes, folding over her belly, and this time, gave a strangled cry that brought Shetri to her side. When her breath returned, she said, "It will be well. I am not afraid."

AS THE LIGHT FADED, SO DID THE PAINS, WHICH SEEMED NOW TO BE AT some distance. Her attention flickered like the fire that warmed her and lit up the night, but she continued to listen to the quiet conversation around her, marveling at Sandoz's voice, so unlike Isaac's—not loud and halting but soft and musical, its pitch rising and falling, its cadences varied and flowing. Ha'anala had forgotten that humans could speak that way, and she was saddened by the years that had passed since she had last heard Sofia's voice.

Swept by mourning, she grieved for the past, and also for the future she would not know, for there came a private moment when she knew that she would die—not with the unfocused theoretical understanding that she was mortal but with the physical certainty that death would come for her sooner rather than later. To her surprise, she slept, waking briefly with each gripping muscular wave, aware that she drew on a diminishing reserve of strength each time she rejoined the living. Once she came fully alert in the darkness, and told the others, "When I am gone, take the children to my mother." Soothing murmurs succeeded shocked silence, but she said, "Do as I ask. Remind her of Abraham. For the sake of the ten . . ." This said, she sank back into oblivion.

At dawn, her husband's snarl brought her back to the world. She was in the house now but warm, covered with blankets the likes of which she'd never seen. Without moving, she could look out the door to a ghostly landscape softened by fog. "No! I won't permit it!" Shetri was insisting. "How can you even *think* of such a thing?"

"Are you giving up then?" she heard a foreigner demand, his harsh accusatory whisper carrying easily in the still dawn air. "You needn't lose them both, man—"

"Stop!" Shetri cried, turning away from Shaan, ears clamped shut. "I won't hear of it!"

Closing her eyes, Ha'anala listened to Rukuei explain why she had to die, his words coming to her in scraps and tatters. "There's no help for it . . . necessary . . . prevent generations of suffering in the future . . . the greater good . . ."

Ha'anala did not recognize the next voice, but it might have been Hozei who said, "This is not a thing of abnormality but weakness brought on by hunger!"

"Shetri, I think you are right and that Ha'anala will die soon," Sandoz said steadily. "I think Shaan is wrong. The procedure he wishes to try will kill Ha'anala. None of us is an adept—we don't know how to do this in a way that will preserve the mother's life, and I think Ha'anala is too weak now to survive it. I am sorry. I am so very sorry. But—among us, when this happens, the child sometimes lives for a very short time after the mother dies. Please—please, if you will permit it, perhaps we can at least save the child."

"How?" Ha'anala called, firm-voiced. "How do you save the child?"

She saw the small foreigner's outline in the doorway, black against gray, and then he was at her side, kneeling, his hands in their strange machines, resting on his thighs. "*Sipaj*, Ha'anala, someone thinks that after you are gone, for a few moments, the child will live on. It would be necessary to cut open your body and lift the child out."

"Desecration," Shetri hissed again, standing above them both, tall and stiff-backed. "No, no, no! If—. I don't want the child! Not now, not this way! Ha'anala, please—"

"Save what you can," she said. "Hear me, Shetri. Save what you can!"

But he would not agree and Suukmel was arguing now, and Sofi'ala wailing, and the foreigners—

Suddenly, Ha'anala knew what it was to be Isaac, to have the music within her drowned out by noise. "Get out, Shetri," she said wearily, too far gone to tolerate the *fierno* another moment, too used up to be kind or tactful. "All of you: leave me alone!"

But she reached out and hooked her claws over Sandoz's arm, and held him fast. "Not you," she said. "Stay." When the room was empty except for the two of them, she told him slowly, in the language of prayer, "Save what you can."

FOR NINE HOURS MORE, HE DID WHATEVER SHE ASKED OF HIM, TRYING to ease her any way he could. Assured that there was hope for her child, Ha'anala rallied, and Emilio allowed himself to believe that she'd manage on her own. Ashamed of himself for panicking, his greatest concern for a time was how he would ever apologize adequately to Shetri for making this birth so much more frightening than it already was for a terrified father who'd lost two earlier children.

But the labor went on and on. Toward the end, thirst was her main complaint, and he tried to help her drink, but she couldn't hold anything down. He ducked outside the crude stone hut to ask about ice, but the small glacier that had formed between two peaks near the valley was too far away to be of use. John ran to the lander and got the oldest, softest shirt out of his pack; soaking a section of it in water, twisting it like a nipple, he handed this to Emilio, who offered it to Ha'anala. She sipped at the liquid this way and did not vomit, so for a time, Emilio simply dipped the cloth into water, over and over, until her need abated.

"Someone likes the sound of your voice," Ha'anala told him, eyes closed. "Talk to me."

"About what?"

"Anything. Take me somewhere. Tell me about your home. About the people you left behind."

So he told her about Gina, and Celestina, and they fell silent for a while, first smiling about rowdy little girls, then waiting for another contraction to pass. "Celestina. A beautiful name," Ha'anala said when it was over. "Like music."

"The name is from the word for heaven, but it can also mean a musical instrument, which sounds like a chorus of silver bells—high and chiming," he told her. "*Sipaj*, Ha'anala, what shall we call this baby?"

"That is for Shetri to say. Tell me about Sofia, when she was young."

When he hesitated, she opened her eyes and said, "No, then. Nothing difficult now! Only easy things, until the hard one comes. What did you love when you were a child?"

He was ashamed to have failed her, and Sofia, but found himself describing La Perla and his childhood friends, losing himself in old passions and simple beauties: the solid smack of a ball into a worn glove, the swift arc into second base, a whirling throw to first for a double play. She understood very little but knew the joy of motion, and told him so in short, breathless phrases.

He helped her take more water. "Music, then," she said when she could. "Perhaps your Nico will sing."

Nico did, sitting in shafted light: arias, Neapolitan love songs, hymns he'd learned at the orphanage. Soothed, her thirst slaked, Ha'anala said once more, "Take the children to my mother." She slept; Nico sang on. Tired himself, Emilio dozed off, and awoke to a song that was surely the most beautiful he had ever heard. German, he thought, but he knew only a few of the words. It didn't matter, he realized, transfixed and at peace. The melody was everything: supple and serene, rising like a soul in flight, obeying some hidden law . . .

All around them, the VaN'Jarri listened as well, children clinging to parents, everyone aware that the time was very near. Opening his eyes, Emilio Sandoz saw the last fall of the chest, drew back the blankets and studied the abdomen; saw the faint movement and thought, Still alive, still alive. Nico, wide-eyed, handed him the knife.

As though from a great distance, Sandoz watched his own unfeeling hands cut quickly and decisively. For hours, he had feared this moment, afraid that he would cut too deeply or too hesitantly. In the event, there was a kind of wordless grace. He felt purified, stripped of all other purpose as this body opened up beneath him, layer after layer, blossoming, glistening like a red rose at dawn, its petals bathed in dew.

"There," he said softly, and slit the caul. "Nico, lift the baby out."

The big man did as he was told, swarthy face paling in the shadowy hut at the awful sound—sucking and wet—as he pulled the child free. He stood then, thick-fingered hands supporting the infant's fragile form as though it were made of glass.

John stood just beyond the door, ready to clean the baby and take it to the father, but when he saw what Nico carried, the steam rising wispily from its fine, damp fur, he threw back his head and cried, "Stillborn!" Nico burst into tears, and there was a great howl from the others that fell away when Sandoz lurched like a madman through the doorway and whispered in direct address, in denial and defiance, "God, no. Not *this* time."

Abruptly he snatched the child away from Nico and dropped to the ground with it, supporting his weight on his knees and his forearms, the tiny body so close he could feel the lingering warmth of its mother's corpse. With his mouth, he sucked the slimy membrane and fluid from the nostrils and spat, enraged and resolved. Tipping the damp head back with one ruined hand, holding the blunt little muzzle closed with the other, he put his mouth over the nose again: blew gently, and waited; blew gently and waited, over and over. Eventually he felt hands on his shoulders drawing him back, but he wrenched his body from their grip, and went back to the task until John, more roughly now, yanked him away from the little body, and ordered in a voice ragged with weeping, "Stop, Emilio! You can stop now!"

Beaten, he sat back on his heels, and let a single despairing cry into the air. Only then, as the sound torn from his throat joined the high, thin wail of a newborn, did he understand.

The infant's squall was lost in the eruption of astonishment and joy. Fine Runa hands gathered the baby up and Emilio's eyes followed the infant as it was cleaned and wrapped, round and round, with homespun cloth, and passed from embrace to embrace. For a long time, he stayed slumped where he was, blood-soaked and spent. Then he pushed himself to his feet and stood, swaying slightly, looking for Shetri Laaks.

He was afraid the father would mourn the wife and curse the child. But Shetri was already holding the little one to his chest, eyes downcast, oblivious to everything but the son he jounced gently in his arms to quiet its crying.

Emilio Sandoz turned away and ducked back into the stone hut, where he was greeted by the wreckage of a woman, as forgotten as he was in the rejoicing. We cremate our dead, Rukuei had said. When? Two days ago? Three? So the Pope was right, Emilio thought numbly. No grave to dig. . . . Drained of emotion, he sat down heavily, next to what had been Ha'anala. If anything could prove the existence of the soul, he thought, it is the utter emptiness of a corpse.

Unbidden, unlooked for, the stillness came upon him: evoked by music and by death, and by the shadowless love that can only be felt at a birth. Once more, he felt the tidal pull, but this time he swam against it, as a man being swept out to sea fights the current. Putting his head in his hands, he let the weight of his skull press down on the hardware of his braces, for once in his life seeking a physical pain that he could rule, to block out what was beyond his control.

It was a mistake. Tears that sprang from his body's hurt now began to bleed from his soul's wounds. For a long time, he was lost, and freshly maimed. It was not his body violated, not his blood spilt, not his love shattered, but he wept for the dead, for the irreversible wrongs, the terrible sorrows. For Ha'anala. For Shetri's losses, and his own—for Gina and Celestina, and the life they might have had together. For Sofia, for Jimmy. For Marc, and D.W., and Anne and George. For his parents, and his brother. For himself.

When the sobbing quieted, he lay down next to Ha'anala, feeling as empty as her corpse. "God," he whispered, over and over, until exhaustion claimed him. "God."

"SANDOZ? I'M SORRY." DANNY HESITATED, THEN SHOOK HIM AGAIN. "I'M sorry," he repeated when Emilio sat up. "We waited as long as we could, but this is important."

Sandoz looked around, bemused by the sensation of his own swollen eyelids. The confusion lifted quickly. Ha'anala's body had been removed sometime during the night; the room was packed with priests.

"You okay?" John asked, wincing at the stupidity of the question when Emilio shrugged noncommittally. "Look, there's something you have to see," John said, and he handed over his own tablet. Frans Vanderhelst had shot a set of data files to his root directory, leaving them for John to discover. A case of divided loyalties, John had decided, looking at the images with growing fear, and working out what they meant. Frans had evidently been watching the show for some time, trying to decide what, if anything, to do about it. A good mercenary has just so much latitude and Carlo was the padrone, but ultimately the fat man had done what he could . . .

"Jesus," Emilio breathed, scrolling through the images. "Do you have an estimate of the size of that force?"

"I make it something over thirty thousand in the main body," Joseba told him. Any picture in Joseba's mind of the stately, deliberative life of the Runa had been swept away by the time-date stamps on the images, as he confronted the reality of an army that had conquered the known world of Rakhat as quickly, and more thoroughly, than Alexander had conquered his.

"This looks like light infantry in the vanguard," Danny said, reaching over Sandoz's shoulder to point at the screen, "backed by armor, maybe two day's march behind them. And that's an image from about four days ago. Can you see how much brighter it looks? We're picking up the glare off the metal."

"There's infrared showing another large group behind them," Joseba said. "Look at the next one."

Sandoz stared at the image and then looked up at worried faces.

"Artillery," Sean confirmed, "and they're headed right for us."

"But we came in above the cloud cover, and John stayed below the sound barrier!" Emilio said. "How could they have tracked us?"

It was Danny who answered. "Can't say for sure, ace, but I could give it a guess."

Emilio thought, and then closed his eyes for a moment. "Carlo sold us out. He gave them the coordinates."

"Looks that way."

Nico stood just outside the door. "So the signora doesn't have to wait for us to bring Isaac to her," he said. "She's coming to get him."

"She doesn't need an army t'do that," Sean pointed out sourly, hunkering down next to Joseba.

"Sandoz, there's something else you should know," said Danny Iron Horse. "When you three first went missing, Sofia Mendes swore she would 'track those *djanada* bastards to their lair and finish this, once and for all.' "

"Yes. You can see the appeal," said Sandoz. A lasting peace, secure borders, an unblighted future for the Runa. . . . He rubbed his face against his arms, and they all got to their feet. For an instant—in a small stone room, surrounded by huge bodies—he felt reality shift, but pulled himself back to the present, which was bad enough. "We have to warn the VaN'Jarri," he said. "They should probably evacuate. Pull back to that Athaansi's settlement, yes? Concentrate in one valley and set up a defense?"

Danny shook his head. "Fish in a barrel, once the artillery gets here."

"Small, scattered groups might have a better chance of escaping detection," said Joseba, "but they may also starve to death, or die of exposure."

"Six of one, half a dozen of the other," John said. "Either way, they're in a real bad place."

"It's not our decision, now, is it?" said Sean. "We give 'em the facts and let the VaN'Jarri make the move." And when the others shrugged their agreement, he moved to the doorway, jerking his head at Joseba. "Come on, lad. Let us go forth and spread the good news."

"I wonder what Carlo got for us?" John mused as Sean and Joseba stepped past Nico and strode off.

"An excuse to quit before he failed," said Emilio, working through the images Frans had sent. "Look at this one. They're taking on cargo. Carlo's going to load up and go home. The drone has been down to Agardi, what? Three times already." He stopped, and then said, "Oh, my God."

"What?" John asked, frightened now. "What's in Agardi? Munitions factories? Is he—"

"No. Nothing like that. Distilleries," said Sandoz softly, looking up at Danny and John.

"Distilleries?" John echoed, confused. "Then he's loading—"

"*Yasapa* brandy," said Danny. Sandoz nodded, and Danny sighed, shaking his head.

"So that's it, then?" John cried, throwing his hands in the air. "Carlo sells us out, stocks up on Rakhati brandy and goes home richer than Gates!" Furious, he slumped down the wall opposite the door and sat, legs out straight, back against the stones.

"And yet," Emilio remarked mildly, "there does seem to be some justice in the universe after all." He was standing in the doorway, and the light behind him lit up his hair, obscuring his expression. "You see," Emilio said, "I never had a chance to tell Carlo, but *yasapa* brandy is—"

Danny's eyes widened. Mouth open, he paused, barely breathing. "Awful?" he suggested hopefully.

"Say yes," John urged, scrambling to his feet and moving to Danny's side. "Please, Emilio, say it's awful! Lie if you have to, but tell me it's the worst liquor you ever drank in your whole life."

Face haggard, eyes seraphic, Sandoz spoke. "It tastes," he said, "just . . . like . . . soap."

HAD ANYONE ASKED, EMILIO SANDOZ COULD HAVE EXPLAINED THE KIND of half-hysterical laughter that can overcome grief and fear and desperation, but no one was listening to the Jesuits in Ha'anala's hut. By the time Emilio went outside, the evacuation of the N'Jarr valley was under way—parents gathering children, bundling possessions, arguing and shouting, making snap decisions, having second thoughts, trying not to panic. There was an island of calm in the midst of all this, and he pushed toward it, knowing somehow that Suukmel Chirot u Vaadai would be at its center, where Ha'anala's pyre was still smoking.

He dropped to his knees at her side. "We have brought trouble on you," he said. "I am sorry for it."

"You meant well," she said. "And there is a life because of you."

"You're not packing," he observed.

"As you see," she said serenely, ignoring the tumult around them.

"My lady Suukmel, hear me: you are not safe here anymore."

"Safety, I find, is a relative term." She lifted her hand, as though to draw a veil over her head, but stopped, midgesture. "I am staying," she said in a tone that invited no argument. "I have decided that if this foreigner Sofia comes to the N'Jarr, I shall have a talk with her. We have some things in common." Her lips curled slightly, and her eyes seemed to him amused. "And what are your plans?" she asked.

"Much like your own," he told her. "I'm going south, to have a talk with Sofia."

38

On the Road to Inbrokar

November 2078, Earth-Relative

HE DIDN'T DARE USE THE LANDER, PREFERRING TO RESERVE ITS REMAIN-
ing fuel for emergencies, so he and Nico went south on foot. The priests
stayed in the N'Jarr to help in whatever ways they could, but Nico would
not hear of being separated from him and Emilio did not protest. It was unlikely that what they'd face in twelve days' time would yield to a handgun
and a resolute attitude, but Nico had repeatedly proved his worth and
Emilio was glad of his company. Tiyat and Kajpin came along as well, to
lead the way through the mountain passes and twisted ravines and
foothills. The plan was to walk back to the ruins of Inbrokar, and then go
on a bit farther south, where they would wait on the road for Sofia and the
Runa army to come upon them.

By second sunset, Emilio and Nico were both bleeding from the knees,
and Emilio was beginning to reconsider the definition of "emergency."
The Garnu mountain strata were thin and fragile, tipped nearly vertical:
an evil surface to hike, exhausting and treacherous underfoot. The Runa
had three limbs to call upon but even for them, the climb was difficult.
"Are you all right, Nico?" Emilio asked, as Tiyat and Kajpin helped the
big man up a fifth time. "Perhaps we should go back for the lander after
all—"

He stopped, hearing the scrabbling sound of sliding rocks behind him,
and turned with Nico to watch a tall, naked human striding down the in-

cline on dirty, storklike legs, a tattered blue parasol held high over his head.

"Isaac?" Nico suggested, brushing debris from his scraped palms as he rubbed the newest sore spots.

"Yes," Emilio guessed softly. "Who else could it be?"

He had expected a mixture of Jimmy and Sofia in their child's face. Perhaps that was the greatest surprise: Isaac was not a child. He must be close to forty, Emilio realized. Older than Jimmy was when he died. . . . The father's coiling hair had been passed on, but Isaac's was a darker red, now shot with gray, and matted into brittle, filthy dreadlocks. There was something of Sofia's delicacy in the long, birdlike bones, and a familiarity to the mouth, but it was difficult to find the mother in this grimy wraith with evasive blue eyes.

"Isaac has rules," Tiyat informed them quickly, when the man stood still a few paces up the incline. "Don't interrupt him."

Isaac did not even glance at the newcomers, but appeared rather to be studying something just to Emilio's left. "Isaac," Emilio began hesitantly, "we are going to see your mother—"

"I won't go back," said Isaac in a loud, toneless voice. "Do you know any songs?"

Baffled, Emilio hardly knew what to reply, but Nico simply answered, "I know a lot of songs."

"Sing one."

Even Nico seemed a little taken aback, but rose to the occasion, offering Puccini's "O mio bambino caro" with floating top notes in a soft falsetto, repeating the song when Isaac told him to. For a time, there was no sound in the world but the two of them together: twin untutored tenors, artlessly beautiful in close harmony. Nico, beaming, would have sung "Questa o quella" next, but Isaac said, "That's all," and turned to go.

No prosody at all, Emilio noted, recalling symptoms he'd studied long ago in a developmental linguistics course. The VaN'Jarri had mentioned Isaac's oddities but, until now, he had not realized that there was something more than isolation that would account for the things they'd described.

"Isaac," he called before the man had stalked away, knees rising high as a waterbird's as he walked through the splintery rocks. "Do you have a message for your mother?"

Isaac stopped, but did not face him. "I won't go back," he repeated. "She can come here." There was a pause. "That's all," he said, and disappeared around an outcropping.

"She's already on her way," Kajpin muttered.

"That lander is too noisy and stinks too much," Tiyat remarked, going back to the topic abandoned when Isaac showed up. "We'll be through the worst of this bad ground by tomorrow at third sunset," she promised.

ONCE BEYOND THE INFLUENCE OF THE GARNU RANGE, THE LAND GEN-tled, rising and falling by little more than a Runao's height. The sapphire hills darkened to indigo with distance, the near country afire with magenta blossoms flaring in sunlight, and Emilio began to be glad after all that they had remained on foot. Repetitive movement had always calmed him, narrowing the focus to the burning of his muscles, the impact of the ground against his feet. He did not try to anticipate Sofia's arguments or his own. It will be well, he thought, hour after hour, putting one foot in front of the other like a pilgrim walking to Jerusalem. Over and over: It will be well. He did not believe this; Ha'anala's words simply matched the rhythm of his pace.

They foraged frequently as they walked; camped in the open, heedless of detection. "If we're arrested, they'll take us to the army anyway," Kajpin pointed out with untroubled practicality. "What difference does it make?"

By day, Emilio could almost match that fatalism, but the nights were bad, spent wandering in charred, empty dream-cities, or pacing in the noisy darkness waiting for dawn. At last, the others would rouse, and they'd break their fast with leftovers from the previous night's meal. Once or twice, Nico brought down some small game, but much of the meat went to waste. Emilio ate very little—his usual response to tension. Pacing rest-lessly until their journey resumed, he would lose himself in the silent chant: It will be well.

Eight days' travel south of the mountains, they saw the glint and flash of equipment in the sunlight, flaring now and then on the horizon. By late afternoon, they could pick out a dark mass at the base of a dust plume when the rolling land lifted the army into sight.

"We'll be there tomorrow," Tiyat said, but she looked west and added, "unless the rain comes sooner."

That night they all slept badly, and woke to haze and sultry air. Leaving the others to their breakfast, Emilio walked up a low rise, gazing out toward the army bivouac. The first sun had barely begun to climb, but even now the heat was making the ground dance and shimmer, and he was already sweating. Screw it, he thought, and called back to his companions, "We'll wait here."

"Good idea," said Kajpin, joining him. "Let them come to us!"

They spent the morning sitting on the little hill, Nico and the Runa eating and chatting like picnickers waiting for a parade. But as the army grew closer and they saw the numbers, they fell as silent as Sandoz, ears straining for the first sounds. It was hard to tell if they truly heard or only imagined the thudding of feet, the clank of metal, the caroling of commands and commentary from the ranks; storm clouds now hid the western horizon with columns of black rain, and the breeze carried away all but the nearest noises.

"This is going to be a fierce one," Tiyat predicted uneasily, standing with her tail braced against a stiffening wind. The lightning in the west was nearly continuous, illuminating the underside of the thunderheads.

Kajpin stood as well. "Rain falls on everyone," she said without concern, but then added the more ominous phrase, "lightning strikes some." Tramping down the hillock to a small dip in the ground, she sat again, lowering her profile, calmly contemplating the soldiers' ranks before remarking cheerfully, "Glad *I'm* not wearing armor."

"How long do you think before the storm comes?" Nico asked.

Emilio looked west and shrugged. "An hour. Maybe less."

"Do you want me to go to them and ask for Signora Sofia?"

"No, Nico. Thank you. Wait here, please," Sandoz said. He joined Tiyat and Kajpin, and repeated, "Wait here." Then, without looking back, he walked without hurry down the road until he'd halved the distance and stood alone: a small flat-backed figure, silver and black hair lifted and blown by the breeze.

By this time the vanguard had also come to a halt, and before long these ranks parted to make way for a curtained sedan chair borne from the bivouac by four Runa.

Emilio tried to prepare himself for the sight of her, the sound of her voice, but gave up and simply watched as the bearers set the chair down gently. With dispatch, they unfurled a temporary shelter like a veranda around the litter, its waterproof fabric the color of marigolds, bright in the sunlight east of the approaching storm. There was a short delay while an ingeniously designed folding chair was brought forward from an equipment wagon, snapped into shape and placed in front of the conveyance. Finally a staircase, hinged at the base of the litter's entrance, was tipped outward, and he saw a tiny hand as it separated the curtains and took a proffered arm as support in her descent.

He had expected her to be altered but still lovely; he was not disappointed. The raking scars and the empty socket were a shock, but the harsh suns of Rakhat had rendered her face so finely creased that it seemed made of gauze; the seams of scar tissue were now merely three lines among many, and her remaining eye was lively and observant, and seemed to sweep her surroundings in continual compensation for her halved field of vision. Even the arc of her spine seemed graceful to him: a curve of curiosity, as though she had bent to examine some object on the ground that had caught her attention on her way to the camp chair. She sat, and looked up, her head tilted almost coyly, waiting for him. Delicate as a wren, with her small spare hands in her lap, she had in repose a skeletal purity: elegant and fleshless and still. "Thou art beautiful," he thought, "comely as Jerusalem, terrible as an army with banners. . . ."

"Sofia," he said and held his hands out to her.

Her's remained quiet. "It's been a long time," she observed coldly, when he drew near. "You might have come to *me* first." She held his gaze with her one eye until his own dropped. "Have you seen Isaac?" she asked, when he could look at her again.

"Yes," he said. She stiffened slightly and took in a breath, and he understood then that Sofia had believed her son long dead, his name used heartlessly to lure more hostages to the *djanada* stronghold. "Isaac is well," he began.

"Well!" She gave a short laugh. "Not normal, but well, at least. Is he with you?"

"No—"

"They are still holding him hostage."

"No, Sofia, nothing like that! He is a person of honor among them—"

"Then why isn't he here, with you?"

He hesitated, not wanting to wound her. "He—Isaac prefers to stay where he is. He has invited you to come to him." He stopped, looking past her to the troops visible beyond the golden tenting. "We can take you to him, but you must come alone."

"Is that the game?" she asked, smiling coolly. "Isaac is the bait, and they'd have me."

"Sofia, please!" he begged. "The Jana'ata aren't—. Sofia, you've got it all wrong!"

"I have it wrong," she repeated softly. "*I* have it wrong. Sandoz, you've been here, what? A few weeks?" she asked lightly, brows up, one twisted by scar tissue. "And now you tell me that I have it all wrong. Wait! There is a word in English for this—now let me think . . ." She stared at him, un-blinking. "Arrogance. Yes. That's the word. I had almost forgotten it. You have come back, after forty years, and you have taken almost three whole weeks to get to know the situation, and now you propose to explain Rakhat to me."

He refused to be intimidated. "Not Rakhat. Just one small settlement of Jana'ata, trying not to starve to death. Sofia, do you realize that the Jana'ata are nearly extinct? Surely you didn't mean—"

"Is that what they told you?" she asked. She snorted with derision. "And you believed them."

"Dammit, Sofia, don't patronize me! I know starvation when I see it—"

"What if they are starving?" she snapped. "Shall I regret that a cannibal starves?"

"Oh, for crissakes, Sofia, they aren't cannibals!"

"And what would you call it?" she asked. "They eat Runa—"

"Sofia, listen to me—"

"No, you listen to *me*, Sandoz," she hissed. "For nearly thirty years, we-but-not-you fought an enemy whose whole civilization was the purest ex-pression of the most characteristic form of evil: the willingness to erase the humanity of others and turn them into commodities. In life, the Runa were conveniences for the *djanada*—slaves, assistants, sex toys. In death, raw materials—meat, hides, bones. Labor first, livestock in the end! But the Runa are more than meat, Sandoz. They are a people who have earned their liberty and won it from those who kept them in bondage, generation after generation. God wanted their freedom. I helped them to get it, and I regret nothing. We gave the Jana'ata justice. They reaped precisely what they sowed."

"So God wants them extinct?" Emilio cried. "He wants the Runa to turn the planet into a grocery store? God wants a place where no one sings, where everyone is alike, where there is one kind of person? Sofia, this has gone way past an eye for an eye—"

The sound was like a gunshot, flat and unresonant, and he could feel the exact outline of her hand, stinging and sharp, form on his face.

"How dare you," she whispered. "How dare you leave me behind, and come back now—after *all this time*—and presume to judge me!"

He stood still, face averted, waiting for the sensation to ease, eyes wide to keep the tears from spilling. Tried to imagine forty years alone and unsupported, without John or Gina, without Vince Giuliani or Edward Behr, or any of the others who'd helped him.

"I'm sorry," he said finally. "I'm sorry! I don't know what happened here, and I won't pretend to understand what you have lived through—"

"Thank you. I am glad to hear it—"

"But, Sofia, I do know what it is to be a commodity," he said, cutting her off. "I know what it is to be erased. I also know what it is to be falsely accused, and God help me! I know what it is to be guilty—" He stopped and looked away, but then met her eye and said, "Sofia, I have eaten Runa, and for the same reason the *djanada* did: because I was hungry and I wanted to live. And I have killed—I killed Askama, Sofia. I didn't mean it to be her, but I wanted to kill, I wanted someone to die so that I could be *free*, one way or the other. So you see," he told her with bleak cheer, "I am the last person to judge anyone else! And I grant you that the Jana'ata you fought got what was coming to them! But, Sofia—you can't let the Runa kill them all! They've paid for their sins—"

"Paid for their sins!" Incredulous, she stood, and left her chair and walked a step or two, bent and hobbled by a coiled spine. "Did they confess to you, Father? Have you forgiven them, just because they asked you to?" she asked, face twisted with contempt. "Well, some things cannot be absolved! Some things are unforgivable—"

"You think I don't know that?" he shouted, his own anger rising to meet hers. "No one confesses to me anymore! I left the priesthood, Sofia. I didn't come here to judge you. I didn't even come back to rescue you! I came because I was beaten senseless and kidnapped by Carlo Giuliani. I spent a good portion of the voyage from Earth drugged, and all I want to do right now is go home and find out if the woman I nearly married seventeen years ago is still alive—"

She stared at him but now his eyes did not drop. "You said that you knew what happened to me at Galatna, Sofia, but you don't know the worst of it: I left the priesthood because I can't forgive what happened to me there. I can't forgive Supaari, who did this to me," he said, holding up his hands. "And I can't forgive Hlavin Kitheri, and I doubt that I ever will. They taught me to hate, Sofia. Ironic, isn't it? We heard Kitheri's songs and risked everything to come here, prepared to love whomever we met and to learn from them! But when Hlavin Kitheri met one of us——. He looked at me, and all he thought——"

He stopped, spun from her, hardly able to breathe, but turned, trembling, and held her uneasy gaze as he said in a voice soft with outrage, "He looked at me and thought, How *nice*. Something new to fuck."

"It's over," she snapped, face white. But he knew it wasn't, not even for her, not even after all these years. "You work," she told him. "You concentrate on the task at hand——"

"Yes," he agreed willingly, quickly. "And you make loneliness a virtue. You call it self-reliance, right? You tell yourself you need nothing, that you don't want anyone in your life ever again——"

"Wall it off!"

"You think I haven't tried?" he cried. "Sofia, I keep stacking up the stones, but nothing holds the walls together anymore! Not even anger. Not even hate. I am worn out with hating, Sofia. I'm tired of it. I'm *bored* by it!" The storm was now only minutes away and the lightning was frighteningly close, but he didn't care. "I have hated Supaari VaGayjur, and Hlavin Kitheri, and sixteen of his friends but . . . I can't seem to hate in the aggregate," he whispered, hands falling emptily. "That one small island of integrity is still left to me, Sofia. As much as I have hated the fathers, I cannot hate their children. And neither should you, Sofia. You can't in justice kill the innocent."

"No," she said, curled over her own heart. "There are no innocents."

"If I can find you ten, will you spare the others for their sake?"

"Don't play games with me," she said, and motioned for her bearers.

With one step, he came between her and the chair. "I helped to deliver a Jana'ata baby a few days ago," he told her conversationally, blocking her way. "Cesarean section. I did what I could. It wasn't enough. The mother died. I want her baby to live, Sofia. There is very damned little that I am certain of these days, but I'm sure of this one thing: I want that kid to live."

"Get out of my way," she whispered, "or I'll call my guards."

He didn't move. "Shall I tell you what the baby's older sister is called?" he asked lightly. "Sofi'ala. Pretty name, isn't it?" He watched her react, her head jerking as though recoiling from a blow, and he pressed on mercilessly. "The child's mother was named Ha'anala. Her last words were of you. She said, 'Take the children to my mother.' She wanted us to march them to Gayjur! A sort of children's crusade, I suppose. I didn't do it. I refused her dying wish because I am afraid to be responsible for the lives of any more children, Sofia. But she was right—those kids have never murdered or enslaved anyone. They are every bit as innocent as the VaKashani children we saw slaughtered."

The rain was beginning—heavy drops as warm as tears—wind whipping the fabric of the shelter noisily, almost drowning out his words. "I will stand surety for those kids and their parents, Sofia. *Please*. Let them live and all the good they do—all the music, the poetry, everything decent they are capable of—all that is to your credit," he told her, desperate now, taking her stillness for refusal. "If they kill again, I'll be the goat. Their sins on my head, okay? I'll stay here and if they kill again, then execute me and let them have one more chance."

"Ha'anala's dead?"

He nodded, ashamed to weep when Sofia should have mourned. "You taught her well, Sofia," he said, voice fraying. "She was, by all accounts, a remarkable woman. She founded a sort of utopian society up in the mountains. It's probably doomed—like all utopias. But she tried! All three of our species live together up there, Sofia—Runa, Jana'ata, even Isaac. She taught them that every soul is a small reflection of God, and that it is wicked to murder because when a life is taken, we lose that unique revelation of God's nature."

He stopped again, hardly able to utter the words. "Sofia, one of the priests I came with—he thinks your foster daughter was a sort of Moses for her people! It took forty years to burn the slavery out of the Israelites. Well, maybe the Jana'ata need forty years to burn the mastery out of them!"

He shrugged helplessly at her stricken glare. "I don't know, Sofia. Sean's probably full of shit. Maybe Abraham was psychotic and schizophrenia ran in his family. Maybe Jesus was just another crazy Jew who heard voices. Or maybe God is real, but He's evil or stupid, and that's why so much seems so insane and unfair! It doesn't *matter*," he shouted, trying to make himself heard through the roar of the rain. "It really doesn't matter. I don't give a damn about God anymore, Sofia. All I know for certain is I want Ha'anala's baby to live—"

She walked out into the rain, its relentless noise drowning all other sound. For a long time, she simply stood in the downpour, listening to its hissing crash, feeling it beat down on her twisted shoulders, work its way through her hair, wash over the ruins of her face.

When she came back from where she had been in memory, Emilio was waiting for her. Soaked and chilled, she walked slowly to her chair, accepting his offer of an arm to steady her climb. When she reached the platform, she sat as heavily as a tiny woman could.

The first violence of the storm was passing, the rain now a steady drumming, and for a time they simply gazed out at the drowning landscape. She touched his shoulder and he turned to her. Reaching up, she placed her hand gently over the mark she'd laid there, minutes before, and then lifted a lock of his hair. "You've gotten gray, old man," she said. "You look even worse than I do, and I look awful."

His reply was starchy, but the red-rimmed eyes were amused. "Vanity is not among my failings, madam, but I'm damned if I'll stand here and be insulted." He made no move to go.

"I loved you once," she said.

"I know. I loved you, too. Don't change the subject."

"You were to marry?"

"Yes. I left the priesthood, Sofia. I was done with God."

"But He wasn't done with you."

"Evidently not," Emilio said wearily. "Either that, or this has been a run of bad luck of historic proportions." He walked to the edge of the awning to stare out at the rain. "Even now, I think maybe it's all a bad joke, you know? This baby I'm so worried about? He could turn out to be such an evil bastard that everyone will wish he'd died in his mother's womb, and I'll go down in Rakhati history as Sandoz the Idiot, who saved his life!" Braced hands limp at his sides, he snorted at his own absurd grandiosity. "Probably he'll just be another poor clown doing the best he can, trying to get things right more often than not."

Then, without warning, his posture shifted. He became, somehow, taller, rangier, and Sofia Mendes heard once more the beloved Texas twang of D. W. Yarbrough, the long-dead priest who'd taught them both so much. "Miz Mendes," Emilio drawled, defeated but not without humor, "the whole damn thing beats the livin' shit outta me."

TALKED OUT, EMILIO SAT ON THE GROUND NEXT TO HER, AND TOGETHER they watched rain turn the world to mud. Before long, she realized he had fallen asleep, propped against the supports of her chair, the crippled hands lax in his lap. Mind empty, she listened to his soft snore and might have slept herself if she had not been disturbed by a huge and sodden young man, clutching a cloth cap and stooping to peer under the awning.

"Signora? Is everything going to be all right now?" he asked anxiously.

"And who are you?" she asked very quietly, glancing significantly at Emilio.

"My name is Niccolo d'Angeli. 'D'Angeli' means from the angels," the young giant whispered. "That's where I came from, before the home. The angels left me there." She smiled, and he took that for a good sign. "So everything will be all right?" he asked again coming in, out of the rain. "The Jana people can live up there, if they don't bother anyone, right?" She didn't answer so he said, "That would be fair, I think. Is Don Emilio all right? Why is he sitting there like that?"

"He's asleep. He must have been very tired."

"He has nightmares. He's afraid to sleep."

"Are you a friend of his?"

"I'm his bodyguard. I think his friends are all dead." Nico gave this some consideration, but looked unhappy. Then, visibly struck by a thought, he brightened. "You're his friend, and you're not dead."

"Not yet," Sofia confirmed.

Nico stepped to the edge of the shelter and watched the lightning play for a while. "I like the storms here," he remarked. "They remind me of the last act of *Rigoletto*." She had been thinking, He is retarded. But this gave her pause. "We found your son, signora," said Nico, facing her again. "He wants you to visit him, but I think he should put some clothes on first. Did I say something wrong?"

She wiped one eye. "No." She smiled then and confided, "Isaac has never liked clothes."

"He likes songs," Nico reported.

"Yes. Yes, indeed. Isaac has always liked music." She sat as straight as her contorted body would allow. "Signor d'Angeli, did my son appear well?"

"He's skinny, but they all are up there," said Nico, warming to his topic. "There was a lady who died having a baby before we left. Joseba thinks she was too skinny and that's why she died—because she wasn't strong enough. We brought food, but a lot of people were so hungry, they threw up from eating too fast." He saw the signora's distress but didn't know how to interpret it. Turning the brim of his hat around and around, he shifted his substantial weight from one foot to the other, and squinted a little. "What should we do now?" he asked, after a little while.

She didn't answer right away. "I'm not sure," she said honestly. "I need some time to think."

HOURS LATER, IN THE FIRST MOMENTS OF CONSCIOUSNESS, LYING IN A bed of unaccustomed comfort, Emilio Sandoz believed himself to be back in Naples. "It's all right, Ed," he was about to say. "You don't have to wait up." Then he came fully awake and saw that it was not Brother Edward Behr but Sofia Mendes who'd spent the night watching his face as he slept.

"I have spoken with your colleagues in the N'Jarr valley," she told him without emotion, "and to a woman named Suukmel." She paused, face neutral. "I don't rule here, Emilio, no matter what your *djanada* friends told you. But I have some influence. I will do my best to arrange safe conduct for a delegation of VaN'Jarri to speak with the Parliament of Elders. It will take time and it won't be easy, even to get you a hearing. The elders remember what it was like, before. There is a woman named Djalao VaKashan who will be difficult to convince. But I will tell them that you and the priests are good men with good hearts. I can't promise more than that."

He sat up, and groaned at the stiffness, but said, "Thank you." The rain was gone, and sunlight was pouring through the awning. "And you, Sofia? What will you do?"

"Do?" she asked, and looked away, to think, before she answered, of well-run cities, of lively politics and burgeoning trade; of festivals and celebrations; of a joyous appreciation of the novel and the untried. She thought of the florescence of theater and explosion of technology, the vigor of the art that had sprung up when the dead hand of the *djanada* was lifted from Runa lives. She thought of the Runa Elders, who now lived long enough to add real wisdom to raw experience; and of imperfect children, permitted to live, who brought unexpected gifts to their people.

Certainly, there had been a price to pay. There were those who thrived in the new world—liberated in every sense—and those who had been cast adrift, unable to adapt. Illness, debilities, failure, dispute; poverty, displacement, bewilderment—all these were a part of Runa life now. But what they had already accomplished was admirable, and who knew what else they were capable of? Only time would tell.

All that, balanced against tiny crescent claws, and amethyst eyes blinking in the sunlight . . .

She had read Yeats in Jimmy's memory, and thought now of the Pensioner: I spit into the face of time / that has transfigured me . . .

"Do?" she asked again. "I am old, Sandoz. I have spent my life among the Runa, and among them I shall stay." She was profiled against the light, her blind side toward him, and she was silent for a long time. "I regret nothing," she said finally, "but I have done my part."

39

N'Jarr Valley

December 2078, Earth-Relative

AFTER MONTHS OF CONFINEMENT ABOARD THE *GIORDANO BRUNO*, Daniel Iron Horse found the mountains surrounding the N'Jarr as seductive as certainty, and set his sights on a high ledge east of the settlement, hoping for perspective of one kind or another. He had no equipment and his shoes were all wrong, and it crossed his mind that a fall in this terrain could easily result in a very fancy death. But Danny needed to be alone, craved the sense that only God would know where he was, and so he left at dawn, telling no one of his plans.

From the moment Emilio Sandoz left the valley to meet Mendes on the road, Danny had felt the man's absence like a shedding of weight. Now, as he began to climb the main rockface, he was happier than he'd been in a year. Calm claimed him, his attention absorbed by the delicate, tactile search for purchase. Hooking his fingers into cracks in the stone, he saw the sturdy bone of Grampa Lundberg's wrists, thick as fenceposts; felt in his chest the heart of Gramma Beauvais, strong and steady in her nineties. Funny, he thought, how his grandparents had always tried to parse him out. He'd resented their urge to divide his DNA, particularly when his father's family warned him, with tragic justification, about having "that Lakota liver." Now, finally, he was in a place where none of that made any difference, where he was simply an Earthman. Only here had he come to understand that he was not a battleground—to be divided and conquered by his grandparents—but a garden, where each person who'd contributed to his existence longed to see that something of themselves had taken root and grown.

For a time, he abandoned himself to a pure enjoyment of strength and agility, but altitude was a factor. Winded, he gave up a few hundred meters shy of the target ledge, and found instead a rubble-filled indentation that had collected enough debris to provide a humus cushion. Swinging into it, he sat quietly awhile, studying the layout of the evacuated village—alert to clues about social structure—and prayed for the well-being of the refugees who'd left it two weeks earlier. It had been a long time, he realized, since he'd felt like either a political scientist or a priest.

Chagrined by the time it took for his breathing to come back to normal, he admitted to himself that altitude was not the only thing slowing him down. The words of Vincenzo Giuliani came to him: "You are young, Father Iron Horse." Not all *that* young, Danny thought, filling his lungs with thin mountain air and remembering that night in the Naples garden. "You are young, and you have the vices of the young. Short-sightedness. Contempt for pragmatism . . ."

High above the valley, the only sound was the roar of water falling from a cataract so near he could feel its mist when the breeze shifted. Alone now and able to think, Danny forced himself to be still, to picture the chessboard, assess the pieces, see the long game. Unknowingly, he asked himself the very question that had formed the basis of much of Vincenzo Giuliani's career: So, who have I got to work with here?

Nothing came clear. Judging by the outcome of the first mission, catastrophe lurked behind the smallest mistake; muddled impasse seemed the best that they could hope for. That's Sandoz talking, Danny thought with sudden insight. But this is politics. We just have to find a way for all the players to get at least some of what they need.

Hardly aware of his movement, he stood and began again to climb toward the ledge he'd set out for, and by the time he reached it, the solution had come to him like the revelation at Cardoner, and seemed so obvious that he wondered if Vincenzo Giuliani could have foreseen this situation. That was impossible, and yet . . .

You win, you old fox, Danny thought, and he seemed to hear the sound of a soul's laughter as he pulled himself onto the ledge and stood like a colossus overlooking the valley. Suukmel first, Danny thought. Then Sofia Mendes. If she agrees, then Carlo. And from there to the others.

The irony of what he was going to propose was palpable, and he knew that he would not live long enough to see the outcome. But at the very least, he thought, it might buy time. And time was all that mattered.

JOHN CANDOTTI WAS SITTING ON A TREE STUMP, SURROUNDED BY THE pieces of a broken pump he was trying to fix, when Danny strode buoyantly into the center of the village late that afternoon. "Where the hell have you been?" John cried. "Sean and Joseba are out looking for you—. What happened to your knees?"

"Nothing. I slipped," Danny said. "What time is it on the *Bruno*?"

John pulled his chin in, surprised by the question and by Danny's air of enterprise. "I don't know. I haven't looked at a watch in days." He glanced up at the suns and worked it out. "Must be about eight in the evening, I guess."

"So it's just after supper, ship's time? Good. I've got a job for you," Danny said, jerking his head in the direction of the lander. "I want you to get Frans on the radio. Tell him to try the *yasapa* brandy." John didn't move, reluctance plain on his open face. "I could ask you to trust me," Danny offered, small eyes dancing, "or I *could* just tell you to do as you're told."

John blew out a breath and put down the gasket he was making. "Ours is not to reason why," he muttered, and followed Iron Horse to the edge of the valley where the lander crouched. "I don't suppose you'd like to explain?" he asked, as they climbed inside.

"Look," said Danny, "I could do this myself, but I promise you it'll be more fun if you help. Just suggest to Frans that this would be a very good time to have a nice little postprandial drink, okay?"

Frowning, John said, "But then he'll tell Carlo—"

Danny grinned.

Lips compressed, John shook his head, but sat down in front of the console and raised the *Giordano Bruno*.

"Johnny!" Frans cried moments later, a shade too heartily. "How are things?"

"We, um, got your message, Frans," John said, not sure if Carlo was monitoring the conversation. "Sandoz is taking care of it." He coughed and looked up. Danny was making "Go on" motions. "Listen, Frans, have you tried any of that *yasapa* brandy yet?"

"How'd you find out about that?" Frans asked warily.

"Lucky guess. Had a taste yet?"

"No."

"Well, Danny Iron Horse thinks this might be a very good time to give it a try, okay?" John suggested. "Feel free to tell the boss what you think."

"Beauty," Danny said, when John signed off. "Now: wait ten minutes." It took five.

"Nice to hear from you, Gianni," Carlo began affably. "I should like to speak to Iron Horse, if you please." John stood up and waved Danny into the console chair with a look that said, You're on your own.

"Evening, Carlo," Danny said sociably, and waited.

"Business is business," Carlo said, by way of truncated explanation. "No hard feelings?"

"Hell, no. This is all going to shake out fine," Danny said confidently. "The question is, Do you want to discuss terms with me now? Or would you like to try your luck with Sofia Mendes again? I should mention that I've had a little talk with her, and she seems to feel you've misrepresented a few facts when you made that last deal with her. She sounded kind of pissed off." Countable seconds went by, marked by the gradual dawn of understanding that had begun to light up John Candotti's face. "Or you could come on back down to Rakhat and deal directly with the Runa," Danny suggested helpfully, when Carlo failed to respond. "Just keep that anaphylaxis kit handy. Course, you'll have to hope you can explain to some Runao how to use it, because we won't be around to help you. Your call, ace."

The silence from the *Bruno* didn't last long. "And your terms are?" Carlo asked with admirable dignity, given that he could probably hear the small, blissful noises John was making.

"You off-load all your trade goods here in the N'Jarr valley," Danny began, "and don't try to bullshit me, because I've read the manifests. We keep the manned lander and all its fuel—"

"The lander cost a fortune!" Carlo protested.

"Yeah, but by the time you get back to Earth, that plane'll be older than most second wives," Danny pointed out as John began to do a little victory dance featuring Italian gestures aimed at a position in the sky somewhere above the 32nd parallel. "Now, then," Danny continued, "our cut will be one hundred percent of the coffee trade, but we'll broker the rest for you—"

"What guarantee do I have that you won't keep the drone after I send the last shipment down?" Carlo asked suspiciously. "You could leave me with a half-empty hold."

"Which is exactly what you deserve, you miserable SOB," John sang joyously, wiping tears from his eyes.

"I guess you're just going to have to trust me, ace," said Danny, stretching his long legs out luxuriously and settling in for what promised to be a very satisfying day's work. "But if you think you can get a better deal from somebody else . . ."

Carlo didn't, and negotiations began in earnest.

"ARE YOU SERIOUS?" EMILIO CRIED DAYS LATER, AS TIYAT AND KAJPIN shuffled off with Nico to find something to eat. "Danny, the reservations were a disaster for the Indians—"

"Sandoz, this is not the United States," the Canadian said firmly, "and we are not the BIA, and we have the benefit of hindsight—"

"And a reservation is better than extinction," Joseba pointed out with chilling accuracy. "I estimate that even an increase of ten additional deaths a year over present rates could kill the Jana'ata off in a couple of generations. If you have to choose between apartheid and genocide—"

"And Danny knows all the ways a reservation system can be awful," John started, "so he can—"

"Desperate measures for desperate times," Sean was saying. "And as much as I hate partition, it's a way to stop the killin'. Gives people time to get over their grudges, or at least stop accumulating new ones—"

"Wait, wait, wait!" Emilio begged, his mind so fogged by fatigue that he found himself wishing they'd speak Spanish—a sure sign of exhaustion. Countless hours on a treadmill had prepared him to some extent for the month he had just spent on the road, but he was wrung out from seeing Sofia again, and hadn't reckoned on being mobbed by men full of news and anxious for his approval the moment he came within sight. "All right," he said finally, deciding he could manage another few minutes of this. "Tell me again . . . ?"

"I see this as politically independent territory," said Danny. "The Jana'ata are already isolated up here—it's just a matter of getting the government in the south to formalize the situation! And Suukmel thinks this may be a workable solution. She's convinced Shetri, and they're off trying to get Athaansi's faction on board."

Who the hell is Athaansi? Emilio wondered dully. He probably looked like shit, but then again, he always looked like shit, so nobody was attaching much significance to it. "Have you spoken to Sofia about this?"

"Of course!" said John, his happiness still barely containable. "We talked to her a few days ago. It's not like we were sitting here sucking our thumbs while you were gone—"

"She said she'd float the idea," said Danny, "but it'll be up to the Runa Parliament in Gayjur. It's going to take time, but—"

"The problem right now," Joseba said, "is getting the word out so the VaN'Jarri know that the army's turned back and it's safe to come home. We should have set up some kind of signal for that, but nobody thought of it."

Nico arrived with two mess plates of food from the lander. "Don Emilio," he interjected quietly, "I think you should sit down. Are you hungry?" Sandoz shook his head at the question, but sat on a stool.

"—going to rebuild their numbers, they'll need food," Joseba was saying, "and plenty of it, but that central plains region is a meat factory, and perhaps the Runa would be willing to provide game in exchange for coffee or something. Eventually we'll find something new to domesticate." He didn't even notice that he'd begun to think in terms of "we." "The Jana'ata think kha'ani could be bred to lay eggs all year round—"

"In the meantime," John said, "we go out and shoot something big every so often—"

"I can help with hunting," Nico offered, not fully understanding what was being discussed, but content to be of service to Don Emilio and the priests, now that Carlo was going to desert them.

"Ah, I'm sure y'could, Nico," Sean said, "but you and Sandoz'll be goin' home after all."

Nico's mouth dropped open, and an expectant hush fell. Sandoz looked at Sean sharply, then stood and walked a few steps away. When he turned, his face was unreadable. "It's a long walk back to Naples, Sean."

"Well, it would be, ace, but we already booked you passage home with Carlo," said Danny. "We got him to agree to wait a while before he goes back. You'll be on the drone with the last shipment of trade goods from Rakhat."

John was grinning. "We arranged for Frans to sample a little of the yasapa shampoo. All of a sudden, Carlo decided to reconsider his business arrangements. It was amazing, Emilio. Danny cut the VaN'Jarri a beautiful deal—"

Resilience now utterly gone, Sandoz shook his head. "No," he said flatly. "Nico can go back, but I gave my word. I told Sofia that I'd stand surety for the Jana'ata—"

"Christ, she told us," Sean said. "Now there's a woman who'd feel at home in Belfast! She's a wee hard bitch, but y'can do a deal with her, if she gets what she wants. I'll be the goat, Sandoz. You go home and see if y'can find that sweet Gina and her Celestina."

It was Danny who broke the silence. "You're done here, ace," he said quietly. "We got this covered."

"But there's more," John added excitedly. "Rukuei wants to go back to Earth with you—"

"I tried to talk him out of it," Joseba said. "They need all the breeding pairs they can get, but it turns out he was neutered, so—"

Sandoz frowned, now thoroughly confused. "But why does he want . . . ?"

"Why not?" Sean shrugged, unsurprised by yet another example of wayward sentient willfulness. "He says he needs t'see Earth with his own eyes."

It was all too much. *"No puedo pensar,"* Emilio muttered. Pulling his eyes wide open, he shook his head. "I've *got* to get some sleep."

WAITING FOR SANDOZ IN THE FOREIGNERS' HUT, RUKUEI KITHERI PACED and paced, helpless against imagination, burdened with possibility, like a pregnant woman who cannot know what she carries within her.

"Go back with them," Isaac had told him. And Rukuei heard in those words an echo of his own yearning.

He feared that Sandoz would refuse him this. All of the foreigners had argued against it, and Sandoz more than anyone had reason to hate the Jana'ata. But everything was different now, and for days, Rukuei had planned the plea he would make to a man he hardly knew and barely hoped to understand.

He would tell the foreigner: I have learned that poetry requires a certain emptiness, as the sounding of a bell requires the space within it. The emptiness of my father's early life provided the resonance for his songs. I have felt in my heart his restlessness and lurking ambition. I have felt in my own body the violent exuberance, the almost sexual exultation of creation.

He would tell the foreigner: I have learned that a soul's emptiness can become a place where Truth will dwell—even if it is not made welcome, even when Truth is reviled and fought, doubted and misunderstood and resisted.

He would tell the foreigner: My own hollowed heart has made a space for others' pain, but I believe there is more—some larger Truth we are all heir to, and I want to be filled with it!

He heard the footsteps then, saw Sandoz rounding the corner of the hut, followed by the others, talking among themselves. Blocking the foreigner's way into the hut, turning swiftly, Rukuei swept out a circular swath of pebbly dirt. "Hear me, Sandoz," he began, throwing back his head in a gesture that offered battle. "I wish to go back with you to H'earth. I wish to learn your poetry and, perhaps, to teach you ours—"

He stopped, seeing the color leave Sandoz's face.

"Don Emilio needs rest," Nico said firmly. "You can talk tomorrow."

"I'm fine," Sandoz said, not that anyone had inquired. "I'm fine," he said again. Then his knees buckled.

"Is that normal?" Kajpin asked, sauntering over with a bowl of twigs, just as Sandoz hit the ground. The foreigners just stood there gawking, so she sat down to eat. After a while, she told them, "We usually lie down before we fall asleep." Which seemed to wake everyone but Sandoz up.

THE FAINT SEGUED SEAMLESSLY INTO A SLEEP THAT WAS VERY NEARLY coma, as he began to pay the toll extracted by weeks on the road, months of strain, years of bewilderment and pain. He slept through the day and into the night, and when he opened his eyes, it was to starlit darkness.

His first thought was, How odd—I've never dreamed of music before. Then, listening, he knew that what he heard was real, not dreamt, and that he'd never heard its like—not on Rakhat, not on Earth.

He rose soundlessly, stepping over and around the sleeping forms of Nico and the priests. Emerging from the hut into still night air, he picked his way between stone walls glowing with moonlight and the shimmer of the Milky Way. As if drawn by a thread, he followed the uncanny sound to the very edge of the village, where he found a ragged tent.

Isaac was inside, bent almost double over an antique computer tablet, his face in profile rapt: transfigured by a wordless harmony, as delicate as snowflakes and as mathematically precise, but of astonishing power, at once shattering and sublime. It was, Emilio Sandoz thought, as though "the stars of morning rang out in unison," and when the music ended, he wanted nothing more in all the world than to hear it once again—

"Don't interrupt. That's the rule," Isaac said abruptly, his voice in the quiet night as loud and flat and unmodulated as the music had been softly nuanced and chastely melodious. "The Runa drive me crazy."

"Yes," Emilio offered when Isaac fell silent. "They drove me crazy sometimes, too."

Isaac did not care. "Every autistic is an experiment," he announced in his blank and blaring voice. "Nobody like me exists anywhere else." He watched his fingers' patterning for a while but then glanced briefly at Sandoz.

Not knowing what else to say, Emilio asked, "Are you lonely, Isaac?"

"No. I am who I am." The answer was firm if unemotional. "I can't be lonely any more than I can have a tail." Isaac began to tap his fingers on the smooth place above his beard. "I know why humans came here," he said. "You came because of the music."

The tapping slowed and then stopped. "Yes, we did," Emilio confirmed, falling into Isaac's pattern: a burst of talk, perhaps three seconds long, then a silence of thirty seconds before the next burst. A longer pause meant, Your turn. "We came because of Hlavin Kitheri's songs."

"Not those songs." The tapping started again. "I can remember an entire DNA sequence as music. Do you understand?"

No, Emilio thought, feeling stupid. "You are a savant, then," he suggested, trying to follow this.

Isaac reached up and began to pull a coil of hair straight, over and over, running the tangled rope through his fingers. "Music is how I think," he said finally.

"Then this music is one of your compositions? It is—" Emilio hesitated. "It is glorious, Isaac."

"I didn't compose it. I discovered it." Isaac turned and, with evident difficulty, looked for a full second into Emilio's eyes before breaking contact. "Adenine, cytosine, guanine, thymine: four bases." A pause. "I gave the four bases three notes each, one for each species. Twelve tones."

There was a longer silence, and Emilio realized that he was supposed to draw a conclusion. Out of his depth, he guessed, "So this music is how you think about DNA?"

The words came in a rush. "It's DNA for humans and for Jana'ata and Runa. Played together." Isaac stopped, gathering himself. "A lot of it is dissonant." A pause. "I remembered the parts that harmonize." A pause. "Don't you understand?" Isaac demanded, taking stunned silence for obtuseness. "It's God's music. You came here so I would find it." He said this without embarrassment or pride or wonder. It was, in Isaac's view, a simple fact. "I thought God was just a story Ha'anala liked," he said. "But this music was waiting for me."

The lock of hair stretched and recoiled, over and over. "It's no good unless you have all three sequences." Again: the glancing look. Blue eyes, so like Jimmy's. "No one else could have found this. Only me," Isaac said, flat-voiced and insistent. "Do you understand now?"

Dazed, Emilio thought, God was in this place, and I—I did not know it. "Yes," he said after a time. "I think I understand now. Thank you."

There was a kind of numbness. Not the ecstasy, not the oceanic serenity he had once known, a lifetime ago. Just: numbness. When he could speak again, he asked, "May I share this music with others, Isaac?"

"Sure. That's the point." Isaac yawned and handed Emilio the tablet. "Be careful with it," he said.

LEAVING ISAAC'S TENT, HE STOOD ALONE FOR A WHILE, EYES ON THE sky. The weather on Rakhat was notoriously changeable and the Milky Way was rapidly losing custody of the night to clouds, but he knew that when it was clear, he could look up and, without effort, recognize familiar patterns. Orion, Ursa major, Ursa minor, the Pleiades: arbitrary shapes imposed on random points of light.

"The stars look the same!" he'd exclaimed years earlier, standing with Isaac's father, seeing Rakhat's night sky for the first time. "How can all the constellations be the same?"

"It's a big galaxy in a big universe," the young astronomer had told him, smiling at the linguist's ignorance. "Four point three light-years aren't enough to make any difference in how we see the stars back on Earth and here. You'd have to go a lot farther than this to change your perspective."

No, Jimmy, Emilio Sandoz now thought, gazing upward. This was far enough.

Like father, like son, he thought then, realizing that Jimmy Quinn had, like his extraordinary child, discovered an unearthly music that changed one's perspective. He was pleased by that, and grateful.

• • •

EMILIO WOKE JOHN FIRST, AND LED HIM A LITTLE DISTANCE AWAY FROM the settlement to a place where they could listen to the music alone; where they could speak in privacy, where Emilio could study his friend's face as he listened and see his own astonishment and awe mirrored.

"My God," John breathed, when the last notes faded. "Then this was why . . ."

"Maybe," Emilio said. "I don't know. Yes. I think so." *Ex corde volo*, he thought. From my heart, I wish it . . .

They listened again to the music, and then for a time to the night noise of Rakhat, so like that of home: wind in the scrub, tiny chitterings and scratchings in nearby weeds, distant hoots, hushed wingbeats overhead.

"There was a poem I found—years ago, just after Jimmy Quinn intercepted that first fragment of music from Rakhat," said Emilio. " 'In all the shrouded heavens anywhere / Not a whisper in the air / Of any living voice but one so far / That I can hear it only as a bar / Of lost, imperial music.' "

"Yes," John said quietly. "Perfect. Who wrote that?"

"Edward Arlington Robinson," Emilio told him, and added, " 'Credo.' "

"Credo: I believe," John repeated, smiling. Clear-eyed and clear-souled, he leaned back, hands locked around a knee. "Tell me, Dr. Sandoz," he asked, "is that the name of the poem, or a statement of faith?"

Emilio looked down, silvered hair spilling over his eyes as he laughed a little and shook his head. "God help me," he said at last. "I'm afraid . . . I think . . . it might be both."

"Good," said John. "I'm glad to hear that."

They were quiet for a time, alone with their thoughts, but then John sat up straight, struck by a thought. "There's a passage in Exodus—God tells Moses, 'No one can see My face, but I will protect you with My hand until I have passed by you, and then I will remove My hand and you will see My back.' Remember that?"

Emilio nodded, listening.

"Well, I always thought that was a physical metaphor," John said, "but, you know—I wonder now if it isn't really about time? Maybe that was God's way of telling us that we can never know His intentions, but as time goes on . . . we'll understand. We'll see where He was: we'll see His back."

Emilio gazed at him, face still. "The brother of my heart," he said at last. "Without you, where would I be now?"

John smiled, his affection plain. "Dead drunk in a bar someplace?" he suggested.

"Or just plain dead." Emilio looked away, blinking. When he could speak again, his voice was steady. "Your friendship should have been proof enough of God. Thank you, John. For everything."

John nodded once and then again, as though confirming something. "I'll go wake the other guys up," he said.

Coda

Earth: 2096

ONCE AGAIN RADIO WAVES CARRIED MUSIC FROM RAKHAT TO EARTH, and once again Emilio Sandoz was preceded by news that would change his life.

Long before he arrived home, reaction to the DNA music had rigidified. Believers found it a miraculous confirmation of God's existence and evidence of Divine Providence. Skeptics declared it a fraud—a clever trick by the Jesuits to distract attention from their earlier failures. Atheists did not dispute the music's authenticity, but they considered it just another fluke that proved nothing—like the universe itself. Agnostics admitted the music was magnificent, but suspended judgment, waiting for who knew what?

The pattern was established at Sinai and under the Buddha's tree; on Calvary and at Mecca; in sacred caves, at wells of life, amid circles of stone. Signs and wonders are always doubted, and perhaps they are meant to be. In the absence of certainty, faith is more than mere opinion; it is hope.

Emilio himself had read once of a savant in Lesotho who had memorized every street in every city in Africa. If such a person made names into notes, would he have found harmony in addresses? Perhaps—given enough material and enough time and nothing better to do. And if that happened, Emilio asked himself on the long voyage home, would the music be any less beautiful?

He was a linguist, after all, and it seemed entirely possible to him that religion and literature and art and music were all merely side effects of a brain structure that comes into the world ready to make language out of noise, sense out of chaos. Our capacity for imposing meaning, he thought, is programmed to unfold the way a butterfly's wings unfold when it escapes the chrysalis, ready to fly. We are biologically driven to create meaning. And if that's so, he asked himself, is the miracle diminished?

It was then that he came very close to prayer. Whatever the truth is, he thought, blessed be the truth.

The *Giordano Bruno* was nearly halfway home when Nico noticed that Don Emilio's nightmares had ended.

WITH ONLY SIX MONTHS OF SUBJECTIVE TIME BEFORE THEIR ARRIVAL ON Earth, Emilio Sandoz concentrated on the task at hand: teaching Rukuei English, trying to prepare the poet for what might await him. It helped to worry about someone else, to put his own experience to work in Rukuei's behalf. Suspended in time, Emilio refused to listen to the transmissions from Rakhat that Frans intercepted, ignored the responses from Earth. It will be well, he told himself, and let the universe take care of itself while he took care of one apt and eager student. So when Frans Vanderhelst finally docked the *Bruno* at the Shimatsu Orbital Hotel high above the Pacific, Emilio Sandoz was, in many ways, a man at peace. He was, therefore, completely unprepared for his reaction to a letter that had been waiting for him nearly four decades.

Handwritten on a fine rag paper, selected because it would not crumble during his anticipated absence from Earth, the note read: "I am so very sorry, Emilio. I will not stoop to the scoundrel's defense—that I had no other choice. I was simply acting on the principle that it is easier to beg forgiveness than to ask permission. Because I trust in God, I trust also that you will have learned something of value on your journey. *Pax Christi*. Vince Giuliani."

The middle-aged Jesuit who handed Sandoz the note did not know its contents, but he knew its author and the circumstances under which it was written, so he could take a pretty good guess at what that long-dead Father General must have said.

"One last jerk on the chain, you goddamned sonofa*bitch*!" Sandoz cried, confirming the priest's hypothesis. The rest of the commentary was heartfelt and in a splendid assortment of languages. When Sandoz was done, and he did not finish quickly, he stood in the curving air lock, the letter in one braced hand, arms at his sides, limp with exasperation. "Who the hell are you?" he demanded in English.

"Patras Yalamber Tamang," the priest replied, and continued in excellent Spanish. "I'm from the Nepal province, but I taught at El Instituto San Pedro Arrupe in Colombia until recently. I have been the Rakhat mission liaison for the last five years, working with governments and international agencies and a number of sponsoring corporations to coordinate the reception for Mr. Kitheri. And, of course, the Society would like to offer you yourself any assistance you are willing to accept from us."

Still fuming, Sandoz nevertheless listened to Tamang's summary of the steps that had been taken to make Rukuei comfortable, and to ease the return of Sandoz and the crew of the *Giordano Bruno*. The hotel staff consisted of carefully chosen, highly trained volunteers who'd studied the history of the Jesuit missions and who all spoke at least some K'San. A medical team was standing by; the travelers would be isolated for some months, but the entire hotel had been booked for them and the facilities were quite nice and very extensive. There was a customized suite set aside for Frans Vanderhelst in the center of the hotel, near the microgravity stadium, where he would be able to breathe without strain. Endocrine experts were waiting to examine him; they had some hope of reversing the genetic damage that had unbalanced his metabolism. Carlo Giuliani's cargo had, of course, been impounded, pending customs decisions. Giuliani himself was being detained—there were complex legal issues to be settled, not the least of which was whether Sandoz wished to file charges regarding his abduction. Signor Giuliani's elderly sister had been notified of his return, but seemed in no hurry to provide him with legal representation.

The accumulated news from Rakhat was mixed. Athaansi Laaks had been overthrown, but his faction still refused to agree to the reservation solution; Danny Iron Horse sympathized, but continued to press for negotiations. Some kind of illness swept through the N'Jarr in 2084 but, by that time, the Jana'ata were better fed and the toll wasn't as high as everyone first feared it would be. John Candotti had written of Sofia's death. Shetri Laaks was well, and had remarried. Two more sons had joined the one Emilio had delivered—now a young man with a child of his own. Shetri's second wife was pregnant again; they hoped for a third daughter. Sean's latest census of the Jana'ata reported a population of nearly twenty-six hundred souls. Joseba added an analysis indicating that if birth and death rates and other conditions held steady, this was enough for stability. Some forty Runa had joined the VaN'Jarri in the year of the census. These did not quite balance the number of old VaN'Jarri Runa who had died, but it was a slight increase over the inflow from prior years.

"And Suukmel still lives?" Emilio asked, knowing this would be Rukuei's first question.

"Yes," said Patras, "as of four years ago, at least."

"And the music? On Rakhat?"

"There are disputes over adding lyrics to it," Patras told him. "I suppose that was inevitable."

"Has anyone asked Isaac what he thinks about that?"

"Yes. He said, 'That's Rukuei's problem.' Isaac is studying library files on South American nematodes now," Patras reported dryly. "Nobody has the faintest idea why."

Sandoz asked more questions, received thorough answers, and agreed that it sounded as though everything was under control.

"Thank you," Patras said, gratified by the recognition. He had, in fact, worked himself to exhaustion trying to make things right. "Let me show you the rooms we've prepared for Mr. Kitheri," he suggested, and led the way down a toroidal accessway. "As soon as you've gotten some rest, the Mother General would like to speak with you—"

"Excuse me?" Sandoz said, coming to a halt. "The *Mother* General?" He snorted. "You're joking!"

Patras, already a few steps down the hall, turned back, brows up curiously: Is there a problem? Sandoz stared at him, dumbfounded.

"Well, yes, as a matter of fact, I am joking," Patras said then, delighted when Sandoz burst into laughter.

"You know, it's not nice to tease old people," Emilio told him as they resumed their walk. "How long have you been waiting to use that line?"

"Fifteen years. I have a Ph.D. from Ganesh Man Singh University— mission history, with an emphasis on Rakhat. You were my thesis topic."

For the next few hours, they concentrated on the process of introducing Rukuei to new companions and new surroundings. In the press of duties, personal considerations were laid aside, but before the end of that long first day, Emilio Sandoz said to Patras Yalamber Tamang, "There was a woman—"

Inquiries followed; databases were searched. She had, evidently, remarried, changed her surname; had shunned publicity and lived as private a life as wealth could buy and guilt enforce. It was remarkably difficult to find even a minimal actuarial mention of her.

"I am so very sorry," Patras told him weeks later. "She passed away last year."

ARIANA FIORE HAD ALWAYS ENJOYED THE DAY OF THE DEAD. SHE LIKED the cemetery, tidy and rectilinear, with its stone paths freshly swept between rows and rows of high-walled burial niches—an island of grace amid the noise of Naples. The vaults themselves, stacked six high, were always brushed and dustless on November first, golden in autumnal sunlight or gleaming in silvery rain. She was an archaeologist, accustomed to the presence of the dead, and savored this orderliness, taking pleasure in the sharp scent of chrysanthemums mingling with the deeper musk of fallen leaves.

Some of the loculi were simple: a polished brass plaque with a name and dates, the tiny luminos kept burning for a time after the death. The proud and the prosperous often added a small screen that could be activated with a touch, and she'd have liked to go from vault to vault, meeting the inhabitants, hearing about their lives, but resisted the impulse.

All around her, there were low voices and the crunch of footsteps on gravel paths. *"Poveretto,"* she heard now and then, as flowers were placed with a sigh in a loculo's little vase. Old affections, grudges, attachments and debts were silently acknowledged and then put aside for another year. Adults gossiped, children fidgeted. There was a sense of occasion and a formality that appealed to Ariana, but the cemetery was not a scene of active grief.

Which is why she noticed the man sitting on the bench in front of Gina's vault, gloved hands limp in his lap. Alone among the mourners on this cool and sunny day, he was crying, eyes open, silent tears slipping down a still face.

She had no wish to impose herself on this stranger, had not even been certain that he would come today. His first months out of isolation were a circus, a whirlwind of public interest and private receptions—every moment accounted for. Ariana had waited a long time, but she was patient by nature. And now: here he was.

"Padre?" she said, soft-voiced and certain.

Solitary in sorrow, he hardly glanced at her. "I am not a priest, madam," he said as dryly as a crying man could, "and I am no one's father."

"Look again," she said.

He did, and saw a dark-haired woman standing behind a baby stroller, her son so young that he still slept curled, in memory of the womb. There was a long silence as Emilio studied her face—blurred and shifting in the dampness—a complex amalgam of the Old World and the New, the living and the dead. He laughed once, and sobbed once, and laughed again, astonished. "You have your mother's smile," he said finally, and her grin widened. "And my nose, I'm afraid. Sorry about that."

"I like my nose!" she cried indignantly. "I have your eyes, too. Mamma always told me that when I got angry: You have your father's eyes!"

He laughed again, not quite sure how to feel about that. "Were you angry a lot?"

"No. I don't think so. Well, I have my moods, I suppose." She drew herself up formally and said, "I am Ariana Fiore. You *are* Emilio Sandoz, I presume?"

He was really laughing now, the tears forgotten. "I can't believe it," he said, shaking his head. "I can't *believe* it!" He looked around, dazed, and then moved over on the bench and said, "Please, sit down. Do you come here often? Listen to me! I sound like I'm trying to pick you up in a bar! Do they still have bars?"

They talked and talked, as the afternoon light washed their faces with gold, Ariana filling him in on the barest outlines of the years of his absence. "Celestina's the chief set designer at the Teatro San Carlo," she told him. "She's been married four times so far—"

"Four? My God!" he said, eyes wide. "Has it ever occurred to her that she should rent, not buy?"

"That is exactly what I told her!" Ariana cried, feeling as though she had known this man all her life. "To be honest," she said, "I think perhaps—"

"She leaves them before they can leave her," he suggested.

Ariana grimaced, but then confided, "Honestly—she is such a drama queen! I swear she gets married because she likes the weddings. You should see the parties she throws! You probably will, before long—she's on tour with the opera company right now, and that's usually bad news for her current husband. Now, when Giampaolo and I got married, we had five friends and the magistrate—but we really earned the party we had for our tenth anniversary last year!"

Roused by the talk and the laughter, the baby stretched and whimpered. They both watched, quiet and in suspense. When it seemed likely that the child would not awaken, Ariana spoke again, very softly now. "I finally got pregnant just after Mamma died. You know what we say at New Year's?"

"*Buon fine, buon principio,*" he said. "A good end, a good beginning."

"Yes. I was hoping for a girl. I thought it would be as though Mamma had come back, somehow." She smiled and shrugged, and reached out to touch the baby's plump and downy cheek. "His name is Tommaso."

"How did your mother die?" he asked at last.

"Well, you know she was a nurse. After I started school, she went back to work. You left us very well provided for, but she wanted to be of use." Emilio nodded, face still. "Anyway, there was an epidemic—they still haven't isolated the pathogen—it's all over the world now. For some reason, older women were hit hardest. They called it the Nonna Disease here in Naples because it killed so many grandmothers. The last coherent thing Mamma said was, 'God's got a lot of explaining to do.' "

Emilio wiped his eyes on his coat sleeve and laughed. "That sounds like Gina."

For a long while, they did not speak but only listened to the birdsong and the conversations around them. "Of course," Ariana said as though no time had passed, "God never explains. When life breaks your heart, you're just supposed to pick up the pieces and start over, I guess."

She glanced down at Tommaso, sleeping in his stroller. Needing the comfort of his warm, little body, she leaned over and lifted him carefully, one hand behind his peach-fuzz head, the other under his little bottom. After a time, she smiled at her father and asked, "Would you like to hold your grandson?"

Kids and babies, he thought. Don't do this to me again.

But there was no way to resist. He looked at this undreamt-of daughter and at her tiny child—frowning and milky in dreamless sleep—and found room in the crowded necropolis of his heart.

"Yes," he said finally, amazed and resigned and somehow content. "Yes. I would like that very much."

Acknowledgments

ONCE AGAIN, I WOULD LIKE TO MAKE KNOWN A FEW OF MY SOURCES. John Candotti's insight into Exodus 33:17–23 is from the Chatam Sofer (quoted in *Sparks Beneath the Surface*, by Lawrence Kushner). The geneticist Susumu Ohno has, in real life, converted the genetic code for slime mold and mice into musical notation; the results reportedly resemble something by Bach, although harmony has yet to be discovered in the sequences. The extraordinary autobiographies of Temple Grandin and Donna Williams were windows into autism, as was a searingly honest and beautiful book, *The Siege*, by Clara Claiborne Park. The poem whose refrain is "The meat defiant . . ." is "Counterattack," by Wladyslaw Szlengel, quoted in *I Remember Nothing More*, by Adina Blady Szwajger. Sean Fein and I learned all our chemistry from Bettye Kaplan and from *Water, Ice and Stone*, by Bill Green, whose prose is as translucently beautiful as the Antarctic lakes he studies. Two songs were often on my mind as I wrote: Robbie Robertson's "Testimony" and Richard Strauss's "Beim Schlafengehn."

Maura Kirby was there at the conception of this book. Kate Sweeney and Jennifer Tucker helped me on a daily basis during its gestation and stood by me during the long labor to bring it forth; they have both taught me a great deal about the ferocity of the artist. Mary Dewing not only taught me to write, she also taught me (and Nico) to appreciate opera.

David Kennedy, Aitor Esteban and Roberto Marino helped with details of Belfastian English, Euskara and Neapolitan Italian, respectively. My initial reaction to criticism is always to hide behind the furnace and suck my thumb; nevertheless, the following people told me what I needed to know about early versions of this book, and each of them showed me ways to improve it: Ray Bucko, S.J.; Miriam Goderich; Tomasz and Maria Rybak; Vivian Singer; Marty Connell, S.J.; Ellie D'Addio; Richard Doria, Sr.; Louise Dewing Doria; Rod Tulonen; Ken Foster; Kathie Colonnese; Paula Sanch; Judith Roth; Leslie Turek; Delia Sherman; and Kevin Ballard, S.J. One of the great and enduring benefits of having written *The Sparrow* has been the friendship offered me by many members of the Society of Jesus; I hope they will forgive me for the kidnapping in this book. Vince Giuliani and I knew it was a lousy thing to do, but we just couldn't think of any other way to get Emilio to go back to Rakhat!

No one could ask for an agent more resourceful and canny than Jane Dystel, and I am so glad that her associate Miriam Goderich finally talked her into taking a look at *The Sparrow*! Leona Nevler and David Rosenthal took the initial leap of faith that made this book and *The Sparrow* possible, and I will always be grateful to them. The staff at Villard and Ballantine have been uniformly wonderful, but special thanks go to Brian McLendon, whose skill as a publicist is matched by his humor and good sense, and to Marysue Rucci, who accomplished a seamless editorial transition, and to Dennis Ambrose for his cheerful patience with my last-minute changes. Thanks also to the salespeople at Random House and in bookstores, who hand-sold *The Sparrow*, and to the many readers who were kind enough to tell me that they were glad I quit anthro and took a flier at fiction. I know how much I owe you all, and I hope *Children of God* lived up to your expectations.

Finally, immeasurable love and gratitude to Don and Daniel, my very best husband and my very best son, whose support and affection and patience and laughter nourish my soul. Thanks, guys.

M . D . R

Children of God

MARY DORIA RUSSELL

A Reader's Guide

A Conversation with Mary Doria Russell

Q: How would you describe the themes in this book?

MDR: *The Sparrow* was about the role of religion in the lives of many
      people, from atheist to mystic, and about the role of religion in
      history, from the Age of Discovery to the Space Age. I suppose
      that *Children of God* is about the aftermath of irreversible
      tragedy, about the many ways that we struggle to make sense of
      tragedy. It's about the stories we tell ourselves, and the ways we
      justify our decisions, to bring ourselves to some kind of peace.
      And I guess it's about the way time reveals significance, strips
      away self-serving excuses, lays truth bare, and both blunts pain
      and sharpens insight.

Q: **In describing your reasons for writing a sequel, you were
      quoted as saying, "I left my main character impaled on the
      horns of a dilemma, and I wasn't able to let it go at that."
      What was the dilemma to which you were referring?**

MDR: Well, Emilio articulates this at the end of *The Sparrow* and in
      the Prelude to this book: If he accepts that the spiritual beau-
      ty and the religious rapture he experienced were real and true,
      then all the rest of it—the violence, the deaths, the maiming,
      the assaults, the humiliations—all that was God's will, too.
      Either God is vicious—deliberately causing evil or at least
      allowing it to happen—or Emilio is a deluded ape who's taken
      a lot of old folktales far too seriously. That may not be good
      theology, but at the beginning of *Children of God,* Emilio
      believes those are his only choices: bitterness or atheism,
      hatred or absurdity.

Q: **How is that dilemma resolved in *Children of God*?**

MDR: About a millennium ago, Maimonides wrote that whenever
      anything in the universe strikes us as stupid, or ugly, or absurd,
      it's because our breadth of knowledge is too narrow and our
      depth of understanding is too shallow for us to perceive God's
      intent. That was the theology I was drawing on in *Children of
      God.* To me, it meant that God works on a vast canvas, and He
      paints with time. It's only with hindsight, sometimes many
      generations after an event, that we see the significance of some
      tragedy or the importance of some obscure turning point in his-

tory. Or perhaps it just takes us that long to think up a convincing rationale for why things happened as they did, and then we ascribe it to Providence! Anyway, unlike those of us who live a normal life span, Emilio Sandoz's life span is almost tripled because of the contraction of time during the voyages to and from Rakhat. He is given the unique opportunity to see the outcome of events that seemed to be unredeemable when they happened.

Q: **Why did you choose *Children of God* as the title for this book?**

MDR: On one level, the title refers to the powerful notion that if we are all children of God, then we can become one family over time. It's very subversive, that idea—it undermines hierarchies, erodes aristocracies. It makes the discontent of the powerless and the rebellion of the disenfranchised sacred, because it implies that each soul is sovereign and of value. And it challenges its believers to build a world where the inequities of the past are less glaring and brutal. It doesn't matter if God is real or not—once the idea exists, it can change history. On another level, this book is about the revolutionary effect of children. The story begins with babies and ends with babies. There are babies born throughout the story. Even Cece the guinea pig has babies! There are children who are rejected, who are difficult to love, who are sure of their significance or ashamed of their heritage; there are children we get to know and others whose potential is only guessed at. Over time, each of them has some role to play in this unfolding drama, and on that level, the title implies that they are children of destiny, children whom God needed to complete the creation of the world He has in mind.

Q: ***The Sparrow* received lavish praise, won numerous awards, and is still selling steadily and well. How much pressure does such success generate for you as a writer?**

MDR: A ton. A ton of pressure! Now, I put most of the pressure on myself, and did so long before there was any hope that *The Sparrow* would ever be published. But I admit that I was terrified of getting reviews that started out, "What a disappointment after such a promising debut . . ." So the reaction to *Children of God,* particularly from readers, has been a great relief. Personally, I like *The Sparrow* better than the sequel, but that's evidently a minority view. I get a lot of mail, and about 80 percent of the people who write liked the second book better, as did a startling number of critics. In some ways, that's scary because I don't know what I did differently that made most people like the sequel more. Maybe it's the sense of closure—*The Sparrow* left you hanging. *Children of God* has a more peaceful ending.

Q: **What's the toughest thing about writing a sequel?**

MDR: I thought of *Children of God* as the second half of one big book. So the hard part was harmonizing the plots, letting the characters change but in ways that were consistent with who they were in *The Sparrow.*

Q: **Novelists frequently describe how their characters take on a life of their own, moving the story line in entirely unexpected directions. Were there any similar surprises for you as you wrote *Children of God*?**

MDR: Well, Sean Fein kind of walked into my head and started kicking butt. He was a real surprise to me, and he turned out to be just what Emilio needed. Shetri Laaks was great fun—he showed up late in the book, but he had such a strong individual voice, and he kept making me laugh. But I'd have to say that the most striking example of characters taking over was in *The Sparrow.* I practically made Sofia Mendes for Emilio—I was just throwing them together and I had this whole scene in my mind where Sofia would go to Emilio and say, "Serve God. Love me!" And I had a big dramatic confrontation planned, except that Sofia turned around and said, "I would never do that. I'm not stupid—I know what he'd choose, and I'd never expose myself to that kind of rejection." I'm hearing her say this, right? And I'm mentally sputtering, "But, but, but—" when Sofia says, "On the other hand, Jimmy has grown up quite a bit . . ." I swear, my honest reaction was, "He's too tall for you!" I was just completely flummoxed by that turn of events, but Sofia was right. And Isaac was born! Just goes to show. . .

Q: **What do you think will be the most surprising to readers of this book?**

MDR: I hope that they'll be startled by how wrong they were about Supaari when they finished reading *The Sparrow*. I admit it: that was a set-up. I gave readers an opportunity to make the same mistakes about Supaari that people on Earth made about Emilio Sandoz when he first came back. Everything you knew about Supaari indicated that he was a decent, honorable man who was doing his best to cope with this wholly unprecedented situation—first contact with aliens. Then he gives Emilio to the Reshtar, and you think, "That scum-sucking social climber! That miserable, no good—" But you're just as wrong about Supaari as Johannes Voelker was about Emilio Sandoz.

Q: **Do you consider *Children of God* a darker story than *The Sparrow*?**

MDR: Yes—it's a long dark tunnel, but it ends in the light. In *The Sparrow*, I had Before and After. I had the leavening of the hope and plans and the anticipation of the mission to lighten up the story. But in *Children of God*, it's all After. Emilio is a very angry, very bitter man, and he's much harder to love, although Gina manages it. Many of the characters from the first story spend most of the sequel hardening their views, closing their minds, more and more seduced and comforted by certainty. There is a real difference in the mood of the two books. In *The Sparrow*, there are a lot of one-to-one conversations. People aren't really sure of what they think, and they're willing to reveal their confusion to a friend, in order to get help in sorting things out. In *Children of God*, there are an awful lot of people with their minds made up, and they know that if they exposed their reasoning and decisions to anyone the least bit objective, their private cover stories would be blown. They fear disclosure, and with good reason.

Q: **In *Children of God* Sandoz is kidnapped and dragged to Rakhat against his will. And yet, at the end of the story, he**

makes his peace with God and with his past experiences on Rakhat. Is one of the lessons here "the end justifies the means"?

MDR: No! A crime is a crime! The fact that the victim ultimately survives the experience and redeems it somehow does not reflect glory on the criminals for providing the victim with an opportunity to grow! Guiliani and the Pope and Danny Iron Horse are guilty of an act of utter moral bankruptcy, but each of them has managed to find a semi-plausible theological reason to justify their collusion. And they certainly aren't the first religious figures who undertake terrible deeds for high-minded reasons.

Q: **Do you use any real cultures as the basis of the civilization on Rakhat?**

MDR: In part, I had Romanov Russia in mind. A while ago, there was an exhibition of Faberge eggs at the Cleveland Museum of Art, and they were exquisite—just stunning, really. But even while I was admiring them, I thought, How many thousands of peasants' lives are represented by each of these eggs? How many human beings' bodies and souls were squandered in the accumulation of wealth by a single family, so that one man could give these things to his wife as Easter presents? I mean—there was a reason for the Russian revolution in 1917! The social injustices in pre-Revolutionary Russia were mindboggling. And yet, the high culture of Romanov Russia produced literature, art, music, and dance that have never been exceeded, and the culture that replaced it has been just as brutal with nothing artistic to show for its own bloodshed and injustice.

So, you can see the point here, I hope—the Runa revolution unquestionably ends an abusive and exploitative relationship with the Jana'ata, but at the cost of terrible suffering and of the brutalization of the Runa as well. And it's unclear what will replace that high culture. Even so, I meant to imply that the Runa are doing just fine, thank you. Here, I had in mind the invasion of North America by European settlers. That was unquestionably a catastrophe for the native peoples of this continent, but at the same time, it was the best damned thing that ever happened to an awful lot of immigrants from around the world. The analogy is to the fall of the Jana'ata and their replacement by the Runa—this is a catastrophe for the Jana'ata, but at the very same time, it's the best thing that ever happened to the Runa. And therein lies the tragedy.

Q: *Children of God* **uses parallel narratives to tell its story—that of Mendes and that of Sandoz—and also jumps backward and forward in time. As a writer, what's the hardest thing about moving between these different times and narrative lines?**

MDR: Trying to keep the reader oriented, and to make the jumps informative, not annoying! Chapter 21, where we listen to Danny and Suukmel's conversation, is probably the most difficult—I rewrote that chapter a dozen times trying to figure out how to encapsulate 20 years of Rakhati history as quickly and efficiently as possible. I tried a straight historical narrative, and that didn't work. I tried a lot of stuff, and ultimately the least bad solution to this narrative problem was to convey the information in a conversation between the two canniest political minds in the story. That way, in addition to describing the effects of the Kitheri revolution, I could peel back a few layers of those two characters as well. It wasn't a perfect solution, but it was the best I was able to come up with. Writing novels is not an easy game. Aside from that chapter, however, I was pretty pleased with how varying the timelines could be used to project a slanting light on events. I meant for Time itself to be, well, almost a character, in both *The Sparrow* and *Children of God*. I wanted to show how time changes perceptions, to demonstrate how little we understand things when we're in the midst of events, how much perspective the passage of time can bring.

Q: **By the end of *Children of God,* Sofia's son Isaac makes a discovery that gives certain meaning to the entire Rakhat venture. Does this meaning justify the suffering sparked by the mission to Rakhat?**

MDR: There is a simple message to be found in that music: You are more together than you are apart. Did anyone have to suffer or die for that message to be heard? No! (Just as an aside, the Buddha's message was heard and is heard, and he didn't have to be martyred to make his point!) Isaac might just as easily have become obsessed with DNA and music while living in a peaceable Runa village. The beauty of the harmonies he discovered would have been there for the hearing, the implications of the harmony would have been there to be interpreted, even without the revolutions that took place during the same years that Isaac was involved with the DNA music.

But there is such great power in a story—and I imagine that the Rakhati of both species would be drawn to any story that made sense of the upheavals and deaths and suffering and change. They too come into the world hardwired to hear noise and make language out of it! The stories of Genesis and Exodus are so powerful that they've been told for 3500 years among Jews and adopted by Christians and Muslims all over the world. Similar stories would probably take form and take root on Rakhat, and who knows what they would sound like a few millennia down the line? I'd be willing to bet that there would be at least three versions of the story!

Q: **Is there a moral to this story?**

MDR: Don't be so damned quick to judge! The less we know about someone, the easier we find it to make a snap decision, to condemn or sneer or believe the worst. The closer you get, the more you know about the person or the situation in question, the harder it gets to be sure of your opinion, so remember that, and try to cut people a little slack. Like Emilio says, "Everything we thought we understood—that was what we were most wrong about." So the moral of the story is to be suspicious of your own certainty. Doubt is good.

Steven Oppenheim created the reader's guide to *Children of God*.

Visit the Reader's Circle website at
www.thereaderscircle.com

Reading Group Questions
and Topics for Discussion

1. How have the unforeseen mistakes of the first visitors to Rakhat influenced the history of the planet? Are there any parallels from our history? What does this story say about the gap between intention and effect? What do you see as the themes of this story?

2. Russell has constructed *Children of God* using a three-tiered story line: Earth and its standard time; the ship, *Giordano Bruno*, and its Earth-relative time; and time on Rakhat. The story also contained two parallel narratives: that of Mendes and that of Sandoz. Do you think this make the story more interesting? Did you find it easy or difficult adjusting to the time jumps?

3. Russell never tells us what happened to the UN party that showed up at the end of *The Sparrow* and sent Emilio back to Earth. What do you think happened to them? Why does Russell leave the fate of the rescue party a mystery?

4. One reviewer describes the characters in this story as "rather too forgiving to be wholly human." Do you agree? If you were in Sandoz's shoes, would you be able to work with the people who kidnapped you?

5. At the end of the book Emilio Sandoz makes it very clear to Sofia that he can't forgive what was done to him. He is ashamed of that—he wishes he could, but he just can't let go of his hate. Do you think that will ever change for Sandoz? Sandoz also realizes that he can't hate the children of the men who harmed him, he can't hate the Jana'ata in general for what Supaari VaGayjur and Hlavan Kitheri and seventeen other men did to him. Is this a moral triumph for the former priest?

6. What price does Danny Iron Horse pay for agreeing to do what feels like a wrong for the right reason? Eventually Sandoz comes to understand the pressures Danny caved in to, but he never misses an opportunity to rake him over the coals for it. What sort of pressures was Danny subjected to? And how does Sandoz make him pay for his decision?

7. History and religious literature are both packed with examples indicated that God's favor brings not wealth and happiness, but agony and torture. How could Sandoz, a Jesuit priest inculcated with stories of martyred saints, feel so betrayed by God? Is there a difference between what happened to Sandoz and what happened to martyred saints throughout history?

8. Sofia has had all the same traumas as Emilio but unlike Emilio, she did not have sympathetic supporters to help her overcome what happened to her. How does she survive her experiences? How would you describe her reaction to the traumas she has suffered? Why does she become so blind to the suffering of the remaining Jana'ata?

9. In the Coda, Emilio muses that we come into the world hardwired to hear noise and make language, to see a chaos of color and find patterns, to experience random events and make a coherent life out of them. Is it possible that the idea of God is simply a manifestation of that biological drive to impose structure on sensory input?

10. How would you compare Children of God to the first Sandoz/Rakhat book, The Sparrow? Some reviewers consider Children of God a much darker story. Do you agree?

11. Even when he appears to be getting on with his life, Sandoz is caught in the larger machinations of a battle between Fate and Providence. Which do you think wins out in the end? Is there a clear winner? Does this novel provide the answers to Sandoz's questions about faith?

12. This story forces us to face the task of accepting the less theological and more ethical possibility that God may be merely an idea, yet one that still drives a people to live like children of God who place as much faith in a universal family as they do in the divine. Do you think God is merely an idea or does God really exist?

13. Beyond its determination to see Sandoz fulfill his destiny on Rakhat with or without his consent, why does the Church conspire to kidnap Sandoz and send him back to Rakhat? What purpose does this act serve? What would your reaction be if you were

in Sandoz's shoes? Does the result—Sandoz's reconnection with God and his coming to terms with what happened to him on the planet—justify his kidnapping? In other words, do the ends justify the means?

14. There were extraordinarily important children born because Emilio was on Rakhat, including Isaac, Ha'anala and Rukuei. So, whether it's Providence or dumb luck, Emilio was the catalyst for everything that happened on Rakhat in the generations that followed the first Jesuit mission. Do you think Emilio realizes this? Does this make the suffering he lived through worthwhile?

15. What do you think of Danny Iron Horse's plan to save the Jana'ata by establishing reservations? Do you think Danny's plan will work in the long run or will it be as disastrous as America's reservation system was for Native Americans?

16. Sandoz faces a dilemma at the end of *The Sparrow*. If he accepts the spiritual beauty and the religious rapture he experienced as real and true, then all the rest of it—the violence, the deaths, the maiming, the assaults, the humiliations—all that was God's will, too. Either God is vicious—deliberately causing evil or at least allowing it to happen—or Sandoz has been deluded. What do you think of the way Russell handled this dilemma in *Children of God*? What is the place of evil and pain in the world ruled by a benevolent God?

17. Isaac composes a song based on the DNA for humans, Jana'ata, and Runa. He says it is God's music. What do you think he means by that?

Excerpts from reviews of Mary Doria Russell's
Children of God

"Immensely satisfying . . . *Children of God* engages readers with Russell's provocative themes because it is a fine novel, with a compelling plot, intriguingly complex characters and enough poetry in the writing to convey the heartbreaking tragedy that even the best-intended actions can cause."

—*The Cleveland Plain Dealer*

"Even more ambitious in scope than *The Sparrow*, the sequel addresses issues of peace, justice and belief, handling complicated spiritual and moral questions with depth and sensitivity."

—*USA Today*

"[Russell] SPREADS THE STORY OUT OVER TIME AND SPACE, drawing in every possible character with beautiful logic. . . . Sequels often stumble. This one soars."

—*Detroit Free Press*

"A GEM . . . SWEEPING, OPERATIC . . . Russell's gift for dialogue and the novel's questioning of our very souls at the dawn of a new millennium give *Children of God* a quality that transcends genre."

—*The Globe and Mail*

"A sequel that will please even readers new to her interplanetary missionaries . . . Misunderstandings between cultures and people are at the heart of her story. It is, however, the complex figure of Father Sandoz around which a diverse interplanetary cast orbits, and it is the intelligent, emotional and very personal feud between Father Sandoz and his God that provides energy for both books."

—*Publishers Weekly*

"The slow return of [Sandoz's] faith brings pain nearly as great as the sudden rending of it. Russell's exploration of the psychic rift and its healing is eloquent, illuminating all the dark corners of the mind in great novelistic style."

—*Cleveland Free Times*

"A brutal and deliberate tale . . . that will challenge and sometimes shred the reader's preconceptions."

—*Kirkus Reviews*

"This is not a book about easy faith, or God as a nice guy. This is the God of Job, and his world is a moral thicket, a vale of tears, a place of terrors and wonders almost beyond human understanding."

—*LOCUS*

Widely praised for meticulous research, fine prose, and the compelling narrative drive of her stories, MARY DORIA RUSSELL is the award-winning and bestselling author of seven novels. In addition to the science fiction classics *The Sparrow* and *Children of God,* she has written two novels set in the 20th century: a World War II thriller about Jewish survival in Nazi-occupied Italy, *A Thread of Grace,* and a political romance set in 1921 Cairo called *Dreamers of the Day.* With her novels *Doc* and *Epitaph,* Russell has redefined two towering figures of the American West: the lawman Wyatt Earp and the dental surgeon Doc Holliday. Her latest novel, *The Women of Copper Country,* tells the story of the young union organizer Annie Clements, who was once known as America's Joan of Arc. She holds a Ph.D. in biological anthropology from the University of Michigan and taught anatomy at the Case Western Reserve University School of Dentistry.

MaryDoriaRussell.net